THE MIRIYAMA

Tracy deMercleden

The Miriyama

Published by The Conrad Press Ltd. in the United Kingdom 2024

Tel: +44(0)1227 472 874
www.theconradpress.com
info@theconradpress.com

ISBN 978-1-916966-26-0

Typesetting by: www.bookstyle.co.uk
Jacket design by Charlotte Mouncey with artwork by Tracy deMercleden and Maria Deane Williams.

The Conrad Press logo was designed by Maria Priestley.

Printed and bound in Great Britain by Clays Ltd, Elcograf S.p.A.

THE MIRIYAMA

THE FIRST SIX BOOKS

ALSO CALLED 'MIRIAMRING'

MiriamRing is the story of Miriam, in and around Palestine;
with the master Yeheshua, his mother Mary and Mary Magdalene,
Peter and the Apostles, and many others.
Told by Mary Magdalene, and firstly how she came into it all.

Tracy deMercleden

CONTENTS

BOOK 1: MAGDALENE'S BLOG

Miriam wants to go to the East where Yeheshua had been travelling and teaching earlier in his life. To go to places he had spoken to her about; to renew his message to the people there.

I cannot bear to see her go; she who has been like a second saviour to me in these past few weeks.

When all the work of the master with me had seemed to be unravelling like a badly sewn shawl.

And I cannot help feeling that her going has a lot to do with the attitude of some of the brethren.

*

Where should I start with the story?

That day in Galilee that meant so much to me perhaps, where the voices of confusion were lifted from my mind? Around the very same time that Miriam re-found her Love and her Lord?

Or maybe those fateful few days, or weeks, around the crucifixion?

Yet, who is able to hear the deeds of others without being all too ready to give judgement?

If you can allow, stay with me and I shall go back to what was the beginning for me, of my search.

Then hopefully all the rest will make some sense.

As a young girl, everything was so clear and simple. Life was good because God made it that way. There were hurts and upsets too of course, but put there perhaps just to be overcome.

Then, almost imperceptibly, a thin cloud came to cast a veil across my sun. What was this cloud and where did it come from?

I don't know; I only knew that something had started to slip away from my grasp. The happiness that I needed, as food and sleep, had become half a step removed from me.

I sought hard to regain it, looking to our scriptures and prophets for the way as I was taught.

Great Solomon and his father David knew, being beloved of the Lord.

Their songs and prayers helped keep my spirit winging forward, and encouraged, I threw myself onwards into my studies and devotions; until I met the wall.

I was a girl fast becoming a woman and not permitted entry to the mysteries of the God of the Jews.

The magic, mystery and mastery opened to Elijah and Elisha would always be closed to me.

I was told that there was another way for me through being a loving wife and mother; once a good match was found for me. For me as an accepting woman but not as a rebellious child!

Something nearly died in me then... if I would have accepted that my God was this 'God of the Jews' and not the true 'Most High God' of all my childhood.

But I couldn't.

I rebelled in my heart, determined that I would not follow this path dictated to me by others.

Then my father died; victim of a gang of thieves.

Though he could see the rebellion growing in his daughter and admonished me often and severely, he had never withdrawn his love from me. I loved him too, even enjoying the fighting between us, right until he was taken from us so suddenly; for it was not his fault that the world was as it was.

But with our father gone my brother was not so patient, looking to offload me into marriage as soon as possible.

And he found a market trader willing to take me on.

So I ran away.

Luckily or through Grace perhaps, it was made easy for me.

I had always loved the comings and goings of the trade caravans to Magdala and had become friendly with a few of the route-masters, plying them with questions of the lands they travelled between.

The particular caravaner about to leave Magdala at the time of my flight was one of those I knew and he agreed to help me.

Within his camel train was a woman of wealth and substance travelling back from Egypt to the far-off city of Ephesus.

She was of Greek origin, travelling overland because she could not bear the sickness of the sea and was wealthy enough to manage things her own way.

Several maids travelled with her as well as guards and other servants. Maybe this lady, called Dianaela, would take me on to earn my passage.

She was intrigued by me I think, and it must have amused her to help me escape from the zeal of the Jews.

So it was I found myself setting off into the desert night, watching the glorious display of stars arrayed around us, as Dianaela's newest handmaiden. I was almost as happy as the little girl who used to point at those same stars from the arms of her father.

My mistress was an ample, kindly woman who also had a keen business sense and a wide knowledge of the customs of different peoples of the world, which she loved to display when given the chance.

In me, she found a very willing audience. Partly as this allowed me respite from other tasks, which in truth were not very onerous; but also for my love of all such tales and knowledge.

It was her that told me of the Great Goddess, and how she was worshipped far and wide. Isis and Astarte, Ishtar and great Diana. All encompassing was Her realm, stretching back to the beginning of time; but not in Judea or Galilee.

"Yet even great Yahweh must have a consort, but you Jews keep the secret very close;" and she laughed.

I was shocked at her but it made me wonder; now that I was travelling through another country with companions nourished on such different ideas.

M.B. #03

We travelled north, going quite close to the sea, crossing slopes where magnificent cedars grew. Past Tyre and Sydon and where Ancient Byblos lies, the centre of Astarte's realm, and on towards Antioch in the north.

Lady Dianaela also told me the tale of Adonis, Asarte's love. Born so beautiful and carefree that goddesses vied for his love and feted him as their delight.

He was fated though to perish through his own delight in hunting and the lamentations of the women have never been surpassed. Yet he came back to life in spring, bringing beauty and freshness ever new as the harvested seed brought forth new life, perennially returning for the rites of Astarte's love.

Something of this struck a chord in me, young as I still was, and liking the idea of renewal and of life being refreshed.

We passed through Adonis's especial valley; but we journeyed on northwards and I was saddened to be leaving all this romance behind.

Venus, Astarte's sign, still shone bright in the western sky following the sun down toward the sea and I knew I didn't want to leave this land. More especially I was filled with a great desire to know more of the ways and mysteries of the Great Goddess and her loves. That missing piece that I had been searching for, I could see that now.

My mistress told me much of Ephesus of course, and the young boys who held Adonis as their model; for she sensed the interest she had aroused in me.

She had large estates in and around the town and claimed to be descended through her mother's line from a princess of the Amazons.

Her father had apparently been a famous physician from Corinth, yet I thought I felt a kind of loneliness in her and discovered that her husband had been killed in the wars of Rome. She had not married again but thrown herself into her businesses.

Maybe she did wish for me to stay with her but once she knew I had developed another longing, to devote myself to the Goddess and Adonis, she helped me in every way she could.

There were not many places where she didn't have influential connections and Antioch was no exception.

There was a great temple of Astarte there, where she knew the High Priestess and could recommend me to her as a likely neophyte.

Which was how I entered into the new phase of my life and search.

M.B. #04

My former mistress Dianaela had not long left when I was called for interrogation by the High Priestess herself.

A fine-featured woman of indeterminate age; mostly perhaps because she was wearing beautifully applied make-up.

She asked me questions in Aramaic with a heavy Assyrian accent which I could barely understand; but I gathered enough to know I would be required to learn many things quickly if I wanted to stay in the temple; it wouldn't be an easy ride.

Then she took me by the arm and led me to stone steps that circled up around the inside walls of the tower that stood at the centre of the temple. Stairs that led up to a wide flat space surrounded by a wooden parapet that formed the top of the tower. From here there was an uninterrupted view over the roofs of Antioch and across some of the surrounding fields and hills; and of course, up and out into the sky.

Night was just drawing its velvety depth from the completed day with the strongest stars shining high above the oval roof area. The two furthest ends of this space each boast a tall alabaster pillar, curved and pointed like a horn of purest ivory. In the centre, where a broad circular platform had been raised to knee level above the rest of the roof, a deep bowl of incense was burning and letting sweet smelling smoke drift into the cool evening air.

This passed by me as a series of fleeting impressions for the woman had led me over to one edge of this stage to where a clear crescent moon lay suspended in a fine glory that heralded the melding of day into night.

Floating close beside the moon fair Venus shone with amazing intensity and they were all that seemed to exist out over the city.

It was a sight that made me gasp with its unexpected impact.

I turned towards the High Priestess whose painted face shone faintly. The beautiful mask smiled and said how auspicious it was for me to have applied to serve the Goddess on this night when Her signs were brought together in such a way.

So it is, I have been accepted to learn the ways of Astarte's Priestesses.

M.B. #05

I sleep in a dormitory with many other girls but they treat me with some suspicion. The Jewish girl from Magdala. What does she want in the temple of the Goddess?

Indeed, I do feel quite out of place with these laughing, pretty creatures of polished smiles and sliding glances.

Instead of worrying though I am throwing myself into service, eager to please the Goddess Herself if not her young handmaidens.

My first duties, with other new neophytes, are to clean the dormitories, toilets, washrooms and kitchens of the temple complex. These are laid out around the sides of the main courtyard, which has openings on the south, leading down a hillside where the gardens and orchards of the community are spread out.

These cleaning tasks are the most menial service in the temple but it is work that I am well able to do and take some pride in. Several of the other young neophytes obviously hate it but I hate rather the mess of it being left undone.

We all prefer helping in the kitchens as this gives opportunities to go out into the farm gardens where a group of the oldest priestesses are responsible for all that is done; or who actually spend much of their time sitting round under the trees and snoozing. Quite a happy retirement, it seems to me.

Out on those southern slopes there are many different areas. An ancient olive grove is separated from a citrus orchard by equally ancient walls, along-side which a tangle of fig-trees and prickly pear cacti compete with each other.

On the other, rockier side of the olive grove are rough pastures where our goats and straggly cows wander, whilst in the better tilled ground beside the citrus orchard there are a swathe of well cared-for vines.

Closer to the temple buildings lie the vegetable and herb gardens which occupy most of the elder priestess' working hours, and water brought from the kitchens and the washrooms keep the vegetables growing in the peak of condition.

On the other side the effluence from the toilets is diverted into covered pits, away from all the rest, but which will eventually change into something more useable, I am told.

M.B. #06

Fetching and carrying for the kitchens has led to us joining classes with the ancient crones, to learn about the usage of the herbs which is their great delight.

And every day we all gather in the 'Courtyard of the Tower' for morning and evening rituals; just before the sun rises and then as it sets. Rituals led by one or other of the senior priestesses from a balcony built around an opening that is near the base of the tower.

I haven't got to climb the steps of 'Adonis Tower', as it is called, since that first magical evening. It stands at the northern end of the great courtyard close by an arch that leads to the grove and an ornate door to where the high priestess has her apartments with a few others.

That is called Temple Court and it is from here that Billel commands her 'empire' within the city and district of Antioch.

Temple Court is quite grand; its sides being three stories high with golden columns on the ground floor. They are arranged around a central water-pool, which extends within the columns on one side of the courtyard, to form a heatable bathing area.

There are rooms for receiving important visitors, teaching and other purposes, all dedicated to the Goddess in her different guises, particularly Aphrodite and Isis who are the most popular at this time.

Tower Court has a simple colonnade on two sides, and communal buildings for eating and sleeping, with an arch going to the Goddess Grove in the east and gates to the west that lead to the fetival grounds, neither of which we neophytes can enter until we have passed through our Acceptance.

Our dormitories are in single story complex on the western side of Tower Court with access to the flat roofs which we use a lot.

And gradually I am becoming used to the workings of the great temple and feel more a part of it all. My fellow neophytes called me 'Magdalene' and it is a name that has stuck with me.

M.B. #07

There is so much to learn before a neophyte can even be considered for 'Acceptance'. One by one new duties and tasks are being added as the weeks go by.

We work hard in every aspect of the temple life in a series of rotas, but none of these allow us outside the temple and its gardens.

We wash all the robes, shifts and winding cloths and dry them on lines strung from poles on the flat roofs above the dormitories and washrooms; but the priestesses do all of their own under garments themselves. Then there is the sowing, mending and pressing to do as well.

Our 'discoveries' within the herb garden have become more formal instruction into making them into ingredients, some of which are for the kitchen but there are others that have quite different uses.

We are learning about them all.

Potions, powders and different sorts of mixtures are sold to the women of the town for personal and household use, and we do much of this.

Certain ointments and potions are used only by the temple priestesses, and these we are learning to prepare as well, except for one that is a great secret. Even its use is only to be revealed to us after we have undergone our 'Acceptance'.

We keep a record of our bodies, especially around our times of menstrual bleeding; and how this affects our moods in relation to the phases of the moon and other heavenly bodies.

And now we are learning the arts of beautification; such as face-painting and arranging our hair for this or that occasion; which can take quite a long time for it is sometimes very intricate.

Then there are the dances that are so important and of course there is the proper way of dressing and holding ourselves, and even walking. All of these create certain effects that a priestess needs to be mistress of.

Beyond that we shall also be learning about massage and other womanly arts. Some of the priestesses are skilled midwives, much in demand amongst the noblewomen of Antioch.

There is a very great need for priestesses that excel in any area of women's life and such talents are always looked for amongst us neophytes.

I don't think I am very special at any of them.

M.B. #08

I am fascinated by the lessons we are getting about the Goddesses. Many of these are represented in the temple and some others aren't.

You may reproach me for turning my back on the one God I professed to love so much, but it isn't like that.

The Almighty is still everything, as much as ever I have felt, it is just that my views are expanding, allowing for other versions of that truth than the ones I had previously been taught.

In fact, I am starting to wonder how much of their knowledge our Priests and Scribes have deliberately been keeping hidden from us, the ordinary Jewish people?

At just fifteen I am neither the youngest nor the eldest of the thirty or so neophytes at the temple, and of these thirty there are four or five of us that hang about together, when we can.

Sarita is the first that I have got to know well. She has dark, glossy hair and golden-brown skin. She is beautiful, though some would say too thin.

Her family had come from the east where they worshipped the Goddess Durga. They came in a trading caravan and lived here for some years, but they fell on hard times.

It was Sarita's choice to serve the Goddess at this temple. Dance is her passion and she has real talent. She was welcomed by High Priestess Billel. In many ways Sarita and I are both outsiders which is maybe why we befriended each other.

Perhaps too this is why Aella and Helen latched onto us for support. These two sisters came to the temple a few months after I did.

Whereas Aella is older than Sarita and me, Helen is a year or so younger. They are the daughters of a Roman auxiliary whose wife has died and who have no other family.

Both Aella and Helen are tall and fair haired, making a striking contrast with Sarita.

They hated the endless rounds of menial tasks that they had to do at the beginning and I took some pity on their misery, helping them when I could. For this they were very grateful and together the four of us make quite a happy gang.

The other sometime member of our group is Carmel who I think likes to be with us just because we are different to most of the others.

Carmel doesn't like to miss out on whatever is happening and she keeps us involved as well.

She is a lively soul to have around.

M.B. #09

There are many occasions for communal singing and dancing in the temple but nothing is quite like the late summer festival. This is the timeless celebration of the harvest and one of the two great rites of the temple when Adonis and Astarte are especially honoured.

The autumn rite is about the death of Adonis and the spring rite brings his rebirth. It is for these that the High Priestess takes the name Astarte-Billel, when she portrays the Goddess, and the 'Adonis' is chosen yearly from the young men of the city.

Carmel and Sarita have been involved in the official dancing arrangements, whereas 'the sisters' and I are free to wander around the ground, dressed in the dark red cloaks that declare us promised to the Goddess but not yet fully in her service.

Great tents have been set up in the ground and coloured streamers festooned everywhere, strung from pillar to post; and many rugs are spread inside these tents where musicians have practiced all the afternoon.

Toward the end of this first day huge pots of steaming food: fish, meat and vegetables, were prepared to join the baskets of many different breads, spread out on the makeshift tables to welcome the townspeople in; just as the sun sets over the western edge of the world.

The day has been very calm and there is hardly a cloud above to interrupt the pale evening sky that is spread from horizon to horizon. Caught in the magic of the moment I walked away from all the tents towards the rim of the festive ground.

The moon is half grown, sailing in the southern quarter, soft and beautiful. I moved back, slightly away from the bushes and trees, instinctively peering toward the western sky, knowing that when night came Venus would be riding peerless amongst the stars.

But the Queen of Heaven was already shining bright in the still pale blue sky. No other star would be visible for a good while, but there she is, with a magnificence that is all her own, displaying an unearthly beauty I could hardly fathom.

Held in my reverie I was caught by surprise to hear the voice behind me. "Look well Magdalene…" the High Priestess Billel had been watching me and I had been unaware of her approach. She has the knack of being able to do that kind of thing, "See truly and you are seeing the Goddess herself. The sky is hers alone this evening."

I knew she spoke the truth for I could feel it in me and wished to let the Goddess in completely. "Your studies will be starting in earnest soon and her realm will open to you as it has for me. Come, join back with your companions, for there are other things you should observe this night as well."

We went back to the tents where the feasting had nearly started, for the great and rich men and women of Antioch and around had come to pay their homage. The handmaidens of the Goddess were arrayed in white festive gowns to meet and entertain these worthies; for the autumn rites had begun in earnest.

I rejoined my friends who asked where I had been, scolding me for being a neophyte out alone amongst the bushes. Didn't I know the risk?

Until a neophyte is accepted by the Goddess, she must not have relations with a man, but remain a virgin. If she flaunts this rule then she would lose her chance to become a priestess, even if it hadn't been by her choice that it happened. High Priestess Billel has been vigilant on my behalf.

Sometimes there are men driven to make rash attempts to ravage the unwary neophyte, and if caught at this in olden times, such creatures would be hunted and slain by the priestesses with their slim but deadly bows and arrows. Nowadays the town guards are asked to pursue them and deal out Roman justice.

The festivities went on late into the night, on this, the first day of the rites. There was still a slightly formal order to the proceedings and only the priestesses picked by Billel would lead their high paying guests away into the night.

Tomorrow it will be slightly different.

But tonight, we neophytes approaching Acceptance were taken to special places in the outer wall where we could view the intimate rites in play; the first time we have glimpsed how the Goddess will work through us.

I am fascinated but rather shocked, though of course I know there is more to love-making than kissing and cuddling. No topic has been more discussed amongst us 'virgins', but I was not expecting to witness it quite yet; the time for our acceptance is coming soon.

M.B. #10

The second day's festivities start in the western outskirt of the city where there is a temple to the God that rules the earthquake and the sea; Ba'al-Poseidon.

Many youths are out there, testing their acrobatic skill and courage against that of the chosen bull, rushing up behind it and bouncing off its rump, if they dare. And as the animal whirls to confront the insult, others jump in from the other side. Not quite the feats of ancient Crete, and quite often there is a goring of one or other youth, but the excitement continues to grow stronger and deeper.

Eventually, when the bull becomes sufficiently tired or confused it will be brought to the ground by the use of ropes and then sacrificed to the great God by the temple priests.

Later the triumphant young men will bring two parts of the dead animal to be the offering to the Goddess; the head and loins.

All the priestesses of the temple, including us neophytes, have spent the morning bathing in the sacred grove and readying each other for the day ahead; gossiping about the young men they eyed the night before and offering to help each other net the lover they desire. For today there will be much revelry once the offerings have all been brought, and this year's Adonis chosen.

Many, many offerings were brought before the Great Goddess. From the field portions of grain and fruit and wine, and from householders, small bottles of oil were the favoured offering; to be blended into the balms and potions of the priestesses skilled designs; or used to make some tasty delicacy and resold again into the marketplace.

Last of all came the offering of Adonis. One of the youths that brought the offering of the slaughtered bull would be chosen for the role.

They could not tell who it might be, or what approach was likely to make their suit succeed. Only the High Priestess knew, and she would say it was the Goddess herself who made the choice.

All the young men's bravado had drained away, leaving the group almost naked to the scrutiny of the circling priestesses. They met the enquiring glances as best they could, not knowing which was Astarte-Billel, for she had disguised herself for this special task, being hard for even us neophytes to distinguish.

Then suddenly the choice had been made, and one young man was being carried shoulder high by his comrades to the centre of the arena, amidst great cheering from the crowds of onlookers, and the youths themselves.

With him were brought the bull's head and loins which were placed before the altar of the Goddess and her sacrificial fire.

The chosen Adonis knelt before the Goddess's statue but Astarte-Billel raised him up and embraced the youth, signalling to her aides to deal with the bull offerings.

They took the head and fixed it by the horns to a pole that enabled them to lay it across the sacrificial fire. But before fixing it there they expertly plucked, with short curved knives, the eyeballs from the shaggy head and placed them on the lowest step of the three-tiered altar in a silver cup.

Then they took the loins, cut into sections, and arranged them around a grid of iron that formed the lower ring of the fire.

Once this was done the moment arrived for the Adonis to perform his trickiest task. He had been armed with a sharp short-sword, given him by Astarte-Billel, and whilst the other priestesses tilted the bull's head to present its under-neck, he had to cut out the great tongue which had been roasting over the top of the fire.

A tough task in front of all the crowd, but one helped by the earlier preparation of the head by Poseidon's priests. Confidently the youth pushed his sword into the animals opened neck and after just a couple of slicing cuts was able to pull out the bull's great long tongue.

Again, great cheers went up in the crowd as Adonis raised high his trophy before placing it on a copper salver held out by Astarte-Bel. This she laid on the second tier of the Goddess's altar.

On the topmost level of the altar there was inset a shallow golden bowl, and now the moment had arrived for Astarte-Billel to complete the magic rite and offering.

Two doves were held out by her priestess aides; and she received their offerings; one in each hand. Raising them high to either side, she propelled one dove up into the sky in a noisy fluttering of wings. The crowd watched hard.

In that brief moment a small curved silver handled knife appeared in her emptied hand and with one quick motion she cut the neck of the other dove and laid the bird on top of the altar, holding it there as the blood drained into the golden dish from the severed neck; and its wings flapped feebly.

It was a moment of awed hush, for once again the Goddess had shown her rule over life and death.

Adonis led the cry that was taken up by the crowd. "Hail Great Astarte; Hail;" and she took the Goddess' crown of disc topped horns and affixed it on her own head.

Then as he knelt again before her, she smeared a bit of the dove's blood onto her Adonis' forehead.

M.B. #11

Today, being special to Adonis, the feasting started in the middle of the afternoon, rather than after sundown. The Adonis-chosen was led away by a group of virgin neophytes clad in short scarlet tunics, to be bathed and dressed ready to lead the feast.

I was part of that group and was fascinated to see how the young man would cope with our attention. He didn't seem sure at first as two of us tried to take his clothes from him and others awaited around the pool of warmed water we had prepared for him.

He was handsome I suppose, clean cut with curly black hair, but not quite the young man that I would have chosen to be Adonis. There was something in his demeanour that made me think he expected our admiration. But once he knew he was to lose every last vestige of clothing before entering the pool he lost something of his haughtiness.

The splashing and playing that ensued helped him to laugh and relax. The changes that this brought softened him and made him seem younger. Closer to the role I felt he needed to portray.

I was one of two given the task of arraying him in his godly robes. We passed him the under-tunic of golden yellow and then helped him with the covering robes of cerise and purple, trimmed with many silver threads.

His dark eyes locked momentarily with mine and I beheld the questing hunt that drove him on and felt an answering pull from within me. I smiled and his returning one lit up his face.

We took him back out into the arena, a young Godling fit to take the arm of Astarte-Billel. She was now dressed in a shapely white dress with trimmings of gold and on her head a curved gold and silver tiara set with precious stones that also indicated her to be high priestess of the Goddess Aphrodite.

She welcomed him with a warm smile of her own and set on his head a thin circlet of gold. Honoured and encouraged he stepped forward to acknowledge the cheers of the assembled crowd and to signal the feasting and music to begin anew.

*

As the sun set and the evening drew in, Astarte-Billel took the arm of her young Adonis and led him back into the tent, to the whistles and acclamations of the well wined revellers.

17

We neophytes were still his attendants at this point and the great tents were laced closed and Roman guards posted on the outside. A tough job for even the most seasoned of soldiers, not to partake in the evening's revelry; but they would get their rewards later.

In the inmost sanctuary of Astarte's tents two priestesses, skilled in the arts of massage, worked their arts upon the youth with perfumed oils, from head to foot, as he lay upon a spacious cushioned couch.

Then after some time Astarte-Bel herself came in and sat down next to the youth, to finish what her aides had started.

They made way for her and joined the few neophytes watching from behind surrounding drapes. We had been instructed to watch and learn everything we could, for there would be no better way, time, or teacher to receive it from; an opportunity we were not to waste.

*

M.B. #12

Before first light the young lord was awoken and we took him back inside the temple gates and out into the sacred grove. Priestesses bathed and sported with him anew, in readiness for his final trial, when once we re-entered the arena.

That day many, many of the town's women were at the festive ground, as was the custom; dressed gaily for dancing and merriment. This was the day for them and their Adonis.

Once the singers and musicians had done their job of working up the expectation of the crowd, the Adonis finally entered the arena with his entourage of young comrades and attendant priestesses, all carrying baskets of sweetmeats and cakes that had been specially baked for the occasion.

These delicacies were as much sought after for their aphrodisiacal qualities as their renowned taste, and it was a major task to distribute them to all who wanted without being completely mobbed. But distribute them they must, far and wide.

Gradually the baskets started running out and, and the priestesses one by one retired to take their place around a big ring of drums in the centre of the arena, giving their last few sweetmeats to Adonis to give out, ensuring he would be the last to finish.

The drumming from the central arena grew stronger as the priestesses worked up the tempo and the crowd responded. Adonis moved as fast around the throng as he could, and girls would catch at him to steal a kiss or any contact they could make as well as grab the cakes he offered out.

It became increasingly hard for his entourage to protect him. His helpers themselves became engulfed in the mob of women and only Adonis remained, pushed and hugged until he half struggled and was half chased through the ring of priestess drums into the centre of the ring.

There he stood alone whilst flutes and lutes joined in the swirl of sound to urge him on.

And at the very centre of the ring stood a nine foot pole, newly stuck into a freshly cut mound of earth.

On top of the pole were the charred remains of the sacrificed bull's head, with horns still proudly jutting up into the sky. The youth had nowhere else to go and six priestesses stepped into the ring, swaying to the music and dancing around him within the impenetrable ring of onlookers.

His responding dance weaved in and around the priestesses, round the mound, again and again, out towards the pounding drums, where the crowd were stacked many deep, back to the centre and out again. It had a well-worn traditional form but it was the Adonis that imparted to it the energy needed for the dance's impact.

On and on it went until the six central priestesses produced three long lengths of cord which they included in the dance, holding the ends in pairs and restricting the range of Adonis' dance, bringing him back towards the central mound.

Adonis mimed the chase of a chosen ibex, springing on and off the mound and all around, embellishing the display with acrobatic handstands and tumbling leaps.

Then he appeared to notice the horns atop the central pole and made strenuous efforts to jump and reach them, though they had been carefully placed beyond his reach.

Again and again, he leapt high in the air until he paused for a minute to regain his breath and strength, leaning against the pole.

At this point the priestesses moved in, each pair having their cord stretched out between them as they circled out and about each way, around the mound and pole.

The first cord caught him round the top of his thighs, and as the dancers crossed behind, they pulled him back against the central pole.

He started to pull at this binding but the second pair, with arms aloft, circled him and caught his arms against his sides, pinning them there and him to the pole, unable to struggle free.

To complete the task the third priestess pair circled lower, taking Adonis around the knees and with swift counter circulations of all three cords he was bound securely to the post.

The youth tried, with renewed vigour and pulsing strength, to break his bonds. The music drove on wilder and stronger until, in a climax of clashing symbols the Adonis finally collapsed and slumped against the pole, hanging in his bonds.

A great moan went up in the crowd as they witnessed the conclusion of their hunt. Other priestesses dressed all in white now crossed the ring and went up to the spent form. They unbound the cords and as they brought the youth down from his post, they gave him a long drink of what included a sleeping draught.

By the time that they had carried him back to the tents, he was as still as death itself.

It had been a magnificent performance and I found myself strangely moved, as was the whole audience, though most of them had seen the rite enacted many times before.

Astarte's priestesses washed and oiled the sleeping youth and used their arts to give his face a deathly palour that emphasised his natural beauty.

They clothed him in a fresh purple-red tunic and laid him on a litter that had been prepared as a bed and arranged all manner of fresh flowers, leaves and fruit around him.

Whilst this was going on the moans of the crowd had increased to a kind of wailing that was very hard on the ears, until suddenly the High-priestess stepped forth and signalled all to quiet.

She was very strikingly dressed in a long robe of gold, green and black, looking taller than ever. Pale and beautifully painted she now had the upturned crescent of Hecate set upon her brow. Her demeanour was neither sorrowful or glad, but entirely commanding. She crossed to where the mortal Godling lay, looking down at his recumbent beauty, whilst the crowd stared on in hushed silence.

She signalled to the youths who had been his entourage to come out of the crowd and pick up the litter, instructing them to carry him and follow her.

She led the procession out of the festive ground and down the route that took them through and past the town and out to the temple of Poseidon once again.

Many priestesses accompanied the body, bringing further offerings to accompany their Adonis into the Underworld.

A wailing recommenced amongst the townswomen and many were allowed to reach out to the body and touch it with little terracotta statues of Adonis as he passed.

The god would give them favour.

… and by the evening the procession had been received back at the temple of Ba'al Poseidon, and then on to a nearby cave entrance of the Underworld where the great autumn festival was brought to its completion.

M.B. #13

A lot has changed after the autumn festival.

It has left me with so much to think about, so much to work out in myself and I didn't know how to begin.

Eleven of us have been told we should be ready for our initiations after the longest night has passed. So, sixteen weeks to understand what we are taking on…

And now we are starting to learn much more directly with the trained priestesses; both inside the Temple's sacred grove and outside in the city of Antioch itself.

The grove is where we celebrate the turning of night into day. Priestesses who have tended the rites of night, plotting the passage of the planets, stars and moon around the sky, come here to relax before they retire; whilst the early rising team that will take the temple produce to sell at market also like to spend this hour here… and those who are taking over from the kitchen's early bakers.

Then, after the morning rite of greeting the Lord of the Day, there is another hour when the rest of the priestesses can enjoy the grove, often joined by B'el herself.

These hours have become our favourites of course.

We have been divided into pairs. Sarita has been put with me and Carmel with Aella; whilst Helen was thought to be not quite ready, which has really upset her elder sister.

Our pairing suits Sarita and I quite well for she is my oldest friend at the temple. We have already shared most of our secrets and helped each other in many ways.

We all talk about the things we will be required to do as the Goddess's priestesses and Sarita seems quite sure of herself and the path ahead. Of course, the subject of sex is foremost in most of the discussions of our group.

To Sarita the arts of love are the highest gifts that she can perform for the Goddess, to be her vessel in the world of men. Each time it would be a sacred act performed to make men love the Goddess more, to raise the desire to the higher level where beauty rules.

I am not so certain. I think I would need to feel attraction and some kind of love first, before committing myself in sexual union with any man.

I was lying naked on my tummy in the grove, whilst Sarita's slender hands kneaded a surprisingly powerful pattern across my back. She laughed at my objection to her argument.

"The only choice we women have is to take control of every situation. Use the power that the Goddess has placed in us; for Her, but also for ourselves."

I considered this. It made a sense, but was very different from the romantic notions that still lingered in me.

"Could there ever be a combination of personal love and sacred sex?" I asked.

"Our personal love can be for Adonis of the Goddess," Sarita answered, "which is hidden in every man, and our task at these times is to help him gift his love to Her."

She seemed really pleased with her explanation and I rolled over to see her expression.

"But this is going to be real; as real as us talking here. Can it be deep and yet so casual at the same time?"

She looked at me with her quizzical brown eyes gleaming.

"Only with the Divine grace. That is why we serve Her, Maddy."

I sighed and turned back onto the mat, studying the edge of it through one eye of my side-turned head. If only I could find it so simple.

A priestess came over and started giving Sarita instructions on the massage she was doing, which was really unnecessary as the Gandharan girl was as accomplished at this as she was at dancing.

I let my thoughts drift away. Today is the first time that Sarita and I are going out to the city market.

M.B. #14

Aella and Carmel have already been into Antioch.

They came back full of tales of boys and men and boys and a few descriptions of the city and its market places thrown in as well. Now our time has come to venture out and see the city we have lived so close beside but never visited.

We have helped each other with the final touches to our makeup and dress. Both of us are in the ochre working dress of neophytes and our dark red cloaks. The priestesses wear green cloaks, in all shades from almost yellow to arguably blue. Somewhere beyond the temple walls a cockerel is crowing.

Mario was waiting with the four donkeys at the gate to the sacred grove. Sarita and I followed the two priestesses Nereyn and Selene through onto the dusty street where a dog scavenging in a pile of rubbish and an old lady was cleaning the doorstep of her house were the only other beings around.

The sun was yet to rise but the cool air breathed the fresh promise of a lovely day. Gaius the grizzled old door guard and the black eunuch Bocca watched us go down the street and round the corner before turning back to the gate-house and some hot mint tea.

The environs of the temple are in New Antioch, although there has always been some sort of temple on the site of the spring.

There are quite a few rich people living in the area and the streets are relatively well tended.

Today we are making a couple of stops at local houses before going into the city proper.

Delivering rolled lengths of cloth and collecting finished garments from the women who have made them to the customer orders they had been given.

The priestesses act as intermediaries for many women who work within the textile and clothing trade, having all the contacts needed to keep a thriving little industry going.

As we approached the south-west gate of the city wall, two guards that would accompany us to the market came out to meet us. Part of a longstanding arrangement between the temple and the city guards, who are also some of the temple's best customers in other ways at other times.

The inner streets were already awake with activity. At one corner a group of merchants were haggling with the owner of an inn about the storage of their goods.

At another some children were being berated by a mother to get back inside whilst a group of beggars lurched along the other side of the road.

There were cages full of chickens stacked up by a wall beside one doorway, whilst song-birds sang from smaller cages out on higher balconies or roofs; between lines of washing strung out to catch the early sun.

It was colourful, not yet very noisy, but certainly smelly in places and both Sarita and I had to watch carefully where we stepped as we followed the clip-clapping hoofs of the donkeys towards the market square, avoiding the detritus of city life.

The closer we got to the centre the more the bustle of early morning city life intensified.

Mule drawn carts carrying goods of every kind passed us down the centre of the way whilst hand-carts were pushed out to the sides jostling one another and us until we all spilled out into the centre areas of the town.

The forum is a large rectangular space with the twin temples of Zeus-Jupiter and Hera-Juno set back up several wide banks of steps at the farthest end. Today the market activity extended from the market square through the surrounding streets and into the forum itself.

Two of our donkeys carried on to Market Square with Selene, Mario and the produce from the temple. Speciality vegetables on the one with breads and all manner of other freshly baked products piled high upon the other.

In the Forum Sarita and I stayed with Nereyn at two stalls being constructed side by side. One has clothes of every sort that we have brought, and the other is smaller but stacked with a myriad of glass and terracotta vessels of all shapes and sizes, variously filled with lotions and potions; individually marked and sealed closed.

Many of these are ready to be claimed by the person bringing a token with the same sign, for they have been re-filled at the behest of their owners, to be collected at the stall.

There are also larger pots on display containing the range of cosmetic and other speciality products that Astarte's priestesses make; ready to be decanted into smaller ones, from boxes on the cart.

This is where we spent most of the morning, greeting and seeing to the needs of our customers, who are mainly well-to-do women of the town, but also the occasional man on a mission for their wife or other lover.

There were a number of young men in the Forum too. Some were engaged in a debate upon the steps of the temples, whilst others were less discernibly involved in anything.

Both Sarita and I were aware of being assessed at different times by these little groups and we were as actively involved as them, looking to see what the young men around were like; anyone that could spark our interest? It didn't look completely un-promising.

The sun was warm, despite the time of year and a travelling band of musicians had set themselves up a near one side of the Forum. Our business had slowed and I was allowed to stroll over and watch the performance at closer hand.

The musicians seemed to have come from a different world for they were from a tribe that wander in the semi-desert lands, children of a mysterious tradition. Their music is simple and yet I think more beautifully constructed than anything I have heard. Entranced, I moved closer amongst the encircling audience.

M.B. #15

Rather loud laughter, coming from nearby, interrupted my enjoyment and turning round I realised it came from the youth who had been Adonis at the autumn festival, laughing with his friends.

Somehow it rankled more, coming from someone who I felt should have known better, but then another movement caught my attention. A man was walking over to the stall where Sarita was still serving any customers who might come.

I watched as he went over and started studiously looking at the things we had to sell. It wasn't long before he was asking Sarita questions, and as they talked together, they seemed to grow in animation. Could they really still be discussing cosmetic lotions?

Nereyen came over to them and he parted from Sarita's side as he addressed the priestess, quite formally.

The music behind had reached a particularly poignant turn and reluctantly I tore myself away from watching what was happening at the stall to immerse myself in its final passages.

Once it had ended, I returned towards our stall and I caught 'Adonis' watching me. Deliberately I raised my chin a bit and swayed my hips a little more, chastising myself all the while for doing so.

By the time I got back, Sarita's admirer had disappeared and I had great difficulty in prising any information from her. It was Nereyen who said "He has got a big desire for Sarita. He saw her dancing at the festival and she has apparently been constantly in his thoughts. What are you going to do Sarita?"

"Don't be silly," answered Sarita. "He is just like all the others; trying to impress us with his fine talk." But she looked down as she said this, pretending to adjust some pots that were fine just where they had been.

"Really? Well, he looks very rich," I couldn't help adding, for the young man's hair was well oiled and he sported a finely worked cloak-like coat.

"Yes" said Nereyen, "and he has asked to meet us formally. I said he could join us when we go to our town-temple at midday."

The temple in question was Aphrodite's, situated a few streets beyond and uphill from those of Zeus and Hera. We had packed up the stall and left it under the guard of the two stall-keepers who worked partly on a wage for the temple but also for their own separate business.

Not much was done in the hottest part of the day and they also retreated into the shade to have their provisions and enjoy a nap.

We climbed the last few yards to the modest entrance of our sister temple, glad to be let into its cool interior by the little old woman in black who was the doorkeeper.

In the middle of the courtyard we had entered, was a pool where a statue of a youth let water fall from a shell onto the reclining form of a goddess.

Two priestesses greeted us, dressed all in white and obviously well known to Selene and Nereyen.

Sarita and I were introduced and much to Sarita's embarrassment Nereyen explained about the possible arrival of Kasver, the aristocratic suitor that Sarita had attracted.

After that we all sat down to a selection of spicy dishes that had been prepared, together with some fine red wine, relaxing on Grecian style divans whilst the priestesses enjoyed as much fresh gossip as there was to tell.

Sarita must have been mortified by the realisation that she was about to become a major topic of gossip, or I certainly would have been.

I told her about the musicians and their wonderful music, hoping to take her mind off the subject of Kasver, but as I recalled how I had also seen 'Adonis' our thoughts both came back to the young man who might be about to join us.

It was not till after the meal was over and we were drinking sweet mint tea that the doorkeeper came in to say that there was a visitor at the gate.

I was encouraged to stay but Aphrodite's two priestesses left Selene and Nereyen to deal with whatever they had arranged.

M.B. #16

Kasver came in, bearing gifts. He presented some bracelets he had bought, two to the priestesses and one to Sarita, before realising that I was there and he had not included me.

He seemed genuinely distressed and wanted to give me something of his own, but I declined, smiling as encouragingly as I could.

He had a handsome face with a bronzed complexion, slightly lighter than Sarita's own. His manners were very courteous and he asked whether he could talk a while with Sarita. The priestesses said he could but that they must stay within the bounds of the court of the fountain.

I did not know what the customs were for this situation, for clearly Kasver had more than just a passing fancy for Sarita. He was serious in his intentions, whatever they might be.

Later, when we had got back to our own temple, she told me all about their conversation and how stricken he appeared to be. She also said that she really

25

liked him and had noticed him more than a little at the autumn festival; as he had her, and her dancing.

"You've kept very quiet about him then," I said. "I thought you were about to embark on a quite different path... you know, to help every man who came your way."

"Maddy you are terrible," she retorted. She was the only person who didn't call me just Magdalene. "If the Goddess wishes that I serve her with this man, then that will be the path that I embrace. If not, then I won't."

I gave her a hug and told her how jealous I was. Kasver seemed to be really nice, "though not my sort at all," I added, as she looked at me from behind her defiant lashes. She laughed and hugged me back.

I think she was almost frightened to dare believe something could come from it. But something did; for he approached Billel and declared his wish to take Sarita for his bride.

Kasver was a younger son from a noble family and for them to know that the girl he had fallen for was a virgin, promised to the Goddess but not yet consecrated, made the possibility of the match acceptable.

B'el was wise to all the business angles and she made much of the loss to the temple this would mean, of a dancer that they had not seen the equal of in many years.

Negotiations continued and within a couple of weeks the price of compensation was settled and the release of Sarita to become Kasver's bride was agreed.

Emotions warred in me for though I was happy for Sarita, as she seemed so pleased herself, I was really sad to be losing my best friend at this time of severest trial.

"You shall all come and visit me," she told us as we helped with planning her part in the wedding. Aella was pleased because Helen was now rejoining us in our 'Acceptance' group. Helen was paired with Carmel and Aella was working with me, and Sarita too for a while.

"What! We could all entertain your husband?" jibed Aella and Sarita punched her arm. "No, you shall not!" and she paused, "at least not until I am very bored with him;" and we all laughed.

M.B. #17

The wedding came and went in a grand manner, close to Winter Solstice, following the Zaroastrian customs which Kasver's family adhered to.

I missed Sarita so much. Though there were only a very few weeks to go till the 'Acceptance ceremonies' it seemed to be an eternity without her.

She followed her path with such a simple faith that it was hard to believe she really meant what she said; but I am sure that she did. To me she was a little golden Aphrodite, Goddess of love, and I was not surprised that Kasver had fallen for her so completely. Well, he had better appreciate what a jewel he had gained and to be fair to him he seemed to be a man that might. I sighed again and again inside; where to for me now?

My mind turned to the Goddess herself. I needed to comprehend what it meant to follow her path, rather than just blindly blundering on.

What had I really understood about Her? Them? The questions continued to circulate in my head.

Astarte must be the greatest, embracing motherhood as well as all other aspects of womanhood; Queen of heaven, lover and even warrior. Surely this is why the temple is dedicated to her?

Aphrodite is and yet isn't the same; all consuming is her pursuit of love and beauty and in this alone she is perhaps the greatest force. Certainly, she seems to be the goddess most widely honoured in this modern world.

The goddess Isis is another that high priestess Billel seems to esteem most highly, but the reasons for this are still a bit secret, and not much shared with us neophytes.

Thrn of course there is Hecate; peerless in her own right. No God cared to contend her greatness; yet the one most often overlooked. None escaped her power, curled hidden in the underworld, expressed in the crossroads of life and death itself.

The winter, with Adonis in the underworld, seemed to belong most particularly to Hecate and with that thought I found myself wandering towards the herbal gardens where the eldest priestesses stayed, that understood so much of Goddess' lore.

Maybe they could help me; though I didn't quite know what with.

It was the middle of the afternoon and though the day wasn't very hot the sun was bright and most of the temple was still enjoying a lull in the day's activities.

I crossed the outer courtyard, trying to think what question I might ask of the ancient sisters.

Perhaps about the rite of Acceptance? Except we pretty much knew now what to expect. After a day of preparations Astarte-Billel would take the exploration of our bodies into its most intimate areas and herself play the part of Adonis by opening our channel to the cup of Venus with a tool of polished marble. There would be pleasure because the priestesses were expert in bringing this about, and pain because our bodies were as yet untried. So much we had found out.

Then again, I could ask about the great secret; the potion that was called Hecate's knife. Only these ancients knew its whole, apart from the high-priestess herself and perhaps her closest aides. Yet though we didn't know its formulation we already understood its purpose for nothing could be kept completely secret in the temple.

The potion is what the priestesses took that stopped them from getting pregnant; and B'el would prepare it for each of us.

I stepped through the lower gate and down the stony path towards the corner of the gardens favoured for a quiet rest. Still undecided about what I might ask but looking for the one I most hoped would be there.

We called her Grandmother Beth or just Granny-Beth and she was the oldest, most bent and most wrinkled of all the priestesses. She hardly ever left the inner gardens where she had her own hut, and was the only one excused from attending morning and evening rites.

I found her dozing on a bench against the outer kitchen wall. Her eyes were closed and I bowed my head as I sat down on the ground near her, keeping quiet so as not to disturb her.

I waited, listening to the sounds of the hillside until I realised that Granny-Beth had opened her cloudy yellowish eyes and was watching me with a look of curiosity.

"Are you alright dearie?" she asked, "you seem a mite troubled".

"Oh, I am fine thankyou grandmother," I replied; "but I did want to ask a question, if I could."

Granny-Beth inclined her head a bit to one side but said nothing. Her smile told me though that she was happy to let me go on.

I still didn't know what the question was exactly so I just reached inside and tried to formulate what I was feeling.

"Which is the greates; that... the Goddess we seek to serve?" It didn't quite make sense, but Granny Beth replied as though it was the clearest thing.

"Kindness" she said firmly.

"Erm," I started to reply because I was thinking this wasn't quite what I had meant; "er, but which of the goddesses…?" and I trailed off, slightly confused.

"Hecate, Hecate, Hecate" chuckled Beth, and I was quite put out. No-one did a triple-appellation to Hecate out loud. Not lightly at least.

Granny-Beth must have noticed me start because she chuckled again and displayed a toothless grin. "Don't worry dearie, I am so close to her realm now that she doesn't mind me taking the odd liberty, see."

I nodded out of politeness mostly, but she was rocking gently with her eyes closed. I couldn't move. She opened her eyes again and fixed me with a clear but distant look.

"Kindness," she said again, clearly. "You shall be blessed with knowing very great kindness, and in great abundance;" she added, stopping and closing her eyes again.

There was a long pause. I was thinking of getting up.

"But first," she said, not even opening her eyes this time; she sounded very tired. "But first you will find the need… a very great need… for that kindness".

I sat a long while wondering what she meant and whether there was more to come, but she seemed to have nodded completely off to sleep.

The distant sounds of the hillside joined us back again, and eventually I got up and silently thanked her as I backed away.

I felt that the Goddess had spoken to me. This was the start of all that followed and I tried to open myself to accept what would come.

M.B. #19

The weather got really cold in the weeks following on from my Acceptance, with ice and snow blowing in on a persistent north wind. Life in the temple became introspective, with only essential trips being undertaken into the city and its markets.

There was one casualty too, as a direct result of this cold. The senior priestess of the library, Mistress Astel, was found dead one morning in the little cell of her reading room.

She was not one of the priestesses that I knew as she had hardly ever ventured out from Temple Court but others felt her passing keenly.

The funeral procession took her tiny, empty body down to the caves and graves at the bottom of the southern hillside, where she was cremated and her ashes placed in a little pottery urn that was buried in a place of honour there.

B'el herself led the procession and the tributes to the woman who had been one of her own teachers. A number of wealthy women from the city also endured the cold to attend her passing. Quite a surprising number I thought.

It made me think of the influence she must have had and this prompted me to visit the library. My new status of novice priestess allowing me entry and the cold weather gave me plenty of opportunity.

There were two other priestesses who worked there. Phillipa was one; a middle-aged woman who had been involved in teaching us as neophytes; telling us some of the stories of the Gods and Goddesses. I had thought of her as a rather fastidious lady and she hadn't been a very inspiring teacher.

It was B'el herself who had taken our most memorable lessons about the roles and stories of the Goddesses.

But Phillipa was friendly enough, and in the library she took a special interest in keeping the star records. Every night, when conditions allowed, observations were made on Adonis Tower concerning the positions and movements in the heavens. These were given to Phillipa who incorporated them into the records, updating the current positions for B'el and other senior priestesses to use in their deliberations and predictions.

The other priestess in the library was called Arianne; a young Armenian woman with curly brown hair and a round face. I would not have described her as pretty but nevertheless she had a sort of inner glow and a jolliness that I associated with cooks and cooking rather than the fusty rooms of a library and scriptorium.

We liked each other the moment that we met, the morning that I knocked rather nervously on the library doors.

Arianne was glad of a visitor and I of the welcome I had not expected.

She had come to Antioch from the temple at Tyre, specifically to study under Mistress Astel. She worked mainly in the scriptorium, maintaining its collection of ancient texts or deciphering and copying those borrowed from other temples and libraries.

She also sometimes wrote letters for B'el, or one of the other senior priestesses, especially when they needed to be in Greek.

She had an insatiable desire to know: what was going on; what had happened, in this and other places, and what might yet come to pass. She liked to be involved and thought this was a good place to be so.

Some days after my first visit we were sitting side by side at a table in the scriptorium, enjoying some welcome sunshine coming through the un-shuttered window, when I told her about my Acceptance ritual, and how it had gone disastrously wrong.

"I don't know why B'el likes to bring in the 'chosen Adonis'," she responded as we sat with our hands around our cups of hot tea. "It nearly always goes wrong in some way. I think she wants to make the initiation more real for certain of her chosen pupils. So perhaps she has high hopes for your future."

"Or uses fate to weed out those for whom the stars of destiny don't shine," I answered wryly and she laughed. "Shame on you, Magdalene. That he couldn't exercise control with you shows in your favour, rather. You must be her special protégé."

It was my turn to laugh. "I don't think so. Not when I remember her expression when she gave me that awful concoction to drink. She was furious… and I have never been so sick. It seemed to go on for hours."

We giggled a bit and I sat, remembering the dawn of that new day as I lay in the sacred grove, recovering from the night's events.

"That was when I first saw Venus rising before the sunrise," I said after a while; "but I didn't know then what that bright star was. It was special to me because I was so weak, and it seemed so beautiful and full of…" I couldn't think of the right word but Arianne looked sideways at me, nodding.

"Mmm" she said, not trying to name the magic quality either.

"Yes, purity." I answered myself.

We finished our tea and got out the document we had been working on together. It was a Hebrew scripture and I understood the context better than she did, and for once I was able to help her by explaining some of its references. I had worked hard in my youth and was glad of that now, but of Enoch's travels I knew very little.

She was teaching me so much about all of the different schools of learning there were, and had been, in the world; that she knew about. And I was glad of this chance to try to return something.

Then out of the blue Arianne suggested the possibility of sending a message to my mother, to let her know that I was well.

Up until the time of my 'acceptance' I had given hardly any thought to my family in Magdala. Now that event had passed, I somehow felt that I could think of my former home again. I was no longer just running away. There was time to access now where I had got to, and where I might be going.

I wasn't sure whether to make it a long letter, or give any details of what I was doing. Would anyone other than my mother care? I didn't know. In the end I settled for a short note sending my love and saying that I was all right and living and working with friends in Antioch. I didn't give any details but no doubt she would be able to guess a bit from the way the letter would reach her.

When the weather improved Arianne would arrange for the letter to go on one of the regular routes to Tyre, where she had a friend called Rachel. They had worked together in the temple there, before Arianne had come to Antioch. Arianne also wrote a letter of explanation to Rachel and included a little money to help her get the letter on to my mother.

A little kindness that would go a long way.

M.B. #20

Those early days of feeling part of the Goddess's world were mostly very sweet.

It was a very individual thing; a personal feeling that nestled in the vitals of my being; that my life was on the verge of being included in something greater. But the feeling of connection was there more intensely when we, her priestesses, worked together for her cause. B'el had taught us that through conscious work our mind-soul would absorb the influences from the Gods and Goddesses invoked. Our choices would mould our mind-soul's texture and our efforts would bring it strength and depth.

One day Aella and I carried firewood out to the shrines. We were helping the priestesses who attend to the shrines, where male supplicants were received. Those who came because they needed the Goddess' touch and paid homage to her there.

These shrines were small rooms set into the perimeter wall, behind the bushes and occasional trees that lined the outer areas of the festive ground. Aella and I swept the floors and hearths and lit fresh fires in them. In this cold weather the hearth-fires would provide just enough welcoming warmth for the priestesses to perform their duties as the Goddess-chosen.

We had our new green cloaks wrapped around us and could feel the package that marked our passage into priestesses hidden in their folds. A small, curved, silver-bladed knife was tucked into one pocket of the leather pouch whose other pocket held another protection. Hecate's potion that B'el had worked into a small, unappetising cake for each of us, held in cloths that had magic symbols on them.

There were not many visitors to the shrines in the bitterness of this season's chill but Anna was on duty and there was a captain of the City Guard, called Karaster, who braved the icy snow for his and Anna's customary rendezvous.

He was let into the North-western gate by the eunuch Bocca and went to the covered area at that corner of the ground where Aella and I were ready with a warming drink. He accepted it gratefully as he shook the frosting of snow from his cloak.

Another priestess, called Felicita, was with us but she knew that the tough captain would have been told by Bocca that Anna was here.

Aella's hood fell back, revealing her long fair hair. Karaster appreciated it with a wink and a joking comment. "Are you on duty tonight as well priestess? Perhaps I should ask for the Goddess's favour through you?"

"Kras!" Anna's voice cut across the intervening space from where she had entered the scene, "Don't mock the Goddess."

We all turned to look at where she stood, tall, with a presence about her that I wouldn't have guessed. A radiance was enhancing her natural femininity. Maybe she wasn't the greatest beauty but there was no doubt that at this moment she was the chosen.

Karaster immediately crossed over to greet her as he always did, kissing the palms of both her hands that she outstretched towards him. She hugged him briefly and then they moved off together to one of the shines we had prepared.

I had felt a charge of energy within me and Aella had too. Quite soon now it would be one of us being hostess for Astarte-Aphrodite. It seemed we would be ready, and I hoped we really would.

We walked back together for the evening meal. I was on kitchen clearing duties, but Aella would be going back to the shrines after mealtime.

I knew she had started taking a portion of Hecate's poison and wondered what she was planning.

The next day she told me that players had been coming to the north-western reception and practicing their music. Carmel had been out a couple of times and they were going out again that night.

I joined them and Helena came along as well.

The day had been a bit warmer and there was the feeling that a party was happening out there.

A myriad of stars were out in a clear sky as we made our way across the festive ground, and music emanated from where the glow of several braziers were giving their light and warmth into the night.

Two torches we carried made the shadows flicker about us as we walked and across the space ahead we could see people dancing; some early practicing for the spring festivities.

At the edge of the light Carmel called out greetings to a couple of the musicians, and Aella turned to say, in hushed delight, that there were more people there tonight than the night before.

The musicians had set up their instruments and some were already playing snatches whilst singers tried out their voices in improvised accompaniment; it was fun to be there with them.

A couple of the watching men we recognised as regular visitors who came to obtain the favours of the Goddess.

And others were there who didn't appear to be either musicians or suppli-cants, but who had somehow succeeded in bluffing their way past Gaius and Bocca at the gate. They had wine with them which they were drinking quite freely.

M.B. #21

One of these approached Aella and spoke with her in tones that told me they had met before. Aella introduced him to us as Krippa and he offered us some wine too. He was a smooth talker and he seemed to take a special interest in Helena.

A couple of his friends also came over to talk to us, but I was more interested in watching the dancing and listening to the music. There was something very presumptuous about them that I didn't like.

Carmel was practising with one of the dance groups, and watching them and the musicians working together was exciting. I sipped the wine and enjoyed the atmosphere.

Helena was still talking to the one called Krippa and I noticed Aella looking rather irritatedely at them. She obviously had no interest in his friends either, but instead flounced away towards another couple of men that were sitting watching the dancers.

I could feel Aella's jealousy as she drank down her wine, glancing back at her younger sister, all the while flirting with one of the dance-watchers.

Then she joined the dance herself... at the end of the line, removing her cloak and swaying her hips before the men; she oozed allure.

Helena and Krippa were watching her now and Krippa had slipped an arm around her younger sister's waist.

I watched transfixed as well as one of the least pleasant of the seated men got to his feet and moved over towards Aella. Being passive watchers was not going to be enough; she had encouraged their attentions and now she had to deal with them.

She turned away from him making it clear that she wasn't interested in him and I felt a strong urge to go and help her; to pull her away whilst I still could.

Crossing quickly over to them I tried to show as much authority as I could pretend to have.

One part of my mind told me to get the silver bladed knife from the pouch inside my cloak but instinct told me my voice was my best resource.

Out of the corner of my eye I saw one of the musicians sliding away, sensing possible trouble. 'Coward,' I thought, feeling anything but calm myself.

The man had grabbed Aella by the arm, pulling her to him

"Release the priestess," I said in what I thought was a commanding tone.

Aella's expression was that of any frightened young girl. The man looked dangerously drunk. He looked at me and sneered. "Harlot" he said, spitting the word at me.

"I shall have this one." Another man had come up behind me, trying to put an arm around my waist. His breath stank.

"Take your hands off me," I said as loudly as I could, but my mouth had gone dry and the words were hardly more than a squeak.

Others had moved towards where we were stood, Krippa being one of them, clear concern showing on his face.

The man holding me had pulled out a concealed knife from within his clothing. No men were permitted to bring weapons into the temple grounds. He reached towards Krippa and would have cut him with a vicious swipe if the boy hadn't jumped back.

"Stay away and we won't touch you," he said as the other pulled a terrified Aella away towards the bushes beyond the torch and brazier light.

I was stunned and the man holding his knife menacingly close to my face started to push me in the same direction. I thought of my own little curved blade that was really meant for cutting the woody stems of herbs and my shaking fingers struggled uselessly to penetrate the folds of my cloak.

Bushes scraped against my thighs as I was pushed out beyond the brazier light. Fear was like cold fingers clutching in my chest.

From behind us came a barked command. "Drop that knife!"

The man holding me swung towards the intruding voice, knife outstretched, as a short club-stick came down on his inner forearm. The knife fell from nerveless fingers.

Gaius had been alerted by the musician and it was he who disarmed the knife-man.

Bocca, following close behind, chased after the other man that had now deserted Aella, heading for the gate at a sprint… and was gone.

The knifeman wasn't so lucky. Gaius and Bocca led him away.

The 'party' broke up quickly. Everyone dispersed and Carmel took me under her wing whilst the two sisters clung to each other sobbing.

Nothing very much was made of the incident. Once Gaius had made some sort of report, B'el gave us all a strong lecture about the meaning of our service, taking Aella away to admonish her more privately. Aella was on kitchen duty for every evening of the next week.

Dance practices carried on under stricter supervision with no 'extras' joining in. The game must go on. Small incidents like this were to be expected when novices were involved.

We had our important uses though and as the weather had turned milder, we were once again encouraged to join the trips into the city.

Spring rites were not too far away.

M.B. #22

Sitting in the library taking a break from our copying work, Arianne and I were discussing things that had and were shaping the world we live in.

Different cultures continued to contribute to the complex web that make Antioch, and Astarte's temple in it, what it has become.

Traditions of Egypt, Assyria, Persia, Greece, Syria, and Israel too; blended in the cauldron that is the Roman world.

Mostly it is the strongest that make the rules and take the spoils but to us it seems that something else drives us on to greater ends as well.

Some say that the Gods and Goddesses are the rulers, whilst others that we have to find the way for ourselves.

What is the greater meaning that we are a part of? Had the Gods once walked the earth like us and lead its peoples still?

Or did it happen through specially gifted ones, able to be in touch with the Divine? Such as our prophets of Israel.

It was our business to find out and understand how all these were woven together; what the pattern was; so we could do our service better.

Arianne told me how Astel had been continuing the ancient work of reading this from the heavens themselves. The 'Starry Revelations' she had called them, where all things were made plain to those who knew how to see.

I mentioned that I had seen Sarita in the marketplace the day before and that she had invited us around to her new home in a few days time.

I was wondering if Arianne would be interested in the many stories of her homeland that she often used to tell when we were novices together.

B'el had come in and crossed to where we were. She had a knack of somehow catching a moment and taking it to another level. I had a fleeting impression that she might have been listening.

"Isis," she said. "Isis, is the Goddess that is also the priestess. She is our pattern and is the secret of the highest level of our revelation, Magdelene. When you are ready; when you are ready, she could be your guide."

We had been working on copying a tableau with Isis in it.

"Is the tablet ready?" asked B'el, as though she was reading my thoughts.

"Not quite B'el," said Arianne. "Is the lady here?"

"Not today," answered our high priestess. "Today I only need the star charts for the five friends of Desmina, councillor Gregory's wife. But I shall need it tomorrow when I go to the Governor's palace. It is his lady that is the keen devotee of the Egyptian mysteries."

Philippa had also now joined us, bringing the required charts.

B'el thanked her as she took the scrolls and turned to me again. "Isis wears the veil that separates the mortal from the immortal," she said.

I was like a sponge, soaking up this vital information; then I remembered Sarita.

"High priestess," I began; "when we saw Sarita yesterday …. who was married recently to Kasver, the Zoroastrian nobleman…" B'el nodded, showing me she knew of whom I talked, "she invited a few of her former temple friends to visit their house, at the evening of the next new moon. Is it all right if we go?"

Billel considered, realising that Aella was one of these friends, and had also been central to the recent troubles. "Our work is just as much with the women of the city," she said. "We have a duty to make the most of our connections."

Her expression softened; she even smiled. "Of course. you must go." Then adding with steely seriousness, "but there are not many chances given on the way. The Goddess will not be mocked. Your lessons, and those of your friends, must be learnt quickly."

*

When the day came, we set off from the eastern gate with Arianne and Nereyen, and one donkey to carry our gifts and baggage as well.

Carmel led the donkey and Nereyen led the way.

Aella was in good spirits and closer than ever with Helena.

Arianne and I walked at the rear, happy to be out in the town and I to be going to visit a dear friend.

We had been to Sarita's wedding but since then had only had messages from her till the day I saw her at the market.

She had looked really happy and had been accompanied by two other women, one of whom I took to be her mother-in-law: a fine-looking woman of noble bearing who had also seemed very proud of her new daughter-in-law.

The route we took this time was different from the way to the central market areas yet no less fascinating. Firstly, there was a district of quite large and impressive houses straddling the hill that bordered the southeast of the city. Then we passed through a guarded gate into a crowded area of narrow streets of mixed housing and every sort of working shop you might need.

In one was a blacksmith's that exuded greater heat and noise than even our temple kitchens and several carpentry shops that had many lengths of dressed wood leaning against the walls, and the rich, dusty smell of wood shavings.

Another was full of stalls where cloth and clothes were stacked on trestle tables and in the next street the un-shuttered openings declared all manner of foods for sale.

Some cooked, some not, and all the streets had awnings of every colour stretched out across the way.

Women were standing at entrances, some with babies wrapped to their backs, arguing with each other whilst young boys play-fought around them; and a couple of men passed carrying loads that donkeys might have been proud of.

Then we crossed a wider spcae where many people were sat around eating and drinking in the shade of a small stand of palm trees.

A full day of activity in the suburb of one of the world's greatest cities with straw and dirt and rivulets of smelly water, spilling down into gutters to join the sundry rubbish there.

Occasionally an outcast of some description interrupted progress on the road, whom everyone would try to avoid; a deranged soul or with some incurable illness; leprosy perhaps or being possessed by a restless, evil spirit. We would also close our ranks and hurry past.

Then the streets opened out and the activity lessened. Locked gates and grander house frontages indicated that there was less need here for frantic struggling, and the places where the traders displayed their wares were finer, like those whose dresses beckoned to the richer women and where cobblers worked on their accompanying footwear, out the back.

Even the taverns here looked to afford better elbow space.

We passed a synagogue and a butcher's shop nearby that had an entrance strung with a colour-beaded curtain.

Young men walked together down the road, clearly Jewish. One glanced at us and then away again, with interest only for themselves. Unusual amongst the young men of Antioch, and I recoiled a little at their haughty indifference.

Then another group joined our street from a side alley, engaged in lively conversation. One young man in particular caught my eye, his handsome face animated with whatever they were talking about.

He seemed to smile in my direction as we passed, and I thought in that moment that he looked familiar too. Then they were past and he was gone.

Walking on, the afternoon seemed a little brighter. Arianne was talking to me about something but I missed the meaning.

"This is the Jewish quarter of town," I told her.

"I know" she answered, looking at me sideways, "and your friend Sarita's husband lives on just the other side. Is it like Magdala at all?" she asked.

"A bit maybe," I answered lightly, savouring our walk in this marvellous city.

M.B. #23

Sarita's reunion with us, her old comrades who were now priestesses, was a joyous one. There was no mistaking how well married life suited her and how easily she seemed to fit into her new role of noble-lady.

She hugged us and gave us each a present; in little boxes tied shut with coloured string.

We gave presents too; to her, her husband and her mother-in-law; from B'el and the temple, but chosen by us.

There were many other guests and we went out to join them on the covered veranda that jutted out from one side of the palatial mansion, with spectacular views over the city.

Lights flared up across the hillsides as the evening turned towards night and a thin new moon settled over the rooftops of the town.

Around the edge of the terrace copper lanterns were being lit, selected by Sarita especially for the occasion.

Kasver asked a servant to show us to rooms that had been set aside for the six of us and where we were able to spend a little time arranging ourselves for the evening.

Putting on our best white dresses, freshening our makeup and re-dressing our hair didn't delay us too long. We knew we were expected and rejoined Sarita, Kasver and their other guests as soon as we could.

Some were Zoroastrian, easy to distinguish by their clothes and the way they liked to arrange their hair in complex coils and whirls; and their enjoyment of unusual perfumed oils.

Others were more Roman in appearance; two being legion legates in full uniform, one of whom had his young wife on his arm.

Finely dressed women there made me feel rather naive at first... till I looked at Nereyen and the other priestesses. The way we had arranged ourselves was equal to that of any of these rich people; eloquently simple but stunning.

Musicians played at one end and long tables were prepared for the banquet down the other; set also with flagons of wine and Roman style glasses.

B'el had given us a little talk to tell us what she expected from us in this visit; preparatory advice that did make socialising with these friends of Sarita and her husband easier.

She impressed on us the purpose of representing the Goddess and her temple in everything we did, but with subtlety... the effect of which tonight was to prompt a kind of formal flirting throughout the evening... with invitations being offered out to join us at the temple for the Spring festivities.

The food was delicious and varied and the drink flowed easily.

Music accompanied it and other entertainments followed.

Dancers from a professional company of players whom Sarita encouraged Carmel to join in with. Carmel was good but we knew that Sarita was even more talented and we couldn't help ourselves from pleading with her to dance as well, as if she was still our temple comrade.

She looked over to Kasver who smiled back at her, gravely nodding his approval; and I think she blushed.

She called over the chief of the musicians and whispered a request for a different type of song.

After a few adjustments they started playing and for a while she listened intently before getting to her feet and gliding to the centre of the floor.

Her dance was not quite like anything I had seen before; so beautiful and full of angular poignancy that everyone else stopped to watch as well.

She danced for all but clearly somehow just for her husband, expressing so much, so eloquently, that all we could do was applaud. I felt so proud of my lovely friend.

At the end she got up from her final position curled at Kasver's feet and came to me, pulling first me and then Helana and all the priestesses to join her in one of our favourite temple dances, that had everyone clapping to the rhythm.

Finally other guests got up and joined in as well, including some of the men. Sarita pulled on Kasver to stand up but he drew her down into his embrace instead, to enjoy watching all of us dancing for them from the vantage of his couch.

As the evening wore on the mass of guests broke into smaller groups and then some went to thank their hosts for a wonderful evening, before they took their leave.

More and more drifted off but there were quite a few who were staying at the mansion, including us priestesses.

Aella and Helana were at the centre of a group of young Zoroastrians whilst Carmel and Nereyen were amongst a few guests that were mixing with the remaining musicians.

Arianne and I found ourselves in lively conversation with Kasver, Sarita and a Roman officer of the garrison, called Marcellus. Fine drinks and exotic sweetmeats were laid around, which we were enjoying, draping ourselves on the couches as though we always did this.

Kasver asked Arianne about the work she did, and I was surprised at the enthusiastic interest he displayed in what she told him. It seemed that he had a great knowledge of these things already and was fascinated to hear a different side.

M.B. #24

Arianne wondered whether Sarita had told Kasver any of her own store of tales, that I had told Arianne of.

Sarita said she hadn't but then, in answer to Kasver's repeated requests, she did relate one about the Goddess Durga and another of the God Vishnu.

It was Arianne's turn to be fascinated and then Marcellus joined in too. He had been based in Egypt before coming to Antioch and had been amazed at the ageless magnificence he had witnessed there.

Arianne knew much of Egypt's past and hearing of their ancient myths Sarita was entranced with the resonances to her own stories.

Osiris who conquered the whole world with his music and his goodness; Osiris the dusky skinned was rather like Vishnu himself or perhaps an incarnation of him.

Vishnu rode on the fabled bird Garuda; a swanlike eagle, whereas Osiris had the wonderful phoenix. Were these the same bird and they the same person?

Had they been real living people? They were both meant to periodically return. Was Zoroaster one such return? And what of Mithras too?

Then the talk turned to what the stars said? That there were different ages as the sun moved through the heavens. That one age that was now completing, that 'of the fiery ram', and one that was due to start: 'of the fishes'.

I had never experienced quite such a flow of conversation that seemed to have a life of its own, fuelled no doubt with beverages, but sweeping us magically through the night. The stars were all around, testifying to our truths and filling our spirits with their own glory.

Marcellus and Kasver had told of their own countries and lives, and Sarita and Arianne of their journeys, which were amazing to me; yet they all still wanted to know about me as well.

So, I told the tale of my escape from Magdala and they seemed really astonished at it, but to me it was just what had happened.

It was later than late when we noticed that Sarita had almost nodded off. In one final confidence before she and Kasver retired to their rooms, Kasver told us quietly that she was carrying their first child.

Sarita smiled languidly under her long dark lashes as we congratulated her, and Kasver too. "It is very early days yet, but she has moved beyond the sicknesses and we will be ready to announce it soon. For now, please keep it to yourselves, but this evening has been a kind of celebration of the coming event, and we are so glad to share it with you."

I hugged them both good night and Arianne and Marcellus did as well. The three of us left, walking over to the veranda edge, looking out into the dark countryside.

The night was old and familiar star patterns were arrayed across the sky.

Instinctively I looked to where the sun would soon be edging a pale light over the horizon, and sure enough the morning star was already bright in her glory.

Arianne and I looked at each other and Marcellus noticed it as well, as if for the first time.

"Venus," we told him and he seemed genuinely surprised or impressed. Probably the effect of being up all the night and talking, but there she shone as if to confirm that everything we talked of was still in play. Still happening now, just as immediate as the armies of Rome themselves.

"I have seen her in the evening sky," he said, "and now being born into the morning light, as if in the myth itself. Unblemished beauty" he said and I noticed, not for the first time, that he looked very handsome too.

He put an arm around each of our shoulders and pulled us gently to him, one on either side. Neither of us resisted but we nestled against him, gazing silently into the soft face of the day's dawning light.

For long minutes we stayed that way and then we moved over again to settle on a couch. He was almost asleep himself and Arianne and I laid him down and covered him with his own cloak and another curtain drape. He closed his eyes and slept.

We went back to our rooms. I shared with Aella and Helena, but neither were there.

I leant for a long while at the open window, listening to the sounds of the new day stirring.

My thoughts travelled around the events of the evening, thinking of all the people we had met, wondering if I would see them again soon, at the Spring festival perhaps.

But the face that sprang most strongly to my thoughts was not Marcellus or any of the other guests. Rather it was the face of that young man we had passed on the way. Not from the first group of earnest young Jews, but the other one with the ready smile and the laughter in his face. My heart pulsed a bit stronger and I stared out at Venus silently seeking her sympathy and approval.

M.B. #25

The spring festival came and went.

We had heard that Marcellus probably wouldn't be able to be there because he was away with his legion. He only joined Antioch's city garrison for portions of the year. I confess I was a bit disappointed.

When it came to the springtime rites Apolinus, which was the name of the autumn 'Adonis' who B'el had 'included' in my 'acceptance ritual', singled me out because of the unfinished business between us.

In some ways he was the last person I had wanted to be with. He and dozens of others had issued from a low dark tent representing the underworld, set up on our festive ground.

All dressed in short white tunics, each of this troupe of young men started hunting out the partner they wanted from the large throng that was processing around the tent in a loosely winding dance.

Spring had come and Apolinus was leading it out, and with a rush of mixed feelings I realised he had noticed me and was seeking me through the dancing throng.

I expect I should have been grateful. He was not unpleasant to be with but I hoped that he didn't think that there was something special between us; there wasn't.

It was difficult because I found his expectations did make him behave arrogantly, though I knew he wasn't really. I had seen him when his guard was down, but now I had to look hard to find that new-born Adonis that had sought the Goddess's favour.

On the other hand my body did react to the attentions he was giving when he had got me away from the dance, beyond the bushes. Kissing me in an embrace with one arm, his other hand was moving over my front, giving firm caresses around my breasts, and lighter ones over them, pulling a reaction that I could not deny.

He continued to probe my body's softnesses, who's responses swept me along.

A knee between my legs, hitching up the front of my dress, and his hand sliding up my inner thigh, triggering a surge of sweetness that drew me to follow.

This didn't feel right though. I was a priestess, trained for the Goddess's service. Yet now apparently the plaything of this man's lust.

I called to Aphrodite to aid me; to give me the strength I needed.

Apolinus' hands were now grasping my buttocks and his urgent phallus was pressing against me, through his tunic.

His need was obvious and this helped me; to take control, to place this whole encounter upon Her altar.

My sweetness was Her gift. His desire for me must become for Her. I had the strength and the training, and I used it.

Firmly parrying Apolinus' advance I turned it back to him. My hands tracing the paths on his body that they had been taught. His back, his sides, his belly. Taking his one-pointed desire and spreading it through his body. Kissing his face, his lips, his eyelids. Bringing him to greater heights of unexpected possibilities.

Apolinus became pliant to my wishes, with a vulnerability pleasing to the Goddess, turning his overwhelming desire into some kind of offering… aching to be accepted.

And in my own time I took him within me and let him give all he had, my hand caressing the back of his neck as his body thrust and thrust into me, loosing a stream of sobs and fluid convulsions.

It was easier and more pleasant than I could have hoped. I did not feel used or abused but rather that my Goddess had been served.

The day was warm and we were at ease with ourselves, lying close on the couch within one of Aphrodite's shrines.

I remembered how B'el had sported with Apolinus at the autumn festival, with us neophytes watching from behind a drape.

Now I thought to do the same, and once he had rested, I resumed my attentions. Slowly and carefully bringing him to an ecstasy again and managing to collect some of his semen in one of the cloths with Hecate's symbols on it.

Inwardly I rejoiced that this first assignment, the hardest, had been successfully accomplished.

The spring festivities were held all around the city, with many venues involved. There were competitive events where the young men strove against each other at running, throwing and wrestling, and another place where chariots were raced as well as horses without chariots, and of course the feasting and dancing spread throughout the town.

Apolinus was one of the most skilled wrestlers and he assumed that I would watch his assault on the championship, and though I was comfortable enough with him, his assumptions and expectations still rather grated on me.

I did not want to be paraded around as his personal trophy but needed to find a way of releasing myself from him. I was a priestess and not his trophy.

We saw a few of my other friends in our festive ground and went to join them. Helena was sitting with one of the young Zoroastrians we had met at Kasver and Sarita's party. She looked really pretty, like a true spring flower. She told me that Aella, her sister, had been claimed by Krippa.

Carrying on, leaving the festive ground we headed for the garrison barracks where the wrestling tournament was being held.

M.B. #26

Carmel was there already and I was glad to see her. Her young man was also a competitor but I knew she had an eye for Apolinus.

Apolinus went to join the preparations and left us together.

I watched one or two of the bouts but had no particular desire to stay for the whole event. Aella also joined us and Krippa with her. He started to explain some of the rules and techniques involved in the bouts. I left Carmel and Aella with him and slipped away.

When I saw Apolinus later in the day he was the wrestling 'champion', with Carmel on one arm and another girl on the other. He was clearly enjoying himself and that was fine by me.

The next day was when the Gods were taken through the streets of Antioch as large sculpted statues, pulled along on special wheeled platforms attended by hundreds of priests and priestesses.

Our temple joined with Aphrodite's town temple to prepare the Love Goddess' image and to be in her retinue as she was pulled around the streets. I didn't mind doing this, partly as it was a reason not to be expected to be with Apolinus.

It was a hot and dusty day and a long march. Eventually all the platforms were assembled in front of the foum steps of Zeus and Hera's temples ready for the party to begin afresh.

Performances in praise of respective Deities were sung and danced and it was whilst engaged in this that I noticed a dashingly dressed Roman officer watching us from the front of the crowd. It was Marcellus.

He smiled and for the first time in ages I felt self-conscious and a little silly to be doing what I was.

He had bought food and drink from one of the stalls that had been set around the outside of the square. When we had finished the formal rites he came over and asked me to join him.

So different from Apolinus, Marcellus hid any expectations he might have had and behaved in every way like a true gentleman.

There had been a battle many leagues to the east in which Marcellus' legion, the sixth Ferrata, had arrived to reinforce the Romans already engaged with the Parthian forces; which had broken off when men of the legion's 1st cohort had crashed into their flank.

Marcellus was refreshing company, invoking in me the presence of the greater world far better than any of these little ceremonies of the city and temples.

Carmel spotted us and arrived with Apolinus, who looked at me rather darkly. I greeted him formally, kissing him as the new wrestling champion which helped to soften his glare; and introduced him to Marcellus.

Marcellus congratulated him warmly too, which seemed a little strange to me; that a soldier come from the heat of battle would fete the play of a wrestling champion; and nor did Apolinus seem to quite grasp the importance of the battle with the Parthians either.

The party continued into the evening but Marcellus didn't stay as late as I would have wished. Torn, it seemed, between us and some un-named duty, he returned to his barracks; as I did to the temple. The night was beautiful, full of stars and I went up onto Adonis tower to watch them.

The full moon was riding high and majestic over the hills to the east but Venus had long gone below the western horizon.

I gazed up towards the stars but something in me felt troubled. A loss that I couldn't explain.

Nothing to do with Marcellus or Apolinus, but a grief that was my own.

All the beauty around couldn't quite touch me; disconnected from their singing in the silence of night; isolated from the familiar comfort that they gave me.

Two priestesses were doing their observations up there and I felt the need to get away, to be alone. So I turned to go back down the tower, a private acknowledgement of the tumult stirred up inside.

The flat roofs above the dormitories provided me with the place I needed… to think, to try to feel the source of my loss, my need to grieve,

My thoughts went somehow to my father and he was saying, "My Mary, what are you doing? What are you doing?" And I had no answer other than the pain in my heart and the lump in my throat.

I pulled in breaths to clear my chest that instead brought more undeniable grief into my throat.

And curled up in one corner of the roof, out of sight of anyone but the stars themselves, I cried soundlessly, tears streaming down my cheeks.

"Mother," I mouthed into my prayers, "I am so sorry; I am so sorry."

I didn't know what I was sorry for, except for all the pain I must have caused her, be causing her.

No, it was more, I was sorry to myself that I had lost, could be losing… everything.

I rocked back and forward on my heels, my arms clutched around my knees, crying for all the pain there was in the world, till eventually I was empty of everything and lay down on a pile of linen sacks we used to carry the washing.

And slept…

*

I awoke in the early light of morning, wondering for a few moments where I was, and why there was pain in my left side, until I started to remember my heart's ache of the night, before and lying down on these sacks.

The grief had gone now, and I remembered something of what it was, might have been… that the glory of the stars, the sky, the night, seemed to be saying that something great was happening, but I felt I wasn't a part of it, could never be worthy of reaching there.

This morning I vowed to redouble my efforts, and watching and recording the movements of the stars is one of the new duties I am to be learning.

First there is the background of the fixed wheel of stars that turn around the hearth-star in the north. Then there were the planets; the heavenly seats of certain Gods and Goddesses, together with the earth, moon and sun.

Of course, I knew something of the movements of our own Venus, how sometimes she was the evening star and sometimes the morning star. Her change from one to the other I had already witnessed without realising it.

Now I was to start being one of the recorders of the way all the planets came and went, sometimes combining with each other and sometimes not, in a wide dance of heavenly influences.

How these influences were lined up was of importance to more people than just the rich women of Antioch, planning their love affairs or the marriages of their children. Even the military generals took an interest, coming to B'el for monthly or even weekly reports.

When Astel had been working in the temple scribes from many places would come to consult with her. Arianne kept up the tradition and herself was preparing to make a journey to Egypt; a return visit to Alexandria and Heliopolis. I would miss her but was not allowed to go with her, there being too much training for me to undergo.

Of course there was still the ongoing business of being a temple courtesan, based on the reported liking of the great God Baal-Zeus to wander on earth in human form.

We priestesses were required be ready to treat any stranger as though he might be that God.

In reality this custom grew into a very profitable business for the temple, both as an income and as an influence, particularly with the soldiery of all descriptions and their officers.

If we harboured doubts about how we could cope with this aspect of the priestess's work we needn't have worried unduly. In practice we were introduced very carefully, but also in a way that brought more business to the temple.

Our time as novices at the festivals and our forays to the markets in the city had all been a part of keeping the profile and reputation of the temple fresh and desirable. Now the experienced priestesses made sure that we met with such guests that would suit us.

They did this with the help of the door guards, Gaius and Bocca, and in general it was a well-controlled process with little or almost no trouble. The incident with Aella had been an exception.

It seems that she learnt her lesson well though and now Aella had become one of the stalwarts of the shrines which I suppose did not entirely surprise me. Helena on the other hand preferred to tend them as little as possible and I was somewhere in between.

Apolinus still asked after me but I had managed to miss him so far; Carmel being still eager to take that burden from me for which I was grateful.

It was a situation that we priestesses were becoming well prepared for. The supplicants came, sometimes full of their pride and manhood, but we knew that they really needed someone who could touch more than just their flesh but who could recognise and understand their need inside.

Generally we could, and we tried as honestly as possible to enrich the lives of our visitors with the womanly gifts the Goddess had entrusted to us.

Then one day Marcellus came to the shrine and my world went into a spin.

He came on a day that I was serving the Goddess there and he asked for me. Maybe he already knew I would be there but I don't know how. I was nervous in a way that I'd never been till then.

He greeted me just as a friend would and we went and sat in one of the shrines and talked.

I tried to feel how to get where the need he carried must take us but it seemed to be complicated.

We talked about some of the same things we had at Sarita's party and particularly about Mithras. He went to the Mithras rites regularly and said he would have told me about them if he had been allowed.

Instead, we talked all around the subject as it was clearly important to him. Redeeming the world; a job he seemed keen to take on, within the embrace of Mithraism.

I moved over to him and he flinched as I touched his arm. I could feel a struggle going on inside him and tried to smooth it out, but something else was working against me. Friendly as he was, I think he was undergoing some private test which I couldn't help him with.

Eventually he left and all we had done was talk... but he seemed really pleased with this, and let me know that he would be back.

When he did things went very differently.

M.B. #28

When he came back to the shrines Marcellus was so passionate; completely unlike before. This time he swept me off my feet, literally; into an embrace that took my breath away. There was no room for applying my training but I didn't

46

want to either. I became a willing participant in the flood of some release; and when he left, I think we both must have been glowing.

It was another few days before he came back again. I was on tenterhooks every evening, and it was only the kindness of Bocca and Gaius that got me through, assuring me that I would not be assigned a different visitor.

It was then I first realised that the south western gatehouse was where Bocca lived, had his home. The large gates with their pillars of Adonis and Astarte were only used at festival time. The smaller door next to them led into the shrines' anteroom which was the entrance to Bocca's house as well. The wall next to his doorway had a large mural that was dominated by a raised relief portraying the Cow image of the Goddess Hathor, complete with the Sundisc between her horns.

The door to the outside was tended by either Gaius or Marius, who checked the visitors and took any weapons to look after for them. Then they passed on to Bocca and the priestess in charge, who received them together in front of Hathor.

The priestess' duty was to know how many and who would likely be needed to attend the shrines but when it came to the moment to decide for the visitor, she would defer to Bocca.

When he came next, Marcellus was more controlled but still a passionate and welcome lover; for such a short time it seemed to me, though we must have passed an hour together.

I wondered how things would go from here but then I didn't see or hear from him again for quite a few days.

My heart was in turmoil but I carried on all my duties, trying to let nothing show how much I was affected, but I did go out earlier than needed to the shrines, as much as anything to talk to Bocca; and Aella came with me too sometimes. Together we would press him to tell us his life story.

Then once again Marcellus called for me. Such a quick visit, full of ardour but something seemed to be on his mind that I couldn't reach; then nothing again for weeks.

I was obviously presuming much too much.

By then Aella and I had learned much about our tall handsome eunuch; how he had been born in a small village far to the south in Upper Egypt and how even in his youth he had wanted to serve the Goddess, whom he knew as Hathor. He went to offer his service at the the temple in Thebes, and it happened that the temple guardian, a huge old crocodile, had just died, which was to dramatically change Bocca's life forever.

The priests took his arrival as a sign, and in a feast of welcome Bocca became overcome with potent drink. When he awoke he discovered they had cut his testicles off of him.

Distraught beyond belief, he next discovered they had fed them to the new young crocodile, which was to be the temple guardian, and that Bocca was supposed to be linked forever to that service.

They feted him but it made no difference; he was just angry and inconsolable.

His new status did have certain rights however, and he used these to travel from temple to temple downstream and up again on the Nile, being received everywhere with some deference.

In those temple visits he learnt everything he could, especially about the Goddess Hathor, who in his heart he still served.

It was on one of those trips to Memphis that Bocca met mistess Astel, who was visiting Heliopolis and Memphis.

He was assigned to guard over her, and it was her kindness to him that once again changed his life.

For the first time, when being with her, he felt his status as a eunuch was almost a blessing.

She was to travel back north to Byblos, and Bocca asked the Hierophant at Heliopolis if he could travel with her, both to guard her on the journey and to serve the Goddess there; to learn more of their understanding of her as well.

To Bocca's surprise the High Priest gave his blessing, and so it was he came up north with Astel, first to Byblos and later here to Antioch.

And Fate struck again, for they arrived here soon after the death of another temple guardian, a man called Tariffe.

Tariffe was Mario's father who was married to a senior priestess and who worked alongside Gaius for many years.

He had a house in the street opposite the temple where Mario still lives, with a wife who is not a priestess but works with his mother as a seamstress.

Bocca was welcomed warmly and struck up an enduring friendship with Gaius, and for Bocca's part he felt he had come home, to be able to serve Hathor through all the priestesses.

Listening to his amazing story quite removed me from my own little trials and I sensed that it was having quite an impact on Aella as well.

In fact, she clearly seemed to be falling in love with Bocca, which was a marvel in itself.

Then Sarita's baby was born, quite soon after the autumn rites; a beautiful little girl. And as her old temple friends, we were there to help, together with the temple's most skilled midwife.

M.B. #29

Little Leila's birth was a time of celebrations for Sarita and Kasver's family and friends, and at one of these Marcellus re-appeared.

He acknowledged me but there was something remote in his greeting. He was a hardened soldier now, I could see that; with no further room in his life for temple games. He was a man with his own mission.

Yet, to my surprise, he did come again to the shrines, to talk mainly though he was attentive and affectionate as well.

I was confused and he seemed less sure of himself, trying to articulate something. An apology for his behaviour; or a regret; and a wish to be with me again, but not here, like this.

The temple had ways of allowing priestesses to meet with special lovers; not in the shrines but in the morning at the sacred grove; after the other priestesses had spent their time there.

Gaius or Bocca would let them in by the north-eastern gate; those blessed to greater intimacy with the Goddess and her handmaidens.

Marcellus became such a one for me, and I learnt it wasn't unusual.

Gaius had been the chosen companion to the High-priestess before B'el, but B'el did not take a permanent lover, preferring the younger Adonii of her choosing, but she was reasonably sympathetic to me.

Sometimes the man would indeed become a lifelong companion but more often these affairs just ran their course. Occasionally the pair would get married and the priestess would leave the temple, but not very often.

Sarita's case had been different because she was still a neophyte at the time.

Marcellus and my liaison could be special. I believed it was and gladly gave my heart to it, through all the months and twists and turns of its course.

He was hard to read though. Sometimes he was as passionate and attentive as though I were Aphrodite herself. At others he was distant and difficult to please.

Then suddenly one day I found a letter awaiting me in the grove.

He had returned to Rome, in advance of his legion. He was so sorry that it was like this, and was not what he wished, but he had no choice in the matter. He had been called and did not expect to return. He could only wish that I would be happy without him, but that he would always hold me dear to him.

That was it.

I was distraught for weeks, especially as there had been no warning that this might happen. We had been making plans for the coming summer, how we might escape the confines of the temple. Then just two days later he left that letter for me and was gone.

All the talk; all the loving; all the sharing; gone.

I didn't understand. I had no concept of how lost I could feel. No-one could help me.

I cried into my pillow for what seemed like hours, several nights in a row, with the refuge of sleep impossible to find.

Why? Why? Why?

Eventually I was able to get back to something like my normal life but the scar was always with me.

The Love business had pitfalls and I had barely begun.

I remembered what Granny-Beth had said about kindness and the need I would have for it, and wondered if that time was now?

During my affair with Marcellus, B'el was not only sympathetic but almost actively helpful.

She even wanted to coach me in certain methods of invoking the Goddess' presence and pleasure during lovemaking. Her interest wasn't easy for me to accept but neither was I able to deny her completely.

Thankfully she mainly satisfied herself with discovering what inquiries Marcellus made into the secrets of the Goddess temple and helping me by supplying both suitable answers to his lines of enquiry and probing questions in return about the Mithraic cult.

She already knew most of what I was able to discover of course, but I could now see how important it was for her that this game of power and influence was played out to the full.

The cult of Mithras was a growing influence in the Roman army, and as such was a real rival to Astarte's temple, which benefited considerably from the support of the military. How we might forge a partnership with a cult that would let women play no part was a tricky puzzle for our High Priestess.

Despite this apparent anti-female attitude some followers of Mithras had a fascination with our temple, part of which was certainly bound up with sex, even though it could be as much about denial as passion, like it had been with Marcellus. Then again, our knowledge of the heavens and the movements of the stars was second to none, which appeared to be the added attraction.

The way that Mithraism excluded women from their mysteries reminded B'el most closely of the Jews, and of course it wasn't lost on B'el that that was a huge part of what led to me running away from Magdala.

Then Arianne returned from her extended visit to Egypt and B'el wanted to hear all about what was happening there and the details of her many meetings.

Arianne and I were sitting in the library sharing a pot of our favourite fresh mint tea to celebrate her return when B'el called us both to her inner sanctum. I was slightly surprised but really pleased to be worthy of including in these discussions.

B'el hugged Arianne warmly when we entered her apartment, pleased to have her priestess back; the one who was continuing Astel's vital role. She had obviously missed her a lot.

There followed B'el asking after the ardours of the journey and offering refreshments to Arianne as an important returning colleague, which I was glad to enjoy as well.

Arianne relayed the main points of her visits to Alexandria and Heliopolis and her longer stay at the temple of Isis where Astel had come from.

"And have they seen anything of the adoption of Mithraism into the Roman army?" asked B'el after a while, glancing across at me.

"Yes, it did come up," answered Arianne. "I think because of the echoes it brings of the invader Cyrus and the slaughtered bull of Apis."

"What do they think of this version of Mithraism then?"

"That it is more about the changing of the Age than anything else, with the sun's unstoppable procession through the heavens," answered Arianne, "and they asked me everything I knew about the cult when they realised I came from a region where Mithras' influence was part of ancient truth and customs.

I told them that I believed its resurgence to be because of King Antiochus of Commagene, the brilliant son of King Mithradates. Antiochus had sowed the seed in the Roman army through his association with Pompey, whom he called the heir of Hercules and Alexander the Great; with himself being a son of Mithras. The possibility that legionaires could play their role in establishing the New Age of the Invincible Sun was sown, which they took back with them from that campaign.

Then I related how, strangely, the seed really seemed to have sprouted most strongly when Crassus tried to repeat Pompey's feat but when everyone knew this was only for vain-glory and booty. He and his army were annihilated at Carrhae; the worst defeat of Rome since Hannibal's victory at Cannae and one that I believed reinforced the idea of needing to be true to Mithras' virtues to attain victory."

"Yes," said B'el, "that could well be; and tell me please, what did you find to be the prevailing thoughts in Egypt on the coming Age?"

"Many think that Osiris will return but no-one is agreed on how this will come about. Some others that I met think the Messiah of the Jews will come and unleash the power of the Tetragrammaton against the Romans, driving them away."

"Maybe the followers of Mithras would rally round such a Hero and lead him in triumph to Rome itself," said B'el.

"What do you know of the Tetragrammaton?" I asked. I had felt a small thrill run through me at the mention of it, the veiled power behind everything.

"It is what you Jews claim as the true name of your God Jehovah," answered B'el. "Your people are not the first to lay claim to the Great Word of Power that cannot be resisted. But if the Jews are the true heirs, then it surely must be time to bring it forth."

"Is it somehow contained in the Ark of the Covenant then?" I asked.

"Maybe so, but it seems that a Messiah is needed to wield it. But tell me Arianne, what do our sisters of the temple of Isis have to say?"

"They say She is come indeed and brings her Lord with her," answered Arianne and again I felt the thrill that reached to the heart of me.

"What was the precise utterance?" asked B'el.

Arianne took out a small scroll from which she read, though I knew she would know it off by heart. "My holy presence will be in three, for so is my will and love. The mother Divine is the first. Sister and consort is the second, and the priestess of Light is third. Yet this must be earned, even as my Lord will win His reign anew."

B'el's eyes were closed and yet her smile shone all the stronger. For a long few minutes she remained thus, and I also closed my eyes and seemed to see the figure of the Goddess Isis, as I had copied it many times on library scrolls, drawn against my eyelids with a fine golden light.

"This is good, very good," said B'el at last. "You have done very well, Arianne. Astel would be proud of you also. Let us go now and eat with all our sisters and let them know of your return. We shall talk more of this tomorrow."

When we were next alone, I got to ask Arianne more about her travels.

Some of the places she described sounded marvellous and incredible and I wondered if I would see them one day.

Of all the people she had met she told how she had been most impressed by one man, surprisingly, for he had been quiet in much of the discussions. He was quite an elderly man called Philo, a Jew living in Alexandria.

He had been a friend of Astel's before she had come to Antioch and had influenced many of our former priestess' views. Arianne had taken a small wooden box to him, as Astel had wished. It contained a letter and an intricately worked amulet that Astel had had made to her own design.

Philo had received Arianne kindly and listened to the discussions that her enquiries had sparked amongst his circle of friends, but he didn't say much himself.

Arianne remembered that this group had been proclaiming that a Messiah could be for more than just the Jewish people, but could not say quite how this would come about. Philo had clearly enjoyed the lively debate but would not be drawn to enter in, though many urged him to.

It was a subject that Arianne wanted to be able to ask him about as well, and before she left Alexandria she did get her chance.

He smiled at her and his brown eyes sparkled as they took in Arianne's earnest gaze.

"When your need is deeply felt, then what you want will be drawn to you; such is the law; but no one can say exactly how or when this will happen.

Therefore, our task is to uncover our heart's truest desire and hold onto that alone, not becoming confused with all the other seemingly important things.

Do you think you can do that?"

"I must try at least," Arianne had answered.

M.B. #31

"So what did you really want to ask me?" Philo had asked.

Arianne had tried to frame that one question from her heart but couldn't find the words that fitted the feeling buried within her, so she said nothing for long seconds whilst she struggled with herself.

Philo had smiled again. "You will find your answer even though it may not come in words, because I know you are being true to yourself. That is all that counts in the end. Hold out for the key that opens everything for you."

"That's what remains with me strongest, Mary. Even though so many greater things happened, especially at the temple of Isis, it is this that somehow stayed with me… that I shall find the answers that I really want and need, if I can clear the space in myself, in my life, to receive them."

I was excited about the news that Arianne brought and it was the first time that I could truly say that I no longer felt regrets about Marcellus, or wished that things had worked out differently.

There were always the ongoing labours of our life in the temple to temper my enthusiasm though. Things had got easier for me certainly, but we still had to take our turn in the kitchens and with the washing, and in the gardens and the cosmetic and clothing industries, and in the shrines too.

And of course, there were still our visits into the city.

From amongst my friends Helena, or Helen as she was to me, was the one that had got involved with trading in the city. More specifically she worked within the cloth and clothing trade that the temple had a big share in.

Her Zoroastrian friend, Liemonedes, was also in the trade, bringing in silks and spices from the furthest east. Such connections were invaluable to the temple and won Helen greater freedom than others might enjoy.

Aella on the other hand, had gained a pre-eminence in the shrines and she jealously guarded her status as the favourite amongst Aphrodite's maidens.

Cara, as I called Carmel, was involved in everything as ever. Always knowing what was going on. She was being groomed I think to be a temple administrator.

We all still got together when we could, after the morning rite or at an evening meal, but it was with Helen that I spent a few weeks working as springtime arrived anew, for my workload in the library had lessened with Arianne's return.

We went out quite frequently and especially as Sarita was with child again and always welcomed our visits.

I was over the novelty of being about in the great city and was rather shocked at what it was starting to reveal. Now that I wasn't totally involved in looking for my Adonis in every young man we saw.

The poverty and misery of many of Antioch's citizens was plain to see, together with so much disease that everyone tried to be push out of view, as though that cured it.

Leprosy was one of the worst burdens we faced and also the number of people possessed by evil spirits. They were all declared 'unclean' and were avoided.

One day Helen and I were going through the suburbs withthe senior priestess Selene, looking for the house of a new dress designer that Liemonedes wanted us to use. The partnership with Helen's businessman was flourishing.

We used routes that we knew to be safe and relatively pleasant, but we hadn't been this way for a little while and a new building program was underway, forcing us to detour around it.

These streets were much less familiar and well appointed. Rubbish abounded and the smell from the open ditches was awful. In fact, we had just decided that we were going to turn back when this wild, unkempt looking young woman started calling out and hobbling towards us.

I could see that she was an 'unclean' and it soon became clear that she was a 'possessed', with many self-inflicted cuts and bruises on her upper arms and shoulders.

As we turned and backed away, she shouted obscenities at us and even called out our names. This wasn't altogether unusual as the evil spirits could know things others wouldn't but something made me turn back towards her.

Did she know me? Did I know her? I couldn't decide, but hands were pulling me away and the woman, whoever she was, had picked up a fair sized stone and thrown it at us, though it landed quite wide.

We escaped and found a better route to get to where we were going, but I was haunted by what had happened.

The woman's voice had at one moment been full of taunting hatred, but in the next it called with heart-rending pleading, and this had cut me to the quick. I even thought I should have recognised her and this impression wouldn't leave me.

Then, with a kind of horror, I remembered who she was; a girl named Rassilda who was a friend to one of the young men who had been in the wrestling tournament at last Spring Festival.

Realising this made it all become so much more personal.

I would look out for her whenever we went out and about the city and couldn't help noticing all the other 'outcasts' on the edge of society. There didn't seem to be anything that could be done though, except strive to keep ourselves out of the mess.

A mess where crime thrived and only the strong arm of the Roman army prevailed to keep the rest of us secure.

"Why should it be this way?" I asked B'el one day, and she replied that it was because proper worship of the Gods was not observed, and therefore the people had to endure the results that were visited on them.

'Meanwhile,' I thought to myself cynically, 'our duty to the Gods seems to be to align ourselves with those who hold the power. And to gauge where that power and wealth was going next.

It wasn't that I was disillusioned with temple life, but I was able to observe how B'el had developed a multi-facetted empire within the greater Roman world.

An empire that also involved many of the wealthy women of the city, and I couldn't help admiring her for her skilful use of her powers to achieve this.

But more and more I also wondered how such a large portion of the population could just be discarded and, because of Rassilda, this troubled me like a personal wound. I couldn't help but remember again what Granny Beth had said about finding the need for kindness, and this need seemed to be growing ever closer and stronger.

It was later that summer when I had my next real chance to put this question again to B'el.

She and Arianne were up on Adonis Tower with Philippa and myself. It was well past midnight on a clear and warm night, with the stars spread in amazing glory across the whole sky.

The late waning moon had not yet risen but we had been there to observe the great constellation of the Hunter rise into the sky, followed by the special star of our lady.

"That is the sign of our Adonis, and Osiris too" said B'el "being raised up by the light of the Heavenly virgin and priestess."

It was so calm; so inspiring, I felt I could almost fly up into the heavens and join in the celestial singing of glories to the Most High there.

"It is truly beautiful," I said.

"However many nights we spend up here, recording the movements, it never ceases to impress anew. Yet…" I hesitated, not wanting to break the spell it had cast on me "yet, how is it that our world is allowed to teem with disease and evil? This glory above is such a contrast to what we saw today, down by the river. I found it hard not to try to do something to help the poor stricken creatures we came across there."

"There is nothing that you could have done, you know that," said B'el, looking back to the horizon where the yellow crescent of the old moon had just lifted itself into the night sky. She gazed at it for a few moments and then seemed to make a decision; "but I tell you what we shall do. Tomorrow we shall consult the Goddess herself, and you can ask the questions, Magdalene. Arianne; you and Magdalene should meet me in the back of Temple Court at midnight tomorrow and come prepared to record our meeting. You, Magdalene, come clothed in your best white robes and bring your silver priestess knife. And three pertinent questions."

*

M.B. #32

It was dark when Arianne and I arrived in Temple Court, and cloudy, leaving only a smattering of stars to see reflected in the wide, pillar-lined pool we crossed behind.

A small door was tucked into the furthest wall that we knew led down to a subterranean hall but I had never been there. Arianne said that it was the entrance to our temple of Hecate and her sister Queen of the Underworld.

B'el was waiting by the doorway, tall and severe in the lantern light, dressed in her gold-trimmed robes of green and black. She reached into an alcove and brought out three torches which she proceeded to light from the lantern, giving one to each of us.

She looked me up and down as if to make sure I had made proper effort to dress for the occasion. Arianne had helped me and B'el nodded in satisfaction.

Arianne was dressed in darker robes and carried a stylus and clay tablet to write upon. B'el nodded again and we turned, following her through the door into a passage.

At the end there was another door which B'el opened with a heavy key. Beyond were stairs leading down into the blackness of earth and rock.

B'el paused at the top and turned to me. "We are going down to Hecate's Temple," she said. "When we get there, I shall explain what we are going to do and you must follow my instructions carefully. Ask if you are not clear on any point. It will not be difficult and you need have nothing to fear as long as you do exactly as I say."

Nevertheless, a shudder of fear went through me as we started descending down and away from the stars and lights of our normal life. The darkness closing over and behind us was an oppressive weight but the need to concentrate on where I was going was just enough to keep the fear at bay.

I followed in our High Priestess' huge shadow, my heart pounding in my chest.

Stopping at last at the entrance of a dark cavern, B'el turned and explained clearly to us; what she would do, and what she expected us to do. I nodded that I understood and heard Arianne's whispered answer that she did too.

"Speak clearly Magdalene," said B'el. "Let me hear you say 'you will'".

"I… w..ill" I answered, finding that my throat was dry and my voice cracked. I understood now why B'el had asked me. I swallowed, cleared my throat and spoke out clearly "I WILL," and B'el held up her hand.

We moved out into the underground hall and our torches spread a guttering light that barely reached the edges.

A carven high-backed chair on a wide stone plinth drew the eye immediately. The circular outline of the plinth was interlocked with two other circles made from small white stones. All three circles were inside the red painted figure of a square which itself had a circle scraped around outside it, almost reaching out to the rock-hewn temple walls.

We walked once around the outer circle, our torches lighting the crudely painted symbols and figures that adorned the rough-cut walls as we passed. Brief glimpses of naked bodies interspersed with images of the moon in her phases and then B'el had crossed to the plinth to place her torch in a holder at its front before taking to the throne. She signalled us to fix our torches and take our places too.

I put mine into a torch-ring to one side of the throne chair and went and stood in the left-hand circle facing straight at B'el, and Arianne did the same in her circle.

B'el's eyes were closed and she appeared to be swaying slightly from side to side.

I glanced around into the shadows where the painted figures danced disconcertingly in the flickering light, strangely lifelike as though coming through the walls.

B'el had started to hum, lightly at first and then with growing strength. The time had come… and when she opened her eyes and looked directly at me, and then Arianne, we knew this was the signal for us to join in…

My throat started to vibrate scratchily, till something released in my chest allowing the out-breathing hum to vibrate out of me and around the cavern, joining with those of the others, growing and growing into a crescendo of sound… an encompassing wave, washing around and back at us form off the temple walls where the moons shimmered between the dancing figures.

I was starting to feel a little dizzy and then B'el raised both her arms and we fell silent.

Her eyes were closed but her voice was vibrant when she strongly spoke out the name of the Goddess we were there for: **"Hecate"**

I had drawn out my priestess' silver knife and raised it in the air and "HECATE" I called in a loud clear voice, which Arianne completed to the rhythm of our breathing. "*Hecate.*" she intoned with skin prickling finality.

"Come to us Great Goddess." B'el invoked, quieter now, but with intensity. I saw her eyes were still closed. "Come to me thrice great Queen, come to me."

Whether a breeze wafted through from the doorway or what it was I don't know, but the torches felt something that made their light gutter and shake.

I thought I felt something like a cool wave stroke across my shoulders but it could have been my imagination. My attention had slipped for a moment from B'el, but now it struck me how incredibly pale she had become.

Her face had changed as if to become a living marble statue of Hecate herself, with her white face framed with jet black braided hair, caught into three coils on her head, revealing a beauty… strikingly severe.

B'el had said that when Hecate came to her that I was to point the knife at her breast and ask the Goddess whichever of my three questions that came first from my heart-soul to ask.

She had said that I would know the moment… and I did. The hairs were sticking up on the back of my neck as I stretched the knife directly out in front of me and opened my mouth to speak.

"Great Goddess," I started. "Why is the world overburdened with so much suffering, and how can it be relieved?"

B'el's eyes opened but only the whites were visible, giving her face an over-powering sense of otherness that sent tingles of awe through me.

"That is two questions, young witch," came the quiet response, and I sensed Arianne starting to write on her tablet. She only had to write the responses.

"But I shall answer them. The suffering, disease and all the rest comes from you people yourselves, for you have been given this power to create what you wish to have. Yet you have no understanding of the consequences. Thus, you err."

57

"To cease from suffering you will need to understand the way to bring your desires back to where the Divine is waiting for you, and the Divine itself comes to teach you that. When you are truly able to listen then your sufferings will leave of their own accord." A palpable silence followed. "What is your final question then?"

I felt stunned by her answers and cast around to find the right words for my final question, reminded in that moment of Arianne's story of Philo in Egypt.

"When will your real Lord Adonis, the Messiah come to us?" I blurted in my customary muddle when I tried to put everything into one thought or sentence.

The cavern was utterly quiet and then I heard what sounded like an unearthly laughter reverberating all around that was more unnerving than anything that had come before.

I couldn't tell whether it was loud or soft or where it came from; it might even have been in my own head.

Not directly menacing, yet some element of it did appear to be coming from Hecate-B'el and the laughter subsided when she spoke; her words thudding into my head:

"What makes you think that is not We that are waiting for Him to come to Us? We all get our chances;" she said, and then in a low hiss that seemed aimed directly at my breast, as my knife was at hers. " And you need to make the most of yours."

I knew she had gone for B'el's head had slumped to one side against her shoulder.

Arianne was looking at me "What?" she asked, and I knew she had missed the last whispered utterance.

"I will tell you after," I said as I had moved forward to check on B'el. Some colour had already come back into her face and she was opening her eyes.

"I need to write it now," said Arianne.

"She said 'you need to make the most of yours' or rather 'and you need to make the most of yours'. That was all."

"Are you sure," whispered Arianne. "Yes, I am sure," I replied and nearly found myself laughing. Somehow the whole tension was breaking and a kind of relief was flooding through me.

B'el looked at us and I could see she was completely drained. Arianne and I took the torches, and quietly we helped B'el to leave and lock the temple. We had been blessed I thought, but didn't understand how or why.

M.B. #33

By the time we got B'el back to her apartments she had already recovered considerably. She wanted us to go over everything that had been said; several times, till she had every detail fixed in her mind.

Then she took some food from the altar of one of her personal shrines and gave it to us. "Eat this now, and rest awhile," she said, "and then if you want, we can go up to see the dawn from Adonis tower. Actually, I think it right that we should go."

When we climbed the spiral stone staircase it was so different from the steps down to Hecate's cavern, going out instead onto the starlit platform. Philippa was there and the moon had already risen over the horizon and climbed part way up into the sky. It was more slender and yet whiter than when we had seen it the night before, riding higher, between some remnant clouds.

But what made me start as I moved across to one of the alabaster horns was how two bright planets were riding there too. Venus shone well below the moon and Jupiter was high above her in the arch of the sky.

"This is the time," B'el was saying. "This is the time for us."

Somewhere over the other side of the town a cock crowed and I could see the light was growing in the east, turning the sky pink and then pale blue where it reached up towards the morning star, touching me as well with the promise of it's coming.

As we stayed and watched, near and far more signs of life started to join in; birdsong greeting the new day, the odd dog barking out in the town and priestesses readying the temple's wares to take to market.

At last, the sun poked its golden red rim above the distant hills and B'el indicated that it was time for us to attend the morning rite, and tired but exhilarated I climbed back down the Tower to join the throng of gathering priestesses in Tower Court.

Thankfully I didn't have to attend my allotted duties for the day, as B'el asked Philippa to find a replacement for my shift in the washrooms that morning.

Later on I did go to the gardens where I was due to be gathering herbs, and heard the news that there had been another break-in from the southern slopes; and this time one of our goats had been stolen.

'Uncleans' apparently had been seen around the lower end of the valley and it was generally thought they were responsible or some criminal elements that used them for cover.

The city guard had been called but there was little or nothing they could do; only suggesting that we build a better wall on our southern boundary.

This sparked a train of ideas that echoed what I thought the Goddess might have meant, and I resolved to speak of it to B'el at the time of the new moon in a few days time.

Down at the bottom of the southern slopes were the graves of former priestesses and a shrine here and there to one or other Goddess. The sacred ground was bounded by a small stream thickly overgrown with thorns and bushes and it was on the other side of this that a small shrine to Hecate had been made, over where a narrow crevice cut into the ground. It was quite near here that the break-ins seemed to be happening.

I asked B'el if we could enlarge the shrine to Hecate and at the same time help reinforce our boundary. But most of all I asked her if by doing this we could find a way to take offerings to the Goddess there and leave them for the wretched 'uncleans', giving them some other chance than that of stealing for their needs.

I could see B'el didn't like the idea much but she also was freshly affected by the encounter in Hecate's temple, which had left a puzzle in the Goddess's answer to the last question which B'el admitted that she had not fully understood. Whether or not the Goddesses were awaiting the same changes as we were hoping for, it was clear to me I had to make the most of my own situation.

B'el gave limited approval for my scheme as long as other duties were not affected; but I should have to find the funds myself to make it work.

I threw myself into my project, first of all just spending time down at Hecate's cemetery shrine, seeing and thinking about what could be done.

Then Cara came down with me for she was worried by my being there alone in the evening. Together we were able to move small rocks to clear a bit of ground in front of the shrine, piling them instead across the broken-down stretch of wall.

"You are mad," she said. "What good can come of this?"

"Well, if we make a proper shrine and leave some of our cast off food and clothes and things, maybe the 'uncleans' will be able to take them, rather than have to steal," I replied. "At least it is worth trying, Cara. I cannot stand seeing the misery and doing nothing. B'el has given her permission, if not her blessing. Do you know of anyone who could help us build a wall around this area?

"Maybe," she said and was better than her word. There were a couple of half-grown boys she knew who came and helped. They were a bit wild but actually proved more useful than I first thought. They didn't do much themselves but they got the message out to the 'uncleans' that someone was trying to help them. In the end it was the 'uncleans themselves that did most of the enlarging of the shrine, working in the night and guarding what they had done.

M.B. #34

We took left-overs from the kitchens down there as planned, and other materials as well. Things got better and better. To my surprise some priestesses got involved of their own accord, especially a few of our 'retired' sisters who saw the southern slopes as their special domain.

They supervised the building of a buffer zone we called the 'middle area' and took responsibility for taking some of the 'offerings' there; deciding which should go to the shrine and which to the goats.

Once curiosity and sympathy had been aroused the scheme pretty much ran itself and by winter time the new arrangements were in place and working.

The rebuilt shrine had three parts: outer, middle and inner.

The 'inner' was Hecate's shrine proper, still over the crevice in the rocks but increased in size. It had two outlooks, one towards our temple and the other out over the rough land outside our walls which was part of the 'outer' area.

The 'middle' wall joined the shrine proper from our side to the outer and it was here that Hecate's offerings were placed, in small openings in the now higher wall that could be reached from the other side.

The 'outer' area had a partial boundary wall but with some places built in where people could take shade and shelter.

And of course, the openings through which the offerings were received. Much of it done by the 'uncleans' themselves. Even B'el was surprised and reasonably satisfied with the results.

It had taken food and kindness but also a lot of goodwill and effort. I was really impressed because after the initial impetus from me most of it had been taken on by others. Cara was the true star but she wouldn't take any of the credit. She put it down to the older sisters wanting to take care of 'where they were going'.

I looked at her, trying to see if she was joking and I think she was. We laughed anyway.

For myself I was spurred on by the activity on our southern slopes to see if there were other places in Antioch that the same could be done. This wasn't quite so easy as I had to find new partners wanting to help but I did have some success.

The largest area where the 'uncleans' gathered was outside of the city walls to the west, down the river. They were left to scavenge on the town's rubbish dumps that were cited out that way or else starve or die of any number of causes.

The biggest source of unused foods was the market, particularly on Fridays, because much of market food that went past Friday was likely to be thrown away.

And I found my supporter in Sarita's Kasver.

His normal worries in this area were dealing with the criminal gangs that would break into his warehouses, given the chance. He had been forced to get one of the gangs to protect his businesses from the others and give them a share of the profits in the process.

When Sarita told him what we wanted, he agreed that we could use one of his ox carts, together with a driver, to transport what we wanted down to the 'uncleans'.

The City guards even said they would provide an escort to keep an eye on things in the encampment.

All we had to do was get the left-over goods from the traders and get them onto the cart; and off at the other end.

Cara and myself managed it on the first week, with help from the ox driver, and afterwards we travelled back to Sarita's house to celebrate. We even thought we had been able to get a bit more from the traders than they would have normally rid themselves of.

The next week we were loading up again when one of our 'customers' from Aphrodite's shrines got involved. He didn't like the idea of us priestesses going to that encampment alone and so he came along as well. Then he arranged that he and a couple of his friends would take it in turns in doing the loading and unloading instead.

They might need payment of a pleasanter kind but I knew someone who could help. Aella particularly liked one the three.

What we hadn't known was how the distribution of the goods we brought would be dealt with by the 'uncleans' themselves. As it turned out it wasn't too hard, for several women amongst them seemed to be controlling the supplies and soon we were able to make our weekly arrangements with them.

B'el however thought I was spending too much time with this 'hopeless work' though I assured her it was not taking me from my other duties.

"It is about control," she said; "that is what makes the difference, not all this giving away of rubbish."

"Food" I said, "it's not rubbish; and it only takes a little kindness from many people to make a huge difference. It is not my efforts at all."

"Magdalene, I am serious," replied B'el. "It is in greater control that the answer lies. Isis brought prosperity to Egypt because of Her law giving.

Isis was even able to bring Osiris back to life because she had such control of power. She is your true model, or should be.

Look at your Moses, he had control of such great power that the Red Sea parted for him; never mind the Egyptian priests bowing down to him. Isn't that what your Jewish priests say?" she paused, letting her words sink fully in.

"That is what makes the difference and that is where you should be putting your efforts."

M.B. #35

It was difficult to argue with B'el and I had to do as I was commanded but I was particularly glad the projects were now running on their own.

Though I still hadn't seen Rassilda I heard from someone that she had been chased right away from the city; which was often the fate of the 'possessed' when their spirits were violent in nature.

I did get down to studying with Arianne in the library again. I thought that if the Goddess Isis was spreading her influence in some special way, then I should try to understand Her more, to be able to recognise this happening.

Arianne had brought back with her some of the works of Hermes-Thoth, which she was studying and translating… and she shared her understanding of these with me.

"Holy is God, the Progenitor of all things, the One who is before the First Beginning…"

I was excited at what we found because it struck such a chord in my heart.

Here was an exposition on the Most High God that was both the God of my childhood and of my own people. Yet from another people. The same feeling of simple, certain Truth.

"Holy art Thou, who by Thy Word hast established all things."

Could this Word be the same as God's Name that cannot be spoken by mouth I wondered?

And there amongst these writings Isis and her Lord Osiris played major roles in establishing civilisation, including *"devising the training of an inspired priesthood to nurture men's souls with understanding and their bodies with healing arts when they might fall sick"*.

"Wow," I thought, "that's fantastic. How I wish I could have studied with them." Yet here were Arianne and I trying to follow in their footsteps; and the work with the 'uncleans' seemed to fit. If only I could get to know how Isis used her healing arts. Maybe B'el was right after all.

Thinking of Isis, Goddess, Priestess and Queen of Egypt led my thoughts down other paths that I had heard told of as a child. How the Queen of Sheba had been a queen of great knowledge and understanding, from the furthest part of Isis's realm, who had visited the Great King Solomon and studied from him the ways of the Living God. The same tradition, I was thinking now, as Isis and Osiris had brought, and Moses and Hermes-Thoth too.

Yes, and Solomon had been the successor and possessor of these great powers. He was able to control the spirits and even reputedly had healed the Queen of Sheba of her afflictions.

Enlightened Jewish masters, as the successors of Solomon, should be carrying forward these abilities into our time. What were they doing with what they had inherited?

The inspiration of my studies gave me an energy that I was able to channel into other work, and especially with the 'uncleans' at our southern boundary and at the river encampment.

I no longer felt so threatened by them. Somehow even reading of the healing powers of old had given me a certain confidence that I would be protected.

These were some of my happiest days: my heart felt as light as a feather.

M.B. #36

My travels around the city often took me through the Jewish quarter and though I saw no great signs of enlightenment I did again see the man who caught my eye on that first visit to Sarita's; who had made my young heart beat the faster.

Then one day as I was crossing by the same area I saw him again, whom I now knew was a young lawyer called Thomas. He was engaged in debate with another man in the forecourt of the synagogue which was raised a little above the road.

There was a small throng listening to the arguments and attracted mostly by the chance to see Thomas again I joined the crowd to listen from the back.

"What I would wish, is to understand how and why these things are done." Thomas was saying, "because…" he held up his hand to stop the other's instant reply, "because in *understanding*, the best way forward can be achieved. Otherwise, it is just blind blundering along."

"You should not concern yourself with why," the other man replied. "Only with the how? That the Great Magus *can* control the spirits is all that matters. And that he will teach us this power also."

"So, you say that he can fly because of this control he has over spirits of the air?" asked Thomas.

"I have seen it with my own eyes. The most incredible thing I ever saw," answered the other.

"Undoubtedly," Thomas was saying, as my own thoughts recovered from the shock, "yet I cannot see where it all leads, or how it makes him or you a better person for it. To work on some arcane formulation of power is not for me. Besides I have already found the teacher I have been looking for. I wish you well but I have no desire to come and meet your Simon Magus."

Who was this that could teach one to control the spirits? I could see a use for it, with so many 'possessed' people like Rassilda affected by them, even if Thomas couldn't.

I was torn at which way to go; attracted by Thomas and the way he spoke on the one hand, but by the possibility of using the powers that the Magus seemed to promise on the other. I stood transfixed in thought.

Before I realised it Thomas and his friends had gone away down the road and the other's group was starting off in the direction I had been going minutes before.

I couldn't let the opportunity pass by completely and with a few quick steps I succeeded in catching up with them.

"Can I ask you about the things your friend was discussing back there," I said as I walked beside the last in their group.

He looked sideways at me, 'probably a Jew' I thought and he seemed surprised at my bold approach. "You mean Saul? What about him? Saul," he called, "there is a woman here wanting to know about the Magus".

The five of them all stopped and turned to see who had accosted them and the one called Saul tool a few paces back towards me.

"What do you wish to know, *priestess*?" He seemed to sneer the last word at me.

I could see no point in beating around the bush. "I wondered whether the Magus would teach the powers you spoke of to a woman?"

Saul studied me with some disdain and answered with a curl of his lip, "Women are important to him. All can receive his mission… except the harlot-priestesses who turned against his Helena. She who is the Bride of the

Chosen. You witches in your green cloaks would be well advised to stay away when he shows his power tomorrow."

Too late I realised how much a priestess of Astarte was not welcome and I hastily made my excuses and went back along the way to the synagogue; there was no one left around there; Thomas and his friends were long gone.

I stopped for a minute, wondering what I should do. I felt alone and rather stupid, no longer wanting to go on to Sarita's because of the chance of meeting that same group further on.

I looked into the entrance of the Synagogue wanting desperately to go inside but I felt even this was denied to me. A lump came in my throat and I fought back tears that I didn't know the origin of. Had my God rejected me or was it I that had deserted Him.

My heart called out a prayer of feelings without words.

Reluctantly I turned my back on the Jewish temple and made my way back to the one I lived in. I would have to drop off the package I had been taking, another day.

Tomorrow. Tomorrow I would go again. Tomorrow I would go and see what this Magus could do as well I decided.

Helen was not surprised or bothered that I had been unable to take the package because of an unexpected disturbance en route, saying that if I could do it early the next day that would be perfect.

I didn't have other duties till my kitchen shift in the evening so I could make my own arrangements.

Perhaps it was foolhardiness but I thought my determination to follow through the investigation into Simon's powers was worthy perseverance; not to be put off by Saul's ill-informed prejudice.

I would go and see and hear the Magus for myself. Then… well, I would work that out later.

The journey to the dressmaker's house was uneventful. The day was full of promise; there were chickens pecking around outside her front door which I decided could be taken as a good omen. I delivered the new dress-pattern and the materials to make it from. It was still early in the day; time to stay for a drink and a chat.

Camina's house had a well-appointed wash room and I stopped on the way out, for a few minutes, to adjust my appearance. In the bottom of another bag, I carried an old brown-black travelling cloak that I had borrowed from Arianne. I swapped it for my own green one and also spent a couple of minutes adjusting my make-up and hair; greying the russet tresses that might escape from under the hood.

Stepping out into the street I was a slightly bent, older lady. Possibly a widow I decided.

The synagogue would be a good place to wait if I saw no other signs of the forthcoming 'display' on the way there, which I didn't.

There was a gnarled old olive tree just within the low perimeter wall that offered a bit of welcome shade. I sat down under it and waited.

It seemed like an age but no-one bothered me. One young man called me 'mother' and asked if I was all right. I nodded with a slightly vacant expression and told him I was waiting for my daughter. She would be here soon I assured him. He even brought me out a drink of water and I blessed him for it.

Eventually I came by the information I was waiting for. One of the group I had accosted yesterday went by in lively discussion with another young man. "Come and see, come and see. He will be in the fruit market square shortly before noon."

I knew where that was; we sometimes both bought and sold produce there.

M.B. #37

I got up and hobbled to the square, trying not to be too quick for an old lady and pushed my way into the middle of the crowd to watch what was going to happen, but not wanting to get too close,

There were pawn-broker shops set along one side of the square but scant evidence of the fruit market that happened on different days of the week. One or two of the Magus' followers could be seen talking to little knots of people; you could tell them by the black band they had around their heads, whether or not they wore a scarf underneath to keep the sun's rays at bay.

Others had formed a wide semicircle in front of us. The atmosphere was sharp with expectation. We waited, and the heat beat down on us. Still, we waited.

Suddenly a few of the Magus' followers that included Saul and some highly painted ladies came into the square from the other side, moving to the back of the semicircular area. Our flagging spirits lifted palpably.

One of the newcomers stepped forward to address the crowd, whilst the others scoured us to see what kind of people had come. The speaker introduced himself as David, 'Servant of the High God'.

I noticed Saul seemed to be particularly vigilant in searching through the faces of the crowd, as if this was his special job. I deflected his probing gazes and missed most of what the speaker was saying, except for gathering that he was telling us how lucky we were and that Simon the Magus was about to arrive.

For my part I scanned them back to see what kind of people they seemed to be; apart from the belligerent Saul. There was another, fresh-faced, young man that I noticed amongst the new arrivals who looked quite pleasant. He was smiling and joking with a friend which partially renewed my hopes about the Magus.

Then he was here. The Magus swept into the square with his Helena on his arm and a darkly clothed couple following behind. He wore a long, pale cloak over dark robes and a turban headdress that had a moonstone in a silver setting pinned to the front of it. He carried a short black staff that added to his commanding air, like a chieftain coming from the desert I thought.

His piercing eyes swept the audience as he stepped into the circle that had been formed. He raised his arms, staff held high and started…

"You think you are here to see a spectacle, but I am here to tell you that you are living in a spectacle."

"Yet the powers of this world wish to hide the truth from you; keep you oppressed. I have come to be the power of God amongst you…"

"What happens in this square is to be a glimpse for you behind the veil of the mysteries. I am the one to pull back the veil but the mysteries will be yours to live in…"

His darkly flashing eyes seemed as though they must be penetrating all disguise; surely, he could read our thoughts even.

"Once I have shown the way, you must make use of it."

"If you listen to me, I will show you the route to paradise. And if you listen to what my sons tell you, you will be able to go there.

For as I represent the will of the Almighty, so they will represent mine. And mine is the power, which you can share in."

The way he spoke it wasn't hard to imagine that he could do these things. What a huge difference it must make to have this power to direct events in the world. No wonder there were so many ready to listen. Now it seemed he was ready to offer proof of what he could do for us.

He had gestured to half a dozen or so young men that stood behind him, stepping aside to give the crowd a good look at the young men he spoke of. Saul was one and so was the other young man I had picked out before.

With a sweep of his staff the Magus gestured them forward.

Three came with a wide cloth and placed it on the ground in front of the circle.

"My friends, come and give your offerings to the Almighty and I shall transport them thence, even as you watch. Give to my sons as they come amongst you and you shall see the proof of what I am saying."

Seven of his helpers went through the crowd taking all that that we had to offer. They placed these on the cloth that had been laid on the ground even as the Magus explained further what would happen.

"As you give so what you have given will grow in paradise and as you follow me so your prize will await you there; but everything you hold back will hold you back."

Quite a lot of money and valuables had been collected on the rug. There were even a few coins and a small piece of cloth from me, that were taken with a bit of a shrug by one of the followers. 'Only a poor widow', I could almost hear him thinking.

The collecting went on for a while but once the Magus was satisfied, he waved his helpers back and traced a circle in the dust around the rug-like cloth with the tip of his staff. He was mumbling words and making gestures with his hands as he did so.

He then marked out another circle slightly away from the first, and four of the Magus' painted women came forward and stood at points around it, where he directed.

He took his position in the centre. Not anyone said a word but the build up in tension was palpable.

He started his incantations, quietly at first, but as he raised his volume a buzzing noise seemed to be growing in my ears. Others too were obviously feeling the same for they had put hands up to the sides of their heads.

The Magus' words grew loud but I could not make them out because of the buzzing. He held out his staff, pointing directly at the pile of offerings. Words became commands and the edges of the cloth raised up into the air. Commands that were repeated twice, thrice and the cloth was pulled up, as though by unseen hands, weighed down in the middle by the weight of offerings.

The Magus moved his staff, held in both hands, as if the great burden of the offerings were balanced on the end. Slowly he swept it around watched by an amazed crowd; and the bundle moved higher and higher as he drew it round the circle; twice the height of the tallest person there.

He brought the staff back towards the front, crying out as though with one last effort. A sharp 'crack' of noise accompanied a momentary appearance of a dark crack in the air and the cloth bundle and everything it contained disappeared.

The mesmerised crowd gasped as one.

"Thus, what you have given has been taken to paradise," he said. The buzzing had gone and his words were easy to hear, "and there they will multiply as now you witness", and another commanding word was followed by a small shower of coins falling out of mid-air to the circle on the ground where the cloth had been.

One or two people started forward to grab the miraculous coins but he waved them back. "These are to be given to the poor," he said, gesturing to one of his chosen. "Gather them up and take them to the synagogue, for the poor."

He moved back into his circle and once more addressed the whole crowd:

" You have the power in you, and I am the one to release it. Give me now your faith and I will show you how the power will raise you up also. Give me your faith; open yourselves and let me show you the power that is for my chosen ones. Give it now," he said. "Open yourselves to me".

He was moving his arms slowly out from his sides and up, his short black staff still in his hand. As round and up they swept, imperceptibly at first, he seemed to rise as well. Then with arms held high he had definitely risen a foot or so into the air.

Some of the followers had started to chant "Simon Magus, Simon Magus" and the crowd joined in. The cries grew and the Magus rose higher still and apparently lifted his Helena into the air as well, to float towards him.

"Thus, the beloved are raised up," he said and the crowd stretched out their arms towards him along with all those near him too. He permitted his close disciple to get a hold of him now and to the tumultuous applause and cries of the crowd his entourage carried him and Helena shoulder high from the square.

M.B. #38

As soon as I realised that the Magus was leaving, I started working my way through the crowd towards the same corner of the square that he was going. Those of us that were following struggled our way through a narrow arch that led into an alley beyond, that itself fed out to a larger street.

Turning left into this wider way I could see that the Magus was no longer held shoulder high but he and his entourage were some distance ahead. Then they turned left again into a residential area of larger houses, and were gone from my view.

When I reached the turn, I had become just one more person in a large straggling procession. I could see the house where the Magus was apparently staying, a short distance up that street.

As we got closer, he seemed to be giving some kind of audience in the entrance space in front of the house. Though I couldn't see the Magus what I could see was the aquiline profile of Saul searching through the crowd over the retaining wall.

With the press of people ahead of me I could see that it would be very difficult to get to the front, and with Saul scanning the people for undesirables I knew I would not get inside the house let alone to get to speak to the Magus himself. 'What should I do?'

My mind was in an excited state with thoughts flying this way and that like a weaver's bobbin… and as a pattern started to emerge it suddenly became clear what to I needed to do.

I turned back the way we had come.

The Magus had said that he was going to work through his 'sons' and we should learn from them. Well, there was one of those that I thought I could maybe get along with; the youthful seeming one.

He had also been the one that the Magus had told to pick up the 'magical' shower of coins and take them to the synagogue.

A new plan had formed fast in my brain. Much better that I should approach my task through the disciple of the Magus than the Magus himself, who it seemed had particular problems with Astarte's priestesses.

I had started to retrace my steps to the square when I realised there was a quicker way to the synagogue where I must try to meet the young disciple. Hopefully he really had gone there with the coins as instructed.

A long flight of steps led down from the main roadway to a street that led roughly in the direction of the synagogue. I rushed down the well-worn stones as fast as I could and onto a curving way, then crossed through a narrow connecting alley and into another main street.

Turning a corner I could see the synagogue, along ahead at the end of the road. I ran and walked and ran again. My thoughts flew ahead but my breath was labouring, so I slowed to a walk to let it recover. I would need to be clear headed and composed when I found the one I was looking for… if I found him.

It was the other side of the street that ran along beside the synagogue. I crossed quickly, aiming towards the front entrance past a side door that opened, just at the moment to throw me into the path of a man coming out.

To my great surprise I found myself being held from falling over by the Magus' apprentice I was seeking.

My thoughts were thrown into confusion by this sudden stroke of fortune; but I hadn't worked out yet what I would say.

"I'm sorry," he said, "I didn't see you at all. Are you alright?"

"Fine" I answered. "I'm sorry, it was my fault."

He looked at me and I at him. My hood had fallen back and I must have looked slightly strange. Not that he gave any sign of thinking that, rather the reverse; and I thought he was still as pleasant as my first impressions had suggested.

"Actually," I said, ready to plunge into the unknown again, "I was looking for you."

"Me?" he said, astonished. "Have we met before?"

"Not exactly," I answered, "but I was at the Fruit Market Square today to listen to Simon the Magus. I noticed you there as one of his close disciples and also that he sent you here with the coins."

"Oh. Yes." He looked at me again, obviously trying to gauge what I wanted. "Are you very poor?"

I laughed. "No; that is not why I sought after you." Perhaps my disguise as a poor youngish widow was lingering longer than I imagined. "It wasn't that at all."

"What then?" I think he may have blushed a little. He still seemed nice enough and I didn't want to embarrass him.

"The Magus said that we should seek the way through his sons," I answered; "and seeing that there was no way to get to speak to him personally I thought to seek you out."

He looked at me questioningly. Certainly, he had not been expecting this. "My name is Mary," I added. "My friends call me Magdalene".

"Oh really, are you from Magdala?" His look changed to surprise; "I have family at Bethany in Judea. I am called Johannus."

An old lady in black shuffled past us by the synagogue wall, and we both glanced at her though she didn't look up. He looked back at me, with one eyebrow raised.

"How come you are in Antioch?" I asked quickly before he asked me the same question. I wasn't sure how I was going to answer this yet.

"I live here. My father is a silversmith and I help him in the shop mostly. His family have been here for three generations. He met my mother on a pilgrimage to Jerusalem." There was a short silence as we both wondered where this was going. A fly was buzzing around him and he flapped at it, till it came and started flying around me.

"What does he think of the Magus and his teaching?" I asked, but regretted it immediately, as it was none of my business and was almost certainly going to be a difficult subject.

"Not a lot actually. I have had to move out of home. We were arguing too much." He dropped his gaze and his face took on a melancholy look. I had unwittingly touched a raw nerve.

"It is none of my business. I'm sorry." I moved forward to touch his arm but thought better of it. He glanced up again and smiled, a little ruefully.

"It is nothing. I have my own life. But what do you think I can do for you?"

I hadn't found a better way of broaching the subject than hoping he would be sympathetic to my aims. I thought he might. I went straight to the heart of it.

"I want to be able to help people who are possessed," I said, "and I believe that the Magus holds the key. I believe he controls the spirits in the same way that Solomon could and that is what I want to learn myself." Could I tell him I was a priestess and that Saul had warned me off? I wasn't sure at all what was best.

I didn't want to frighten him away but did want to be as honest with him as I could.

M.B. #39

"What are you doing here in Antioch?" he asked as if he read my worries. We were walking along, away from the synagogue and I hadn't thought to ask where we were going.

"Well, I ran away from Magdala when my brother tried to force me into a marriage," I said, and then decided I had to tell him, if anything was going to work out, "and I work as priestess in the temple, of the Goddess." Then added, "but I am thinking of leaving." I bit my lip, what was I saying?

Johannus didn't react in anything like the way Saul had. If anything, he seemed rather more sympathetic. He nodded. "Well, that would be tough; where will you go?"

"I don't know yet; I would like to do this without leaving the temple if that were possible" I answered, "and I do want to continue the work we have been able to do with the 'uncleans'; but I also have some very good friends here in the city. So, I don't know."

We said nothing for a while, walking along side by side. Suddenly he said

"I am taking you away from where you were going. I have to get back to the Magus's residence. Do you want me to try to get you an audience with him?"

"From what Saul said I don't think he would look very kindly on the idea," I answered.

"Don't take any notice of Saul; he would say that." He thought about it for a few paces then added, "you might be right though. But perhaps we could work together, if that is what you wish?"

Strong tremors were coming from him, for I could feel he was drawn to the Goddess deeply.

"We could," I said, "and if you agree we can bring some hope, then I think we should."

"When would you come?" he asked. "I have a room in a house not far from here. We could meet there or at the Synagogue or maybe a tea room somewhere?"

I thought about all the duties I had lined up. "A week today I shall have a free day. Would that work for you?"

"That would be very good, I think," then added, "Simon Magus will probably have left, but I should have completed my training. What time would you come?"

"Let's meet at midday, at the Synagogue," I said.

"Okay Mary… Magdalene, and I promise I won't say anything to Saul," he said grinning.

M.B. #40

The week went by rather slowly giving me plenty of time to reconsider the course of action I was embarking on.

The first thing I was sure of was that I wasn't doing it because I thought Simon the Magus was the Messiah as the claims of some of his followers seemed to suggest.

To believe it my heart would surely have responded to him and his message; but it didn't.

I was reminded rather of stories that both Sarita and Arianne had told… of magic practitioners and sorcerers from the east, that used their powers in displays like these; but powers that I believed could control spirits… and therefore were just what I needed to help the many people possessed by such spirits.

Arianne was working on the documents from Egypt but we also talked about what Hecate-B'el had said to us that night; especially Her answer to my third question.

Arianne thought that the Goddess' meaning had to be that the one we awaited was on the earth already, for them as much as to be here for us.

B'el had thought otherwise. She said that Hecate was angry with my presumption to ask about the things beyond my understanding. She was telling me to mind my own business which is what the last phrase *'and you had better make the most of yours'* literally meant.

Certainly, I thought, Hecate was telling me that I had better make the most of opportunities that came my way. My mortal span was brief and I would have to make my chances count… if I could recognise them.

More than that I didn't understand; B'el was probably right; I was asking questions about what I didn't understand.

She did more audiences with the rich women of Antioch this week than I could ever remember. Whether they came to seek her advice or she called them to her I don't know but somehow her unavailability made me feel more isolated than usual.

I ought to have consulted her before doing what I was planning but I couldn't, for whatever the reasons were.

It was hard to see what the temple might gain by my seeking the powers I did and this venture was not something I could share with even the best of my friends.

I knew it was risky but also the sort of thing I believed needed to be tried if greater gains were to be had; yet to think of what I was about to dare sent little tremors through me.

B'el herself had said that I should be looking for the control of power in the manner of Isis.

So, in fact I was following B'el's direction; but conversely the rebel in me found it exciting to be attempting it in my own way.

Torn by these many different thoughts the week gradually slipped by and I had not made great headway in my planning; but it had to be better to try to improve the lot of the many suffering people than just not to bother.

I decided I would go and see what Johannus had learnt. There was no harm in that at least. Why was I making all this fuss with myself?

I couldn't sleep that night so I went up Adonis Tower. As assistant librarian I was allowed up whenever I wanted, which was a privilege I loved to enjoy. Priestesses Theresa and the faithful Phillipa greeted me asking why I was up so early.

It was between midnight and dawn. The growing moon had long since set and Venus was in her changeover period between being the morning and evening star.

"I couldn't sleep and I am doing the early run to market," I said pulling my shawl tighter around my shoulders. The balmy warmth of summer nights had not yet quite arrived.

I searched up into the sky, feeling for what the stars could tell me. Many familiar patterns were there and Saturn was prominent in the western sky. Mars too was high above my head. I craned back my neck to take in its reddish hue.

Shivering slightly, I looked again to Saturn, oldest of the great ones. "Father and Mother hear my prayer," I whispered.

I sat in silence with the priestesses and they knew I was troubled by something but did not press me for answers. Their presence was a comfort though, and I hugged them each before going down to the Sacred Grove to do my ablations and purifications.

Later, as I helped sort and pack the fresh baked loaves, loading them high onto the patient donkey, my mood had considerably improved, sustained by one of my favourite herb flat-breads. It was still warm and exuded fumes of such pungency; no wonder that bread-making was one of the favourite jobs within the temple.

Narissa was with me and she was happy too to be going to the city market. She had a long-time lover who she hadn't seen for a while but who had promised he would come and meet her there.

It was a long but pleasant morning. Half way through we were joined by a few priestesses who were promoting a new range of our cosmetics by doing free coiffures for anyone who bought the products. They became such popular items that more of Aphrodite's priestesses were fetched to help.

I had finished doing a young girl's hair, watched by her lovely mother who had bought our most expensive new perfume. That was my last job. I had the rest of the day off.

I made my way amongst the pigeons in the square to where the wide spaced steps became a sloping way that led a winding course up past our sister temple. Turning right there were more steps to another street that led to the Jewish quarter where, in the distance, I could just see the top of the white-painted synagogue outlined against the bluest of skies.

M.B. #41

Johannus was waiting for me in the entrance court, pacing rather nervously around. I had taken my green cloak off and wore a sober dress such as any good Jewish woman might wear; and a head shawl. He greeted me with a smile, which I returned, addressing him as 'cousin'.

He bowed slightly, "Mary," he said. "It has been too long," and held my outstretched arms in a token of a hug.

"Maybe we could take some refreshment?" I suggested, "it has been really hot in the square today."

"I know just the place," he said and led the way into the shady road that ran down the side of the building.

We passed a tea house and would have stopped but I spotted Saul sitting inside with some friends. He seemed to look at me for a moment but showed no sign of making a connection between me and the green-cloaked priestess he had been rude to a week before.

I wanted to move on just in case, and pulled Johannus by the arm. He had seen him too and agreed that it might be prudent to move straight to where he was living. He could brew some tea there and he had enough provisions for a light lunch as well.

"Lead the way then," I answered, amused by the solicitous way he phrased the offer.

The room that he lived in was a reasonable size with a table in the middle and alcove-spaces around the edge for various uses. A bed was pushed into one; another was the washroom with a door into a communal yard. The cooking fires were in a third, complete with oven; and the fourth was the store-area.

Johannus went to his stores to get the ingredients he needed and then fetched some water from the washroom. I settled back into one of the two comfortable chairs that were in addition to the four stools around the table.

"Not a bad place you have here."

"It does the job well enough for me," he answered from the room where he was re-kindling a small fire behind the oven that was exclusively for cooking and heating water but was a part of a larger fireplace, which would only be opened up and set with a full fire in winter.

He was easy to be with and soon we found ourselves bantering about the different strengths and quirks of the people we were involved with.

He conceded that the Magus did make the offerings re-appear and re-use them for himself, but argued that as he was God's mouthpiece this was quite in line with everything he had said. They *were* in paradise being used for the future of the people who gave them. All of them would be the beneficiaries if they kept faith with the Magus.

On the other hand, he questioned our temple's offering up of young women for sexual practices in order to bring in an income.

I countered that it was an ancient custom that had brought many young and even older men closer to understanding the Divine.

"I don't necessarily disagree exactly," he said, "but there are always different ways of seeing the same thing. It is not always easy to judge; or sensible to try to, I think."

"Well how otherwise could we be contemplating working together?" I joked.

We ate the food he had made and then he prepared his tea, which was not too bad considering that he hadn't access to the abundance of fresh herbs that we did at the temple.

"it is really strange that you approached me at this time," he said after a space of silence; "because this is the point in the Work where I have the need of a partner in the rituals." He paused. "Extraordinary that you have arrived just like this."

I nodded, thinking that it did indeed seem very fortuitous for my purposes as well. "Isn't that the way it is meant to work? That the need brings the answer?"

"You know that it will require quite a lot of intimacy," he said and blushed, not able to keep his eyes on mine. "More than quite a lot, actually."

"I am a priestess of the Goddess, you know," I answered gently, feeling the delicacy of the topic between us. I was glad he was sensitive to it. I couldn't work with him if he were not. This needed to be a collaborative venture.

Possibilities were beginning to frame themselves in my mind. This might indeed be able to be a collaborative venture, in an ongoing way. Where both magician and priestess could work together on solving the problems of controlling spirits and related illnesses.

Johannus was apparently thinking along similar lines. "It will be easier when Simon and his travel companions have left the city. There is so much going on around him at the moment."

"He is still here then? I thought he had already left."

"He will be leaving tomorrow, with a caravan going east."

"Oh," I said, and then added "maybe at some time you will be able to come to the temple as well. Maybe there is a way co-operation can be achieved. If we approach it carefully."

"I wonder if that would be possible…" he was saying when the door from outside into the washroom burst open. Saul pushed into the room with the Magus and other followers just behind. Apparently, they had been listening to our words through the nearby window into the yard.

"TRAITOR." Saul spat the word at Johannus. "WHORE, WITCH!" he shouted at me.

The Magus gestured Saul aside and moved into the room. His face was a black cloud of anger. His silence was far more menacing than Saul's shouting.

Finally, "Get out; get out!" he said quietly but emphatically to Johannus, "I shall deal with you later."

M.B. #42

Johannus was punched and pushed by several pairs of hands out of the door, that was then barred, leaving me alone to face horror.

"You should be killed," it said, "but maybe you will wish to die and no-one will bother to try and stop you." I backed off, but only into the table. The 'others' had crowded around either side of me.

Trying to recoil away; back inside of myself was the only way to go. There was no reasoning with this Magus. No empathy to be had, of any kind that I would wish for.

"Instead, we will give you what you want," he continued mockingly. "Seven times over you will get to know the spirits. This is our kindness to you. We shall see how you can cope with that." He paused dramatically to let it sink in then barked, "gag her and hold her arms."

Everything he said and did was a desecration of what I held dear. Inside of myself I recoiled and recoiled again, down corridors of mind and soul to a place where this could not be happening.

I could not change what they did to me, brutal and vile, or what that brought, but my memory of it is of watching it happening, as if to another person; mercifully detached.

The Magus made what preparations he deemed necessary. The shutters were closed, circles drawn and powers invoked.

I was held face down over the end of the table and my skirts pulled up over my head. Then each of the group sodomised me in turn.

The monstrous Magus took the lead. With demonic laughter he was calling on the spirits by their names to come and take possession of me. To my watching mind he looked like the devil himself and his followers his attendant demons.

My body felt the invasion of lust and pain and I the jeopardy to my soul. My heart cried to the Almighty for shelter but my mind to the Goddess for vengeance against my attackers.

Spirits entered me.

I knew they had as surely as I felt the seed of the demons enter me but not in the same way. My watching mind saw the features of the perpetrators horribly twist as the spirit forms passed through them.

At last, the Magus had had his fill of hate and lust and everything else he conjured for my defilement. They pulled me up from the table and I felt my spirit-mind jerk back into my poor abused body. Only for a moment before I lost consciousness completely.

When I came around, I found I was lying in a ditch some way from the building. Hands were pulling me again and I struggled against them. As I tried to cry out other things were pulling at my mind. Inside and out, I was in turmoil.

"Mary, Mary." Someone seemed to be shouting what I knew was my name. I tried to look to see where the call was coming from but found the way blocked by the person that was pulling at me.

Eventually some semblance of normality returned to my brain. I recognised that it was Johannus; both the voice and the hands.

Images were flooding back into me; disjointed and awful but the presence of Johannus was important as well. I stopped struggling against him and let him help me regain my feet.

"What have they done to you? What have they done?" He looked almost as distressed as I felt.

My mouth was like a pipe blocked with rubbish and filth. It refused to open to let the words out. This was something that had been done to me as well I knew. I couldn't tell Johannus what had happened.

Then I knew there was another thing to do, to say, and found that words would come at last. "You must fly. Get away from here; as far from them as you can. He is a devil: EVIL. You must escape. You do not deserve; you do not... GET AWAY."

Johannus had put an arm around me and inside I felt my mind getting pulled aside by other spirit forces. Confusion was fast overtaking me.

"But what did they do to you Mary?" Johannus asked again, even as he turned half away, undecided what he should do. "Come with me; I shall look after you. Come on, you are in no state to be alone."

One last effort welled up from my heart. One word that was like a build up of flood water behind the blockage. Neither the Magus' spells nor the spirits in my mind-space could in the end deny it.

"ABOMINATED; abominated!" I cried with all my strength again and again and it was from some other place that I watched as Johannus turned to flee the woman who was flailing around with the strength of someone seven times possessed.

M.B. #43

They wouldn't let me back. They had my body now. The more I raged against them the more they laughed at me and the stronger they became. I feared for my poor abused body and I would have broken down and wept, if I could. Even that was denied me.

The horror kept on unabated until I think I must have fainted or collapsed again. When I awoke, I found that I was in a desolate part of the town that I did not recognise. My first hope and thought was that I was in a nightmare dream from which I might still awake.

Lying in a waste ground from some building project I was surrounded by nothing but rubble and puddles of murky water which made me realise just how thirsty I was. That didn't seem like a dream.

I must have been chased out there or maybe I had just followed my own self-destruct mission. My shins were bleeding and bruised and all of my body hurt one way or another. My thoughts were my own though and that was more important than anything else.

Just as I thought this, I started to feel a buzzing in my head. I tried to stand up thinking this might help but felt overwhelmingly sick and dizzy and sat down on a rock; head in hands to try to stop the buzzing.

Then the voices began. The buzzing noise had resolved itself into separate noises that became discernible as voices. They seemed to have full use of my thinking space. Mentally I crouched down as small as I could as if I was not there.

They laughed at my attempt at concealment and goaded me but seemingly could do no more than put thoughts through my mind that I had no wish to think.

Somehow, I knew or guessed that they would use my own strengths against me. If I got angry again, as I had been before, this would have been theirs to use. So, I did my utmost to deny them any reaction.

Instead, I adopted a kind of clouded stupidity and getting unsteadily to my feet lurched in a direction that I thought was away from them.

The sun was going down and I badly wanted to be home... home that the temple was to me.

The desperate hope that came to me at the thought of the temple was a perfect opening for them. They rushed in to tear it down with images of B'el shouting curses on me; throwing me down the rocky hillside to where the 'uncleans' were. I couldn't go there. Hope vanished amongst demonic cackling.

The spirits of despair danced on my dashed hopes, dragging me once more across the city in the growing darkness. Nothing I did made much difference but an overwhelming tiredness eventually did the job for me. Somewhere on the outer edges of the city I fell over some unseen obstacle and didn't get up.

I don't know exactly when they found me, but sometime in the night a patrol of city guards came across my unconscious and battered form. One of them amazingly recognised my face and they carried me back to Astarte's temple.

Gaius and Bocca received the guards. They and the priestesses on duty on Adonis Tower took me to what had been Astel's cell near to the library and tended to my wounds; then they let me sleep.

Early morning Arianne was the first to visit and my voices were already prowling through my head. I couldn't and didn't dare respond to her concerned enquiries that came to me as through a haze. She obviously thought I had been drugged, beaten and abused, and with kind words she bade me rest whilst she went and talked to B'el.

When Arianne came back it wasn't with the B'el I had come to know as friend but the High Priestess Billel. It didn't take her long to find out some of what had happened. She tried to question me and my attempts to answer were pushed aside.

"She is ours now," another's voice said from my mouth.

I could see Billel's eyes narrow and her face take on a palour that resembled fury.

"Leave her or I shall bring down the Goddess's wrath on you." Billel looked quite capable of doing just as she was threatening but my oppressors were less than impressed.

"She belongs to us," came the answer with a cackle of obscene laughter.

"The laws are being fulfilled," said a second voice.

"The seals are set," and "she has to pay for her transgressions," and then the most ominous of all; one deeper voice, full of menace: "We shall tear her apart if you try to expel us, as is our right."

Billel's face had gone even paler as she faced the spirits and then: "Magdalene!" she commanded. "Answer me..."

Pulled back to centre stage I looked back into the face of the one I feared most. "WHAT have you done?"

I couldn't speak the words. They wouldn't come. My head was shaking from side to side and tears were streaming down my cheeks. It cut no ice with the High Priestess. "You fool. You stupid, headstrong, little idiot. Look where your meddling ideas have got you. You have ruined everything that could have been. Thrown away everything you have been given. Lost; all lost."

She turned away from me and my heart slumped, all hope gone. At the same time the spirits got hold of my rising despair and started an awful cacophony of wailing.

"Silence," barked Billel. "She is finished but I have not." To my surprise they stopped their triumphal howling.

"Why shouldn't *I* kill her, as is *my* right?" demanded Billel, who had turned to face the spirits again. "What would happen to you do you think?"

Silence continued as her words were digested and understood.

"We would destroy your temple then. Not the walls maybe but we would be free to terrorise the world of your little witches."

It was Billel's turn to laugh, "I don't think so," she said. "Rather we would extinguish you at the same time."

I was beginning to think that my High Priestess had the measure of them. I caught sight of Arianne's face and was transfixed by how involved she was in the struggle. The balance was finely set.

It was Billel's voice that broke the tension. "Take her," she said, "she is no use to us anymore."

"Noooooooo…" the denial was torn from Arianne's throat. "You cannot mean that."

Billel turned on the young priestess, fury etched upon her face. "How dare you question me?" she barked. "Magdalene has betrayed us in the most profound way. Don't you travel down the same path. Do you wish to join her?"

Arianne backed away slightly "No High Priestess. I am sorry."

My heart clenched in despair as my final refuge left me. Not even enough strength to pray.

"But please can we send her to someone who might help?" Arianne didn't wait for the answer but continued, "Rachel in Tyre is a healer of great skill. Not the priestess Rachel in our temple there, but another, greatly respected. Could you possibly allow me to send Mary to Tyre?"

Billel's face had softened slightly. She needed Arianne; even more so now that her protégé had desecrated herself.

"Alright, you may. But do not take anything from the temple, except some food and drink. Enough for three days. That is all."

M.B. #44

Arianne bowed her head and left the room, leaving me alone with Billel. If I or any of the spirits might have thought she was vulnerable now one glance at the curved blade of silver that had appeared in her hand dissuaded resistance.

"Sit down there," she ordered, pointing the blade at the chair against one wall.

The spirits were not fond of being ordered around and had no care for my physical safety. I sensed that they wanted to try the High Priestess' mettle. The darkest one took the lead, building on the fear that I was drenched in.

"Don't prattle at us Billel. We know you are nothing but hot air."

Billel moved forward, her hand clenched around the handle of the knife pointing at my chest. "Azrael-roth, stay quiet or I shall bind you with chains of fire." She seemed to have made her point; the devil-spirit backed away.

When Arianne returned a few long minutes of tension had passed. She was hastily pushing a sealed letter into a side flap of a bag that clearly contained some of her own travelling clothes.

She took my arm and between her and the temple's eunuch guard Bocca they guided me to where Gaius was stood outside the north-eastern gate, beside a donkey.

It was not one of the temple's donkeys and I don't know where Gaius had got it from; maybe it was his own.

At the time what I could understand was that I was being torn away from the place that had been my home for several years. An outcast...

An outcast that no-one would want to know; and with nowhere to go, to belong.

Bocca walked with me and the donkey that had been loaded with some provisions. I could hear him repeating something and was glancing sideways at me every few seconds but he stayed steadfastly with me all the way to the camel park.

There he spoke for a few minutes to a train master, getting me accepted as a trail follower.

I was managing to remain impassive and the spirits could do no more than jabber inanely in my brain, making thoughts of every unpleasant kind. I knew that if I struggled with them, they would use that against me.

"I have told him you are a bit simple but are going to Astarte's temple in Tyre. You must..." he trailed off, knowing there was nothing he could say, but he kissed me on top of my head and whispered in Coptic Egyptian 'the Ankh protect you' in my ear. Then touchingly he gave me a hug and there were tears in his eyes as he released me.

Earlier at the temple's gate Arianne had also hugged me tearfully and for a second, I had lost the slim control I had of myself. But the sisterly love I felt for my friend was not something that the spirits could use immediately to their advantage.

Arianne had sensed the danger and she let me go quickly, reaching into the pouch of the bag she had given me. "Here this is a brown travelling cloak that will do you well." B'el had told me I would have no green priestess cloak. Then Arianne pulled out the letter she had written and turned towards me, her face intent and serious.

"Magdalene!" she commanded my attention. No mistake could be afforded.

I stood before her. "What?" I answered glumly.

"Take this letter to the temple in Tyre and ask for the Priestess Rachel. There is another Rachel as well that will help you. This letter explains it so you must keep it safe above all else. Do you understand?"

I nodded. She made me put it in the safety of the pocket of my inner garment. Then she hugged me very quickly, turned and went back inside the temple. The shock of her going nearly unhinged me again. Bleakness was all that was left.

As the donkey I rode upon followed the caravan out through the city walls the bleakness was the best of what was left to me. The rest I didn't want to know.

M.B. #45

The caravan moved at a slow relentless pace but my donkey needed a lot of encouragement. Getting left behind was another thing I couldn't afford to happen.

Keeping myself together during that whole day's travelling, with the demon voices circling around in my mind like vultures was exhausting. I was semi-consciusly repeating the word Ankh over and over, trying to get to its meaning which I had learnt through Araianne.

Looking back, I know that my training and experience as a priestess was giving me some means to detach myself from what was happening inside me; but the effort was rapidly consuming my reserves of strength.

Effort that brought no release but only managed to keep me in a kind of limbo; a stalemate with no purpose and one which I had no idea how long I could keep going.

By the time 'camp' was reached that evening I almost wished to be dead, leaving this pointlessness behind, except I didn't even dare acknowledge this; for death itself didn't guarantee any release, maybe quite the opposite.

I stayed by myself away from the communal fires and ate flat-bread from my provisions. Someone at the temple had provided me with more than I would need for B'el's proscribed three days

Once again Granny-Beth's words came back to me and I knew my time of need was here; and hope almost grew in me at all these little kindnesses.

It wasn't too cold but I checked all the items that Arianne had packed in my bag. There were spare under-garments and a dark dress as well as my other pair of sandals.

Most surprising, at the bottom, folded as flat and small as possible, was Arianne's old green priestess cloak. She had two others but this further act of kindness, in defiance of the High Priestess herself, meant the world to me.

I wrapped myself in the green cloak underneath the dark travelling one, trying to get some scrap of comfort from it; without much success.

Falling into exhausted sleep brought menacing dreams where the evil spirits were dragging me down long dark slopes that evoked huge dread in me.

Every time I was about to reach what it was I so feared, I awoke in a sweat of terror; only to find that my reality was much the same as the dream.

There was no escaping this darkness. No simple rest or sleep without returning to the slopes of fear. It was an awful night with no prospect of a better day to follow.

The pit of my stomach felt knotted in despair. Clenched like a fist around what I wanted least. Aloneness that had driven everything else away except the demons of my wrongness.

This and they remained to gnaw away at me; to ensure that I understood how I deserved to suffer.

Trying to keep things going on the second day was worse than the first.

I could feel the devils awaiting their moment, living off the little crumbs of emotion that my human condition automatically provided. Despair mostly but any of the feelings that we took for granted became their food.

Their hunger for the basic stuffs of life was palpable. I knew and they knew it was only a matter of time before I would break down and they would be able to gorge their hunger and thirst on my unguarded mind and soul.

This inevitability became my torture; not knowing how and when but certain of what was going to happen… unless; if only I could reach the temple at Tyre.

The approaching storm within me held off until the evening and I started to think that if I could get through another night, then maybe…

I remembered as I tethered my donkey with the rest of the animals, just how terrifying last night's sleep had been and I recoiled from the idea of travelling those paths again.

The claustrophobic feeling of constriction and being locked in with the devil spirits got the better of my vigilance and I pulled the hood back to better feel the coolness of the evening against my face and hair.

Too late I realised there was a driver watching me and his features registered some surprise that I was not the elder priestess they had believed was travelling with them.

And I couldn't stop my mind couldn't help noticing how he looked as well: young and free and quite handsome too.

That very moment of exposing my fatal weakness was my undoing.

In my pride as a priestess I would have relished the moment, knowing each nuance and look, controlling where the encounter would or would not go.

Not now though; I pulled the hood over my head again as I turned and hurried back as quickly as I could to my secluded spot.

Away from the dangers that other humans were to me now but nothing had gone unobserved by my inner attendants.

They hungered for flowering lust to grab onto and the glimpsed pride was enough to get to it perhaps… whilst I scrabbled inside myself for self possession, no matter how.

The driver had decided to take my coyness as an invitation for him to come to me, out where no-one would intervene; and my balance was all gone, no chance to defend my mind from what was coming.

His approach was confident but not brash and I tried to turn away and show no interest; but instead, I found myself staring towards the tall form, searching out his dark eyes in the moonlight.

The waiting spirits had overpowered my feeble resistance and pushed themselves to the fore.

The driver didn't immediately realise there was anything wrong, only that his advances were being readily accepted.

M.B. #46

From apparent shy recluse this woman had changed to rampant slut in no time at all and I watched his hestation as the ugly demon worms of lust in me reached out to suck at his life.

Pulling away was not what the spirits would allow and the poor young man quickly realised that he was up against some sort of demon possession as black anger joined the outright lust venting through me.

Raw distaste turned to sheer horror and alarm.

Desperately he pushed away my clawing hands, calling out for help as he struggled and finally managing to disengage enough to turn and flee to where his shouts had aroused the other drivers.

Together they did what they were good at and drove me out of the encampment with sticks and stones. They chased me as I ran wildly, leaving everything behind except the clothes I was in.

I had no choice. I don't know how long it went on but every time I tried to rest, they were there again beating at me if they could get close enough, or throwing stones that bit me like stinging bees when they hit.

Worst of all the spirits seemed to delight in the fear and anguish this brought to me and they rode a wild cacophony of emotion within my tormented frame.

In the end I think I must have lost the drivers for when I collapsed on the ground there was no-one trying to hurt me anymore.

Perhaps they had got me far enough away from the camp for me not to find my way back, even if I tried.

Nothing remained to me but a wretchedness that would become my normal condition in the days ahead. A shivering, relentlessly miserable night followed with no better promise in a cold and dreary dawn.

When I finally did find my way back to the camp that next day the caravan had long gone and my donkey too. Nothing was left of my possessions. My bag was gone and my supplies with it. My travelling cloak must have been discarded in my early state of passion. Even the old green under-cloak had been torn from me in my flight; I remembered that.

84

I sat with my head in my hands and let the spirits feel my anguish. No surprise that they wallowed in the taste of it and I had not the strength to deny them; better rather to drown in the loss there.

Eventually I got up and wandered away from the camp having no wish to be found by another caravan or even other travellers. I trudged roughly in the direction that I had taken the night before with little or no hope left for anything good.

Which was when I found my priestess' cloak hanging on a thorn bush by the side of the path.

Such a small mercy but one that I accepted gladly, wrapping it around me like a defence against the world.

Except that my troubles were on the inside… accompanying me with an incessant stream of thoughts that were not my own; or were they?

If anything changed in the weeks that followed it was that it became harder to distinguish what was me and what was actually them; the devils.

I knew their hunger and their thirst almost as my own. I would even have pitied them hadn't it almost immediately left me drowning in pity for myself.

To die would be welcome except that I knew I would end like the ghosts; pitiable creatures without a home of flesh and bone, warmth or feeling.

I followed paths that went south and skirted straggly villages where people made a hard living on the rocky landscape with a few goats grazing and rough tilled fields that yielded only a little of anything they planted. There was not much water and I felt the lack of this more than almost anything.

People that I encountered easily recognised my possessed state and either shunned me or drove me away. Occasionally I managed to scavenge for something I could eat, whether it was discarded as rubbish or put out for animals. Well I remembered the dumps outside the walls of the city of Antioch where the 'uncleans' roamed and now I understood; understood wretchedness.

I also remembered everything I had lost, although distorted by my attendant demons.

Remembered the kindness of my friend Arianne and then too the ancient crone who told me that I would know the need for great kindness.

What an explicit truth that was to me now.

All the wonderful ideas I had played with as a priestess of the Goddess boiled down to just one thing; the need for release; a release that could bring me peace.

Nothing else really mattered when it came down to it.

My body took more than just abuse and many beatings; it suffered awfully from lack of any kind of proper care. Half starved and with sores breaking out in many places I got into a terrible state. It couldn't go on like this.

Memories of what was done to me never left me, they were all too present and maybe were the reason that I couldn't give my poor body the attention it needed.

Too painful to allow any relief that benefitted the Magus' demons as well;

so much better to give them nothing but suffering as their reward.

A huge and unpleasant burden that for some reason I had to carry around and couldn't be discarded because they were attached to me and I held onto them too.

Their fear was my fear; their lust was my lust; my anger was theirs, escalating it out of all proportion but I didn't know how to let it go or to let go of them either.

I was completely lost in every way.

M.B. #47

Something unknown kept me going; something greater than me or the devils that tormented me.

I would have prayed constantly if they hadn't delighted in making mockery of this; and only silently did my heart cry out to my God.

The end must be close I knew; I couldn't fight for much longer.

I cannot remember many details of that long dark tunnel that was leading steadily down into the chaos of madness but one day, or part of one day, remains etched clearly in the mists of unreality.

I had stayed in a derelict building just outside the edge of a village for several nights and managed to find food; but one morning there were moves afoot to get rid of me.

I tried to make my escape as soon as I realised the villagers were preparing to run me out or worse.

Hobbling along a rocky path I stumbled frequently. The remains of my sandals provided almost no protection but hard skin had developed over most of what had been blisters. New cuts hampered my progress only a little.

Shouts from the direction I had come told me that the pursuit had started in earnest. Anything that could be struck together to increase the noise was being. They wouldn't want to do half a job; but fix me permanantly I was sure.

I could smell the pungent smoke of a building that had been set afire drifting in the air.

I slid down a sandy slope where the path I was on joined the wider road.

When I had awoken the day had still been relatively cool but it was hot now.

Faster progress could be made on the road but they would be able to see me too easily; so, searching for another path, I half limped half ran along the side of the track.

A thorn got stuck in one foot and it was really painful; I wanted to stop but didn't dare. I could still hear the villagers somewhere back around a bend.

Scrambling between rocks allowed me to get off the track and out of sight from anyone on it. The land I found was strewn with rocks, scrubby bushes and the occasional scrawny tree. No relief anywhere I could see and the day was going to be unbearably hot.

I had not even any water with me and after my exertions my throat was already parched with thirst. A thirst that never seemed to go away in those days but the waterless plain ahead was more than I could attempt.

There was no other option than to try but my strength failed me.

I staggered towards a rock to lean against, tripped and fell instead, grazing my arm on its rough edge as I slumped to the ground.

Movement at the edge of my vision caught my eye and I looked across the rough ground at a viper that regarded me impassively a few feet away, its tongue flicking in and out as though it was trying to tell me something.

The silence between us for a few moments was more solid than words. Then it turned away and wove sinuously across the ground to disappear behind another set of rocks.

I also crawled across the stony ground, in the opposite direction from that the snake had taken but with much the same idea. There was one slightly larger boulder that looked as though its overhanging side could offer me a little shade.

Once I had got there, I collapsed; I could go no further. This was the end.

M.B. #48

The sun must have worked its way round to penetrate the shadow of my rock.

I could see the light but I couldn't even open my eyes, let alone move.

Brightness that was more pleasant than burning and it moved; not much, but enough to define itself into a shape. A man was standing in front of me.

He was part of the light and yet within it. He was saying something to someone who I couldn't see.

"No harm will come to her," he said and I felt warmth and security in the authority of his words.

He came closer and I could look into his face; his eyes. Kindness is what I saw and what I remember.

"Come to me and I shall give you peace," he said. The words penetrated through all my layers of misery, seeping to the parched world within me like rain into a desert.

"Seek me and you will find what you need most. Come home… Mary." With this last word, my name, the vision faded but the feeling didn't. For the first time since, since the abomination… my heart breathed fully and easily.

I lay there not even caring. Not wanting to move, just savouring the hope-giving words that my soul had drunk; now I could die.

The noises of people on the road came to me again. I was much nearer to the track than I thought. I must have crawled back towards it without realising.

Involuntarily I groaned aloud at what I knew was to come.

*

The three travellers came across villagers on the road who appeared to be in the process of chasing someone or something out of their area, their lives.

Johannus recognised the signs of frightened people banding together and he and his companions were quite concerned for themselves. The last thing they wanted was to get caught up in the villagers' business.

One man, a village elder probably, came forward to talk to them. He warned them that there was a woman possessed by demons nearby. She possessed the strength of several men, was extremely cunning and apparently had a wicked beauty that made her especially dangerous.

One of Johannus' companions told the elder that they would not interfere with their driving the demon-woman away from their village. All they wanted was to travel on to the south.

The elder had his doubts and told them they risked much but seeing there were three of them he looked as if he might be persuaded to allow them past.

Reluctantly Johannus's friend produced a few coins from a leather pouch under his cloak, letting the elder see the short sword he carried for protection.

The man took the money with a rather surly expression and let the men and the four donkeys with them go by.

They carried on along the way, followed for a while by several of the villagers. These carried sticks and who wanted to use the travellers to push the way forward or so it seemed.

Others spread out to check the land on either side of the road and the companions pretended nothing unusual was happening, but then suddenly Johannus noticed that the three of them were on their own again; the villagers were somewhere behind, out of sight as though they had met some unseen boundary.

He couldn't help but remember Mary and the part he had unwittingly played in her abomination. He wondered where she had got to, what had happened to her. His conscience could never let these thoughts entirely leave him.

They trekked on warily. "Keep a lookout Mark," he was saying, "we don't want to have rocks raining down on us from an angry demoness."

"What do you think I am doing?" said Mark, "I am not sure why Plotinus even persuaded them to let us pass."

"Shut up, for goodness sake," answered the one called Plotinus, "I at least want to get to a decent campsite tonight; not get stuck in this god-forsaken place."

Mark was just raising his voice in a reply when Johnnus thought he heard a moaning sound from the right of the track, just beside the corner they were going around. "Sshh… I think I heard something".

They were almost past the rock when Johannus saw the form of a woman, prone upon the ground, covered in a tattered green cloak. His heart almost stopped. Carefully he turned her over

*

I knew the face that looked into mine though I couldn't remember why; but the calmness within me allowed me to be glad.

Tears came to my eyes as I closed them again, letting go, to dying.

"I know this woman," said Johannus, "we have to help her."

"You are mad," answered Plotinus. "You know she is a possessed. How could you know her?"

"I knew her in Antioch where this thing happened to her. It is part of why I am leaving that place. I must help her."

"You are on your own then," said Mark. "There is no way I am having her travel with me."

"Help me get her away from these villagers and I shall leave you alone. Otherwise, we shall all be in trouble. I promise you that."

They looked at each other but realised they had to decide quickly.

"Alright," said Mark angrily, "get her on your donkey; quick."

Johannus didn't need telling twice. Swiftly they laid Mary across the back of the donkey. Mark and Plotinus mounted theirs and Johnnnus led his with its new burden as fast as he could along the track.

After a mile or so they felt they were safe enough to stop and reassess their plans.

"What are you going to do Johannus?" asked Plotinus.

Johannus was already giving water from his waterskin to the now waking woman whom he had managed to get off the donkey.

Her body was so scrawny and what were left of her clothes were torn and tatty. Lifting her down his arm had felt the scrunched-up letter.

"There is something in her garments; I think it's the paper of a letter scroll. Yes, I'm sure it is."

Mary had forgotten about the letter but released the rolled up crumpled paper to Johannus from within her garments. She was in a terrible state and he didn't want to stress her any further than she already was.

The letter had been sealed hurriedly with a priestess' seal. Written beside this on the outside was the address: "To Rachel, Priestess of Astarte at Tyre".

Johannus wondered for long seconds whether he should break the seal, but decided he couldn't.

Resolve set in his heart and mind. "I am taking her to Tyre," he declared.

His companions shrugged, not seeming to care. "More fool you," said Plotinus.

"There is a place not far along this road where you can follow the way to Tyre, if you must," said Mark. "For my part I am continuing on to Caesarea Philippi as we planned."

"How far is it to C.P. do you think?" Johannus asked.

"Well, I don't think we shall get there till about noon tomorrow," answered Mark.

Johannus thought about trying to buy the baggage donkey from Mark and

Plotinus but quickly realised that it wasn't going to happen. He hadn't enough money to make it an attractive proposition.

He turned to Mary to see how she was. Her eyes were closed and he could see how horrible her general condition was.

Obviously, she would need to be carried on his donkey. He would have to go the whole way to Tyre on foot.

He wondered if she was well enough to travel even on his donkey. They would have to go as fast as they could manage.

Mark and Plotinus were eager to get on their way. They took Johannus's baggage from the fourth donkey and gave him some of the shared food supply, which he was later grateful for.

Then they repacked their loads and were gone, almost before Johannus knew it was happening; he was really stuck now.

M.B. #50

He tried to feed Mary some food before getting her onto the donkey but she didn't respond, so he loaded the donkey with his baggage instead, packing it to be able to secure Mary against it once he had got her back up.

He was acutely aware they needed to move off as soon as possible.

With a big effort and only a little assistance from the woman he was trying to help Johannus managed to get Mary up onto the donkey, sitting her sideways and strapped as best he could to the load beside her.

Grateful for this success at least he took the donkey's leading rein and started to pull her down the road, wondering all the while what he had committed himself to.

The splitting of the roads seemed an age to reach but eventually they came to it and took the turn to the right, towards the west.

It was a day of hard toil for Johannus, trudging single-mindedly on this road, avoiding any kind of contact with people whenever possible and when it wasn't he would hurry through the place before the urchins who inevitably came to pester him for whatever they could get would realise what the donkey's burden was and hurry off to tell some grown up.

When he stopped it was to check on Mary and give them both something to drink. He worried that she appeared to have fallen into a fever. Maybe it would be more than he could do to get her to Tyre at all.

At least he had enough water for both and was able to stop at a small stream to fill his skins up; and he ate some of the provisions his companions had left, though Mary would take nothing.

It was his feet that were starting to suffer quite badly; sore and blistered from the relentless trek that was unlike anything he was used to; and with little relief from the fierce heat for the rest of him.

He didn't doubt what he was doing though; there was no other option than to help get Mary to Tyre after what she had done for him. Without her he would still be following after that so called Magus, Simon... How completely changed his view of that man was now.

Somehow, he had managed to escape the venomous attacks that followed on from Mary's night of horror, but his family had then been targeted as well.

His father had stood strong with the aid of his friends and contacts in the city guard; and as a result, he and Johannus grew closer than they had been in years.

For this and for opening his eyes to Simon's real nature, Johannus felt his debt to Mary deeply, and he wouldn't relinquish it; no, he couldn't.

The troubles with the Magus' disciples had fairly soon died away, but it had still seemed a good idea for Johannus to travel to Bethany in Judea, and pay an extended visit to his aunt and uncle there.

'Now this', he thought ruefully. 'A chance to put things right, maybe.'

As the afternoon wore on each hill, each up-slope, got harder to climb than the last and they stretched out seemingly interminably ahead of him.

Eventually the road passed beside a small stand of trees and gratefully Johannus took advantage of the shade they provided like countless travellers before him on this road.

He knew they would need to travel through the night but first he must let the donkey rest and eat and drink; and himself and Mary too. Carefully he lowered her from the back of his donkey and propped her up against the base of a tree before trying to do something about his feet.

Under the trees on the road to Tyre the small fire he managed to make helped him relax and he must have slept because he woke up with a start, from a dream; but one that slipped quickly out of his memory's reach.

Mary was sleeping fitfully as well and the stars were beginning to break through the darkening sky. This was as good a place as anywhere to camp and normally he would have been glad to have stayed the night here.

Right now though, he feared for Mary and he knew that they couldn't rest for long.

She was quiet but so pale as though all life was draining out of her. He couldn't bear to see her livid sores and other hurts.

The more he looked the more everything about her was telling him that she wouldn't last much longer.

Sudden desperation seized him and forced him to get up from the comfort of lying by the fire; to get them going again.

It took a great effort to get her dead weight to lie face down across the donkey's back but eventually he succeeded. Panting and sweating he set about final preparations, kicking dusty soil over the last embers of the fire. Feeling stiff and tired down to the very boot-sandals he had strapped his protesting feet into, he proceeded to push one of them in front of the other into the gathering coldness of the night, pulling the donkey and its load behind him.

There was a growing moon that would make following the way easy and gradually Johannus's legs loosened enough to make the progress quite brisk.

In the night he stopped as they reached the crest of one ridge, allowing himself and his donkey a break from their labours. Mary seemed hot one minute then cold the next and had been groaning on the upward climb though she showed no sign of gaining consciousness as he lifted her off her donkey's back. He would need to arrange her in a better position.

Able to use the lie of the ground, he got Mary up sideways again like she had been in the morning but couldn't find a way to strap her there securely.

Again, he struggled with her shivering body and managed to swivel her around, getting one leg over the rump to sit her astride the donkey's back and leaned her forward onto the baggage behind the donkey's neck. Swiftly he pulled out a couple of woollen shawls to help secure her in place, and keep her warm as well.

The moon was still riding high in the sky whilst dipping low onto the western horizon resplendent Jupiter pointed the direction they must go. Despite everything, Johannus' spirits began to rise.

The downward slope allowed a good pace which he was able to continue up to the next ridge. Mary was still more or less fixed in the same position but that was the only good thing that Johannus could see about her condition.

This was his moment to give his best effort and he was glad to be doing so; despite the tiredness nagging at him, telling him he should stop and rest or even sleep; he carried on; he simply had to get her to the temple at Tyre.

Eventually a welcome dawn crept up the sky behind as they passed through a village waking to the new day. Cocks crowed from out in the countryside and Johannus decided it must be time to take another break.

The morning that followed was a continuing trial for man and beast as the heat of the sun once again started to beat down on them. Traffic increased on the road and the countryside looked much more prosperous. Johannus sensed they were getting close.

Those last miles into the outskirts of Tyre hurt the most; for instead of reaching his goal and being able to rest he continually found out there was further to go; always further. Much as he might want to give up, he couldn't; not now.

Mary was unconscious and Johannus didn't dare look at her for fear that she had in fact slipped away from this life completely.

He trailed seemingly for ever down one street after another, shunned by all around, which made it difficult to get directions. Once or twice he even had to turn back the way he had already come… and that was very, very hard.

But finally, he did round a corner and knew he really had got where he had spent day and night striving to reach; had managed to get them both here.

Enormous relief poured through him, even though his feet were so sore and his legs ached in every muscle and sinew. Almost joyously he knocked on the ancient wooden doors as loudly as he was able.

The woman that opened them surveyed the dishevelled state of the traveller standing there and wondered whether she shouldn't just close them again; but then she noticed the crumpled letter-scroll he was clutching in his hand and relented.

The minutes passed like an age as Johannus waited for a response to the letter he had delivered, sitting slumped on a low wall. He had got Mary off the donkey and was relieved to find her not only alive but willing and able to drink some water. That was all he could do.

The priestess Rachel came hurrying to the gate as soon as she had read the letter from her old friend Arianne. It had obviously been written in great haste and told of a friend in great need.

Seeing Mary for herself, Rachel could see that things were worse for the one-time priestess than even Arianne could have imagined. Rachel knew that the best chance of saving her was indeed to get her to the house of the other Rachel; the healer, her friend.

*

M.B. #51

'Rachel the Healer' lived in a house near to the coast.

She had inherited it from her mother, together with the trading business that her mother had taken over when Rachel's father had died in a shipwreck.

Rachel had sold the remaining ship to its present sea-captain, but she kept a share in it, and one of the two warehouses, to use in a quite different way from before.

Since young adulthood it became clear to her parents that she didn't wish to marry, at least not to any of the prospective suitors they had come up with, so they had reluctantly but indulgently allowed her to pursue her passion.

Her passion that was to understand everything about how the world was the way it was; what it was; what life itself was.

A passion that brought her into contact with many wonderful and sometimes strange people and finally led to her meeting the two women who taught her the most.

Melody was the chief herbalist at Astarte's temple in Tyre, when Arianne had been working there and Rachel's friend, another Rachel, gained acceptance to be a priestess.

The same summer that Astel travelled up from Egypt and stayed some months in the temple before going on to Antioch.

It was Melody that introduced Rachel to so many of the quiet wonders of a parallel world where plants gathered and expressed the elemental properties for life.

The temple cooks used many of course, and the trained priestesses knew some others but Melody was so happy to find that her extraordinary ability to feel a plant's uses, purposes, somehow seemed to rub off on Rachel. She had

93

found someone who could receive her knowledge, take it on.

Of all the learning Rachel had gained it was this branch of herbal lore and medicine that she came to love and practice most, making a garden at her parent's house near the sea that became an expression of her and her abilities.

Astel was perhaps an even greater influence on Rachel than Melody, for this extraordinary, wiry, little old lady started her on the path of being able to read people; to know what they needed to gain wellbeing and balance.

It caused a great ache in Rachel when Astel told her it was time for her teacher to travel on, and forbade Rachel to go with her.

"You have all you need, here. Use it!" she said as they walked together in the temple grounds. "I cannot teach you more, you have to learn it by your own practice." Rachel said nothing but it was as if the elder woman read her concerns, "and nor can the sisters of the temple. Don't be persuaded to join them." She stopped and turned to look Rachel straight in the face. "Your destiny is something else, full of hope and happiness, yes, of your own sort, and making."

And she did find happiness and wellbeing of her own kind.

Using the warehouse of her father's business in Tyre she created a kind of refuge there for many people who came to her for help.

It started as fulfilling something she had wanted to do as a girl, to help the families of the sailors with some of the hardships they faced and it turned into somewhere that all sorts of people came with their troubles and illnesses.

She was able to improve the health, and the state, of many of them and some of them stayed, though she would insist they worked to support the refuge.

Others went on their way, but always her reputation increased; as the healer.

The house at the coast was her refuge, where she could get away from all the people pressures. Its large walled garden was where she grew nearly all the herbs and things she needed, as Melody had taught her; and the gate at the further end led to paths that wound directly along the shore itself.

*

She was watching the sun go down over the sea, thinking about a strange person she had dreamt of the night before; a beautiful lady, lying very badly hurt, with vultures flapping around her.

Rachel took note of such dreams and had become good at recalling the details. She remembered that one of the vultures had looked at her before turning back to hack its beak into the woman's wounds. A demon face, such as possessed so many troubled souls.

The woman was alive; she moved her arms as if to try to brush the things away, to push them back… but to no avail; and her voice called out as her eyes searched around for help.

Rachels' heart went out to her and yet she knew she could do nothing for people possessed by spirits; that it was beyond her skill. That was when she had woken up.

She wondered now, as she sat watching the sun slipping down into a hazy reflection of itself in the sea, if having had that dream was anything to do with reports of a great healer working in Capernaum in Galilee. He was able to cast out devils from people it was said, and she had been thinking of going to see for herself.

Going back into the house, she passed a window that faced down the road on which her house was set. Down the other end a donkey and two people were struggling their way up the track, and there might have been another person lying across the donkey's back; she couldn't be certain.

It would have been slightly comical, the way that one of them, a man, was staggering about while the other, a woman in a green cloak, was pulling on the donkey's leading rope; would have been if she hadn't felt the urgency that was propelling them, and recognised that the woman was a priestess of the temple.

Watching the scene in fascination, a shiver ran through Rachel.

M.B. #52

She was suddenly sure the priestess was her friend Rachel, coming to her because she needed her help; and the hairs on the back of her neck spoke to her that this was connected to her dream.

She hurried to the door.

Johannus finally felt that he had gone as far as he could go, but the priestess handed him the donkey's rope and hurried forward to meet the figure that had come out onto the road.

"Rachel, Rachel; thank heavens you are at home. This is Johannus," she said, "who has brought to us a friend of a dear friend; in direst need."

She was trying to press a letter scroll into the hand of her friend, but Rachel ignored this or didn't see.

Her attention was rooted to the figure on the donkey; a face pale as death, yet with auburn hair that looked on fire as it caught the rays of the setting sun, where it wasn't matted with dirt.

Rachel went to her and quickly checked her over, feeling her forehead and pulse, listening to her breathing and noting the sores that she could see.

She became completely focussed on the clear needs of this woman in front of her, ushering the party through a gate beside her house where she called for someone to come and help them.

"How did she get into this condition?" she asked her priestess friend, who shook her head.

"Only what is written in this letter. It is from Arianne, who remembered you. She says this woman's name is Mary, called Magdalene and she was abominated with devil spirits, by someone evil. That is all I know. Maybe Johannus who brought her here knows more."

"Yes, I remember Arianne of course," she replied, finally scanning through the letter she had been given. Knowing now for certain that this was who the dream had been about… who she must help.

Turning towards the man Johannus she asked rather sharply. "If you brought her to Tyre, why is she in such an awful state? That is not what spirits have done to her."

He coloured as he stuttered a reply, feeling a guilt that went further back than the last few days. "Sh..she was like this when we found her on the road from Damascus, ap..pp.proaching Caeserea Philippi. B..but… I had known her in Antioch. I had to help her."

"I'm sorry," said Rachel. "I didn't mean to be angry with you; but this girl has been badly beaten, has sores, and looks not to have eaten properly in weeks. She has a fever and may not be strong enough to get through the night."

"I know" said Johannus. "I didn't dare stop for long last night because of that. We came here as fast as I could manage. It is as that letter says; there was a Magus in Antioch who she crossed and who caught us, her… and did this awful thing to her. W..we lost contact till I found her on the road…"

Rachel looked at him again and saw how clearly exhausted he was. She could read quite a lot between his words and his pained and worried expression; there was probably no use in trying to prise more from him now.

"I really am sorry," she said again, her voice softening. Then she called for her house-girl to come and show Johannus to a guest room and to get him what he needed to refresh himself. "You will stay as long as you wish," she said.

Johannus bowed his head as he accepted her offer, but couldn't immediately shake off the feeling of her early probing question.

"Come Rachel," his hostess was saying, "please stay and help me. We have work to do to get this poor girl through to see the light of the morning sun."

Then she also came over to Johannus as he was leaving with the maid. "Well done. I think you have saved her life. It is a higher power that made you find her. You have done well what you were given to do. Now I must do the same. Be sure to ask for anything you need. Sleep well. We shall talk in the morning."

A huge sigh of relief went through Johannus. "Thank you," he said. "Thank you." He felt a heavy weight, hard to bear, had been lifted from him.

*

M.B. #53

The places I became immersed in belonged to no reality anyone would wish to imagine.

The spirits dragged me into levels of darkness in their desperate rampage through my unconscious being, that were beyond my worst nightmares.

But even in those dreadful times I felt somehow protected.

Protection that flowed with me because the hope that had come in the light and voice of another soul had warmed me and would not be extinguished.

Ice froze my blood and fire burned my flesh but neither quite reached where I was.

Serpents coiled in every orifice of existence but could not bite into me with their fatal poison.

Darkness rushed throughout me but never succeeded in engulfing my soul.

Hate, lust, anger and despair washed over the fabric of my being but could not leave their residue in me.

Then, after an unknowable time amidst the hunger and thirst of that desert of the soul, a rain began to fall.

A rain that reached me, where the darkness hadn't.

Washed me.

Woke me.

*

Rachel again washed the sores of the woman Mary, and with another sponge brought water to the parched lips.

For a moment her eyelids fluttered and opened. She appeared to try to raise her head, but having looked for moments into the eyes of this person nursing her she settled back and closed her eyes again.

Johannus had left and so had Rachel. Both had stayed the first night and then Rachel had gone back to the temple, with the intention to return later.

Johannus stayed half the day but felt more and more that this was no longer his place, his business. Rachel understood this and gave him provisions, making sure he had everything he needed to travel on to Bethany.

Then her friend Rachel returned and told of another time that Arianne had sent her a letter for this Mary, a few years ago. A letter that they had sent on to Mary's mother in Magdala; but Mary had made it clear that she hadn't wanted to take it further.

Clearly, if mother and daughter could be re-united that would be good thing; but to have a daughter returned, possessed by spirits? Wouldn't that be almost impossible to bear?

But... what of that healer in Palestine who was reputed to be able to cast out evil spirits and devils? He was said to be living in Capernaum; so close to Magdala where her mother lived, and maybe still was.

Rachel decided she would travel there with Mary to try to see him, once she was strong enough.

*

Coming around to this real world again was almost harder to bear than the inner dreams that I had just endured for what seemed an eternity.

The spirits were still in my mind and their natures were still as much a part of me; of what I had become. It filled me with an overwhelming sadness for all the beauty that had gone from my life; and a terrible tiredness from having to bear this tormented destiny.

The healer Rachel was very kind but I could not respond as I would have wished but only with a guarded lethargy that I had learnt was able to keep at bay the worst of 'their' interference; but so foreign to my own nature.

She seemed to understand my problem but said there was nothing she could do to help except tend to my physical well-being.

Despite the terrible depression that weighed me down and highlighted my helplessness, having my body's needs looked after was a wonderful kindness.

Then one morning Rachel sat with me and said she was going to travel to Capernaum to visit a Master Healer there and wanted me to come as well. His name was Yeheshua.

Some little spark of light seemed to strike my heart as she told me this; a chord that struck a resonance in my soul.

Yeheshua; Yeheshua. A face from a vision or a dream came to my mind and the spirits could not forbid it.

"Yes, I will come with you if I may," I responded with what seemed like the first smile I had ever managed.

Rachel hugged me and the spirits returned, howling within my mind. Feeling my renewed distress she released me quickly, her face mirroring the concern for what was raging inside me.

So, she prepared for the journey and I treasured the new hope that had joined me in my place where the spirits could not reach, allowing it to endure and be nourished.

*

Rachel chose the mule cart as best for travelling in, with comparatively little to burden them; and Abrineth to accompany them on a small horse. He was a young man, dark, wiry and completely trustworthy. His father Ashembindar was a ship's captain and she had known this son since he was a child.

Rachel had several competent people to help run her business and her home, which gave her the freedom she desired. She liked to involve herself in all of her inheritance but not to be tied to it completely.

She managed this so well that she had the freedom to make journeys such as they were now undertaking, with few attendant worries.

The day was hot and travelling was pleasant, though Mary, undercover in the back of the cart, appeared to be as glum as ever.

Rachel couldn't imagine what it was like for her, though she had had glimpses of the seven spirits, hungry to possess her completely. Glimpses too of the real Mary that still struggled not to be overwhelmed; but most of the time there seemed a kind of stalemate.

Rachel felt genuine pity and a slight desperation in this venture they were embarked together on.

"Brin," she called to the man riding slightly ahead of them, "can you remember how far it is to the inn we want to stay at?"

"About an hour's ride, at the speed we are making, I would say," he answered, letting the mule come up beside his horse.

"Do you think you could ride ahead and check that they have rooms for us then?" she asked. "Then get back to us? I want to know if we are going to have to travel further."

Abrineth said that he could be back with the answer within the hour and that the horse would like the chance to stretch his legs a bit.

They made the inn Rachel wished for and stayed at another on the following night, before they came within sight of Capernaum and the Sea of Galilee.

*

M.B. #54

The thing I remember most was that with the growing hope the thirst also grew; so closely entwined that they were almost the same thing.

Their tangibility gave me something to hang onto but at the same time the demons in my mind-space became increasingly agitated.

Almost as a counter-action to my jabbering spirit-thoughts, the rumbling sway of the cart along the road became pleasantly familiar; together with the clipping of the mule's hooves and the faint grinding crunch of the wheels when the track became stony.

Some part of me wanted to reach out to Rachel in thanks for all she was doing, but it was as much as I could do to not vent out some cry of doom or rant of hatred against the world and all its inhabitants instead.

Both inns we stayed at were serviceable enough with travellers of every sort, either staying in one of the low lodges like us or else camped out in the area beyond. Their similarity was obviously suited to the purpose that they served.

Each had a central building or area where food and drink could be had and whatever entertainment was passing along the road sampled.

I preferred to stay away from as much of it as possible; and although I knew Rachel wished to sit closer to the fire and where the music was being played or songs sang, she stayed with me instead.

I could not help it; I had to guard myself against what had happened before. We made good progress on both days and an unspoken excitement grew as we travelled on, understanding that we shared perhaps, of deeper hope that we could not have put easy words around.

In the silence of the days journeying, we sensed something important was happening, not just for me, but for us both.

Then on that third day we came close to our destination and I caught sight of sunlight glinting on the inland sea. So much my home that I began to cry and even the wailing of the spirits seemed to be the same thing.

Rachel looked at me and was able to put an arm around my shoulders without invoking any adverse reaction from my part.

Further ahead we could see the beginnings of the town sprawled out, and as we approached the mule speeded its pace as if it could sense its labours were nearly done.

Before long we were amongst the buildings and passing people in the road or by its side. Rachel selected someone to ask the way.

"Excuse me," she called to a woman carrying two pails of water suspended from a yoke across her shoulders. "Can you tell me where the healer Ye-he-sh-u-ah lives?"

The woman looked back at Rachel, across to me and back at Rachel again. She lowered her burden to the ground and wiped her forehead with the back of her hand before replying. "Yeshua you mean." It was a statement rather than a question. "He lives in Lakeside way; not far from here, towards the sea. A house called "Mirimion"; but I think you will find it full today."

She chuckled to herself and then looked me over again. "She need his help?" she asked, not unkindly but slightly wary at the same time.

"Thank you," replied Rachel, "we had better get going then. We both want to hear him speak today if we can. What street did you say to take? Which way?"

"Keep going down here towards the waterside but fork left when this road reaches a small square. You will soon then come to Lakeside way and you won't miss it. It has trees down one side and that is where Yeshua's house is. Set back a little from the road. I've been there" she added, quietly then: as if a little shy.

We thanked her again and carried on in the direction she had pointed. Would we really be getting there soon? The sun was getting low in the sky behind us and we sensed we must hurry.

Once we passed the square, Abrineth was sent to sort us out some rooms that we could stay in for a few days. Rachel had used them before and they had places for the horse and mule a well.

We walked the last part to Mirimion, crossing other streets and catching glimpses of the Galileean sea. The sun was only just above the hills that we had travelled through and the sky was streaked in pink traces.

The woman we had talked to was right about the trees and it was easy to pick out Yeheshua's house as there were many people crowding around in front of several open windows; trying to listen to the words being spoken in the front room.

We joined the back of the throng outside the house. We couldn't quite see the speaker because we had the least favourable spot but we could hear the words he was saying:

"… and the Kingdom of Heaven is no place on this earth. It is the Kingdom of the Soul. It is within you.

To go there you must have the eyes to see, the ears to hear and the heart to thirst, to feel, to know.

There is an eye to see the inner Truth; an inner ear to understand the welcome within; and yet we need not feet to walk the path where Life is breathed anew with every breath, for to open wide the doors to Love it is our hearts that must gratefully accept the gifts that flow from God's own store.

The Master comes to clear the way; to help remove the obstacles we have become entangled with. The snares that have been set to catch unwary souls; these traps have done their work. We see it all around and for our part we must learn to avoid them before they can take their hold.

Not all are obvious as the cruel ailments that affect so many in this time. Most are subtle traps and flaws that claw at the fabric of our minds and souls, to drag us down some darker road than we were meant to go.

These shadows must be swept away if we are to make the doorway clear, to bring the Kingdom near; and the master comes to help you so the King can reach out from within to guide you through.

Peace and joy are yours in great abundance; waiting for you to claim as your own inheritance. Stand up, arise, shake off these crumbling chains of sin and come to know your home within. Not within these houses of stone and wood but rather prepare to go within that human house that God has made for each of you with loving care. Be ready, for your day has arrived, your time has come… Blessings to you all."

Yeheshua must have finished with this blessing of the crowd. Shouts of joy and cries for him to stay and speak some more mingled from the front room.

I was home; I didn't want to go anywhere else, just stay and soak in the feeling of the approaching evening and its blend of warmth and cooling balm.

We had only just arrived, but now many people were leaving. Yeheshua had apparently gone from the front room but there was still an atmosphere of rich calmness remaining.

Everything felt just right in those minutes as we leaned against the wall beside the entrance gate. We said nothing and didn't need to. Both Rachel and I felt the same.

A woman came up to us and started talking to Rachel. I didn't listen to what they were saying but then an older man was there and talking to me as well.

He must have noticed we were late arrivals for he was telling me about what had been happening earlier in the day. How miraculously people had been healed of many things.

I couldn't concentrate on what he was saying for the all too familiar buzzing was starting in my head again. Only then did I realise that the spirits had been driven away and now were clawing back into me again. Things had just seemed so right that I hadn't even noticed.

Now that they were again pervading my spaces I had to turn away from the man. It must have seemed very rude of me but luckily Rachel noticed something was happening and broke away from her conversation to help me.

She raised a firm hand and consoling glance in the direction of the man, coming to my side to guide me from the very place we had journeyed so long to reach.

There was nothing more we could do that night and we made our way across half the town to where Abrineth had secured our stay.

The angry buzzing of my attendant spirits was lessened enough for me to continue almost normally, but the joy I was starting to feel at Yeheshua's house was now replaced again by the sadness of my appointed lot. Not wholly so, for the hope that had flowered in that joy within me had left its indelible impression.

M.B. #55

I sat on my pallet in the place we were staying while Rachel was making something for us to eat.

The visit to Mirimion had ended sadly even after the initial beautiful promise of it, and now my devil laden mind was convincing me that I would never be able to partake in what was being offered.

All of it snatched from me again and the more I tried to hold onto it the more the chance seemed to drain away, leaving nothing but an awful hollowness.

A central emptiness that belonged to the demon-spirits, yet my limbs were filled with a horrible jangling of nerves; both a residue and warning of their return.

Food held no interest for me, nor lying down any prospect of rest.

Thinking was the worst thing because my own thoughts were fully merged into those demons who possessed me.

'I deserved all that was happening to me; disobeying my parents, deserting the Most High God,' my mind ranted at me. 'Deceiving my high priestess and the Goddesses too; always continuing to flaunt my pride before anyone else's wisdom,' and here my fall was being accompanied by the taunts echoing back from within the misery; *there was no-one to save me… a fool's dream… give it up… eat what I had truly earned.*'

Rachel knocked on the door and came into the room carrying a tray of spicy smelling food. One look at me told her things were not well.

For a while I had forgotten the devils' very real powers, but now they were back in full strength and consumed with a terrible desperation.

Dark wings flapped in and around my thoughts, clawed talons eating into my vitals as I doubled up in pain. Everything was buzzing in my head.

"Mary are you alright? This food is just what you need. Would you like me to leave it here?

"*Go away,*" I heard an ugly guttural voice utter the words out of my mouth, "*go and shrivel your dags elsewhere, witch-whore.*"

Rachel almost dropped the food in shock, just managing to place the tray on a low table beside the door as she hurriedly ducked backwards out of the room.

The leading devils swung my arm at the tray of food, scattering the contents across the floor.

'*Down on your knees, bitch,*' that harsh and vile voice sounded within and ouside and my legs crumpled under me, leaving me scrabbling around in the mess.

102

'*This is all you are good for, making food into faeces. Excretia is what you are, and what you will get.*' My hands pushed into the filth and smeared it over my face, and it did truly smell as the demon described; making me cringe and retch.

'*Eat your death*' and I turned to face the presence of darkest dread, the shadow of evil. I knew my death was here; the demons' play had reached the finish.

Yet… "No harm shall come to her," the voice-memory came back to me, quiet but distinct, despite Death's demons presences. The irrepressible kindness in those words was everything the devils were desperate to blot out; but hadn't quite managed to.

I knew, absolutely, that this was the moment I had to act, and without hesitation I grasped my vision and dived inwardly to where the voice was somehow shining at the heart of me; careless of anything other than getting there.

A dreadful wail sounded all around and the fearful buzzing threatened to engulf me, but I clung to the candlelight of compassion that shone in the void, and I wouldn't leave hold of it.

It was still a long night that I faced, holding intact whilst the cacophony of terror continued, that turned eventually to whisperings and coaxing; for me to be sensible and face up to the real world.

And normally I would have heeded what sounded like my own good sense, but the unexpected gift of my possession was that I knew beyond any doubt what it was I really needed.

What I felt here in the deepest part of me could not be gainsaid by any amount of smooth and clever thinking.

So, I managed not to listen to those disparaging voices, and even slept a bit before the dawn light woke me again.

M.B. #56

Rachel had stayed the night outside my room in heartfelt prayer, and had set Abrineth to guard the door to the alley lest any of our noises drew unwelcome attention.

Thankfully, the ensuing outbursts weren't so loud as the first.

Eventually she had fallen asleep as well and now awoke stiff-limbed and sore. For a few moments she couldn't remember where she was, but as her memories of the last night returned, she got up hurriedly; there were sounds of movement from within the room.

Hesitantly Rachel's hand stretched out to open the door and she started in shock as it opened in front of her. I was stood there, and to Rachel's immense relief my eyes didn't have the mad glare she had seen there before.

"Have you some water?" I asked, "I am so thirsty."

I wanted her to hug me but was frightened of the turbulence that still stalked inside my mind. She smiled broadly though and scurried off to get us both a drink.

As we sat together, I described my feelings of urgency to go back to Mirimion, before unpredictable streams of thoughts could return to confuse and confound me again.

Rachel explained there would be no healing done that day as it was the Sabbath and Yeheshua was spending the day teaching some of his close disciples. This much she had been able to gather from the woman she had talked to last evening.

I still wanted to return. I didn't care if there was nobody else around. All the better in some ways. I dearly wished to see that it was real; yes, to try and recapture the moment when he had been speaking there.

Reluctantly Rachel agreed to accompany me, but when we reached Mirimion neither of us wanted to go too close to the house. We loitered beneath the trees, enjoying something of the shade they gave and watching the house for signs of life.

I could feel Rachel wasn't altogether enjoying it and was on the point of saying we should go when a flurry of activity came down the road.

One man was leading a few others at a fast pace. He was talking to the two directly by his side and they were laughing. The sun was warm but the day hadn't yet reached its full heat.

Before the group turned into Yeheshua's house I already knew that they were going there. I recognised the Master from my vision in the desert. When I had been driven from the last village and had thought my death was upon me.

The same kindness shone in his face; the same tawny hair and beard; the same feeling of, of sureness, is what I saw. Then he was round the corner and had gone into his house.

Just for a moment his eyes had taken in the two of us, stood underneath the trees. Dark eyes across the intervening shadows and the bright lit road.

When he had gone, we looked at each other and both had the same thought, I know. He saw us standing here. He saw us and we saw him.

One of the men came out and started sweeping out the front yard where all the people had been. Then he thought better of it and put the broom away.

It was the Sabbath after all.

He got out a wooden chair and placed it in the shade and sat there instead.

I think he must have seen us standing where we were but it didn't bother him. Instead, he himself defined a kind of boundary for us. Yeheshua would be teaching in a room behind, somewhere in the house.

Two men and a woman came up towards the house, to the doorway where the man we thought of as the guard was sat. They talked for a few moments and then the visitors turned and left.

We were just thinking of doing the same, of going back to where we were staying, thankful for what we had seen already, when two women came out of a side door in the house and came across towards us.

Both had shawls over their heads, as we did. One was slightly older than the other and it was her that came forward and addressed us both.

"Hello, my name is Mary, and my son has asked me to make sure you are alright. He is the teacher Yeheshua who lives in this house."

Something about this woman's presence was totally engaging. She was relaxed and made feel at ease as well. "My name is Mary too; Mary Magdalene," I said, "and we have come looking for Yeheshua's help. Well, actually Rachel has brought me here because of my problem."

I had never talked like this since the time that I had been abominated, and Rachel looked at me in shocked surprise.

"There are these presences in me that I cannot break free of. They control much of my thinking, and anything I feel they latch onto and feed on if they can… leaving me helpless to stop what they do."

This was the first time I had spoken of what was happening to me and I could at the same time feel stirrings of protest from the spirits themselves.

It seemed that Yeheshua's mother was herself a kind of shield against their malicious power; but which I knew still lay coiled, deadly and ever watchful within me.

She turned to talk with Rachel next, asking her where she had travelled from and where she stayed. They seemed to me to have a natural understanding and Mary asked us both whether we should like to come inside and take some refreshment.

The other woman introduced herself as Salome and it was with a little trepidation that I followed them towards the side door of the house. The balance of control within my mind was finely held and it felt like I was taking a cage of wild and dangerous animals in there with me.

The inside of the house was like others I had seen but there was something a bit different. It wasn't plush but there was an almost shining cleanness. There were other women busy inside. A working harmony prevailed. Certainly, no place for unruly spirits to be let loose.

I knew my job was to be carrying them, containing them, and this I concentrated on doing.

Yeheshua's mother smiled at me and gave me a glass of hot sweet mint tea which was my favourite. I could smile in reply and enjoy the drink. Her face emanated serenity and was quite like her son's, except with grey eyes and streaks of grey in her dark hair.

There was a knock at the side door and one of the women let a traveller in. He looked as though he had come a long way and took off his cloak and exchanged his boots for soft sandals.

Mary greeted him as a dear friend; embracing him; "Lamaas; welcome," she said. "The master has been hoping you could get here. He is teaching in the inner room. Will you have a drink with us, or will you go straight in?"

"Dear lady mother," the man replied, who reminded me a bit of Sarita's Kasver. He must have travelled from the East I thought. "How could I not accept your offer? But how can I delay going in either?"

Mary pressed a glass of tea into his hand and he took his time savouring it. "Thank you, that was like a whole day's rest," he said, and laughed. "I shall not delay any longer then."

He had looked around the room and smiled at Rachel and me. Then he had gone further into the house, and Mary went with him.

I looked around and saw that we were in an anteroom that seemed to be also used for meals. Off this room, towards the back of the house, was the kitchen where most of the women were working.

I was just beginning to wonder what we should be doing when Salome came over and sat with us, offering us some biscuits that had been freshly baked. I took one and nibbled at it, ever fearful that each new activity would tip my balance. It was made of almonds and probably tasted delicious but I couldn't spare the attention to notice.

Then someone else knocked on the side door and Salome opened it to see that a woman had brought some fruits as an offering. I glimpsed the man who had been out the front stood just behind the woman; Salome nodded to him that it was all right.

He went away and Salome let her in. She came and sat at the table I was at.

By now mother Mary had come back into the room and the newcomer rose quickly and gave the offerings to her, and she accepted them gracefully. Mary gave them in turn to Salome who had just returned with a drink for the woman.

Yeheshua's mother was clearly in charge of the household and made a few quick arrangements. She suggested to Salome that the newcomer might like to help prepare a dish with the fruit she had brought then, turning to Rachel, asked: "Please could you both stay for a while as well. The master wishes that I spend some time with Mary?"

"I would love to," said Rachel. "Is there anything I can do to help?"

"I think that you could stay with us, Mary and I, if you would. Let's go into the front room. I'd like to show it to you. We call it the long-room. Yeheshua has been working on it to make it suitable for his work."

The long-room had been made from what had previously been two front rooms, either side of a central corridor that had led from the front door into the centre of the house.

The corridor walls had been replaced by sturdy wooden arches that completely opened up the space.

There was a graceful armchair set with a cushion at the far end, facing back down the length of the room and also slightly to the window at the front. Down that end the windows had been widened in a similar way to the arches, so that the space outside the front of the house could almost be made to become a part of the room.

As we entered sunlight was streaming through the furthest open-shuttered windows to where the chair was; with tiny dust particles glinting in the rays.

On the stone floor there were many rugs and cushions where people obviously would sit and listen to the Master speak.

Down the side of that half of the room, close to the inner wall, was a long bench and behind this a gap wide enough for people to walk down to a door.

Next to Yeheshua's chair by the far wall there was a small table and a short bench with a wide rack, full of scrolls, mounted on the wall behind.

There were three doors into the long-room. One, at the furthest end near to the chair, led back into the house; obviously for access, to and fro, particularly by the master, but others too.

Another, down this end, was where we had come in, from the anteroom and kitchen beyond. Then there was the main double door, towards the street, which was where most people would enter and leave by.

In this half of the room there were chairs and several couches; mostly by the central arches where sickly people could easily be placed.

We went over, still with our drinks, to four chairs that were by the window, set around a low table. My heart gratefully sensed the purposeful peace that the room inspired, even though the wings of darkness still flapped menacingly around the back of my mind.

Mary asked me how long it was since I had been in Galilee, and so I started to tell her my story.

Her face stayed serenely beautiful, though there were clear concerns being etched there as well. Her attentive nods pulled me to say more than otherwise I might have.

At first it was remarkably easy for me to talk, although I could still hear the spirit mutterings, but as my story came closer to the point of seeing the Magus Simon, things got harder and harder.

It was as if my tongue was getting tied in knots and the volume of the noise inside my head grew impossible to ignore.

As their clamour to shut me up became intense, Mary put a hand on mine and turned her questions instead upon Rachel.

Rachel had heard much of what had happened to me from Johannus and was able to fill many of the gaps I had left, but the struggle still raged on within me.

At the point where I thought control was being ripped from my will, a sudden light shone brightly, just for a brief moment, forcing closed the opening breach.

In the respite that this gave, I looked down the long-room to see that the Master Yeheshua had entered in and was walking up to where we sat.

An endless moment yet he moved in certainty, bringing that presence of serenity that had come to me in that desert vision.

He was smiling as though this was a reunion of old friends rather than an urgent rescue of the demon crazed woman that I was.

I turned towards him, leaving my chair to kneel upon the floor as he approached.

The spirits had again stirred a frenzied buzzing, but somehow I managed to ignore them.

He wore the softest of robes, that I felt brush along my outstretched arms as he placed his hands at my elbows to lift me up.

His hair brushed against mine and as I rose, he breathed into my ear; spoke the Word in Holy Breath.

There was a sound that came with the breath that was like a thousand million tiny stars, tinkling together. This noise was more encompassing than the buzzing, rolling it up like a mighty rushing wind might gather leaves; growing, till nothing else was there and then receding out and out and out into the furthest recesses of my inner world; little rippling waves going on to the end.

Then stillness. I stood there, amazed and transfixed. There were no more spirits in my mind; I knew for sure. Gone, and I was free.

It was impossible to take in at first. Instead, I collapsed gently to the floor at the feet of the one who had rescued me. There I felt entirely happy and at peace.

Yeheshua was talking to Rachel about where she had come from and whether she wished to stay. She briefly said she was from Tyre and had brought me there because she had heard of his abilities.

She said as well that she very much wanted to stay and learn from him anything he might wish to teach her.

I had somehow managed to get back up from the ground and Yeheshua turned to me again.

"Mary Magdalene," he said and those two words were like a welcome and acceptance. "It is done. You are free." Do you wish to learn the way to the peace eternal within as well?"

"I do," I said, "with everything I am." The answer came easily. There was no question.

"Well, first I would like you to go and make your peace with your mother. She must need to see you very much. Then, when you are completely ready, come back here again and find me."

Being given a task to do was like another release. A purpose to fulfil and a promised return. I bowed my head in assent and said I would.

Rachel cleared her throat and asked whether she could take me to my mother and then come back as well.

Yeheshua beamed a smile that meant more than words, then "Thank you," he said, "and please do come back as soon as you are able."

Somewhere in the house a gong had sounded and the master took us both by an arm and moved towards the ante-room door. "You must come and eat with us. Mother, is there room for two more with you ladies?"

"Of course," she answered, like a gentle wind to his strong sun. "Plenty of room and plenty to eat as well; and then I would like to show you both our garden as well. Once all the men have finished their repast out there."

They laughed together as at some unseen joke, and we went through to taste our first meal in His house. Food had never tasted so good before.

N.B. #01

We didn't in fact travel to Magdala till the next day, as we spent most of the afternoon at the Master's house as well.

After the meal mother Mary had taken us around her courtyard garden and then Yeheshua came out again and invited us all to come and gather there. He wanted to speak to us together.

It was a wonderful time for me. I could have sat and listened forever. I felt like he was talking just to me.

"Sometimes the way of Truth seems like a gentle, peaceful path; like now, like being in this garden; and sometimes it seems filled with the hardest things for us to overcome.

What we have to give, the efforts we have to make, seem huge at the difficult times but once they pass it is as though they were but a minor thing to bear.

We can never do enough, give enough, to have earned the gifts that our Father God wishes to bestow upon us. Simply to accept them is our greatest task.

And when I say Father God, you must understand that I could as well say Mother God. These distinctions are a fiction of our human thought. Love does not recognise the boundaries of form; it reigns supreme, the same in every heart, and we must show the way to everyone who has the ears to hear..."

It was like a new day had dawned for me and I travelled to Magdala the next day with a glow in me that was greater than the sun on my skin and the wind in my hair.

A glow that was throughout my being and Rachel was the same.

I wanted to shout out to the world that the Messiah was here.

Sing out the glory of the Most High God.

Dance the dance of loving the Lord.

I might have annoyed Rachel with this sudden transformation from her former morose companion, but she didn't show it. Instead, she joined in when I sang a song she knew and told me how thankful she was that our journey had turned to so much good.

And Magdala was not far away. We would only need part of the day to reach it.

Rachel drove the mule cart quite fast. She wanted to get back to Yeheshua soon. Though she understood why release from the spirits was so exciting for me, she also knew the real journey had only just begun.

She wanted to learn whatever the master would teach, having realised he was a healer through knowledge of the Soul of things; and she was so happy for this chance to learn.

"This is only just beginning for me too," I acknowledged. "I need to be able to experience for myself."

"Yes, and certainly we must be before we can think to help anyone else in this way," Rachel mused. "It must take great dedication," she paused and in it I felt the quietness of my breathing. "Now that I have found the Master, I know I have waited for this all my life."

My heart sighed in complete agreement.

"Should we get something to eat in Magdala before we go to your mother's house? Or is it really your brother's now?"

"No, she will want to feed us, I'm sure;" and then, "yes, I suppose it is his, but I can't say I'm looking forward to seeing him again. I shouldn't say that but I don't think I meant anything to him, other than being a total nuisance."

When we made our way up the road that led to my old home on the outskirts of the small town, something had changed. A lot had changed. I hardly recognised anything.

In the first place one of our former neighbours seemed to have gone, house and all. Then the area around the house seemed overgrown. I started to be worried.

We went down the path to our door and saw the house, I understood at least why the neighbour's house had gone. Our house had large extensions built onto that side.

Yet this sign of prosperity was incongruously offset by the already shabby state of the surrounds.

We knocked at the door and after a while we knocked again. Just as I was going to go around the side, someone came to open the door. Jacob; not my brother or my mother but someone who had been my father's close friend and business partner.

He looked at me for long seconds. "Uncle Jacob," I said, "don't you know me?"

"Mary? Is that you? Can it be you? Wait till I tell Ruth." He moved first back and then forward, apparently undecided whether to go first and tell my mother or to come forward and greet me.

Suddenly he was giving me an embrace like he used to and then he turned to Rachel too. "Uncle Jacob, this is a friend of mine; Rachel from Tyre. Rachel this is a dear family friend, Jacob Ben Geddon."

"Welcome my dear," said Jacob to her. "I must announce your return to your mother, Mary. Give me a couple of moments, please."

We went in and could hear Uncle Jacob talking to someone in an inner room. Would my mother be happy to see me? I worried for the hundredth time.

Or would Benjamin be here? I wondered, but blocked the thought out quickly.

She hurried, hobbling as best she could to the hall where we stood, not quite the way she might have bustled a few years ago but even now she couldn't wait any longer than necessary. Her daughter was home.

She embraced me with tears in her eyes and words clogged with emotion. I too was unable to stop from breaking down and crying.

She had grabbed my robe and was pulling me through into the inner room and I just managed to beckon Rachel to follow.

Mother turned to acknowledge her too. A scrawny hand grasped and squeezed Rachel's in way of greeting and thanks.

"What a day; what a wonderful day," she was saying in her gruff voice. She had only a shadow of her former strength. She was quite bent and shrunken but still her spirit shone through.

"Welcome home my naughty girl: welcome home. Come and tell me how you have been, away so long. Look Jacob, what a fine woman she has become. A bit skinny but we can fix that perhaps."

N.B. #02

I laughed with relief to see how happy she was, in this moment at least. I could see that recent years had not been kind. "Where is Benjamin? Will he be home tonight?" I asked.

It was Jacob who answered me: "Your brother died, over two years ago now;" he said. "It has been very hard on your mother."

He carried on: "First Rebecca losing her life in childbirth with my grandson. Then your... own disappearance and then her only son dying of a wasting disease. All that and losing Joseph too. Hard years, very hard; but now you are back again, beyond hope. It is a miracle."

"Benjamin dead. Oh Ma! My poor, poor Ma," I said going forward to hold her sobbing shoulders. I couldn't tell which emotion she was shaking with most but I could at least try to comfort her.

Rachel had asked Jacob if she could help by making us all something hot to drink, and Jacob agreed to help her, leaving me alone with my mother.

Some time later we were sat around with our drinks talking about the intervening years.

Jacob told their side of the story, with little interjections here and there from Ma.

They didn't know which came first, his great success or the onset of the disease. Business had boomed for him once he had gained control of much of the olive oil trade in the area. Mostly just shrewd good sense had won him a small fortune, though some complained at the ruthlessness of his dealings. No pot was made without the potter's hands working it.

Then even as he was planning to get married it became clear that something was wrong with his health. Coughing was how it started, and in the end he had gone without anything the doctors or his money could do to help. In between he had built the fine hall onto the house, that we had seen from outside; to hold the wedding celebration that never happened.

Jacob had been securing the family finances since then, to make sure Ruth was all right. She still had a good income from the olive and other distribution businesses and also had two servants here at the house. A married couple who helped run things, but Ruth hadn't the will or the energy to do much more than get by day to day and Jacob had his own affairs to deal with.

When it became my turn to share my story it was hard to tell them that I had been a priestess in Astarte's temple. I could see it in uncle Jacob's face that he thought it unthinkable. My mother thoughts also seemed clear: 'what would your father have thought?'

Rachel had put a hand on my arm and I found the strength to continue and relate how in trying to help the city outcasts, lepers and those possessed by unclean spirits I had myself gone against a black magician who conjured devils to possess me.

I faltered here, even more affected than my audience, who themselves were clearly horrified by my described predicament. Both my mother and I were crying.

Rachel carried on the story to tell how the temple scribe Arianne and a silversmith Johannus had helped get me to her in Tyre, and how she had heard of the healer Yeheshua in Galilee, so resolved to bring me there.

"Who is this Johannus?" asked Jacob.

"Someone who himself was in trouble with the 'so-called' Magus, and who was leaving Antioch to visit relatives in Bethany," I answered.

Rachel continued, "in Capernaum we found Yeheshua, who drove the devils from Mary when no-one else could do so. I myself do some healing in my country, but never have seen such a master healer. I shall be travelling back there as soon as I can. You might have heard of his great works."

"We have indeed," said my mother; "the 'miracle worker'; but we didn't know how much to believe. So, it is true then, he can really do the things that people say?"

"Incredible and wonderful," I replied. "I am living proof of what he does. Rachel has told you a little of how bad it was with me. I could carry on no further without help. He has brought me back to this life, as if from death."

Jacob was looking slightly sceptical, but my mother was clearly moved. "If only we had been able to take Benjamin to him when he was ill," she said; "but then again, he probably wouldn't have gone. It seems that some faith is needed to get Ye'shua's help. Benjamin put his faith in whatever his money could buy him."

She looked overwhelmingly sad again but then she turned, stretching out her arm to pat my leg as I sat beside her. "But you are back Mary; God be praised. Twice and thrice praised for He has brought you back to me whole and shining. We must put the past behind and I will live thankful to have you for whatever time is left to me."

"Jacob, I now give my share of the businesses directly over to my daughter, Mary. You two must work together for the best for both families. Mary, if you wish to, I would love you to make this house our home again. Make it shine like your brother tried to, but died before he could even have his wedding feast here."

I nodded and said that I would, but I knew that my mother recognised my faltering when she mentioned my brother's wishes. "Mary, you know he changed in those final weeks of his illness. He told me how much he regretted trying to marry you off, driving you away. We had never spoken of it for several years. You had become a forbidden subject, but in those last days all that changed. It hurt him most deeply that he had taken you from me, and that he was leaving me old and alone. Please forgive him too."

A lump came up into my throat from deep within. Somehow, I couldn't hold back the emotion that was rising through me in a wave. I had to cover my face as it crumpled once again into the tears of a hurt child.

It was my mother's turn to comfort me, and we sat together for a long while letting things pass between us in the silence that renewed our bond and healed our hurts.

Rachel and Jacob were talking in the other room, no doubt about business, as there they had much in common. When they came back to us Rachel was saying that she must get back to Capernaum.

My mother did her best to insist that she should stay as our honoured guest and I did too, but it seemed she wanted to give some instructions to Abrineth to take back to Tyre, about her staying on in Capernaum.

Jacob said he had wanted to introduce her to his family as well, and she seemed to be weakening for a moment. I tried again. "Rachel I would be so grateful if you could just stay tonight and meet my new business partners as I think there could be a tie up with the businesses that you have. No-one could give me a better helping start." Then added: "except for you, Uncle Jacob."

"I should really love to stay, Mary," she said, "and meet Daniel" she said to Jacob; "but apart from talking to Abrineth, the master said for me to come back quickly."

"You are right, he did;" I replied, "and maybe sometime there will be things we can do together that will help him too."

"Yes, I'm sure;" Rachel smiled, "that we will. Meanwhile, I think your uncle Jacob is the best help you could have in business. I really would love to stay, but I need to be back".

I understood, and I would miss her comforting presence so much. She had been such a tower of strength to me. How could I ever express what her taking me to Yeheshua meant to me? Except that she found him too…

We caught each other's glances, like thoughts that needed no words, yet said our farewells nevertheless, knowing that we should meet again very soon. I had some work to do first, but I would be retuning to Mirimion as soon as I could.

N.B. #03

There was a lot of work for me to do in the days that followed but I had been given the energy to do it. It was such a huge uplift to have had my life given back. I had to make the best use of this opportunity.

The words of the goddess Hecate about opportunities were starting to make sense I thought; here I was, a woman of substance and I had found the Master as well.

Even more so the words of granny Beth who had said I would find great kindness, but first I would have great need for that kindness. Her words had come true; I must never forget just how deep that need had been.

The house was not in bad condition, but I needed help to get it to be what I wanted. Cleaning it, airing it, these things I could do, but there was heavier work needed too, like clearing the outside where the surroundings had got overgrown and wild.

It was such a pleasure for me to open up rooms, to let the sunshine into places that hadn't seen it for ages. Just like what was happening to me. Free; free to breathe in the air, full of the glorious scents of the day's passing moments.

Benjamin's hall was a large, impressive space but was by no means the only or even the greatest improvements that he had done to the house. There were new bedrooms set around another courtyard and improved kitchens and wash-rooms too.

Once I had met up with Daniel who had been married to Becky, my eldest sister, I was able to assess the funds available and the people to help me with the house.

Daniel was Jacob's eldest son and had been devastated by the double loss of his wife and unborn child. After a year he married again but I could see even now how hard he had been hit. He was much quieter than the brashly confident young man I remembered.

His second wife Sarah was really sweet and the two boys they had were quite a handful; obviously the pride of Jacob's eyes. Jacob had a daughter too, with three children, but she lived away in Tiberias and he seldom saw them.

There had been another daughter, Elizabeth, who I had known quite well and who had never been strong. Apparently her health had got worse and when she was bitten by an unknown insect she got a fever that she didn't recover from. I was sad to hear this.

Daniel was very helpful with all the arrangements I needed to make. He had the businesses well under control and yet wasn't resentful at all of the fact that I was now involved, rather than my ailing mother who hadn't interfered at all.

As far as the house was concerned, he knew people I could hire to do the things I wanted and also someone who would make an ideal gardener; an older man who had recently lost his wife and who also needed a room to stay.

I found Hilda myself in town, a girl to help look after the enlarged house, and her mother came along too, which pleased Ruth who found they had much in common.

Many of the people I spoke with were very interested to hear about Yeheshua but there were some who were much more disparaging, warning me that he was nothing but a trouble-maker and a fake. I wondered how they came to this opinion as it didn't seem founded on anything more than rumour.

More challenging to me in some ways was people's attitude to my past; my life as a priestess of Astarte in Antioch.

Clearly most close family friends would prefer that it was not mentioned or, as far as possible, even known about. Uncle Jacob had great difficulty with it and Daniel was much the same. They obviously felt that it tainted them.

I was not prepared to be ashamed and play the disgraced penitent. I still had dear friends in Antioch who I wanted to see again. Arianne and Sarita particularly.

How would they react I wondered when they heard that the Messiah was really here; was real; was travelling around preaching and healing. That even now he was living in Capernaum.

Wouldn't they want to hold a festival as for Adonis reborn? Why should I turn my back and deny all that these people believed just because of what another people believed?

What about Isis? Was she come too, as was foretold?

I thought of mother Mary and my heart skipped a beat: 'First is mother'.

At least my own mother backed me up. I didn't feel that she wanted me to deny my past. She seemed to understand something about fate and destiny and her love for me opened her to possibilities that others rejected.

The path I had taken had led me to my Master, even though I had been attacked and possessed by demon spirits on the way there; but he had wiped my slate clean.

What was it the Master had said about all the barriers that we had in us? That some were obvious but most were not?

The spirits were obvious but I could see now that there were so many other little prejudices, habits and things that pushed us away from that which Yeheshua called us to acknowledge; in others certainly, but in me as well.

If I hadn't been so violently damaged by that Magus and the spirits, would I have ever got to the house Mirimion? Would I have found my Master?

Even now I could sense how I contained some of all that I fought to avoid in the spirits. Anger, hate, lust and, and something in me that felt a trepidation about returning to Capernaum.

Thankfully though, my heart and soul were pulling me too strongly to be denied.

I went to see my mother and told her that I would be going back to be with Yeheshua. I wanted to know the Truth he talked about.

She smiled and said that if she was younger, she would come too. I was surprised.

"If it is possible, I shall ask him to come to Magdala; to preach and to stay with us here."

Her face was creased with wrinkles that told of her delight at the idea. "I shall make sure that the house is ready," she said. "If you bring him, how wonderful that would be. If you go with him elsewhere, then so be it. I shall keep the house ready for you, whenever you want to be here."

It was my turn to show my happiness. That she accepted me so completely was truly more than I could ever have expected. I hugged her to me. "I shall ask him, for you," I said.

Before I left, she brought me something that she had been working on in the days that I had been busy with the house and businesses. It was the old priestess cloak that I still had with me.

It had become almost un-wearable because of tears and threadbare areas, but now it looked quite different. It was neatly sown and patched with a rather fine green material that almost matched the original. At the neck she had worked in a gilded chain and fastener that transformed it into a quite respectable cloak; old but well loved.

I didn't know what to say.

She chuckled and then sighed deeply. "You know your father was a good man", she looked at me and I thought I saw a much younger woman behind her eyes, "but that doesn't mean he was always right. Nor these ways we live under. I cannot say I have always agreed with them but didn't speak up. Not the way you have; I should have supported you better back then."

"Mother, you did all that you could. I just needed to understand these things for myself."

We looked at each other. "I cannot say that I totally regret the life that I have followed though; not now that it has led me to this," I said; "and thank you so much for all you are doing for me, with me; It means more than I can ever tell you."

N.B. #04

Daniel and I left for Capernaum early. It had been nearly two weeks since I had come back to Magdala with Rachel, and I had done all that I could there for the moment.

Our small train of asses left early, before the sun had risen, but still my mother had been up to see me off.

The asses belonged to the distribution business that Daniel ran and I had a share in. The donkey I rode was nearly white. She was very huggable and was called Cara.

It made me think of Antioch, the early trips to market, and the girl I called Cara, who was probably a temple administrator now; or soon would be.

The difference in this scenery to those city streets and alleyways that we travelled though was immense. Only the sky was shared and today that was already a fine light blue with hardly even the hint of a cloud. The inland sea was spread out to our right and dipped in and out of sight as we passed around the rocky outcrops.

We reached Capernaum after only one tea-stop where we also shared some herb bread that I had baked with my mother.

Daniel was going to come to Mirimion with me to hear Yeheshua speak, though how much he wanted to was hard to read.

First though, I wanted to leave my things at the room I would be using, as our business owned a few rooms there; and a storehouse. These were close to the marketplace and to where Rachel and I had stayed.

It felt a little strange to own things like this but Daniel made sure the donkeys were stabled and then joined me for the walk to Mirimion. Later he would be rejoining the others who had taken the wine and olive-oil jars on into town.

There was no one at Yeheshua's house except a girl who pulled the view flap back on the side door and told us that the Master had left early in the morning to go up the shore to where he was teaching and healing.

She explained how the crowd had swelled in recent days to make it impracticable to be teaching from the house.

We thanked her and I worked out that it wouldn't take us too long to catch up. The place she spoke of was a lakeside bay, but not too far away to put me off walking there.

Daniel decided not to come as he needed to meet with the team before midday. I didn't really mind as I didn't want to be dragging him anywhere. He could make up his own mind in his own time.

The walk was longer than I thought, and the day had really warmed up but I loved every step of it, despite the heat and dust. I was going somewhere I really wanted to go.

Following the track around a promontory I saw the first signs of lots of people milling around the water's edge.

There was a fishing boat pulled up to the beach and a small group working around a fire nearby. Cooking fish I guessed. I thought I recognised Salome there.

There were a lot more gathered close to where a small stream snaked its way through the scrub. I would have gone there except that I was drawn to the further side of the inlet where the track came right near to the edge of the lake. There was a low ridge covered with people who were watching something going on just out of view.

I knew that was where Yeheshua was and quickly skirted everything else going on to see what he was doing.

The crowd was larger than the hollow there could contain and I couldn't make out much through the swarm of heads. Clearly though, from snatches of conversations I heard around me, Yeheshua had already spent a couple of hours teaching and was now healing the many suffering people that had made their way or been brought to him.

I wormed my way through the crowd, wanting so much to be close and to express some thanks for myself as well.

And I managed to reach a place where I could see him bending over a make-shift bed onto which an elderly matron had been put. His hands were working around her ankles with a palpable gentleness.

She pushed herself up into a sitting position and Yeheshua placed first one of her feet and then the other on the ground next to the bed. He took her hands and pulled her gently up whilst she looked in wonder down her black dress to her ankles.

She stepped forward and a couple of her family reached to catch her but she didn't need them. Instead, she turned to the man who had healed her legs and cried into his shoulder with happiness. He whispered something to her and she nodded her head, several times.

Then Yeheshua moved to another man who was bent and ill with coughing. He rubbed the man's back quite vigorously and drove the illness from him with force of word and will. "This coughing has no part you," he said. "Fear not; take your herd back to the high pastures; you are whole and well."

The man gingerly unbent himself, his breath coming easier as with each inhalation his lungs filled more wholly than before; no longer sending him into convulsions. Yeheshua moved on to another person, out of my sight. Two disciples went with him and another checked that those who had been healed were all right to carry on.

Even with the two healings that I saw, I loved how he was able to recognise their need; giving each person his whole attention in that moment. You could feel the connection.

Behind me I heard the stirrings of conversation from of few men who sounded as though they came from Judea.

"Do you think that they are planted, for effect? For us?" asked one voice.

"Probably," answered another, "but they are not even very impressive miracles."

"His speech was quite impressive though, I thought," said a third. "Untaught in the finer points but he certainly reaches the common people. Raises their aspirations, but where will that all lead I wonder?"

I couldn't help turning a bit to look at these men. Pharisees I realised; but couldn't they see what was happening here? Couldn't they see and feel the genuineness of the care and concern being given? Apparently not.

I wanted to say something to them but they were completely oblivious of me and continued on another tack.

"Then there is that 'baptism' rite," said the first man. "What would possess a sensible man to get ducked in the water? Especially by some follower of this rabbi and not by the man himself. What do they think it is doing?"

"Purification, like the Baptist on the Jordan," answered another voice, "but only the most gullible would believe that nonsense. That years of impure behaviour can be eradicated that way is ludicrous."

"How hard do they think it is? We have spent a lifetime following the correct ways. Does he think we need 'purifying' too?"

I was struggling to keep my mouth shut. I had turned to face them completely now. They were definitely Pharisees. "Is that what is happening at the other end of the beach?" I asked. "The baptism rite?"

They seemed to see me for the first time and were clearly horrified that they had been accosted by a strange woman. Almost as if touched by an 'unclean', and looking around I realised I was indeed the only woman nearby.

I didn't need or wait for an answer, but I couldn't help myself from giving one parting shot: "So maybe it isn't complete purification," I said, "but a demonstration of some humility before the Most High would be a good start, don't you think?"

N.B. #05

I had left the Pharisees, not wanting to wait to hear what they might say or think. They made me so angry. What did they think was so great about them? They were everything I had left Magdala to get away from.

Cross as well that they had driven me away from being near to the Master, I realised. However, that baptism was something I hadn't yet received, though Yeheshua himself had driven the devils from me.

Huffing, to and at myself, I topped the rise and went back along the shore to where the other crowd was scattered. I had calmed down; the day was still glorious and as I walked, I watched a few little white clouds strung high above the lake enhancing the deep blue around them and being reflected in the water beneath.

There was a line of people waiting in a queue and others sitting back from the sides of the stream, and on the rocks that fringed the lakeside.

Just before the stream reached the beach it formed a kind of natural pool where the water flowed out over a shelf of rocks. This was where things were happening and now that more of the crowd were seated it was easier to see what was going on.

Two of Yeheshua's close disciples were stood up to their knees in the pool and baptising each person in the queue as their turn arrived. I watched a young man that had reached the front, step rather gingerly into the water.

The first disciple asked him something and he replied he would. Then the two together lowered the supplicant into the water just where it flowed into the pool, splashing water all over his bowed head and torso.

Then they had raised him up again, one at each side saying, "Lord we come to you to be cleansed of our sins and receive new life. We beseech your help for our brother Michael to accept your Grace."

Then the second disciple explained something to Michael as he left the water, directing him to someone who was sat under a tree. Meanwhile the first disciple was addressing the next in the line.

Michael looked uplifted as he walked over to the tree and I went to join the back of the queue to be baptised. A woman took my sandals and told me they would be placed on the other side of the pool.

The quietness of the people in the queue was like a gentle rocking. I was reminded of mothers or fathers carrying their babies; except we were cradling our hopes instead.

The calmness was a balm that I valued all the more because of the time I had spent invaded by restless spirits. Time could come to a stop and I would be complete. Someone was singing a song. Almost a lullaby I heard myself think.

The queue moved slowly on, with an occasional shuffle in rhythm to slowed thoughts.

Then out of the corner of my eye I caught a commotion coming along the beach. Yeheshua was walking at pace down the waterline, with disciples and the crowd strung out behind.

I was nearly at the front of the queue and we couldn't help but turn and watch. He stopped briefly at the cooking fire but before the crowd could gather round again, he carried on towards us at the stream.

The two disciples, with some difficulty, carried on what they were doing. The man in front of me was asked if he wanted to receive new life. He said he did and the first disciple said, "Then come and be washed free of the grime of this world," and the man went forward into the water.

Then before I knew it, it was my turn.

The disciple was asking me "What is your name"; "Mary," I replied "called Magdalene".

"Mary, do you want to come to the Lord and receive new Life?" I was looking at Yeheshua who had taken his sandals off and was paddling upstream in one of the rivulets.

It was just as he had been as he crossed the front room in his house. "Yes," I said. "Yes please, I do."

"Come and be washed of the sins of your life," he said and I saw Yeheshua looking at me for a single clear moment as I half stumbled into the pool.

Arms took me as I fell to my knees in the cold water. I bowed down and water was washed all over me. Refreshing, cleansing, all encompassing.

As I was pulled out of the water, baptisers giving thanks to God and me with them, I saw that the crowd had come up around the master and that a half ring of disciples had formed to give him space; I could still just see him.

One of the baptisers reminded me of where my sandals were and asked me to go and give my name to Levi who was sat under the tree. He told me too that his name was Nathaniel and the other was called Philip.

The sun gave a welcome heat that shimmered on the scene. I felt like I almost floated over the ground to where I picked up my sandals but my attention was all focussed on what was happening nearby, around Yeheshua.

N.B. #06

The four Pharisees had got near enough to ask Yeheshua a question.

"Do you expect that we should go through your baptism rite?" one of them asked. The others stood behind him like reinforcements waiting to pounce.

Yeheshua continued cooling his feet in the stream, looking down at the pebbles under the glinting surface. At last, he answered.

"When we are accepting food from His table, first we wash our hands. Is this not our way?"

"It is," answered the Pharisee.

"Then when we are asking to accept His own presence into our life, is it not right for us to wash ourselves, inside and out?"

"Yet this baptism cannot do the purification that is needed, surely," answered the persistent Pharisee. "It is a lifetime's work to try to be ready. Is that not also true?"

"More than can be done in any lifetime," answered Yeheshua. "It is not by our own efforts that we can become worthy to receive His greatest gift. Yet He wants us to come home, and He will make us ready. The rite of baptism is only a token offering of ourselves to receive His Grace."

There was a long pause as they thought about this; no one could find anything to add.

The Pharisee questioning tilted his head forward in acknowledgement of the wisdom. Then suddenly he asked: "May I receive that Grace also?" to the obvious consternation and surprise of the other Pharisees around him.

"Certainly Simon," said Yeheshua, gesturing to where the disciples Nathaniel and Philip were still standing in the Baptism pool.

The Pharisee Simon discarded his outer garments and his sandals and went over to the pool. Philip took him in, asking him his name and whether he sought to receive the presence of His Lord. He did and the two disciples took Simon and laid him in the pool, covering him in the water's flow, then helped him to his feet again.

Water was draining off his face and he was grinning like a boy. It was hard to tell it was the same man picking up his pile of clothes as the one that had stood out proudly to question Yeheshua.

His companions had left in disgust. They hadn't stayed to watch but he didn't care.

Yeheshua had put his sandals back on and was going back to give instructions about the food that had been brought and the fish that had been cooked. It was lunchtime and everyone seemed to be ready for it.

Simon, I and one or two others went over to where the disciple Levi was still taking the last names of the people baptised that morning. He gave us each a little square of cloth which he said to keep.

Simon asked why and Levi said it was to show we had received baptism that day. I thought Simon was going to ask why again but he obviously thought better of it. He took no notice of me at all, not appearing to link me to the querulous individual at the healing in the morning.

A woman came over from a group that was standing around nearby and offered me a shawl because all my clothes were completely soaked and I had found myself shivering despite the heat of the sun.

Yeheshua and two of his disciples waded out to a second fishing boat that had arrived at the beach with provisions, and after helping pass these to others who had followed, they climbed up into the boat and it was slowly edged off out into the lake. Word was that he was coming back later.

There were lots of people who had been baptised that day still sitting around the area of the stream.

Some were eating under the awnings that had been erected to provide some shade. Others had made a bit of their own shade from drying their outer robes on poles that were available from the place where the cooking was being done.

I wanted to walk up the shoreline and went to give the shawl back to the girl who had lent it to me. She insisted I kept it till later and another gave me some bread chunks and a small rounded lump of goat's cheese.

They also told me that the newly baptised would be brought to the front when Yeheshua returned; that was what the little squares of cloth denoted.

Thanking them both, I headed for the path I had spotted that wound on around the rocks.

Out on the sea was the boat with the master aboard.

Its sail was fully unfurled, catching the breezes over the water, pulling it along.

Something on the boat glinted in the sun like a signal.

From my seat on a flat rock atop a small knoll I shaded my eyes with my arm, looking for movement out there on board.

He was there; I could make out the paler colour of the robe he was wearing. He had taken the tiller.

Back on the beach more people were arriving, anxious to hear what this powerful young Rabbi would say; this man who was changing how the people thought about their lives; how they could live their lives.

I was one of them and feeling happy. My clothes had dried and I ate one piece of the bread I had been given.

When I scoured the sea again the boat was further out on the water; its sail was lowered and it seemed to be bobbing on the water out there like a beautiful lake-bird.

I chewed some more bread and cheese, thinking nothing except that this was a special day.

N.B. #07

We gave our baptism cloth-bits to the disciples that were letting us come to the front, to be close to Yeheshua as he spoke to the large crowd.

They told us that we could come back early in the morning to learn more about the journey we had embarked on. This was just the beginning.

I could hardly sleep and rose early at the first hint of dawn in the darkness. I washed, dressed and went to the underground room where the goat's milk was kept in a large pot but after a small sip, I realised I didn't actually want much; or much bread either.

Outside in the cool morning air the light was growing in the eastern sky.

I walked past Yeheshua's house, pausing to take in the feeling. There was a light in an upper room and though I couldn't just stay and watch I didn't want to leave either.

Someone came out of the side-door followed by another two and I started to walk after them as they appeared to be heading towards the lakeside.

They saw me behind and one turned round and called to me, inviting me to join them. I think he must have recognised me either from the day before or from Yeheshua's garden a couple of weeks ago.

They introduced themselves as John, James and Andrew and I walked with them, sharing in the enjoyment of a new day.

By the time we got to where the baptisms had been the day before, some people were already there and others were joining along with us.

The sun was rising majestically over the other side of the sea and there were a couple of fishing boats already out on the water.

Andrew stopped at the stream but James and I walked with John to the other end of the beach, to where the sick would be brought.

From the discussions along the road, it was clear that the arrangements for today were different from yesterday. Yeheshua was staying all morning at the house to give specific instruction to a number of disciples.

John would be dealing with the sick, working out who were able to wait for another day and who should stay to be seen by Yeheshua later.

James would be talking to the newly baptised with the view to readying those who wanted to know what full discipleship meant.

There were about ten of us that James gathered by the beach, waiting for any more to arrive. Then a boat sailed in close and two men jumped into the water and carried some supplies in to the beach.

With a bit of a jolt, I recognised both of them.

Lamaas was the first, a master from the east, joining in all the work with a good will. The other had dark curly hair and a handsome face that I had seen before.

It was on the way to Sarita's house for a party that he had made an impression on me and now did so again. It was definitely Thomas, the young lawyer and sometimes philosopher from Antioch.

Two women had come from the house as well and they took control of the supplies, calling to some young helpers to carry the baskets over to the food preparation area.

Thomas and Lamaas went to help John and after a while longer on the beach James asked us all to follow him to a quieter spot away from the water where a few trees would provide some welcome shade.

He talked for a while about the opportunity it was for us that the Messiah had come and of the things he had witnessed since meeting him. We listened and listened and I was surprised to find that I just wanted to hear more.

Thomas had come and sat with us as James was speaking of his own personal experiences. It was easy to be drawn into and held by his story.

Thomas had also brought some water with him and when James finished, we were grateful for the opportunity to have a drink; it was turning into a really hot day.

Then Thomas sat where James had been and asked what questions we might have. Into the pause of silence, I suddenly heard myself asking him how he himself had come to Yeheshua.

He looked at me and smiled but I don't think he remembered me as I did him. In the ensuing pause he closed his eyes for a few moments before he started to speak.

I was fascinated to listen to how he had searched amongst philosophies and philosophers too, to find one that lived up to what he taught. Some had been genuinely good men. Some had been charismatic and powerful speakers and one even performed miraculous feats that Thomas couldn't explain.

But not anyone had brought to life the wisdom Thomas loved; not like Socrates and Plato had been able to do, until he had met Yeheshua. Here was a man that lived the truth and backed it up with teachings of such clarity.

Thomas looked at me along with all of us sitting there but I still didn't think he remembered me, and I scolded myself for even thinking it. Clean-shaven in the Greek style he carried his handsomeness easily and yet, listening to him, he wasn't affected by it as many good-looking men were; for it was his honesty and openness of thought that shone through.

When we finally broke up for the morning we went to see if there was anything we could do to help in the rest of the activities going on.

Lamaas and John were still working amongst the sick. Lamaas was doing some of the healing that Yeheshua himself might have done. The care and attention that this visiting master demonstrated was helping many people. He was obviously a very gifted man.

John too was doing all that he could, especially looking after the ones that Lamaas couldn't help, taking them to an area apart and making them comfortable.

I wanted to stay and see what they could do for these people, because we had tried some similar things in Antioch.

James suggested it would be more useful to go and help with the cooking. Slightly reluctantly, I did.

N.B. #08

The next day we returned to take another step towards discipleship.

Simon Peter was asking questions and doing some sort of selection. Several were chosen to go to the same place as yesterday, where Thomas was; and the remainder of us stayed with James.

Then Peter asked the few women in the group to go with Salome who had come over to join us. She recognised me and we greeted each other warmly.

Glad as I was to be there, a part of me was felt that women were somehow not expected or able to pursue the same teachings as the men. I hoped I was just imagining it…

But I dared to ask Peter whether women would sometime be allowed to go with the other group and he answered that women had an equal role which was organised by Yeheshua's mother Mary and the other female disciples.

My heart dropped, crying to me that it thirsted for the teaching of Yeheshua himself; yet my sensibility told me I could have no complaint; that to be with the Messiah and to work beside mother Mary was more than I could have ever dreamt of.

She had helped me so much on that first fateful day at Mirimion that I felt very close to her. I held my peace.

As we walked together Salome told me that Rachel had gone back to Tyre to sort out some business matters but was expected back any day, and looking back we saw that the master had arrived at the lakeside and was very soon surrounded by a crowd of onlookers as he oversaw the care and washing of a group of lepers. They had been here the day before when John had done the same and asked them to come again today.

We heard later that Yeheshua was pleased with their improvement, telling them to keep their faith and purity of heart for wholness to grow anew in them.

It was so incredible to be here and to witness everything that all else was driven from my thoughts, but the crowd had grown deep around the master healer, and we had our appointed duties to attend to.

Returning to Mirimion along the now familiar and dusty road. I told Salome how wonderful it was to no longer be filled with those hateful demons; the hungry spirits that had inhabited me.

How sweet it was to be able to be, to feel life's freshness again in every moment, and how the reunion with my mother had brought a renewal of my worldly fortunes as well.

Our Magdala house could accommodate quite a few guests; and it was my mother's dearest wish that Yeheshua might visit and even stay there if he was travelling by that way.

Entering Mirimion by the side door we found Yeheshua's mother and several other women working inside. She greeted me with a hug, creasing my being into smiles, and introduced me to another woman called Susannah who I thought had the mark of being wealthy but was still humble with it.

About the same age as Yeheshua's mother, yet she was happy to be helping in the house, even just to be washing clothes. In fact, she was shining with contentment.

Listening to their talk I realised how little I knew of these women.

Afterwards I found out that Susannah herself owned large estates to the north and was able to give quite a lot of money in support of Yeheshua's work.

She had known Mary before the master had returned from abroad and so already had received some insights about him, more than confirmed by everything she had experienced this last year, freeing her from the trap of believing in this world; transforming her life.

It became clear as well that the younger Salome was a talented organiser, much relied on by Yeheshua and his mother, whilst my rescuer Rachel was not only learning so much from the master but she also had the means in Tyre to help him in her turn.

For he had made plans to send disciples all over Galilee and these were the ones that the master had been spending extra time instructing.

Yeheshua would follow after them to bring the Kingdom within to all who were awakened to the possibility.

It was my pleasure now to be in a position to offer material support as well, and to have it gratefully received. And Mother thought that perhaps Magdala could be an early stop along the way around the lake to Tiberias. She would mention this to her son.

He worked so incredibly hard; it seemed there was hardly a moment when people didn't surround him. His close disciples protected him when they could but his work amongst the sick, and all those he was teaching, was more than any other could have maintained.

And I also wanted so much to receive the master's teaching, to be his disciple; yet this idea persisted in me that others were deciding who could or could not receive it.

Here, now, was an opportunity to ask Mother about it, but it didn't feel right to suggest to her of all people that some of the disciples didn't want women to be taught like them.

To me though, the customary barriers were still there; raised against women, not to be as acceptable to God as men were.

This had always been such a personal issue in my life; one that I knew I must face up to myself; and somehow in a way that would be filled with joyfulness.

I don't know what Mother saw in my face but she laid a hand of kindness on my arm and said, "the day is coming very soon…"

N.B. #09

I got no chance to ask the master directly for his teaching but the thirst grew as each day I saw others joining the group under the trees. Simon the Pharisee was one of these and my heart felt it would burst with the aching.

Then I heard that this Simon was arranging a great feast at his house where Yeheshua would be the guest of honour, to meet all the men of influence that the Pharisee knew.

It set me to thinking of the festivals we held at the temple of Astarte, as priestesses of the Goddess. How we welcomed the return of the God Adonis every year with a great feast and lamented his departing too. Adored Him even in the pain of separation.

Who could have feted their Lord more? Was that love not worth something?

Yet what these women are doing here is so much more I thought, because this is all real, though it seems they are always pushed into the background by the men.

Who am I to judge? I have been everything they would be horrified about.

Should I be ashamed of what I have been and done?

Sarita's sweet face came to my mind and Arianne's caring, joyful one. I would write to her as soon as I got the chance. First, I must do something for them all and for myself; to try to demonstrate the gratitude I felt towards this special man, this master soul I had been given the chance to find.

A gratitude and love that was changing my life dramatically, even though 'how' was beyond my understanding.

The morning of the feast-day I was out at the lakeside to see if Peter had asked the master about women receiving the inner teaching. He replied again that it wasn't his place to ask it. That women had their own way.

Had our own way; what was our own way? Strangely enough Peter's words sounded like a gong in me. I was a woman and I should understand our way. What Peter was telling me, could, if I had enough faith, be taken as a direct instruction.

I laughed inwardly, suddenly feeling freed to follow the way we women had, that I had too; and now I knew what preparations I needed to make.

I visited the centre of Capernaum to find and buy the things I needed. Clothes, perfume, make-up. I had my hair cut in the way I wished. I would dress it up myself, later.

There was someone I had heard about who had a very good bathing pool. It was a reminder of the grove at the temple and the many, many women who would have given anything for this chance I had been given. I went to meet the owner and she let me bathe and prepare myself there, doing my best to purify my body and mind as offerings.

Returning to my lodgings I washed my hair again in the cool water, rubbed it dry and brushed it out to make it soft. Using all the arts we had become expert in, I dressed and decorated myself as perfectly as I could; to be presentable, acceptable.

I had brought my most precious jar of oil oil I could from home, packed in an alabaster box for safety. Almond oil and subtly scented; I would take this for Yeheshua.

Anyone could recognise my training for what it had been, but I didn't want to hide that. All who knew the master's touch would wish to praise him, celebrate his being here; man or woman, saint and sinner alike. My whole being trembled with the idea of taking my love and gratitude to him in person.

I stepped out into the street as the sun was sinking in the west. The night sky was going to be glorious. A fine crescent moon was chasing after the sun and further beyond the moon, Venus, the queen of heaven, hung in early splendour.

Emboldened I walked along the street, feeling the rush of energy that drove me on.

The desire to be complete, without pretences. Maybe I was no demure Jewish girl, for I had travelled paths that had shaped me in other ways and whether there was shame or not I would not lie to my saviour and my master.

I would give him all that I was. Somehow express my thanks to him.

And alongside this was my deep desire to learn the Great Mysteries that were central to the great prophets of my people.

N.B. #10

I had always thirsted so, even as a girl. To know the source of life and death; and love; everything. What else was there to thirst for? I had never let go of my hopes for this and the master who could take me there.

And how was I to ask him, to ask him for his kindness? What had granny Beth said? I would find the giver of great kindness. Then I must make the most of my opportunity Hecate had told me. I thought, not for the first time, I might be starting to understand.

I reached the area of town where Simon the Pharisee lived and it felt almost as if it was a dream. No-one had invited me to this feast. I had not expected to be; but somehow, I had to try to fulfil my quest.

Getting past the servants into the feast hall wouldn't pose a big problem. The role of priestess had equipped me for this much at least, with a bearing that was difficult to turn aside.

But what I had forgotten till that moment was how it felt to enter a house where the master was. It had a kind of aura that lifted my soul within me, with hushed breath.

The ideas running through my head abandoned me and I stopped trying to figure it out; just pushed forward into the aura of special-ness.

Carrying my little box, I told the servants at the door that I was to go to the Master of the Feast.

They didn't question the air of my authority, but to me it had become more a heartfelt plea than any kind of command.

Luckily it didn't make any difference; they let me through just the same.

The feasting hall stretched out on both sides of the door; with lots of men sitting there at a long table.

To the left was an arch through to where a table of women were eating.

I caught the eye of mother Mary; she smiled slightly though other faces there seemed slightly horrified. She had known me I knew. Others I thought probably hadn't.

Back down the hall of the men I sought for Yeheshua. Some faces were familiar and others not. The familiar ones were his disciples, whilst the others were probably the great and powerful people that Simon had thought to introduce to him.

They certainly looked intimidating but then there was Yeheshua at the end of the table, smiling gently. How could I have seen anyone else there besides him? And next to him was a pleased looking Simon, the host.

Faces had turned to stare at me; but not in friendliness. Some were like high walls of intellectual might. Others were full of disdainful indifference.

But the master was also there and that was the only way I could go. The only way I had ever wanted to go. But in this moment, there was no other option anyway.

Walking behind the row of guests was like going down a hostile corridor, yet I didn't care. It led to where I was going; to take my small gift; to give my heart.

My breath took me there, where my legs were growing shaky.

Finding myself at his feet I remembered only that this is where I had found that peace where unwanted thoughts and presences couldn't reach me, and seeing the kindness in his eyes I had a sudden insight.

By these feet he travelled the world to give people the chance to find what he himself already knew. He had the peace and love we sought; had them in abundance. Not for himself was he in mortal flesh; he had come for us.

Overwhelmed in this understanding and what I come for I poured out my tears and thanks together. At his feet, onto his feet, I let it all flow out of me, and I washed the tears with my hair and cried the more for being able to.

He let me stay. Others looked put out and made disapproving noises. He took no notice.

I broke the seal on the alabaster box and poured ointment on the blessed feet. That my hair could spread this balm on them was the most any woman could have ever wished.

"Your sins are all washed away," he said.

Yeheshua turned to his host, explaining something about washing of hands and forgiveness of sins to him. I noticed Simon Peter amongst the faces of the nearby guests, and next to him was Thomas.

I didn't think that Peter had recognised me but I knew Thomas would have.

This was the crux of my whole life. I had my chance with the Master now.

As the conversation stilled and he turned back towards me I quietly asked my heartfelt question. "May I receive the way to your inner truth?"

He looked at me and all else dissolved away for me except his face, his eyes. "Yes, you shall," he said. "Go in peace."

N.B. #11

The morning was beautiful and full of promise.

What had happened the evening before lifted me to high expectations of what this new day would bring.

The master had been so kind that despite the apparent disapproval of every other guest I had been able to leave feeling that he had been there just for me.

Out at the lakeside Peter was once again vetting the aspirants coming forward from various baptisms to take a larger part, to enter the path to the Kingdom within.

This time I knew Peter would say I could come. The master himself had accepted my application. Peter looked slightly tired I thought.

"Can I join the group with Thomas now?" I asked.

"I think we have been over this haven't we?" he replied; "just yesterday?"

"Yes but last night at the feast; when he accepted my anointing his feet, he said…"

"That was you?" he asked, looking genuinely surprised. Clearly, he had not recognised me.

"Yes, it was me." I felt myself blushing, which took me aback a bit. Peter seemed equally flustered.

"I remember him pointing out to Simon that he hadn't even offered him water to wash his hands before the meal and the surprise of the other guests when he said your sins were washed away but, but I cannot say I remember anything specifically about this."

He was rubbing the top of his head with one hand, eyebrows raised, obviously trying his best to recall the exchange.

"I remember it." Thomas had come to join us, unnoticed by either of us. "He did say she could join the inner path. Mary asked quite specifically and he gave his assent."

Peter nodded and shook his head almost at the same time. "Well then," he made a little worried sigh. "In that case, I suppose you may join them, but I cannot see any good coming from this."

I felt both relieved and deflated at the same time. Somehow Peter had made this wonderful thing for me seem like a bit of a nuisance; but Thomas had helped my case. I was grateful to him. He smiled encouragingly.

"They will already be at Mirimion," Peter said. "Thomas, you had better take her over there and explain it as best you can."

Peter was still shaking his head a bit as we walked away, back to the Master's house.

Thomas chatted easily as we walked the coastal road into Capernaum. I told him he didn't really need to escort me and he laughed. He said that he was coming to make sure that I would be allowed to join the group. This would be the first time this had happened. Thomas seemed quite happy with the situation but I was starting to feel concerned. Was I just causing trouble? Trouble for Yeheshua as well? It was too late to back out now.

"Are you alight?" Thomas asked. He must have noticed I had gone quiet.

"I don't want to make trouble for our master Yeheshua," I said.

Thomas gave my shoulder a little encouraging squeeze. "Don't be silly Mary. I saw how he beamed with pleasure when you came to him at last night's feast. Some Jews are so bound up in webs of laws and institutionalised ideas. You were a breath of fresh air. It was funny to see how these supposedly great thinkers couldn't cope with devotions to the master of a beautiful woman."

I blushed for the second time that day.

"Peter has actually taken it a lot better than many of the others might though." He was more serious now, "but I have absolutely no doubt that Yeheshua means for you to join the group," and he laughed again, as if at some private joke, "and that is quite unusual, for me to be so certain."

Nevertheless, I was quite subdued when Thomas introduced me to the group in the front room of Mirimion.

There were about twenty or thirty men sitting in that large room and all of them seemed unsure of how to react to my coming to join them.

James and Nathaniel were the disciples leading the group and they also seemed slightly taken aback. Where should I be sat. At the back? At the front?

I looked to see where there might be a space. I couldn't let the situation get worse. There was a young man to one side who looked less concerned than some of the others and there was an unused cushion on the floor behind him.

I walked quickly to it and sat there. I didn't want any more fuss. The day had turned awkward enough already.

Listening to James talking I still couldn't help noticing some of the men turn to glance across at me and others that stared more openly.

James was talking about the needs for entering the path. "Purity of heart is the only thing we need for the gift to take root. This is our job, whether we have just arrived or have been treading this path for years. Our task is to prepare the ground, and uproot the weeds that try to choke the growing experience.

Weeds that are fed by our lazy tendencies, to settle for the comforts of this world. Sins are not necessarily what we think they are. The roots go deep into the way we think and treat those around us; and most of all the way we treat our own life, as though it were something we ourselves have made."

I could feel the discomfort in some of the people listening. One seemed to have an intermittent cough and another kept shifting his sitting position. Others just kept looking around whenever this was happening.

James stopped talking and asked if there were any questions that anyone wished to ask.

There was a short silence and then the one who had been unable to sit comfortably spoke up. "If this is about purity of thought James, why have you allowed a woman into the group. Isn't this bound to achieve the opposite result?"

If I had been working as a priestess there were several observations I could have made. There were some there whose glances told me of their need, that a priestess of the Goddess might have drawn out. They would have not been a problem but that was in a different life. Now I chose to ignore it.

The man who had spoken out though was not like this. His makeup was complex and I sensed a conflict within him that was bound up with his question.

"It is not purity of thought that I was suggesting," James had replied. "Rather purity of heart. We cannot uproot impurities in our thinking. That would be an endless and impossible task. But we can search our hearts and uproot the causes of these problems, once we can recognise them. These recognitions are most important. Most important," he stressed "because that is where the thirst is, that when accepted for what it is, will bring us to receive the truth. So, we should not fear this process."

N.B. #12

Would these brethren be able to recognise purity of heart? I couldn't worry about them as I needed to gather it for myself.

When the time came to take a break there were a few that stood together discussing the turn of events. One of these was the man who had spoken out and I had no doubt they were talking about me.

Someone came over and brought me a drink. It was Nathaniel. He smiled kindly; then mother Mary was there. She gave me a hug and invited me to go with her. Gratefully I accepted.

I wanted to apologise, knowing my presence there had caused a disruption but she wouldn't hear of it. "They will have to understand one day," she said. "The Lord has so much patience with them but sometimes an outside push is needed."

I looked at her questioningly and she continued: "This whole nation is so stuck with its rules and laws and ideas of sacredness and sin. Yeheshua so much wants to shake them all, to wake them up to what they have. Each breath coming from the fountainhead of Life itself. Even those who want to understand, even they are still so stuck."

I felt a lot better and she laughed. "I mustn't judge them though, because this is all very new to them. Even for the disciples who have been longest with him it has only been a couple of years at most." She paused. "Except for Lamaas," she added; "he has been a good friend and co-worker of Yeheshua for many years."

She had caught me by surprise and I looked anew at her. What must it have been like to have watched the baby she nurtured at her breast grow into a youth so full of love and wisdom? Then to let him go out into the world but recognise the master that returned and learn from him.

She told me more than I could have asked as we sat there, out in her garden, letting the others worry about the preparations and arrangements for the midday meal.

She told me of the angel that had come to her as a girl and Yeheshua's birth and the flight to Egypt and something of the early years in Nazareth. In a street called Marmion Way.

And she told me how Yeheshua had travelled as a guest to Orissa to learn the wisdom that they had to give and how he travelled through as many lands as possible to give and receive all that he could.

All those years of travail had come to fruition, as now was the time for more sowing and the new harvest to be brought in too. I could see that she was so happy to be a living part of the unfolding story. For her there was no argument; she seemed to be relishing every hour of every day.

After the meal she came back into the front room with me and we sat together at the back listening to Nathaniel speaking. He told of the kindness of the Master and the joy he felt in living with the experience of peace Yeheshua had brought to him...

And later Simon Peter returned with John, and Peter came and spoke in the front room as well.

No-one sat in the Master's seat but rather on another chair placed to one side. Listening to Peter speak though, we all hoped that it meant Yeheshua might be coming soon. He talked passionately of the need to grasp the moment and live the truth with every day that came. A living truth for living people, not of the kind that could be put into books. He was inspiring and we needed it after a long day sitting in the hall.

He looked at me several times sitting at the back and seemed satisfied that all was as it should be. Mother Mary had left the room by then, and I wondered if the Master was due home; but it seemed he was working harder than ever and he didn't get back till later.

I was hoping that the next day would be easier amongst the group but I was wrong.

Simon the Pharisee had not been there the day before but he was this morning when I arrived and looked into the front room. He was talking to the two men that had seemed to have the biggest problem with my presence the day before.

I ducked out of the women's door and into the kitchen area where a woman called Joanna was working. Both mother Mary and Salome had gone out to the beach early and she was quite short handed. I said I would come out and help her if no-one else arrived.

Back in the hall there was another little stir when I entered the room, but there appeared to be divided opinion for a couple of the men, called Joseph and David, solicitously invited me to sit up at the front, possibly to annoy the group that the Pharisee was in.

I started to decline their offer, preferring to be at the back, but then decided to accept it, as Yeheshua was expected to come. Why sit at the back if I could be at his feet?

This obviously annoyed Simon who would have to see me sitting in front of him, and half way through the morning he got up and left.

At lunchtime several close disciples returned; Simon Zelotes, Judas and Philip as well.

John had done the morning talks and I had found myself absorbed in all he said. There was an aura about him that spoke to me of all the magic and mystery that the Temples strove to possess and which he really did.

But in the break times more discussions were going on with Simon Zelotes and Judas Iscariot being collared by what I thought of as the Pharisee group.

I went out to work in the kitchen. Joanna was at least glad to have me there and I glad to be able to help.

N.B. #13

It would have been easier and more pleasant to stay out of the hall and find other tasks to fill the afternoon with, but I remembered what mother Mary had told me the day before and I would have been letting her and myself and even the Master down not to go back in.

I felt as though all eyes turned on me but thankfully most returned to their own discussions. It seemed that these weren't all about me as my fears were trying to convince me, but rather about the divisions amongst the town's elders.

Most were very unhappy about the extreme popularity of Yeheshua amongst the people but they had had no success in trying to woo him to their way of doing things. They would have liked to enhance their status by taking him on as a protégé but they said he kept deliberately going beyond the bounds, even almost insulting them.

This is what the Pharisee Simon had reported and was trying desperately to bring the two sides together. Having me in the group was one aggravation too much, even for him. He expressed his exasperation to Simon Zelotes who seemed to have some sympathy.

Judas came over and asked if there was something else that I could be doing that would be more useful than fuelling the problem by insisting on staying in the hall; but John came to my rescue by calling the room back from these discussions to continue the work.

I sat close to him at the front and he talked of things that I found hard to understand. The world was an illusion created out of the elements for our senses to enjoy, he said, and that the powers of darkness strove to make us think it all there was. He said that in reality it only existed by the Light and the Word that dwelt in the heart of everything; which Yeheshua would reveal to us as a tiny seed; yet which was also the most powerful force in all of heaven and earth. This mystery we could know.

Whatever arguments might have been stored up for this afternoon, John quashed with his complete conviction. He spoke with a strength that came from a living experience that hushed the room into quiet expectancy.

At the break though, it became clear that some element of dissent still hadn't been completely dispelled. I felt eyes looking at me that turned quickly away and the persisting flavour of gossip in one corner from where the phrase 'possessed of spirits' carried to my ears. I had assumed that was known by most people already but then maybe not as widely as I'd thought. I shrugged inwardly.

Then the word 'whore' was whispered just within my listening range. I wanted to run away but John had come up behind me and placed a hand on my shoulder.

"Take no notice," he said. "They don't know what they are saying."

"They do," I answered. "I was a priestess of the Goddess; in Antioch."

"I know that," he replied, "but they cannot see what is in your heart. The Master can. He has accepted you; more than you know."

I looked into John's face and saw that he thought no bad of me.

"Thank you," I said. "Thank you for not judging me; but it is not right that I come here and cause discord; is it?"

"'Everything that is hidden will be revealed.' He has said this. We see it happening. There is no place for hate to be held in the heart; not when we come to the fount of Love."

I sat back in my place as John took his in the chair again. The hall was quiet but I thought I felt a tension in the room. John seemed totally unaffected.

"We must come to this truth with the heart of a child; this is our Master's requirement. It may sound simple but to achieve this is not at all easy, in my experience. We are full of all the prejudices that the world has fed us with. I still cannot claim such purity; though I have been with the master for many months."

John was tackling the issue head on and yet I could still feel the unrest in the hall.

"But it is the Grace of God that allows us to approach, not our own efforts…"

At that moment the door behind John opened and Yeheshua walked in.

Everyone's eyes went to him and John slid to the floor beside me.

Yeheshua sat in the master's chair and looked around. I thought he looked severe, until his glance rested upon John. Then he smiled, just for the briefest moment, and I was caught into its beauty.

"It is true what John was saying," he started. "This Life is such an incredible gift, that we have received without having to appreciate the Giver; This Giver who is presenting us this gift moment by moment, with every breath. This is not something that happened somewhere else, long ago; this is happening now."

"We think we know what is meant to happen; know how God's plan should be accomplished. We think we can help Him do it right. You think that the master should do this or that, and act this way or that. But God does not need our help. The master does not need the approval or patronage of any man. The Lord provides his needs."

"Your task is about emptying yourselves of what you have learnt, not trying to make the Truth fit what you already think it is. You bring so much baggage with you that you have no space for what the master wishes to give."

He stopped for few moments, looking around at us piercingly before continuing on in the same vein.

"There is no help you can give the master; he has to help you. If you cannot understand this there is no point in approaching him. He does not have to try to fathom the secrets of your hearts for he can see them clearly written in your faces. Nor can you conceal anything from your Father God, He already knows every detail."

"Therefore, when you come, look not at the others around you but to your own heart. For therein lies the greatest mystery of all. Nowhere else; here; here." Yeheshua's pressed his open palm to his chest. "Are you ready to receive it? And to be received yourself?" He searched all the faces in the room. I felt his gaze and everything else disappeared for me. "What state do you come in, to be received into His Kingdom?"

What state am I in? Bits; but happy to be in bits, I thought. At your feet in bits is where I want to stay.

"These are the things you should ponder on tonight, for tomorrow there is the chance to take the next step. If you wish you can come. I shall be here to answer those questions that you have."

"If you search your heart and find that you are not ready for the next step, then that is fine as well."

"Far better that you should wait till you are ready than to try to pluck the fruit before it is ripe. For the fruit would indeed be hard to pull from the tree and bitter to the taste."

"Come then or wait with my blessings, and the sweetness you shall know will be worth your commitment and your patience."

The new day dawned and I couldn't wait to get to Mirimion.

I really didn't want anything to eat but had bought some fresh figs the day before and thought instead to take them with me.

Washed; dressed; out into the street and along the ways that were becoming so familiar until reaching the tree-lined avenue where Mirimion lay nestled, I paused, taking stock. Was I too early?

There seemed at first to be no-one about. Then I noticed two other applicants, already waiting under a tree; and a man sitting on a low wall, almost out of sight.

As I approached this man rose to meet me. I recognised him as one that was often on the gate; his name was Jude. He asked if I would wait with the others as the front entrance was still locked.

I went over to the two young men beside the tree and they nodded in a not unfriendly way, though none of us felt the need to enter into conversation. It was nice just to be there. Waiting was a pleasure in itself.

Several others arrived and it wasn't long before the double doors were swung open and we went inside.

Mother Mary herself greeted us and I gave her the fruit I had brought which she asked me to take through to the kitchen. A woman was brushing this end of the hall and the girl Sarah arranging things down the other.

In the kitchen Susannah took the fruit from me and smiled. "Are you here preparing to receive the truths?"

"Yes, I am," I answered, but felt there was more behind Susannah's question. Otherwise, I would have been asking for something to do to help, I supposed. So, I added, "are women not generally accepted, then?"

"Yeheshua accepts us all," she answered. Then, after a slightly pregnant pause, "but none of us I think have challenged for this right to be known amongst the men. We are all hoping it goes well for you. Our hearts are with you, at least."

I thanked her, for I felt the genuineness of her good wishes and wondered, not for the first time, what had I taken on?

Coming back into the hall, Jude had opened the outer shutters, letting the light stream in with the morning air. The scent of cedar wood from the pillars of the room reminded me of the breezy slopes where these trees grew; remembered from my journey up the coast to Antioch. Long ago it seemed now.

Looking back, I reflected that I had always been pushing the boundaries; literally at that time; not really knowing where it would take me. All leading, incredibly… to being in this room, in this house; on this day.

More people arrived. Mark and Joe both together who greeted me warmly.

Susannah came from the kitchen with a wide plate covered in small slices of two different melons, passing amongst us and offering us what we might want before placing the plate on a table to one side. I took a slice, enjoying the refreshing taste of the watery fruit.

Names were being taken by the door and several of the Master's close disciples had joined us in the room. The brothers James and John were there and Simon and Judas too.

Thomas and Peter had left a couple of days earlier to join up with disciples who were going town to town in Galilee, spreading the news of Yeheshua's mission of healing and renewal. Preparing for the Master to follow after.

All this had been happening in the last couple of weeks.

The pressure had been building in Capernaum and we were thought to be the last group awaiting initiation before the master went abroad in Galilee again; and maybe even to Judea.

Then almost before we knew it, we were all once again sitting in the front room waiting for Yeheshua to come.

James took the seat beside the master's chair, giving thanks in his calm and measured tones for the opportunity to be there.

Thanks for the new day and for the chance to understand its value more, to go deeper into the beauty that is clearly with us, but which we struggle to hold on to.

We try, though it never quite works. What we want elude us, time and again until we get dispirited that real fulfillment can ever be ours; all with our lives drifting past.

"When hope is at its lowest ebb the master comes and offers us the way to go inside to where our home is, as ever it was. Complete, untouched, awaiting our return."

He paused and hesitated, looking to where mother Mary and the women sat, at the back.

"This gift he brings is like a drink of purest water to a man dying of thirst in a sea of salt. It may look similar to the salty water, but only when we drink it can we realise that it isn't. Only after trying it do we know it is good and can slake our thirst."

He looked again at the back and nodded slightly.

"To drink the first sip, we must have some trust. How many times have we tried the salty water and been sick? How many times have we tried to refuse the temptation to try it again? Then comes this person saying 'why do you not drink the pure water you have with you? In your own water-skin' and we say 'what nonsense are you talking? We know all about the right way to drink; when water is pure and when it is not; and the correct times to drink it. Go away, we don't need your help'. But, you know, we do, we really, really do. Just the simple kindness of showing us what we already have, but have forgotten about"

One or two people had turned around because James' concentration seemed firmly fixed on the back of the room; I did as well.

Yeheshua had come in the other door and was standing at the back, listening and watching. Perhaps he had been there for a little while.

Everyone turned around and the Master walked into the middle of the group, looking immaculate in a robe of palest cream; smiling and relaxed as being amongst friends.

He stopped and asked a man's name and what he did and another where he came from, a third how long he had been waiting and where he had heard the call to come. He wandered easily about but I think he managed to speak to everyone. He stopped a moment by me, asking how my mother was. I told him she was well and hoping he might visit some day. He nodded smiling and moved on.

"You are all welcome to the entrance hall of the Kingdom," he said. He had reached his customary chair and sat down, filling the room with his presence. "There is no amount of money that can buy admission; only your sincerity will suffice. Bring true sincerity and you will be able to share in the bread of life that has no end."

"The uncreated Power is everything; is in everything. Nothing exists but by its will."

"Its nature is that of purest Love which the Master comes to demonstrate."

"By Holy Breath the Power of Life is spoken into man."

"When man can unite with Holy Breath through Love Divine… that is the sacred marriage from which issues the new birth into everlasting Life."

"Receiving the Master's gift, you are truly re-born in spirit, and your task is to stay at that point of clearness; of simplicity. There is so much to do, that needs doing; and to be able to stay in that simplicity whilst doing whatever is needed is what brings the Kingdom of Heaven to earth."

"This is not a task like any other, and only meant for those who want the Truth in their lives. For that Truth is the Love that takes everything to itself."

Sitting listening to Yeheshua was like listening to my own heart talking back to me. No room for unwanted thoughts; just the wish to listen.

N.B. #15

"What we begin with is just a seed. It is called that because a seed contains the final tree, waiting to come into being. Only our care and attention is needed. That is the warmth, light and water that the seeds need to grow. We ourselves are the soil."

I was focussed on absorbing his words.

"Now is the time to come, to know and to receive, and first, are there any questions that anyone still needs to ask?"

Quiet filled the room for long moments. Then Simon Zelotes spoke up;

"Master, people have been asking me a question and I don't know how to answer. 'Is it fit that at woman should receive the sacred truths?' they ask, 'for it is against our Holy Law,' they say. Please help me how to answer this."

"Are these people here Simon, so that they can ask this for themselves?"

asked Yeheshua. I felt frozen to the spot.

Simon looked around for a few seconds. "No Lord; I don't think that they are."

Yeheshua got up from his seat.

"That is good," he said, "because this question has no place here."

I felt myself frowning angrily; in sympathy with him as much as for myself.

He stepped forward, his robe brushing past me like a refreshing breeze filled with springtime, dissolving any anger away.

"You Joseph and you David, and you..." he picked out half a dozen people by name, the kindness in his voice completely dispelling the disruption of moments before. "Please go with my mother and await in the appointed place. Prepare yourselves in quiet and I will come to show you the way within, this very day."

When they had gone, he turned back to the rest of us, taking up the point again with near weariness.

"That was the sort of question that the lawyers and Pharisees bring to me, not someone who has started to understand their own need; for peace, for joy, for truth; for knowing real love."

"Why do we think our Father would not care for all His children just the same but instead subject us to such laws?"

"Where is the person who will come with simple humility to their God?"

Had I been the one to bring this question? I asked myself, concerned at the passion that this issue had caused and that I was not amongst the chosen. Was it my mistake?

"What counts to me is what you have in your own heart. Your thirst; your desire; your yearning. This is the only thing that counts to me. God's Law is written in our hearts not in scriptures. Only when our hearts become closed to ourselves do we need these books and even then they are a poor substitute. Not even a substitute at all in fact."

What was he saying now?

"Look," he said, "if a prophet were to write {God's Law is in men's hearts} wouldn't that be true? Exactly what I have just said. Then a priest comes along and says 'Ha-ha! It is written {God's Law is in men's hearts}, so definitely not in women's hearts. They are different from men in this respect'."

Slightly nervous laughter went through some parts of the room. The master stepped forward again amongst the aspirants, touching several on the shoulder one by one, saying quietly to each: "Go with the others and await my coming." Then to John: "Take these and show them where to await me."

Again, he waited for a few moments after they had all got up and left.

"Can it ever be possible to untwist the thinking of the priests and lawyers, who have spent so much time twisting the strands of their rope together to make it strong. Little knowing that this rope is to go about their own necks."

He was serious. The whole room went quiet, attentive.

"Let your thinking be straightforward and it can be as a soft garment for you and yet strong to protect you from the wind and rain of life's trials."

"Work from your own experience and you will make real progress."

"Feel what this life has to bring, for yourself, not what others tell you. Then you will start to distinguish the real from the unreal."

There were noises at the front of the house. It sounded like some sort of delegation wanting to speak to Yeheshua, full of demands.

He turned to a young man sitting to one side. "If I give you this gift today, will you guard it carefully and tend it with love?"

"I will," replied the youth soberly.

"And will you," he said turning to one sat next to me;" give it a real chance to flourish in your life?"

"Yes, I will".

"Then go with James both of you and I will give you the keys to enter in by."

He paused and said to Simon "Debating points of Law is not going to win the day, Simon. You can do better. Find out what the person wants and if they just want to argue then walk away. If they are actually trying to understand, then offer what you have learnt from your own experience. That is all ."

Half raised voices continued to intrude from out the front of the house.

"Judas, please deal with the council's representatives that we can hear outside. You know how to talk with them. Don't alienate them deliberately but I shall not speak with them today."

Judas went out to do the master's bidding.

"Today is a special day," Yeheshua continued, "in the way that every day becomes special when we make time to sit in the company of our own soul. For those who are ready there is nothing more to be asked."

I felt I would burst with the aching for him to choose me too.

"Simon has that answered your question?"

The room was very quiet but I could feel the doubt still lingering there; the back of my neck prickled but I couldn't look around.

Yeheshua returned to his seat and sat facing us again, drawing the tension to himself. Finally, he spoke out with quiet force: "If God's Law is that women cannot receive this teaching, shall I make Mary into a man so that she can receive it?"

Stunned silence. No-one would have imagined such a thing.

Who would dare suggest that he could not do this or that he was joking either?

N.B. #16

The room's tension fell in on itself in hushed whisperings as people asked each other what he had said, what had he meant? I heard at least two people get up and leave; then another quickly followed.

Arguing voices could still be heard coming from the front and Yeheshua asked Simon to go and help Judas. "Please ask them not to disturb us now; we will soon be going away from Capernaum and have preparations to make." Simon left.

"Mary, I want you to go to Magdala today and get ready for my coming. Will you do that for me?"

At last, he had asked something of me. "Yes, yes I will." Unexpected joy flooded into me.

Then to all the room: "Tomorrow I shall be leaving Capernaum," he said, once again catching everyone off balance. "There are many souls in other towns that are crying after that which can quench their thirst."

And turning back to me, "maybe there would be room for some women to stay with you and your mother?"

"There is plenty of room, master," I replied. "My brother enlarged the house before he died and my mother has been making it all ready in case you could come."

"I'll ask Salome and John to go with you, Mary. They know what shall be needed and what will be possible there. Matthew you should go as well, to make sure funds are available for what is needed."

Yeheshua moved around the room asking one or two more to come to Magdala and to the others he said "keep faith and come on to meet me in Tiberias in three days time. Go now and get yourselves and your affairs ready for the journey."

As the room cleared James and John came back inside. "Ah John, I want you to go to Magdala with Mary here, and Salome, to prepare for my coming tomorrow to stay with Mary and her mother, and to be ready to continue this work there."

"And James, you and I have it here to do today as well."

Simon and Judas had come back into the house. It seemed that the delegation had gone way and that all was quiet out there now.

"Thank you Judas, Simon; that at least was well done; It need be that we remain completely undisturbed today."

"They will not return and anyone else will be directed to go to Tiberias," answered Simon.

"I am going to Magdala on the way, Simon. People may go there also, and whilst I am away, I would ask both you and Judas to stay and look after affairs here in Capernaum; for a short while, until I get word to you."

"James, it could be that my brothers will come from Nazareth, later today or more likely tomorrow, and I would like you to help mother with whatever she needs for their visit."

Mother Mary came in at that moment with Salome and Susannah. "Thank you," she said.

"Is everyone settled mother?"

"Yes."

"Thank you," he said, and looking back at him sitting there with his eyes closed, I knew it was time to go and do as he had asked.

John and I walked together over to where I had been staying.

The day was getting really hot and we dodged gratefully beneath the trailing foliage that framed the entrance way.

We were going to go ahead on donkeys, whilst Salome, Matthew and the others came slightly later, in Andrew's boat. This would give them all more time to collect what they might need, and Salome extra hands to load some supplies onto the boat.

Cara was still housed in our stables with several other donkeys. We had briefly checked if we could take one of these for John and found that there were a few due to return to Magdala anyway.

We loaded on my things, some water for the journey and some bread, cheese and fruit as well, then headed out of town. Me in my mended green cloak and John swathed in a loose robe, all but ready to cross a desert.

We talked of many things, amongst which of course was how Yeheshua had threatened, or offered, to turn me into a man and how the shock of his words had cut through the debate that had been quietly raging in the front room.

"Yes, he does that; so many times I have seen it now," John was saying. "He will not be dragged into trying to discuss the nature of people's ignorance and confusion. He has that ability to completely come at it from a different perspective; and make people understand something crucial in the process."

I agreed. "I couldn't imagine any way to silence what had been rumbling on since I joined the group. It seemed so deep rooted in quite a few of them."

"Did you ever hear of Alexander of Macedon and the Gordion knot?" asked John.

"The conqueror of Asia who solved the problem of the impossible knot by cutting through it with his sword? Yes," I laughed, "the master was a bit like that, completely chopping the argument to bits, without taking part in it. Not that I think it is finished with yet. There are all the other people who will think the same thing."

Our donkeys carried on up the path, sure-footed and surprisingly quick. We had been going for a while now and I knew there was a group of trees around the bend at the top of the slope where we might stop to give them a break.

We cobbled them where there was a little grazing to be had and gave them some water in a wide shallow bowl.

The view over the sea of Galilee was magnificent. The cicadas were noisy and the day hot. It was a good way to travel, especially when there was a place like this to stop at.

My thoughts strayed to what was still happening in Mirimion. "It must be incredible to receive the Master's gift," I mused out loud. "I cannot imagine how wonderful."

"It is nothing that you can think or imagine, Mary," said my companion, quite seriously, "it is far simpler than you think. That is why he calls it a seed. Many people get the wrong sort of expectations."

"The way I sometimes think of it is as writing. All our thoughts and ideas are like the words we write on a papyrus scroll and we are so involved in this writing. Then comes the Master and says there is something more basic, more fantastic that we need to know than all the things we are writing, writing."

"Mmm…" was all I could answer.

"So, we start thinking what fantastic words the Master must wants to show us. Because that is what we know, we do."

"All right, I can see that."

"But he wants to draw our attention to the papyrus itself. Not by writing more but by showing us the unblemished surface itself. Giving us the chance to realise this is something fantastic that has been given to us."

"Oh."

"Without the papyrus there would be no writing, just a useless pen and ink. They are also gifts of course, but without appreciation for what we have been given to write upon, what would be the point of them?"

He paused, "It is not a very good analogy," he added, laughing at my serious expression. "But in some ways, I quite like it. Seeing the paper may not seem so exciting as all those words, to most people; but really special to those who want to know; to know what is real. You shall see for yourself, anyway."

I laughed too because something in me warmed to what John had said, even though he succeeded in bamboozling my thinking.

We carried on after our break and in a surprisingly short while we found ourselves winding down the track past the fields that signalled we were nearing the outskirts of Magdala.

There were quite a few large properties out here, but not always visible as they were surrounded by olive groves and vineyards. Conveniently close to the small fishing port of Magdala yet within reach of Capernaum, with the further opportunities offered there.

Opportunities that my brother had been successful in exploiting.

Our house was further in towards the town, on a down-slope that gave it a fine view. Normally there would not have been room for a big house this close to the centre of town, but my brother had been lucky to have the chance to buy the neighbouring house when the owner died, giving him the space he wanted.

My mother was having her rest after lunch when we arrived, but she was so excited to see us that she insisted on showing John around the house immediately.

He was suitably impressed, and so was I, at all the work she had been able to get done in it.

John seemed particularly taken with the suite of rooms that Ben had built for himself and his bride to be, overlooking the gardens and with a view through to the sea itself.

"Could these rooms be made available to Yeheshua, if he was staying in Magdala?" he asked my mother.

"Of course," she answered. "When do you think he could be coming?"

"Well, tomorrow actually," said John, and my mother made an audible gasp.

"I have to get started immediately," she said. "Mary, come and give me a hand. How many others will be with him? There is plenty of room. Let me show you the guest rooms."

She was doubly excited now as we followed after her through the new courtyard that had been formed from the extra rooms built around two sides.

"Ma," I said, "there is no rush. There is help coming from Capernaum even as we speak. It was Yeheshua's request that the women of his house might be able to stay as well. Salome is his housekeeper, and he has sent her out with supplies and people to help you."

"My goodness," answered my mother. "That is very kind; but there is no need, we will manage; we will manage."

"Well actually, mother," said John respectfully, "the master is making this the start of a tour of the towns of Galilee. There will be very many disciples and followers passing through Magdala, and Matthew and Salome and others are coming to make all sorts of arrangements in the town. But if Yeheshua could stay here, with the women who look after so many of the practical needs, then that would be wonderful."

"And you, master John" said my perceptive mother, "You must stay here also, to look to the needs of your Master. He shall need another man amongst so many women."

"I doubt he needs anyone at all," laughed John, "but if you can squeeze me in, then I will not refuse your kindness."

"Done," said my mother.

N.B. #18

After leaving our house we went to see Uncle Jacob and Daniel, to give the donkeys back and let them know what was happening as well.

They wanted to play their part and John arranged that certain disciples would be able to stay there. Philip and Andrew amongst others.

Leaving the donkeys, we walked on down into town to see what else there was and to meet up with Matthew and Salome when they arrived.

After having lived in Antioch, and more recently Capernaum, Magdala didn't seem to have much going on in it. The market square dominated and there was a street leading on down to the docks that had permanent shops and services.

A blacksmith and carpenters, a general food store; a cloth and rope merchant; and of course, places where the fish were displayed that had been brought in from the boats.

The synagogue was on the side of the square furthest from the sea and we passed by without seeing anyone outside. There were just a few people around the square as the afternoon heat was still strong. Quite soon there would be many more.

We walked down to the jetties where several fishing boats were tied up. Andrew's boat had not arrived yet but there was a sail out on the sea. John said it was Andrew's boat for sure, though how he could say at that distance I didn't know.

We sat and waited under an awning attached to the front of a closed shop. It was quiet and beautiful and the boat sailed closer quite quickly. It was Andrew's.

When it arrived, the first person I saw was Rachel. What a surprise. What a fabulous surprise. We hugged each other in greeting. She had arrived at Mirimion soon after we had left it seemed.

Salome was there of course, organising the supplies and she had brought Sarah with her too.

Also Matthew, and six aspiring disciples, that included Joe and Mark.

Matthew and Mark were related and they had a mutual cousin living in Magdala.

They were staying with him and his family, whilst the four other aspirants would be at Jacob and Daniel's, and would be helping us carry the supplies up to Ma's house.

We should have brought the donkeys I thought, but we managed the bags and packages between us.

Salome met my mother and they got on well, luckily, for I didn't know how Ma was going to take to the assistance being offered; but Salome seemed to understand her and I think her seeing Rachel again helped as well.

Having taken set their things at Jacob's house, the four young men came back with Daniel; and all together we went back down to the square.

Matthew, Joe and Mark were already there, talking to some men and women at an evening tea bar. We went over and joined them.

There was such a difference between Yeheshua's followers and most people in the square in Magdala.

Was it just a question of happiness, or purpose, or more than that? Maybe it didn't matter what it was, but the people certainly were responding to being told about the master's message. Hope for the promised land which he said could be fulfilled in them.

The Kingdom was at hand, and all were being invited to come to the banquet, where even the sick could be healed, so they could partake of the peace he brought as well.

There were some clear candidates for this healing help in evidence in Magdala. I talked to a woman who was in a bad way but mostly I think because she had lost her husband and little boy. Talking about it helped her a bit. Rachel was looking after another woman with more obvious, physical ailments.

One man seemed oddly dangerous and no-one could approach him. Blind and dumb though he was, the demon that possessed him did not seem so helpless, quite the opposite in fact. It was unsettling when he was anywhere around, exuding tormented hatred.

I did meet up with some people whom I had known as a girl. I hardly recognised them as our lives had travelled such different paths. Yet meeting again was a kind of amazement in the context of Yeheshua coming to Magdala that held great joy for me; to tell them this wonderful news.

Almost everyone was interested and would come and hear the Master speak when he came.

Then there were the Pharisees.

They came into the square together; there were three of them. I wondered if one of us should speak to them but before I had a chance to go and ask John, who was on the other side of the square, they had gone over to Joe.

He seemed relaxed enough and chatted to them easily. Maybe I was being silly. I just felt there was something ominous about them.

Matthew had wandered over to Joe as I watched and in a little while the Pharisees all turned and left.

What had they wanted, we asked Joe. He said they seemed interested in finding the Kingdom that Yeshua proclaimed. Joe told them that he would be in Magdala tomorrow.

It wasn't good news but the master didn't seek to avoid the Pharisees, just not to play their game by their rules, John said.

Rachel said that when she had arrived at Mirimion earlier that day, there had been been a group of Pharisees outside. They had been quite unpleasant, she said, and Philip, Simon and Judas had had their hands full in containing their abusiveness.

The sun had almost gone down and the shadows were melting into the dusk. I was at the furthest corner of the square nearest to the sea, looking back at the town of my youth.

This place evoked so many memories in me; so much that was wonderful and some that was painful too. It was as if this was my life laid out in front of me.

Everything had a place, a meaning, that I accepted somehow, without really knowing why.

People busy with their lives, trying to make some sense out of the efforts needed simply to deal with all of the burdens piled upon them. That was how I had found it was everywhere.

Then there was the possessed man. How terrible it must be for him; caught in an ongoing horror, just as I had been. Could there be a way out for him too?

Even the Pharisees. I had been a priestess. My mind was trained to follow the ways of religion too. They were a part of what I was and this frightened me because only my heart could truly understand the master, because it had felt his great kindness. Only that was taking me where I needed to go.

Tomorrow he would be here, coming to my own town, to where my life had been formed.

My greatest hope was to continue to be with him and learn from him. Continue to make use of this chance we were having right now; and that the people of this, my town, could also benefit.

N.B. #19

The new day dawned. I woke up in my own old room, early. It had been a pleasant sleep with dreams I couldn't quite remember. I got up and went down into the garden.

The sun was still below the horizon. There was a seat in the new garden where I thought I might watch it rise. Uncle Jacob had put it there for my mother when Ben died.

The ground was still a little damp with the early morning dew and the bushes of bougainvillea were resplendent with their purple and mauve flowers. Recovering from the overgrown state the garden had been in.

Sitting there breathing in everything; the sights, the sounds, the smells; filling me up, body and soul.

A rim of orange-red peeped through the thin veil of haze at the edge of the world. I watched entranced as the sun grew into a completed orb, its light reflecting in golden sparkles across the surface of the sea.

The arrival was a signal for me to go and make sure everyone got breakfast.

Perhaps no one was particularly bothered about breakfast that day but I enjoyed doing it for them anyway. Then it was down to the jetty.

There were a lot of townspeople already gathered by the time Andrew's boat arrived, but due to the press of people it didn't dock immediately. Yeheshua was on board and he directed the boat to a small bay around from the jetty.

The crowd surged around on the shore, us along with it.

The Master spoke to us from the boat, telling us that this was an opportunity to receive the seeds of joy and peace, and to sow them in our lives. That there was a field to plant within us where we could harvest everything we wanted; the very things which we had searched so hard for in this world.

That field is our heart and we should let the farmer come and do his work because this was the way to claim our promised inheritance. For so long that promise may have seemed an empty one, but not any more.

"You have it all with you. The Love, the Grace, the understanding. All is in you, waiting for you; and you can enter the Kingdom of your heart. If you can put aside your carnal mind for a moment, and see instead what it has covered over. See what you have always been and come to your God as that."

There were many very unwell people at the back of the crowd; that were too sick to come to Yeheshua in that rocky cove. He pointed over to them.

"The sickness that this carnal world visits upon us is not always so obvious, but however we are, whatever has happened to shape our existence, our duty

148

to our own heart is to try to prepare ourselves. Maybe these sick people need more obvious help perhaps, but all of us come to His table needy."

"Bring these stricken ones to the square in front of the synagogue. I shall meet with them and you there."

He signalled to Andrew to turn the boat around again and we all turned as well, to go back to the square.

John and I had been near the front but now we were at the back of the crowd. They were rushing to the jetty again to meet the boat as it arrived. I was worried at what the crush would mean, with no chance for us to help.

"Don't worry Mary, it is fine," said a voice at my shoulder. I looked around. It was Lamaas, and behind him, head partly covered under a shawl, was Yeheshua. They must have got out of the boat after everyone had turned the other way.

John laughed, and we reached the top end of the square before the crowd had even realised Yeheshua was not on the boat.

He lost no time in getting to work on the sick that were there, and the gathering crowd formed a respectful circle around, watching.

I loved watching the master working, giving his love to all who needed; we all needed it.

Then I became aware that the Pharisees were there. Not just the three that had been in the square the night before but others as well.

They were not causing trouble but watching, along with everyone else, and talking softly among themselves and with others around them.

I moved a little closer, to hear what they were saying.

Innocent enough discussions, apparently. Fair seeming words that yet belittled all that was going on in front of them.

"There is nothing unusual or difficult about that."

"Unfortunately, she shall not continue to get better; I have seen that before. It is illusory. If they only knew, no-one would bother."

Then they were circulating around the fringe of the crowd but I couldn't hear what they were saying. There were quite a few and I recognised some of them from Capernaum. They had probably come to discredit the master if they could.

I went a bit further out to see what they were saying.

The voice of reason, telling the people that this was just a 'flash in the pan'. Here today and gone tomorrow. Promising all sorts of impossible things and then leaving without delivering anything worthwhile.

Raising expectations in people that were clearly unrealistic and nothing to do with the real lives people had to lead, where hard work and attention to the laws of God and religion were the only ways to make things better.

Miracles that any trickster could perform. Making people think they were better and leaving us to pick up the real burden.

So, they went on in their reasonable voices, sowing doubt and poison at every opportunity as to what Yeheshua was about. Even trying to stir some people into anger I realised, when they found someone who would listen.

"He shouldn't be allowed to do this. He is taking advantage of everyone's goodwill. We come here and listen and what does he give but a load of prattle. I bet you he doesn't go hungry. I bet he has never known the suffering that you and I have. It makes me mad to think how gullible he thinks we are."

And I struggled to remain calm myself.

Yeheshua had finished talking to the woman who had lost her husband and her son; the lady I had spoken to the night before. He still knelt beside her and she looked quite different now. Thoughtful but not miserable as she had been.

He looked up, a hand still resting on her shoulder and I knew he saw what the Pharisees were doing, trying to undo all his work.

N.B. #20

Yeheshua got up and addressed the crowd. "There was a farmer who sowed good seed in the field," he said. "Then in the night his enemy came and sowed tares in that field. What should the farmer do?"

"He does nothing, but let the wheat and tares grow up together, because he knew he would also harm the good seedlings if he tried to get rid of the bad. Then, when it came to harvest time, he told his servants to gather up the good wheat and store it, but to also gather up the tares and burn them."

"Sowing good shall bring forth goodness and joy. Sowing evil shall bring forth evil and pain. We have the way to know the difference. It is our nature to love what is good and which brings us joy, but to hate what brings us pain. It is obvious even to a child but when the deviousness of the enemy makes us confused, even the simplest truths become hard for us to see."

"Therefore, strive to become pure and simple as a child and once again it becomes easy to turn the evil one away, and welcome the sweet happiness that is our true birthright."

The Pharisees had stopped to listen also but I heard a sneering in some of their low spoken comments. There were more of them coming into the far side of the square, making noise.

The possessed dumb and blind man went before them as though they were driving him into the square. The crowd parted to get away from him, pushing the unhappy individual further towards where Yeheshua stood.

Crouched there the tormented man seethed with menace, the demonic quality of which made him almost totally unapproachable. The Pharisees formed a wide arc behind him.

Yeheshua was to his front. We all watched, rooted to the scene.

Yeheshua stepped forward and the possessed man cowered more. The master closed his eyes and held out his hands, as though blind himself. "Come out of him," I heard him say. "Leave this man to himself. You have no business here."

I swear it was as if I saw a great shadow rise about the crouching man, towering high, menacing the master. Yeheshua took another pace forward, eyes still closed. "Leave this place," he said. "I command you by the Word of Life, go from here; back to your own realm. Go and leave this man in peace!"

Even as he spoke these last words, he had reached the blind, dumb man and touched him with his hands. One on his shoulder and the other on top of his head.

There was a kind of shudder in the air about them or so it seemed to me. Like a dagger stroke that divided the shadow from its victim, forcing it away.

There was a loud cry, and I wasn't certain where it came from, but then another that was certainly from a watching Pharisee.

"See you people." His words were almost a scream. "See how this Yeshua commands his own devils. He is the one that creates these devils and now sends them away. By the power of Lucifer he does these things. Have nothing to do with this devil in human form."

"Aye," cried his comrades in an echo. "He certainly is in league with these fiends and that is why they do his bidding. He is the very heart of evil come to plague us. Let us drive him out of our town."

Yeheshua said nothing but bent low to the man in front of him, holding his head between his hands and bowing his own head close to that of the dumb, blind man.

No-one moved and even the Pharisees were caught into the intenseness of the moment. The master whispered in the man's ear and, lifting him up, he kissed the man's closed eyelids.

"Open your eyes," he said, "for you can see, even as you can hear me speak. Open your eyes, for that which oppressed you and turned you to hide away has gone. You are free again. You are free to see, to hear, to live again."

The man straightened up and opened up his eyes blinking.

Yeheshua put an arm around his shoulder and led him to where Lamaas stood nearby, then turned and spoke directly to the Pharisees.

"If I do these things by the power of all that is evil, then certainly that kingdom will crumble, being divided upon itself. But if I do this by the power and will of God then you should understand that His Kingdom is at hand and make yourselves ready to receive it."

The faces of the Pharisees said it all. They were livid with fury but could find no way to attack him.

Most people in the crowd however had made up their minds and had had quite enough of these Pharisees and their disruptive unpleasantness. They turned on them and drove them away.

N.B. #21

Yeheshua turned to me, "Mary, is there a larger open space than this market square around here?"

I knew one, the camel train park where the caravans stop; often more convenient and pleasant to stay here than at Capernaum's dusty site.

Beside it was the ground where we used to play as children. They still did as I had seen the day before when I had visited it out of curiosity. Nor had there been a caravan camping in the park.

"Yes, master the caravan park is close by. It is wide and stands empty today."

"Good; please show me the way," he said, and so I did.

The confrontation with the screaming Pharisees had shaken most of us. I wondered how Yeheshua could carry on without rest, especially as I knew the healing work to be very draining.

But he was oblivious to such needs as though he knew his time was limited, striding on to explore the space I'd brought him to.

He saw our play mounds at one side of the park and decided to use them as a place to address the people. Many had followed and word got around quickly to him being there and it wasn't too long before he was speaking again:

"Today we have a chance to understand something that can help us for all our life. No more rules and formulations and things that are good or things that are bad. Nothing like that."

"Not what you should do or should have. Not things to better your human lot compared to others. How much of our lives do we spend pursuing all of that?"

"What I want to tell you about is much more incredible than that, yet lies completely hidden by our many fears, anxieties and desires. All those things tell you of what you lack; what you don't have and what you are not."

"What I want to tell you of is what you are and what you do have. For with every breath you are being given everything; the whole world; to be alive. What I bring is the wakening to that knowing, that feeling, that experiencing of this great love, being given to us in every single breath."

The people loved to hear him speak because he revealed a world that was theirs as well but which they seemed to have lost touch with. He brought back the freshness and magic of childhood and made it live for us again. Even to the old and infirm.

"Every person should know what they have and everyone who has felt this joy, given to us moment by moment, will want to let others know as well. First to feel the joy for ourselves, then to let others know as well. That is all it takes; as much as any person could wish to have and do."

The people were like a sea all around him and I was so happy to be sat at his feet as he spoke. It was entrancing and most other people were seated on the ground as well, especially those anywhere near to the front.

Someone was working around the side of the crowd to try to find a way to get to Yeheshua. I recognised him; it was Jude who often guarded the front door at Mirimion. The master saw him too and signalled to the people to let him through.

"Master," he said when he had got close. "Your mother and brothers are here and asked me to request if they could speak with you; for they cannot reach you through the multitude."

"Who is my mother and who are my brothers?" answered Yeheshua. "Every person who takes this message to their heart is my brother and my sister; and every person that works with me to let others know is my mother and my father."

"This is the reality of the universal love we are invited to know, to feel its touch every day."

"I will be over presently," he said to Jude, looking over to the raised western entrance where a group of people were standing. "Do you know if the food is ready?" he added.

"I don't know. Would you like me to find out?" answered Jude but the master shook his head. I looked over to where the road from the market square entered the park and thought I saw disciples just arriving, carrying baskets of something and skins of wine or water.

N.B. #22

"Friends" said Yeheshua, raising his voice again for all the assembled to hear. "Food and drink has been brought so you can stay here if you wish. You do not need to go and seek refreshment. If you stay seated the food and drink will be distributed...

And I can see there are also shady areas down the furthest end of the park to get out of the sun."

"I shall return after this break, for those who want to stay and listen... to learn more of what we can do in this life to help ourselves."

John and I followed behind and to either side as he crossed to where his relatives awaited him.

He greeted his brothers James and Simon cordially, embracing each and asking after their families; and they asked after his health as well.

"The Pharisees are liking my message less and less," he said, "but that cannot be helped."

"We wish you would be more careful in what you say to them. Is there such need to stir them to fury? They are becoming like a nest of angry, disturbed bees." James was the eldest after Yeheshua and felt responsible for the family.

"Bees were never as poisonous as they," answered Yeheshua. "There is no way that what I have to say and do will wash with them. It is as well to confront their hypocrisy head on as try to mollify them. It would make things worse for everyone in the long run. You will not be involved though; or your families."

"You can always come and stay with us if things get bad," said his youngest brother.

"Thank you, Simon. There will be times when there is nowhere to lay our heads and I shall remember that there is a place to rest with you and be thankful." He put a consoling hand on the young man's shoulder

Mother Mary was behind the brothers and Yeheshua turned to her as well.

"There is another here; I would like you to meet... Miriam," she said and stepped aside to reveal a young woman who had been standing behind her waiting.

She was dressed in a robe of mauve, edged with silver threads, with a fold draped lightly over her head.

Though I saw only a portion of her face, yet I knew a rare beauty shone there.

But something I felt in that moment overrode any other impression; for between Miriam and Yeheshua flowed a recognition that was so tangible that it shook through me like a personal earthquake.

He greeted her with outstretched arms, "Miriam, how wonderful… that you are here," he said, and John and I looked at each other for a moment. He felt what was happening too, for I could see the suppressed amazement in his glance.

"Master," she returned simply. "I heard you were teaching and hoped to come and learn as well."

Nothing in what she said betrayed what passed unsaid between them but I could see something of it in her face. An openness that revealed the beauty of purity within; the one thing that the master responded to most.

Mother Mary was beside Miriam and she also looked into her son's face. She was smiling with real happiness, knowing that these two were meant to be together.

Whatever her son might deny for himself, heaven itself had sent its queen to be at his side.

"I am staying at Mary's house," he said, turning to me for a brief second, then to John added, "will everything be able to be done there? Can we continue in Mary's house?"

"Yes Lord," answered John, "it is very suitable."

"Tomorrow Miriam, we shall be at Mary's house where I hope you can join us; but today I would ask you for one favour, if you will. To sing one or two of the songs of Israel to the people assembled here, such as you sang to me when first we met."

I think she may have coloured just a little, and she took a deeper breath, "it will be my honour, my lord" she answered, "if you will be close by to me".

"I will," he answered and he led her gently to where his mother was insisting he should come and take refreshment and rest from the midday heat.

Afterwards they went back together to the 'field of souls' where Yeheshua taught the assembled people more about the way to happiness, and Miriam sang the songs that had inspired the Israelites in days of old.

Together, side by side, they gave from their hearts and I watched the expression of that love in the park of Magdala, sitting close beside them.

Full circle for me. This is where I had run away, trying to find this, this wonder that I witnessed and enjoyed here today; happiness complete.

BOOK 2: KADESH QUEST

CHAPTER 1.

It was the hour before dawn, the windows showing just enough light to see that the day was coming, but there was hardly any noise in the house, besides the creak of the wooden stairs as I went down into our hallway. Cool flagstones met my bare feet; first the old familiar worn stones, and then an area of wide, sharper edged ones by the new front door.

I took a broom automatically from the cupboard there, but put it away again; the light wasn't strong enough yet to see properly by anyway.

This was a special day and I wanted everything to be perfect. All the arrangements were made but it had been made clear to me that there was no need for me to get further involved in them; not today.

Perhaps I could go out into the garden and pick a few fresh flowers though.

We had a full house of guests and Yeheshua himself was sleeping in the master bedroom. Rachel, my friend and benefactor, had got back from Tyre, and I was so glad she was here. John was the only one of the twelve staying, sleeping in the dressing area adjacent to Yeheshua's room. All our other guests were women from Capernaum.

My thoughts were interrupted by slight noises from outside the front that sounded like the hooves of a donkey moving on the road. I unlocked the front door to have a look.

There, out on the road, was the outline of mother Mary sitting on the donkey, with a boy at its head. The sky beyond held a smattering of stars above a pale line of morning light.

But my eyes were drawn almost immediately to the other figure coming down the path towards me. Quite tall yet slightly built, with head covered, her presence struck me like an open hand pressed to my chest. I caught my breath involuntarily; it must be Miriam.

She pulled back her head-scarf, letting her dark glossy hair free to frame the honey pale features in her oval face. Whilst the glory of the sun slumbered still awhile, here the beauty of the moon had come to my door.

For a moment I stood dumbfounded, and then a clarity washed through me. This was not my door, nor my house. There was no owning of anything here; there was just this day, just this moment, just the incredibly good fortune to be alive and to be here.

She waved goodbye to the figures at the other end of our entranceway before turning again to where I was standing, a reminder of the excitement of the coming day shining in her face.

Was it all right to have come so early, she whispered? Undoubtedly it was the same consuming passion that brought us both here.

"Of course," I answered, also whispering. "Come inside; I don't think anyone else is up yet... I am another Mary," I added as she took my offered hand in hers.

"Yes, I remember," she said, "and I am too, though I prefer the old form of Miriam. Probably a good thing, Yeheshua's mother being called Mary..." and her quiet laugh reminded me of her singing of the day before.

I waved towards the figure on the donkey, which was being turned around by the boy leading it. Mary waved back to me. "She said she would be back slightly later in the morning," Miriam said, "if that is alright with your mother?"

"Of course," I answered again, and Miriam took my arm as we went inside. She was only a couple of years older than me but had such a presence about her, imbued with purpose.

"What can I do to help?"

"I was just thinking of getting some flowers to put in the room we will be using, but perhaps it would be better to get some water heating up first."

"I can the get the embers going, if you like; l love doing that."

I left her kneeling by the still warm remains of last night's fire and went out into the garden to select some colourful blooms to decorate the inner room that used to be the house's largest.

That was before my brother had built the fine wedding hall.

Miriam and I arranged one vase each, to go either side of the master's chair, and then swept the rugs, plumped the cushions, and rearranged the low stools and a few chairs around the edge of the room.

Salome had already come down and taken over in the kitchen, setting the fire under the oven to get the bread made she had left proving in the larder.

I introduced her to Miriam over a cup of tea, and in a while several others had joined us for an early breakfast, but not yet Yeheshua or John.

My mother bustled in to reclaim control of her kitchen and she was grateful that they had waited before coming down, and that she was able to offer them her hospitality in person.

It wasn't long before John's form filled the kitchen doorway and my mother hobbled, almost nimbly, over to him, realising Yeheshua would be close behind.

On her recommendation John and Yeheshua sat out in a garden alcove where the view and the early morning sunshine combined to make it her favourite breakfasting spot.

Honey cakes and soft goat's cheese were taken to them, and cups with juice squeezed freshly from fruit as she had waited for them to come down.

A few of us ventured out to be close by to them and Salome produced some of the master's favourite herb bread, fresh from the oven. He shared it around with all of us, especially calling my mother out to join him.

John gave up his seat with alacrity.

"Today, we will start as soon as all the others arrive," Yeheshua said. "This is our time, where each of us, each of you, has the opportunity to focus on that which is most important... that is the meaning and purpose of our lives, but which the business of our worldly round hardly gives us the chance to remember."

"Even if we were to somehow understood of our great need for it."

"Unless… unless by exceptional good fortune, a possibility is somehow brought about where the truth can be revealed… and then to reconnect us with that."

"That is what today is all about. I am here to help make that possible for every person who comes to me, who recognises their desire for that joy."

We sat and soaked in the meaning… feeling the warmth and comfort in it.

Yeheshua retired again upstairs and it wasn't long before others, invited from Capernaum, arrived to join us. We reassembled in the prepared room.

Everyone had already spent hours listening to one disciple or another trying to prepare us for today; to understand the kingdom that the master brought; except possibly Miriam.

At times Yeheshua himself had led these sessions and now was the culmination of all the preparations.

He joined us a few minutes into the quietness we were sitting in, taking his place in the chair provided.

The shutters were closed but the extra curtains John and Sarah had rigged up were still drawn open, leaving the room in a half-light.

Miriam was sitting near the front and the master welcomed her. "Many won't know of the time you have spent hoping and praying for this day, but I do," he said. "Let me spend a few minutes laying out what everyone else has already had explained, and this can be a check for all."

"The eternal is, and has always been, inside of us, but we are unable to be there. This is because our attention is drawn into everything else, and this attention becomes used to the forms and plays of this temporal world."

"But our hearts cannot find true contentment in these carnal things for it has the memory of something else which it still holds most dear. Each of our hearts has the key to knowing; to feel that heaven that has been placed inside us."

"This is the most simple thing, because we are not required to do anything, other than allow ourselves to feel what is already here. To be led into the kingdom, to meet the king."

I watched the interplay between Yeheshua and Miriam as he spoke to her and all of us. It was particularly poignant because I knew something of the personal love he felt for her and she for him. I could see it in his face and felt the thrill that he should share even this with us.

"Purity of heart is what you have, and what you need to bring to this meeting," he continued, looking at Miriam and then all around at each of us, deep eyes glancing over our expectant faces.

"Purity is the child in you that is welcomed home."

At that moment mother Mary and Lamaas slipped into the back of the room and Yeheshua nodded over to them.

"Please come in and sit down… and close the curtains," he added to John. "No-one else should come in. This is between each of you and the master only."

CHAPTER 2.

I didn't find the practice of what the master showed us easy, though I could find no obvious reason for it; except perhaps because I thought it would be different than it was.

Despite every warning to have no expectations, it was impossible not to. What was shown in that inner room was very simple, as we had been told. Now I needed to spend the time to work with what I had been given.

It was my thoughts that made this difficult. They were so much more unruly than I could have imagined and to try to quell them by my own efforts seemed impossible.

Thoughts had never before been so distracting, almost separate from who I was. Sometimes this could be helpful in recognising what was real, in contrast to their shifting impressions; but it was also a source of some fear to me. They echoed the demons that had once invaded my life, but were even more personal, as this was my own mind at work, not some other entity.

The fear of some kind of re-occurrence of my previous possession may have hampered my efforts, but every now and then the wonderful inner experience would flower for me, just when I had given up on it, and this kept me going.

It seemed that, except from when I was deliberately trying to immerse myself in the practice, the presence of the Word was somehow with me, joining me in some subtle way with everyone and everything else. This revelation was amazing and uplifting, making up completely for the struggle I was having in my private meditations.

This Word brought my breath, and was my breath, just as the master said. Feeling this truth filled me with an up-welling of joy, enough to overcome anything else that might come, and was the basis for the love that flowed.

Being with the master though, was what brought the whole thing to life, making it all real; infusing every day with the excitement to be a part of what he was doing, who he was.

This excitement and love that all the disciples, followers or whatever we were, lived with, was infectious, and continued to boil over into any town or village that the master Yeheshua visited.

I threw myself into all the activities, no longer finding the opposition from the brethren that I had experienced before. It seemed that they accepted me as one of them, an anomaly perhaps, but nevertheless a kind of breakthrough had indeed happened.

Miriam had a different experience. For her the practice of the hidden path was a joy and a glory from the start. She encouraged me also to persevere with my own efforts, just as Yeheshua encouraged her strongly to make the most of this time to experience the inner world.

Our master exhorted and inspired us all, of course, and from time to time he would take a group apart for a day or two, to spend time in contemplation and specific teaching; and after that special day in my house in Magdala, we women were included more openly.

But mostly the master allowed separate time for us; partly as a time to relax, and usually in the evening.

What was clear was that certain disciples did not understand Miriam's appearance and how she had become so close to the master in such a short space of time.

The first time, when Simon Peter came back from Tiberius, Miriam was with the master and his mother and I can remember Peter's puzzled expression on being introduced to her, and his discomfort in the way she waited so personally on Yeheshua. I could tell he wanted to ask 'who' and 'why', but he never managed to; not then.

Others were not so discomfited; John and Thomas obviously liked her a lot, and James too, seemed to like having her around. Philip was definitely an admirer.

For some though it must have been like a big hole being rent in their ideas of what it was the master was teaching. Holiness, purity, love; what did these mean exactly? Where did Miriam fit?

But when she sang people, whoever they were, stopped and listened. Her singing truly moved everyone, and in this she received more than acceptance. She could have found a following of her own, except she had no wish for one.

There were many people who would bring instruments so that they could play along as she sang, and the audiences loved it. Yeheshua took the greatest pleasure in her singing and she, for her part, created new songs that spoke directly of this time and the wonder of what was happening; what he was doing:

"Bring forth the harp, the vina and the lyre; bring forth the highest sounding cymbal. All you choirs of heaven; join in this song, this brand new song."

"The Lord of All has bended down at hearing the cries of men; the Prince of Darkness' stronghold is shaking like a leaf before the wind. The sword of Gideon is again unsheathed."

"The Lord, with his own hand, has pulled far back the curtains of the night; the sun of Truth is flooding heaven and earth."

"The demons of the dark, of ignorance and death, are fleeing fast; are disappearing as the dew beneath the morning sun."

"God is our strength and song; is our salvation and our hope; and we will build a house for him anew."

"Will cleanse our hearts and purify their chambers, every one. We are the temple of the Holy Breath."

"We need no more a tent within the wilderness; no more a temple built with hands. We do not seek the Holy Land, nor yet Jerusalem."

"We are the tent of God; we are the temple built without the aid of any tool. We are the Holy Land; the New Jerusalem. All joy and praise to God our

Lord; all praise."

And then Yeheshua would speak, and the words of the songs were brought to life.

Afterwards, in the evenings, Miriam would apply the ways to ease the strains the work wrought on his physical frame. Massaging his feet and shoulders, she knew, better than any priestess, the soothing touches of the caring heart. What is more she was unafraid to offer these to Yeheshua, when others may never have dared.

I loved her for this, so much. It made me feel that everything was being made whole. That which the world might judge to be impure, if given the chance, were not necessarily so; all was in the heart. Purify that, just as she sang, and everything was... re-born, anew.

All of the disciples strove to give back to our master for what he gave to us. In this we were the same, and recognised each other. There was an extraordinary brotherhood even though we were very different types of people. We all loved him and so each other as well.

It wasn't always easy to fit in a private life within the immediacy of the work being done, except for the time trying to tread the inner path. That all belonged to me, as much as I wanted; whether there were struggles or smooth sailing, whichever came.

Miriam could share the master's love in this outer life in a way no other could; making it easier for him to give to the world that needed his kindness so badly; to have Miriam's love to help with the burden.

Mother Mary loved her for this too, I know. She wanted the best for her son and Lord, and worried when he spoke of trials to come. 'Sister' she called Miriam and this was also because they were related, through the marriage of her cousin to Miriam's father.

"Sister" is what Yeheshua would call her sometimes too, especially when they were with 'the twelve', and I was reminded of what I had learnt of Isis and Osiris, in the temple at Antioch. Isis had been, amongst other things, the virgin consort and sister of Osiris. Surely the myths were being played out in front of us.

CHAPTER 3.

The momentum continued in all the towns and villages of Galilee, and beyond; the impact of the master's work growing all the time. His message reached more people in more places, and his kindness touched all that came to him.

Every disciple reacted differently to what was happening, trying to gauge where the master was taking them; the destination of our journey.

The questions that seemed to hang on every lip was 'when do we go to Jerusalem again?' and 'when shall he declare his claim?' but Yeheshua never hinted that he planned to do this.

He always stressed the 'Inner Kingdom' and the 'King within', but however much he did so there were those who saw the multitudes gathering after him and thought other routes to power were being laid down. Even some very close to the master.

Several times he warned that worldly powers would come to take him and put him to death, but this was hard for us to understand, for all clarity and righteousness were his; and all the power, strength and support of the people lay behind him too.

It felt instead as if this must refer to events of some future time, an eventuality perhaps, that those who found their power undermined and threatened would somehow seek to use violent means to halt our progress; his message. We would be surely ready for them when that time came.

Miriam listened closely though, and spoke to me of her worries for his safety. "There is no demon that could stand against his Word, but in the hidden places of man we can hide things away from the light. We have even been given the power to destroy ourselves. Though Yeheshua seeks to help every living thing, or perhaps because of this, he makes himself vulnerable. He has no thought to protect himself from what man can do; I do not know what we can do ourselves; those of us that love him."

She pointed to the imprisonment of John, the Baptiser on the banks of the Jordan, who had proclaimed the master's mission at the start.

I had no answer for her, but I felt how real her fear was, and saw that mother Mary did as well.

I am sure it was nothing to do with that, but I had started having quite difficult dreams, where the spaces of the underworld and those that ruled there were calling out to me. I usually did not remember the details but a feeling of disquiet sometimes persisted until my daily practice set it aside.

In contrast I was getting along well with all 'the twelve'. There were one or two that I was nervous of, Judas and Simon Zelotes in particular, but then again there was also Thomas. The one who I liked the most, and who had come from Antioch; as I had.

He was a little different from the rest, being almost Greek in character, and clean-shaven. One time he did return from a tour of Decapolis sporting a bit of a beard, such as the others of the twelve wore. Yeheshua had laughed; "if our wisdom depends on the length of our beards then we are all in trouble."

Thomas had gone away and shaved his beard off, at which there had been more general laughter, till Yeheshua appeared with his cut off as well; and kept it thus for many weeks.

He looked younger without it, I thought, but it was Miriam, I think, who persuaded him to grow it back. A beard made him look less vulnerable she said to me one day, and anything that gave some protection, even the semblance of it, should be encouraged.

It was said she could get him to do anything, and sometimes disciples would go to her to ask her to plead with Yeheshua on their behalf. This was as it had always been with his mother too, and Miriam laughed with her about it.

There was even talk of 'betrothal'. Mother Mary may have been the one to have started the rumour, but many would have been happy with the arrangement. Some not so, perhaps.

And all the time she sang the songs that soothed the hurts and inspired the hearts of the multitudes that listened. Yet her many singing performances took a lot out of her, and there were times when her throat was too sore to perform. On these days Yeheshua was as concerned for her as she had been for him; but it was difficult, even for him, to stop her.

There came a day, when we had just got back to Capernaum, that I went early in the morning from my usual lodgings, to Mirimion; to see if I could help with the preparations for the welcome home feast Mary was preparing.

I had a key to let myself in and was surprised to hear a slight sobbing sound coming from the front room. I put the bag I was carrying down and moved quietly to the adjoining door and listened for a second or two. My heart was pierced by the sounds coming from inside and I opened the door to go within.

Miriam was there, sitting on the floor, sobbing quietly; and, astonishing to me, Yeheshua was kneeling there as well, with an arm around her shoulders. It was hard to tell whether he was just consoling her or crying as well.

I hardly knew what to do at all, and was rooted to the spot; the emotions of the scene starting to engulf me as well. Then Yeheshua looked in my direction and I know I blushed bright pink and turned to go, but he called my name; "Mary, stay. Your help is needed. Please come to us."

Like dragging myself through treacle I went over to where they were and Miriam saw me too and threw an arm around my neck and cried the louder, or so it seemed.

"Mary." It was the master speaking, his composure recovered, "I need to ask you to do something for me that only you can do."

"I have asked Miriam to seek answers in Kadesh, that mean more to me than I can explain, and only she can do this. It means a long journey into the wilderness and though we can make provision for the journey, I cannot come with her, as I have to stay in Galilee a while longer. But please, will you go with her where she has to go and bring her safely back again to me?"

I was non-plussed. On one hand it felt wonderful to be asked to do something for Yeheshua that he was saying no-one else could do. A very great honour; but on the other hand didn't this feel somehow like a betrayal of Miriam? She was obviously in great distress about it.

In slight hesitation, I looked at her and her brown eyes looked back into mine. Somehow through the tears of pain she smiled at me and nodded. "You don't have to come," she said, in seeming contradiction to her nods; "I will be fine."

"Of course I shall go, master, if you wish" I said, then added. "It would be my greatest delight, Miriam, to go with you to the furthest depths of the desert if that is where you go."

She smiled at me, but I felt rather that her tears were easier to bear, and I started crying in response. Yeheshua put an arm round my shoulder too and I could not tell joy from pain, it all seemed to coalesce in me.

I knew that Miriam's pain was because she had to leave her Lord, but her joy was that he was here now, comforting her. Yet it was his wish that she should go, and on a journey of unknown length and outcome. This I understood, and knew as well that Yeheshua shared the pain of asking her to do this.

If there was any help I could give then of course I would, but I didn't really believe I could. More a kindness given to allow me to think I could.

Anyway the preparations he asked me to make were easy. The donkeys, tents and other things we would need. I set off to Magdala to arrange them from the business resources I had there, and would meet Miriam and the master again in Nazareth.

There was a festival happening there, where Miriam was going to be singing.

And so she did. All the week she sang the songs of Israel that everyone knew but had never heard sung in such a way; and also her new, new songs that told of what was happening now.

Everyone was amazed and touched by the power of these songs and the beauty of Miriam singing them.

No-one in Nazareth had known who Miriam was, though the master had taught and healed there too, with mixed reception. They found it hard to accept a teacher who had once lived there amongst them; in Marmion way; and the son of a carpenter of all things.

The impact of her singing was greater here than anywhere, creating much wonder. Usually, Yeheshua would have continued conversing with the audience after her singing, but he didn't do this in Nazareth. All week she had centre stage and the master attended on her afterwards.

Then, on the last night before the Sabbath, Yeheshua did get up on the stage after she had sung, and himself started extolling her praises for her singing and the purity of her vision. Clarity had blessed them with her own sight and song.

Miriam was stood beside me as we listened to him, talking in a way that neither of us had heard before. She turned to me and said "Mary, it is time for us to go. Now; tonight."

Quickly we went to round up the others. Philip and Nathaniel of the twelve were travelling with us, together with several other brethren they had picked to come. All were ready for a sudden departure, and by the coming of night we made our first camp just a few miles south of Nazareth.

CHAPTER 4.

The journey down through Samaria to Jerusalem was a pleasure

We travelled in quite a leisurely way, stopping at many villages on the way down. There were nearly always people around that Yeheshua had met and taught a year or so earlier, and that we were able to spend some time with.

Nathan and Philip would also perform baptisms when there were new people that wanted to start following the master's teachings, and Miriam and I spent pleasant hours telling the stories of the work Yeheshua had being doing in Galilee. Helping anyone too, wherever we could.

Sometimes we would stay the night, sharing food that we had brought and Miriam would most often sing some songs whilst I liked to help prepare the meal.

Other nights we might make our camp along the way, enjoying the glory of the late summer nights from round our campfire. Miriam and I shared a tent and she told me more about the mission Yeheshua was sending us on.

"He said that we would get help from the priestess of Isis at Rekem. Her name is Leila, and I think I may have met her at Heliopolis."

"Did you spend a long time there?" I asked, fascinated to be able to hear more about that extraordinary place. My friend Arianne had visited there, and received the prophecy about the Goddess Isis.

"I met the master in the temple there, and gave my heart to him." She went quiet and I didn't want to intrude into her memories.

We were sitting in the outer entrance of our tent and we gazed up at the sky laced with a million pinpricks of heavenly light. The three stars of the Hero's girdle had risen above the southern horizon, the first time I'd seen them in many weeks and Miriam smiled as we both beheld them. She placed a hand on my arm. "Mother Mary will be missing us you know; she has been telling me how much it means to her that you, and now I, have joined her and the master."

I felt honoured to be told this and the quiet spaces between my breaths filled with the joy and knowledge of being able to serve; in some way; in any way.

The sun beat down fiercely in the daytime and we took frequent breaks; for us and our mounts to be able to drink. We each had an ass and there were several others that carried our gear, and the food and water.

Miriam and I rode along side by side as I continued the conversation of the night before. "Where is Rekem, Miriam?"

"On the caravan route to ancient Sheba," she replied. "It is a wonderful city carved out of the living rock. Being carved still; rose coloured temples of... great wonder."

"And Kadesh?" I continued my line of inquiry, trying to put the pieces together.

"Kadesh is Rekem and other places in the wilderness, where Moses's sister

Miriam lived the last years of her prophecy, her service and her life. She was buried there. It is more than just a single place though; it is where water could be found, and that was Miriam's special skill."

She stopped, as if thinking of other times and places. "Water is a symbol of the spirit, as in the baptism rite; as Kadesh is the symbol of that which I am to seek." She went quiet again.

"There was also something Yeheshua told me," I volunteered, in return for the questions I was asking. "He said that I would find someone in Bethany who might want to join us in our quest; and that if he did that, we should accept him to accompany us."

"Really?" said Miriam, looking sideways at me from the back of her donkey, "That is a surprise. I know that the master's friend Lazarus lives in Bethany, with two of his sisters, Martha and Mary; but his health is frail. I don't think this journey would suit him. Are you sure the master said a man?"

"Yes; I am sure of that. Definitely."

"Well, we are visiting to tell them that Yeheshua will be in Judea around the autumn festival time. I cannot imagine any of them wanting to come away with us." She looked slightly puzzled; "we shall have to wait and see, then."

When we got down into Judea we headed straight for Jerusalem, but Miriam wouldn't go there. Nathaniel, Philip and two of the others went to the holy city, whilst Joseph and Mark came with us to Bethany.

We stayed with Lazarus and his family and they looked after us tremendously well. Even though we had enjoyed the trip down to Judea, staying with them was like being in an oasis of Yeheshua's special love. We could really relax.

We talked a lot with Martha and Mary about all that was happening; including the concerns for the times to come, because of the opposition and hatred harboured by the Pharisees to the master. We also discussed the journey that we were embarked on; more even than we had been able to with Nathaniel and Philip.

Miriam asked them about the best way to go to Rekem, for she was drawn first to go south towards Bethlehem and Beer-Sheba; yet she was being told that the best road was down through Nabatea on the other side of the Jordon: the incense route from Damascus.

I could tell that Miriam wasn't sure, and that the wilderness where lay the Kadesh she sought was calling to her soul. Should she go the direct route to Rekem, and then go into the desert, or the longer way round, down through the Judean wild lands, close by her goal?

We made a trip down to Bethlehem to spread the master's news. Not just that he was coming soon but that we needed to keep ourselves ready and fresh in the joy and love he taught.

We returned again to Bethany just as Philip and Nathaniel came with news from Jerusalem. Apparently, many of the priests were expecting trouble at the autumn festival and were fearful of the people's support for Yeheshua.

Nicodemus had said as much, and we wondered at it, and worried about it, for this was the worst time for us to be away from our master.

Philip suggested that if we went the route over the Jordan, we could visit Ruth and Asher on the way, in Jericho; and this seemed like a good plan.

We also needed to decide what we would be taking with us, and arrange the camels that we would travel on to Rekem.

I had made contact with the local dealer and done some haggling for the asses we had brought. Now that Philip and Nathaniel had joined us, we could finalise the deal, for they all still had to get back to Galilee.

Bethany was a pretty town, nestled in the Judean hills and the walk to the camel dealer was invigorating. Close to the compound I passed a smithy where the heat and noise of metalworking could be felt through the open doors to the workshop. I paused a moment, watching the two men bent over pieces of iron they had been heating and beating. Something was familiar about one of them, though his back was mostly turned to me. As I watched, fascinated, he turned his glance to the doorway and our eyes met.

Johannus was as surprised to see me as I was to see him. He lost his concentration for a moment too long and almost burnt himself.

"Johannus; watch your iron," called his colleague and Johannus turned away from me.

"Sorry," I heard him saying. The other man looked at me and frowned. He was an older man with a full beard; black, streaked with grey.

"Excuse me Beor," said Johannus, "this is someone I must stop to say hello to."

"I'll come back Johannus. I cannot believe it is you. How marvellous; I'm going to the camel dealer. I shall come back within the hour."

"Fine, fine. Will that be all right Beor?" The other man grunted as he hit his working piece with a large hammer.

We had made a good deal with the asses. Some of them would get back to my business partner Daniel in Magdala, carrying goods for another trader to Capernaum, led by Mark and Joe. We would only buy two camels but planned to keep one of the asses as well.

After sorting the details with Ahmed, I walked back down to the smithy, wondering at this meeting with Johannus. He must have told me, during our extremely short association in Antioch, that he had relatives in Bethany, but I hadn't remembered. That whole journey to Tyre, when I was at the height of possession, had just been a nightmare to me.

Of course, I had heard from Rachel the huge part Johannus had played in rescuing me from that terrible situation. Yet so much had happened since then that I never thought I would get the chance to thank him. Now I had.

CHAPTER 5.

Johannus had been working in the smithy for a while now. The hard physical nature of the work suited his frame of mind, since the awful turn of events with the so-called 'Magus', Simon; and the flight from Antioch.

His ability to help Magdalene had somewhat saved his self-respect as well as her life, but still he felt the tinge of shame for what had gone on before.

He had been completely helpless when Mary, his guest at the time, had been defiled and abominated by his former friends and teacher; and this helplessness gnawed at his honour.

Then a very strange thing had happened as he travelled to Bethany from where he had left Mary with the healer Rachel, at her home by the sea, near Tyre.

He was travelling on his donkey, making his way across some rocky desert terrain, when he decided to stop and take a break. A thorn tree that had put out spindly branches that would provide enough some shade for him and his donkey.

Probably not a recognised resting area and maybe not the best place to stop, but the day had got hot and he had enough water to spare for this break.

He tied the donkey to a low branch on the tree, providing her some water in a bowl, and slumped himself against the other side of the rock, which the tree seemed to be partly growing through.

He pulled his cloak over his head and lay down on one side, propping his head on one elbow, his other hand scuffing over the stony ground in front of him.

There was one large dark pebble that was mostly buried in the ground, but so evenly smooth to his tracing touch that it intrigued him. His fingers rubbed the dust from its surface, revealing a polished regularity that might have suggested human craftsmanship.

Johannus tried to prise the stone out of the hard ground but it resisted his best efforts. He was slightly frustrated, but he knew he had a knife that would make the work easy. He felt his belt pouch for it, opening it and searching inside, but it was not there.

Slightly annoyed with himself again, he struggled to his feet and checked his baggage. Not there either. He must have left it at Rachel's house in Tyre.

Everything seemed to be working to nullify his wishes, magnifying the sense of personal helplessness he had been struggling with. No knife. Damn. He looked for something else to scratch the ground away around the half-buried stone and came up with nothing except his silver working tools that he kept wrapped in a leather cloth.

Normally he wouldn't have dreamt of using them for such an activity, but out in the desert things had changed. He attacked the ground at the edge of the stone with precision, as though he was working in his father's workshop. To his amazement he uncovered first a band of metal around the stone and then another, and a whole setting like a wide round brooch, but going deeper into the ground than that.

Finally, he had in his hand a black, shaped and polished stone, secured by bands of gold and silver to a bronze holding piece, a setting for something but he didn't know what that could be.

Having broken open the hardened surface, he now found that a part of a fallen branch was sufficiently strong and sharp to open a bit more of the ground, but he found nothing more. Eventually he gave up and sat back down to work out what he had found.

On the under-side, away from the stone there was a slot in the bronze. It was clogged with earth, but he decided that the bronze setting must be hollow and that something was designed to fit in this end, probably being twisted and fixed in place, once inserted through the slot.

Suddenly it hit him what it must be. The pommel of some old and ornate sword handle; or maybe of a large ceremonial knife. Either way it was an extraordinary find and it lifted his spirits in an immediate way.

All the way to Bethany he pondered over what he might do with the pommel and these deliberations seemed to come together when he found the chance to work at the blacksmith's.

He would fashion another handle and blade to fit the pommel he had found; then use the crafts he had to finish it. Silver-working and the arcane skills he had studied. His mind recalled Gideon's sword and he sought in his way to make this a symbol for something greater, something he aspired to be.

Of course, he needed to learn to use the sword as well, so that never again would he feel the helpless inability to protect those he cared for.

Beor had laughed at him a bit in his gruff way but hadn't tried to stop him making the weapon; even though it could have got him into trouble with the Roman authorities.

In fact, Beor helped him fashion the blade and haft, to fit into the pommel and also made a cross-guard and bronze strap which he heated and wound around the wooden piece that Johannus had carved to make the grip.

Over the bronze Johannus stretched a piece of goatskin which he bound in place with a tight spiral of silver wire, pulled in under the pommel as he fitted and locked it in place. The polished black stone in its gold and silver setting looked very fine and even Beor was quite impressed.

Beor himself worked hardness into the blade, following the slightly leaf-like shape that Johannus designed for his sword. It was not as long as Beor would have imagined, to go with this pommel, nor yet quite as sturdy as the Roman gladius. Nevertheless, it would be very useful.

Johannus had made a plain leather and wood scabbard for it and after Beor had worked the blade to sharpness Johannus engraved the tri-flamed letter

'Shin' onto the side of it. He used all his skill to inlay some gold into the letter, the letter for spirit and truth.

The smith's own tastes were simpler. He was not a man of letters or learning but had a depth of earthy wisdom that Johannus had grown to admire.

It was Beor that first told Johannus about the teacher Yeshua, who had visited Bethany and shown incredible power and bravery in rescuing a little child trapped in a burning house. The smith had been there and had not forgotten how the flames had lessened at Yeshua's command, as he stepped in amongst them.

Nor had he forgotten how the young master had shown great kindness through the whole community and this impressed Beor almost more than anything.

Beor had no time for the high and mighty Pharisees or priests but nevertheless he had sought baptism from this teacher, much to his own surprise.

Johannus was still reeling from his troubles in Antioch with the so-called Magus Simon, in whom he had put so much faith and trust, and he resisted the interest that Beor's stories aroused in him. He had seen power before and he was slightly sceptical about Beor's talk of kindness. He couldn't forget what had happened to Mary; what was done to her.

The smith didn't mind at all, but seemed to enjoy everything that happened to him, in his singular way. Talking about things like this with Johannus was just one way in which things in his life were changing.

"I feel like I am being shaped myself, day by day. Even as I myself shape the metal with my forge and hammer," he said. "What I thought I was, I see is not quite true. I am a part of the greater whole, and that is what I am coming to accept. We shall see; we shall see. Who knows what an unlearned man like me can come to understand?"

Then Mary had re-appeared and nothing would be the same again. She had recovered from the abominations. Not just recovered but seemed to almost shine with well-being.

When she told him how Rachel had taken her to Yeheshua and that he had driven her demons out, he was astonished. First Beor and now Mary. It was as if this teacher was showing something directly for him; without even being there himself. His heart skipped a beat as he asked her about being given the teaching. He never thought he would do that; not after the Magus thing.

Mary told him that there were several close disciples of the master, living right here in Bethany, and that if he wished to receive the way to the kingdom within, then he need go no further. The master himself was coming to Judea again, very soon.

Surprised and inspired, he agreed to go to Lazarus' house to hear more about the master Yeheshua and his teaching.

CHAPTER 6.

I was really glad that Johannus agreed to come back to meet the others at Lazarus' house, and Beor came as well.

Johannus was a little shy, it seemed to me, but that was completely understandable. I also saw that he was hugely struck by Miriam's beauty. I doubt this was an observation that anyone else would have made, but I had been trained in these things, and knew a little about Johannus as well.

Then again, the only time most people saw Miriam was when she stepped up to sing, and everyone was always struck by her beauty. Otherwise, she generally liked to cover her head; but not in Lazarus' house.

She was kind and polite to Johannus, telling him how much she missed being with Yeheshua and he nodded and made noises of sympathy as if he understood, but I could see he was awestruck, smitten by her.

Philip asked if he wanted to take the initial baptism, which was a symbol of seeking to be accepted in the spirit. Johannus replied that he did and Philip said there were others coming as well, to the place called 'black springs', in the morning. The black was a simply reference to the colour of the rocks there, and it had always been considered an ancient holy place.

We were going to eat supper and Beor agreed to stay but Johannus said he wanted to fast and prepare for the rite on the coming day; which was accepted of by us all as appropriate, if that was what he wished.

Beor was fun to be with, and was full of praise for his young helper. He did tell us of the sword and Johannus' work to make himself competent in using it as well, which surprised me hugely; until I came to see how badly affected he had been by what had happened in Antioch; to me mostly, but also to him and his honour.

That next day we all went to the stream where the baptisms were being done. Philip walked with me and he told me that soon it would be more than just the water baptisms that the twelve would be doing. I looked at him, the question of 'how do you know?' rising to my lips, but I thought better of it and mumbled something like "I wonder when that will happen?"

Philip glanced across at me. "I guess he will make it happen when we are ready; so, Nathaniel and I need to be back as soon as possible. We shall leave to go back to Galilee tomorrow. Will the asses be ready for Mark and Joe to come with us?"

"Yes, I think they will. I finalised the agreement yesterday. Ahmed would like us to take them from his yard as soon as we can. Otherwise, he must continue to feed and water them with his other beasts. Joe is using one to collect the merchandise, and should be set for a departure by the end of today. Mark is arranging supplies for the journey."

Philip smiled and asked me about the arrangements for our journey, to

Rekem. About this I couldn't be so certain. I looked round to Miriam who was behind us, walking with the sisters Martha and Mary. She was laughing with them and seemed totally unconcerned with such thoughts, though I knew from talking to her after supper that she was still undecided.

She had joked about "my nice young man" and I hope I had not blushed when I had assured her that he was **not my** young man, which made her laugh the more. "Well, he is very gallant, Mary. I think he should be somebody's young man."

Nathaniel led the baptism rite, with Philip's help, and Lazarus talked to each person that came dripping from the stream, greeting them to the fledgling community of Yeheshua's followers in Bethany. Martha and Mary had brought something for them to eat and drink and Miriam and I helped with that as well.

Johannus was the last to get to the stream and I watched with interest as he addressed himself intently to what Philip and Nathaniel were asking of him. I was reminded of how young he had looked when I had first seen him in Antioch, and now it seemed as though many cares were lifted from his face again. He smiled with a freshness that made me happy for him as well.

The day was spent with the new disciples taking advantage of the presence of Philip and Nathaniel, in particular, to ask questions about the path they had started upon, listen to the answers and spend time in quiet reflection as well. It was a lovely day and the news that we gave that the master would be coming quite soon to Bethany and Jerusalem added to the sweetness of it.

Martha and I went back to their house and made some food for a light afternoon break for everyone; particularly the newly baptised. Miriam sang some songs and Mary accompanied her with a lyre.

Eventually Philip and Nathaniel needed to go and make preparations for their journey the next day. Lazarus went with some of the new followers to their homes but Johannus accepted an invitation to eat at Lazarus' house, which he had passed on the day before.

The conversation turned inevitably to Miriam and our journey to Rekem. Clearly Miriam wanted to travel south through the wilderness rather than join the commercial route across the Jordan, but there were obvious concerns expressed by Nathaniel, and others as well.

"You say that you have travelled that route when you returned from Egypt, Miriam," argued Nathaniel, "and that you also travelled there as a child with your father. But each time you were with a group of merchants. That was not the same as two women travelling alone."

"It is a safer way than the bandit infested route across the Jordan," answered Miriam; "and I know how to live in the wilderness as well as any man."

Nathaniel didn't look convinced, and Philip added to the argument. "How can we tell the Lord that we let you go alone into the wild?" Miriam shot him a fiery glance and I sensed that she wanted to remind him who had sent her thither, but said nothing. The silence lingered. Neither Miriam nor I wanted to ask for anyone else to come with us either; so, a kind of stalemate hovered in the room.

"I could travel with you if you like, if I could be of use."

I looked round, realising that it was Johannus who had spoken up, most surprisingly.

"I have crossed the desert from Beersheba to Egypt and back again. If I can assist you as a guard, it would be my great honour to do so."

My immediate thought was that that was ridiculous but I bit my tongue, and for a moment or two no-one else said anything either.

It was Miriam that broke the new silence. "That is a very kind offer, Johannus." She was looking at me, questioning; "and one that I think we shall be delighted to accept. Magdalene?"

My mind was empty of replies. "Remember what the master… " Miriam was adding, aside to me, and I suddenly realised she was reminding me that Yeheshua had said we should accept the offer of someone we met in Bethany.

Strangely, I hadn't put this prediction together with meeting Johannus again, but now I had to admit this was a possibility.

"If you come with us Johannus," I said, "you could well miss Yeheshua coming to Judea you know?"

He appeared to consider this for a little while, then replied "I can go to anywhere that he may be, there is nothing holding me here in Bethany. First of all, my offer holds to see you through to Rekem and back, or wherever you and Miriam need to go."

"Thank you Johannus," said Miriam, and looking at me again, "then we accept?"

"Yes. Thank you Johannus," I rejoined.

Nathaniel was frowning a little, but he made no objection. Instead, he took Johannus by the arm and asked him to go out into the garden and discuss the needs for the journey; which he did.

A little later Johannus came back and told us that he would need a day or so to make preparations, which was fine with Miriam and myself.

Most unexpectedly the way lay clear for the next leg of our journey.

CHAPTER 7.

Beor was a great help with the preparations. Far from being cross with Johannus for leaving his employ after so short a time, he delighted in coming up with all manner of gifts for each of us travellers.

He helped repair the tackle for the horse that Johannus had been able to borrow. Johannus had ridden horses on several long journeys though he made no claims to any great proficiency; but a camel he really had no wish to try. He was happy to leave that to Miriam and myself.

His uncle had bought this animal for his own use, but had not actually ridden her for quite some time now. He was feeling his age, but did not want to admit it. Johannus taking her on this trip served him quite well, though the bridle, saddle and carrying bags had fallen into disrepair.

For Miriam, Beor had a small earthenware censer, encased in a fine metal fretwork frame, designed to carry still burning embers from a previous night's fire. Perhaps more importantly he gave them a stock of wood that was the best type to retain this heat. Johannus had a good flint and iron striker for starting fires, but Miriam was thrilled with the gift and spent time enjoying it, testing it with fiery fragments from the smithy's furnace.

I was even more surprised when Beor turned to me with a package that revealed a small bow and quiver of arrows. A woman, who was no longer as rich as once she had been, had given it to Beor instead of payment for the work he had done replacing a rusted and broken axle on her carriage.

He liked it but had found no real place for it and seemed slightly embarrassed as he gave it to me.

I had practiced using such a bow a bit, as a priestess in Astarte's temple in Antioch. Traditionally the priestesses had them to chase off, wound or even kill trespassing and otherwise offending men; but not anymore.

I passed them through my hands, enjoying the shapes that were so beautifully crafted to fulfil their design. A master craftsman had fashioned the bow and I thanked Beor for it. "I will bring it back to you, when we return," and he nodded, surprised I think that they had found favour with me.

Martha and Mary were also skilled at making many things. They had been working with a weaver in Bethany to construct a fine woollen robe for Yeheshua, a garment that would have no seams. Cunningly constructed with painstakingly joined edges, single thread by thread, they would be ready to give it to him by the autumn festival.

For their newfound friends and comrades, they made us some wonderful flatbreads for them to take as provisions. Each one was made with different spice and vegetable fillings and cleverly cooked into a package.

They were first baked for about two thirds of their normal time and then wrapped in thin, oiled pastry before going back into the oven again to finish them and seal the pack. Stacked into a woven basket with layers of cloth between them these loaves formed the basis of many good meals, heated on firestones that cracked off the outer layer, revealing the freshly warmed prize within.

When everything was ready Lazarus led the party to see us off on the road, himself riding his donkey, for a mile or so along our route, before reluctantly turning back again. He, perhaps amongst everyone, empathised most with Miriam and would have really wished to join us, had his health allowed.

If there were any doubts about who was leading the mission these were soon dispelled. Though Nathaniel had spent some time questioning Johannus on his experience of travelling and explaining his responsibilities in taking us safely to Rekem and back, when it came to the actual journey clearly Miriam was in charge.

She had spent quite some time helping me get used to the way a camel needed to be handled and cared for as well as reviewing all our provisions for the journey. Johannus soon saw that her expertise in the whole travelling business was much greater than his and he set himself to learn as much as he could from watching her, rather than trying to interfere, however well-meaning his intentions would have been.

This was a good thing, dispelling any unnecessary friction that might have developed once we embarked, and I was particularly thankful that there seemed to be a harmony of purpose between us. I had been worried that introducing Johannus might have been disruptive, but it didn't appear to have worked out that way.

I generally rode along beside Miriam, or just behind her, and Johannus followed on his horse, leading the donkey as well. He said he loved to see us on our high mounts, commanding the view of the way, equal to whatever the sun or the wind threw at us, looking for all the world like nomadic men of the desert, wrapped in our long travelling robes.

He had never felt so completely at ease with his life, having a purpose that he carried with him like a badge on his heart; to protect and help these special women. He had to confess, to himself at least, that he felt real love and admiration for them.

Johannus was surprised at the routes that Miriam chose to take over those days, travelling south, down the wild places by the great salt sea. She didn't seem to mind whether we were taking the quickest or most direct route and would sometimes deliberately go off the road to explore some side valley, rather than go by the larger towns and villages.

On a couple of these occasions we encountered small Essene communities, hidden away in the caves of the rugged hills. She even knew one of the hermits in one of these, from travels with her father, and we stayed a whole day sharing their lives.

Miriam liked to spend more time in inner contemplation than Johannus had been expecting and I joined her in that too. It meant that the journey would take longer but he began to get the feeling that speed was not the essence of the trip. Each day had its part to play in reaching an understanding and he began to feel he had some share in this learning.

After a couple of the unexplained diversions Johannus stopped worrying about them at all but concentrated on making sure he kept the water and food levels as high as he could, as well as looking out for any kind of trouble.

There was no trouble. It seemed that he, with his sword would perhaps be the most worrying person around, so he hid it away and just followed Miriam as inconspicuously as he could, a younger brother in learning.

Except that some of the Essene elders we met also had some issues with me. The contact I had had with heathen gods and evil spirits apparently left some mark on me, which they did not understand and were fearful of.

Miriam explained that the master Yeheshua had cleared me of the troubles that had happened to me and that the master trusted me implicitly.

Clearly Miriam had a close affinity with these people but their initial antipathy to me made her realise that these were not places to tarry too long and that we should push on to Rekem.

Johannus was fascinated at the people we met but was never happier than when being on the trail; and soon we were pushing on, ever closer to the road between Gaza and the town we sought: Rekem.

The way Miriam had chosen took us well east of Beersheba, and though we had managed to replenish most of our supplies, we now entered the desert proper, feeling how much we were on our own.

The next campsite was the first for a couple of days where there was no one else around, nor was there likely to be for a few to come.

We enjoyed everything about the camping. Loved setting up the tents and arranging the fire, Johannus collecting fuel to burn if we hadn't come by enough during the day, which we always tried to do. Both Miriam and I would cook, improvising from our supplies, together with whatever we had managed to collect or gather that day.

Johannus loved us telling stories around the campfire, mostly of the master Yeheshua but also other people and places as well; and sometimes, most special of all, Miriam would sing.

Johannus knew these were her own personal devotions to her Lord, and his heart opened up to the love she shared.

They had reached a point near the spice road where they must decide what they would do next, and that evening Johannus felt that he was receiving almost personal instruction, listening as closely as he could to every word.

"Purity of purpose is what is required to bring success."

"Earnestly seeking to gain understanding of the Truth will hone this purpose, clearing away unnecessary baggage."

"Learn to love Purity itself, for this will become a flame that will burn away any obstacle."

"Once that fire of Devotion is lit, nothing can stand in its way, but even the hardest trials become the fuel for Love."

Johannus knew Miriam was speaking of her own experience and whilst he felt it to be quite natural to be learning from these women of wisdom, somewhere in his brain he realised that many others couldn't have contemplated this.

"But not the kind of purity that the Pharisees talk of," I said after a long pause, in which Johannus had been trying to take it in properly.

"They are so concerned with what other people think of them," I said, for I knew he might reproach himself for not meeting Miriam's heights.

"The master says: 'Judge not and you shall not be judged'. That is a kind of purity of purpose that cannot be touched, where we are not looking for the faults of others but just wanting to receive our own experience from Life's bosom. This is what I am learning and it is freeing me from so much of the anger I have been carrying around with me."

Miriam nodded and we sat thus for a while looking into the flames. Then she spoke again.

"Many people think that God is a power that will come with an army of angels to change the world. Many more think that that the Messiah will claim the thrones of worldly Empires so that the Divine Kingdom will be established. Little do they know that He works within and through the hearts of mankind; has always done and always will. The master comes as a human being for us, that are also human beings, and brings His Kingdom to our hearts. This is the secret that men and women may find, or not, within their own lives."

The web of ideas that Johannus had woven around his life was starting to unravel. He didn't understand exactly how it had come to him to be following these women into the desert. He did feel there was a purpose hidden just beyond his view, but wasn't sure whether his efforts were perhaps nothing more than a desire to be with their beauty that he was drawn to like a moth to flames.

He asked Miriam about the journey we were embarked on and she smiled as she told him of the master's request, to seek that which was needed for what lay ahead.

"He is asking us to do this for our own sake. It is always that way in the things he asks. And it is my task to fulfil it, and if I can do that, then I will know why."

"We have nearly reached the Rekem road from Gaza," Johannus said. "How will you wish to go?" he asked. "We could go west to Beersheba. This may be the best way to pick up a caravan."

"I don't want to go back to Beersheba," she said. "If our supplies are well enough stocked, I would prefer to turn to the east at this junction."

Johannus considered this, but could not help feeling uneasy at the idea of travelling that road without the support of a caravan train. It was a very different prospect from the infrequently travelled ways they had been taking so far, and he tried to express something of his concern.

Miriam looked at him and he felt the honour of being taken seriously. Was he worried for himself? She knew that he cared for her and my safety more than his own. Yeheshua had put him there to help keep us safe.

We waited in what we felt was a safe campsite near the road, for the two and a half days until a caravan came by travelling east, that bore whatever form of goods and payment that was to be exchanged for the next spice shipment.

Days during which Johannus fretted whether he was advising the right thing, but Miriam and I relaxed and enjoyed the break. Miriam had found the buried cistern of water in the rocks that was the secret of the nomads who visited and used this site.

Water available so we could spend time cleaning ourselves and our clothes, careful to be as sparing as possible.

We ate little though, as we didn't know for how many days the wait would be. Miriam and I spent most of the time in our quite roomy tent, itself in the shade of one of the thorn trees which typified the site, leaving Johannus the main duty of scouting out for the caravan's arrival and any other danger. In the end it was the donkey that gave the game away one morning, braying at the smell on the wind of his fellow kind, somewhere on the road nearby.

There was a Roman guard, led by a young officer who amazingly Johannus recognised from having been stationed in Antioch, a couple of years before. What was the chance of that happening, he wondered?

The officer remembered Johannus and welcomed him and his companions. Apparently, there had been some local troubles at Beersheba and the caravan had skirted it without stopping. It was fortunate they had waited where they had.

Thankfulness flooded through Johannus that he had been able to successfully complete this part of whatever this task was he had been given.

CHAPTER 8.

The new day dawned in the special way it did in the desert, with the brief and precious time when the balance of warmth and moisture and comfort enabled its creatures to get themselves set, before the long day's heat truly set in.

We caravan travellers were no different to other creatures. Once we had enjoyed the start of the day, eating and striking camp, we cocooned ourselves in our robes, climbed upon the backs of our faithful camels, or in Johannus' case his faithful mare, and settled into the rhythm of their languid walk as they followed the line of the march set by the company of soldiers.

They were on horses as Johannus was. The rest of the caravan was a mixture of burden camels and asses, but there were also a few local guides and drivers riding their camels as well. We fitted in quite well, following along at the back of the train.

Miriam was in high spirits to be on the move again and Johannus shouldered his responsibility with great seriousness, wearing his sword openly in a way that he would never have done in Judea. The Roman officer of the guard, Antonius, spent time travelling with us as well. I hadn't known him personally in Antioch, I was glad to say, but enjoyed his conversation, being reminded of my friends from those days.

Mainly though, I liked to look out from my cocoon, matching my breathing to the languid movements of my camel as the glory of the desert landscape gradually rolled around us. The leisurely journey down through Hebron had given me precious time to practice the harmony of all things, and I felt that my experience was gradually growing.

Antonius asked Miriam what had brought us on this journey and she plainly told him that the master Yeheshua had sent her to consult with the priestess of Isis in Rekem.

Antonius had heard of the Hebrew Sage Yeshua and said he had heard him spoken of very highly, as being a wise and kind man, with a great gift of healing. "But," he added, "he is also reported as having a problem with his own God's priests, which cannot be a helpful state of affairs, is it?"

"Priests of any religion jealously guard their power, Antonius; but yes, you are right, the laws given by God are closely enshrined in the temple of my people, making any challenge to their spirit, or form even, difficult to countenance. Yeheshua seeks to set all men free from the priestly interpretation of these laws, by giving access to the actual Love of the One who has created us all and who is giving us this Life, moment by moment."

Antonius was silent, pondering her words. Finally, he spoke, "Is it possible that such can be for us Romans as well?" "Certainly," Miriam replied. "In just a little while the whole of the Roman world will hear the Truth. Carried by men of faith such as yourself, Antonius."

He looked at her and saw the look of prophecy upon her. "We shall get you safely to Rekem then," he said.

"That may be beyond your power" she said, "but every valiant effort will endure."

I was surprised myself to hear Miriam talk like this, not having connected her with the gift of prophecy before, but realised it must be bound up with the quest the master had set her upon; and entrusted me to bring her back safely.

I asked her later what she had meant about it being beyond the power of Antonius to get us safely to Rekem, and she would only say that it was God who protected us, rather than the Roman army, and I had to be content with that, though I kept close to her whenever possible.

I was glad to see that Johannus was being very cautious as well. He posted himself as a guard near our tent at night and I don't know how much he sleep he got, if any at all. I noticed that he dozed sometimes on horseback during the day, and I was torn between staying close to Miriam and going over to check on Johannus.

Antonius came back to talk with us again the next day, as we rode along a narrow valley between the steep sides of the hills that were fast becoming mountains. He urged us to ride towards the front of the caravan where he could better protect us from possible bandit attack. The pass ahead was sometimes guarded, but not always by the Nabatean King's guards.

The conversation turned towards the priestess of Isis at Rekem, whom Antonius had seen but did not know. "Her name is Leila," said Miriam, "and she has met the master Yeheshua before his work in Palestine began. The master respects the truth that is enshrined in other religions, as well."

He nodded in response and they rode on in silence for a while.

"Isis has become very popular in Rome, in recent years," he said at last. "An alliance between her and the Great God of the Jews would be a powerful force indeed."

"Is there some rift in the bosom of the Divine that we are needed to fix do you think Antonius?" she said laughing. "We humans are good at making divisions, not fixing them."

"I meant the religions that are here, not the… " he trailed off.

"I know what you meant sir," she replied, "but this is about something that is real, known in the heart; not the power games of men, however clever or great they are, or we they think that they are; for a brief span."

The pass was clear of any opposition and a few Nabatean troops gave us clearance to proceed. Antonius rejoined the head of the caravan and we went back to the rear. We should reach Rekem the next day.

Johannus kept guard on us again that night and I was glad he wouldn't have to try again for another night. When the day dawned, I stepped out of our tent, over his sleeping body and down to the supplies to wash and take a drink. It already felt this would be a stiflingly hot day and I wanted to wake up properly now.

Miriam was still sitting upright in her bedding when I lifted the entrance flap and went back in. I had brought some water for her too, but later we would go down to where the guides were brewing the tea before setting off.

Johannus managed to pack up all his things and help us with ours as well, so perhaps he had got enough sleep, though he still looked tired. I made sure he had the last of the flatbread that Martha and Mary had given us, and he thanked me, smiling. He was fine.

The morning's ride was just as hot as I thought it would be, soporifically so, but we were getting closer to Rekem all the time. The mountainous terrain was hugely impressive but I would be glad to reach our destination.

My eyelids were heavy and it was easy to let them close, just for a second or two. I jerked upright as I realised that I had been asleep; but only for a moment and I set myself to resist doing it again. Easier said than done. Several more times I found myself jolting back from slumber to wakefulness.

I turned to look around and the faithful Johannus was riding up towards me. He had obviously noticed the difficulty I was having, and he pointed out that Miriam was slumping in her saddle as well.

She responded to our call and we decided to ride up to the front of the caravan as something to relieve our tiredness.

The soldiers were suffering just as we were and Antonius agreed that it would be good to take an early break, which helped us all, and afterwards we retired to our accustomed place at the rear of the train.

Then mountainous terrain had flattened out into a wide plain stretching left to right with further hills and mountains on the other side, where we were heading. The train was still quite spaced out and Miriam urged her camel forward to catch up.

Johannus and I followed her lead and once again we settled into the pace of the others as we bunched up with them. Once over the seemingly endless and scorching plain we would soon be there, for somewhere in the hills and mountains ahead the city carved from living rock was there to greet us.

This thought kept me awake because the soporific quality of the day was overtaking me again. The air felt very close, as though there was a storm brewing somewhere closeby, but the sky showed no sign of it. We kept pace with each other, all eager to be across the exposed heat of the plain and amongst the hills again.

Eventually we were on the other side and winding our way through the rocky landscape, always climbing. It was well past the middle of the day and time for another stop, surely?

I watched Miriam for she was clearly struggling a bit, and she looked to me as well. "Do you want to ride ahead?" she asked.

"We could take it in turns to be in the lead," I answered, "that would help us all, I think. What do you think Johannus?"

We looked around for our companion but he hadn't come around the rocks of the last bend yet. We sat and waited for a few moments but he didn't appear. Suddenly I was worried and Miriam was too. She turned her mount around and urged it back along the route. I followed but rather more clumsily.

Johannus was nowhere to be seen on the road behind.

Miriam rode back, calling Johannus name; her trained voice carrying clearly across the windless spaces. There was no response.

"When did you last see him?" Miriam asked, reigning in her camel as I came up to her.

"He was definitely with us after crossing the plain. I think I last turned around only two or three bends ago from here? But I am not sure," I answered.

"Yes, I think it cannot have been long ago. Maybe he drifted off to sleep and has gone off the road. You ride on and tell Antonius and I shall go back and see if I can pick up his tracks."

"I am not leaving you Miriam," I said. "If you are going back then I am coming with you. The train will have moved away by now; I cannot leave you alone back here."

"Mary…"

"I won't, Miriam. I could not bear it…"

"All right then, lets work together. You look for tracks going off the road to this side and I shall search on the other. We mustn't waste any time."

CHAPTER 9.

Johannus had sat late into the night outside his tent which was set a little way away and at an angle towards the women's tent; intent upon carrying out his watch.

He knew from experience what how the beauty of women could affect a man's thinking, and though he believed the Roman soldiery were well disciplined, he wasn't altogether sure about the others in the train.

Miriam, in particular, was careful to keep her head and face mostly covered whilst she was in general company and Mary was following her example; which was usual for women travellers and respected by the desert guides.

Whilst alone with Johannus, Miriam and Mary did not keep their heads covered, but treated him as a brother, which honoured him greatly.

At no cost would he do anything to jeopardise their trust.

As he sat on the one of the wood and leather camel-saddles, outside his own tent, he pondered on the instructions Nathaniel had given him, that formed the core of his service to the master Yeheshua, and which he accepted. To protect Miriam and Mary with his life. Not in theory, but here and now.

He got up and walked over to near where the horses and camels were settled in for the night, and where two or three drivers were still sitting together around a couple of fires. He acknowledged one group and they him, but he didn't join them, rather turned back, walking along the edge of the site, drinking in the beauty of the desert night.

Stars spread wondrously across heaven's expanse, which the new crescent moon had recently vacated, giving space for their glory. Magical; such a wide, full silence that seemed to be calling him, pulling at his soul.

Back on the camel seat out front of his closed-up tent, he mused on the things of his heart and mind. Starting with whether there was danger here, and whether he was best prepared to deal with it.

If there was, then this last night before getting to Rekem was when it would strike. He began thinking about in what way it might.

If anyone wanted to get at Miriam and Mary, even with him here, the best time would be very late at night, maybe an hour or two before dawn. He would be struggling to be alert and so easy for them to creep up on and probably slit his throat.

The women would be in their deepest sleep so they could likely silence them before taking them from their tent…

They would have to have previously dealt with the two Roman guards set on the merchandise and the beasts that carried it during the day; camels, asses, donkeys and the horses.

They will have had several nights to watch the routine of the night guards, who even he knew rotated the watch amongst the six of them, every two hours through the night.

Johannus thought of those three men he had seen earlier, sitting around the fire. He had made out their faces; one of the drivers was one he didn't like the look of; which as much as anything was why he hadn't joined them.

Suddenly he was reminded of Antioch and how things had gone so bad.

He got up again, taking his travel staff as well as the sword to go and check around a bit. Make sure he wasn't a sitting target. They had gone from their fire and all seemed quiet. He went a bit further till he could see the Roman guards; all was well.

As Johannus turned back around, he thought he saw a glimpse of movement around to his right. He stopped, crouching down, and looked for any more. Nothing. He straightened up and sauntered back towards his tent like nothing was wrong but keeping half an eye out; that way, his left side now.

Maybe, just maybe, there was another movement at the edge of his vision. He decided he might be just imagining it; but he was spooked.

He couldn't settle at his own tent so took the camel-saddle and set it in front of the women's tent instead, where the other camel seat was.

Was he being stupid? Was he just being there because he liked to feel close to them? Was he just weak and no good? Doubt, creeping up his spine, was worse than attackers.

So, he thought hard about the master whom he had not yet met, but on whose behalf he had received his baptism from Philip. All he really knew about Yeheshua was from Beor, Miriam and Mary and yet the feeling conveyed was so loving, so kind, that recalling their words, particularly Miriam's, made him feel stronger in himself, and that what he was doing… was real.

He moved one of the camel saddles away from the tent to be in front of a thorn tree, that was still reasonably close and gave him a full view of the women's tent, but was in open ground that would be very hard sneak up on.

He spent time on one seat, sword drawn, as long as he could without getting too drowsy, and then walked around a bit, stretching and observing as much of the camp site as he could make out in the starlight, then settling again at the other seat, with renewed wakefulness, looking out from a different perspective; and repeating the process at intervals.

The easy part, but also the hard part, was to feel the preciousness of those he was guarding, which also showed him how likely they were to be targeted.

Being a cold night, the rest of the watch was a torture of self-imposed discipline, but which fulfilled something in his soul, like Beor had said of the sword's blade being worked to hardness and sharpness, keeping any trouble at bay.

As the light of dawn crept into the eastern sky Johannus knew he had broken the back of his watch, and allowed himself the added warmth of another blanket, knowing it would soon be safe; to sleep just a little while, hand still clutching the pommel of his sword; the sword which he tried to imbue with all the good qualities of strength that he knew he needed.

As he slept, he had a dream in which a tall and daunting lady was telling him something that he knew was really important. It was still with him when he woke, but all too soon the meaning had escaped his mind, and then the memory of the dream had gone, try as he might to bring it back.

That day was the hardest yet, because something in its heat seemed to cling to them, making the distant haze shimmer in their vision like a veil between wakefulness and sleep. Crossing the great basin was more than Johannus thought he could achieve without succumbing.

Mary and Miriam were wonderful in helping him through that heat haze, and he reciprocated when he felt he had any excess energy to give. Once they were again amongst the rocky hills, the oppressive atmosphere lifted a bit and they all felt they could relax.

Johannus was leading the donkey he called Sarah along the track and the heat was not as bad as it had been, despite it now being the middle of the day. She was pulling a bit to the left though and it took him vital energy to pull her back onto the road. She had not played up like this before and something in him was telling her to stop behaving like Balaam's ass. It didn't help, she seemed determined to misbehave, but he would prevail; and he did.

He needed to catch up with the group and he urged his mare forward. He didn't understand why the road was so bumpy or why his horse was picking her way amongst rocks.

"Miriam, Mary," he called, "I am coming. I'll be with you in a minute."

Miriam was there in front of Johannus, much taller than he remembered, but of course she was on a camel. Except that she wasn't; nor was her voice as melodious as it should have been.

In fact, it was not Miriam or Mary, but nevertheless something in him recognised her, tall, beautiful and yet severe. He had dreamt of her; he remembered now.

"How will you find your way when you cannot control your mind," she was telling him; "or even your ass."

"I can control my donkey; look I have," Johannus replied, pleased with himself and trying to turn around to Sarah.

Moving around in the saddle was so hard to do. He strained to see his donkey but she wasn't there or he couldn't see where she was. The rope he was pulling on was the scabbard of his sword, and not the rope at all.

Panic threatened him but Johannus called to Miriam again. "It is alright," he said, more in hope than anything else, "Where are you? Where are you?"

He felt he was falling and awoke to find he was slipping from the back of his horse, and he clung to her neck as his boots cracked onto the ground.

Awful reality started to hit him. He had gone to sleep and had been dreaming. Sarah was not with them. He had let go of the rope. Where? What? How? What was he going to do?

Looking around he found he was in a large bowl-like hollow, strewn with sculptured, pink rock formations and drifts of sand that had blown into it. There was no indication of which way he had come from, but he had to find out.

He led his uncle's horse, called Melody, up the nearest slope, but there was nothing to see but a long gradual ridge. He could have continued that way, but could see no advantage to it either. He stopped and turned Melody around. He had to think.

Whilst still on the higher ground he called out for Miriam and Mary as loud as he could, until he felt stupid. There was no reply. It made him realise how thirsty he was though, and it was then he remembered how little water he was carrying. Most of the supplies were on Sarah, including the water bags. He did have a small amount, but suddenly he also knew he needed to conserve it.

His mind was racing and as he struggled to slow himself down. He could hear the words of the lady in his dream, which had been more than a dream. 'How will I find my way if I cannot control my mind?'

He put his head in his hands and prayed. 'Help me keep strong and focussed, please God'. He sat and breathed, not expecting any answer but just listening to the noise of his heart beating.

He needed to find his tracks that led into this hollow, and retrace them back to the road. It was as simple as that.

Except when he went to look for them it seemed that Melody had walked at least once all the way round the basin before he had fallen off her back, making it hard to find the actual entry point. He climbed higher up the side and started his work again.

Then he found them; clear tracks where the sand was only slightly covering the rocks and stony ground, or strewn around the sparse grasses. There was something else though that made him think again; a trail of marks amongst the tracks that spoke volumes. Dried blood.

These were not his tracks at all; but Johannus pulled out his sword and followed them. They were important.

Instinctively he felt it was a man trying to get away and that he was struggling to keep as straight a course as he could, neither climbing up unnecessarily nor yet going down into the basin. Looking ahead Johannus realised he was heading towards a slight notch in the slope ahead.

The bloodstains seemed mostly on the right side of the tracks and there were signs of that foot dragging over the ground. The man was wounded in that leg and losing blood fast. How much further would he be able to go? Johannus knew the man was slowing down and everything was more of an effort.

Even as he followed the trail, he felt the great effort the man was undergoing, felt the strength draining from him.

His leg was caked and painful but soaked at the same time with a steady stream of blood. It wouldn't work properly anymore. And his strength was draining away with the blood into the sand. Hot sand that soaked up his blood and his will to go on.

He desperately needed water, more than anything and Johannus drained the last drops from his leather water bottle. He struggled to contain his anxiety, losing control over his reality for precious moments. He staggered forward and caught himself. There on the ground ahead, just through the notch in the side of the basin's rim were the remains of the man; the man he had been becoming in his mind.

Jolted by the sight of the bones that had been spread around and picked clean of any flesh by vultures, jackels and other disposers of carrion, Johannus sat on the ground and wondered at himself. He had left Melody somewhere behind him. Why had he risked this? He should have stayed where he was.

He looked back and saw from where he was the long range of mountains rising just above the hills that had kept them from view. Of course; these were where they were heading and he knew that roughly he must go that way, except that they stretched all along one side of the hollow's rim.

Then again, he knew in himself that the man he had been tracking had been fleeing from something that had happened on the road. Instinct or whatever, he knew this was the case. By retracing the steps that he had taken and continuing roughly that way, towards that end of the mountains, he would find the road.

Relief flooded through him and he was about to get up and get going again, to collect Melody, his horse, when something fluttered behind him as an unlikely gust of a very welcomed breeze caught some part of the dead man's clothing.

It was a sash that had once been pink or ochre perhaps, like the wonderful colour of the rocks around them. The man had probably been a priest and Johannus felt it was some badge of office. But it wasn't the sash itself that particularly caught his attention, but the rock that was holding down one end of it.

This rock was much darker than the surrounding ones, almost as black as the one that formed the pommel of his sword. Johannus went over and bent down on his haunches and looked at it. It was a baetyl, or bethel stone; this much he clearly knew. Not large, but one that clearly had a power, or at least a great value to the priest. This man had given his life to protect it.

It was fairly even and rounded, particularly at one end where it was smooth as if from prolonged handling.

Johannus picked it up and hefted it in his hands. Quite heavy for its size, but easy enough for him to carry with him. He wrapped it in the priest's sash, and making a fold in his robe to carry it in, he set off back along the way.

Perhaps he should have done something with the bones he thought, and he struggled with this idea for a few steps before he reluctantly went back to the body again.

He wrapped the priest's bones that he could immediately find in the remains of the man's robes and did his best to bury them by placing a few loose rocks over them in a little pile. That was the best he could do. He said a little prayer for the man's soul and set off again, feeling slightly foolish but also quite a bit better too.

Soon he realised though that his troubles were not yet over. Even when he managed to get hold of Melody again and climb back on the saddle, he was acutely aware both of his need for water and also of his complete lack of it.

He really didn't know how far he had to go to reach water or whether he could or would make it. Perhaps he had already over-reached himself.

Miriam and I scanned along both sides of the road, searching for where Johannus might have left it.

After two or three bends we came to a spot where the ground showed signs of widespread disturbance. We hadn't noticed anything when we had crossed over it the first time and our caravan's tracks clearly dominated the trail's markings. But we now observed the surrounding ground, beside the road, that told a quite different story.

There had plainly been a considerable skirmish of some kind here, and there was still evidence of the blood that was spilled. We looked at each other, our thoughts concurring; this was not a good place to hang around.

It was easy to see that it would be an ideal spot for an ambush and others had obviously recently taken advantage of this. Not that we thought this disturbance had anything to do with Johannus' disappearance, for the marks of the fighting had occurred before our train had passed by. Still, it made me feel very uncomfortable.

We scanned the surrounding ground leading up to low ridges that had higher ones behind them. Would we have to go out into that country? We were horribly exposed.

"Miriam; would it be here, or should we go further back along the road?" I suppose I sounded hopeful for the latter, for she sounded so apologetic when she replied.

"I am certain that it was here, Mary. We have to try looking from here, but I don't even feel like calling for him, let alone going out there."

"Well, I am only going where you go. Which side must we try?"

"To the left, over here," she said. She had dismounted from her camel and was leading it through the scrubby ground beside the road, where a few wild tufts of grass somehow survived, amongst the wide scattering of rocks and stones.

Reluctantly I followed her, also dismounting from the great camel that had almost become my friend. He tried to nip me as he always did, but I was used to him now and smacked his nose softly. He relented and followed me off the road.

Miriam pulled back a bit, came over and put an arm around me. She was obviously feeling the same sense of dread that I was.

Suddenly she flinched. "I saw something," she said. "Over there at the top of the nearest ridge."

From the way she spoke, it hadn't been Johannus. I wanted to turn around and get back on the road and ride away, as quickly as I could; but instead, I froze by her side and searched the rocks where she was pointing. I saw nothing.

I was about to ask her if perhaps she had seen a bird or even if it had really been her imagination, when I saw a movement as well. "There," I said. "I saw it too. Let's get back to the road."

I pulled at her arm but she resisted. "Wait," she said, "there it is again. Mary look; look."

I turned back to where I had spotted the movement and did see it again; and this time I could see what it was. Sarah, our donkey, was picking her way through the rocks at the top of the ridge.

"Sarah," I exclaimed, and then again "Sarah, Sarah." I felt like crying, after the fear. How wonderful to see her.

Much less reluctantly we made our way up the slope to meet the donkey. Neither of us spoke of it; of the hope that Johannus would follow just behind her, but he didn't. The cold dread began to creep into me again.

"If anyone had attacked him, Mary; they would certainly have taken Sarah as well."

Miriam was right. She took the donkey's trailing rope and tied its end to one of the camel straps. We carried on, turning Sarah around in the process and going back over the ridge.

There was no sign of Johannus though.

Johannus did his best to retrace the tracks the priest had made in trying to escape from his attackers. The lack of water was Johannus' biggest worry, and the sun beat down on him relentlessly. With no end in sight, it was a whole different story to the carefully paced journey along the road that they had been following.

He wondered to himself how delicate the balance of safety was; right now, he felt very much on the wrong side of it.

He recognised nothing of the surroundings but he carried on, keeping his path as straight as he could. With the mountains to one side, he was either going in the right direction, or exactly the wrong one. There was no sign of the road though, and his suffering was starting to stretch out because of the slowed pace he and Melody were able to maintain.

His mind returned to the vision of the Goddess, and the dream he had had. He decided, somewhat hopefully, that it must be Hecate, the keeper of the crossroads, wearing the crescent on her brow. Also, dweller in the underworld his mind reminded him, more worryingly. Putting that thought aside he tried to recall her words and suddenly, unexpectedly, he remembered his dream that he had been unable to hold onto when had had woken up that morning. It seemed an age ago now.

"You must stay close to Miriam and Mary, otherwise you will find yourself in grave danger," she had said, and he remembered also how he had deliberately set himself to remember her warning, even as he slept. He had failed.

Later she had mocked him. "How can you find the right way when you cannot control your mind, or even your donkey?" Well, he had lost Sarah and now felt less sure of any decision he had made.

Even as he thought this, he had the distinct feeling he had recently passed the same rocks that he now drew level with. He shivered slightly at the idea he might be going around in a large circle. Surely this was not possible, his mind was just playing a trick on him.

He kept doggedly to the task and direction he had set himself, but moving so slowly now that he made little progress. His doubts on the other hand were growing apace, and the small breeze that had started blowing seemed against him as well.

'Surely you must be going the wrong way.' He had topped a little rise but there was no sign of the road, only another little dip and rise ahead. 'You should turn around and retrace the way you have come, before it is too late.' The agony of indecision clutched at his heart. He had been so sure when he found the dead priest and his precious bethel.

The stone now weighed heavy in his robes, banging sometimes against his right hip. 'If the road is the other way, then you might just make it if you go back now. Otherwise, you are doomed.'

As Melody wound her way to the bottom of the dip, Johannus again slid off her back, but deliberately this time. He was completely undecided and set himself to pray for guidance. He set the bethel of the unknown God upon a shelf of rock and bowed his head. A confused mixture of thoughts strove in his brain and prayers. Yahweh, his God. Yeheshua, the master he had not yet met. Miriam the prophetess and Hecate the Goddess. Perhaps this stone was for Hecate or more likely the God of the Nabateans... his prayer went out from his heart... just for help, in his need.

"Johannus." His name rang out from seemingly angelic lips and he looked for the source, seeing again the Goddess there, above him on the higher ground ahead.

"What are you doing?" Another Goddess had joined the first and spoke again, "Johannus, Johannus, we have found you."

Groggily Johannus realised that Miriam and Mary were the Goddesses and his prayers had been indeed been answered, miraculously.

*

I was so relieved to see Johannus. We had only climbed a couple of ridges from the road but had gone slowly, being careful not to miss Johannus if he had fallen from his mount.

It was strange to see him kneeling in front of a 'God-stone', out in the wilderness. His reaction to my 'what *are* you doing?' was confusion but I went forward and embraced him as he struggled to his feet. He started to explain that he had found it on a dead priest, but Miriam brought him water to drink and he gratefully accepted it instead of talking.

A little later, after he had eaten as well as drunk his fill, he told us his story and showed us the baetyl he had brought back with him. "Is it wrong? Should I have got rid of it?"

"Not at all, Johannus." It was Miriam answering. "The stone is a symbol, that is all. It is a symbol that has been used all round the world, for the power of the God that is unseen. The time has come for us to understand what this symbol really means, and that is why the master comes; to show the real. Yeheshua will show you the meaning of the stone, the cornerstone of everything that is."

We sat under the small canopy we had erected, and let Melody and Sarah have some precious water as well. The breeze that had sprung up had blown a few clouds up from the South, bringing the scent of possible rain. "We shall return the stone to the people of Rekem. I am sure that is where it would have come from and will have certainly been missed."

CHAPTER 11.

Once again, we were all up on our mounts and almost back to the road when a large company of soldiers came riding down it, out of the mountains. Their captain reined in his horse at the sight of us and the other horsemen spread out along the way, spears at the ready.

Antonius was at the shoulder of the Nabatean officer and presumably telling him that we were the travellers that had gone missing. There was an undoubted wariness about the Nabateans though and our camels didn't like the confrontation either. My beast felt as though he wanted to hightail it back down away from the mountains.

As I struggled with him, Miriam went forward slowly to meet the officer, with Johannus just behind her. She was talking directly to the captain and gesturing towards Johannus.

Johannus, at her request, brought out the stone that he had wrapped again in the priest's sash, and the Nabateans gasped audibly when he revealed it. The tension of the situation transformed from suspicion to wonder.

I rejoined them again as Johannus was explaining how he found the priest's body and the precious stone. Then one of the men started pointing at me crying, "Al-Uzza; Al-Uzza; she brings the God. The prophecy is come true; Al-Uzza and Al-Lat have come."

Belatedly, I realised that my head had come free of the encircling robe and it appeared that the mass of my auburn locks, caught by the breeze and changing light, had caused this conclusion. His cry was taken up by another soldier or two and we soon found ourselves encircled with awe, and being escorted back, up towards the city in the mountains.

The way gradually became extremely narrow and we had to make our way up the track in single file, following the soldiers ahead, with others behind. The path zig-zagged up the side of the high ridge and it was easy to see that no army could attack this way.

We started to pass tiny plots of land, shelves cut in the mountainside where people made their habitations. Any available space was being used although the dwellings here, on the outskirts of the city were all very insubstantial.

Soon goats and chickens started to be in evidence, showing an increase of wealth as we travelled closer to the city proper. The people we saw seemed to be in a state of hightened activity, but that had nothing to do with our arrival, though later both things became as if linked.

Everyone was making hurried preparations for the coming rains. The clouds had gathered heavily above the mountains to the south and west; already the gods were striking their great blows of light and sound that were the precursors to the deluge that crept towards us.

We could see where the run-offs of the mountainside would be channelled and many women were brushing and clearing these channels, ensuring all the ways would be ready to guide the most precious gift of their god into their keeping.

We reached the top barely before the coming storm made the passage impassable; the mountaintops to the north bathed in a wonderful, pink light that streamed in from the sun in the western sky; and those to the south were blanketed in massive, dark clouds.

Where we sat atop the world on our camels we could survey all the jutting peaks, stretching north and south; and there on the edge of the storm was an extraordinary city, seemingly suspended in the wide valley within the mountains.

Fine buildings shone in the disappearing light, that I had not seen the like of since leaving Antioch; no, not even there. How could such a marvellous place be sustained in the middle of these desert mountains?

There were also a myriad of tents and other semi permanent housing that looked like a vast encamped army, and areas of ground cultivated with rivulets of vegetation. The whole effect was an amazing patchwork of living, struggling, variety.

We wound our way down the side of the heavily populated hillsides with the rain now teeming heavily down on us and starting to bounce and stream off the rocks; into the rock-cut channels prepared by the people of the city.

Amazing to see such a relationship played out magically around us; an ageless dependency between man and the Giver being celebrated, thankfully.

The captain of the guard delivered us to a fine building in the midst of the many columned ones that seemed to comprise the heart of the city. It was a temple of the Goddesses and a priestess took us into her care, whilst the rain still poured down all around and the thunder and lightening played out their might and majesty in the mountain crowns further north.

What an incredible day it had been. It was as though I was in a bubble of grace, both inside and all around. The feeling was still with me when I awoke and realised that there were things that had to be done that day. The events of our arrival had grown into something of an event within the city.

We were going to have to present the God-stone to the temple of the God Dushara, whence it had come, apparently being taken with two other stones to consecrate a site in the north. The priests and their escort had been ambushed and up till now it was thought that all three stones had been lost. The recovery of this one, the most important of the three was being heralded as a great event.

Miriam was in audience with Leila, the priestess of Isis who had come to Rekem from Heliopilis in Egypt; a working together such as we had done in Antioch. Indeed, life in the temple was very familiar to me, and somehow I felt that I was being given a precious opportunity; that now I had something much more real to contribute, since coming to Yeheshua. I had found 'the Annointed', the Messiah who had come to fulfil the promise.

Two priestesses were helping me bathe and get dressed in ceremonial robes, for they told me I was to represent the Goddess Al-Uzza in the ceremony to return the bethel. Johannus would be the bearer and he was still guarding the stone within the precinct of the temple itself.

Miriam was still with Leila when the priests of Dushara came to accompany us to their temple. They were earlier than expected and I thought we should wait for Miriam and Leila. I asked the priestesses to call for them but Leila had said that they were not to be interrupted.

For a while there was a stand-off, but we could feel the pressure mounting, not only from the waiting priests but also of a gathering crowd, arriving from all over the city.

Goodwill was of paramount importance, I knew, because relations were badly strained between the Jews and Nabateans, particularly King Aretas and Herod. What if they discovered where we had actually come from? It wouldn't take much to turn the acceptance we had seen so far into suspicion and accusations.

The temple priestesses were getting nervous as well. I realised that we needed to perform the task we had been given, sooner rather than later. Johannus was looking tired and drained so I took the lead, accepting the offer of the priests to head the procession to Du-Shara's great temple.

Cries of 'Al-Uzza, Al-Uzza' went up again from the crowd as they had the day before; the Goddess by another name; familiar yet strange as well to be her representative; the power was with me; given for me to know by Yeheshua, coursing within my breath and blood.

Johannus carried the stone, still wrapped in the dead priest's sash, walking just behind me, with priests on one side and priestesses on the other. We processed up to the huge columned temple of Dushara and there the High Priest of their God was at the front to greet us.

I had been carefully painted, made up, and with braided hair set into the style the Nabateans portrayed for their Goddess. The High Priest bowed slightly as we met and I realised how much of an impression our arrival out of the desert must have made. He was being careful in front of this strange woman who the people were hailing as their Goddess, fulfiller of the prophecy.

It was a moment of great celebration when Johannus stepped forward to give over the shrouded stone, which the High Priest unwrapped, holding up the dark rock to the cheering people.

In the moments that followed a tension of expectancy grew. More was being asked of us than just to hand the stone over, I was sure. I also felt that there was more I could give.

The crowd was very many people deep in a wide arc around the temple doors, straining to get a sight of 'Al-Uzza'. Instinctively I stepped up to a higher plinth where I could see them better, and they me.

The priests and priestesses made way, also, as if this was what they were waiting for as well.

"The God-stone that is received here again by Du-Shara's priests is a reminder of that mighty power; a symbol of God's home that we keep within our temples. We are glad to bring it back to you today, from where a faithful priest died to preserve it, out in the desert." A ripple of calls of praise went round the crowd, and the priests seemed pleased.

"And we also need to remind you that the real home is actually in our hearts. You know that. Had you forgotten it?" The words were coming as if of their own volition. "God sends help to us, to bring us home. Yeheshua is the name of the master that has come to bring this truth to us, which is the Kingdom of God revealed." I felt the drawing of interest in the silence; in the pause that followed.

"Everywhere he goes the master finds that we are tormented with many ills, doubts and obstacles to our understanding. These he patiently helps us overcome as well." The words tumbling out were of my own experience. "Evil spirits abound and torment us, as do all other manner of diseases. These he can clean away, but we ourselves need to try to open up our hearts, so that our God can take us to himself…"

I am not sure that any of the priests had been expecting this kind of speech, and I was surprised as well. From the side of the temple some people joined us, and I recognised one as being Miriam, walking tall, her head covered with her customary shawl. Once again renewed strength flowed in me and I continued. "My name is Mary, called Magdalene. Not a Goddess, but just as you are. We are the ones that can feel the presence of God within. We are His children, all of us. It is our time; in this life, our lives."

The priests were no longer looking very pleased, but I was glad to have spoken the words of my heart. Miriam had reached me and was smiling broadly, doubling my joy.

Murmurs were coming from the crowd to the right and there was something happening there; a woman who was not as others was causing a commotion, shouting as she thrust her way through the yielding crowd, towards where we were stood.

Possessed, I knew immediately; and by a spirit that was keen to challenge the threat. Priests drew back as well but were watching keenly to see what would happen.

'Poor woman,' I thought. I remembered what it had been like to crouch out of the way in some corner of my being as demons had control of my senses. Yet now I felt the strength of my wholeness, through every pore of me. This was her right as well.

The crowd had scattered from the area between us and the possessed but I went forward to meet the woman, determined to reach to where she was, despite the thing that was abusing her, using her, controlling her body.

I felt no fear, just fullness of life; as it is meant to be; and outraged that something sought to deny this woman access to hers, to the joy of her own breath.

We confronted each other at the base of a pillar, where the steps that I walked down met the paved street. 'Her' face was twisted in a way that it was never meant to be; but somewhere in there, the real person still exited, though cowed away in fear.

Despite the raised demon within her form, I reached out with my hands and soul to find her, believing I could sense the woman's own presence, faint but real; a touching of our hearts.

The thing possessing her screamed abuse and tried to claw at me, but somehow was strangely powerless to halt the simple contact we had made. We, the lady-soul and I held to each other. "Begone!" I told the possessor and again, louder. "Begone to where you belong; leave this woman alone." I felt the Word's power in me and that the demon could not hold out against it. "BEGONE."

Its hold on the woman withered, faltered and was released. She collapsed into my arms. The crowd gasped as one.

Calmness was in and around me, though I felt tired now. Miriam was at my side lifting me and the woman both, her hug bringing renewed strength.

There was nothing to add to what had been said and done. The priests were stunned and the people called out the names of Al-Uzza and Al-Lat, but also Du-Shara too.

We processed back to the temple of the Goddess, surrounded by her priestesses.

CHAPTER 12.

Johannus needed to get rest, and as soon as we got back to the Goddess temple and its surrounds, he was taken away to Leila's guest suite, which offered all the private seclusion he could have wished for.

Miriam and Leila apologised for being late for the 'handing over' ceremony but this didn't matter any more. Our concern was now for the woman who had been possessed, but whom we had brought back to the temple with us.

That we had been able to drive the spirit from her was viewed with a degree of awe by the priestesses, and Leila herself seemed to regard me with an unasked for deference. Miriam stayed close by me though, for which I was very grateful.

Normally, when the midday heat took hold of the city, its inhabitants retired from strenuous activities until the later hours; but this was the day after the great rains and the invigorating freshness meant that work continued on, to make the most of what had come. There would be more rains yet, but today was special; the first storm of the season had come.

Leila, Miriam and I retired to the inner courtyard where there was a pool adorned with lotuses and fish; a little oasis of wonder. Leila explained that the rainwater was channelled here from off the roofs of the temple and surrounding buildings. It fed a rock-cut and sealed cistern, deep and wide under the temple buildings. The pool in the courtyard was just a reminder of the miracle of water from the heavens.

There was a lot for us to discuss because so many strange things seemed interwoven with our arrival; a complex picture which we needed to untangle quickly.

Djinn-demon worshippers had been raiding villages, striking from out of the desert. It was they that had attacked the priests and stolen the bethel stones, the chief of which Johannus had miraculously recovered. Never before had they been bold enough to reach over the west side of the Shara mountains.

These evil tribes were reported as drinking the blood of their victims; the most horrendous desecration imaginable and a plague upon the kingdom.

So the King himself had taken a part of the army to pursue and destroy them after that attack. Even now he was reported on his way back to the city after a short but successful campaign.

Perhaps the worst thing was that it was rumoured that King Herod was behind the increase in power of these demon worshippers, and that he encouraged and provided for them to attack King Aretas' kingdom; so that they wouldn't attack him and his. This, coupled with the dishonouring way that Herod had treated Aretas' daughter, his erstwhile wife, made the Jews prime enemies of the kingdom at the moment.

John, the baptiser, had criticised Herod for divorcing her and marrying his own brother's wife, Herodias, instead. As a consequence, the tetrarch had had him beheaded. That John had also been an advocate for the Master Yeheshua, us being disciples of Yeheshua might go in our favour; but this was not a certainty.

On the other hand King Aretas was as fond of having beautiful women available to him as King Herod and many other powerful men. Leila feared that King Aretas would make it hard for us to leave Rekem, especially with this stuff of the return of the bethel stone, not to mention the earthly appearance of Al-Uzza.

The temple could give us sanctuary for a while, but the priests of Dushara would likely poison the king's ears, once it was discovered we were actually from Palestine.

I was sorry to have probably caused this problem but Miriam would hear nothing of it. We would declare the truth as long as we lived, but that did not mean we should stay and endanger ourselves stupidly.

A priestess came and told Leila that many people were waiting outside the temple, trying to catch a glimpse of their 'Goddesses'. Miriam said that if possible we should leave Rekem very soon, but that we would also make the most use of the time we still had here.

Leila and Miriam had already discussed Miriam's mission to Kadesh and Leila had offered her own personal aide, a man called Kardun. He came from southern Egypt, but had long served as travel guide and escort to the priest-esses of Isis and knew the desert regions as well as any man in the city. Miriam accepted the offer of help gratefully.

It was decided that we would leave early from the tomb of the King of Kings; a new and wonderful building that was being cut into the living cliff-side. It was close to the exit way and Miriam wanted to stay the night there, before leaving early in the morning.

We would go down there later on. I asked that Johannus should be allowed to sleep until the evening meal was taken, and afterwards be brought to join us at the Tomb Temple.

We actually left the temple just when the main heat of the day had passed and went as quietly through the city streets as was possible. Nevertheless a small crowd of people followed us. I thought of Yeheshua and all the people that kept after him, trying to get his attention. How hard that must be; going on all the time.

I also noticed that there were lots of others heading the way we were, mostly paying us no attention. Many had children in tow, all dressed in their best; for festivities of some sort, I presumed.

"Where is everyone going?" I asked Leila.

"To the amphitheatre; assembling to give thanks for the coming of the rains. Many of the temple priestesses are already there. Also for the news of the King's victories over the demon-worshippers, clearing all the routes around Rekem."

Then she added, quietly aside to me, "though I have heard other reports that they found very few to oppose them, and that the main body of attackers had just melted away into the eastern desert."

There was singing coming from ahead. Then the impressive façade of the amphitheatre came into view. Leila said we should join the celebration. it was a special occasion and our appearance would be greatly valued. She would keep it as low profile as possible and arrange an early exit for us.

Miriam stepped through the entrance portico slightly behind Leila, holding my arm tightly. I could feel her heart beating as we got to see the wide auditorium filled with all the city's finest.

Several priests, and others, recognised us amongst the stream of people arriving. Word travelled fast, and suddenly it became clear that we would not only have to attend but also take some part as well.

The story of the healing incident of the morning must have reached many ears. I hoped that more of the same wasn't expected. The priests leading the celebrations looked slightly put out as they indicated where we should take up our places, and Leila looked rather worried.

The singing had started up again, after a short hush, probably caused by our arrival. We could join in with these, for we understood them.

First the ancient calls for rain, ringing around the auditorium again and again; a chant of pleading and of need. On and on, and on till one by one the priests raised their arms and the chanting faded into silence; becoming a pause instead; of tense expectation.

Then the great drums started up, quietly at first but soon growing loud and demanding before fading again as cymbals, trumpets and horns took up the call. Then the drums took the lead again and the trumpets and cymbals answered; back and forth in imitation of thunder and lightning in a storm. But gradually the intensity slackened which was the signal and chance for the people to renew their singing. New songs: the rain songs; the celebration songs.

With these underway, priests and priestesses started to process around the circular stage carrying long lengths of coloured material between them. As the tempo speeded up so did the dance in the centre, rippling in a multicoloured suggestion of clouds and whirling water.

When the long chants of thanksgiving finally ended silence and stillness descended within the amphitheatre. All eyes seemed to turn on us, sitting in the places of honour. Would we respond? How would we?

It looked as though it might be up to me, because some sort of connection had been made between me and their favourite goddess, Al-Uzza.

Miriam turned to me. "Mary, I have a song I would like to sing. What do you think?"

It was like a prayer answered. "That would be wonderful Miriam." Then I thought if there was anything I could do. "Do you want me to introduce you?"

"If you could, that would be perfect."

I stood up and raised my arms. "Friends; people of Rekem," I started. "My sister, Miriam and I are honoured to be here with you at the arrival of these precious rains…" I paused, looking across at Miriam; how could I introduce her? "and we ask your indulgence if you would stay for a song that Miriam would like to sing for you. It is my privilege to have this chance to share this with you all."

Miriam had moved forward towards where the priests and priestesses were making room for her on the central stage. "This is my dearest sister Miriam," I called across the amphitheatre, as loudly as I could, and sat back onto my stone seat.

She pulled her head-cover back off from her dark hair, revealing something of her beauty before the instrument of her special talent, her voice, drew everyone's rapt attention, as it always did.

It was a song I had never heard her sing before, starting with a couple of verses in praise of the wonder of the unfailing rains that come to us and nourish us in our need.

Then she sang praises to the mighty mountains that drew the clouds about them and gathered and stored their precious cargo; to give it out slowly for us, till the next rains came.

Then her lovely voice sang out in gratitude to the boundless ocean that was the source of all the water and whence it returned as well; suggesting that this was what we were all doing as too, going home to our source just as the rains returned to the ocean.

Each verse was like a hymn in itself, sweet and achingly pleasing to all of us listening.

The final verse was of the desert flowers that waited for this water to arrive, but when it did put on such a display that brought tears of joy to the eye of Beauty herself.

There was a deep hush after she had finished, and I think we all longed for her voice to continue on. A few calls of "Al-Lat, Al-Lat" could be heard punctuating the persuasive silence. When she spoke again it was almost like a continuation of her song.

"Just as we need water to drink for our body's thirst, my friends… so we need the water of love and inspiration for our soul's thirst. Our hearts are the seeds waiting in the desert. The rain of love divine comes from heaven when we need it most, when we cannot wait any longer. Not just once. No, but again and again; age after age; the rain of love comes, for we cannot live without it."

"Even as you gather the water so skilfully off the mountains side, if you can gather the rain of love when it comes, then your true thirst will be fulfilled. Make your hearts ready, for Love is here and you are called to receive it. Listen to the call of your heart, and surely the rain will come for you as it does for the seeds waiting in the desert soil. If you do, then truly, the Lord of all will bow to bestow blessings of joy on you."

As quickly as she had reached the stage she left it, and the crowd was stunned.

I could see a priest reach his arm forward and open his mouth as if he wanted to ask her a question, or perhaps make some request, but she had already moved out of the central arena, and was making her way back to where Leila and I were.

Except Leila was no longer sitting beside me. I saw her calling several priestesses to her; she nodded towards me; I understood urgency and got up in response. Out of the corner of my eye I saw Johannus standing at the back, by the exit point. He had already seen me and was coming towards me, even as I went to meet Miriam's return.

I hugged her and a man dressed as an officer of the King's guard stepped up to us. "Would you like to come to the palace tomorrow, for the King's return? he asked. "Please come and sing for him." I suddenly realised the need for urgency.

"Tomorrow will bring what it will," she answered enigmatically. "Please excuse us for the moment."

Johannus had reached us. "Are you ready now, my lady?" He sounded just the right note and tone to make Miriam's departure easy and I was grateful to him for being so in tune with our need.

Johannus ushered us to the exit point where Leila and the other priestesses were. Leila drew us into a recess and handed us each a type of over-robe her priestesses wore. There was another priestess in darker robes. Leila called to her.

"Bishmi; go quickly with our guests. Take them to Yresmin in the great tomb. Tell her I sent you. We shall join you later. Okay?"

"Yes, Leila," said the dark-clad priestess. "Come on Mary" said Miriam, "we don't want to stay for any more pleasantries."

"Johannus, you come with us," said Leila. "As if you are still accompanying Miriam and Mary"

"Yes. Yes, if that helps. Let me escort you. Where are we going?"

"Back to our temple. Let's get going."

We left, carrying on along the road as anonymous priestesses.

I glanced back once to see the other procession going back towards the city centre. More people were leaving the amphitheatre now as well; following them.

CHAPTER 13.

Yresmin had been a priestess of the Goddess Manat for over thirty years. She had come to Rekem as a young woman, at the time of the appearance of the star of Destiny, and been quickly drawn into the service of Manat.

Very few priestesses dedicated themselves to Manat, because most were attracted to serve Al-Uzza and Al-Lat, perhaps to take on something of their glamour. Yresmin wasn't; she had wanted to pursue the clear answers that service to Manat offered; for Manat was the Goddess of Destiny and her realm encompassed old age and death as well.

Manat didn't require more than one special adherent, and Yresmin had fulfilled this role for as many years as she cared to remember.

She had been 'married' twice; the first being a temple assignment to a priest of Dushara, which had been more or less required of her as a novice priestess. He had died quite young through some unknown disease. She had mourned his passing, as much as anything for the pain he had gone through.

Her second marriage had been of her own choosing. He was the greatest architect of the city, and they came together in the designing of the 'temple tomb'. They shared a secret belief in its higher purpose, that it would be for the King whose star they both followed.

To be a palace as much as a tomb; to be a celebration for life before and after death; for eternity. The pain she suffered when her Rakkim fell from the cliff's face, in the early cutting phase, was as long-lived as his was short.

Ever since his death she had stayed in that tomb-temple and overseen the continuation of its creation. For eight years she had not gone far beyond its confines, except for certain important ceremonies and celebrations; such as the rain-coming ones.

Yet her reputation had increased, and none in the city was more respected than her. Even the King would consult with her and it was said that after such a meeting he had started styling himself the 'friend of the people'; probably on her advice.

Yresmin was a tall woman with steely grey hair that had once been jet black, and which she most often wore scraped severely back from her face in a tightly wound knot, pinned on the back of her head. This was her personal preference, though most people saw it as a signal of her mood and thought twice before approaching her. It rather amused her that no one wanted to risk unfavourable answers from her.

When she was feeling particularly open to the beneficence of the Goddess she would brush her hair out into a free-flowing style that, because it was naturally curly, became like a wide halo around her face. When she appeared thus, people loved to fete her Goddess with offerings of all kinds, and she most often responded freely with her blessings.

The day after the rains came was usually such a time, but something held her back this year. She didn't attend the celebrations in the amphitheatre and there wasn't anyone who dared to remind her. She laughed to herself, glad to be left in the quiet of her sanctuary. Even the building workers had all gone.

She spent a while brushing out her hair, thinking of the news that she had heard of the coming of Al-Uzza and Al-Lat, or rather Mary and Miriam and a priest of the un-named God.

She heard all the goings on in the city, without even leaving the temple. Bishmi, her hand-maiden, told here most things, but there were also several amongst the craftsmen who kept her informed of other sorts of things. All stone masons were fiercely loyal to her, enjoying a kind of protection that no others could boast of.

But having brushed her hair out and considered the changing events from all angles, she absentmindedly scraped it back into the familiar knot, wondering what she would say when she met them.

The drape that hung across her deep-set little alcove was shaken gently and its bells tinkled. Bishmi's face poked around one edge of it and the lamplight flickered.

"What is it, Bishmi?"

"Visitors my lady. Leila asked me to bring them to you. Their names are Mary and Miriam, as you know."

"And the priest? Is he with them?"

"No, my lady. He has gone back to the temple with Leila; to draw the crowd that way. They... we wished to come to you alone."

"Have you taken them refreshments?" Bishmi shook her head. "Then ask them what they would like, from what we can offer. I shall join them in the middle room. Please bring me some water and for yourself too. Whatever you like."

She let go the un-pinned knot of her hair and ducked under the edge of the curtain as she left her inner room, her heart skipping a little beat as she did. She felt the familiar tingling in her spine that spoke to her of Manat's influence; she relaxed. The excitement of the moment of contact never failed to inspire her and she had learnt to savour it.

Miriam and I had already entered the high inner space of the 'beauteous temple' and climbed the steep, wooden steps that rose to the raised area of the middle room. It was carpeted, and had four spiral-carved pillars, one in each corner of the square. There was a low table in the middle and cushions set all around, two of which we sat upon.

We appreciated the sumptuousness of the precious cedar wood used in the construction. The pillars at each corner were beautifully carved and smoothly elegant, with a lamp set on top of each, as yet unlit because daylight still streamed through the huge doorway.

But it was the marvellous ceiling space that drew our eyes with wonder.

There, still being constructed out of silver rods, gilded with gold, and filled in with finest Roman glass, was a marvellous pyramid canopy.

The mauve-purple glass was of rare quality, looking like facets of a jewel, each in a golden setting. It would be a fitting place for a deity, bringing together as it did the ancient knowledge of Egypt with the newest and richest technology of the Roman Empire.

Yresmin climbed the steps, eager to join her guests in the meeting room. We rose from our cushions as she entered and she waved us back again. How natural and gracious she was, I thought.

Bishmi came in through a side drape carrying a tray of two jugs and several glasses. She poured some drinks into the glasses and handed them around. Yresmin took a sip of her water and looked at her women guests. She certainly noted Miriam's beauty and smiled at me, perhaps conscious of her own advancing years and the way she had let her own hair loose. She ran an elegant hand through it as if to try and re-exert some element of control.

None of that mattered though. She stepped forward and spoke. "Welcome; welcome to the temple of the beloved. My name is Yresmin. I serve the Goddess Manat."

Miriam answered. "This is indeed a most wonderful temple, that neither Mary here nor myself have ever seen the like of. My name is Miriam and we are come here on the request of our beloved master Yeheshua."

"I have heard that you have both made quite a stir here, already. How were the celebrations for the rain-coming? Bishmi tells me you have just come thence, on Leila's suggestion."

I answered this time. "It was very fine. Afterwards Miriam sang a truly lovely song and spoke to the people about the coming of peace; and the Kingdom."

The tingling that had started up Yresmin's spine was also in her ears. She let the Goddess speak through her without further preamble.

"Where you seek is within where we call the 'Cauldron of Manat'. Also known in Egypt as the 'Breath of Maat'. It is 'The Wilderness of Zin'; wherein lies the place that the tribes of Israel call Kadesh Barnea, for it sustained them in their need."

Miriam had stood up and crossed towards Yresmin. Answers had come without her even voicing the question. She stopped a couple of paces from her with hands clasped in front of her. "Can you help us reach there, lady Yresmin?" she asked.

"Yes, it is not far. Bishmi will go with you; even with her husband, Kardun."

Miriam moved forward and took the priestess' hands in hers. "Thank you," she said.

Yresmin faltered, slumping forward into Miriam's outstretched arms. Bishmi also leapt up to help catch her seemingly fainting mistress.

But Yresmin recovered herself almost immediately, feeling the strength coming through from the steady arms of her guest. She allowed herself to be sat upon a cushion and Bishmi gave her some more water. Relaxation engulfed her in the aftermath of delivering her message.

"Bishmi dear. Is there some food you could bring us, as well?" she asked her younger priestess and friend. "I haven't eaten all day, and I am sure our guests would like something too."

"Of course, my lady," said Bishmi, and she glided swiftly out of the room.

"Well what do you think of this dwelling place? Would it suit your master Yeheshua do you think?" asked Yresmin.

"He would love the way the wood has been used. He worked with his father as a carpenter, and understands it well," Miriam answered.

Yresmin was surprised and asked to know more of this teacher, which Miriam and I gladly told her. Not just of the miracles and the healing work he did, but also of the teaching of the Kingdom; how all human beings could reclaim their divine inheritance.

She listened carefully to all they said, not as the high priestess of Manat but as a seeker after Destiny. He had come, she knew. Again, she knew the tingling in her torso but this time it was more of a glow around her heart. She breathed her first question again; quieter this time, rephrased. "Do you think he might come here?"

"He might," answered Miriam, "but there is no guarantee. He is very involved in the work he has set his heart upon in Palestine."

"Then I must go to him," said Yresmin with finality.

CHAPTER 14.

Johannus walked through the streets of Rekem, marvelling at the buildings, many cut directly into the rose-coloured rock. Leila was by his side and Kardun had gone to organise the camels, the horse, donkey and supplies for continuing the journey.

The sun had dropped over the mountains but there was still a wonderful light illuminating everything, and he revelled in it. The fame of the returned bethel stone followed him in the form of curious townspeople and he wondered how Leila planned to get him unseen to the place where Miriam and I were.

She took him on a bit of a tour, showing him many of the splendid, impressive sights that abounded at the turn of every corner; which had to include the nearly completed façade of the temple-tomb of the King of Kings, of course.

In front of the massive temple doorway and pillars, a garden had been created, that even allowed for a trickling stream. Johannus stood awestruck before the temple, and it was several minutes before Leila could drag him away from the little oasis there.

As they set off to wind their way to Dushara's temple Leila whispered in his ear. "Remember the way back here; this is where you must come in a few minutes time."

Returning alone, robed inconspicuously as one of Dushara's priests, Johannus slipped through the half-light back to the cool of the garden in front of the magnificent temple. 'Wonderful' he thought, and remembering his instructions he approached the huge entrance, knocking three times at the leftmost of three temporary doors stretched across the high gap.

He waited, and was about to knock again when Bishmi opened the door and ushered Johannus inside, bolting it after them. The marvel that greeted him within was every bit as fascinating as the greatness of that outside.

A living pyramid appeared to be opening open up before him; the lower steps of which climbed up to veils strung between two pillars. Bishmi told him to wait at the base of the polished wooden steps whilst she finished lighting the lamps.

Carrying a lit taper she went to the left-side of the pyramid base where steeper steps were cleverly constructed to rise gracefully like a trailing vine up beside one of the grooved pillars. Nimbly, despite her slight rotundness, she set off up the carved ladder and stopped about half way up. There she placed a loop of the cord she was wearing around her waist over a little wooden knob and then continued on up. At the very top she lit the lamp there, its light joining the radiance of the three she had already lit upon the other pillars.

Light that sparkled off the top half of a crystal pyramid that Johannus saw as if magically raised, glowing as a purple roof over a veiled cubic space.

"Come," said Bishmi, who had clambered down again, taking his arm to lead him up the steps and through the veils.

Miriam and I turned to greet Johannus as Yresmin got to her feet as well. "This is Yresmin, the High priestess of the goddess Manat," said Bishmi, "and my lady, this is Johannus who found the bethel stone that was taken."

Yresmin looked at the slightly awkward man that had entered the room. Young seeming but neither quite a warrior nor yet a priest. She smiled at him to put him at his ease and noticed the pommel of his sword sticking through the front of the borrowed priest's tunic.

"Can you show me your sword please?"

He started guiltily; "I am sorry, I shouldn't have brought it in here. I didn't think." He took the sword out of its sheath and offered her the handle.

She took it from him. "It is all right," she said and held it up to the light.

The pommel shone like a dark jewel held upon a spiral of silver, and the letter 'shin', on the down-turned blade, glowed golden in the light, as well. "You have a well-wrought sword," she said. "It will serve your purpose truly. And this is a fine stone pommel; a bit special."

"I found it, half buried by a roadside; when I was travelling from Tyre to Bethany." He remembered when it had been and blushed slightly.

"Was that after you took me to Rachel?" I asked.

"Yes. Yes it was. Beor helped me make the sword and handle. We put it together and I had the silver wire from working as a silversmith, and some gold from a ring to emboss the letter with. It might be a bit fanciful, but I am glad to have it, just in case..." He remembered his helplessness when I had been abominated and said no more.

Yresmin looked over to me; I had already told her half the story and I nodded. "What do you think of our temple-tomb?" She asked Johannus.

"Incredible," he replied, looking up again to the pyramid top. Seen from the inside, with the lamps, standing lit outside the four corners, the quality of the workmanship, glass and colours shining through were even more striking.

"It is fantastic," he said again. "To what design is it constructed? I have never seen the like before."

"Everything we know has been made with all the love we have to give. The knowledge comes from everywhere, but Egypt in particular. We might say that this is the temple of Isis for her Lord Osiris. The God who rules the dead, but also the God who returns, and whose star is Destiny."

Miriam rose and crossed to Yresmin, and touched her on the arm. "A wonderful job has been done. It will be a monument to beauty and love for ages to come. Maybe never to be surpassed."

"It is designed to be a place for the King of Kings to stay when here in Rekem, and for his body to be placed after he dies. Under where the table is, there is a space where a stone sarcophagus can be brought. Then the crystal crown can be lowered to make the pyramid, and a place of pilgrimage, complete."

"A wonderful idea Yresmin," said Miriam; "but still just that, something based on ideas. He tends to work to another plan."

"Yes," said Yresmin. "I know you are right, but there was nothing else to go by, and it has brought us to today, so I am glad and thankful; that I still have the chance to go to where he could actually be. Bishmi, when you return with Kardun, you shall be Manat's priestess. Unless you wish to travel on to Palestine as well?"

"My lady, my greatest wish would be to complete this temple here that you have spent so long working on. Please grant me this, and I will be Manat's priestess too. Nothing else."

"I shall come here again, Bishmi," said Miriam, "and I think your mistress will return as well."

Everyone turned to listen to her; it was something in here voice. "The next time I come this way I shall be travelling on to Sheba and beyond."

"Are you sure?" I said. "Will that be soon?"

Miriam shrugged slightly and continued. "That is where it must be thought we are going now, and it can rightly said we have been discussing this." She paused, looking to Yresmin, who nodded.

The pause continued and when she spoke again, she looked unsteady on her feet, "I feel the ground shaking here," she said, and her face had turned quite white, drained of blood; "…and so it will come to be." Another long pause followed and Mary was getting up to go to her friend when Miriam continued. "Yet there will come another in this land, a greatest one who will truly shake the whole world." Her palour had receded and Yresmin had got to her feet as well, "to wake the people up, even up to the end of the age." it was Yresmin's turn to steady her as she half stumbled sideways.

The older woman put out an arm around the shoulders of her visitor and guided her back to her cushions. There was a stunned silence.

A tingling shiver ran through Johannus, and he found himself asking: "Are you saying that the master Yeheshua will come here soon?"

After a few seconds Miriam responded. "Our Lord Yeheshua is bringing in a new Age and in this age masters will come again and again to help the people along the way, in many lands. This will not be an easy age, but one which will bring the highest prize within the grasp of all mankind."

Miriam was tired. There was still much to discuss; so Yresmin and I got Miriam to rest until Leila arrived.

Bishmi sat and talked to Johannus, asking questions about the journey they had made so far, explaining that Yresmin wanted her to go with them to Kadesh because she had been to the bowl of Manat before.

When Leila and Kardun did get there, Yresmin went over what had happened, repeating the prophecies that Miriam had made. Leila hugged her old friend, hearing that she was going to leave her temple sanctuary, to travel on her special pilgrimage.

"I shall not leave till Bishmi and Kardun get back, for I know they will."

Kardun was initially surprised and then rather pleased that his wife, Bishmi, would be joining them on the journey into the wilderness; and proud that she was the appointed High Priestess of Manat. He had more reason than ever to make the task they faced successful.

Leila laughed at the predicament they were in. "The King has indeed returned, and is encamped with his army outside the Siq; the narrow way that leads up to the temple here. Goodness knows how we shall get you past his guards."

"We cannot risk being held up with demands to attend upon the King; however well meaning they may be," I said, knowing that Miriam felt the same.

"Then we must move out very early, before he gets to hear about the return of the bethel stone and those who brought it. After all this is what made him set out after the assailants in the first place. He will want to know…" added Kardun.

"He won't like it that you have gone before he could meet with you either," said Leila. "I suspect he will send out a party of soldiers to bring you back."

"Miriam has told us she will be travelling to Sheba," I said, "and that there are special places on the way she wishes to visit as well, that are sacred to the goddess Al-Lat."

Leila started to ask more and then stopped, taking note of my intense expression. She nodded and said nothing.

Kardun said he would need another camel for his wife and left the temple without delay. Suddenly it became clear that the time was upon them. Whatever preparations they needed to make they would have to do now before grabbing a very few hours sleep, and Bishmi bustled around, finding blankets and whatever her guests needed for the night, and to pack her things for the journey ahead.

Johannus felt the excitement of the impending flight, wondering what part he would be able to play. Certainly, his sword had no use against an army and he chuckled to himself at the ridiculousness of the thought.

'How could they get past the guards?' The question circulated again and again, before he slipped into a restless unconsciousness in which lifelike dreams had him wrestling to remember the way out of a maze of temple tunnels; a problem that he continued to struggle with even when he woke up.

Finally realising that the maze was not real Johannus heaved himself off the pallet he had been tossing and turning on. Finding he was apparently up before anyone else he continued to get himself dressed and ready to go.

Bishmi had put his bed into one small alcove that fed off from the main room of the temple. Miriam and Mary were in the main area where they had all spent the previous evening. His eyes and ears strained in the pitch blackness, neither able to see nor hear anything.

Just as he was feeling his way back into his alcove, a glimmer of light from the far side of the middle room made him realise that another person was up and about. It must be Bishmi. He waited on the lower pyramid steps and the light rose, entering the veiled room above him.

Bishmi woke Miriam and Mary before coming out of the room on Johannus' side. He whispered her name so that she wouldn't get a shock when she found him there. Quite soon they were all bustling about, getting ready for the off.

Kardun arrived and knocked on the same door as Johannus had, in a pattern that told Bishmi who was there. She opened the door just as Yresmin also came out of her alcove, fully dressed and there to wish them a safe journey.

Kardun had the camels, horses and donkey outside, ready to go except for the loading on of their luggage, which didn't take long. The star strewn sky was still dark as they set off, and Yresmin hugged each of them in turn. Johannus felt her caring concern when she clasped his arms. "Hope to see you in Palestine soon, then," he said, and she nodded with a tight smile.

Bishmi was also riding a horse and she took the lead as they entered the narrow passage through the cliffs that led from the temple place. Johannus followed next on his mare, the donkey's lead rope tied to his saddle and the three camels came behind with Kardun taking the rear. They expected to meet the King's guards and Bishmi was happy to do the explaining. Her position in the temple gave her a fair amount of authority.

By the time they had wound their way along the incredible passageway through the cliffs that led out from the city into the eastern desert a light had started to grow up the stripe of sky ahead. From time to time they had passed a silent sentinel by the side of the way, which made Johannus tense with fright until he came to see that they were carved into the rock.

As the way broadened out, they passed real living city guards, facing out into the desert, who hailed Bishmi, recognising the priestess as she nodded to them, letting her and her group past.

The tents they saw, probably backed by caves into the cliffs, spoke of a strong enough force for most defensive purposes, and all of the travellers were grateful that leaving the city had been so easy.

But some distance beyond, on the outskirts of the desert, part of the King's army lay encamped, and the party was soon stopped by soldiers on the roadside.

Bishmi rode towards the burly and helmeted officer who had stepped into their path. His beard was curly and impressive, as was the sharp-pointed spear he hefted. "Armedeus," she called to him. "How did the King's campaign go?"

"Very well priestess Bishmi," he replied. "The King has left much of our numbers in the north, strengthening the garrisons along the desert wall; and he will be leading a procession into Rekem today."

It was reassuring to those listening that Bishmi knew the man, but he showed no sign of moving aside, though he had lowered the heavy spear, cradling it diagonally across his body.

"Where are you going, mistress, and who are the members of your group?"

"We are priestesses who travel to the sacred sites, upon the command of the Goddess Manat; with two guides who long have served the Goddess as well." She paused a second then gestured back to the others, "Kardun, my husband, come forward and meet Armadeus, captain of the king's guard."

Kardun brought his camel forward and forced her down onto her knees beside Bishmi. Armedeus nodded in recognition then spoke again.

"We shall need to inform the King of your passing. He has commanded that all transits be reported to him. He will be awake within the hour and so the delay will not be long. Will you join me for some refreshments?"

Just when the invitation seemed impossible to avoid Miriam urged her camel forward to the other side of Bishmi. She stayed high but pulled down her travel scarf as she spoke to Armedeus.

"Sir, I am Miriam, of Al-Lat; and this is Mary, of Al-Uzza," she said, indicating me. "We would like you to convey our regrets to your King that we shall miss his procession, but the Goddess bids us make all haste. The boat will sail for Sheba at noon today."

He looked up at her and seemed slightly dismayed. Her voice carried complete certainty and her beauty was disarming.

"Bishmi," she continued, "you and Kardun should accept the officer's offer of refreshments, but the rest of us must remain mounted and ready to go, lest we bring the Goddesses' displeasure on us."

Suddenly it was Armedeus' turn to seek for an honourable way forward. His face still displayed doubt, which he cast about to lay somewhere. He called to one of his soldiers to bring some tea from the tent beside the way, looking around at the travellers in front of him. "And this man," he said; "who is he?"

Johannus pulled on the donkey's rope as he kicked his horse forward. He dismounted, standing squarely before Armedeus. "I am Johannus, sir," he declared, "and am here to serve these priestesses with my life."

The captain of the guard was a huge man who looked Johannus up and down, taking him in, noting the pommel of his sword at the gap of his cloak, approving the determined, but not unduly arrogant, set of his eyes. He nodded briefly.

"All right," he said, returning his gaze to Miriam. "You may travel on, and I hope the King is not angry with me. I shall report your passing and give your regrets to him as you have asked. God speed and a fair wind." He turned to the soldier who had brought out a tray with drinks on it, took it from him and offered the drinks up to each of the travellers himself. They were free to go.

With half held breath they set off again, skirting the wide encampment of hundreds of pointed tents, grouped around three large pavilions in their midst. They passed other guards beside the road, but only the last outpost of these stopped them. Bishmi answered their captain's questions and they were allowed to proceed once more.

With huge relief they quickened their pace until it was as fast as the donkey could go, carrying them on along the cinder strewn road till the only sign of the tents was a distant spark of light, reflected by some shield or spear from the newly risen sun.

*

A hawk hovered over scrub ahead, wheeling away as we got close; free as the desert breeze. Our road swung round to the right heading south and then we took a lesser way, towards the south west. We pressed on, enjoying the glory of the new day. This was the best time to be travelling and we made the most of it.

We stopped once and decided to redistribute some baggage from the donkey, so we could go even faster if the need arose. We hadn't discounted the possibility of King Aretas wanting to call us back, and we were going to do our utmost to avoid any confrontation of this nature.

So much had changed since Johannus found the bethel stone and someone had seemed to recognise us from the lines of prophecy; an upsurge of activity around everything that we were doing. A growing wave that it was easy to become swept along by.

Only Miriam seemed truly able to retain her calm focus, never wavering from what she had been given to do. For my part, after all the hiatus in Rekem I was now just trying to stay in a bubble of quiet, and to support my friends as I could.

After some miles along our road, passing only the occasional goatherd tending their widely spread flock on sparse grazing, we came upon a small settlement where we left the main road, once more filing up the into weather-worn hills on a narrow track.

Struggling our way up to a gap in the ridge we then wound down and down towards a wide flat plain that bore beautiful witness to the recent rains.

214

A wonderland of flowers greeted our descent.

"You can see why it is called the 'Breath of Ma'at' when you see it decked out like this," said Miriam as we loped gently along, side by side.

"Why the 'Cauldron of Manat' though?" I asked her.

"Here the rivers don't run out to the Ocean, though the port of Aila is not many miles to the south of here," said Miriam. "Instead, they run north, down to the salt sea of Palestine and Judea, sunk like some great long bowl in mother earth; where Destiny is stirred up, again and again. That is why."

Bishmi slowed as we reached the floor of the basin and came back to consult with us. "Are we turning back north here?" she asked.

Kardun had joined us as well. "What is the chance of them following us here Kardun?" asked Miriam; "if the King did order a pursuit."

"The people at the settlement back there would confirm our passage. There was no point in trying to conceal it. They would come this way."

"Well, we could be still going to Aila or back north to the wilderness. We must try to make them believe we have turned south again."

We made some false tracks in the wadi, tracking up along a wide area of pebbles, crossing and re-crossing rivulets of water, heading to the south; then we re-traced our way down the watercourse again. Further down the valley we found a platform of hard rock to leave the stream by and Miriam urged us to follow her as quickly as possible across to the other side of the plain.

There was an urgency in that rush that we didn't ask about, but followed her at a gallop with the wind of our flight streaming through our garments.

Eventually Miriam drew up in the shelter of a large mound of rocks, at the beginnings of a narrow valley that stretched up into the hills on the other side of the great wadi.

Johannus and Sarah came up last and we laughed to see them, mostly from the exhilaration we were feeling, but partly because of the scant control of the two animals Johannus had been able to exert, hanging on as they had chased after us.

"We shall climb this track till we can watch the plain, but leave quickly and invisibly if we need," said Miriam, and so we did, just as soon as Sarah had drunk her fill of what was offered her.

We found a ledge that served our need and lay there looking out over the plain.

"Why do you think the King would send soldiers to chase after us? Would he really bother?" I asked; it was a thought that kept recurring to me.

It was Bishmi who answered. "You have created a myth in Rekem; in just a couple of days. You came as Goddesses, with the God-stone, fulfilling a prophecy, and then confronted a demon and stirred up the people with your words and songs."

I hadn't seen it like that, being caught up in the events themselves. "But worst for the King," continued Bishmi, "was that he wasn't there and had no part to play in it. He will want to remedy that; and the priests, they aren't at all happy, either. You have rocked their ship and they will be stirring the king's mind with the need to cut the myth down to size. You come from Palestine; Herod's land; that won't sit well with the King either."

I glanced across at Miriam, but she didn't seem to have been listening, concentrated as she was on gazing out from our vantage point.

"There," she said suddenly, shaking my arm; I had started to yawn. "Dust spreading from the other side. Horsemen." We strained our eyes and Kardun soon confirmed her sighting. "Yes, twenty or so men on horses; they are nearly at the river. We shall soon see if we have succeeded to mislead them."

Even I could see them now and how a few followed our tracks in the wadi but others started circling out and around in wider and wider circles, searching for signs. They would find our tracks for sure. We didn't wait; we quickly got off our ledge and set off again, trying not to be panicky.

CHAPTER 16.

We made good progress over the tough terrain, trying not to think of our pursuers.

After what seemed like an age, we reached a road that ran up from the south. Left or right, which way should we go? Miriam would decide.

"Do you know this road, Kardun?" she asked.

"Yes, I know it well. Left would take us to Aila; going right would take us to Kuntillah, the north of the country, and towards Gaza; or Beersheba."

"Yes, but is there a place you know where we can get across it, unnoticed?"

Kardun stopped, thinking hard. He smiled as he realised that Miriam had a different plan. "Here is a good a spot as any. We could make our way down to the road to Egypt. There is a good chance they won't pick up our tracks if we are careful and I clean the area; with your help, Johannus."

So, we crossed the well-used road and waited whilst Kardun and Johannus spent precious minutes brushing away the evidence of our movements.

Grateful to be away from the main thoroughfare, we followed instead a goatherd path amongst the bare hills, never entirely certain that we were safely away, even then.

The day was wearing on when Miriam called us to stop. "We shall turn right up this valley, get over that ridge and find a good place to rest."

The little dip we found was ideal for our camp and the small fire we made to cook our meagre meal; flat breads with additions that Kardun had packed from Leila's kitchen.

Johannus went back to the ridge top to keep a lookout, in case our pursuers had succeeded in following us. There was no sign of anyone and we called him down to eat as soon as Kardun was free to relieve him.

As the sun started to dip over the western horison we thought we should be putting up our tents but Miriam said 'no' we should just rest for a little while longer, because we would be travelling through this night.

The growing moon was high in the sky as we un-tethered our mounts and readied ourselves again to continue on. Kardun had questioned Miriam as to where we were headed and she told him that we would re-cross the Kuntillah road again, to shake the soldiers off our trail for good.

Stars began to show overhead, the sky deepening through purple into a sparkling darkness and the moon lit the rocky ground that we picked our way across.

The going was slow but we were not in a hurry. We had circled round to rejoin the Kuntillah road some way northwest of where we had first crossed it. Kardun and Johannus crept down to check it out on foot, whilst we waited with the animals, out of sight.

It seemed hours before they returned, sustained though we had been by watching the beauty of the starry heavens. We had already dismounted and now we led the animals down to the road. Apparently, there had been a lot of recent horse traffic up and down, which seemed to indicate they had searched the road thoroughly.

Johannus and Kardun had checked some distance both ways along it, but had not found their camp or any sign of them close by. So, we carefully re-crossed the road and took our time to erase our traces. Kardun was a stickler for details and he got Johannus to ride his mare up and down the road to ensure it looked just as it had before we were there.

Tired, but glad for having made the effort to do a thorough job of our escape, we carried on, finally stopping and making camp again before the moon dipped completely over the horizon.

We slept till the light of day was fully developed and we could feel the warmth of the sun from inside our tent. Kardun was already up and had checked the vicinity of our camp, even re-tracing much of our late-night journey from the road. He reported that any pursuit was now very unlikely.

Nevertheless, we struck camp and set off once again into the wilderness, heading in a generally northerly direction. Miriam herself took the lead and I thought I could sense a change in her mood; a lightness as though this is where she had been wanting to reach for many weeks.

She led us in a meandering route that didn't appear to make any particular sense. By midday it was very hard to tell which way we were travelling and when we stopped to rest and refresh ourselves it was a puzzled Kardun that asked her about this. I had noticed how hard he had been trying to adjust to every change of direction.

"I do not know the paths of this part of the wilderness well, Lady Miriam," he said. "Nor do I know where the watering places are here. I think I can still find the best way back to Rekem but I cannot guide your way if you wish to stay in these hills."

"Kardun, you have done your service well. You have got us to where my lord has sent me. All I ask of you is to stay and enjoy our few days in the wilderness. Be at ease and have no concern for where we are. It will be my task to locate the water sources."

I don't know what Kardun made of her reply because I sensed that he was still trying to work out what direction we were going all afternoon; and it seemed to me that Miriam took us all over the place, wherever her whim took her.

As we sat around our evening campfire Miriam took the issue up with him again. "Kardun, my friend, I am going to ask you to do something for me tomorrow. It will need your trust, that is all. Will you do it?" He paused.

"What is it," he asked.

"Nothing hard at all. In fact, the reverse; it will be easy, but just require you to trust me. Will you do that?" Again, there was a long pause; we could sense he was worried.

"If you want me to, I'll try," he said at last.

"Good, good, thank you. It will really help make this expedition a success. No need to dwell on it now; let's get some sleep. Tomorrow I am sure we will succeed."

After our usual breakfast, when nothing further was mentioned, we started packing up the animals. Miriam turned to Kardun when he had got his camel ready and presented him with a black scarf, which, after explaining her intentions, she tied, firmly around his head, binding his eyes.

"Can you see anything?" she asked. "No," he answered.

"All you have to do is keep it on, and allow us to lead you, blindfolded, through the day. Can you ride blindfolded, as long as we keep the going easy?"

"I think so. I am willing to try anyway; if this is what you want?"

"OK, let's go then," and we all swung onto our mounts and got them up and ready to move off.

We rode out of our sheltered camping area onto a plateau amidst the surrounding hills, and set off across it. On this flat ground we were able to ride abreast and Miriam took her camel alongside Kardun's, talking to him as we went.

She was telling him of the flight of the Israelites from Egypt and we all got our mounts as close to them as possible so we could hear as well.

"Sometimes it is when you fail that you learn the most important things," she was telling him. "So it was for Miriam, Moses' sister." We waited, wondering what she was going to tell us about her namesake.

"She was a great prophetess, given many things to see and know. Then she made a huge mistake when she thought to make judgement on her brother. As a result, she found herself confronted with the reality of her own purity, more dreadfully than you can imagine. Confronted with being completely leprous."

She let the idea sink into us, what it must have been like. "Facing up to that was a watershed for Miriam. Her purity itself was a gift from on High, and in finally coming to understand this it was given back to her again. This time she really knew… accepted and loved this gift… this being given; and the Giver most of all."

We all knew the story of Miriam of course, but it had never been brought to life so vividly before, at least for me. Kardun coughed under his blindfold; "have I made a bad mistake?" he asked.

Miriam's response showed delight and concern together. "No of course not, Kardun. How are you managing in there? At least you haven't fallen off yet," and she giggled mischievously.

"You are making fun of me now," he said, still unseeing.

We stopped in a valley, off the edge of the flat plain and Miriam gently removed the scarf. It was a different wadi, yet similar to many of the other places we had been in. We made tea and drank it with some of the bread we had left over from breakfast.

"Where are we?" asked Kardun. "Have we got where you wanted yet?"

"Not yet, I am afraid, and we need to get on as soon as possible; but rest a little while first."

We travelled on, faster than we had in the early day. The sky had got cloudy and none of us had any idea which direction we were going. Least of all Kardun, who had accepted the blindfold scarf again.

When the way got harder, we travelled in single file, with Miriam leading Kardun's camel and mine following his. Then it started to rain; not hard but enough to cool us down and prompt us to stop again. Miriam took off Kardun's blindfold. We sheltered under the lip of an overhanging cliff, enjoying the feel and smell of the air filled with raindrops.

Kardun said nothing but reached his arms out into the rain like the receiving of a blessing. "It is good here," said Miriam, let's find the best campsite we can." We carried on up the valley, leading our mounts, and came to a natural bowl in the surrounding hills and stratified cliffs. At the base of one of these, several caves attracted our attention. We stopped and unpacked our gear as the sun broke out once again from behind the clearing clouds.

"Here we are then. How does it feel, Kardun?"

"It is a lovely spot. There is enough grazing for the animals. I reckon this is as good a place as any to be." She waited for him to go on. "That is it; I feel like we have got there. Wherever we are, I don't care anymore."

Miriam smiled broadly. "OK, we are here; this is where I wanted us to find. Let's set up camp and explore the caves."

CHAPTER 17.

Bishmi and Kardun selected which one they would stay in for its broad dry shelving interior and wide view across the valley. Little signs told them that it had been lived in before, a long time ago.

Miriam chose a cave that went deep into the cliff and gave plenty of space for both of us, though it had a narrow entrance that afforded it less light than Bishmi's.

Johannus preferred to set up his tent on a shelf between the caves and where the animals were tethered. There he kept the cooking fires ready to spring to life.

Kardun went looking for water but could not find any. He was sure there would be a supply close by, because of the caves having once been tenanted. He searched around the next morning as well and decided to wait till after the midday meal before asking Miriam's advice.

She had spent the morning in seclusion; precious hours to herself after the days of intense activity. She appeared on the slope outside the caves when the sun was high above the southern hills.

Johannus had some tea brewed and was working on cooking the lunch. Kardun had produced a couple of quail and Bishmi had helped prepare them. Johannua decided to spit cook them and they were almost done.

Miriam accepted the tea he offered and sat beside him looking at the fire. "I will just have some bread, if it is ready baked," she said. "I won't be eating any meat for the next few days."

Kardun came up and sat down with them. He was easy mannered with Miriam and Johannus felt awkward by comparison. She sat there, her beauty framed by her long dark, wavy hair, her slight build belying her inner strength, which they all had felt the mettle of.

I had been washing out some underclothes when Bishmi told me how little water we had left. I looked over towards Kardun, sat by the fire, and asked Bishmi whether he might have found a source today, because I knew he had been out looking. She shook her head. I was about to say something more when I remembered what Miriam had said about it being her responsibility to find it.

I finished putting out the cloth to dry on sun-baked rocks before walking over to the fire and sitting down in the ring. Bishmi followed as well. Miriam was talking to Johannus and Kardun about how wonderful it had been to spend time with Yeheshua, doing the simple things like cooking and cleaning and yet finding oneself bathing in his love in the process.

She paused for a while after our arrival and I glanced over to Kardun, wondering if he had already broached the subject of our shortage of water. I decided that whether or not he had, I had better ask the question, after what she had said the day before.

"Miriam, Bishmi tells me that we have little water and that Kardun has had no success yet in finding any. Do you think you would be able to help?"

Miriam looked at me, her dark eyes revealing nothing, and then at Kardun and Bishmi too. "Yes," she said. "I think I can. Let us eat our food now and then Kardun should take Sarah with the waterbags over behind that hill."

Kardun started to reply what we all could tell was going to be that he had already searched behind that hill, when he cut himself short. Miriam smiled at his effort. "You will be successful this time," she said.

Without further questions Kardun finished eating his portion of the quail and then collected up the waterbags, loading them onto our faithful donkey. I decided that I should go and help him.

We went out along the path leading to the wide rocky hillside that afforded little hope of a secret supply of water and Kardun dutifully made another search, hoping that he had missed some secret opening.

I couldn't summon the energy to help him much. There were hardly even rocks enough to provide any shade, let alone a water supply. At last, I found a passable spot and sat there watching Kardun. After a little while he joined me.

"It will be here if she says so," he declared and I marvelled at his faithfulness.

"You trust her completely, I can see that," and I paused thinking about it. "Certainly, she has led us well, but she could easily be mistaken about this. It would be quite understandable."

He looked at me, his dark face impassive, unreadable, his eyes glinting. "I remember her in Egypt," he said to my surprise. "She came to Heliopolis with her father; when she was quite young."

It took quite some questioning for me to find out much more but I gathered her father had been a far travelled trader, dealing mainly in spices, and had been a much respected, personal friend of the High Priest at the great temple. Miriam used to stay at the temple of Isis and Kardun had, even then, had the feeling that she was special; everyone seemed to have thought so.

Down below where we sat Sarah was taking interest in some scraggy thorn bushes and I idly speculated as to whether they could magically produce some water for us. Her bell tinkled and I wondered why Kardun had tied it on her?

*

Miriam stayed by the fire ring, talking with Johannus and Bishmi. Johannus was happy and grateful that Miriam seemed unaware of his awkwardness, or that in her kindness she could see beyond it.

"I know you had a bad time in Antioch, with that Simon Magus," she was asking him, "but how did you manage to find Mary when she had been possessed?"

Johannus found himself telling her and Bishmi much of his story and surprised himself at how extraordinary it had been. The emotion was high in him and as he drew to an end Miriam put a hand on his arm.

"Johannus," she said, "there is something that you could do, that would benefit you, I think. Would you like to try?"

"Yes," he answered. "If you think I can."

"It is a simple breathing exercise," she said, "but powerful." He turned towards her to give her his full attention.

"When you breathe in draw the air deep into your belly; push out your tummy to do this, rather than filling up your chest. And again, as you breathe out, push down into your tummy. Can you do that? Look, put your hand on your belly and feel it expand as you breathe in. Yes?"

Johannus did as Miriam was recommending, soon finding it quite easy. "I think I was told this exercise before, but I have never practiced it much."

"You could think of it like pushing your sword into its scabbard," said Miriam. "You wouldn't leave your sword only half sheathed into the scabbard, waggling around in a dangerous way. Your breath is such a sword that can cut through any obstacle, and it needs attending to as well."

Johannus sat there thinking about it as his breath resounded within him, upholding him, with or without his help. Bishmi was watching him and he smiled at her. She had a plain face, not quite pretty, but she displayed a sensitivity that made him know he could trust her.

Miriam was still talking to him though. "Use this exercise as a rope to pull you to the feet of the master. That is where we get the true help that we need."

She turned to Bishmi and gave the priestess something that looked like two short rods, about the size as would fit in a closed hand, and far heavier than wood. "This is the rod or rods of Ma'at…" Miriam told her, "and I would like you to have them. They were given to me in the temple of Heliopolis and I was told that I would know who should use them".

Bishmi said that she couldn't accept them, that it was a gift far too great for her. "They are for you," Miriam repeated, "it is you that can use them. You shall not only be a great priestess but a healer too. We need that."

For a few minutes Johannus and Bishmi sat with Miriam, not needing anything but to soak up the feeling of the day; minutes in which Kardun and Mary plodded up the valley, with Sarah carrying freshly filled water bags.

They were laughing as they came up to the fireside; happy that they had accomplished their task.

"Kardun never doubted your word, Miriam, but I must confess I had not seen a less hopeful place to find water."

"You found it though?"

"Sarah found it; or rather she found goats and their goatherd took us to the place. It is further than the other side of the hill, but now we know where to go…"

The water was unloaded and stored in a cave, out of the sun, before they returned to the fire.

"Kardun was telling me that he saw you in Heliopolis, when you were young."

"Yes, I used to go there with my father." She paused and no-one said anything and the silence took our thoughts to the gates of a great temple. "That is where I met Yeheshua," she said. This time I knew she was ready to tell us more of her story.

"I had often stayed at Isis' temple before. My father was expected soon on a boat from India. Then I was called to the great temple, to see the High Priest. I was worried that there had been bad news about my father, but I was wrong. He wanted to ask for my help."

"There was a Hebrew Sage visiting the temple; they wanted me to sing the songs of Israel to him; in a very particular way. He gave me precise instructions for what I was to do and what not to. It was a personal service to the Divine and a favour to him."

"I agreed to what he had asked, for it was like a beautiful play, to sing for him as though I didn't know he was there, listening. That was all. Then when I walked into that room where Yeheshua was, everything changed. I sang the songs, but they had become more special than I could have dreamt."

"For I had dreamt of him. Not in the dreams of sleep, but in my heart. His presence was that of my own love, my everything; and when I did what the High Priest asked it was everything that my heart desired. It was not for the High Priest or Isis that I sang, but for this man and for my love."

"I could not think of anything or anyone else for days. Then I saw him again, briefly; just enough to express that. In a moment, in a touch, that lives with me to this day. A few words of feeling, then I had to leave him, against every fibre of my being."

The High Priest gave me no further direction; the outcome of our meeting was beyond him.

"The next time I saw Yeheshua I believed we could transcend all the limitations of our situation, for I felt that every thought in my heart was already shared with him. That is what the contact had become to me."

"We did talk and I offered him my self, wanting nothing other than to be with him. His answer frames every moment of my life.

'Fair one, your very presence thrills me with delight;
your voice is benediction to my soul;
my human self would fly with you, and be contented in your love.
But all the world is craving for a love that I have come to manifest.
I must, then, bid you go;'

Go, go? Go where? I could not bear to go. There was nowhere. Standing frozen in my personal devastation, I heard his voice continue:

'but we will meet again; our ways on earth will not be cast apart.
I see you in the hurrying throngs of earth as minister of love.
I hear your voice in song, that wins the hearts of men to better things...'

His kindness to me could not stop the tears of grief washing through me like a flood, and I ran from the room, not wanting him to see; and yet those words upheld me through the many months that followed, till we did meet again, in Magdala.

I have seen the work he does and now I marvel that he took that time with me. Who he is... is beyond description. It is a revelation for our souls... to nourish.

CHAPTER 18.

When we were alone in the cave Miriam told me something more of those intervening months.

She went to the port to meet her father; seeking refuge from her feelings. His ship came in eventually, but he was not on it.

Instead, the captain faced her with tears rolling down his wide brown cheeks and told her of the storm that had taken her father from this world. He had been on deck to help because he always shared the dangers of the whole crew. A freak wave had washed him overboard... the captain lowered his eyes and wrung his hands, shifting on his feet in front of Miriam.

Miriam had placed a hand upon his shoulder, though a fresh surge of grief rose up to envelop her. She told the captain what she knew; the thing that he didn't. Her father knew he had not long to live; the priest-healers had confirmed what he knew in himself, and he had confided this to his daughter.

Despite that knowledge and the time to prepare, the hurt went very deep and she mourned his loss with all her heart.

There were two men who always travelled with Miriam's father and who offered to take his personal things back to Magdala with her. She bid them go without her; she needed to make her own way, on another path.

She considered going back to Heliopolis to try to see Yeheshua again, but her heart told her he would no longer be there.

A kind of bleakness descended that was alien to her. Where normally she saw people as souls striving for a greater joy, now they seemed to her to be all caught up in weirdness. Weirdness everywhere and she thirsted to breathe purity and peace.

She took her camel out into the great desert, craving the vastness of the universal nature. She stayed at an oasis that she had visited before and had found enchanting. Instead of peace, this time Miriam encountered fear amongst the people. Fear of the ghosts and ghost worshippers that had started to terrorise the area. Stories of their atrocities abounded as though their numbers were swelling like a tide of darkness.

Miriam gave them what strength she had, but found herself wanting. Unhappy and undecided, she left the oasis, setting her course to follow where her heart pulled her, whereto her master would call her.

The path she took left her dangerously short of water and she almost didn't care. The keenness of her thirst delighted her.

After a long ride Miriam came upon a low wall that she followed beside until she came upon a guarded tower. The sentries there were very surprised but gave her water, some food and directions to the King's Highway.

Knowing where she was, she was able to make her way to the country of the Essenes, that was the closest place that she could think of that might supply a link to Yeheshua. Her chosen route skirted the lands we now were camped in, and though she had wanted to come here because of the other Miriam, she had declined to stir the ghosts of the past to gratify her personal wishes.

A small community of the Essenes welcomed her and wanted her to stay with them, which she did for several months. Their austerities suited her and she gladly set her life to follow their ways. Yet something still was incomplete; for she had glimpsed a state of being, a love that needed to be followed and fulfilled. She would or could not hide this knowledge away.

The Essenes were aware of the tide of darkness rising about them and their reaction was to turn in on themselves, more desperate than ever to follow the rules of their covenant.

She had asked the community's leader about Yeheshua but he didn't know of him. He told her that everything she needed was right there. No other teacher was needed. Her singing set her apart and he let her know her that several communities sought after her to be their dove-convener. No greater honour could be had.

Miriam had poured out the question foremost in her heart. "Can you make manifest the love divine?" The rabbi had been taken aback, being asked something like this so directly and had hedged around the subject. Miriam knew then that she had to move on.

A young woman had come up to her as she packed her things. She had heard her question to their rabbi and told her about the Baptiser by the Jordan. John was his name and he professed the coming of divine love. Surely, he could help her.

Miriam found John and he had greeted her and embraced her as cousin. She was surprised and he had laughed. "You are kin to me in more ways than one," he had said mysteriously. He had remembered her from when he was young, having been in the Essene community when she had passed that way with her father.

Her father had recognised the young John as the son of his cousin Zacharias and now John returned the favour. He also told Miriam that Yeheshua had been to see him, some little time ago; described how the spirit had manifested and led to the divine master embarking on his teaching mission.

John saw Miriam as a kindred spirit and he knew that she was meant to be with Yeheshua. How he knew this she had no idea but to spend time with someone of John's purity of spirit was like being cleaned from the inside out and she insisted on being baptised as well.

Miriam stayed with the disciples of John for a while, bathing in the clarity she felt, but he was humble and expected her to go to and find her lord. He had already told her that Yeheshua had been teaching in Jerusalem and when she was leaving, he embraced his cousin again. "You know," he had said, "I am related to you both. You on my father's side and Yeheshua on my mother's. You will love Mary, his mother. Please send her my greetings as well, when you see her."

Miriam had gone to Jerusalem but Yeheshua had already left. It was a shock to her, after being with John and his spirit of light, to be in the city where the darkness seemed to be crowding into every corner. It was harder here to identify what the darkness was, for there were no ghost-worshippers like in the desert, but she felt it working as an undercurrent, everywhere.

She left quite soon and resolved to find Yeheshua as quickly as possible. Some said that he was in Samaria and some said that he was in Galilee and wherever she went it seemed that he had been there not long before, but had moved on.

Many people testified to the great works of healing that he did, a revelation of the power of love divine if ever there was one. She was in awe of what she heard and the love she felt drawing her on, growing day by day.

Around Passover time she found his house in Capernaum, but he had returned to Jerusalem, to celebrate the feast there. She met his mother Mary, who told her that he had only decided to go at the last minute.

Miriam could not wait for him there, though Mary had asked her to, if she would. Something about Yeheshua being in Jerusalem unsettled her. She had to try to go, but, once again, when she got there, he had already left. She turned around and wandered village to village as he was want to do.

The urgency of reunion was so real and strong that by the time she got back to Yeheshua's house in Capernaum she indeed felt reborn. Even then he had been back, but moved on already to Magdala. Mary was going there as well, together with other family members.

Magdala had been Miriam's home, so close by to Capernaum, and after all the travelling and searching she had been doing to find Yeheshua she didn't know whether to laugh or cry. He had gone to stay in her town. So, she and mother Mary set off for Magdala together.

That was how she had got to be there that day when Yeheshua was staying at my house.

Out in the desert, so far away from Yeheshua, it became clear how vital the practice of what he had shown us that day really was. I found it hard to devote a much time as Miriam did, but it was wonderful to get this chance with no distractions and I made the most of it, in my own way.

The next day I spent quite a lot of the morning with Bishmi, while Johannus and Kardun were out hunting and gathering firewood or fetching water. We enjoyed each other's company and made me think of my friend Arianne, at the temple of Antioch.

Talking to her reminded me so much of my time as a priestess and I was fascinated to hear of the unfolding events from her perspective. They knew that the confrontation of Light and Darkness was happening; they could see the signs in the world around them; the terrorisers and the possessed abounding. Leila and Yresmin were ready to fight for the Light and so was Bishmi.

For me the battleground had been made more personal; my own being having been invaded by the Darkness. Bishmi shuddered when I told her some of what had happened to me; and was amazed at my rescue and Johannus' part in it as well. He had come back with edible roots to cook, that Kardun had shown him how to find.

As we cooked lunch Miriam came out to join us, shining like a goddess it seemed to me. Our individual small endeavours were coming together to make our living here really enjoyable. Miriam talked about some of the things that the Israelites had done in this desert and in the afternoon; we had our own taste of it as well.

Making music had been a dynamic and important aspect of their worship and celebration. The tribes had inherited much of the ways of the ancients, whose understanding of music and sound had been employed to aid the Egyptian builders. Their temples in the western isles were energised, especially at the times of coming together of their peoples for celebration, by the power of sound and music.

Miriam took us to a cliff-bounded corner of the valley where echoes resounded unusually strongly. She set us out at four points and instructed us in our parts to sing. "All hail; the king. All hail; the king" was all we said, each one of us taking two words of the phrase, picking it up with the next as the echoes returned.

The repeated refrain swelled as our phrases, and their echoes, built on each other. We were getting immersed in the effects being created when suddenly Miriam joined in with the words of her song feeding in and out of our chanting.

"He comes with love, to set us free; the deaf to hear, the blind to see.

He charges us to dwell in light; showing us where to place our might;

And utilise what we've been given, to open on Earth, the door to Heaven…"

Changing the words as her heart led her, she continued on again and again

"He comes with light to help us see; the lame to walk, the hurt to feel, how peace lies here within our grasp, and set our hearts into the task… He is the song we are to sing, with hearts that open wide their wings, so soon the world will know of him, and the glory of that he comes to bring."

The beauty and strength of her voice was unparalleled anyway, but the way she was able to weave her words into ours, and all the echoes, orchestrating us at the same time, was quite amazing.

We were totally caught up in it, listening to the song pouring from her into ours, such that I had never experienced before. We were carried along on the wave that grew and grew till Miriam allowed it to gently dissolve into a potency of quietness.

We sat in the stillness for quite some time after we had finished, no-one wanting to break the spell. Eventually Miriam tapped me on the shoulder and said that we must get out of the sun, and so we made our way back to our camp.

Around the campfire that evening Kardun asked her about it.

"When the tribes of Israel made their music, there were enough of them to make their own echoes; but the effects were similar and astounding," she said. "So much of that ancient power has disappeared today, maybe never to happen again."

"How do you know about it?" asked Bishmi.

"It is in the memories here, that I am given to be able to read, and so much more as well. The Israelites spent forty years or more in these wildernesses, living much as we have been. What we are told to believe is that it was all about reaching the 'promised land'. Don't they realise that most of the people who left Egypt with Moses, spent all their lives here with him? Do we think their lives were a waste, that they never entered Caanan?"

We thought about it, but she didn't wait for our answers or questions, she carried on. "It was the most wonderful way to spend their lives. Living under the instruction and shelter of the Most High, with their living Prophet. Accepting, day to day, their life as it was given to them."

"Of course there were times, over the period of forty years, when things got tough, water was scarce or disease was rife, and the people got disgruntled. History finds it hard to understand the wonder of what they had, because all it cares for are the problems that arose, rules that were made or lands that were won in battle, but most of those 'chosen people' found real joy in their lives and a heritage of contentment. It is that same heritage that the world needs to know and grasp. Contentment in the life that is being given, as it is given, not in what we think is our due, and are still to get."

"That is the task being handed over to us, to see that all the peoples of the world know of the love they have waiting for them, in the heaven that is within them."

CHAPTER 19.

Kardun left Bishmi sleeping when he went out of the cave, on their last morning in the valley that had so quickly come to feel like home.

He still had a few snares out that he wanted to collect; otherwise, some animal or bird could get caught and be left wounded in one.

Johannus was up as well and Kardun welcomed his offer of company. They had quite different outlooks but Kardun had grown to value the younger man's sincerity.

The day after the musical episode Kardun had described to his new friend how he saw the world, and Johannus had listened with real interest. Then Miriam had told them they would be leaving the next day and they had spent the evening packing up camp.

The sun was not yet up and there were remnants of dew on the ground. The light had grown up into the lower part of the sky whilst the rest was still managing to hold onto most its stars.

They worked around to the eastern slopes and picked up the two snares that Kardun had left there. The rim of the sun was about to creep up over the horizon and they watched for it, sitting back on their haunches, side by side.

"Did you really mean that when you said yesterday that the Empire of Rome is destroying belief in the true Gods?" asked Johannus after a little while.

"Yes, because the Gods are becoming nothing but puppets in their eyes. Worldly power and wealth is what Rome worships."

"I heard that the cult of Isis has become massively popular amongst the Roman aristocracy," said Johannus, provocatively.

The little man spat into the dust beside him. "Exactly," he said after a short pause; "they think the Goddess is theirs to toy with; to make her the Emperor's harlot. They know nothing. The power of the Goddess is here in the desert; here with us. Miriam and Mary have the true power of Isis in them. So much so; so much.

"Bishmi as well," said Johannus. Kardun continued scratching a pattern on the sand with a short stick. "Hmmm," he said. "Maybe yes; Bishmi too."

Bishmi and I had got up and found the men gone; we set to making a pre-journey meal. Bishmi talked of our apparently immanent return to Rekem and her concerns about facing the priests and the ministers.

Miriam came and joined us, much earlier than she had in the last few days. She quickly gathered the essence of Bishmi's worries and addressed them. "You won't be going back empty handed, to face the king's wrath for evading his army, Bishmi my dear companion. You will go with a gift he will appreciate."

"I am so grateful for your gift of the rods of Ma'at, Miriam," answered Bishmi.

"Not that, not that;" said Miriam. "We haven't finished what I was sent here for. My time is approaching though… and we must keep ahead of the Darkness."

Bishmi and I looked at each other. We were worried by the tone of our friend's statement, but aloud we wondered where Kardun and Johannus had got to.

The two men were approaching the area of the waterhole where they split up to dismantle their traps. This is where Kardun had taught Johannus his methods and so Johannus had set some of his own.

There was nothing caught in his and secretly Johannus was glad. Crouching down behind the rocks, filling in the hole that formed the bottom of his trap, he heard a stifled cry from somewhere beyond the rocks, shocking him into alertness.

Slowly, carefully, he raised his head enough to be able to see the track beyond the waterhole. There were people coming along it; dark-robed men, strung out along the path; fifteen or twenty of them.

He froze; the leading ones were pushing the goatherd before them. It was the boy's cry that Johannus had heard.

Something about them made the back of his neck prickle. Their armed and shrouded forms looked dangerous enough, but there was something else; something sinisterly familiar.

Their long dark robes of greys and browns; the confidence of their swaggering; something. The hint of cruelty. Then it hit him like a blow. It was Simon the Magus and his desert henchmen that they reminded him of.

Johannus gripped the hilt of his sword tightly and nearly sprang up as the goatherd was sent sprawling across the ground to the laughter of his captors; but with his heart pounding in his chest, he ducked down again, behind the rocks, and backed carefully away.

It didn't take him long to find Kardun but his urgency was desperate. "What?" said the expression on their guide's dark face, before he even got close. "What is it?"

Johannus described what he had seen; the goatherd being forced to reveal the watering place; the dark robes and callous faces. "Ghosters," said Kardun. "Djinn worshippers from the great eastern desert; they shouldn't be here."

Johannus thought Kardun would want to see them for himself, but he didn't. The description was plain enough.

"The boy…?" said Johannus.

"He will be safe enough," replied Kardun… "as long as he tells them everything; particularly about us."

Realisation sunk in quickly; it was Mary who had first befriended the boy and his goats. Mary and their donkey, Sarah. They must get back and warn them…

Bishmi and I had cleared out and cleaned the caves and completed the loading of the baggage.

Miriam brought the horses over, handing the reins to Bishmi. "Let's get mounted up," she said, turning around to go back for the camels. I felt her urgency like a blow and hurried to join her.

Bishmi was about to ask about waiting for the men to get back, when she saw Johannus and Kardun hurrying up the wadi, dodging around the scrub bushes, running.

Miriam and I were already astride their camels, urging them to rise. "Come on," said Miriam as she rose up into the air above the two panting men. "We have no time to lose."

Johannus tried to say something, but found hardly enough breath to spare for speaking. Kardun shook his head. "She knows," he said and his comrade nodded, astonished but half expecting it as well.

They got onto their respective mounts as quickly as they could, appreciating as they did all the work that the women had done in clearing the camp. He noticed that once again Sarah was only lightly loaded.

Without further delay they followed Miriam's swift retreat out of the other end of the valley.

They moved fast, travelling directly and determinedly southwards, as the tracks allowed. Not meandering as they had previously, but Miriam led the way with unruffled certainty and kept the pace brisk for long mile after mile.

We stopped briefly for water and continued on again, slower but steady, late into the morning.

Eventually Miriam called a halt, drawing us into the shady areas of a craggy hillside. "What do you think Kardun?" she asked the guide, "Is this far enough?"

Kardun knew exactly what she meant, though they hadn't discussed Johannus' sighting of the Ghosters. "Yes, I think so," he said. "They have no reason to chase far. They will only be looking for easy pickings."

We rested in the hottest hours of the day, eating first the food that had been intended for our breakfast. Kardun left us to keep watch of the land we had passed through; careful to catch sight of anything that might contradict the confidence of his words to Miriam at the earliest possible moment.

Miriam bade us rest as much as we could, because she needed our strength for the night ahead. Bishmi and I heeded her warning but again the tenor of her words worried us. What did Miriam know?

When Kardun had returned with the good news of no sightings we made ready to travel on again. This time Miriam picked her way round rocky formations that fringed the ridge, and down into the start of a narrow ravine, away from the relative smooth territory that we had been traversing.

We had to lead our horses and camels over another stretch of broken ground. The sun was still pretty high, but behind them now, pushing their shadows ahead as they went.

'East,' thought Kardun. 'After three hours riding southwards of where we were.' His mind was already piecing together a view of their location. He frowned to himself, 'I don't like the way this wadi is turning back towards the north again. Desert devils could be anywhere, but north of here is where we found them; or they nearly found us.'

Bishmi followed behind Kardun, the last of the three camel riders; Johannus followed behind her, with Sarah too. His thoughts were also of the men he had seen that morning, and of the priest's body he had found, the one with the bethel stone. The sense of the man's desperation had come to him when he had followed his death trail. Now he sensed that somehow 'they' were tracking his thoughts. He shook his head, knowing he was being stupid and concentrated instead on the exercise that Miriam had taught him. It helped.

"I wonder how long before we get back to Rekem,' said Bishmi, over her shoulder. She couldn't help the sinking sensation in the pit of her stomach. 'I must be strong, for Miriam' she thought, but she didn't feel it. She had never wanted to be a High Priestess but now she knew that she would have to be. How could she represent the Goddess Manat? How could she? Please Goddess help me; please Manat help me, she repeated again and again. She breathed a little freer.

Miriam looked back at us, following her trustingly down the valley. We must have all looked a little troubled. She smiled encouragingly. "Come on Mary, we can get up and ride here."

I had been watching the shadows dancing over the surface of the rocks in front of me as I walked. Something in my thoughts was trying to suggest the Darkness was already with me; that it didn't need any help from the interlopers from the eastern desert that Johannus had told them about at the break. I banished the thoughts without too much difficulty though, looking for the presence of every breath within me instead.

Miriam noted my returning smile and she checked back to Kardun. He didn't seem quite so at ease as usual and Miriam asked if he was all right. "Just a bit of a headache," he answered, "I have drunk some extra water; that should do the trick."

"I think you need to take a break soon," answered Miriam. "You probably stayed out too much in the sun back there, whilst we rested. Once we are down the valley a bit, we shall take another break; and you must rest."

When they did stop again Miriam put her hands to the back of Kardun's neck and head. It seemed to be burning hot and she allowed the heat to come out of him. Bishmi took over, and after a little time he was able to catch some rest.

Miriam came over and sat with Johannus and I; to see I think how he, in particular, was coping with the unseen pressure. She obviously knew it was there for all of us and she started to explain what she was experiencing, hoping this might help us too.

"The past and future are pressing in on me hard; the past tries to envelop and suffocate, whilst the future threatens to rend and tear me apart. Only in this precarious precious moment is there freedom to choose, and this is becoming a single pinnacle, a single step, a single breath as we reach closer and closer to our given goal."

Johannus was really worried, asking what he could do what to help.

"The greatest gift we can have is in fact, this time, this life. The greatest thing you Johannus will ever be given to know is already within you and in fact is you. When you are ready to know that, then all things will start to fall into place for you. Until then it will be a struggle; but be of good heart for it is a worthwhile struggle. That you can do for me, if you will."

Johannus didn't mind a struggle. He knew he was in one, to make himself worthy of the prize; and if Miriam was telling him that it was good then he was happier. Right now, he felt ready to confront any Darkness that might try to stalk them.

Bishmi came over and joined in too, and Miriam turned to her with a revelation and a request. "Tonight, I go to walk with my Lord, beyond the greatest crossroads, where the past and future cross with life and death. I will ask you to call your Goddess, for protection. Can you do that?"

"Call Manat?" said Bishmi, "I don't know if I can; even with the rods of Ma'at."

"I called Hecate once; the Goddess of the crossroads and Underworld. Perhaps I could assist you, Bishmi," I said quickly.

"Mary, I think you should just stay with His Name and not be the active partner in the calling," said Miriam, and after a moment's thought I realised just how right she was.

"Hecate and Manat are essentially the same," said Johannus. All the women turned to regard him, quizzically. "I could help; I also worked with these things; remember, Mary?"

"This is real Johannus," said Miriam. "Are you ready to face the true Goddess? She may not accept your call; you have to know her to call her."

He sat and wondered what he had offered, because he knew that they would be relying on him if this offer was accepted. He turned to Bishmi. She was the one who would be Hecate-Manat if her calling succeeded. He knew she could do it without him; she just needed confidence. "If Bishmi is ready then I will be too," he declared.

"This is why Yresmin sent you Bishmi," I said. "This is your time to become Manat's own priestess. Yresmin wanted that for you. Are you ready?"

"I don't know; but I must be," said Manat's high priestess-to-be. "Manat will protect me."

She realised what she had said and they all laughed. "Yes, Manat will protect me from Manat. How ridiculous I am."

"Not at all," said Miriam. "Surrendering to divinity is not a joke. It cannot be done without divine help. All of us are going to need that help tonight. Me maybe most of all."

CHAPTER 20.

Soon after Kardun awoke we were on the way again. He rode up-front with Miriam and I following them on my trusty, if a little grouchy, companion. 'Crusty' I had come to call him.

The shadows had lengthened and I wondered how long we had left of daylight. A couple of hours perhaps till the desert twilight took us into itself.

Bishmi and Johannus rode behind me and the sounds we made travelled clearly in the still afternoon heat of the valley. I heard the odd snatch of their discussion about the goddess we would be calling. I was glad that they were supporting each other now, because I was worried about what the night would bring.

I thought back to the night that Hecate had manifested in Bel, the high priestess of Astarte's temple in Antioch. How I had stood in front of her with my priestess' silver bladed knife pointing at her breast. The hairs raised on my arms and back, just remembering it.

"Johannus," I called, drawing my camel back to within talking distance of the horse riders. "That pommel and the handle of your sword, coiled with silver thread, would be the thing to use."

"We are wondering whether we should call for Hecate or Manat," said Bishmi.

"I would say to call for her as you know her best. If that means you use both names, fine; or different ones, fine too. It is the spirit essence that counts and opening up to her; both of you."

"Yes," said Bishmi. "I shall call for Manat, but I think you know Hecate better, Johan. Let's use whichever names come strongest to us at the time. Mary, have you got any idea where we are going? Has Miriam said anything?"

"Not directly, no; but I think it will be somewhere of importance to the Miriam of old."

I urged Crusty forward again, linking back up with Miriam and Kardun, wondering if I should finally ask her where we were going. Kardun had apparently recognised something in the scenery and regained his bearings for he was talking of what lay ahead.

"There is a hill straddling the entrance to this valley where there is a large village. Do you mean to stop there?"

"It was an important place in the days of Moses. The tribes congregated there, but no, we shall not go there now. I believe there is a way to cut through the hillside to the right." She turned on her saddle towards me. "Are you and the others all right, Mary?"

"Yes, fine," I replied. "You know where you want to get to tonight then?"

She nodded several times, rather gravely, but said nothing.

I fell back a little, allowing her and Kardun to ride side by side. The track had widened out a bit but it was still far from being an easy descent.

I was worried about Miriam, naturally. Up until this morning all that was good in the world seemed to be growing in our venture, but now that had changed. Perhaps I should have realised something but obviously Miriam had known. Darkness was gathering and Ghosters were out hunting. What did she know about the coming storm?

My mind ranged back to when Yeheshua had asked me to bring her back safely to him. At the time I had not believed that there would be anything I could really do to help but now it was the request that I was taking more seriously than anything in my life. He had said I was the one person who might be able to, and it occurred to me here, riding down into the shadows, that maybe it was the intimate contact that I had once had with that other world that would somehow be useful.

Bishmi and Johannus were still following, but quietly, no words breaking the tensions in the air around us. The concern I was feeling for Miriam encompassed them as well. 'Dear companions' she called them and if anyone else had said that then I would probably have ridiculed them, but it fitted exactly what I was thinking. Did they have the strength to hold the Goddess in an alliance against the dark tide. As much help as I could give, I would, to the last drop of my strength.

We were far from Yeheshua, yet I was still able to feel his kindness within the presence of his Word. That unspoken Name; his gift; shown to us that day in my house. Yet on top of even that he had given me this task to accompany his Miriam and to bring her home safely. This immediate purpose in my mind gave me an inkling of unshakeable calmness.

The tops of the hills were still bathed in the incredible pink and orange hues of those sunlit rocks, but the track that we followed led further and deeper into the cooler tones of evening. We passed one herder with his flock and Kardun went to speak with him awhile, before returning to us with a report that all was quiet.

Further on, just before a bend in the valley, Miriam pulled her camel to one side, stopped and dismounted. We did the same. In the near gloom we shared leftovers from the morning meal. Venus shone in the pale sky overhead, the only star shining there. Never before had I felt so close with people; and felt the love returned. Where were we all going next?

Miriam pointed out a track that led up the hillside we were standing beside. "This way."

Surveying the track she had indicated, the rough terrain of the hillside looked a lot less inviting than the comparatively smooth valley floor we had been travelling down.

Before anyone else could react Johannus sprang forward and started up the stony track, pulling on the reins of his horse.

We toiled up the slope till we crested the ridge, looking suspiciously at every bush and rock we passed. There was another slope ahead, and probably another and another after that. It was a daunting thought.

Johannus paused and Miriam came up to him, taking him by the arm. "This is far enough," she said. "There is another path to the left here."

We looked where she showed us and there was indeed some sort of way leading down through a narrow ravine, that angled away from the main valley; a very dark looking path.

Johannus didn't hesitate, though I almost wished he had. He drew his sword and set off down the way Miriam had found. Reluctantly I went next and Miriam followed me. Bishmi followed her and Kardun brought up the rear.

It was slow going in the deep shadows but above there was still a gash of clear mauve sky that lifted our spirits, just as the dark pools around us invited terrible thoughts to come to our minds. Thoughts of inner and outer demons, both; but we persevered and came through the ravine, right up to the edge of a wide plain.

The light of the world had changed and the reason was clear before us; a full moon had lifted above the rim of the mountains that framed the floor of the desert ahead. We stopped and stared across it, mesmerised by the bewitching light.

The bark of a jackal, out there somewhere, cut into our reverie. Another answered it, from over to the right of where we were. We strained our eyes but saw nothing. Miriam answered our unasked question.

"Out across this valley is a large formation of rocks rising from the valley floor. That is where we must get to, as soon as we can. Kardun, we need your best guidance to get us across unseen. How can we do it?"

"I fear that there are bands of Ghosters about my lady. Though none have been seen today, the herder confirmed there have been sightings, but no attacks on their village, but I…"

A distant human cry stopped him in mid sentence, despite its faintness. We were obviously very sensitive to such sounds and stood there straining every sense to catch any further clues. Nothing more came on the still air.

Our breathing was noisy in our own ears and our hearts beat hard within our breasts. How indeed could we go out onto the plain? Even though the night had descended, its cover was shredded by the low moon.

"We shall have to move like Ghosters ourselves," said Kardun suddenly. "I know how they work; we can imitate them and maybe… no-one… " he trailed off and surprisingly Bishmi took over his thoughts. "Yes, husband. You of all people could make it happen. Show us what we must do." She sounded business-like and ready.

We were all surprised, I think, by the strength of Bishmi's resolve. Maybe she sensed that Miriam would baulk at asking us to endanger ourselves on the uncertain way across; across to the rocks she sought.

"Well…" continued Kardun, as caught off balance by his wife's response as any of us, "well, first of all we should stretch out in a line, side by side, making a shallow vee." He paused listening for our response. We said nothing and he continued. "I will lead in the middle, with Miriam and Mary riding on either side. Johannus, you take the left flank and Bishmi you take the donkey with you on the right."

After a few more instructions we all understood what we were about. "We shall go slowly and purposefully, as if looking for something; not ourselves looked for or at. Our strength must be in our self-assurance. Nothing can dare to challenge us or even think of trying. We shall ride tall and dangerous, from the start."

Bishmi had mounted up and Johannus followed suit. They spread out to either side of the ravine, inviting us camel riders to take the central lead. Taking deep breaths, we followed.

Kardun put out his right arm, holding us back till he himself would start forward. He stared out at the far horizon where clouds rode around the moon. One large one edged in front it, dimming the world, which was what Kardun was waiting for. He dropped his arm and rode out from the protection of ravine's mouth. Determined not to show the nervousness I felt, I followed, out to Kardun's left. We all went out from our cover, keeping to the formation that Kardun had explained to us.

The air was cool and smelt of desert myrtle bushes. Slowly we rode out, not flinching when the light of the moon returned, but looking ahead and some-times to the sides, scanning the ground and the land around us.

We had moved a few hundred yards out onto the valley floor when another cry came from our left, in the distance, followed by shouts and sounds of commotion. Kardun put out his right hand to stop us, and signalled us with motions of his arm to wheel around him, keeping the source of the noises to our left. He signed us to move on again, which we did, but now we knew for certain there were… 'the others' out here.

Some sort of attack seemed to be happening at the village. Kardun held up his arm again and we all stopped. He spoke to Miriam quietly, who turned her camel towards Bishmi and edged her forwards. I watched in fascination as Miriam said something to Bishmi, until Kardun startled me by whispering close beside me, "Go, after Miriam. Keep her in sight, but don't rush up behind her; keep a gap. We are heading just to the left edge of the moon. Go!"

We fled in a long line, directly away from the commotion. The new urgency made it feel like there were people chasing us, even though they probably weren't. Any sound was to be feared. Crusty veered slightly as a low shape flew across our path, and I had startled; a desert owl, out hunting.

The veil between the inner and the outside worlds stretched to near tearing point. Demons rushed within the spaces of my mind even as their human counterparts were, somewhere nearby; but Crusty moved on in rhythmic faith-fulness like the movement of my breath within me. Onwards we went, across the dark, yet moonlit plain, closing on the up-thrusting rocks that I could now see as distinct from the mountains beyond. We were nearly there.

Miriam led us into the darkness where huge shapes loomed high over us. She dismounted quickly and led her camel up through a narrow defile, with Bishmi close behind. Somewhere in the distance I heard a jackal's bark answered by another and then a third. I glanced around to see Johannus and Kardun leading their beasts up the track. Their faces were tense and Kardun also turned his head to search the moonlit stretch of desert we had just crossed.

We worked our way deep into the rocky fastness where Miriam found a little dell for us to gather in. Kardun was asked to take the animals on into the foothills of the Sharra mountains, but first she took him with us to show him where a narrow crack in the cliff-side ran down behind scrubby bushes to form the narrow entrance of a cave. "This is where we shall stay till the light of the sun returns. It is deep in many ways. You keep yourself safe in the ways you know best. We shall see you in the morning."

CHAPTER 21.

Johannus conferred with Kardun, spending a few precious moments making a makeshift torch. The last place the little Egyptian had wished to be, with the Djinn worshippers about, was confined within caves, however far back they went. He was a man who loved the open desert and he had an idea of where he could get the animals to. If the Ghosters followed him, then so much the better.

The last to squeeze through the cave's entrance, Johannus took the torch from Kardun who was setting it alight with a coal from his censer. They clasped wrists and each withdrew to deal with whatever the darkness might throw at them.

With the torch in one hand and his sword in the other Johannus rejoined the three women in the cave's interior. His first glance showed him that the space inside was wider than he could have expected from the outside, and went quite high above them, tapering to follow the line of the fissure.

He handed the torch to Miriam who took it slowly around the full perimeter, showing up a couple of alcoves that had been hewn into the walls and a low dark passage that went beyond the torchlight into the furthest end of the cave.

Near the middle was a stone plinth, raised to nearly knee height off the cave's floor. The light guttered slightly and Miriam passed the torch to Bishmi. "This is the crossroads, Bishmi. You three are strong enough; hold firm; hold true; be in his love."

Bishmi climbed onto the plinth, handing the torch to me as she went. "I have traced the circle, Mary," said Miriam; "I must go now, through that passage to another chamber. Stay strong dearest sister; stay strong."

Almost as soon as Miriam had stepped outside narrow circle of torchlight, it guttered even more and then went out. The blackness was complete.

Johannus and I had taken up our positions; Johannus directly before the plinth and I was back a bit and to one side. Bishmi's view of Johannus' encouraging smile vanished with the light.

She turned her thoughts to her mistress Yresmin and the things she had been taught. Surprisingly to Bishmi, this cave reminded her of the great temple tomb at Kadesh-Rekem, partly because of its height but also because the narrowing roof-space was reminiscent of the pyramid within that temple.

She stood, tall as a pillar that stretched from earth to sky, a column of air circulating to the rhythm of her beating heart. The calm smile of Yresmin warmed her from the inside out. Gone were any thoughts of the terrors they had fled away from.

It took a few breaths to set herself, to ready herself, to open to the possibility of receiving her Goddess. She opened her mouth and started the hum that began her call, "mmmm…" Her voice gained strength as the "maAA…" raised high into the heavens, then "nn…aaaatt" brought it settling down to deepest earth again. "Hail great Goddess; please receive my prayer."

240

Bishmi was aware that nearby Johannus and Mary were aiding her call, each in turn fuelling the invocation she had started within the cave, but her mind was absorbed by her own task.

"mMAA…nnaaaatt; great Goddess, hear my call," she said again, not shouting but still with all her being, "Manaat, come to us in our need." The sky seemed to ripple like wavy black hair spread out all above Bishmi; and in the middle of it all shone a single jewelled star as crown. Vaguely, she wondered whether her eyes were open or closed but she also new it didn't matter.

Another breath raised high within and round below as Manat's aspiring priestess opened the wings of her heart to fly. "MMAAnnaatt, receive the offer of this life," and the cave beat an echo to support her.

She felt something of a rush of energy, lifting her, lifting her from within, up to where the light and darkness were rushing down, to where the greatness of the goddess stooped to enter her mortal form.

It took several seconds for our eyes to adjust to the darkness of the extinguished torchlight and to realize there were still glimmerings of light around. I gazed at where I knew Bishmi stood and the outline of her head was faintly visible. Further to any light coming through the cave entrance some moon or starlight gleamed through a section of the rocky fissure above, filtering directly down onto the area of the plinth.

Bishmi stood there, high and imposing, and now I could make out Johannus standing before her as she started her call to the goddess. It grew and then fell back again. Johannus took up the call "Hecate, great goddess; hear our voices" he said in vibrant tones and unexpectedly I found my voice breathing the words, "ISIS… heed our call."

Twice more Bishmi's invocation was echoed by Johannus' to Hecate, and twice more my breaths intoned my heart's call to Isis.

As Bishmi sounded her final giving to the goddess I felt the kind of breath of wind that I remembered from once before, coming seemingly this time from the sky beyond the rocky walls.

Johannus tensed, straining to stand taller, still clutching the sword in his hand.

"Who dares bear iron in my presence," said the voice that came from Bishmi's mouth.

Johannus panicked, belatedly, turning the sword point down and lifting the pommel up towards the figure on the plinth. He had grasped the blade tightly in both hands and the sharp edges cut into his fingers but he paid no attention to the discomfort. His eyes were straining to take in the features of the goddess in front of him.

The light had grown and we could see the clear silvery features of a beautiful woman that was not unlike Bishmi either.

Johannus stammered as he put his prepared question to her. "H… h… ow can we d… defeat the Darkness, g… great Goddess?"

241

An unnerving, tinkling laugh came back, that spread out around us like waves on a beach.

I thought there wasn't going to be an answer but then she spoke with steely sweetness. "Stop creating darkness, and you will be free of it. It is you humans that create the terrors that plague not only you yourselves but threaten to engulf the three worlds. Seek instead to love the Light rather than to fight the Darkness."

Johannus gazed up at his goddess. "What about you? What can we here do now?"

"Now it is for you to learn the way to freedom. You must learn what is kindness. You must learn what is affection. You must understand the difference between what love is and what is lust. You shall have to know both respect and trust, to become free."

Johannus' head dropped and as it did Manat-Bishmi reached forward her left hand that held the rod of Maat and touched him on the wrist. He jerked his outstretched hands away and stabbed himself in the hip.

Lurching forward with a cry of pain Johannus dropped the sword and fell onto his knees in front of the Goddess. He stayed holding onto Bishmi's robe for a couple of seconds before he slipped down to bow at Hecate's feet, banging his head on the edge of the stone plinth as he did, and ending prone upon the floor of the cave.

It was quite a comical scene and I would have laughed in other circumstances. The profile of the Goddess that was Hecate looked down upon Johannus' form and then, as she lifted her head and turned to me, it was Isis that I saw returning my stare.

We regarded each other and I felt a shiver of recognition going through me as she softened her features with a smile. She reminded me of Yeheshua's mother.

"Mother;" I started, my mind returning to the task that Yeheshua had set me. "Where has my sister Miriam gone?"

"This is the Kadesh that she has been seeking, and now she has gone beyond the veil to walk with her Lord, where time and place have no more hold."

Despite the calmness of her voice, I felt a great apprehension rise and shake my whole body. I couldn't not do anything, but I had no idea of what I could do. "Can I follow her there?" I asked at last.

The figure on the plinth shrugged slightly. "Maybe, if you can persevere." Then she spoke again, without any preamble. "Mary, you shall have a child, and because you have invoked me, she shall be known as 'the Egyptian'."

"No!" The denial came from me before I could think but she had already turned away to regard the unconscious form of Johannus on the floor. I was torn for a few moments, wanting to tell her that there was no way that Johannus and I would have a child, which is what seemed to be the implication.

This new assumption was something I just had to put out of my mind. Whilst I was worried about Johannus and leaving my companions of the appellation, I was still more concerned to fulfil my promise to Yeheshua and to follow after Miriam.

The Goddess turned to look at me once more, her features closest to those of Bishmi-Manat now. "The boy is all right with me. Have no fear."

I hesitated a little, wondering what I was taking on and still a bit shaken, but then turned and started towards the dark passage. I had to leave the ring of starlight that the Goddess had brought with her. Looking back, I saw Bishmi sat upon the edge of the plinth and reaching down to help Johannus.

Just ahead of me was the fulfilment of this journey's task, and yet all the troubles that it had apparently attracted wanted to block the way. Ghoulish horrors seemed to be lying in wait and my mind railed against my choice of entering this path. Yet Miriam had definitely gone this way, because I had seen her, out of the corner of my eye, and this image helped to quell my fears.

I started to move forward into the low entranceway, having to duck my head down to do so. I reached out with my arms to touch the sides of the passage, feeling the reassuring rough solidity of the rock on both sides.

I still found it incredibly hard to move forward, crouching down, my eyes straining ahead into the blackness. The ground felt smooth and almost pebbly under my bare feet; I had taken my sandals off when we got ready to call Manat. 'This passageway must be where water runs down through the rock'. The thought reassured me, helping me to focus on the image of Miriam being somewhere ahead.

Little by little I edged down the tunnel, my hands trailing along the edges of the walls. It seemed like passing through an eternity of fear but I expect it was only a very short way till my feet encountered larger rocks on the floor, just as my fingertips could no longer reach either wall.

I stopped, my heart beating hard. I found that I was holding my breath and I made a deliberate effort to let it go, feel it return and let it go again: to feel the comings and goings, and take comfort there. I was shaking I noticed; alone and out of touch with anything. I needed to pull myself together.

Most of the rocks were on the left side of the passage floor and so I moved a bit to the right-hand side, trying to find a way round them. The right wall bulged out into what must be a little alcove; it wasn't deep.

Managing to skirt around the rocks I then discovered that the tunnel roof sloped rapidly downwards until I could go no further. I was on my hands and knees and could feel the solid rock ahead of me. Blind in the darkness, my hands searched frantically for a way forward, but found none.

I felt myself starting to panic. I turned and sat on the ground, staring back up the passage I had come down. Not that far away was an oval of faintest light that described the entranceway. Where was Miriam though? It could only be there was another tunnel, probably where the rocks were strewn across the floor. I had to check.

Even though the other end of the passage was freedom and light, getting up from that floor was perhaps the hardest thing I had ever had to do. The wall behind me glued me to it as if it was the only place that really existed and all the demons of hell were arrayed around the tunnel, or about to break through the fabric of my mind. I prayed to God and my master Yeheshua to help me.

This seemed to hold them back, just a little longer.

Pushing myself forward onto my hands and knees I felt my way the couple of yards to where the rocks on the floor were, following the tunnel around on that side this time.

There were a lot of the stones, but none of them were too heavy for me to lift out of the way and I found enough space to crouch and explore the other alcove, where the stones had been taken from. As I studied the back, I could definitely see a jagged opening; there had to be light coming in through from somewhere.

Stretching forward I was able to peer into the space where the rocks had been. Though I couldn't quite see the source of the light I could see a figure that it faintly lit; part of the profile of Miriam, sitting in the middle of a small chamber, with her back mostly towards me. She was still and upright, emanating peaceful concentration, as though this is where she was quite at home.

A great relief flooded through me to see her there, and I relaxed back against the side.

The next thing that Johannus knew was to hear the sounds of the sea coming through the other end of the cave, as waves came and went in the entranceway.

He turned sideways towards the girlish woman who was sitting beside him. She was impishly attractive with a curvy smile that set off her green eyes. He realised she must be one of Hecate's maidens, sent to look after him.

He remembered what had happened in the ritual, how he had discovered his impurity standing in front of Hecate and how embarrassed he had been. With this girl though it didn't seem to matter, for one of the few times in his life.

The girl had put a hand upon his shoulder and he felt they shared a sense of intimacy that needed no apology or fear.

They were sitting near the back of the cavern where no sunlight could reach, though Johannus could see signs of it glinting in water at the cave's mouth.

The girl spread a kind of light about them and they could see each other clearly, which seemed perfectly normal. Johannus leant against her and she put her arm around him.

"Where are we exactly?" he asked, because he knew this was not the same cave as the invocation had taken place in.

Before she could answer him, Johannus heard a flurry of noise behind them that was like the beating of large wings.

With lithe movements the girl was up from his side and had jumped towards the back of the cave. Johannus turned, jaw dropping as he saw her visibly grow and the girl's face transformed into the severe profile of Hecate, ancient goddess and queen, looking back into the shadowy blackness.

The back of the cave still appeared to Johannus to be solid rock but nevertheless it definitely also contained a space where much movement was happening.

Hecate walked purposefully towards the wall and it opened to the light she gave off, surfaces becoming whole vistas of possibility. She put out a hand and pointed to where the flapping noise was coming from. For a brief moment Johannus saw a creature framed by her wide hand gesture, its dark wings beating strongly and giving it erratic movement. A very large bat he thought.

She spoke words of command, not loudly but easily and quickly as though she did this all the time, and the bat creature was gone.

She moved further into the wall space and Johannus found that he had got up and was following just behind her. She paused, bent and picked something from the ground. Her light made its vegetation go all blue and green, with purple rocks, yet she herself seemed to be suffused with a golden glow. Johannus saw she had picked up a ball of some sort and smoothed it into a shape that half-crawled, half-hopped away as she set it back on the ground.

Somehow the ferns and mossy rocks revealed were just what he would have expected on such a dank hillside he found himself on, though they were unlike anything he had ever seen. He was fascinated and peered out around to try to see further.

Hecate turned and saw that he was there. "Come," she said, "the Shadowland is not for you."

He dared not look her full in the face but allowed himself to go back to where they had been sitting and his companion was again the young maiden, though he now had no doubt that this was in fact the Goddess Hecate.

"They think that because they can fly, they can do anything they like, but that is not the case," said the girl in a business-like way, as if by way of explanation. "If they get to the water everything is a mess… there are just too many now to deal with them all properly… they have to be shown that the rules exist to be obeyed."

Johannus shuddered slightly; whether because of the rather fearsome creature of the dark he had seen or because of the revealed power of this being beside him, he wasn't quite certain. He looked at her again, more intently.

She was very attractive and feminine and she smiled disarmingly back at him, but he wondered if there wasn't still a touch about her of the haughty severity of the older woman, queen of the Shadow-realm. 'No' it wasn't that, it was just her natural reserved-ness, he realised. A shyness that was almost a loneliness.

They regarded each other and the connection of their original intimacy started to grow again between them. He looked deep into her and found a question that might have come from her.

"Are you alone here?" Somewhere in the back of Johannus' mind were memories that told him the Goddess Hecate always remained without a consort.

Something changed between them. Her face had changed, but not in the way it had before. She was still the same except that she was grown into a fully mature woman. Caring eyes looked back at him; full of a mother's love and compassion.

Then, "Do you have any children?" he asked, before he had thought the question through.

"This is not a place for children" she said and Johannus had the feeling that the complexity of the being he was with was far greater than he could comprehend. He was a simpleton by comparison, but she was treating him as an equal for this moment, this place, and he appreciated that.

"Whom do you love?" This question came from her to him, wordlessly

He knew he couldn't lie and the first person his mind went to was Miriam. The beautiful Miriam who so loved and was beloved of the master Yeheshua. It was their love he sensed most strongly and his thoughts turned next, by association, to Mary Magdalene, with whom he had shared so much, in some ways…

Her love was also for Yeheshua and she had done much to help him understand why this was so. The master was helping those who came to him to uncover true love, and indeed he was worthy of love, Johannus' love, for everything that had come to pass. He had felt that love as real.

"Yeheshua," he replied and the woman by his side started slightly by this declaration.

"You have not even met him," she pointed out, and Johannus felt slightly ridiculous.

"No, but he has helped me to understand more about love and myself than any other, even though it has been through Mary and Miriam."

"What woman have you loved most then, in all of your world?"

Johannus sighed and a deep hurt pulled at his chest. He closed his eyes, for tears had come to them. Saltiness that made him screw them up... as if the sun shone too brightly...

He was lying on a beach; down at the coast from Antioch. He was here with other friends; all aged around fourteen. The sun was very bright and they had already swum in the sea, and now they lay drying themselves on the rocks.

Girls had joined them, a couple of whom Johannus knew. They stood around the rocks, not wearing much, as was the Greek fashion. There was one new girl to whom Johannus was irresistibly drawn. Fair of hair and face he thought her the most lovely person in the whole world. Her name was Jasmina.

The girls called to them to come and see a boat that had landed up the beach, but Johannus found that his young unruly manhood made getting up impossible. He feigned nonchalance and stayed where he was, but one of his friends made a comment that was close to the truth and others had laughed.

Jasmina had shot him a smile that melted his resistance and he forced himself to be able to join them and run down the beach after them. It was always a close thing though, keeping his body in check.

They had stayed on the beach well into the evening and made a fire from driftwood they collected. Someone produced a flagon of wine that had come with the boat, and someone else had caught a couple of fish that they cooked and shared out small mouthfuls of, around the group.

Jasmina had come to sit beside Johannus and he passed her the morsels of fish to eat. Her lips sought to take the bits directly from his fingers and he felt the immediate response from his loins. She seemed to know and he melted to her advances.

She pressed her knee against his thigh as they sat together and his hand slipped sideways to take hers. He could only follow the trembling promise of his heart. They kissed and he allowed his world to dissolve into the contact of their mouths, the soft sweetness of her lips and tasting tongue. Deep into the warm summer night they each gave their bodies over to their young love, sleeping through to a chillier dawn in each others arms.

She left with her friends in the morning and he vowed to her and himself to see her very soon. She smiled, enigmatically, and it was with great difficulty that he was able to follow up on this promise, finding that the girls he knew were very reticent to tell him where to reach her.

When he did manage to see her again, she had thrown her arms around him and broken down in tears. It seemed that since her return she had been promised by her family to another, in marriage.

She was much too young for that, Johannus had protested, but it seemed that it was the custom. She claimed that she had not known when they had met on the beach, and Johannus wished whole-heartedly to believe her; he had to.

Would she run away with him? he had asked, but with no real plan as to where or how; and she had seen that it was only a dream. He cursed himself and all the Gods of the Greeks that seemed to want to taunt him. Being Jewish was hard enough without this.

He never met anyone else that he could love as he had felt he could Jasmina, utterly brief though it had been. He tried, with several short liaisons following, and then he had sought rather to discover what forces shaped this universe and his being in it. Eventually this led to him following after the Magus Simon and all that had brought; though never with healing of the original wound of love.

"Jasmina" his heart grieved with the resurfaced pain, and his mind and mouth protested, "my Aphrodite".

"You cannot always trust Aphrodite," said the voice of Hecate close to his side and then "Johannus; Johannus." His name was being called over and over, several times.

CHAPTER 23.

Everything in my head became clearer. I realised that Miriam must have pulled down a part of the stacked stone wall herself, enough to get through to this chamber. I moved as far as I could to the side of the entrance hole to try to see where the light was coming in. It was softly beautiful but I still couldn't see the star that must be shining through some gap in the rock face opposite.

Breathing easier I settled back against the side of the alcove. The partly demolished wall next to me seemed to have stones that I could move aside, and so I tried. I didn't want to disturb Miriam but managed to move enough of them to see that the star shining past her left shoulder was Venus herself. She must be very low in the sky, close to dipping down over the horizon.

I stayed there, absorbed in the wonder of finding this magical moment in the place I least expected it, watching till the star did indeed disappear and the chamber went quite dark. I was no longer terrified though and I settled to my contemplation practice, just as we had in the cave that had become our home, for the last few days.

It wasn't as easy as it had been there because so much was happening and I was really tired now, but happy to have found Miriam. I closed my eyes and the blackness lessened, but my focus was weak and without realising it I slipped into an in-between state of dream and vision.

Miriam was there and so was the beautiful light, just on the other side of her, but the darkness all around was a tunnel of menace.

I was a spectator, not threatened by the Satanic darkness that appeared to be fully engaged in trying to snuff out the beauty of the light; and Miriam holding that light.

The harder I looked the more I was able to see. At first it had been as though Miriam was moving off, a long way down the tunnel, but as I gazed I got closer and saw that she was not holding the light but had her hand upon the shoulder of a figure she was following.

The figure contained the light and was the light. Miriam protected the light and was comforted in turn by its presence as they went on into the depths.

On and on, down and down; it seemed an eternity to me watching. How much further could they go without being engulfed? Unspeakable, unseeable, unthinkable entities rushed in on them but they could not reach the light. They fell back and others came on but the light was not diminished.

I watched, entranced to see the light live and grow, in despite of any surrounding evil and death.

Grew and expanded, living and full of love. Grew till it filled all space and became a sky; a sky that filled my sight as my ears were with the song of the stars; and Miriam was in the middle of it still. The darkness was entirely banished.

I don't know if I awoke or went to sleep but there was peace that I was lifted by and rested within.

When I opened my eyes again there was a tinge of light in the normal darkness, both up the tunnel and from the side chamber. Not much, but enough to show me Miriam lying on the floor.

Being able to see the rocks made it easier for me to move them, and so enlarge the hole to the side chamber. Then to crawl into the space where Miriam was.

Inside I could see that there was another narrow slot that had been cut into the rock, over the tunnel, when the chamber had been first formed. It was via this hole that some early morning light was entering, joining the last vestiges of the full moon's rays from the crack in the opposite wall.

There wasn't enough light to see anything clearly and not much room to move either. Miriam wasn't moving at all and I couldn't hear her breathing; everything was deathly still.

I wasn't worried at first, because the stillness was filled with peace, with no scent of the fears that had plagued us during the night. But when I failed to feel any of the movement of Miriam's breathing on her chest and then struggled to find her pulse, the dread of losing her became very real again.

Had she gone so far into the eternity of her love that she wouldn't return? I couldn't bear to think it and I whispered her name, close to her ear, with no result.

My pulse was racing again, even as I slowed my thoughts down and checked her more closely. Her breathing was shallow but I could just feel it on my cheek, when I put it close to her face. Her pulse was very slow and rather faint, but regular.

I did not dare shake her or anything like that but called her name a little louder and more urgently, still with no response.

Suddenly I felt the weight of the rock and darkness all around, pressing in on our little casket of space and air. I knew I must get Miriam out before she went further from us.

I manoeuvred her around onto her back with her head pointing towards the opening; which was hard to do in the restricted headroom. Getting behind her I was then able to lift her head into my lap and hook my hands under her armpits, edging backwards towards the tunnel.

We made some progress but I found it very tiring because of the cramped space I was working in. Once I got by back into the hole though, I got completely stuck. I couldn't go back or forwards either.

I was breathing hard from the exertion and glad to take a break; but Miriam seemed to be almost completely lifeless and this soon galvanised me into renewing my efforts. Still unable to go backwards, I found that I could shift Miriam to my left side and twist my torso forward into the chamber again.

Once free I wriggled backwards on my tummy and pushed myself into the tunnel, scraping my knees on some of the rocks. I could now reach back to

Miriam but couldn't get a good enough hold to be able to move her.

The light was slightly stronger from the other end of our black tunnel and I called out to Johannus and Bishmi; with no response; and then louder and louder again, but still getting no answer.

I didn't want to leave Miriam, but I definitely needed some help, so reluctantly I set off back up to the main chamber. My mind was trying to tell me that if I left, I could never get back to Miriam again, but I banished the thoughts forcefully.

Coming through the entrance I saw Johannus lying on the floor in the central space next to Bishmi who was leaning sideways against the raised plinth. Both were clearly fast asleep.

I remembered how Johannus had banged his head and I went over to see how he was. The light wasn't good enough to make a good inspection, but he seemed to have a bit of a gash on his forehead.

I turned to Bishmi and tried to rouse her but she was deeply asleep and I knew how the night's work must have exhausted her. I let her rest and went back to Johannus, calling his name over again as I tried to wake him as gently as the urgency I felt allowed.

He responded quite quickly, although the groan he let out as he tried to raise himself from the floor testified to what must have been quite a sore head.

I had found one of our water-skins and gave him it to drink, which he did, sitting on the floor.

I explained that I needed help to get Miriam back and asked if he would be able to. His worried expression told me all I needed to know. "Where is she? Is she all right?"

He had struggled to his feet and I put my hand on his arm. "She is all right, I think," I said, "but I am not certain. I really want to get her back here."

"Where is she?" he asked again, and I led him towards the entrance of the low passageway, that sloped down into darkness.

He hesitated, pulling back from me, and I understood his fear, only too well, though in the half-light of the outer chamber it didn't seem quite so ominous to me as it had in the night earlier. I saw his hand search for the sword at his side, but it was somewhere back on the floor behind us.

"It is all right; I know the layout now," I said. "The master said that you would help us with this task; and now is our moment..."

He looked at me with a slight look of wonder on his face and said, "I will be all right. I have never liked dark holes of this sort, that is all; but I shall be fine, with your help."

We got down the passage with me leading Johannus with one hand and both of us trailing our other hand along a wall until I reached the rocks on the floor.

Johannus crouched there whilst I squeezed my way back into the chamber. "Follow me as far as you can," I said, "then I shall get Miriam through to you from the other side, if we work together."

Inside the small side chamber, I found Miriam, and found again that her vital signs seemed very faint. 'Were they lessened?' I asked myself but put any doubt aside as I set myself to what I had to do.

I was able to position myself over Miriam's body and move her head and shoulders a little towards where Johannus was. "Can you reach her?" I asked, putting my hand out to him, and guiding his to her shoulder. "See if you can get both your hands under her arms, and I shall move her by her hips," I said, and he did as I instructed, after squeezing himself as far as he could into the gap.

We made good progress and in the near complete darkness were able to get Miriam's body through the hole and out into the passage. With Johannus' help the task of getting her back to the main chamber was relatively easy, but we were still pretty exhausted as we carried her and placed her limp body next to the central plinth.

Bishmi had awoken during Johannus and my exertions back into the chamber and she was soon fussing around Miriam, checking how she was. There were cuts on her hands and feet that weren't too serious but apart from these she seemed okay.

We washed the cuts and grazes and wrapped them in strips of soft clean cloth. There wasn't anything else we could do till she awoke, which had to come from her own self.

We laid her so that she was bathed in a halo of light from through the cave's mouth, a rolled up cloak under her head and another over her. Bishmi put one of the rods of Ma'at in each of her hands, placed by her sides. I kissed her on her forehead, which was colder than I would have wished.

"Where is Johannus?" asked Bishmi as we raised ourselves from off our knees.

"Outside I think," I answered, for I knew he had been hankering for the light and fresh air.

"Perhaps we should join him. We have done what we can for the moment." I nodded but I was rather loathe to leave Miriam thus; but looking down on her she was completely at peace, and I knew Bishmi was right.

We squeezed around the thorn bush that almost concealed the fissure that formed the cave entrance and came out blinking into the early morning light. The sun was shining on some nearby mountain tops, but not yet here.

Johannus was not around the cave entrance, but we stayed close, still mindful of the commotions of the night before. Indeed, strangely, we heard what sounded as if the commotions were still going on or had been renewed for sounds of what sounded like distant fighting came to us there.

Just as we were wondering what we could do and what had happened to Johannus, he came scrabbling down the side of a rocks. "I am sorry to have gone off without telling you", he said, "but you seemed to be busy and I had to try to see what the noise was about."

"Well, what did you find out?" I asked him.

"There is fighting going on, further to the north, but not far away. I could only see the dust clouds and hear the cries; and the occasional horn blowing; but whilst I was watching it was moving off, away towards the west I'd say."

We wondered what it meant, and Johannus asked how Miriam was. We could only say that we didn't know and a slight glumness fell upon us, the morning suddenly feeling rather chilly.

We were standing there like that when someone said, "Kardun will be here soon." I looked around to who had spoken to see a figure in a cloak standing beside us. For a moment I was thrown but as the hood fell back, I recognised the gentle smile. From beyond hope Miriam had come back to us.

Kardun went back to the animals and strung them together in a line he could lead across the remaining gap from the rocks to the real foothills of the mountains.

It was impossible for him to tell if there were any Ghosters about and onto his trail but as soon as he got to the foothills he headed north along their lower reaches, confident that he could escape their clutches even if they spotted him now.

He knew these mountains well. He knew how far he had to go to find the goat-track that he had once climbed down, and first of all he knew where he could leave the horses and camels, and Sarah.

Once satisfied that they were well enough hidden and secure Kardun was able to strike out on his own, a free man in the night. The full moon shone down, showing him all the way-signs he needed.

Looking out across the plain there was movement in the dust, and far-off calls that might have been either human or animal. There were still a lot of terrible things happening.

The climb was hard and he knew that it would take him maybe several hours to reach the guard-post he sought. He thought he could get there in time... but in time for what?

Making contact with the guards was tricky. There was a good chance he would get killed before he could explain why he was there; especially with the fear that was heavy around this approach point to the city.

He stayed in the rocks close to the guard post, watching for something to lead him in. He had to move from cover soon even though he hadn't decided how to do it. How ironic to have evaded all the dangers only to falter on the doorstep of safety. He broke his cover but hesitated, caught in his indecision.

A plumed helmet crossed in front of the brazier's light; a Roman officer's helmet. Kardun's heart leaped; he recognised the way the man held himself, the set of his shoulders under his cloak. It was Antonius, who had led the guard that had brought Miriam, Mary and Johannus to Rekem.

"Antonius," Kardun called loudly. "Antonius, I come looking for your aid. My name is Kardun, husband of the priestess Bishmi and guide to the priestess Leila."

Guards sprang out from their posts, shields held at the ready and spears pointing into the shadows that concealed Kardun. "Wait," commanded the Roman officer, "I do know this man. Let him come forward into the light, unharmed."

Thankful, Kardun stumbled out from his vantage place, hands wide and empty.

Antonius had found it difficult to sleep. The caravan that he and his men were helping to escort from Port Lucius to Gaza was due to leave Kadesh-Rekem in the morning. But the reports of the desert fighters, the Djinn worshippers or 'Ghosters', having crossed the Sharra mountains was making everyone nervous. The king himself had led an expedition against them but had not been able draw them into a proper fight. Mostly they had evaded his forces and he was not best pleased.

This man Kardun was now telling him that these Ghosters had gathered into an attack on the fortified settlement on the other side of the Great Wadi. Kardun believed the Ghosters had tried hard to set a net that would prevent anyone from escaping across to give warning, but that his party, which included Miriam and Mary, had managed to evade them and cross over the plain.

The news that Miriam, Mary and Johannus were close by surprised Antonius because he had heard the story of how they had slighted the king and how furious he was.

On the other hand, Kardun was presenting a fantastic opportunity to attack the Ghosters when they least expected it, but Antonius knew he would have to be very careful. He had liked Miriam and Mary and did not want to deliver them to the king if they didn't wish that, but neither could he afford to anger the king himself.

Kardun's suggestion was to cross the wadi before dawn, whilst the Ghosters were still terrorising it, and take them from their rear, before they had melted away at first light, which was their way. This meant that the Roman and Nabatean force would have to assemble and set out very soon, in the middle of the night.

Antonius thought he could get his men ready but would need the help of a willing Nabatean officer.

The man commanding the guard seemed reluctant to commit men to a venture without the direct command of his superior and so Antonius decided that he would go and wake the man in question and speak to him directly.

Kardun waited at the guard post and after a while Antonius reappeared with a sleepy looking Nabatean officer who was not much older than a boy.

Antonius was explaining to the young commander why it would take too long to go through the channels to wake the king, which is what Halderas wished to do. "We have to reach them while the night is still here. This is what we have never managed to do; but Kaldrun here can pinpoint their positions for us."

"How can we trust this man? Who is he?"

"He is the guide to High priestess Leila of the Al-Uzza temple; there is no-one we can trust more."

The tousle haired young aristocrat peered at Kardun who withstood his gaze easily but said nothing else. He could have mentioned Miriam and Mary, but stopped himself in time.

Antonius had fetched a piece of parchment scroll and was busy writing on

It. "Here Halderas; I am writing to the King. I offer all the success of this proposed venture to his fame, as we share the essential aim and desire to defeat these raiders. However, I will accept any defeat suffered directly on my own shoulders, as the consequence of my impetuosity. Here, I shall place my seal on this my word. "He was heating some wax over a flame. "Only, we have to dare to win; we cannot hesitate. All I ask is for an equal portion of your Nabatean soldiers to fight alongside those of Rome. That way you, and the king, can claim the victory for Nabatea."

The matter was so important for Antonius because the caravan and all his troops were seriously at risk with these murderous bands loose on the trail. Much better if he could find and fight them before the caravan left the safety of Rekem. Many more troops stayed in Rekem than accompanied the caravans.

Halderas apparently came to similar conclusions and throwing off the remnants of sleepy indecision he threw himself to the task alongside his Roman colleague.

It wasn't long before they had assembled their troops and were briefing them with Kardun's help.

Kardun explained how he believed the Ghosters were arrayed. Separate bands had come together to attack the settlement on the other side of the Great Wadi. Small groups would have been searching out and testing the least defended portions of the town since early nightfall, spreading their awful brand of fear, whilst others patrolled a line across the wadi to ensure no-one could escape to Rekem to raise the alarm. Well before dawn they would amass and overrun the defences, complete their despoiling of all they found, and then withdraw again, before even the first streaks of dawn showed in the sky.

A plan was quickly made to strike with a third of the combined Roman and Nabatean force, straight towards Casa Barnea, but with two flanking groups circling wide around either side and slightly behind the initial attack. It was hoped that the first would split the Ghosters, causing them to flee, but straight into the flanking forces.

A spare mount was found for Kardun and he rode with Antonius back down the mountains, full moon to their front. It was starting its descent towards the furthest horizon but they should have enough time to make their strike,

Kardun had time to explain a few things to Antonius about his need to meet his wife and her priestess guests at first light. Antonius, for his part, was quick to understand and they made an agreement that Kardun should start with the southern flanking group, but break away to ensure that his charges were still safe.

Assuming a successful outcome to the battle, Antonius would sound the horns when Casa Barnea had been secured, and Kardun would meet him there, with Miriam and the others.

It was a reasonably good plan and one that worked quite as well as could be expected. They were perhaps a little later than they would have wished though for Ghosters had started to amass together just when Antonius led his first charge into their confused ranks.

Because they were no longer spread out in groups across the wadi, the ghosters preferred to stand and fight, rather than being split apart as Antonius' plan intended. But they underestimated the numbers against them, seeing only the first third of the attacking force, and when the two flanking columns came around and behind them, they completely panicked, trying to flee but with no way to go.

Fighting was fierce, the ghosters being caught like rats. Kardun was not a fully trained soldier but he had been armed with a spear and a sword and given a watching brief from the left flank. He wanted to keep an eye on any ghosters trying to escape in that direction; his first duty being to protect Miriam, Mary and the others.

Suddenly a small group of ghosters managed to break out of the vice-like grip of the Nabateans on the left flank and raced for the comparative safety of the hills behind them.

Kardun watched as several of the Nabateans took up the pursuit. He followed at a slight distance. In front it seemed the ghosters would reach the hills, whilst an increasingly long way behind him the battle continued unabated.

He pulled up his mount and looked around. The light was growing and more of the plain was becoming visible, but he was at the limit of his range of sight.

He started to retrace his steps, anxious that nothing should happen without his notice. Ahead he thought he could see a horseman out on the plain. Had another ghoster escaped unnoticed, whilst he was following the other pursuit?

Kardun urged his mount forward, out across the plain, determined to intercept this ghostly figure that seemed to be going exactly where Kardun least wanted.

We all embraced the returned Miriam. Tears of gratitude poured down my cheeks and I laughed as I brushed them aside with the back of my hand.

The morning sun had not yet reached the spot where we stood but its brightness lit up the highest places of the rocks about us.

"Let's move down to where we left the camels and horses," suggested Johannus. "That is where Kardun will bring them, if he is not already there."

We assented to this and he started to lead the way, limping a bit from his recent accident with his sword. "On second thoughts, I think I should go first and check that it is clear," he said.

We followed quietly at a safe distance while Johannus went to the next bend ahead and signalled the 'all clear'. Soon we found ourselves at the spot where our rocky path met the way in from the Great Wadi. Kardun was not there yet, but the sunlight was starting to penetrate the thin layer of early mist that had seeped into the far end of our canyon.

"Didn't I actually say to Kardun to meet us at the cave entrance?" An unaccustomed note of doubt sounded in Miriam's voice.

"I don't think it matters," said Bishmi, pointing to the mounted figure coming up out of the mist. "He is coming here now."

He saw us as well and urged his horse forward, just as we realised that it was not Kardun.

His arm was not upraised in greeting, rather it brandished a javelin-like spear and he was riding directly towards us with menacing speed and intent. There would be no chance to escape.

Miriam was standing tall; not moving out of the way. I grabbed her by the arm and tried to pull her towards some rocks. Our world seemed to have slowed down but nevertheless the rider was closing swiftly, arm pulled back, ready to release his deadly missile, directly at us.

Johannus dashed forward to intercept the attacking ghoster, with little thought of his own safety. At the last moment the rider saw him and adjusted his aim to strike him down, releasing the spear with fierce venom.

But the spear went wide of its intended mark, but only because another had caught the rider between the shoulder blades. Kardun had frantically galloped the last mile knowing Bishmi and us others would be here, ready to greet him.

All this happened so quickly. Miriam was still standing and I was clinging to her arm. Kardun immediately dismounted and came over to us, pulling his horse behind him and praising Isis in finding us safe.

Many horns sounded across the plains. Kardun now explained how he had been able to give Antonius the chance to entrap the ghosters, more completely than any previous attempt, and that the mass horns were a pre-arranged signal of his completed victory. We could join him now, across on the other side of the Great Wadi.

There was no rush and first we found a hollow in which to place the dead ghoster and cover his body with stones, before Miriam left with Kardun, using the ghoster's horse to help collect our own mounts.

We others climbed back to find a secure spot, away from anyone, and it was a chance for me to share with Bishmi the wonder of having found this tomb.

"Not only have you and Kardun brought this victory to King Aretas, but you alone will know where this special place is, and as priestesses will be able to bring the King here. Only the King, and on his own he will experience the need fo some humility. I think this will be the most wonderfully auspicious way to start your term as Manat's priestess."

Bishmi had grown in so many ways. I could see her taking in this gift that Miriam had given her, and which she would only share with Leila and a few others, and together they could bring the King here; no others.

She had no fears now and smiled at me. "Yes, this changes much. I feel most blessed, and can hardly wait to take this news to Yresmin; that all is well."

Meeting Antonius again was a happy moment despite the evidence of the fighting that was still all around. There were many dead and some wounded ghosters and a few soldiers as well, but it had clearly been an overwhelming victory to the combined Roman and Nabatean forces.

Antonius agreed to accompany Halderas, the Nabatean commander, back to Rekem's outer gateway but he wanted Halderas to go with Kardun and Bishmi into the city and claim this victory for King Artetas. Antonius still intended to lead his laden caravan to Gaza, and needed it to leave before midday.

Halderas protested but Antonius was clear about what he was going to do and the Nabatean officer's authority did not extend beyond the city of Rekem. Besides, if Antonius wanted him to take most of the credit for the victory, he wouldn't continue to argue about it.

Bishmi embraced Miriam knowing the anxiety that Miriam felt in letting her take the brunt of whatever the king was going to throw at her.

"I am ready Miriam," she said. "It was Yresmin that sent me on this mission; and I am doing this for her as well. I go back to Kadesh-Rekem in a triumphal procession. What better beginning could the new priestess of Manat ask for?"

"Thank you dear Bishmi," answered Miriam. "Thank you, my lady," answered Bishmi and they hugged each other again for long moments.

Then Bishmi came to me and we embraced as well. There were no words I could find other than the tears in my eyes, and she kissed my cheeks and pressed my hands in hers.

Briefly she went to Johannus who was with Kardun. Johannus embraced them both, and Kardun came over to say his farewells to us as well.

Then she had taken Kardun by the hand and gone over to Halderas to congratulate them both in the great victory and to take her place between them for the return to Rekem.

I saw that she carried the rods of Maat folded across her chest and she held her head high as she shone like a calmness over the field of death. The soldiers cheered.

*

Our ride to the border was swift and relatively uneventful. Antonius had understood our wishes and they worked perfectly for what he wanted as well. Going home.

BOOK 3: CELEBRATION

Yeheshua spoke, "God, the Creator is complete, all-mighty and glorious;
and the creation is also magnificent; wonderful in every detail."
"It is we that see it as broken, tarnished and full of pain and hardship.
This is the inheritance of sin and death which we clasp hungrily to our breast."
"I come to tell you that you can make your world whole again, for in Truth it
has never been broken, and your heart is aching to reveal that fullness to you."

CHAPTER 1.

We rode up into Bethany. Johannus took his horse back to his uncle, leaving Miriam and I at Lazarus' house.

He promised he would join us again for the evening meal.

*

Johannus led his mare along the dusty track that terminated at his uncle's house. There were three donkeys that he didn't recognise tethered in the small paddock; he wondered a little who they belonged to.

His aunt answered his knock on their front door and fussed around him as she greeted his return. "What marvellous timing," she was saying, "there are relatives of mine visiting us from Egypt. We so want them to meet you."

"Why is that?" Johannus asked; he couldn't think why his aunt would want her relatives to meet him.

"Just come and see," she said, patting Johannus' hand between both of her rather leathery, wrinkled ones.

As his aunt ushered Johannus into the house's main room he saw his uncle was talking to another man of about the same age who wore the elegant robes of a person of some wealth. A slighter figure was seated beside him, wearing a loose gauze veil across the lower half of her face.

"Johannus," cried his uncle, heartily; "welcome back, my brother's son. I hope you have returned my favourite horse in one piece." Johannus' uncle had crossed over to him with remarkable swiftness. "Come and meet your cousin's cousin. We were just talking of you."

Johannus felt the eyes of the man, his aunt's cousin, scanning him in a not unfriendly way as they grasped hands. His name was Petrakis and his uncle described him as one of the great businessmen of Alexandria. Johannus took in the sharp intelligence of the older man, who then turned and introduced his daughter Rebecca.

Her eyes regarded him from behind long lashes, her chin lifting with the hint of a smile, which he returned. His gaze slid over the fashionable headwear that hung gold-leafed dangles across her forehead and saw that she was a beautiful girl, with or without the decoration and despite the partial concealment afforded by the loose veil.

Something told him that the businessman Petrakis was looking for a suitable husband for his daughter, and that somehow he, Johannus, was being considered as a candidate.

He had learnt some things about himself in his life and knew of his weakness for feminine beauty, and his fickleness from its influence. Somehow this was different though; it wasn't happening because of his desire and choice. It was beyond his expectations and he felt a bit out of his depth.

At any other time in his life he might have thought this to have been the most desirable opportunity imaginable but just at this point there were other things uppermost in his mind. He was on his way to see the master Yeheshua; and he was escorting the master's own beloved; the lady that Johannus admired most in all the world: Miriam.

He told himself that he could marry this Rebecca and he almost laughed at the wild idea. 'You *will* marry her,' Johannus heard himself thinking but he soberly set this thought aside.

She raised her eyebrows and he bowed a little to her. His errant thoughts were ready to offer her anything in his power to give but Johannus asked her instead whether she was enjoying the travelling.

She said she was and then suddenly Johannus realised her father was asking him how he was employed.

This line of questioning usually left him feeling somehow 'unworthy' but today this self-doubt couldn't touch him, so buoyed up he was with having completed the return journey from Kadesh and its desert environs, and of having helped his friends succeed in their mission.

He told Petrakis a little of what he had seen in and around the Nabatean capital, Kadesh-Rekem, and described some of the troubles that king Aretas had been having with the 'ghosters', ending with what he knew of the battle of Kadesh-Barnea, as Miriam called it; and how their guide and friend, Kardun, had been able to lead the soldiers to pin down the elusive raiders.

Johannus' uncle interrupted him… "but really, John, you are a trained silver-smith, isn't that where you see your future efforts taking you?" Johannus could see his uncle was trying to present him in a more attractive light; as a possible husband for Rebecca, but Petrakis himself was still caught up in Johannus' story.

He had heard there had been similar 'ghoster' problems up near Damascus and that several of the Nabatean trade routes had suffered as a result of them. The news of the victory in the wilderness was important to Petrakis who was involved in the distribution of the goods that came through Alexandria. He looked at Johannus with some respect.

"I am not sure that I will return to silver-working again, uncle," answered Johannus, belatedly. "There are many things going on that I need to attend to; but I am not ruling anything out either."

"Quite right," Petrakis said. "If you face your future with fixed ideas then what you will find is bound to be very limited too." He continued, following the line of their previous discussion, "it is rumoured that King Herod is not blameless of supporting these raiders into Nabatea's flank. What do you think?"

It was unusual for Johannus to find his opinions given so much weight by serious minded people. He felt himself being drawn deeper into unfamiliar territory. "I don't know but it seemed the king was anxious to meet with… Miriam." He almost immediately regretted saying this, as he didn't want to go into explanations of the Goddesses Al-Lat and Al-Uzza, let alone his part in finding the bethel-stone.

"I wonder why that was?" asked Petrakis, stroking his short beard. Johannus mumbled "I… I don't really know," but the visitor was pursuing the lines of his own thinking. "Could it be that the rabbi Yeshua you spoke of is looking for an alliance with King Aretas? We know the Jewish priests already seem to fear his power."

"I would say not; definitely not. We made a considerable effort to avoid being detained by the Nabatean king." Again, he felt uncomfortable to be discussing the Lady Miriam's business but Petrakis seemed unwilling to let the subject drop. "Yet you said that you had contact with Aretas' generals and were able to deliver up the raiders to them?"

"We did, but more through the influence of the priestesses than the army," answered Johannus, and then found himself responding with forceful words that surprised even himself. "The kingdom that the master Yeheshua teaches about is of the heart, not of worldly alliances with kings or any others."

He had spoken with certainty and authority even, yet he also knew he was only really repeating what Miriam and Mary had told him, despite the baptism he had received. Nevertheless, he felt good about setting the record straight, his sense of ease returning.

Petrakis was nodding. "You are going to see him yourself?"

"I am," said Johannus, feeling the whole encounter was somehow in the balance. The moment stretched out and Johannus glanced towards the girl who smiled encouragingly at him. He relaxed and smiled a little in response.

Suddenly Petrakis was changing the subject. "Knowledge is power," he said. "In my business I really have to know what goods are coming into Alexandria; when and how; by ship or caravan. I have to be able to keep ahead of my competitors. More and more I am looking for trusted people to help me. Do you think this could interest you Johannus?"

This question again caught Johannus by surprise. Petrakis was valuing him higher than he did himself. He paused because he didn't know exactly where this was going. "It could do," he said finally, and his answer seemed to some-what satisfy Petrakis.

A glance at his uncle Mikael though, who was shaking his head, told Johannus that he thought him being unbelievably casual about this apparently wonderful offer. He turned back to Petrakis who was speaking again.

"Well, I shall be returning at Passover, Johannus. I should like you to think about it and maybe we can discuss the possibilities further."

Johannus' aunt had bustled around the edge of the group, coming up beside Johannus. "You are staying to eat with us, aren't you Joh…?"

"I am afraid I can't Aunty Jessica," he said. "I have already promised to be at Lazarus' house for tonight's meal."

"Surely you could change that," she said, frowning at him. 'Was there no end to his ability to risk everything he was being given?' was the thought that Johannus read in the lines of her forehead. "You wouldn't want to slight our guests," she added quietly, nodding towards Rebecca, who smiled back sweetly.

"Maybe I could visit again tomorrow morning..." he said, knowing that as Petrakis and Rebecca were staying with his uncle and aunt, he would need to find another place to sleep.

Mollified slightly, his aunt agreed that he should come on the morrow and stay for lunch as well.

CHAPTER 2.

Yresmin had been sitting in her little alcove of the great temple-tomb, a virtual prisoner of the king's displeasure, when the news of Bishmi's return reached her.

She smiled to herself, savouring the reported victory over the terrorising Ghosters and the part her protégé had played in their rout.

The Ghosters were Djinn worshippers from the deep desert who had been terrorising Nabatean villages for months. The king's expedition against them found them to be an elusive enemy, but Bishmi and her husband Kardun had delivered them into the hands of one of the King's brightest young generals.

Yresmin knew that now she would be able to pass her position as High priestess of the Goddess Manat over to Bishmi, without any objection from the King. Her priestess had excelled in every way, earning Aretas' respect and gratitude.

And the re-discovery of the location of the tomb of Moses' sister Miriam was more than she could have dreamed of.

Yresmin would be free to follow her heart's greatest desire.

It was over thirty years since she had come to Kadesh-Rekem, barely more than a girl, to serve the goddess, following the star of Destiny. Following it from her fishing village far down in the south, for her heart had called to her, telling her things that she now called the promise of the Divine; of Hope and Love and a new start.

Yresmin had spent all her life trying to make that Destiny happen. Manat was the Goddess of Fate and Destiny and, accepted as one of her few priestesses, Yresmin gradually became privy to Her most intimate secrets.

The greatest of these concerned the Prophecy of the Divine King.

"He will come to rule through the crux of wood and open tomb of stone;" where 'crux of wood' could also read as 'crossroads of wood'.

Yresmin had spent the best part of her life trying to bring this into reality. On becoming High-priestess of Manat she had married the greatest architect in Kadesh, infusing him with the dream to build the most wonderful temple-tomb of all time.

When he died in the building accident, she had carried on their dream, constructing her interpretation of the crux and crossroads of wood within the great rock cut temple itself; making it into a wonderfully compact dwelling-place, fit for the Divine King's arrival.

Aretas had thought this would be his royal tomb and for a while Yresmin had wondered whether indeed Aretas could be the Chosen One.

He was certainly a great king and she was pleased that he took the title 'friend of the people', even if it was to annoy the Romans. Yet he wasn't the one her heart had spoken of; of that she became sure.

So many years of dedication and devotion had Yresmin put into the edifice that it almost became the purpose in itself; and the years wore on and no Saviour-King had come.

Then, a couple of weeks ago the most unexpected arrival of all happened, fulfilling a favourite, but not entirely un-related prophecy, about the Queens of Heaven. How they would travel the earth and restore a lost stone to its place of honour.

When Miriam and Mary arrived out of the desert bearing the stone that had been lost in a Ghoster ambush, the whole of Kadesh-Rekem had seized the news with fervour. Their favourite goddesses had come to earth and were here for them.

Yresmin was slightly sceptical about the talk of Al-Uzza and Al-Lat being present on earth and, whether it was true or not, she wouldn't be distracted from her own purpose.

What she wasn't prepared for though was how the presence and words of Miriam and Mary rekindled a special feeling in her heart. Their talk of the master Yeheshua struck a chord within her that she recognised as the same pull that had brought her here, from her village, all those years ago.

At that moment, with that clarity, it was an easy thing for her to let go of everything she had put her life's energy into and to decide to go to Palestine, to find Yeheshua.

Since then, the time and days had stretched while she awaited the outcome of Miriam's quest; and to see if the king's displeasure would wane for the part he believed Yresmin must have played in their escape.

She knew it was out of her hands, but felt oddly confident that Fate and Destiny were on her side; almost as though the Goddess she herself served was actually stooping to serve her priestess.

Bishmi had come and knelt before her old mistress, and Yresmin had pulled her to her feet and hugged her. The daughter of her heart if not her womb. She had not succeeded in having children of her own.

Letting go of all this happiness and to follow her resolve to go to Palestine was much harder now after those weeks had passed and the day of leaving had finally dawned.

Yresmin decided to go into town to where Bishmi lived in the house she was inheriting from her mistress. It was a fine house that Yresmin had lived in with her husband, Jeorkim, the architect. But after his fall during the sculpting of the temple façade, she had left their house and taken up almost permanent residence in their nearly finished temple.

She walked up the dusty route into the centre, loosing her great mass of curly hair from the scarf that bound it. It had turned greyer in recent years but it was still the feature she was most recognised for; her signature.

When she set it free, as she had today, it was thought she could be approached by those looking for Manat's blessing and indeed she very often obliged those seekers that came to her then.

But when it was tied tightly back in a great knot at the back of her head she seemed like a brooding eagle and few dared to interrupt her for anything other than urgent business; unless perhaps it was one of her temple builders that she worked so closely with.

Today people seemed somewhat surprised to see her but many greeted her cheerfully. She recognised some but knew only a few to talk to. Bishmi knew many, many more and would no doubt conduct her priestess-ship in a completely different style.

Yresmin passed the amphitheatre and, further on, the great temple of Dushara where several young priests bowed towards her as she went by.

At the crossroads she turned left towards the market and so to the entrance of her house. Bishmi would be surprised to see her as they had planned to do the hand-over that evening, down at the temple; but Yresmin wanted to ask her friend for a final favour.

It was the nut-brown face of Kardun, Bishmi's husband, that broke into a well-creased smile as he opened the door to her. Kardun was the chief scout to the priestesses, ever since he had guided Leila here from Egypt, many years back.

"Is Leila here?" asked Yresmin, though she wasn't sure why she thought she might have been.

"Yes, she is actually," answered Kardun. "Come in, come in, we see much too little of you here in your own home."

"It is your house now Kardun, my old friend; but if I should return, I will ask your favour that you let me have the back room to stay in."

"Of course, Chosen; always. It shall always be kept ready for you."

They went through to the inner courtyard where Leila and Bishmi were sitting together, in the shade of a graceful arch.

"Mistress Yresmin," said Bishmi, rising quickly to greet her; "what a wonderful surprise."

Yresmin hugged first Bishmi and then Leila, who smiled deeply.

Leila had tried to dissuade Yresmin from leaving Kadesh, but once she saw how serious Manat's priestess was, she was glad for her. It was a long journey that Yresmin was embarking on but of them all it was Leila who had actually met the master Yeheshua, a few years back when he was travelling through Kadesh to Egypt.

She was almost tempted to join Yresmin, now that the day had arrived, but she knew that it could not be. Somehow the Fates had cleared the way for her friend but not at this time for her.

Yresmin turned to Bishmi with her request. "Would you cut this great mass of hair off me, before I go, Bishmi dear?"

Bishmi was non-plussed and, as they all took in what it meant, she burst into tears.

"Mistress Yresmin," she said. "Please don't ask this of me. I cannot cut your

268

hair; that means so much to everyone."

Yresmin was shocked. She really hadn't expected this reaction, but before the moment became too painful Leila stepped forward.

"I shall cut your hair; if that is your wish," she said.

Relief coursed round the room and Yresmin gave Bishmi a consoling hug.

They took their places whilst Bishmi went to fetch the cutters, and a girl came into the courtyard carrying a tray of drinks. She was tall and darkly clad, reminding Yresmin somehow of her younger self. She didn't think she had met her before.

"This is Selina," said Leila, introducing the young woman. "She has been chosen to take Bishmi's role in service to Manat and her high priestess." It had been necessary to find a suitable helper for Bishmi, but it had been thought best not to involve Yresmin. Wouldn't it be like rubbing salt into whatever wounds she might be feeling?

Yresmin looked into the serious face of the young woman with her large dark eyes and nodded in approval, accepting the bow in return from Selina.

"And I thought that Selly was coming with me," she said to Leila, who laughed. Selina was also the name of Yresmin's donkey that was going to Palestine with her. "Even as I take my old friend away, she is transformed."

Leila took the cutters from Bishmi and asked Yresmin how she wanted her hair cut.

"I don't wish to be recognised as 'that priestess of Manat'," Yresmin replied. "Please cut it short but not too short."

Yresmin sat there, with Leila cutting off her fine mass of locks and Bishmi kneeling in front of her, holding her hands, and still unable to restrain occasional tears from rolling down her cheeks. Yresmin patted her friend's hands and told her how much she approved of her choice of Selina, which just made Bishmi burst into sobs again.

"Bishmi dear, I shall quite probably be coming back and asking to stay with you and Kardun… so please stop this crying. It will spoil the start of my pilgrimage."

Bishmi accepted the gentle scolding in good spirit and wiped her nose and eyes.

When the job was done Yresmin surveyed her new haircut in the polished mirror. She nodded to Leila and smiled broadly to everyone. "Free at last" she said with a particularly fierce grimace at Bishmi. They laughed and she went off to pack the last few things she had decided it would be useful to take, both for the journey and on reaching Palestine.

She came back with her bag and went out the back to meet with Kardun. He was already there with Selly, whose pannier he had been packed with food and drink and all the essentials he decided that Yresmin needed.

"I don't need all this," she told him, but he answered her with a grin, "then you can give it away or share it with people you meet on your way". She sighed a little, accepting the burden he was giving her, but knowing she would enjoy the giving and be even more pleased when it had gone. Time to get going.

CHAPTER 3.

I was so glad Miriam and I had arrived at the house of Lazarus to stay with Martha, Mary and Lazarus; though I sensed we would not be staying for very long.

After the joyful greetings, involving the giving of some little gifts we brought with us and our taking their offered refreshments, I was shown to a private area where I would be sleeping and the washing place where a special treat of a hot water tub was being prepared for me; a wonderful gift after our long journeying.

I felt that here I was both a guest and at home; a luxury that allowed me to be at ease in taking a private hour after I had lifted my body from the scented bath. Refreshed in every way I went again in search of my host and hostesses.

Martha and Mary were in their workroom, kneeling on opposite sides of a low bench-table, working together on stitching the sleeve of some sort of garment that was stretched between them.

After watching for a little while, I realised they were putting the finishing threads into a wonderful robe that they were surely making for Yeheshua; of soft wool and silks that they had put together in such a way that it would have no discernible seams.

I stood silently to see how they were doing this. Martha stitched a single silken strand across where a seam would have been, weaving it into the other side, through the weft of the sleeve; and Mary threaded the next needle with a fresh silk thread.

Once they had done several of these cross-threads Mary then pulled the shorter woollen strands across from each side, with a slim hook-ended tool; and then they turned it over and repeated the silken stitching on the other side, intertwining with the first side's strands.

Fascinated by their patient skill with this section of the last join, I realised it was no wonder that such a garment would cost a small fortune. Even as I watched, engrossed, a gentle laugh that was now so familiar sounded from somewhere behind me.

I half turned to see Lazarus and Miriam coming to join me by the opening.

Martha and Mary looked up and smiled at us before returning to their work. We stepped inside to join them.

Miriam wasn't wearing her customary headscarf; as she hadn't either the last time we stayed in Lazarus' house. She slipped down onto some cushions beside Martha and to my surprise I noticed how different the colour of her hair was from what I had come to expect. It was a light brown now instead of being the nearly black colour I remembered; and on the top of her head, I could see that it was growing-in fairer still.

If anything, she looked even more beautiful than she had before and I was quite surprised that I had only just noticed the colour change; but then again, she was accustomed to keep her head covered, and in the desert cave that we had recently shared the light hadn't been enough to show the difference.

Martha voiced the thoughts I was having, "Miriam your hair has changed, but how lovely it looks. How did that happen? Were you dying it to keep it dark?"

"Yes, I was," Miriam smiled conspiratorially. "Ever since I lost my heart to my Lord Yeheshua, nothing else mattered after having to leave him in Heliopolis. Dying my hair black became just one way for me to grieve for my loss."

I wondered at this revelation, seeing some kind of sense in it.

"Then, when he sent me on this quest, I thought… I thought to try to let the light back into it; so I stopped colouring it dark."

Mary took the opportunity to ask the question I had been wanting to for days: "And, the quest he gave you; did you find what he sent you for? Are you able to tell us what it was?"

Surely the room itself was straining to listen to Miriam's reply. She had leant forward, apparently studying the garment that the sisters had made, but as she raised her face to us again it displayed a warmth that connected directly with our hopes.

"Yes I did…. Yes, I found more than I could ever have dreamt possible, and some of it I can share with you, I think. I'm not sure how much but I can try if you like."

Happily, we moved closer around her, in unspoken response to this offer; and sat together as if being included in a giant hug.

"We went to the Nabatean capital, Rekem-in-Kadesh, in the mountains of Sherra, as Yeheshua had suggested." She looked at me. "We had many adventures, not least because Mary and myself had somehow been identified with two of their goddesses and King Aretas himself wanted to discover what this fuss was about. Though we were able to escape his attentions we found out for ourselves that there were large raiding parties of Djinn worshippers abroad in the wilderness, threatening all they came across."

I sat there remembering how we had camped in the caves of a steep-sided valley, in just the area where our people might have sojourned when they left Egypt, following Moses all those centuries ago. How lucky they had been to be living directly under his guidance, I had realised.

Miriam had opened our eyes to the meaning of those apparently wasted years in the wilderness and here, sitting with Lazarus and his sisters, it made me reflect on just how fortunate I had been to have met Yeheshua in my life. Not just to be alive here where he is but to have been able to recognise his Messiah-ship and to be sharing in his mission, in some way, however small.

Part of that sharing was to be sitting here with these friends, feeling so thankful for how lucky we were.

How many more people, some who had power to help Yeheshua, instead seemed to prefer to go and argue with him and try to trip him up? Perhaps

I would have been the same except for the trials that had beset me. Strange indeed how things worked out.

Miriam had moved on to describe how we had come upon the tomb of Miriam of old, at the height of our extreme need.

With a little shiver I remembered as well following after where Miriam had gone, down a low dark tunnel into the place to where Moses' sister had been laid to rest; and how my fear had turned to wonder. Small shafts of moon and starlight pierced through slits in the rocky walls, and shone in upon Miriam in that hidden place, as if perfectly arranged to do so by Destiny's hand itself.

"In her chamber I went deeper into vision than ever before. Time and place became no longer fixed around me and I was free to go wherever I would."

"Uppermost in my heart was to know the way my lord is travelling and in my vision I followed closely in his footsteps, visiting the days that are yet to come."

Miriam paused and the tension in the room became intense, as we were realising that she could be about to reveal extraordinary things.

The pause lengthened and I thought that she had decided not to continue. Instead, though she reached out and placed a hand on Lazarus' arm. "It will not be an easy road for any of us," she said at last, smiling at the man of uncommonly fragile health, who was Mary and Martha's beloved brother; "but we can do what will be needed because it is our Lord who asks it of us… and he who leads the way…"

She stopped again but only momentarily; her voice lifted: "Without seeing what I have been shown I do not think I could face these times as now we must. For when the master said he will be taken by the stewards of this carnal world and killed, because they cannot face the truth he brings… I know now this to be a real and immanent thing and not a parable or metaphor."

I sat somewhat stunned by this hard-hitting blow. We all were, I think.

"He walks a path that insists we face this gift of being alive, and that our God is just as real for every person, giving us personally each breath we breathe. This is our true birthright, not the concocted formula that the priestly classes force upon us; complicated rules to their own devising."

Yes, I thought, we all recognised this summary of the root of the struggle that Yeheshua was having to bring his simple teaching of joy and peace to the people of his homeland.

"As I said," Miriam continued, "without this vision that he sent me for, I really should be unable to face at what is to come, but… I have seen that neither Death nor all the Powers of Darkness can stay him in his task; to make a way for mankind to tread… to freedom of the soul, and peace of heart."

She looked down at the garment on the table again and must have felt our need to hear more of what she had seen because she lifted her head again and continued, picking her words as carefully as she could, it seemed.

"We followed Yeheshua's Light into the Darkness and felt the turmoil that was wrought, that threatened to rip mind and soul apart. Giving our hearts into his light was the only way forward; to bring about a wonderful transformation."

I remembered my own vision of sitting in the tomb of Miriam, and could understand how hard it must be for Miriam to put this into words. She carried on though… "Most of all" she said, "was knowing that Yeheshua was moving all of this existence onwards, bringing us out of Ignorance and into Truth." She paused. "It was overwhelming, flooding through and about me, freeing me, bobbing in a sea of knowing, not *anything* but the everything; just as though it was laid out… like the glory of this garment that you have constructed here; for Yeheshua; every thread woven wondrously together. This work of love that you have made describes it better than I can in words."

She sat silent now and so did we, taking in the portent of her words. I was admiring the workmanship of the robe, a tangible and eloquent expression of what we all felt, when Martha voiced a question that lay somewhere within me too… "What can we do more?" she asked quietly.

When finally Miriam started speaking again her tone had changed. "In many ways it will be harder for the men than for us women." I looked at Martha and she seemed a bit puzzled by this answer.

"Men expect to fight for what they see as right, or die in the attempt; yet there is so much more that Yeheshua is offering us. So much we have to still learn about the path ahead; and the brothers need to, in particular; because it is closer to a woman's nature to feel; live in the heart things; than it is for men. They usually want to respond by doing."

We sat, taking this in; for although I thought I sort of understood what she meant, no-one had ever expressed it in this way before. I wondered exactly how this related to my sometime frustration of not being allowed to take a greater part.

"Women take the passive role for, according to the rules of our society, our place is seen as being in the home with the family and bringing children into this worldy round."

I wondered now where this was going to lead?

"It will take an age before man's perception changes, but within the bounds we have been given there is still a huge amount that women will be able to do; and in the kingdom of our souls those barriers don't exist."

She turned to me with a piercing gaze and I felt she knew the stirrings of rebellion in my bones. "It will not always be so, for I have seen…" and her voice trailed off.

"What did you see?" I asked, unable to hold back.

"This I can tell you truly, that in that future time when our Lord comes again in power and glory, as he will, we will not just play the passive role, but also rise to that great harvesting of human love and toil."

"And our changing roles will be a marker of those times, the 'coming of age' for humankind."

"Then his feet will walk in every land and all the peoples will have their chance to join in with him. Women as much as men, in every way."

"Ahhh," I sighed, for something like awe spread through me, on receiving this glimpse of a dream fulfilled. Mary was brimming with smiles as well.

Whilst reflecting on these wonderful revelaltions, I heard myself asking instead, "what about now?"

Miriam shook her head slightly, but after another pause answered. "We are most blessed; there is no more we need to know. Our lord is with us and we have this chance to show him our love." Her hands were stroking the soft fabric of the seamless robe.

Lazarus had been listening intently to all that was said. Now he added his part. "My thoughts are that the best we can ever do for him is to understand that which he gives, the knowledge of our Life and Soul. In grasping this and helping others do the same, maybe his burden would be a little less... hard."

"Yes brother," agreed Mary, "that is the greatest love we have to give. How blessed we are to have this chance, this time with him."

Lazarus continued. "Now he has called for those of us who can and wish to go, to join him in Capernaum; in celebration of his great harvest, successfully brought in. If my sisters could go with you Miriam...?"

"Of course, Lazarus," said Miriam, "we shall leave tomorrow..." but Martha countered quickly, "Mary shall go and take the robe as a token of all our love; but I must stay with you, dearest brother. You are not well enough to go and Yeheshua would never wish us to put your life at risk."

"I would risk more than that even if it could help make a difference; but thank you Martha for your care." He paused, but finally turned directly to Miriam. "Please tell him that I long to be with him, that we all long to be with him, and that, though I cannot travel, I have nearly completed the trials my body sets for me, and that I shall always be listening for his call..."

"I will" she said.

CHAPTER 4.

Johannus went round to see Beor, his former employer and friend, to see if he had a place he could stay the night. Beor was one of the two blacksmiths in Bethany and the first person to tell Johannus about the master Yeheshua.

They went down to the smithy together as this was the only sensible place left for Johannus to have his bed, for the whole of Beor's family were round for the feast-day meal, with several of them staying the night.

"How come you are limping now?" asked Beor as they approached the wide double doors, and Johannus explained hesitantly how he had come to stab himself in the hip with his own sword. Beor laughed uproariously. "That has got to be one of the funniest things I've ever heard; go on tell me again Joh."

"No, I won't," said Johannus; "that wasn't the only thing that day you know. I nearly got killed when a ghoster attacked us. It wasn't all so funny."

"All right, don't get spikey with me; you might do yourself another injury…" and Beor broke into uncontrolled mirth again, which Johannus couldn't help but join in.

There was a pile of leather-working stacked to one side of the furnace, covered up with layers of sacking, which Beor made into a passable bed; and once Johannus' sleeping arrangements were sorted out Beor went back home again, leaving his friend the run of the smithy.

Johannus already knew where everything he might need was located so after a bit of nosing round at the work Beor had been doing he freshened himself up to go to Lazarus' house for the evening meal. He wanted to try to look presentable.

It was Lazarus himself who opened the door to welcome the younger man into his house, and introduce Johannus to the other guests. Apart from Miriam and I, there were Lazarus sisters' friend Ruth, her husband Elias and Simon, who showed all the marks of a man who had once had leprosy. And of course Martha and Mary.

Lazarus himself looked to be in even frailer health than the last time we had visited, which was belied by the easiness of his smile and the vigour of the life shining in his eyes. I could sense Johannus wondering what lay at the root of his unwellness. His thin frame looked as though a harsh wind might blow it apart.

The evening was very relaxed and pleasant, with the sisters Martha and Mary serving a range of spicy dishes that tantalised the senses. There was no segregation of men and women at Lazarus' table and Johannus found himself sitting between Ruth and me, the second Mary. After the meal much of the conversation turned to the journey up to Capernaum, on the morrow. Ruth and Elias were going as well, but Simon, like Lazarus, was remaining in Judea, most especially to help with preparations for the master's expected arrival before and around Passover.

Johannus had to admit that he had promised to go to his aunt and uncle's for the midday meal and that he would have to catch up with the others later on. So it came out about the visitors from Alexandria and the veiled Rebecca.

Ruth latched onto it quickly, ribbing Johannus with the obvious possibilities. Normally Johannus would have laughed it off easily but he caught a glimpse of Miriam's dark eyes regarding him and the colour flushed up into his face.

Martha joined Ruth in extracting as much information as possible about Johannus' romantic liaison and I thought to help him out a bit.

I told him that we had sold the camels back to Ali, and although of course we hadn't made a profit, the result was that we had had the use of both of them for several months, for very little money. I insisted that Johannus should take some of the money for all the time he had spent as our escort.

Johannus was indignant at the suggestion of taking any payment, but his grateful look told me he was relieved that the subject seemed to be changing.

"No, don't take it as payment, we just want you to share in our good fortune. What I was thinking was that you could hire the mare back from your uncle, for the journey north."

Johannus looked thoughtful, but doubtful. Then I couldn't resist adding, "… it would look a lot better than having to beg her off him again."

He shot a black look at me and I laughed back. "Don't worry your secret is safe with us." He shrugged and Lazarus himself came up and gave the young man a hug. "Don't worry friend, there is no shame or guilt. It could well be that this Rebecca is destined to be your future wife."

Johannus felt his confusion fleeing as Lazarus released him. Regaining his composure and the good spirits of being amongst friends he thanked me for my offer, realising what sense it in fact made.

Just as Johannus was wording this acceptance Mary came back into the room carrying some slim packages. She laid one in Miriam's lap. "We would like you and Mary to accept these small gifts, as feast-guests to our community."

She gave another package to me and with a glance at Miriam who was doing likewise I started to open it. I recognised the cloth immediately as the same as they had used to make Yeheshua's robe. What a beautiful head-shawl it would make; perfect for travelling.

In the midst of giving our thanks I noticed that a serious faced Mary had also given a slim package to Johannus, whispering something in his ear. He thanked her formally, matching her look with a probing one of his own, and I noticed too that Lazarus was smiling on good-humouredly.

*

Johannus slept most of the way through the night, untroubled by the sorts of dreams he had been having recently.

Since the battle with the 'ghosters' many of his nights had been visited with dreams featuring the blood drinking marauders. Sometimes they were like the one who rode at him on horseback but just as often they were ghostly male or

276

female figures floating close by, behind or around him.

Always there was blood, as often as not his own, streaming from his wounded side, which seemed to attract them. Sometimes he could see their faces, pale except for the blood trailing from their gaping mouths or smeared on their foreheads.

Frightening though they were, Johannus mostly 'knew' that they could not reach him. They would only come closer if he allowed their approach; which he didn't; and when he awoke he could easily dismiss the dreams from memory. That was, until Simon the Magus, his former teacher became involved in his nightmares.

Simon beckoned and Johannus found himself pulled into darker paths, not at all of his own volition. The ghosters were there and Simon seemed to be in league with them; worse, Johannus' confusion was robbing him of his power to keep them at bay. Both nights it had happened Johannus had awoken drenched in sweat.

Tonight, no ghosters had troubled his dreams; no Simon Magus had appeared to confuse him; and instead, he awoke in a place that was familiar to him. He got up and stretched his back that was a bit stiff. Looking around the smithy in the near darkness he realised there was another figure there.

The hairs on his neck stood up; his back prickled. A ghoster had only ever visited him in dreams before this.

Strangely, he heard Lazarus speaking through him. "In Yeheshua's name begone." The ghoster had a surprised look on her face as she faded and Johannus found that he was still lying on the hardness of the makeshift bed. Even that had been a dream.

He got up, stretching again, and reached for the cup of water beside the bed. Drinking in its coolness he knew he really was awake now. Though something in his head told him that a ghoster might easily appear he also felt confident of his power to dismiss it if it did.

Later in the morning Johannus went to Lazarus' house again to see the party off to Galilee.

Miriam and I had joined with Ruth and Mary and Elias from the night before and couple of friends of Ruth and Mary's. We were travelling in an ass's train.

Martha hugged her sister last, before Mary climbed onto her donkey; and Johannus made arrangements to meet our group at the inn we were heading for, at Jericho.

Lazarus was not well. This morning he had stayed in his bed.

Johannus asked Martha about him.

"He takes other's problems on himself," said Martha. "He always has, but the troubles are getting more intense."

Johannus remembered feeling Lazarus' help with the ghoster, early that morning; and with other things too. "Couldn't Yeheshua help him?"

Martha's grey eyes looked into his. "He is never unwell when he is with the master."

"Then why …?" Johannus wanted to ask why Lazarus didn't stay closer to the master, like others did.

Martha knew what his question was going to be. "He holds the light here in Bethany," she said. "A lit lamp close to Jerusalem herself; Yeheshua wants and needs this."

Johannus thought about it. How deep this runs he realised. How much these people gave of themselves.

"Please wish him well from me, and give my thanks for his help," he said and Martha in her turn thought better of asking him why, but said she would indeed pass the message on.

They hugged briefly and Johannus started out to complete the rest of his morning's business.

CHAPTER 5.

Yresmin loved being back on the road again. She walked when she felt like it and rested when she needed to. There was no-one to tell her different.

The excitement she had felt as a girl, when she had been following the star, was still with her. She was that girl, and her heart was certain of her way.

She sat and watched as a trade caravan went by but she felt no urge to join it.

She loved being alone in the huge expanse of the desert and mountains. She felt truly tiny in every way and she liked that.

In Kadesh Yresmin had lived a simple style that some called austere, despite having been one of the most powerful women in the kingdom.

How she was living now was not so very different, though of course it took her a little while to make up her camp and clear it away the next day.

Every day was a new beginning and as she sat over her fire on the morning of her third day out from the city she pondered this.

Her role as Manat's priestess had been so much about fate and destiny; worthy aims, but somehow 'endings' nevertheless. Now she was enjoying the opposite side of that same coin. Beginning the journey; uncovering hope; discovering the good; feeling renewed.

Selly was a precious companion, carrying the food and water for both of them as she did, along with everything else. Yresmin loved brushing out her tough coat before they set off each day, and she let her stop almost whenever there was the possibility of a bit of useful grazing.

Mostly the area along the King's highway was very barren, once they were away from the watered and tended area in the immediate vicinity of the city. They hadn't come across many places where it was possible for people to scratch more than a very meagre living. Yresmin had already given away half of her supplies in the couple of hamlets that they had stopped at. She was grateful to Kardun for making sure she had this chance.

The people were poor but they too were ready to share with Yresmin what they had. Best of all at the last place she had been able to fill the water skins.

Her feet and legs were more used to the longer spells of walking now and just when she was thinking that her progress was getting quite reasonable, she came across something that shook and shocked her.

The road's course passed a rocky promontory and as she and Selly rounded the bend Yresmin saw movements that she first thought were other travellers; but doing what?

Suddenly she realised what she was looking at was the flapping wings of vultures as they hopped around various piles of remains on the road.

Horror gripped her. Clearly there were corpses ahead and she thought she could smell them now. Flies buzzed around them too, in unpleasant little clouds.

The remnants of a ghoster attack, she was sure.

She couldn't tell how many bodies there were and she had no desire to go and check. She didn't want to go anywhere near them.

Her first instinct was to turn around and go back; back home; away from here, anywhere away from the people who did this.

As she realised this was not an option she would allow herself, her vulnerability on the road ahead became clear. She had never felt so alone and threatened at the same time.

Yresmin dropped back, away from the flies and the smell and the squabbling giant birds.

Out of site of the field of carnage she could breathe and think again. Maybe she should be able to pluck up the courage to pass the half-devoured corpses on the road but, be that as it may, she decided she would find a way around instead.

Not in the direction of the deep desert where the ghosters came from but over and through the foothills of the Sharra mountains that bordered the western side of the King's highway. She was familiar with this kind of terrain and she needed the comfort of that familiarity.

She had never seriously contemplated going back but was very aware of the tides of panic that the fear of these demons sent coursing through her.

Eventually she found the start of what might have been a goat track and Selly followed its route into the rocks. Yresmin followed. She thought that Selly was as eager as she was not to be on the road.

They camped in a small hollow that was pretty well-hidden form the surrounding land, but Yresmin didn't light her usual fire. Instead she curled up, wearing extra layers of clothing, and stared up into the starry sky; desperately hoping that the celestial lights could lift her from the fog of misery that was descending on her.

How free they were of everything that happened here. How dependable and yet ever changing in the pattern that they clothed the great goddess of the night. She prayed to Manat for her protection but found herself staring often at the darkness of the hills and mountains that surrounded her with dread.

Yresmin eventually managed to fall into a light, but troubled sleep, from which she awoke when it was still dark.

She didn't want to move. She listened to the sounds of the day dawning, mistrustful of every little noise. Clinging to her need for rest and safety she ignored any of the signs that would normally have propelled her into action.

The sun rose over the desert and she hid from it for as long as she could.

Eventually her good sense started seeping back into her. She wanted to move but she needed a spur to get her going, to help her regain her purpose, and a little act of defiance of the night before provided the way.

She hadn't hobbled or tethered Selly as she normally would, because she wanted her donkey to have every chance to escape, should she need it. Now she needed to go and look for her.

Getting up, washing her face, drinking a little water and finally dressing was enough to blow away the cobwebs of a night that had left Yresmin's spirits depressed.

It wasn't long before she found her friend munching on the best bit of grazing around; it had been especially enjoyable with the early morning dew still clinging to it, but now she reluctantly allowed her mistress to pull her away and back to the camping place where her day's burdens awaited her.

It was well after midday by the time they had worked their way through the hills and back to the highway.

Nervous at first, Yresmin finally convinced herself that the most likely people to be on the road would be the king's army following up on reports of the attack.

Before the 'badness', as she thought of it, she and Selly had not encountered many people on the road, but today absolutely no-one appeared in either direction.

There was plenty of time to consider the situation as she walked the rutted road, punctuated with its red rock outcrops and overblown here and there with desert sand.

Many had told her the wisdom of joining a caravan when the chance arose and she had been thinking herself foolhardy for letting one pass by.

Now she could only be thankful for not having followed that advice. It seemed very probable that it was that very caravan that had been attacked.

There were no certainties. She was scared of course but somewhere ahead she felt there was still a light that she was heading for. A real haven but it was just such a long way off. 'I am too old' she thought, 'I won't make it.'

But a kind of calmness came to her, different from the exuberance she had felt in first leaving Kadesh, but altogether greater and better than resignation. 'The goddess is with me still' she realised, feeling relieved; 'come what may'.

Still no other travellers had appeared on the highway and a tired Yresmin decided it was time to make camp for the night. Again she went into the broken and hilly ground off to the left of the road, and didn't have to go far before she found a good place, probably used by other travellers in times gone by.

There was enough grass and small straggly bushes for Selly not to need to stray far. Yresmin pulled the baggage off her and sorted out what she needed to make her fire, lugging her bedding and other stuff to the shelter of a slight overhang.

Crouching down over the iron and striker she was using to light the fire, she absorbed her mind into the task. A small flame caught into the ball of tinder. She rocked back on her heels and, wiping the sweat off her forehead with the back of her hand, she blew the dry grass into a fiery response before setting it carefully within the stack of twigs.

The light had changed and the evening was quiet. Yresmin struggled a little to stand back up, her left hand rubbing an old ache in her back. Selly had made a little braying noise and Yresmin looked around at her friend; and froze.

All around the little clearing were figures, with drawn weapons; and she knew they were neither Nabatean soldiers nor friendly villagers. Tribes-people from the deep desert.

'People; just people' she told herself as she straightened up to her full height. She stepped forward to place her hand on the rough neck of her friend, Selly.

CHAPTER 6.

Johannus got to his aunt and uncle's house in plenty of time for the midday meal and was warmly received, especially when he had presented Rebecca with the gift of the head-shawl.

The meal went well and Johannus played his part easily. His request to pay for the renewed use of his uncle's horse resulted in a bidding war, with his uncle at first refusing any payment and then being gradually convinced to take about half of Johannus' original offer; much to the amusement of the other guests.

Honour was satisfied and Johannus also agreed to accompany Petrakis and Rebecca on the first leg of their journey, which they shared, going towards Jerusalem.

The donkeys that Johannus had seen in the paddock were only hired, especially for this family visit, from the inn where they had left the rest of Petrakis' travel gear.

Having said their farewells to Petrakis' cousin Jessica and Johannus' uncle Mikael, Johannus joined them as they headed back to pick up the horses and carriage that had been left with two servants at the inn.

The carriage was an intriguing vehicle that seemed to Johannus to be a combination of a chariot and a litter. There were two horses harnessed side by side to a central shaft that was attached to the litter behind, itself supported on two axles with red painted wheels. On the central shaft there was a raised seat which allowed the driver to hold the reins whilst being in close contact with both the horses.

Petrakis led out ahead, side by side with Johannus, whilst another attendant rode behind the carriage leading a spare hose. The carriage also provided space for stowing the baggage.

Johannus found Petrakis to be a knowledgeable and amusing riding companion, relating as he did so many stories about the great city of Alexandria and the people he knew there.

Johannus had travelled to Egypt with Simon Magus but chose not to talk of that. Instead, he answered Rebecca's father with some comparisons to the city of Antioch, which he knew well.

Rebecca herself left the litter compartment quite soon after they had left Bethany and took the spare horse to ride up front with Johannus and her father.

She had a cheeky sense of humour and interrupted her father more frequently than Johannus would have expected, but he was obviously used to this and took it all in good part.

By the time they got near to Jerusalem and the parting of their ways, the afternoon was wearing on and Johannus realised he was going to have to hurry on the road to Jericho to reach the inn before the night wore too late.

They parted as good friends, determined to meet up again at Passover time.

*

Miriam and I were still chatting next to the inn's fire when a dishevelled Johannus arrived there, that first night out from Bethany. There was still food left over from the evening meal and I went to see the innkeeper for some to be brought for Johannus.

The innkeeper, Zaccheus, was a baptised man who enjoyed having Christine travellers stay at his inn. Yeheshua had actually stayed there one night a year ago and Zaccheus was hoping desperately he would come back again.

Tonight, the inn was overflowing with Yeshua's followers going up to Galilee for the celebratory gathering and Zaccheus was wondering if he could or should be going as well.

"It is certain that he will be coming to Judea and Jerusalem very soon," Miriam had said. I had looked at her then, reminded again of how much Miriam had experienced in vision. Zaccheus had nodded; not revealing what he had decided about coming up to Galilee.

He had realised that this path was continuing for all of his life, but he also knew this was still a special opportunity.

Johannus gratefully accepted the food and was shown where he could make his bed in an unused corner of the inn. All the rooms were already full, of course and I was glad to be able to tell him that Beor and two of his family were here as well. Though tired Johannus was obviously so happy to have caught up with us.

The next day we set off up the Jordan road, close by the sacred river where John used to baptise people and where he had declared Yeheshua's mission.

Miriam wanted us to pause a while and pay tribute to John's memory, which we did; realising how young he had been, how precious his life. What he had done to make us understand our preciousness as well.

We were a varied bunch, some walking, some riding on donkeys and a few on horses. Johannus had dismounted and allowed an elder man to take his place in the saddle, whilst he led Melody on foot.

I walked beside him and asked him how the day before had gone, at his uncle's house. He told me all about the negotiations for Melody's hire and the journey with the carriage to Jerusalem. He still looked quite tired. I asked him if he had managed to get any sleep in his corner of the inn.

"I slept fine," he said. "Well, I had a strange dream; but not an unpleasant one exactly." I said nothing, it wasn't really my business. "It was kind of connected to our journey to Kadesh," he said, looking thoughtful.

We walked along side by side in the relative cool of this late winter's day and it seemed that Johannus was trying to recall the dream. Clouds had gathered in a sky that might later be threatening us with rain. Johannus continued telling me of his dream.

"It involved Hecate," he said, "who first appeared to me when I was lost and maybe delirious; that time I found the dead priest and the bethel stone."

"I remember," I answered. "We all went through so much, and the goddess seemed to play a large part in it…"

I was thinking how Isis appeared to me through Bishmi, Manat's priestess. "Does your hip still pain you?"

"Not yet today," answered Johannus quickly; "but I was told a tale in last night's dream that I wish I could remember. It seemed to be important; which was ever the way," he added, slightly ruefully.

We walked on and I asked whether he wanted to tell me whatever he still remembered.

He waited a while, collecting his thoughts. "I was in the semi-darkness, as I often have been dreaming of late, and there was a storm brewing, but it wasn't like the sky today; much greater and blacker. As it struck, instead of rain, snow blasted through the air, backlit by lightning and thunder… and then Hecate was there but the storm was gone."

"She was different this time." Johannus paused, looking slightly embarrassed. He looked at me, shrugging; "she looked like Rebecca, but I somehow knew it was the goddess. Anyway, I remember asking her how she came to be here and she started telling me a story of… of… well it was about a mirror. No, not an ordinary mirror, but the 'perfect mirror' she called it. The story was how it came into the world, I think… or is still. I cannot remember now."

He laughed. "In some ways perhaps, I didn't get much actual sleep …."

It made me think of when I used to work in the library of Astarte's temple in Antioch. "If it happens again, and you are able to hold onto the story, I can write it down, if you like; if you come and tell me. We used to do that in the temple."

Neither of us had alluded directly to the horrendous events in Antioch that had shattered my life as it had been; and Johannus' as well. In all the time of our travelling together, to and from Kadesh, neither of us had felt it necessary to talk about that other time; when I had been a temple priestess and he a student of Simon Magus. It was a given thing between us that it belonged to the past.

Now it was as though we had already talked it through and it no longer held any power over us. "Without all that happened I cannot see how I could have made it to Yeheshua's side;" I said in the pause that followed.

"Nor I have escaped from the magus' influence," Johannus replied; "and it brought me directly back with my father."

"Really? And it re-united me with my mother too. Isn't that strange?"

"Hmm… yes. Yes, it really is; and if I do have something like that dream again, I shall try hard to hold onto it. And tell you."

"That is sweet of you, Johannus. Let's hope you can then."

Miriam and Lazarus' sister Mary had been walking just ahead and Mary asked Johannus if she could lead Melody for a while; she liked horses.

Miriam came and walked between Johannus and me.

"Actually, there are things I do remember," he was saying; "not her story, but funnily enough it was quite relevant with what you were trying to do in Antioch."

I said nothing, but I was listening. "What I asked was why, as a goddess, she chose to dwell in the shadows of the underworld. Especially as there seemed to be so much turmoil in it; with possessions, ghosters and all the overflow of evil into the world."

"What did she tell you?" Miriam asked, more interested than I might have expected.

"She said the problems are growing. The fears that we cast into darkness have grown and multiplied under the influence of other powers and souls trapped there. It is our own evil that is coming back to haunt us."

"Is that what she meant by a mirror? A mirror of darkness?" I asked.

"No. The mirror she talked of was wonderful, that much at least I remember. It was something Hecate had wanted more than anything else."

"Did she tell you anything more... about the Shadowland?" Miriam asked.

Johannus thought about it. "Yes, she did. I cannot remember exactly but she said something about the borders getting weaker; that the pressures are growing and more and more breaches are occurring. That was about all of it."

It was Miriam's turn to look thoughtful. She turned to me, "Mary I wish we still had the camels. I would really like to get to his side as soon as I can."

"You can take Melody if you like," said Johannus. "She could easily carry both of you; neither of you weigh much... I should imagine," he added a little sheepishly.

Miriam beamed at him. "A lovely offer; thank you" she said, patting his arm; "but we cannot take your uncle's horse."

The older man on that horse's back called over to us. "Johannus, Johannus; can you let me down?"

"Of course, grandfather." We stopped and Johannus helped the man dismount.

"You actually paid for Melody's hire," said Johannus, turning back to Miriam and myself.

I laughed. "Yes, I suppose we did in a way; but I wonder if..."

Beor somehow appeared at my side; The old man was his uncle Ric. "You can take my mare, Nala... if you want to go as well Joh."

I wondered how he knew what was going on but then again, we were all feeling the same, and would all want to help Miriam.

Johannus started to mumble something but I interrupted him. "Beor that would be wonderful. We have plenty of spare space on the asses if you need; and we shall return Nala to you in Capernaum."

*

Some quick rearranging of the baggage and we were on our way again, making fast progress along the rocky road, past the wide outline of the Ephraim hills on our left, heading ever northwards through Samaria; until the clouds opened.

The downpour completely drenched us but we had got far enough along the road towards Galilee that we allowed ourselves to search for the nearest decent inn to recover in; and maybe stay over at, till the next morning.

We had tents with us, as all the travellers on the asses train had, but to set them up in the rain was not much of an option. Instead, we found a reasonably priced travel-stop at the crossroads where one road went back off left, towards Caesarea.

It wasn't a big place but comfortable enough in a sparce sort of way. I shared a room with Miriam, and Johannus was shown to a tiny room that had been built onto the flat roof. It was all that was left.

Having stowed our things and seen to the horses, we headed into the inn's communal areas, where we would be able to get some food and drink.

I didn't like the look of the two men that were drinking in the front room. Not that they were rough looking; far from it. Polished and urbane but nevertheless there was something about their sideways stare, as we crossed the room, that was unpleasant.

Miriam and I sat in the ladies' area whilst Johannus stayed where the men were, seating himself as inconspicuously as possible in one corner, I noticed.

Soup was doled out into bowls with attendant chunks of bread and the warmth and tastiness of the offering made up for its simplicity. I poked my head out of our room to check on Johannus. He had moved from his corner and I noticed briefly that there were a lot of people out there now. Johannus was sitting close to our entrance now; I went out to talk to him.

"Are you guarding us Joh?" I asked, taking up the name that Beor used for his friend. I liked it.

"Hush," he said, under his breath. "There are people here that I am not comfortable about."

Crouching down a bit beside him, I looked over to where the two men who I had thought of as businessmen had been joined by two Pharisees and another, dangerous looking man. I had the uncomfortable feeling they were gesturing back towards me, discussing us.

As I turned away to go back to Miriam, I saw the 'dangerous' one moving over to talk to a group of other rougher types.

"Water is the mirror of life," said Miriam, filling her cup from the table's jug of wine.

"What?" I asked.

"We try to be like the vine that takes water from the apparently dry earth and turns it into the sweetness of grapes…"

I wondered what she was talking about. Hecate's story was all I could think of, but she was continuing, "but there are others that use their lives to turn that water into poison; and these we should all avoid if at all possible. Such as many of those out there…" She said indicating the doorway I had just returned through.

I agreed heartily. "What shall we do?" I asked.

287

She gave me a small purse. "Give this to Johannus and ask him to discreetly pay the innkeeper, but to explain that since the weather has improved, we must press on to Caesarea without delay. Tell Johannus to meet us at the horses stable as soon as he has collected his things. You and I can get to our room through this door over here."

"Some are undoubtedly bandits from the hills," Miriam whispered as we climbed the way to our room, "but I don't know why they are down here by the Jordan road. They know it is patrolled by the Roman army."

She paused and I wondered how much she had seen. "Did you see the Pharisees, talking to those rich men?"

"Yes, I saw them; and the leader of the bandits went to consult with them as well. I could see it in the glass. I think he might be Barabas."

Johannus was already outside our room when we came back out. He had his bedroll and bag slung over one shoulder, and he motioned us to follow him quickly.

We went down the short passageway to a curtained arch that led out onto stairs that led up onto the flat roof. "The innkeeper told me of this way. He said to be careful because he thinks he heard them talking of us; and that they would have posted spies to watch the road. He thought going back towards Jerusalem would be safest..."

Johannus crossed quickly to the roof's furthest edge where there was a sturdy ladder leant against the outside of the parapet. We climbed down to the higher ground behind the inn where the stables were.

"We shall take the Caesarea road, as I said. Let's hope the skills that Kardun showed us will serve our need."

CHAPTER 7.

We saddled the horses as quietly as we could, leading them by rein out onto the road.

The last thing I had expected was to find this kind of danger so close to home; as if deliberately trying to block our way to the master.

"We have got to ride this road, at least for a while," said Miriam. "We must pretend we suspect nothing."

At least it really had stopped raining. Stars were back shining in the sky and a growing crescent moon was dodging between flying clouds, roughly in the direction we were headed.

"You two ride the horses," said Johannus. "I shall stay on foot, between them. I think I know where the spy will be set; just at that bend where he will be able to see up and down the road. If there is trouble, set the horses into a gallop."

"Don't do anything foolish will you Johannus," I said. "Let's just be as insignificant as we can."

We rode at a walk up the long rise towards the corner. There were scrubby trees and low walls on both sides and it was impossible to make anyone out in the deep shadows. Miriam was keeping up an easy chatter about the storm that had passed. I tried to answer in an unconcerned way but felt my heart thumping inside me as we approached the spot that Johannus had pointed out.

We passed the bend and a little further on I sensed Johannus move back and, crouching low, he slipped into some cover at the side of the road. Miriam and I continued on without pause.

A minute or so later a breathless Johannus caught up with us. "We were right," he said; "I saw someone come out from those trees and run back down towards the inn. We haven't got long .... "

'Why would anyone be so interested in who we are or where we are going?' I puzzled to myself. The possibility that they were just after our money didn't comfort me.

"Here;" said Miriam, pointing out a narrow track that joined the road to our right. "This is the way we shall take. It should be fine for the horses."

It was almost certainly a farm track and next to where it met the road there was some sort of small roofless barn or shed, making a low black shape against the darkened hill behind.

"We shouldn't go up the track yet, till we know what they are doing;" said Johannus. "The rain will make our tracks obvious in the soft ground; easy for anyone wanting to follow us."

"What about this dilapidated place?" I said, but I didn't like that idea much either.

"If they check the track, they will certainly check the barn," said Miriam. We paused. "What about behind it then?" said Johannus.

The question was settled quickly because we heard the sounds of galloping hooves coming from down the road to the inn. "Quick," we hissed in unison, starting to lead Melody and Nala along the rough footpath that ran along the furthest side of the decayed out-building.

There was general rubbish half blocking our way, which we managed to get around without making much noise, but there was no way to get behind the barn itself. There was no path, just a tangle of scrub, all in deepest moon shadow.

We stood frozen to the spot we had got to, stroking the horses' necks to keep them calm; listening hard for any sounds coming from the road.

When they drew level with us their party was quite spread out, with the lead riders being followed by a pack of others on foot, strung out to the rear. There were calls sent back from one rider that probably were instructions to check the farm track.

It seemed like an age huddled there, feeling the night chill blowing through our riding cloaks, before we got the next clear signs of what was going on. There was some muffled talking around by the front of the barn and then eventually I saw one pursuer walking up the farm track beyond our hiding spot, intently studying the ground.

As I strained my eyes to watch him, he straightened up and called back. "Nothing been this way since the rains."

"Just make sure," said a loud voice, almost in my ear. Startled, we struggled to keep the horses still, as well as ourselves, whilst it dawned on us that the other man was inside the barn, not more than a few feet from where we were.

Johannus was last in line, standing directly behind Nala, and turning my head that way, I could see the blade of his sword glinting in the moonlight. His fingers were clenched tight around the handle and I felt how determined he was to ensure that it would be the person, or persons, who might find us that would get the nastiest surprise.

Mercifully neither of them looked around the outside of the barn, satisfied that no-one had tried to go this way. It would have been very unlikely that anyone would have had time to make preparations to get away. As far as they were concerned the element of surprise was on their side.

We let several minutes drag by in an attempt to make certain that they had moved on.

Eventually I saw Johannus detach himself from our shadowy bulk and slink off to explore.

"They have definitely gone," he said, returning to us after another short wait that seemed like an eternity on its own. "Let's get going again, before they come back."

I didn't need any encouragement. We kept off the main part of the farm-track as much as we could, so as not to leave obvious tracks, but otherwise wasted no time in putting distance between us and the road.

A dark building grew out of the ground to our left as we crested the first rise. Dogs barked and a man's voice shouted at them to shut up. They were obviously used to things going by in the dark.

There was a torch or fire burning somewhere out of sight that threw its light against an adjacent whitewashed wall, but then we were past, heading up along the muddy track that wound beyond the farm, further up into the hills.

As we reached the real top of the hill the way forked, the left hand seeming to curl back into the farmland and the right way leading on along the ridge. This is the way we went till we came upon a strand of straggly trees and decided to stop and make camp.

It wasn't going to be sensible to light a fire but we raised our shelters against the cold and the possibility of further rain. Johannus made his space a little away from us, nearest to the trackway.

*

The night wore on; I had tried to keep a vigil, focussing within as Yeheshua had shown us, but inevitably sleep overcame my best efforts.

Miriam was down by the stream, that much I knew, so I went down to see what was happening.

There was another woman there as well. Tall, imposing, queenly; facing Miriam from the other side of the stream.

Between them, half in and half out of the stream there was a body lying face down on the grass. Miriam had one foot placed lightly on his back, stopping him from sliding further into the water.

I moved forward and saw that it was Johannus, still sleeping.

Though I was still some distance from them, I could clearly hear their conversation:

"What do you want with him?" said Miriam.

"He seeks me out," replied Hecate.

"Then leave him be. He comes with us."

"Why should I?" the goddess demanded.

"You still seek the true mirror, don't you?" stated Miriam.

"Yes, I do," answered Hecate.

"Amen then," said Miriam, as if that had settled everything; which in my dream it seemed to do.

*

I awoke before the first light of the new day. Johannus was lying half against a tree. He looked most uncomfortable. Obviously, he had tried to keep guard.

Miriam was sleeping curled up in a ball, but peaceful. I thought it cruel to waken her, so set myself to watching the eastern horizon, as we had agreed we should set out again at the first light of the new day.

As I sat watching, the star of beauty raised her light into the promise of morning. Venus as the Romans called her now. Aphrodite, Astarte, the goddess calling once again. She enhanced the magic of the coming day, for today her

291

light was joined with the first rays of dawn.

I rubbed my hands in the little trickle of water that I allowed to flow from my water skin; then took several palms-full to wash my face with. Miriam had woken of her own accord and gone over to check on Johannus.

Soon we were all ready to set off again, but the dawning of the new day had set an entirely different mood from the night before. Hope and good cheer went with us.

Yesterday's path had put us on a roughly parallel course to the main Jordan road, so we knew that if a track crossed our own, turning right down it should take us back to the Jordan again.

It wasn't long before such an opportunity arrived; another farm track, much like the one we had been following. This one went downhill, beside a half-exposed watercourse which today ran with water from the rains of the evening before.

"Keep an eye out, Johannus," said Miriam. I would say we are still in bandit territory.

I felt a foreboding at Miriam's remark, but couldn't think why I should.

*

It happened at a little bridge. The rivulet of water we rode beside had joined a bigger steam and our path now veered left, crossing over it.

He jumped out on us just as Miriam's horse passed the fat willow tree that he had been hiding behind.

He tried to grab the reins of her horse, but Johannus was just quick enough. He pushed the man away, and before the other had fully recovered, Johannus had his sword drawn.

The attacker was unkempt and poorly attired and obviously surprised by Johannus' appearance. It seemed that from his hiding place he had only taken in the two female riders approaching.

It was difficult at first glance to work out whether he was a brigand or just some unfortunate; possessed perhaps. He managed to grab some sort of stout spear from where it was propped up against the willow tree, which must mean he one of the brigands.

Johannus had placed himself between us and the man who was now backing away, his eyes still searching around for something; presumably his own sword that he had put down somewhere.

Johannus pressed forward and the other abandoned his retreat and sprang to the attack, swinging the heavy spear like a staff. Johannus ducked forward under the flailing weapon, receiving only a glancing blow off his back and shoulder.

Changing his grip on the spear our attacker started trying to jab it into Johannus' face, eager to ward off any sword attack; but picking his moment well Johannus managed to duck low under the spear tip just as it was committed to the strike, swinging hard at the outstretched hands that held it.

His blade bit into one arm and with a cry the man let go the spear, trying instead to grab onto Johannus with his unwounded hand. On the return swipe Johannus' sword tip cut across the attacker's chest, forcing him back and to lose balance.

Although on his backside, his one good hand still clutched Johannus' cloak, pulling it from him, and as Johannus raised his sword to cut himself away, Miriam called out to him. "Hold, Johannus; do not strike again. Enough!"

Clearly the man's neck had been exposed to the next blow but Johannus heeded Miriam's call. Breathing hard, he loosed his trapped cloak, levelling instead his sword tip at the man in front of him.

"Why are you attacking us?" demanded Miriam, and I thought that he now looked very ordinary, scrawny rather than stocky, or strong.

"I have to hold this road in case you came this way." He didn't look very pleased that the possibility had turned into reality. "What will you do to me?" he asked.

"Nothing," said Miriam. She had dismounted and picked up the sword that the man had carelessly got separated from. He still had a knife tucked into his belt that he hadn't been able to bring into the fight. "... unless you do anything stupid with your knife. Throw it away over there."

The man obliged with his uninjured left arm that reached awkwardly round to where the knife was stowed. He threw it away under Johannus' careful watch.

Miriam continued to question the man about why the brigands were so intent on attacking us. His right forearm was badly cut and bleeding but the injury to his chest seemed very minor.

I dismounted as well and got some clean strips of cloth out of the saddlebag, together with the water-skin. Miriam and I patched him up, and he turned from menacing brigand into a grateful patient.

"You are free to go anywhere you want," Miriam was telling him, "but I don't think you will be well received by your comrades in arms. Your leader didn't seem to be the forgiving type to me."

"You are followers of that Yeshua," said the man, whose name we had discovered was Seth. "I don't know why we are going after his followers. Bad move if you ask me. We have no quarrel with them. I think the Pharisees say you are supporting the Romans against us. Is that true?"

"So, you are attacking Christines are you?"

Seth shrugged. "Don't know why," was all he could say, and he had lost all trace of menace now.

"Well, I think you are best served by getting as far away from those people as you can," said Miriam. A light seemed to pass across his face, giving it life. "Can I come with you?" he asked.

I didn't know what to say but Miriam was certain. "If you can help us find a safe path back to the main road, you are welcome to do so," she said.

Johannus was clearly unhappy at this, but said nothing.

Yresmin looked at the man who was clearly the leader of the band that had surrounded her. He had stepped forward from the others and up to where she stood stroking Selly's neck.

"You come with us," he told her, jabbing his spear at her belly, leaving her little option but to obey.

Still, she looked him in the eyes, recognising the stare of a man used to command and being obeyed. She held his gaze just long enough for him to know that she was someone who knew power and was unafraid. She nodded, returning her attention to her donkey.

She nuzzled her ear and whispered that she would come and get her; then rough hands were pulling them apart. A few of the band had already finished rifling through her possessions and found precious little to interest them.

One man asked the leader something, with his naked sword close to Yresmin's neck.

She was not afraid to die; she felt the goddess close to her heart. "No," the leader answered, in a negative that resounded, and continued in an Aramaic dialect she understood. "Not yet. We shall see if the Djinn will want her first ."

He was looking at her face, wanting to see what fear this might bring to her; but he was disappointed. For strangely she was thinking of the tales that Miriam and Mary had told her about the master Yeheshua casting out demons from people, and how Mary had reportedly done so in Kadesh. She couldn't think why these thoughts had come to her, but she turned back to the man. "Fine, let's go then."

Her wrists were bound and the end of the rope tied to Selly, before she herself was bundled across her donkey's back, looking down at the ground to one side, purple red in the evening shadows. It wasn't dignified and men's hands had prodded and poked her body but she felt solace in being able to whisper her thanks to Selly for carrying her.

What a funny time to feel thankful she realised, and actually laughed aloud at herself. One of her captors prodded at her hard with a spear, pricking her raised buttock; inflicting sharp pain. 'Ow!' she thought loudly, but kept it in her throat, building her resolve.

As priestess of Manat the approach of death was well known to her, and she was prepared for it in herself. Now her time was coming, and although she didn't welcome it, neither would she shy away.

It was a long journey into the night and the aching pain where she had been stabbed on her bottom was joined by others; especially the old ache in her back. At the end of it, when she was pushed off Selly into a sprawl on the ground, she was so stiff and sore that she could hardly move.

Once more rough hands pulled her to her feet and this time she faced up to the man who was pulling her about. "Desist," she commanded him, and was answered with a hard slap across the left side of her face.

Recovering, she drew herself to her full height, turning away from her assailant, "Great Manat; turn your face from this man, I beseech you."

Laughter came from several other ghosters that were standing around watching the encounter. "Al-Shai-Haffa" called a black bearded man, "that one thinks she can command the gods."

Yresmin ignored them to take in the camp she had been brought to. It was a pitiful sight.

The squalor was divided into two halves; the one side for the ghost fighters, with oily cooking fires and shoddy tents that looked almost prosperous in comparison to where they kept the victims of their raids like animals for use or slaughter.

Common to all of it though was the smell, hanging around everything like a tangible skin. Anything and fear.

Yresmin was just realising there were quite a few ghoster women in the camp when that leader, who she now knew was called Al-Shai-Haffa, came to confront her again.

"On your knees, bitch," he spat at her.

She didn't move. "The Djinn would decide my fate, **you** said." They could kill her now, or do anything they wished, but she was choosing her own death. "I know you can kill me. Go ahead if you like; or let us see whether your Djinn are worthy of your fearful grovelling."

Al-Shai-Haffa was clearly flabbergasted at this response. He spluttered in fury and drew his sword, ready to strike her head from her body, even as she calmly returned his glare.

A wind was whipping up a sandstorm somewhere out in the desert, and in that moment that Al-Shai-Haffa stared, undecided at his impudent prisoner, the moan of it came to them as a fore-taste of the storm itself.

"I think you will be meeting the Djinn sooner than you think," he smiled evilly; "and then we shall see how glad you are to get what you wish for; when they tear you into little pieces and satisfy their thirst from your naked soul."

Yresmin looked right back into his deeply scarred face, sensing an opening that might expose his weakness. "They may tear me limb from limb, that is true; but my soul is not for them. They do not have that power."

A visible doubt crossed his face but he recovered quickly. Furious at her continuing defiance he deliberately swung his sword at her head; not to kill her but to start her on the path to submission, and then death.

Instinctively Yresmin raised her bound hands to protect her ducking head, but the blade still sliced the back of her left hand and cut into the top of her head.

Before she could recover Al-Shai-Haffa grabbed the bowed-forward Yresmin by the hair and dragged her bodily to where other prisoners were cowering in a pen of thorn sticks.

Pushed to the ground inside, Yresmin was too shocked and in pain to do anything but lie there as the rickety gate was bound shut. Outside the ghoster leader turned to two women. "Prepare her for the Djinn; tonight," he said. He didn't want her to have any time to recover and try to influence his people further.

The other prisoners were in no state to be able either to help or bother Yresmin. Clearly each of them had been drained of large portions of their life-fluids, for bloody wounds and older scars were still visible on various parts of them, consistent with such treatment.

Before Yresmin could do much more than pull herself up into a sitting position a ghoster woman had come into the enclosure and over to Yresmin, wiping her hand in the blood that was streaming down Yresmin's arm and neck.

Yresmin closed her eyes, searching for her goddess' help. She thought she heard a woman's voice coming from a very long way off, "Yeheshua is with you; his love is with you." Something in Yresmin recognised it, 'that is Miriam' she thought, and poured all her hope towards the feeling this presence gave her.

"Yeheshua," she said to herself, repeating the master's name again, and again. "Yeh'shua, Yeh'shua;" under her breath; then giving herself into it so the name became her breathing… "Yehe…shua, Yeh…shua, Yeh-Shua; mostly quiet, but sometimes the out-breath was quite audible as she struggled against the awefulness happening to her. The ghoster woman was still exploring Yresmin's wounds, tasting her blood, pawing at her body, but she reacted violently to this whispered chanting, pushing Yresmin away from her and against the thorny fence.

Renewed pains stabbed at Yresmin's arms and back like vicious wasp stings, making her screw up her face and lurch forward again, away from the fence.

The woman dug her nails under Yresmin's chin and forced her to look up into her face. Pale, with straggly hair she was most un-beautiful, but looking into the deadness of her eyes was more terrifying to Yresmin than any contact with Al-Shai-Haffa had been. 'Possessed'.

Despite everything that was happening Yresmin continued mouthing her prayer. The ghoster woman now stood back, calling to another behind her. "Sheba, she calls to Sheba."

The second ghoster woman pushed in front of the first. Yresmin breathed "Ye'shua, Ye'shua" to herself holding onto the faint glow of comfort she felt in her heart, despite the wracking pain of her wounds.

The ghoster looked at the captive, sensing her to be somehow more than any other she had encountered. "She calls the Queen?" she said in a mixture of hopeful and fearful wonder. She turned to the other, "a Queen for the Djinn; they might be pleased."

Between the two women they smeared her with a combination of her own blood and evil smelling stuff they had in pots, making Yresmin retch.

What power that stuff had she never knew but the pain of her wounds receded somewhat and her senses became a little blurred around the edges.

They took away her garments but allowed her to keep her plain undershift, one of two that Kardun had insisted she should always wear. He had said it had a protection for her, but she had no idea what he meant. He had said that she didn't need to; not then.

The picture in her mind of her wiry, brown-skinned friend gave her another bit of hope. If anyone understood these tribes at all, it was Kardun.

She stood, acquiescent, allowing the women to do their work whist she tried to focus her senses for the trial ahead. She was physically drained but some tiny gap of light remained to her within the blot of surrounding darkness. She clung to her breathing chant whilst the moan of the wind grew louder, though the fringe of the localised storm had hardly reached the camp yet.

There were a few women reacting to its approach, hopping around like overgrown vultures, but the men she could see were all flattening and securing their part of the camp, prepared for what was coming. Yresmin searched around to see what Al-Shai-Haffa was doing.

He was on the fringe of the men's camp being attended to by some of the vulture women in the relative shelter of an upcrop of rocks. As she watched he rose and strode forward into the most exposed ground where the other women were cavorting about.

'He thinks he is a Priest-King,' she thought, as if telling Kardun what she saw.

One of the women prodded her hard in the back and she stumbled forward into the gap where the other had opened the thorn gate.

"Ye'shua Ye'shua," she mouthed, a little louder, and once again the women picked up on the outbreath, hearing it as her call to 'Sheba'.

They led her out triumphantly towards the central group and she tried very hard to stand tall and proud; ready to confront the Djinn; to go where Manat sent her; for the ring of light that Yeheshua brought.

"She calls for the Queen of Sheba," crowed one of her attendants, which is what they seemed like to the other women, and Al-Shai-Haffa too. He frowned deeply but the women danced around in renewed anticipation.

Al-Shai-Haffa strode forward, taking control of the situation. "What is this nonsense about Sheba?" he said, glaring blackly at Yresmin.

Yresmin was not bothered about what the women thought or about trying to hide from this man. "Not Sheba," she said, "Yeheshua is who I call to;" she projected the name clearly at him, over the growing presence and noise of the wind.

Al-Shai-Haffa winced; only slightly, but Yresmin read what his fear was, written across his twisted visage. It was as if Kardun was explaining it to her. 'He fears your power with the Djinn will be greater than his. The women will welcome a queen amongst them to be their priestess. He knows you can supplant him, for just so he did himself, to the one who led the tribe before.'

297

They locked eyes and Yresmin knew his mind, but he couldn't fathom hers.

He had heard name she proclaimed so certainly, and recently that Darkness wanted and would destroy him.

He swung away from her and towards the approaching storm where the women flapped wildly, their flimsy garments being whipped around in the wind.

"Not for Sheba" he shouted at them. "This witch calls for a rabble-rousing Hebrew sorcerer. Even the priests of his own God despise him." But he had heard other things about the miracle-worker, which didn't assuage his fears.

A consternation spread through the flapping women, but Al-Shai-Haffa ignored them, striding past them towards the teeth of the storm. He took out a knife and cut himself on the cheeks and forehead, just like he had so many times before, and went forward to implore the Djinn of his cause.

Yresmin watched the strange scene. The women were like ragged dolls, and the storm was like many other she had witnessed. Nothing that she feared, beyond the raw power of it. Two men had come up behind her to hold her arms when Al-Shai-Haffa left her and she had no option but to watch and see what would come next.

*

Al-Shai-Haffa covered his bleeding face with a protective cloth as he walked the familiar route to the Djinn rock, enduring the buffeting he received from the sand-filled wind.

He worried about the outcome of this encounter. Things didn't always go as he expected. Usually, the Djinn accepted the blood and offerings he brought; people who had grown fat off the lives of the poor tribes-people like himself; but not always.

Sometimes captives would be allowed to join the tribe; men who thought it better to serve the cause of the desert people than the unspoken alternative; or women who were receptive to the Djinn and the ghosts who possessed.

Al-Shai-affa was mostly able to guess the outcome and he always tried to carry out the Djinn orders. Sometimes he pleaded with them and they might even allow him what he wished for, but this was a tactic he didn't often employ; only when he was confident of his position, and their mood.

Now, he felt badly unsure of his ground. He wanted to just kill this woman; not to for them take her as a flesh-channel or even to meet with her at all; but he couldn't dare appear in front of them as a whimpering weakling.

Thoughts were whirling around in his head like the wind around him and he put his hands to his face cloth, feeling the sticky blood there. He knelt at the rock, placing his head on the ground at its base; praying for their instructions.

Nor did he need to wait long before feeling their power, but was surprised at what voices were telling him; not far different from his own. They wanted nothing of this woman and were disgusted by any thoughts of the Hebrew sage imposter; 'MalkiTzedek again? No! Not MalkiTzedek, No!' So, they instructed

Al-Shai-Haffa of their will and he went his way back to the camp, leaving his blood face-offering as he always did.

*

Yresmin watched the leader stagger back towards her, bringing the fierceness of the sandstorm with him. She felt it whipping her like flails and tried to turn her face away, but her captors held her firmly there.

"Go" said Al-Shai-Haffa hoarsely, "they want nothing with you."

Yresmin saw a frightened man trying to save himself and his power. "Why should I?" she shouted into the blizzard. "I was brought here to see the Djinn, but now you won't even allow…?"

"They have told me their will," he answered; "and I will tell it to you. *'You are to go to your sorcerer and bear the message of his death. The poison that will kill him is already within his circle. Nothing will avail him now'*. And now you will *GO, and take that message with you!*"

Yresmin felt a chill go through her. Was she, priestess of the Goddess of Fate to deliver such a message from the powers of the dark to the bringer of light and love? Of all things she had not expected this. Her knees went weak but somehow she managed not to sink to the ground.

Words deserted her and Al-Shai-Haffa was enjoying watching her reaction. Finally, she stood straight again and returned his gaze squarely. "Unless you return my donkey, I shall not go anywhere," was all she could say.

Al-Shai-Haffa's eyes narrowed and he jerked his head in command to one of the men holding Yresmin. "Get her donkey," he said, much to Yresmin's astonishment.

The other man allowed Yresmin to turn away from the storm's onslaught as he loosened her bonds, as Al-Shai-Haffa instructed him. Together they took her to where Selly was being untied from her tethering, the donkey also struggling in the storm.

"And a water-skin," demanded Yresmin, but Al-Shai-affa had had enough. "Go!" he screamed. "Go now!"

She left the camp, pulling poor Selly along with her, desperate now to get away from the wrath of the whirlwind, and the fearful misery of the ghosters.

CHAPTER 9.

The dry valley that Yresmin fled down offered precious little protection from the force of the storm. Sand whipped around her and she was blind to anything around her, accept the trusting Selly at her side. She knew she had to get out of the whipping sand, or be flayed alive by it.

She had lost all sense of direction, but allowed herself to be driven where the storm would take her, as long as it was away. Eventually she stumbled over the lip of a slope; a rocky ridge that gave a slight bit of shelter if she could duck low enough.

She rested for a few moments but it was no good for Selly, though the donkey didn't seem quite so bothered by the storm as Yresmin was, attired in only her flimsy under-shift. Suddenly she had an idea and pulling off her shift she put it over her and Selly's heads, to try to keep the flying sand out of their eyes, noses and mouths. It didn't really work until she had tied the top into a kind of knot and then it helped, except her body was taking an almost unbearable whipping, which was opening her older wounds as well.

The blasting sand was coming off the lip of the hill on her right side, and so crouching down behind Selly's body made it possible for them to feel their way along the ridge, just about below the raging wind.

And they did find an outcrop of higher rock that was reasonable shelter for them both, and gratefully Yresmin sank down in the lea of it, pulling Selly in as close as she could get as well.

*

Selly stood over her mistress, her eyes closed against the power of the storm.

Her mistress had taken her shift back but was still in a bad way, she knew. Selly could smell the blood ebbing out of her prostrate form. The night was cold and the wind was worse. She lowered herself onto her knees beside her to give her as much of her own body warmth as she could. It might be enough, must be enough, as she leant her neck across her mistress's shoulders.

She was careful not to press too hard with her body's weight. It was her best effort.

*

There was grass under their feet on the hill they were climbing together and Yresmin saw a marble columned white temple at the top. Selly stopped to taste the grass.

A guide, clothed in white came and caught Yresmin by the hand, and Selly also felt herself being pulled aside.

There was a lip at the side of the hill that plunged into a vast bowl with a huge lake, almost a sea, glinting blue in the basin…

Each of them awoke and knew that the sandstorm had passed or blown itself out, and up above was the majestic sea of stars again. It was cold though, and Yresmin knew this would be the best time to travel, if only to keep warm through exertion.

She really didn't know in which direction they had left the ghoster camp but if the sandstorm had come from the deep desert, then going away from it should have meant they had come westwards, back towards the King's Highway. The stars tended to agree that the ridge they had reached ran pretty much north – south, though their origanal flight could still have been round in a curve, or even a circle.

There was no point in trying to work it out; they would just head west, going as fast as they both could lest the Ghosters, or Djinn even, changed their minds. Hopefully, they could reach one of the Nabatean Army outposts along the Highway, before any pursuit could find them.

They got going at quite a good pace until Yresmin remembered the task that had come as the price of her freedom. The Djinn warning to, or taunting of, Yeheshua, that his circle was broken; poison would enter, spoil all his efforts.

Remembering it was like a poison in itself, spreading awful weakness through her limbs. 'Why me? Why me?' She leant against Selly and cried, such tears of frustration that she hadn't known in many years.

Eventually she gathered her strength to continue but, they not being on a proper path, climbing up seemingly endless slopes and struggling through strength-sapping sand, took their toll. She had to ask Selly to bear her again; allow and urge her to pick the best path for them both, but having nothing to give in return, except her thanks.

Because of the cold Yresmin lay along the back of her friend, hugging her for some extra warmth and once again falling into the strange dream-sleep…

The were approaching a swaying silver bridge, impossibly long spans stretching over blueness

An island swathed in roiling mists… And a gap through to all that is Good

Clots of darkness flew out and around the mists, veering towards them.

The guide could go no further but calmly placed Yresmin's hand on the handrail, pointing the way … she must go there, through the mists.

Darkness came at her and Yresmin tried to shout at it … but no words came to her dry throat.

Faces imprinted on the darknesses were all hers and only Selly was unpeturbed, plodding steadily onwards, pulling at her mistress who clutched at the handrail

bearer of a message of betrayal and death to the one she sought as the bringer of light.

She jerked awake, looking behind her; seeng only the faint line of daylight seeping up into the sky. To the front was a low wall, and Selly stopping at it must have woken her.

And the pain in her head was almost unbearable, mixing itself into the great thirst at the back of her throat. But they had got back to the Highway, and she slid off her donkey, leaning against her, arms around her neck, eyes closed.

She knew she had to open her eyes again, and she tried but without success.

Her face brushed against the furry hair of Selly's back and neck and she focussed her mind, away from the pain and the thirst, willing herself to see her friend, to open her eyes.

It seemed important to Yresmin to find a gap and so she half led, half leaned on Selly, northwards, to where the wall seemed to be deteriorating into fallen piles of stones that could be stepped through.

Which way should they go? Did it even matter?

Northwards to Yeheshua she thought and laughed silently at her madness.

But it didn't matter much. A Nabatean patrol came across the pair, almost stationary and clearly exhausted.

Cupped hands of blessed water was all they needed though, and for Selly to be led back to their base once Yresmin had been helped onto her back.

They had survived. Yresmin gave thanks; they were safe.

CHAPTER 10.

Miriam led her horse and Johannus placed himself between Miriam and Seth, which seemed sensible. Seth moved a bit ahead, and we followed.

I gave the reins of Nala to Johannus and moved up beside Seth. There were things I wanted to ask him.

"Are there many others posted on these roads?"

"A few I think," he said.

"What for... do you think?"

"I think we... they, are targeting you two women in particular; as far as I could understand; but why, I don't know."

"Why should we trust you now? You could easily lead us into further trouble."

"And you could easily have killed me. I probably would have deserved it. I know now that that is not what I joined with Barabbas for; to kidnap women."

"Why did you join him then?"

Seth carried on walking but was clearly pondering this.

"I want to make a difference," he said finally. "The Romans just come in and take what they want. They have no respect for us; everything that we live for and believe in. My mother was killed by them for just trying to protect a neighbour."

"What had he done?"

"I don't actually know. I think he was on the run for stealing." Seth paused.

"So many of us are poor and suffering. I have the strength of my body; I want to help make things better. I don't care what happens to me; I can give my blood for my people."

We walked on in silence. I understood what he had been feeling; his passion. So many young men in particular wanted to do something with their energy to change things. I had been a rebel myself of course, in my own way.

"What I have understood is..." I started. "What Yeheshua has been able to show me is... is that when everything else is stripped away... all the things that we think of as our world; our relationships, our country, everything... and we step back from everything that we think we are; the anger, the cares and loves and hates that bind us to it... when all that is gone, then I have found there is a most beautiful, simple truth... "

Seth looked at me, intently. I concentrated hard to try to communicate the feeling, and deliberately take out all references to God.

"that there is a simple, beautiful... life within us, that is the same in everything, that is called... I am, and in that sweet life we are connected to everything. That is... everything is part of the same, and to really feel it is."

Seth continued to look at me. I wasn't sure what he had gathered from my attempt to explain the simple thing that took away my hates and fears. "It changes everything when you can experience that," I said. "It really does."

He said nothing but I didn't need an answer anyway.

We had reached a spot where we could see clearly across to where the river Jordan lay and there was a distant glimpse of the sea of Galilee. The view was magical but that was not the reason Seth had stopped and we stood around him.

"If we carry on along this track there is a good chance we shall run into Barabbas' men," he said; "but there is a way across this ground that can avoid them."

"I don't trust him," said Johannus. "I think we are putting ourselves in too much danger to go a way he suggests."

"What is the way you say is safe?" asked Miriam.

"Across these grazing grounds. These poles can be drawn back to let the horses through. I know a way to get to the road through here."

Miriam turned to me. "What do you think Mary?"

I was remembering Yeheshua entrusting me with getting Miriam safely back. I could clearly feel how close that goal was now. My heart told me that our master was bringing us home; we only needed to trust him.

"I think we should go across the pastures; the path is too dangerous. If they guard anywhere, it has to be there first," I said.

Johannus still looked doubtful and Seth turned to him. "You can bind my hands and kill me at the first sign of a betrayal." He put his hands out to Johannus.

There was a long moment whilst the two men locked their gaze. Finally, Johannus took Seth's proffered hands. "The offer is enough," he said. "We might need your hands free to aid our cause." Seth bowed his head, and then got on with opening up the wall to the meagre pastures.

CHAPTER 11.

We crossed the wide areas of rough land and got onto the Jordan road and to comparative safety. So, we stopped and took some bread and dried fruit from our supplies to serve as breakfast.

A lot had already happened. Johannus couldn't believe that this time the day before they had just been setting out from Bethany.

A little while ago he had nearly killed the man beside him, whom he was now sharing bread with. He still felt slightly shocked.

Earlier he had woken up after some disjointed but powerful dreams that were probably the combined result of their flight from the brigands and his unsuccessful attempt to stay awake and keep watch.

Hecate had been there; and there was a titanic struggle going on. Strangely he had found himself to be a powerless observer, but one that could get sucked into the outcome at any moment.

*

Hecate was mistress of the underworld; a place of gateways, where choices met the borders of eternity.

Her power kept all beings to their proper course, given by the timeless rules of existence. Consequences were brought upon people by themselves; of dark or light, good or evil. A magic shadow-play where she was both master and mistress.

Now her borders were under siege and she was hard pressed, struggling to keep the buckling boundaries intact; gateways being sometimes rent where they were not meant to be. Wrongness that was growing; troubling Hecate exceedingly.

Death was central in her realm, part of everything.

The wrongness was bound to human fear of death and the resultant terror that this brought to their own lives and all other life.

Something had magnified the problem; whether it was a storing up of this poison or the shear weight of numbers of human souls that had lost their way.

That night Johannus had seen fragments of her in her triple aspects.

Queen of magic and motherhood, keeping the balance of her realm intact. Stretched to the very limit of her caring capabilities, but was nevertheless holding true.

Johannus was in awe of this Hecate.

Fearsome crone who wielded her power and wisdom like a taloned claw. Nothing could stand against her fierce assault, whether of this world or any other.

Terrifying though this Hecate was the notion of her being somehow over-come by the magnitude of her burden was worse, and this fragment of Johannus' dream was the most uncomfortable; for this Hecate could not be in all places at once, and he felt bound to her fate in some way.

Finally, there was the young Hecate, whose girlish beauty beguiled and mesmerised those she turned upon. Lonely but lovely and Johannus wanted to help her, and this is what had brought and held him to the dream.

But throughout the dream he had also known he was travelling to the master Yeheshua; and this had been a flame of hope, even to his awakening.

*

After taking breakfast, we saddled the horses for the last stage of the journey.

Johannus' left hip had been giving him pain all morning and he was hoping to be able to ride for a while. However, it never became an issue because Seth was saying he couldn't go with us; that he needed to atone first for having attacked us.

"You have already done that Seth;" said Miriam. "You have helped us get to this road. You are free to go wherever you want, including to come with us to the master's celebration."

"I need to do something more; I cannot come," he said, "not yet".

We looked at each other and Miriam nodded, knowing what I was thinking.

"We have friends coming up along this road, travelling with an asses train," I said. "They won't have reached the crossroads yet. Maybe you could go back to them and make sure they get safely through. Except, it would put you in much greater danger yourself."

Seth looked pleased.

Johannus turned to him. "If you go, ask for Beor the smithy. Tell him that Johannus asked you to see him because 'you are afraid you might hurt yourself again'."

Seth looked puzzled.

"He will know what you mean and it will prove to him that you come from us and have no harm in you. Miriam, shall I give back Seth his knife and sword?"

Miriam scowled at them; boys and their games. She gave back Seth's sword and Seth repeated what he was to say to Beor. "... then tell him you almost stabbed yourself," added Johannus. "That will make him laugh, and it is pretty much true wouldn't you say?"

Seth still looked a little unsure and Miriam explained, "Johannus here hurt himself with his own sword, and Beor thinks it is really funny. It is the sort of personal thing that will prove to Beor you have our trust."

"Ooh, I see," said Seth seriously, "I'll go and do it then. You all be careful; but I think you should be all right now."

Strangely we bade a fond farewell to the man who had tried to ambush us, and Johannus as much as anyone.

Once more we mounted up, Miriam and I on Melody and Johannus on Nala, and carried on into Galilee with all haste.

*

Johannus hadn't met Yeheshua but he had travelled with the person who he believed was closest to him: Miriam. Still, he was unsure of what lay ahead.

He felt so much for Miriam, though not in the same way as he might for other women; that he was sure of at least. He admired her so that he was almost a little fearful of meeting Yeheshua; yet at the same time the master had hugely influenced his own life, freeing him to be at this place, this feeling.

The worry it caused for him was: would the master measure up to what Johannus had built from what had happened to him and the stories of his companions?

He also didn't know what he was going to do once Miriam and I got back to Yeheshua. For months now his life had been to escort and guard us from whatever danger we might encounter. But that would all be finished with after this and he didn't know what he would be doing then.

But despite even that unknown Johannus really wanted to get to the celebration in Galilee, and was thankful that any misgivings he might have about himself and his life were just tiny ripples compared to a much bigger wave that pulled him along with itself.

The pull that we all adored to feel, to be with the living Lord.

*

Along our way a Roman patrol of about a dozen horsemen met us going in the opposite direction. Their officer stopped us and asked us where we were going.

"To join our teacher Yeheshua at Capernaum," answered Miriam straightaway.

"Have you met with any trouble?" The captain asked, turning towards Johannus. "Any people who could be bandits?"

Johannus glanced at me then back to the Roman officer. "Yes," he replied. "There were a lot ruffians at the inn we stopped at, and some particularly unpleasant types as well. We left early and the last we saw was many of them leaving down the road towards Sychar and Caesarea."

"When was this?"

"Last night, after we had eaten. We stopped there to get out of the storm, but with those people there we decided to leave early. We camped out on the hills instead."

The Roman officer appraised Johannus briefly. If he guessed that Johannus was carrying a sword under his travel cloak he decided to ignore it. Instead, he called over to one of his troopers.

"Gerrant; ride back to the main body and tell Sestius that I would advise him to divide his force into three. The first third to follow us down this way and then take the road to Caesarea; another to make all haste to the west, then cut south to join the Caesarea road at Jallop; and the remainder to fan out and comb the hills between these two flanks like a net. We ourselves shall continue down to take the road to Sychar, and then circle round to meet him."

Gerrant was a bright young man and he joined us for a short while as we rode northwards, then kicked his horse into a faster gallop as we crested a rise. "I shall tell the Commander that you have already given us your information, and to allow you through without delay."

Further on we came to the large troop of soldiers stopped on the road, and many more off its edge. Gerrant was among the first group, obviously discussing things with the senior officer, distinguishable by the impressive plume on his helmet, who waved in our direction and shouted an order to the outermost guard on the road.

We were allowed to thread our way through the troops strung along the road and we felt their readiness. Events were heating up.

Once beyond them we caught sight of the sea of Galilee again, sparkling in the strong sunshine. Here, where Yeheshua had concentrated so much of his time and effort to ignite the sparks, like the light on the waves of the sea. Soon we would be with him, and joining his celebration.

*

We felt the difference. Travelling so close beside the inland sea, passing Tiberius where the soldiers were stationed, and on around my Magdala towards Capernaum. It was like entering into a different country, one where winter had passed and the new spring had come.

The feeling of excitement in the air became even more tangible as we arrived in Capernaum, navigating to the wide road where Yeheshua's home was.

There were many people gathered around 'Mirimion', a big crowd but one that was quiet and ordered with many people seated in groups under the trees on the avenue.

Miriam went directly to Yeheshua. Our horses had already been left at the asses paddock of my business and we walked quickly up to the side of the house where a disciple seated at the gate recognised Miriam and me and let us through.

Yeheshua was sitting in the garden with his mother and his closest disciples. All of 'the twelve' were there.

*

Johannus found himself carrying several bags as he followed Miriam and Mary. Miriam's pace quickened almost to a run as she trod the familiar path up the side of Yeheshua's house and her travel cloak slipped back letting her newly fairer hair flow free.

They passed the corner of the house and into view of the people in the garden. Johannus strained his eyes for his first sight of the master.

They all looked quite similar. There was no halo of light surrounding any of them, such as Johannus' imagination portrayed the master as having. He had sometimes seen, or thought he had, a kind of light around Simon Magus.

The simple difference that Johannus noticed was that one man was the centre of all the others attention. Comfortably so. This was Yeheshua and the master had looked up and was drinking in their arrival.

Yeheshua's face was calm and clear and upon seeing Miriam and Mary it lit up with joy. In a moment he was on his feet and all the others around him were spinning around to see what was happening.

Miriam stopped momentarily as Yeheshua rose and, to Johannus watching, the space between them became a world of its own.

As Yeheshua took a step towards her Miriam glided to him, starting to fall towards his feet, but he caught her in his arms as she did, cradling her head to his breast instead.

His hand was at the back of her neck, fingers curling around golden tendrils of her hair. Smiling he gently he raised her up and looked full into her eyes.

To Johannus their faces reflected their love back and forth, unable to be fathomed.

Yeheshua held Miriam's head in both his hands and kissed her gently, smiling. "How wonderful you are back," he said.

All that was bottled up in Johannus spilled into and from his heart. He had now met the one who was Miriam's Lord… and his Lord.

CHAPTER 12.

Yresmin slept fitfully, her dreams a mixture of nightmares and strange roads that went nowhere or around in circles.

When she awoke, the room she was lying in was blissfully shady with a cool breeze coming in through the open window. The bed she was on was neither hard nor soft. She lay back for a few minutes and then slipped off and walked across the smooth tiled floor to see outside.

*

They were sitting in a large circle under the trees by the far end of the building; on white marble seats around a wide pool that had a golden fountain in the centre. Only a trickle of water was coming from it now.

She followed the line of the pavilion's colonnade, drawn inexorably to the council. She knew she had to be there, to hear the decision.

Looking around her Yresmin saw that everything was covered in a white blanket, purer than any marble, and she wondered how she hadn't noticed this before. The colourfully clad figures by the pool contrasted brightly with it, but the pool itself had changed as one of the figures rose to his feet.

He had a golden circlet round his brow in which a clear white jewel shined, and as he spoke, he gestured towards what was happening in the pool in front of him.

Yresmin gasped at the vision of a familiar lake with wooded shores, lying in the pool. She knew she had seen it sometime but it didn't quite matter. Something was happening in the middle, but it was hard to see what. A light gleamed softly through hopeful gaps in a broiling shadow.

The lord of the council was speaking "… the shadowland is of humankind's making, we cannot interfere with it."

A beautiful woman had also stood up on the right hand side of the pool, asking questions that Yresmin couldn't hear; but she could hear the lord's replies.

"The lords of Hades are not bound by our constraints, no, but we can challenge anything that comes into our realm."

A long pause followed.

"Humankind must eventually light their own way; that is the law. Which is why the divine light, the divine love, is ever amongst them; especially now. Otherwise, there would be no hope."

Another of the Eloi rose to join the standing figures and then another. A clear concern was working amongst them but still Yresmin couldn't quite catch the details.

*The lord raised his hands, calming their distress. "We shall send a message that shows our readiness…. Yes, it very possible that whatever is happening, that he is doing, could change our worlds forever; but I **do** understand it is of paramount importance to all of you … all of us …. that he knows he has our unconditional trust and support."*

"Who can do it?" sounded a deep-voiced question that this time Yresmin heard

clearly.

The lord of the council looked directly at Yresmin from across the image filled pool. "I shall take the message myself; give it to him on behalf of you all," he said with a finality that all the council accepted; and then in the pause he stretched an open-palmed hand towards Yresmin. "Priestess…"

*

Yresmin started and re-opened her eyes. The room's open window let in the hot breeze from the desert, and with it the sound of raised voices.

The palette that she lay on was hard and very real; her body was dotted with pain from unknown hurts.

She shifted her position and felt some relief in her aching side. Her head throbbed and she put up her hand to feel where the wound in her scalp had left her hair matted with blood.

'Urg … that part was real then," she told herself, propping her torso up on her elbow. There was a cup with some water in it set beside bed and gratefully she reached out for it with her other arm.

The water slipped between her cracked lips to answer her thirst; an elixir in itself.

Relaxing back her head onto the bed's thin pillow, she breathed out a deep sigh. How wonderful to be safe. Wonderful… but where was she?

Lying there Yresmin searched her memories and thought of Selly. Her friend had carried her faithfully and she had survived. She must find her.

She pushed herself up again, swinging her legs off the side of the bed and sat there gathering her strength.

Shuffling over to the door she found it closed but not locked and pulled it open to where a platform ran around a square opening in the centre of a squat, square building.

To Yresmin's surprise a woman was walking around to where she was; somewhere in the back of her mind she thought this must be an army outpost and she had only expected there to be soldiers here.

The woman came up to Yresmin and asked her if she was all right, introducing herself as Melinda.

Yresmin was glad to have a sympathetic arm to lean on as Melinda took her to the washroom and stayed with her as she washed and tended her various hurts. She also took out another under-shift from a cupboard there whilst Yresmin set about washing her own travel shift.

Yresmin went back to the room where she had slept and a few minutes later Melinda rejoined her with two hot drinks.

"Where is this place? I thought it must be a frontier fort."

"It is," said Melinda, and then, understanding the reason for the question, "there are several of us wives here as well; ones that don't have families to tend to."

"Ah I see," said Yresmin. "I didn't realise that."

For a while they said nothing, but suddenly Melinda recognised her as Manat's priestess, despite her short hair.

"Not any more, Bishmi is that now," she said. "I am just me; and happier this way, please don't tell anyone." Melinda promised not to but with her prompting her, Yresmin told some of her story, going backwards to the storm and the awful ghoster camp, and then how she had started out from Kadesh on her pilgrimage and found the massacre on the road.

Then she tried to explain how wonderful her donkey had been throughout it all. "I was tring to find her here when I met you," she added finally.

"Let's go and find her then. First, I shall go get you a cloak to wear."

In the couple of minutes till Melinda's return Yresmin hung her travel shift on the drying line across the outside of the window. Heavier compared to the one she now wore, she wondered why it was necessary to have the extra seams that it did. 'Never mind' she thought, 'Kardun had surely meant well.'

Selly was eating hay, happily ensconced in the stables amongst a number of the soldier's horses. Yresmin went up and stroked her friend's forehead and neck and was rewarded with a sideways push from Selly's rounded flank. She was obviously fine.

"I shall go and arrange you something to eat," said Melinda as they watched the animals munching away. "My husband is the officer of the patrol that brought you in. Will you be able to tell him all that you can remember about the ghosters and their camp? It could help to track them down?"

"Yes, I will; whatever I can; and thank you for everything."

Cherandris came and questioned Yresmin. Melinda's husband was an able officer and he quickly gathered that the ghosters had been at one of their many temporary camps and that it would be useless to try to follow Yresmin's trail back to it. They would have already moved.

He wasn't sure what the garrison were going to do with their guest but they couldn't afford to tend to her for too long. They ran a very lean operation. He left her when a meal was brought; she would probably feel a lot stronger after having had some food. Perhaps she would be able to work with the other women quite soon.

Yresmin crossed over to the window where the strong sun had mostly dried the travel shift. Her hands tested the fabric, especially where the seams held onto any residual moisture. She shook her head again at the garment's design, fingers feeling down one side where a loose thread was allowing a seam to come apart.

Something caught her attention; something that was not cotton. She examined the opening seam and an inner thread glinted in the light. What was it? She picked the end of the seam apart easily and uncovered two golden threads twisted along its inner length.

She took the knife that had come with her food and used it to start unpicking another seam, revealing two more twisted gold wires and the same again in a third.

She stood back stunned and then laughed aloud. This explained so much; the seams, the weight, and most of all Kardun's veiled references to its protective power. She silently thanked her old friend for his gift of care; perhaps she would be able to carry on her pilgrimage sooner than she had dared hope.

*

Yresmin dreamed again that night of the Pavilion of the Eloi. Nothing as distinct as the previous night, except that she was with their lord and he was joking playfully with her. She had wanted to give him a big hug and when she awoke, she had the distinct feeling that she had.

Three little coils of gold were sufficient for Yresmin to purchase all the supplies for the journey onwards to Jerusalem, including a new saddle and panniers. Another two bought her travelling clothes as well, together with spare under-shifts. The sixth one was a parting gift to Melinda and Cherandris; they wouldn't accept more.

She collected all her new things and went out to load them onto Selly. Her donkey was certainly completely recovered from any of the elements of her ordeal that she might have remembered. Enough to play up a little as the stable attendant struggled to buckle the panniers into place.

He was a grizzled old soldier, probably quite close to retirement but he had plenty of patience and a ready twinkle in his eye.

"I reckon this girl is quite heavy with foal, you know," he said, displaying a row of uneven and broken teeth.

"No, that can't be true," answered Yresmin quickly.

"Come and feel then," he said and she went forward to feel her donkey's furry flanks and tummy.

"She has always been a bit rounded," declared Yresmin to the upturned eyebrow of the stableman, and then; "how many weeks has she to go, do you think? Should I not travel with her?"

"A few weeks yet, but not many," was his ambiguous response. "She should be fine for going to Jerusalem; as long as she is not too overloaded. No problem at all with what you are taking."

The first thing I noticed was that Yeheshua had shaved off his beard again. It made him look younger, but still somehow kingly; a bridegroom, I realised as Miriam, his destined bride, fell into his arms.

Their kiss was a shock to the twelve I noticed, looking around the familiar faces of the group in the garden. Only mother Mary amongst them all looked truly excited and pleased, and she went over to Miriam even as the master relinquished her from his embrace and turned towards me and Johannus.

He came over to me and hugged me too which filled me with wonder and joy. Releasing me, his kind and smiling face looked into mine and he thanked me for fulfilling the quest. I was speechless, other than indicating Johannus beside me. "This man Johannus played a big part too in keeping us safe," was all I managed.

Yeheshua turned to Johannus, with hands outstretched. "Thank you my friend," he said, and in answer to Johannus' slightly foolish grin he added, "and if you wish to carry on in the same way, giving protection to the women in my following, then I would be most pleased." Johannus' enthusiastic nods needed no explanation.

"What we have been discussing here," said Yeheshua, turning back to indicate the twelve and others in the garden, "are the coming celebrations of all that has been accomplished here in Galilee."

"Invitations have gone out far and wide and we are readying the beach and natural arena by the sea that we used when the crowds became very large. Only this time it will be filled with all of our brothers and sisters who are joined to us in our task."

I looked around again at all the faces intently listening to the master's words, spotting another clean-shaven one, familiar even from my early years in Antioch; Thomas, called Didymus. He caught my eye as well and smiled momentarily, before returning his gaze back to the master.

Then in the background, with a group of the women, I saw Rachel the healer from Tyre and I was doubly glad.

"We will provide extra tents and all of the food, and I wish to have the chance to speak with each and every one who comes."

"That will be almost impossible to arrange," said Peter, ever forthright. "I mean unless… I mean… there will be at least a thousand coming, so we are told."

"Yes, I shall make sure it is possible," agreed the master, almost straight facedly. "So simple that you really could do it if you put your heart into it Peter. On the second day, all the twelve must be ready to distribute the food to our guests sat in small groups of three or four or so and I shall do the rest. Nathaniel, are all the wooden bowls nearly done?"

"The last hundred or so will be ready for you tomorrow morning, sire."

Surprisingly he turned to me again, asking quietly. "Mary will you be able to help Rachel with people coming in need of healing? We want to keep that as separate as possible from the main gathering."

"I would love to," I answered truly and Yeheshua nodded over to where the women were stood, "Rachel, I have found the person you needed to help you."

It was fantastic to be home again.

*

I stayed with my mother and Jacob who had come to Capernaum for the celebration as well. She was older still of course but strong in spirit and happy in her retirement.

She asked all about our travels, for she was one person that I had managed to tell when Yeheshua had asked me to accompany Miriam on the master's quest.

She listened in wonder and then patted my hand, "I am so glad you are safely back, my dearest. I thought you were going to miss this."

"No chance," I answered.

The arrangements for the celebration were well advanced even before we arrived, with pavilions being set up by the shore and boats ferrying supplies to the groups of disciples working there.

Then the day arrived for festivities to begin in earnest.

It was going to last for two days, with people arriving all through the first day and finding themselves a place to be in the festival grounds, lining up for the food and other necessities which had been made ready for them. Many spent the afternoon in catching up with old acquaintances and co-workers or finding themselves a task to help with.

There were quite a few surprisingly important people amongst the arrivals, and I noticed that Miriam and mother Mary were busy ensuring these people were also looked after properly. Not maybe more than others, but so that they didn't feel unnecessarily slighted or left out either. For most of these had arranged places to stay in the town which had its own disadvantages to overcome.

Yeheshua spoke to the assembly that evening as the setting sun lit up the sky. He spoke of all that had been accomplished as the seed for the future age, thanking everyone there for helping bring the light into this world. That their love would feed the people and everyone grow because of that, including themselves; exorting them to rise to the challenge of this new time, and that he himself was going ahead to open the way. At the end he also explained where the tents were that had been provided for those who were staying out at the site, and where the washing and other facilities were as well. Finally, he bade everyone goodnight and said that he would see them early in the morning.

Rachel and I weren't very busy on the first day but we were expecting more sick and needy people to be drawn in by the influx of disciples from around the country. We had set out a nice compound with simple beds next to one of the streams that ran down onto the beach. On the other side of us John had arranged another wide area where any new people would be asked to wait; Yeheshua planned to spare some time for them as well.

This was a new way of doing things for all of us.

The morning of the second day dawned with a beautiful sunrise and I was already out at the site to see it. Rachel arrived soon after, but neither of us were there before Yeheshua. He must have come very early by boat but I saw him in many areas of the site where people had hardly yet awoken, walking around, inspiring them to get ready for the new day.

He visited our area as well and looked at the stock of herbs and things that Rachel had brought. "Very good," he nodded, "and if there are any possessed then Mary you are the first line. You know I am with you;" and then he laughed, "and won't be very far away either."

He was sighted in many places that morning, breakfasting with the Grecian senator Theophilus in one report and several other places in Capernaum as well. Some of these undoubtedly conflicted with how he was seen visiting the activities on the festival site but it would make no difference to try to make sense of it. As it was, he asked us all to be at the main arena an hour before midday. Even we would be able to be at the edge, if everything was quiet.

Quite a few sick people did come to the celebration to try to get the master's help, as would be expected. Rachel was amazing with all the work she did. I felt mostly like a spare part, but helped her in any way I could.

Then there was one moment where we thought that a possessed was indeed causing a noisy problem close by us where the new people were waiting to hear Yeheshua. John wasn't there, but a number of picked disciples from around Galilee were.

The woman fled from the several disciples that approached her, towards Rachel and myself. Neither of us moved until she crashed into one of the beds, and then I went over to her to help her get to her feet. I held her close and hugged her until she stopped shaking, feeling her heart beating like a trapped bird.

"She is not possessed," I said. "Just frightened of the approaching darkness. She is all right. You are all right. Everything will be fine." She quietened down surprisingly quickly and then went to the back of the area she had come from. I wondered to myself how I had known what I had, but Rachel just took me to her and hugged me.

By the hour before midday everything was quite calm and we thought we could take turns in going to the arena, which we did.

Before Yeheshua spoke he asked Miriam to sing some of the songs which all who had heard her sing loved and had missed.

We listened entranced as her voice carried the unspoken feelings of our hearts and laid them in front of the master as gifts of gratitude and love. Never had I felt so completed and included with every song she sung to us and him.

At the end he got up and they stood together for a minute whilst he applauded her. They both looked so radiant and happy; I wondered if this was going to be a betrothal announcement; and then Yeheshua did stand forward and speak:

"If this seems like a marriage feast today, then it is because it is so. For many years I have been betrothed to the task that my Heavenly Father has given me and now I am to share in this marriage of giving His love with all of you. Every single one of you."

"It shall not be an easy path, but once we have put our shoulders to the wheel then let us not step away from it. For in the end it is by the shear persistence of our practice that we shall overcome and reach our goal. No-one becomes perfectly skilled in any art without determination and practice. How much more for the heavenly art of feeling joy and true compassion?"

"Yet every little effort that we make will be rewarded, because that is the bond of this marriage. Every effort on our side is magnified a hundredfold by God's Grace. So, it will ever be."

"And if you stumble, fear not, but get up again. Every one of us stumbles but every time you get up again you will be a little stronger. Yet do not deliberately go astray, for that will let back in other things that you had put away from you, and they will come back stronger also."

As I turned back to go and get Rachel, I realised that she was already beside me. "It is all right," she said. "He is taking care of everything." I could feel she was right; the air around us itself was hushed and attentive.

Yeheshua was telling a story that was making everyone laugh of how a lord eventually had to give way to the persistent pleadings of an aggrieved widow, just to shut her up and explained that we must be just as persistent, and that that on its own will be enough. It was a slightly unexpected idea to me, and then he was giving other examples and parables until he came back to his original point.

"So, all of you know the love that God has for you, and you have His Word to call upon. Do it as often as you breathe and it will be well for you. This marriage will blossom and many, many wonderful doors shall be opened for you. Maybe not the riches of this world, but certainly the riches of heaven, now, in this life, and in the next."

"And whilst speaking of the riches of this world, I have a tiny gift for each of you. A humble wooden bowl; made by Nathaniel and his aides and with a little embellishment from my own hand. Please stay where you are in small groups and these will be brought to you, followed by some hopefully delicious stew to put in them, prepared by Susannah and her wonderful cooks; and bread to go with it which James declares to be his best effort yet."

"Please stay where you are because I also want to come to you as well. Again please heed what I am asking. Stay in the groups that you are eating with, for I want to be able to come and talk to each one of you; but if you were to move around that will become impossible."

Then the twelve started handing out the wooden bowls to all the assembled disciples and Philip brought one each for Rachel and I, standing on the edge.

They were simple olivewood turned bowls, polished to show the attractive knots and grain of the wood, and on the outside of each, four curved lines had been scored that cleverly gave the bowl the appearance of an opening flower. Masterful touches from the master wood worker himself.

"How precious are these?" I said to Rachel.

"Much too good to put stew in," she replied, but we both gave way when our time came and an insistent Andrew, Peter's brother, assured us they would be none the worse for having the stew in them and moreover it was what Yeheshua wished.

The stew was delicious, scooped up by strips of the bread that was perhaps even better than Yeheshua had led us to believe; but our attention was all the while pulled back to where he himself was now moving between the diners, following the pattern that the twelve were making.

Every person had his attention for a sweet brief span. Many touched his robe or feet as well, and he didn't seem to mind. Sometimes he was laughing, sometimes serious, but always progressing around in what appeared as a slow and wonderful dance to all of us watching; knowing that we too were part of that dance.

A procession that took a long time but no-one wanted it to end. No-one stirred from where they were sitting, just as he had asked; couldn't have done I don't think.

When he came to Rachel he said simply, "though it may not always seem this way to you, everything you are doing is making a difference. This world desperately needs for us to care for each other; just as you do. Your example will inspire many and I am proud to work with you."

I couldn't help a small voice thinking, 'what of me?' as Yeheshua turned my way. How could I think this way after he had hugged me? It made no difference to him though, and I knew it.

"You Mary will cast your net wide and bring in a great harvest; this I know." He paused for half a moment, "as long as you keep your light burning as true and as strong as I know you can..." My heart gratefully drank in his words, feeling his strength coming into me. "With your grace and love I will," I said.

"Your love Mary; you have the love in you; and with it you can accomplish everything."

After he had passed us Yeheshua called to Andrew and Peter to go and take the extra bowls and food to the new people who had been waiting patiently through the afternoon in the roped off area John had created.

"Really?" asked Peter, sounding slightly surprised. "Yes, and I shall be over to talk to them presently," answered the Lord and once again Peter felt he should kick himself. "You and Andrew bring James and John as well please, and I shall ask the musicians to play for the assembly, and then maybe Miriam will sing as well again."

We went back to check on our patients in the sick compound and we were pleased that no-one seemed any the worse for our having left them for so long; nor had anyone tried to go away either.

Peter showed no reluctance in giving out all the precious bowls, stalwart that he was once he understood his master's will, and it wasn't long before Andrew arrived, hurrying with James and John and the food.

Before we realised Yeheshua was there as well with a few more disciples in tow as well. "Welcome," he said to the large knot of waiting people, "and thank you for your patience."

"What we are talking about today," he continued without further preamble, "is about knowing the love of God within our hearts. This is the essence of it all; that fills you with every breath you breathe." He paused.

"Why then, you might ask are you not experiencing this wonder? And that also is what today is about."

"There is a work that needs to be done and a path to be followed, which we are gathered here to celebrate. We are not the first, nor shall be the last by any means; it has always been man's need to know this, since the dawn of time itself."

Strains of the music that had started up in the arena carried over to where the master now paused for a moment. Miriam's sweet voice had also joined in, singing songs of Israel of old.

"Moses brought the tribes out of Egypt to reach the promised land. This was the symbol and the promise of the work we all must do, that we need to bring ourselves from valuing everything that this world seems to offer, and to start learning to value what has really been given you to keep; your self; your soul; your life itself."

He stopped for a second and looked around at those of us disciples that were also around him, listening. I looked as well and caught some strange expressions, scowls even.

If he hesitated it was only to take a deeper breath, for his voice resounded stronger as he continued, embracing everyone. "The kingdom of heaven is like a landowner who went out in the early morning to hire labourers for his vineyard. He found men waiting in the market place and he hired all that were there, agreeing with them the price of a day's hire."

Then after three hours he went there again, and in the sixth and ninth hours too, hiring all that were there because he needed many workers to tend his harvest, agreeing the same day's hire as before."

"Even in the eleventh hour he went to the market and found people hoping still to find some work for that day; and as before he took them on."

"When it came time to pay his workers the lord got them to line up and he paid them all the same, as they had agreed. But when the workers that had been toiling in the vineyard all day saw that those that had just worked for one hour got the same pay, they were noisily aggrieved about the deal."

"'Why do you murmur amongst yourselves thus?' asked the lord. 'Do you think I do you an injustice? Did we not agree the price of a day's work? That these other men have only been able to work for the last hour or three hours, waiting in the heat of the day instead, is not your concern."

"'Do not sour the good wine of generosity with the vinegar of your mean thoughts.'"

"'Celebrate with me rather that my harvest has been brought in and that you have the payment we agreed. For the last shall be first and the first last. '"

Turning back to the newcomers more completely, he finished his address.

"And now this is your time too. This is your chance to choose the path that calls you to a wedding feast."

"Today is both a harvest and a marriage too; and I have just one task to ask of you. You see these beds where those who, for whatever reason, are too sick to join in? Come forward and lift these beds and the people on them and carry them after me to our marriage feast and you may stay and join us if you wish as well."

He stepped towards Rachel and myself and Peter, Andrew, James and John followed. He stooped to the man in the first bed and said, "your sins are paid for. Come join us too. Let us carry you to the celebrations," and they lifted the bed with him on it, and other disciples joined in.

Very quickly all the occupants of our sick compound had been transported to the festive field where Miriam was singing one of her new Christine songs, praising the coming of the Prince of Peace just as her Lord indeed re-joined her audience.

He went and sat near beside her, and though she would give the stage to him he asked her to sing on. It was a lovely moment between them and she responded urging the musicians to greater heights as well.

Then when we thought we had heard all the songs, she moved closer to Yeheshua and sang a final one especially for him, for her, for us all. The fruit of what her quest had brought her

"All hail the Day Star from on high!"

"All hail the Christ who ever was, and is and evermore shall be!"

"All hail the darkness of the shadowland! All hail the dawn of peace on earth; good will to men!"

"All hail triumphant king, who grapples with the tyrant Death, who conquers in the fight, and brings to light immortal life for men!"

"All hail the broken cross, the mutilated spear!"

"All hail the triumph of the soul! All hail the empty tomb!"

"All hail to him despised by men, rejected by the multitudes; for he is seated on the throne of power!"

"All hail! for he has called the pure in heart of every clime to sit with him upon the throne of power!"

"All hail the rending veil! The way into the highest courts of God is open for the sons of men!"

"Rejoice, O men of earth, rejoice and be exceeding glad!"

"Bring forth the harp and touch its highest strings; bring forth the lute, and sound its sweetest notes!"

"For men who were made low, are high exalted now, and they who walked in darkness and in the vale of death, are risen up and God and man are one for evermore. Hallelujah, praise the Lord for evermore. Amen."

How many times had the master told us that wicked men would come and put the Son of God to death?

What Miriam sang mixed celebration with events of this hinted terror, putting hard images into song. Yet somehow it was turned to wonder and glory too.

A moment of stunned silence, followed by the noisy applause of enthusiastic approval, we grappled with understanding what was happening; what future we were swimming into.

Yeheshua stood up and took Miriam's hands in his. He couldn't have introduced the subject of his coming trials into the celebration but Miriam had; she knew the meaning of the quest he had given her.

"Please sing this song again beloved, for it points the way. It tells the hope all our destinies. It spells the marriage bond we are to take."

Very slowly she started to sing, her braided fair hair shining gold in the evening sunshine with Yeheshua still stood besides her on the stage. And even then she might have faltered, had not the musicians hadn't found their way to in join the song.

She swayed a little first towards Yeheshua and then back to the musicians and the audience; an impromptu dance of mesmerising beauty, and the tempo of her song increased.

At one moment it looked as though she would sink to her knees in front of Yeheshua but he turned and lifted her again by the strength of his arms, and by his side she continued on:

"All hail! for he has called the pure in heart..." and Yeheshua lifted his upturned hands... once... twice and thrice again, calling all of us to stand as well. "Rejoice, O men of earth, rejoice...", and all of us were jumping and singing the ending, again and again, with the musicians playing their hearts out too...

"Hallelujah, praise the lord for evermore. Amen."

"Hallelujah, praise the lord for evermore. Amen."

"Hallelujah, praise the lord for evermore. Amen."

... and the Lord Yeheshua swayed in dance as well, both a response and joining in our chant of love, his arms spread wide in high embrace.

Finally, he lifted up his eyes to heaven and blessed us:

"All-seeing, all-caring, all-mighty father; I beseech you to let your love, your mercy and your truth rest upon these men and women. So that by your Grace their inner light may always be aflame, even though this Lamp is taken from their sight. Lest otherwise they should tread the ways of darkness and of death, make them know you are always with them."

"Farewell," he said turning from the gathering. "Fare you well, always, now and always."

CHAPTER 14.

Matthew and Bartholomew looked after much of the organisation around Yeheshua and it was Bartholomew that had heard Yeheshua ask Johannus to continue to help protect the women and it was also Bartholomew that took care of seeing that there were disciples available to secure the access to the master and his inner group.

Bartholomew listened to Johannus telling him of the threat to Miriam and me on the road from Jericho and he directed Johannus to talk to Judas Iscariot and Simon Zelotes, who of the twelve were most involved in fending off the political and violent type of threats from outside.

Judas frowned when he heard how the bandit leader had apparently been plotting with rich and possibly influential Pharisees. "Why would they want to kidnap the women?" he asked and then as if answering his own thoughts, "unless they knew they were close to the master and wanted to try to bargain for some kind of an alliance."

Johannus shrugged and Judas asked him to tell him if he thought of anything else that might be relevant.

"Yes, I will," said Johannus. "I shall be with the group taking turns to guard behind the main pavilions, if you need me."

*

The first night of the festival Johannus dreamt again about the goddess Hecate. It wasn't like the other dreams though because he found himself watching her from above her position on her hillside, and yet she saw him not.

He was in the same aura of safety that he had felt ever since arriving in Capernaum, even though he knew he was dreaming.

She was the queenly Hecate, intently watching the river Jordan that ran through the semi darkness of the valley below, gleaming silver in the moonlight.

Johannus looked where she did, and the more he gazed the more he could see. The river was not just any river for its tiniest currents were filled with threads of vision; little scenes of the world following their courses within the main river flow.

He somehow knew that he was looking through her sight, and what she was watching was a road on a hillside that looked vaguely familiar. There was a crossroads and a troop of Roman soldiers riding from it. Johannus could even see the officer's face and with a jolt he realised that he knew him.

Somewhere, high on the hillside behind the Romans, there were other men streaming down towards the same crossroads, and Hecate's attention had been drawn to them.

Clearly nothing was going to happen; they would miss each other. The Romans were riding directly towards Johannus and he saw how tired they were. 'Let them go and get some sleep' thought Johannus at the very moment that

Hecate raised her hand and gestured towards the river below.

A dog started to bark in the shadowy darkness and it was answered by another, louder and closer than the first. This meant little and still nothing would have changed if the dogs had obeyed their owner's command to silence, like a hundred other similar times; but they wouldn't, instead starting another dog off in the distance. Hecate's hand had remained extended and the dogs continued their noise.

The Roman officer heeded the barking and turned his men around and cantered his troop back towards the crossroads, just in case.

Fortune continued with him that night and the leader of the fleeing brigands was captured in the surprise encounter, but Johannus awoke before he saw anything more. He didn't care, the night was nearly over and he knew he was needed to relieve Silas of his watch; to give him a chance of a few hours sleep before joining the celebration.

*

A disciple sat by the gate that straddled the track running along the shore of the sea and up behind the pavilions, controlling access to the master's small private area there.

Johannus however sat on a spot further away from the shore, directly behind but set back from the ladies' tent, guarding them from any intruders that might come from the rough ground in that direction.

His experience with Barabbas' band of rebels led him to believe that a real threat was most likely to come from the most unexpected direction; so, he found himself a shaded spot that gave him the best view of the surrounding terrain, where he could happily spend the whole day.

Susannah spotted him there and drew his presence to mother Mary's attention, who in turn asked Judas to explain it because the women didn't like being guarded too closely. Iscariot explained about the threat Miriam and Magdalene had encountered and Mary nodded.

"I shall ask him to keep hidden if you prefer," said Judas, but Mary shook her head. "It is all right; as long as we understand the need, we shall welcome his service to the master."

Johannus was having a little difficulty not nodding off in the heat, when Judas Iscariot came to talk to him. Judas had intense blue eyes, dark brows and hair and a slightly straggly black beard. He was about the same age as Johannus but exuded a confidence in himself that was palpable.

"So, you think it was Barabbas himself you saw at the inn. What makes you so sure it was him?"

"W… well," answered Johannus slowly, wondering what he should think to say, his memory going back to the vision of his dream. "I did have a very vivid dream last night. I think that was connected to him."

"What sort of dream?" asked Judas, the scepticism clearly showing in his voice.

Johannus sighed. "In it the Roman commander we met on the road, succeeding in apprehending him. I heard Barabbas' name called out."

"That could be anything, especially as it hasn't happened," said Iscariot, getting to his feet, readying to go. "Don't let your imagination run wild out here. We cannot afford to cause unnecessary upset either."

Not too long later Miriam herself came out to where Johannus was, bringing a wooden bowl of stew and some good chunks of bread. He jumped up, excited by this unexpected visit and the prospect of a meal that smelt delicious.

"Hi Johannus, how are you doing; hiding back here, away from all the fun?"

"I'm fine; it's just great to be here," he replied, slightly fazed by the unexpected attention from his favourite woman in the whole world.

"Well, why don't you move your position forward over there where you will get a much better view of what is going on in the arena, as well as be able to hear the master speaking."

"I don't want to intrude any more than I already am," said Johannus, but Miriam wouldn't hear of it. "Everyone is already out of the tents. You are not intruding. Come on, the master wants you to be a part of this as well."

Johannus couldn't hold out against her. He went to the place she suggested and immediately could feel the rising excitement of all that was happening in the arena. It had a magic he could never have imagined.

He didn't want the day to end, but eventually it did and he slept the sweet dreamless sleep of a contented man.

The next day, preparations were already underway for the master's journey to Jerusalem, for the Passover feast.

I was feeling flushed and happy after the previous day when I caught up with Johannus. I was only going to accompany the master's train as far as Magdala turning because I wanted to spend a few days with my mother. We rode together chatting, behind the collection of horses, donkeys and carts carrying the tents, supplies and Yeheshua and his disciples themselves, heading towards Jerusalem and the Passover feast.

The parting of our ways soon arrived, "I'm so glad you are with the master; I'll catch up with you soon, probably in Bethany." I made my way over to my mother's carriage and passing close by Yeheshua, who had already given us his blessing, we left for Magdala.

The road to Jerusalem wound on close to the sea of Galilee, and from time to time Yeheshua would dismount and walk beside the road on foot as they passed through some village or hamlet; often stopping to inspire or bless people that came seeking him.

After the stop at Tiberius, where a lot of people had come out to see the master Yeheshua, Iscariot brought his mount over to Johannus and they rode side by side for a while, following along at the back of the caravan.

"I heard some news back there," he told Johannus. "A contact at the Roman barracks told me that they have captured Barabbas, on a road near Sychar; two or three nights ago." Judas looked meaningfully at him.

Johannus was not surprised but he was secretly glad to have had his dream exonerated in the eyes of one of the twelve close to Yeheshua. He hadn't even told Miriam yet.

"Have you had these kind of dreams before?" asked Judas, but Johannus didn't want to tell him of the interactions that he had had with the goddess Hecate. "Not like that, no;" he answered "but there have been some times when visions have affected me; yes, and some dreams too."

"Well, if you dream about anything that could affect the master and our mission, then I want to know," said Iscariot and Johannus baulked a bit, not being used to taking orders; but he nodded and said nothing. Iscariot looked at him piercingly but said nothing more either.

Johannus was rather thankful that he didn't dream anything that night, at least that he could remember the next day.

Iscariot came over to him again in a much brighter, more expansive mood than the day before and rather than trying to question Johannus he spent time explaining to the new guard something of what he knew was happening.

"You can see, I am sure, the kind of support that the master has amongst the people, everywhere he goes." Johannus nodded in agreement for it really had been a wonderful shock to be in the company of Yeheshua and feel the impact he had made across the country. The people would follow him anywhere and do anything he wished. Such a power that even the Romans wonder at.

"Yes I can, Judas; what do you think will happen?"

"His kingdom is really coming. That is what is happening. This journey to Jerusalem and the Passover is going to be decisive. His time is here and we are going to be with him." He said no more for a little while, letting Johannus take in his words.

"But there are those that fear and hate him too. He speaks of it himself I'm told," answered Johannus, interested.

"Of course there are," said Judas, "but they don't understand the forces in play. They don't realise the power that Yeheshua has to call upon. Anything they do will rebound upon them. It is the law."

Iscariot's enthusiasm was infectious and Johannus wondered at the realisation that he also was going to be a part of this unfolding drama.

That night they camped a few miles past the inn where we had encountered the brigands on the journey up, and Johannus experienced a wholly different side of what was happening.

He dreamt he was standing on the bank of a dark lake, or perhaps it was a wide river, in the middle of which there was an island where a soft and beautiful light was radiating goodness.

Johannus looked along the bank for a boat that might take him out to the island, gazing into the swirling black water as he did. With a jolt he realised that he wasn't looking at water but at dark shapes moving within the solid ground itself. It was all wrong.

Johannus recoiled; the unnaturally moving shapes emanated a horror that rose like a mist, obscuring the light, and instinctively Johannus turned; he had to get away from them, from it.

Struggling to flee he found himself instead moving into a dark desert place that afforded little comfort. There was a familiarity here but not a pleasant one, only a kind of cold dread.

Shapes were gliding towards him across the plains which Johannus thought at first were ghosters but soon realised were something else. Ghoster demons perhaps, though he didn't wait to find out but turned again and tried to run; except his legs wouldn't work properly.

In front of him now was a high black mound that wasn't a mound. It was somehow more fearful even than the ghoster demons. Despite its blackness it was surrounded by an eerie green light, and it moved.

First a terrible head with burning red eyes and yellowing fangs arose, swiftly followed by a necklace of human skulls and outstretched arms, one hand clutching a long, curved and jagged knife; the other a censer exuding a sulphurous smelling smoke.

Despite his fear Johannus was able to see that the face and figure was that of an ancient woman and that the crone was consumed with a dark, fierce rage.

He stood transfixed, the transformation continuing to reveal a dark grey, almost skeletal body, rising with a tremor that shook the ground all around; and Johannus collapsed.

*

He apparently wakened onto a hillside that he knew, watching the river of life where dark shadows were swirling on the banks, unable to touch a light that burned like a bright star out in the middle.

Somewhere further downstream though, things might be different, and that was where the darkness was streaming towards; where the chasm of death awaited.

Johannus took in the scene for just a few moments before Hecate's queenly face turned towards him and a finger reached from her hand and touched his skull.

*

Sitting within the cave, a greenish light entered was flickering on the wall opposite him and an oddly vulnerable young woman was by his side.

This Hecate he knew a little better; was more comfortable to be with; and it felt like the first time that night he was no longer struggling to flee or awaken.

There were a jumble of things going on in his head though; questions that he couldn't quite remember, but the girl Hecate reached around and put a hand on his arm. "Don't worry; just tell me what it is you want to know; what it is that has brought you here to me."

Johannus stopped and everything became clear, and he put the question to the goddess that had had been gnawing away behind his conscious thoughts.

"Why have you chosen to live here in the Shadowland… and alone… rather than in the heights of the heavens where the others are?"

"It is a long story," answered the girlish-woman-goddess after a long pause, which made Johannus realise how close he had come to her, "but I will show you how it has come to be. This is not something that has been told to a mortal man before."

CHAPTER 15.

Hecate's words became Johannus' dream.

"In the beginning, life's river was a fresh mountain stream and my father's kingdom was in the highest peaks.

Before mortal man existed, we were the race that watched the stars wheel in the skies and joined in their dance, for we were the first people and knew no bounds, or even what bounds there should be.

All power was ours; whatever we might imagine we could do; and yet the greatest of all achievements was to be worthy of the gift that was our Lord-King's to bestow.

Only the noblest of our people dared and hoped to gain this, and it was what many spent their entire lives striving to achieve.

What was this gift? The mirror. Not any of the wonderful or magical mirrors that existed in that kingdom but the hidden one that could uniquely show the viewer the uncreated, unchanging face of bliss from which we had come and to where we would return. And there was said that the only limit to what could be known in this mirror was in the viewer themselves.

It was because of having the ability to bestow this gift that my father Lord Vishreus was the high king; and the nature of the mirror meant that though it was singular and never left the high king's possession, once the gift had been received by the blessed, they could call it into use at any time their heart desired; and not just one of them but however many had received it.

These great beings were called Vi-sages and of these few almost all retired into the high caves of the mountain peaks to practice the vision undisturbed.

Only very occasionally would one of these great sages visit our high valleys of the kingdom and when they did Lord Vishreus himself showered them with honour. These were the great feast days and they were my first memories as a little girl.

I had an elder sister, Aythoril, who she was the most beautiful of any person, either within the palace or without. People used to say she was blessed by the mirror and closest to the face of truth.

I would ask her about it, whether she herself also sought to gain our father's gift, but she said she was happy as she was.

I struggled to understand this because it was my greatest desire to know that ultimate, unchanging wonder but I came to see that she enjoyed such love and admiration through her beauty that she didn't feel the same thirst that I did.

Then one day she told me that she had seen the mirror. Not that she had looked into it, only that she knew where it was located, but I thought she meant she had been able to look into it too.

I pressed her to tell me where it was and what it was like but all she had said was that it had been in our parents' private rooms when our mother had called her.

I was wild with curiosity and probably jealousy, but I tried hard to only let this fuel my thirst.

Then came the day when the three eldest Vi-sages came to my father's palace.

There was to be a feast, greater than any other feast that we had known but first the sages spent the day in private consultation with our Lord Vishreus.

I happened to hear a few bits of their conversation that came to me when I was in the bathing room where a hollowness of the joining wall to the council chamber chanced this to occur. The words I heard declared that the kingdom was ready; that the Life water could be let loose over the immeasurable chasm and onto the planes beneath.

Lord Vishreus answered that the sacred mirror was intrinsic to the water of Life. Where Life flowed the mirror's blessing must also go, so that every possibility that it contained would be multiplied; and he asked that the seven sages should be ready too.

I didn't understand all that was said but I knew that the mirror I sought would be going soon and that I must try to find it before that time came.

When I heard that seven Vi-sages had been sighted walking along the snow-line into the high pastures of Io, my self-imposed task became urgent, almost to panic.

I was able to enter my mother's dressing room before she had finished her breakfast and found what could, must be, the mirror.

The case itself was beautiful, though smaller than I had imagined, and being half open I knew it held a mirror inside.

I went across the room and picked it up.

Just as I was realising that it wasn't what I sought, I heard someone coming into the room and quickly closing the case I slipped it inside my robe before turning and facing my mother, the Lady Heralkis, our Queen.

She asked me what I was doing there and I spoke truly that I sought the hidden mirror of the infinite.

She had seen my stupid act of concealing something in my robe and why I had even done that I couldn't imagine. Such a small thing but it changed everything, forever.

Finding her precious compact that could make any desired change real and not just a powdered or painted wish, she was struck with rage and called her husband, my father, to the scene.

Shaking, I repeated to Lord Vishreus that I had been looking for the sacred mirror and had not had any intention of stealing my mother's compact; but of course this didn't help my cause.

He looked at me sternly, yet full of compassion. "The mirror you sought can never be found that way, though you were to search for an eternity," he said, then adding a pronouncement, terrible to my hearing, "and not understanding this disqualifies you from receiving it, from me, in this kingdom."

I was severely shaken, my dearest dream being shattered by his words. I fell to my knees.

"However, you have linked your fate to the mirror itself and even as the time has come for Life's water to flow from these higher bounds and enter into the denser planes of being, so you must follow it for there your quest can be achieved, though how and where is not mine to see."

I was doubly shocked but it seemed that the punishment was not completed yet, for Lady Heralkis now stepped forward.

"For your deception Khaela" she said, for that was my name then, "you shall find no comfort in any other mirror either. They will always fail you, never revealing to you the beauty that you have."

I was hurt, badly wounded feelings tore my heart.

Later my sister tried to comfort me, horrified that something she had said might have led me to this state, and I believed her. I had mistaken what she had meant, I knew that; but the hurt remained uncured still, despite our reparations."

Johannus put his arms out to the young goddess and even as they moved to encircle her, he awoke, the wonders of the night still with him.

CHAPTER 16.

Yresmin and Selly completed their journey to the environs of Jerusalem without any worse problem than Yresmin deciding she needed to walk after one day's journey beyond the frontier fort. She was starting to worry about Selly's growing size, though in every other respect her donkey did seem in very good health and humour.

First, they went to Bethany, as Miriam had suggested she contact Mary, Martha and Lazarus. Martha answered the door and Yresmin was quick to realise she was busy nursing her very sick brother. It was obviously not a good time for Yresmin to stay and introduce herself, so she said she would return another day.

Martha explained that many of the Christines had gone to Capernaum, but most would be back again in about a week's time.

Selly's time was coming sooner than expected and Yresmin needed to find her somewhere she could have her foal; and a place for them all to stay.

She decided they should retrace their steps towards Jerusalem; but before they left Bethany, she found the goldsmith that Martha had been able to recommend, where she changed her golden threads into currency she could use.

The day was getting late when Yresmin led Selly through another little village and spotted a lady struggling to get in a load of washing from a line strung to a tree in the side yard, which itself opened out onto the road.

Something about the lady and the look of her house, which was quite big but rather rundown, told Yresmin that she could use some help; and more importantly that there might be rentable space for Selly and herself.

Following her instincts, Yresmin went and asked the woman if she knew of anywhere that there might be some room for herself and her donkey.

Her name was Rebecca and she looked closely at the strangers before it dawned on her that this could be a great chance for her. "Your donkey looks heavy with foal if I am not mistaken. You shall be needing shelter for the little one." She stated this as if talking to herself and scrutinised Yresmin again through tired red eyes.

"Could you afford the rent then?" she asked.

"You are right about Selly. We will need somewhere for her foal; a small pen should be enough; and yes, I can pay for a room. How much would you be asking?"

Rebecca considered it and named a price. It was low, well within Yresmin's means but she wouldn't accept too quickly as that might be demeaning to Rebecca.

Instead, she took her time to consider the offer and then suggested a lower one, but adding that she could make the difference up by helping with of some of the work around the place.

Rebecca took up the challenge, naming a price between the two and stating the tasks Yresmin would have to do.

Yresmin stuck to her lower figure, but agreed to the additional tasks. She would need to keep busy whilst waiting for Selly and her foal.

Rebecca laughed shortly, spat on the palm of her hand and stuck it out towards Yresmin, who spat on her own and took the proffered hand to seal the deal.

Yresmin led Selly through wide doors into the space on one side of the house that had several feeding stalls built into the walls; but which had not been used for a while; no animals had lived here for some time.

She looked around at the piles of rubbish and rubble; no wonder Rebecca had accepted the lower price. It would take some work to make the room ready to welcome Selly's foal, but she could do it.

A wooden ladder lay across the floor at one end and with its help Yresmin managed to climb up onto a loft platform above the mangers. This is where she would sleep, and could pull the ladder up after her if she wanted.

Happy with the arrangement she had made, Yresmin also found she could get onto the flat roof outside the loft window. Stars were coming out in the evening sky and for a while she watched them getting brighter as the rest of the sky got darker. Eventually she dragged herself back inside; she needed to settle Selly somewhere and then go and ask Rebecca for some food.

Yresmin slept well that night, and in the morning she attended again to Selly who seemed even bigger than ever. 'How much longer have you got?' she thought because this final stage of Selly's pregnancy seemed to have developed very quickly. One day Yresmin had had no idea her donkey was pregnant, next she swore she could see her growing wider day by day.

Selly looked around dolefully at her mistress as she examined her. 'It could be today' Yresmin's worried expression seemed to reply but Selly was hopeful, and glad. The growing of this foal inside her had been a great surprise and something more than she could quite understand.

Yresmin also found the coming of this little donkey more meaningful than she could have thought. Something really special was happening in the world and the coming of this foal was a real part of that preciousness.

She was going to look after it and Selly as well as she possibly could. If for no other reason than the way her donkey had carried her through her capture and escape from the Djinn worshippers; without Selly she would definitely be dead.

Yresmin worked hard that day; first cleaning the stable, then the yard outside it; and after that she went and helped Rebecca in the house.

Rebecca was intrigued by Yresmin's energy and enthusiasm … for everything it seemed; but especially for anything that impinged upon the coming foaling. After Yresmin had completed the kitchen work Rebecca had set they went out together to the stable-byre. Rebecca wanted to see what her new tenant had done there.

What a transformation. Rebecca remembered how it had been when she had first married her husband and the farm-holding had been busy; and now she almost felt excited again… about the impending new arrival. "There is some hay in another store. Come with me and we can bring enough for the foal to have as a bed; and for your donkey to eat."

Rebecca's husband Rabine came back later that day. He was a few years older than Rebecca and had been away visiting their son; but in his day he had been quite a good farmer and was experienced in lambing, calving and foaling too.

He was just in time to be there, sitting on the sidelines giving words of advice, because Selly's labour started close to sunset and lasted through the evening into the night.

None of them had noticed the storm that had gathered from the north because they were so taken up with the arrival of the baby donkey. Once its hind legs had come the rest followed with Selly giving her best effort to help him out.

Soon the tiny colt was up on unsteady feet, nudging his mother's underside in search of her milk.

It was then that Yresmin saw the first stab of lightening through the open door, followed in a few moments by a tremendous peal of thunder. More flashes and booming crashes detonated around them at shorter and shorter intervals, closer and louder. Yresmin looked at the little donkey thinking how terrified he must be, but he seemed totally unconcerned.

Then the rain came; and not just rain but it turned into hail as well, drumming loudly against the roof and blocking out all other sounds.

What a contrast between the power of the storm, threatening to engulf them, and the presence of this charming new life, unperturbed and nuzzling in on his mother. The storm passed on and the little colt remained.

"Indy I shall call him," she told Selly. "What do you think?" Selly shook her neck and ears a little which Yresmin took as a 'yes'. She stepped up to her and hugged her again; "clever, clever girl."

For the next few days, the little foal was the centre of attention at the farm-holding and they all were convinced they could see him growing bigger and stronger daily, and even other villagers would come in and ask about him; such a fine little fellow.

Yresmin was so proud of both her donkeys but had no idea what she would be doing with them; particularly the little foal. She couldn't bear the idea of selling him on.

Nor had she forgotten that she had come to find the master, but then the terrible episode at the Ghoster camp had left her with the task of delivering the Djinn warning to Yeheshua, that the poison was already inside his protective circle; that there was no escape for him. She could see no escape for her either, from this fateful duty.

Caring for Selly and her foal Indy had stopped her worrying about this, but as the week neared its end she started thinking of her dilemma again. Thinking how she could approach the one she had waited all her life to meet but be the person to give him this most unwelcome news.

Indy bumped his head into her as she sat on a stool out in the yard. He wouldn't allow her to dwell on things for long. He had so much life and affection, making her laugh and cry together. How strong he had grown in these few days; how bright and intelligent he was.

Tomorrow she would go out again and see if she could find out any news of Yeheshua; come what may.

She might have fallen asleep in the sun, but she didn't think that she had. It wasn't a dream but there was a voice in her head. "You are the real message; go to your Lord with an easy heart. Another has come who can bear the other load."

She looked around; there was no-one there. Only the little colt and his mother and they gave no sign they had heard anything.

All the same, Yresmin felt something of the unwelcome load slip away from her.

CHAPTER 17.

The air was still cold as Johannus crawled from within his blankets. Earlier he had been on the first watch of the night but since then had managed a scant few hours sleep before the start of the day's journeying.

Others were up earlier still. Hestia, who was one of Susannah's friends or servants perhaps, brought him some warming gruel which he took to eat with Hanif, the on-duty guard.

Judas Iscariot joined them shortly after, instructing Hanif to go and pack up so he could get some rest. He would be able to sleep in the baggage wagon as they moved south.

Soon they would be getting going.

"Have you had any more dreams that might be useful or meaningful?" Judas asked, sitting back and relaxing in the early sunshine.

"Yes, I did actually," said Johannus. "Meaningful I think, though I don't know how useful exactly."

Judas said nothing but looked interested, letting the silence do its work of drawing out the details from Johannus.

"It was quite like where we are now," he said, "and there was a great and wonderful light floating like an island down the river. Except the river was not water but a great tide of many little streams of life and there was something else happening. Clots of darkness were all about trying to blot out the light… but without success."

Judas nodded slowly. "Yes, I see," he said, "that seems about right."

"But that wasn't quite all," said Johannus, "because there was a great chasm coming up ahead in the flow, and the darkness was gathering there, waiting for the light. I had a feeling that a dreadful thing was going to happen."

"Hmm, did you find out what that was?" Iscariot looked curious or worried even. The sun had gone in and a chill wind blew through the camp. Johannus shivered.

Suddenly the warmth returned as the sun edged out from behind the cloud. "No," answered Johannus, remembering something of Hecate's story that had followed, but which he kept to himself. "No, I didn't see what happened then."

Iscariot sat and pondered what Johannus had said. "Well, I think you are right again," he said, surprising Johannus. "There is undoubtedly a great confrontation ahead and the light of lights is here with us heading to where it will happen. It is not without meaning that the master Ye'shua goes to Jerusalem. Every time we are there we can feel it…"

Judas got to his feet. "I shall ride with you today, going on in front this time. We can talk about it then," he said, brushing sand from his hands and robe.

They did indeed set off ahead of the main party, scouting for places where trouble might come from.

A Roman patrol passed, going the other way.

Johannus had warmed to Judas since the early part of the trip to Jerusalem. He had a bright intelligence that drew the listener's thoughts higher with him, and he was reputed to be the best debater of the twelve; his skills often being called upon when people came trying to stir up an argument or cause trouble.

Yet, Johannus found him down to earth as well, being the keeper of the purse strings for the master and his close disciples.

"I used to work with Matthew in the tax office," he explained to Johannus' enquiry, "and I saw the potential of small amounts of money coming from the many. It added up to the power to make things happen. That has stuck with me."

"The Kingdom is coming; it is so close now. I am sure you can feel it, can't you?"

"Yes, I can; I maybe think I can."

There was a track that joined from the hills to their right. Judas urged his mount up it. "We need to get a bit higher if we are going to see what is going on around here. There is a hillock over there that has the best view. I have been here before."

"Shouldn't we be getting back to the others soon?" said Johannus, as they had rode quite far along the way.

"Yes, once we have had a good look at the lie of the land and what people are about. Leave your horse here, and we can quickly climb up this rocky bit."

Scrambling up behind Judas, Johannus found his hip was aching quite a lot. He managed to keep going though, but was very grateful when the slope eased off.

From near the top of the hill they did have a great view of everything around. There were lots of travellers on the road but nothing else of concern that they could see.

"He is going to make something big happen in this land. Something no-one has ever dreamt of. He has been working hard to prepare us twelve, and he says we are ready now. Are you ready Johannus? All of us will need to be."

"I think so."

"That is not enough. You need to be certain; and ready to give everything you have. That is what it is all about; what divides his true followers from the rest."

Ever since they had started climbing the rocky hillock Johannus had been feeling that he had been there before. Looking out across to the river he suddenly realised why it was so strangely familiar. He glanced quickly around to check whether there was a cave behind them. There wasn't.

Hecate's hillside had appeared to be in the other country on the opposite side of the river; hadn't it? Which way had the river been flowing? Actually, it had been just like this, he thought. He looked across at Judas, slightly confused.

"Are you all right Johannus? You look worried about something."

"Well, this is so much like the place where I had the dream I was telling you about; it feels a bit weird that's all."

"A local shepherd told me about it, when I was quite young. It is the best viewing point of anywhere along this road. He said it's called Jacob's hill."

Johannus rubbed his side, trying to dispel the continuing hurt from his hip. An image of a priest carrying a precious bethel stone, hopelessly trying to flee from relentless pursuers came unbidden to his thoughts.

"It does have a fantastic outlook. That is our group just passing the road we took to get up here," said Johannus, concentrating hard to not to allow his imagination to get the better of him; but he couldn't help remembering finding the murdered body of the same priest.

"Yes, that's them. Let's get back," said Judas, and Johannus readily agreed.

They started down the steep way from the hilltop. Johannus' thinking was rather disjointed. He heard a door bang hard at his left ear; it was inside his head, he realised belatedly.

The sense of loss was overwhelming. Nothing held together anymore. He was slipping down the hill and the bright light from the sun was dimming.

"They will see now just what he is all about..." Judas was saying, but Johannus couldn't take it in. For him it was as if his life was being torn into pieces and what was left was falling down upon the sharp rocks.

"Careful, you'll hurt yourself," said Judas, catching Johannus' arm before he fell any further.

Johannus felt dreadful, but couldn't understand why. "Are you alright?" asked Iscariot, rather worried.

Johannus pulled himself together, but he still felt weak. "A dizzy spell," he said. "Don't know why. I'll be all right in a minute."

"Will you be able to ride?" Judas continued in his concern.

"Oh yes; just give me a minute. Everything is coming back to normal now."

They rode back together but Johannus couldn't quite dispel the feeling of what it was to be shattered into nothingness.

"I had a bad experience there," he confided in Judas. "The world was collapsing for me."

"The world will collapse for those that oppose our Lord, Johannus." That is what this is all about. "I think you saw something of what is to come. That must be your gift, my friend."

They stopped and drank from their water skins but would have to get back to the main party to get some food that might help Johannus recover further.

"It was like a warning," said Johannus as they carried on, "and I don't want that to be my fate."

Iscariot listened, letting his companion express his worries. He respected the other's premonitions, but that was all Johannus had to say.

"His kingdom is coming and everyone is going to get the chance to see it;" Judas said at last. "Many are blind; many of those who have the power to help him." He paused. "But not all are. There are some that shall recognise his light and help us raise Israel up again. Those who don't will be destroyed, just as you have so painfully foreseen."

"Stay with us Johannus and you too shall see the Lord's glory on this earth."

At the pace they went it took them a while to catch up with Yeheshua's group again, but when they did, they found them stopped for a rest by Enon Springs.

Judas went to ask for some food and Hestia brought it out to where they were sitting in the patchy shade of a thorn tree. Johannus watched the easy sway of her hips, and she smiled sweetly at him. Iscariot frowned; sometimes he wondered why Yeheshua allowed so many women in his following.

He ate some of the bread, pondering. Matthew had just told him that John and James' mother had been asking the master to specially favour her sons in the coming Kingdom. How could they? But then again as treasurer to the master and the twelve he well aware of how much financial support came from the rich women who followed Yeheshua, and it always irked Iscariot.

Another of the women was coming over to them, well covered against the heat that the day had developed. He saw it was Miriam, the one who Ye'shua treated as his betrothed. She came right up to them, "Judas, the master is calling for you; he wants to see all the twelve, together."

After Iscariot had gone Miriam sat down by Johannus. "How are you doing?" she asked, and then with a mischievous smile added "I thought you were meant to be my guard?"

Previously Johannus would have blushed at such teasing but not anymore. "Not just you, but all the women," he joked back, and she laughed.

She sat and nibbled at some of the bread and cheese, and Johannus was grateful for her comforting presence. "I had a bit of a shock when I was on scouting duty with Judas," he confided, "but it was nothing really; I am all right now."

"What sort of nothing?" asked Miriam.

"Well, when we reached the viewing point on the hill it reminded me strongly of Hecate's hill in my dream of the night before, which confused me; and then when I was coming down, I had the feeling of falling out of the world and into utter desolation. It wasn't good."

Miriam said nothing for quite a while, but when she did, she reached out a hand and held Johannus'. "It is not always easy to be close to the master, Johannus. Everything that we have tried to hide away tends to be brought out into the light. Sometimes this can be quite confronting."

Johannus thought about it. "Yes, I think I can see that. Judas says the Kingdom is coming and that there is going to be a huge confrontation for everyone."

Miriam started to reply but then stopped and looked away; but then she looked back to Johannus again. "Even the twelve can only follow where he leads. They are not infallible, Johannus. He is the centre; we just want to be the petals of his flowering."

They sat together, eating a little more bread and Johannus was surprised but glad that she hadn't gone away yet. He was reminded of a time he had sat with Bishmi in the desert. Miriam smiled, "so what was Hecate up to this time?" she asked.

"Oh, I forgot to tell you," said Johannus. "When I dreamed this time, I was able to ask her to tell her story, as you said I should. Or was it Magdalene? I can't remember."

"I doesn't matter," said Miriam; "but did she tell you anything?"

"Yes she did…" and Johannus told Miriam of how as a girl Kaella, or Hecate, had tried to find the magic mirror of the Divine Presence, that was in the keeping of her father the king, and which had ended in trouble with both her father and her mother, whose precious compact she had pocketed instead. That was how she was banished to the Shadowland.

"There is more to Hecate than the beguiling girl who told you that story, Johannus," said Miriam at the end. "It may well be a true story, but she is also the mighty queen of her arts and crafts, as well as a supreme force of retribution. You should know that she is not someone to be crossed with impunity."

"I have seen something of those other sides to her, Miriam. I don't care to tangle with her any more than I seem to be fated to dream; but I am grateful for the protection she has shown me when darkness has pursued me in those dreams."

"She is bound into the events of these times as well," said Miriam. "The mirror she seeks is not far away. In fact, Johannus, if you ask the master Yeheshua for the teachings of the kingdom, you will be shown that very mirror yourself."

Johannus was astonished. "Really?" he exclaimed. He couldn't have believed that his life was in any way a part of the incredible tale that the goddess had told him of. "Yes really, Johannus. This life we have is very special. That is what Yeheshua is teaching us all."

Ruth, my mother, said that a lot had changed at our house in Magdala, and it was truly spoken. Two families had moved in; Christines that had previously been destitute in Magdala.

I had already met one of the families at the festival in Capernaum, and they had travelled back home with Ruth. There were three of them; the man Hosea with his wife Anna and their little girl, Mary.

Hosea had been a basket weaver, and having our house as a base had given him the chance he needed to properly practice his craft again.

The little two year old girl was really sweet; she loved having the large house to play in and was a real favourite with my mother.

And Anna was quiet and very grateful for the help mother was giving them; there was little she wouldn't do in return, and became a great comfort to her elderly benefactor.

On my arriving home it was Anna that opened the door to me, welcoming me like the younger sister that I had never had.

Hosea was out working in the back yard; little Mary and another woman were with him. Anna and I went and sat with my mother in the arbour, sharing the hot mint tea that had not long been brewed.

Uncle Jacob was still in Capernaum with the twins, a boy and girl who I heard were called Carina and Jarred. They were selling some of the produce that their aunt Felicia had helped Hosea to make; and Anna proceeded to fill me in with the story of how it had happened.

Felicia was one of main reasons they had all come together. She had not only been born deaf but had a trembling disability, despite which she had in recent years struggled to look after her sister's children. Her sister had died of an unknown disease which had also earlier claimed her husband.

Once Carina and Jarred had been old enough they in their turn had helped to look after their aunt and it was them that introduced her to Hosea, who they had met near Magdala, by the sea of Galilee.

Anna herself had been a servant of a rich priest in the city of Tiberius, but when her pregnancy became clearly evident, and they decided she was not going to be so much use to them, they had turned her out.

That had happened at the worst possible time for her and her husband, because Hosea's employer had just had to let him go, having not enough work to sustain them both.

The young family struggled to survive over the next year, Hosea being unable to find good work but turning to anything he could do in order to feed them.

Carina and Jarred had come across them beside the reed beds outside Magdala. Hosea had built a kind of shelter with the reeds which Anna had managed to make into a kind of makeshift home.

Felicia had been really struck by the near-silent Hosea and his deft skills in making things with the reeds. She took a few of his little baskets into the market place of Magdala to sell them, but had met with abuse from the townsfolk there; they didn't want to encourage what they took to be beggars and outcasts in their town.

Ruth's close friend and neighbour Jacob, coming across this bullying on his way back from a visit to Capernaum, went to Felicia's aid, shocked by these people's intolerance to the afflicted in their midst.

Jacob had already surprised many when he took a deep interest in the teachings of Yeheshua. Soon after Mary's departure with Miriam on the quest to Kadesh he had spent many days travelling around after the master.

He arranged with Ruth for the destitutes to move into her house, and when he next went to see the master, he took Felicia with him.

Felicia stayed near Mirimion for several days, returning to Magdala a new person. She could hear again and her trembling was no longer such a disability. Almost every day since she had practiced the art of basket weaving with Hosea and she laughed often at her clumsy efforts.

Laughter had in fact been the key the master had turned to give her back control of her body. Laughter had released wave after wave of suppressed hurt, smoothing out her jangled nerves. Now she found many reasons to laugh; and mostly she loved just to hear its sound, and welcomed feeling it trembling in her.

She had stayed at Mirimion with mother Mary, after Yeheshua had said he wanted her to be laughing freely by the time he got back from a visit to his disciples in Tiberius, where Philip lived.

When he did get back Yeheshua spent time with Felicia and gave her an exercise for her hearing. He told her that if she could feel her laughter within her then she could surely hear it too and so he used this to bring her hearing back into the carnal world also.

All the families' members, even little Mary, though she probably wouldn't remember it, had been to visit the master and hear him speak and spend some time around him.

Jacob became the leader of the Christines in Magdala and the twins loved to work with him and his son Daniel.

Hosea's work as a basket maker flourished with help from his new apprentice, Felicia. Jacob knew what sorts of basket were needed, whether it was for carrying fish, grapes or olives or the many other uses that they had. It became another business amongst the several that he ran, providing a steady stream of funding for the master's work.

And Anna had found her caring nature to be much appreciated in the house; so, it was a happy community I arrived in, and fitted easily into.

Later on that day, I found myself drawn to investigate the garden, which appeared in places to have been a bit neglected and to have got quite overgrown.

There was a small room, a cupboard almost, tacked onto the back of the house, where the gardening tools were kept. The door was rickety and inside the many cobwebs declared that there were some tools that had not been touched since last I was here.

I cleared the room up first, selected the tools I thought I would need and headed out to investigate the garden.

It was a joy to uncover the secrets that lay hid, one by one; many of which were herbs and useful plants that I recognised from my training at the temple in Antioch.

The master had come and cleared away the debris that I thought I had become, uncovering the jewels that were still in my heart. I laughed silently and thought how it must be the same for Felicia and the others as well.

The feeling of spring seeped into every pore, and it went deeper than that too. Our Lord was in the world and this was the spring our spirits had been waiting for. I could feel his presence so strongly here, working in our garden in Magdala. A little bit of heaven inside and out.

The next morning, I went with Felicia to the market in Magdala and found that many people recognised me. Some I think were a bit guilty about the way they had treated our new family and turned away, but many didn't.

We were happy to talk with people and I was surprised at how much interest and how many questions were asked to me about Yeheshua. I don't know why I should have been but I hadn't really experienced this before.

Jacob had arranged meetings for anyone interested and later that day I went along and was even asked to speak. I hadn't a clue what I was going to say but when I did start, the words flooded out of me with a tremendous joy. He was here to help us all feel that which is our birthright and our need. That happiness whose wellspring is knowing we are all a part of the Almighty; included in His great plan.

We gave thanks together in our home as well for each of us had been given the gift of the Word, his Name within, the breath of soul to practice; except little Mary, but she was bursting with enough life and energy for fifty of us already.

A few days passed easily and my mother and I basked in them together.

Then one afternoon I was sitting in the back room where the master had once opened my heart's doors to his inner kingdom, when I heard my name being called.

It was a magical room for me and I loved to spend a quiet hour here when I got the chance and no-one would normally disturb me if they knew I was there. Everyone in the house was very respectful towards me.

I let myself listen to the voice and recognised the caller; it was Daniel. He had travelled the Jordan road with the master as far as I knew and we were not expecting him back yet. I got up and went out to greet him.

Daniel was clearly flustered; he had been riding hard. What could be the matter?

"Its Lazarus," he said without preamble, "he has died."

CHAPTER 19

"What?" I said, horrified. "How? What happened? Was Yeheshua there?"

We all knew that Lazarus' health improved massively when the master was with him, such was their connection. Many thought that Yeheshua should be able to heal him of his frailty, but actually Lazarus never asked for that. Absolute acceptance of everything Life brought him was his way; God's will.

"He slipped into unconsciousness two days ago and never recovered. The Rabbi pronounced him dead yesterday. I left to come and tell you as I knew you'd wish to know."

Obviously, Daniel had travelled up here at speed. No wonder he looked rather dishevelled. "What about Yeheshua," I prompted again, quieter this time. "Was he not there?"

"That was the strange thing. Martha and Mary had sent word to him of their brother's extreme condition, but the master didn't come. They were very upset."

I was shocked again. What could be happening? I would have to make haste and go to Bethany. "Where is Yeheshua then?"

"Over the Jordan; but not so far that he couldn't get to Bethany within the day, if he wanted."

"I must go down there as soon as I can," I told Daniel. "I shall go pack a bag and let my mother know. Have you told Jacob yet?"

"No, not yet," said Daniel, and he might have blushed. "I am going to go back as well. I shall go now and bring horses for a quick journey."

"There is no need for you to come, Daniel. Unless you really want to."

"I never finished the business in Bethany," he answered.

I was doubly indebted to him. "Thank you so much for coming to tell me, Daniel. If you are ready to travel back already, I would be honoured if we could go together."

We left that afternoon and I hardly remember the journey at all. The next day we got to Bethany, to find everyone at Lazarus' house in the height of mourning.

Lazarus was a much loved and respected man in the whole district, and not only amongst the Christines. His reputation for fair dealing and kindness was undisputed and he was one reason that Yeheshua's enemies found it difficult to rally against him in the area around Jerusalem.

I went to see Martha, Mary and their sister Ruth, unable to offer any consolation but wanting to try as best I could. They greeted me kindly and I asked if there was any word yet from the master but Mary shook her head. "Not yet. Maybe he knew he could not get here in time." But she couldn't help herself from crying a bit, and I put my arms around her and held her.

How utterly different things were in Judea from Galilee. It had felt to me in Galilee that we were basking in the benefit of all Yeheshua's work there, culminating in the master's farewell festival of thanks.

After that my days at home had been some of the sweetest I could remember; shared with people that were really caring for each other.

Judea on the other hand was like a bubbling, broiling cauldron of activity and dispute. A vipers nest where priests, Pharisees and their spies seemed to be crawling everywhere, wanting to know about and interfere with everyone else's business.

In some ways I was not surprised that Yeheshua was staying a bit clear of all this poison. Yet it was this poison that had killed Lazarus, or so I felt, and I was more than just surprised that the Lord had not been there when his dear friend had died.

There were a couple of little groups of priestly fanatics hanging around the street corners of Bethany, gloating. The death of this beloved man was a great boost to their cause against the heretical threat from Galilee that he had supported.

It should have been a beautiful spring day outside the house where we were all gathered, still raw in our grief; but it wasn't. Everything was wrong and those gloaters were witness to the wrongness.

'How long before the master would be here?' The prayer for his arrival could be felt all around the house but outside that the thought took on a different meaning, where minds were working to bring about the destruction of the hope he represented.

When a knocking came on the door, the day after I arrived and almost the fourth since the tomb had been sealed, it was Miriam that was there, and behind her other women of Yeheshua's entourage.

Her face was stained by the tracks of tears but her voice was that of prophecy. "The Lord is come, with all power," she said simply.

Martha had answered the door and somehow found this pronouncement easier to accept than further outpourings of grief. "Where is he?" she asked and Miriam answered "He awaits at the village gate."

Martha slipped out the front, sharing brief greetings of grief with the visitors as she went past them to meet the master.

Martha and Mary's married sister Ruth brought the guests into the front room. Mary was out the back. I went to tell her that Yeheshua had come; Miriam followed me.

Mary was sitting by herself under an almond tree, folding a freshly washed robe that had been Lazarus' in her lap; her hands fondling the soft material. She looked up at Miriam and her face had a faraway look.

"Mary, the master is come to reveal the Lord's glory," Miriam said. Mary's expression remained uncomprehending.

"Bring the fresh robe with you; it will be needed."

I understood no more than Mary, but I had experienced the power of Miriam as prophetess before. I stepped forward to help Mary to her feet. "Let's go to Yeheshua, Mary," I said.

Mary accepted my arm and she embraced Miriam as well. Then mother Mary was there and Mary broke down in tears as the Lord's mother came to her. She had loved Lazarus like a son.

We followed Miriam, and Martha met us coming back from Yeheshua. "He is waiting for you still at the village gate. There is a great crowd gathering as well. It is very tense there; we should get him into the house, I think."

Mary ran on ahead and we all hurried to where he was; the twelve shielding him from the mixed crowd that was swelling all the time.

There were lots of mourners; mostly from Bethany but others from nearby hamlets, villages and even Jerusalem herself.

Many others had followed Yeheshua here because they had heard of this teacher from Galilee but hadn't had the chance to see or hear him for themselves; and somehow a whole host of mildly interested onlookers had got draw in as well.

But there were also a good few people who had gathered for other reasons: hoping to stir up the worst kind of trouble; joining those of like mind already there in Bethany.

Mary couldn't help herself from asking the Lord why he had stayed away so long, declaring that her brother would never have died if he had been there.

Yeheshua leant forward to clasp Mary gently to his bosom, and then releasing her he stood upright again, shining like a beacon of light against a stormy sea.

"Death is not the end, for I bring entry to the life that cannot die."

Angry murmurs and some shouting came from certain sections of the crowd.

Mary, as Martha had too, believed Yeheshua talked of the life within, not of this carnal life, but he continued, "I come to demonstrate this day that those who believe in me shall not die but have eternal life."

Walking on towards the house he said to Mary, "your brother and my friend, Lazarus, will be the visible proof of the truth within."

I wondered exactly what he could mean when Lazarus had died so long ago now. Everything seemed to have changed in these last four days.

We came up the few steps to the front of the house where more people were waiting for him, the grief palpable. There was a great hush all about.

Yeheshua stood and allowed their grief to come into him, took it upon himself like a mantle and was visibly affected by it. "Let us go and open up the tomb," he said. "I would see my friend."

Someone was explaining that this was now the fourth day since Lazarus had died and that the body wouldn't be in a good state… when Johannus came to my side. He was being a guard to the women in the Lord's following.

"Mary," he said quietly but insistently, "Mary, I think I have just spotted those Pharisees that were at the inn; when we had those troubles on the road to Galilee. What do you think? Over there?"

I looked over to where he pointed and saw that he was right. "Yes, that is them; and others as well that I wouldn't want to meet. What can you do?"

"I shall go and tell Iscariot," he said.

"Yes, I think you should," I agreed.

Johannus wormed his way to the front of the crowd where Judas Iscariot was. "Judas, I have seen two of the Pharisees who were planning that attack on Miriam and Mary Magdalene, that I told you about. There…" he said, pointing as discreetly as possible.

Judas looked across to where a group of men had partly mingled into the crowd, though they still stood out somewhat by the way they kept talking together and to anyone next to them who might listen.

"See if you can find out what they are about," said Judas, "and keep close to them in case they try to start trouble."

"They might recognise me," said Johannus, "but… but I don't think so."

Iscariot turned to another disciple.

"Aaron; go with Johannus. We need to know what those Pharisees are saying. See if you can get close enough to hear." Iscariot turned back to Johannus, clear about what was needed. "You keep away, a little behind them, but be ready to help Aaron if he needs it. We have to understand what game they are playing."

"Aren't they just here to try to cause trouble for Yeheshua?"

"Probably, but maybe it isn't that simple. Let's find out what we can."

The tension in the air eased slightly as Yeheshua gathered up the bereaved family and set off along the path to Lazarus' tomb. Everyone in the crowd followed, fascinated.

In the steady stream of people, it was quite easy for Aaron and Johannus to get close to the Pharisees who were themselves eager to get to where Yeheshua was going.

"Now we shall see what kind of Messiah he is…" one of the people Johannus was following said to the other man whose sleeve he held. "Do you think the crowd will be ready to turn against him?"

Johannus couldn't hear the reply as the man had glanced around and muffled his voice when he answered, but he had no doubt that these men would cause as much trouble as they could.

The ground opened out in front of the hillside where the tombs were set and Yeheshua stopped in front of one that had been freshly sealed with a large boulder. There was a wide ring of onlookers and such was our Lord's presence that I had a distinct feeling that the whole universe was holding its breath, and watching as well.

Several people stepped forward with levers to move the boulder back, and others joined them with the strength of their arms and weight of their bodies. I noticed that the smithy Beor was one of these.

Mary fell back to my side and held onto my hand as the stone was rolled away, and I put my other arm around her. Despite ourselves we moved forward again as Yeheshua stepped into the tomb. The twelve and other disciples formed an arc around the entrance but let us through where they kept others back.

Martha went in with Yeheshua and we three Mary's and Miriam were just outside, watching as the master found the hand of his dead friend.

He closed his eyes and the light dimmed in the entrance of the cave where the sun had gone behind a cloud. I shivered and Mary clutched me harder.

Yeheshua dived deep into his own heart, and that of all Creation, finding Lazarus there.

For what might have been a moment or an whole age, their spirits communed in the halls of light.

Then gently Yeheshua led him back along the way to carnal life.

Opening his eyes again the master spoke, "Lazarus, awaken…!"

Outside the sun had already come out again and Johannus leaned eagerly forward into the renewed warmth to try to see what was happening. Everyone else was doing the same.

Suddenly there were shouts of joy and jubilation from around the cave entrance, and Lazarus' sister Mary leaned inside, holding out the fresh robe.

Within the tomb Lazarus had opened his eyes and re-joined the world of the living. Yeheshua helped him rise but waved away the proffered robe. "Let him get into the fresh air first," he said.

Gasps went up from all around the crowd as Lazarus appeared at the tomb entrance, flanked and helped by Martha and Mary. "It's Lazarus, alive;" said someone and the shout was caught and echoed by many "Lazarus lives. Lazarus lives."

Behind them Yeheshua emerged into the sunlight. "Allelulia; all praise to the king…." cried a man over to the left of Johannus and others took up this call as well.

"It is a trick," shouted one of the men Johannus had been following, but his voice was drowned out by the others of celebration. He kept trying. "Nothing but a clever trick. The man was never dead… that much is obvious."

"Yes, he is just fooling you with a sorcerer's trick," said another loudly. "Not even a very good one. We should arrest him or better still stone him now for his impudence."

Johannus was just wondering whether he needed to try to deal with them when an old man on their other side answered. "Lazarus was definitely dead. It was I that testified to it and got them to close the tomb; all according to our customs." It was the local Rabbi.

"How much did they pay you, you old fool?" said another of the trouble-makers menacingly.

Johannus stepped forward, buoyed up by the power and presence of the Lord. "Don't you dare disrespect the Rabbi," he said.

"What is to you… ? replied the clever thug. "He is old and obviously foolish as well. I am just telling the truth; which is more than he is."

"Setting up this charade is not the fault of the old Rabbi," said another man, a Pharisee, who pointed at Yeheshua. "It is that charlatan over there that has to pay."

"It is none of your business," said Johannus calmly; "just because something good and wonderful happens you cannot bear to see that, can you? Why don't you just go away?"

Another Pharisee joined the first. It was the one Johannus had seen at the inn. He squinted into Johannus' face. "Have you any idea who you are talking to, you little rat;" he said and then added, "I recognise you; you have crossed me before," and then a couple of the thugs had taken Johannus by his arms and were trying to pull him rapidly to the back of the crowd.

Suddenly there was a wrenching backwards and they stopped. A great, gruff and welcome voice came from behind, "like he said, why don't you just go away and leave us alone?" it was Beor. They released Johannus and were quickly gone.

Yresmin heard of the death of Lazarus but had felt it not to be right for her to intrude on the family at this time either.

So, she had waited a couple of days, expecting to hear news of the arrival of Yeheshua at any moment, but as fate would have it, she had been working in the house, oblivious, on the day the master had actually passed through that village.

Cursing her stupidity when she heard this, she had followed on as quickly as she could, catching up with the back of a huge crowd that had assembled around one side of Bethany.

For some unknown reason she felt rather faint, perhaps because of all the noise and pushing and shoving on the fringe of the crowd, and she drew away a little to sit down upon a stone bench beside the road.

She closed her eyes and the noise was louder almost than before, but pleasanter. She slipped sideways down onto the bench and lay there, listening.

The singing was triumphant and she opened up her eyes again. The high hillsides were filled with a tumult of brightly coloured people, all shouting out in praise. Yresmin couldn't remember seeing such a splendid sight. She blinked and rubbed her eyes but there they still were, innumerable and wonderful. She lay back for a moment to gather her strength and pushed herself up off the bench, opening her eyes again to the heavens... but they were gone. There were only white banks of cloud and a halo of a rainbow framing a bright sun.

The huge crowd on the road stretched ahead of her and they were singing out in praise of the king, as well as that Lazarus had risen. The wonderful feeling was still in the air and Yresmin was buoyed up with joy herself.

She decided to make another effort to get through the crowd when it burst open next to her and a stream of people came out, like puss out of a spot; shocking in their contrast to all the rest that was happening.

They horrified her for they were ghosters, thrusting her back towards a desert nightmare. Maybe not ghosters actually but they felt as bad, worse even. A distillation of evil intentions dressed up in expensive clothes that hid nothing from Yresmin's eyes.

She staggered back out of their path, collapsing again on the ground beside the stone bench. One looked at her as he passed and she recoiled from the unexpected glare of hatred. She had done nothing.

They were gone but Yresmin felt drained of energy. She stayed where she was until some kind person asked her if she was all right and helped her up onto the bench.

She was a local woman, not actually a Christine herself but her nephew was involved, and she was curious. She asked Yresmin if she would like something to drink and Yresmin accepted some water from her house nearby. But she didn't stay long; she was still trying to reach Yeheshua.

Thanking the woman for her kindness, Yresmin set off again along the path to Lazarus' house through the thinning crowds.

The doors were understandably closed to outsiders and so Yresmin asked around to find if Yeheshua himself was staying there. Apparently though, he had already left Bethany, but no-one seemed able to tell her where he'd gone.

What a day, she thought. Incredible things had transpired; amazing and wonderful and yet she was no closer to her goal. She couldn't feel unhappy though, despite it being as if the gods were playing with her. 'So be it,' she thought; she would try again tomorrow.

Back at the farmstead, Selly looked around at her with an unreadable expression and little Indy nudged at her thigh. Rebecca and Rabine were not at home so Yresmin contented herself with relating the day's story to the two donkeys.

She felt rather foolish at first but they seemed to love hearing her speak, so she told them everything and by the end she felt strangely comforted and managed to get off to sleep early, after a cold meal.

*

"Priestess, my faithful priestess; would you serve me one more time?"

Yresmin tried to see where the call came from, feeling the familiar touch of the Goddess' presence. Everything else was grey; dark grey, with no relief; and it was cold. She was sleeping out on the rooftop and strained to open her eyes.

"Look to my stars, priestess."

Yresmin raised her eyes, her eyelids, everything that she could and the mist rolled away gradually, revealing a dark sky where familiar stars were shining; Manat's own constellation.

She was standing in the clearing by the great lake, except tonight there was no lake, no myriad reflections from on high, only the thick grey mist that lapped over everything.

"What help can I give you, Goddess?" In all her time as Manat's priestess the Goddess had never approached her so directly.

"The Eloi have called to me and it is my wish that you accompany me; but as a friend... to my cause at least."

"What cause is that, great Goddess?"

"To preserve the ways of Destiny. To keep the roads of the soul free. To stop the denizens of Fear from over-running Shadowland."

"I will go with you; if you wish it."

"Good. Then let us go; and take this cloak; for it is cold."

Yresmin shivered at this reminder of the cold that was in the tendrils of mist that still snaked across the clearing and between the massive trees that surrounded it

The Goddess stepped forward, detaching herself from the background, taller and statelier than any empress or queen. Yresmin accepted the proffered cloak and put it on.

The way amongst the trees was exceedingly dark and Yresmin concentrated with all her might on following Manat. The grey mist was still around but the cloak did its job and then there was nothing but the trees, punctuated by occasional gaps of starlight shining in from overhead.

Eventually they even came to the end of the trees, just as the dark night sky was turning to a paler shade of light.

Another clearing faced them, or half a clearing. On the other side of this was an endless grassy hillside; and standing in a semi-circle facing the forest were the Eloi.

One stood forward, taller than the rest, to greet Manat. She was a very fine-looking woman, in the zenith of her power, her forehead crowned with a blue-white star, held in a circlet of gold.

"Thank you for coming to meet with us, my daughter," she said.

"This is Manat's priestess, mother. I asked her to come as well."

"That is good, Kaella; for it is about what is happening in their world that I would speak with you. I take it you witnessed the return of the great-souled one to his frail human frame; the man called Lazarus?"

"I did. The Lord scattered the forces of Fear and Death. It was a triumph."

"Yes it was… and yet events have not stayed still since then, either. All the elements of Darkness are re-gathering and the opening of the way from Death has changed things."

"How changed?" asked Kaella-Hecate, who Yresmin called Manat.

"Everything is changing daughter, you must know that. Nothing will remain as it has been after this…"

"Yes, I know, but how specifically after the return of Lazarus?"

"It is your Shadowland that bears the crux of it, Kaella. I fear you are too closely involved to see just how completely the paths of your realm are bound to succumb to the thoughts and wills of humankind. It is their shadow and they will claim it for their own, or it may claim them."

"That may be, but they cannot bear the darkness that is there… and is theirs."

"The Light of lights is with them, they have the way."

"For how long, mother? The whole weight of Darkness seeks to rend that world into the abyss. It seeks to destroy the human being who is the lamp for the Light. Why do you stand back and let it happen?

"We are sworn to our own path, and we invite you to join with us. The Shadowland will not remain your realm; of this we are certain and we beg you now to return to your own."

"Will my father allow me what I sought? Does he want me to return? He is not here with you to ask for it…"

"Your father is being our emissary to the Light. He bears our message of acceptance to the higher will. Whatever changes come, we will accept with gladness."

"So, you do not know the outcome any more than I do?"

"No, now that the moment has arrived all sight is blurred to what may come; but we fear that you are too close to the Darkness to be able to make a clear choice for yourself."

"And the other matter of my own quest? Has my father changed his will on this?"

"I cannot say that he has Kaella, for I do not know; but are you sure that your search is for a real fruit and not the bitter taste of an illusion. Abandon folly if it keeps you from reconciliation with us. You cannot hope to do any good there."

"Thank you for your kind words and your offer of reconciliation. My hope is that it can be between our hearts if not our actual paths; for I fear I must remain true to what I am and where I go. Folly, or the good I might do notwithstanding, and despite being enamoured of the Darkness."

The High Queen realised she had maybe not made the right approach, or found the best words, but she made one final heartfelt plea. "Daughter, it will never be too late to change your will on this. I ache to have you by my side again."

Then turning to Yresmin she said: "Priestess, you must know that humankind is being asked to grow. The time approaches when you must learn to take responsibility for yourselves and not rely on who you call Gods. If it falls on you to choose, please let my daughter come to us, for she has served you long and true."

*"**If** it falls to me, Great Mother," answered Yresmin, "Yeheshua must say."*

*

Yresmin awoke with her joints aching. The cold of night had blown into them and she stretched herself to try to be free of the strange feeling that the world was changing about her.

CHAPTER 21

"What exactly did they say again…?" asked Iscariot.

"The one man said 'We shall find out what sort of a Messiah he is…' or something close to that, but…"

"There you are Johannus," interrupted Judas, "they do recognise his claim at least. They just don't know whether it is true."

"Oh, I think they had made up their minds all right, Judas. The next thing he said was, 'do you think the crowd is ready to turn against him?'"

"What did the other man reply?"

"I couldn't hear, he muffled it. He didn't want anyone to hear."

"So, we don't know anything more about what they wanted?"

"Enough for me; I was lucky to escape them; thanks to Beor."

"Well, keep an eye on the road. Yeheshua has made it very clear that he wants no-one to come here unless they are seeking discipleship."

Johannus kept watch for the hours till dusk, and then was relieved by Aaron.

"James is taking an introduction to entering the kingdom Johannus, if you are one of those expected to go. In the small house around the back; in about an hour; and there is food at the main kitchen."

*

It is wonderful that Susannah's friend has allowed the master the use of this house in the Ephraim hills. It isn't huge but large enough for most of those of us travelling with Yeheshua, especially as there are also two adjacent smaller houses, meant for servants.

Servants that accompany the governor and his family when they get away to this villa for a break. All there are now is, a housekeeper, her husband the vineyard tender, and one young girl who helps the housekeeper.

I have been allowed to join in with the twelve and the coaching that the master gives them. It is an unexpected joy after all the months I had been away with Miriam.

They have all grown immensely, that is obvious, even to me. Deeper and somehow taller; high-souled some might say; but still essentially the same bunch to me. Enthusiastic, sometimes funny, some quite serious; each of them an entirely unique expression of what his love can do, and each one comfortable with that.

Simon-Peter did query my joining them and I explained that Miriam had told me that Yeheshua had said I should.

When the master came to spend an hour in quietness with us, Peter asked for Yeheshua's confirmation and accepted his one word reply: "Yes."

I think my joy is less than Miriam's though. These days are all the time that she and Yeheshua truly have as the lovers that they are meant to be. Not lovers as perhaps we might think but partners nevertheless in that divine love whose limits none of us should try to define.

Her position as his companion is not questioned by anyone; she is just there and like a mirror, a moon to his sun. She never pushes herself forward, always happy to just be somewhere close; not asking for anything else.

He accepts her totally, and if she is not there I have noticed how he looks out for her, and enjoys her return. And she shines with joy at his pleasure, but an inward joy that doesn't seek to take the attention from anyone else.

Even so I can tell that several of the twelve are not comfortable with her being so close to the master; though they don't show it as they used to. But how could anyone question their right, or seek to deny them this time together? Especially if Miriam's premonitions of the events to come are anything to go by.

Of course, there are still all the things going on around the master that there have always been; in particular the unfolding of his teaching about the way to fulfilment in this life.

I had been helping Hestia in the kitchen when Johannus came in. I knew he was preparing to receive entry to the inner path, even as he continued with his guard duties from which he had just come.

I greeted him warmly, and he sat down for some food that Hestia quickly provided. Johannus smiled back at her and I was reminded of his appeal, his sympathy with the feminine.

He ate the food and was getting up to attend James' talk when Judas came through the other doorway. "James is not feeling very well and has asked me to take the session for him," he said, walking across to Johannus. "Is that where you are going?"

"Yes I am," Johannus replied; and it made me think I should go as well.

"Do you mind if I come too, Judas?" I asked, even though I know he didn't really approve of me; but Johannus seemed to like him and I felt I should make an effort.

"That would be fine Magdalene." I thought he sounded pleased.

We walked over together to the house where some of the twelve were staying, that had a useful communal room being used for the preparatory work. The atmosphere was filled with anticipation and a relaxed concentration.

Half a dozen aspiring disciples were there but looking around I could see there were others that had come seeking initiation who were not in the room.

To me that could only mean that these would be the next few to receive the inner sight and spirit, and very soon. The others might have to wait a few days longer.

Johannus sat down on the wide rug in the middle with the others, whereas I found a place next to two of the twelve, Thomas and Philip, who were on a bench at the back.

Judas sat in the chair next to the larger one that Yeheshua would use; just in case he should choose to come and join us. There was always one of these ready for him.

"Good evening, my name is Judas, and I am hoping that this evening I can give you some insight into the voyage that you want to embark on."

"Learning to focus is something that I wasn't expecting to have to do. I thought I could already do it; but when I received this gift it became clear that I had no idea, because this takes a different kind of focussing…"

"Opening the heart and going there, through to where the joyous kingdom lies, is what we must learn to do. It sounds simple and maybe it is, but it takes everything you have to do this, and more. Only because the master gives us the Grace and tools to do the job can we even start."

"and then we must never give up. This is a task that needs to consume us, and it takes a very dedicated person to be able to do this.

Think of all the great minds who want to know this, who are spending all their life trying to find the right way to get God's approval; yet we are the ones, you are the ones being offered this. Why? What have you brought to him?"

I found it a little bit intimidating listening to Judas' talk. It made me think a little bit that I could not possibly do it, let alone be already doing it. I wondered how Johannus would respond, and then realised it might be just the sort of approach that might inspire and galvanise him. We are all different but the Lord comes to touch us all.

"There are so many distractions in this world," Judas was saying as I tuned back into his voice, "that you must purify your thoughts and hearts before any success can be had. Only those who prove themselves worthy can enter the kingdom, and this is what will be asked of you every day; for only those who can give up this carnal world can hope to gain the prize."

Judas' piercing eyes scanned the group and I felt them skip past me rather. He had never hidden the fact that he thought women were one of the worst distractions on the path. I sighed inwardly but continued to listen.

"Others will get their opportunity, be in no doubt of that. The task ahead is there for everyone to take a part. But now it is for us to be the ones to lead the way. We must take the reins our master gives us and drive our wagon forward.

What is being given can take us further than any other thing. The power of the great Word within is what all else must bow to. You have already witnessed this many times and in many ways, but now you must ready yourselves to be the instruments of this power."

I listened but found it difficult to follow it being described thus. I never felt that I was exactly an instrument of the Word, but maybe that is how Judas did.

"Where the master leads, we must be able to follow, and the gift you may soon receive will be the way that you can do this; and where the master leads is to the kingdom of heaven, and here on earth…"

Just at that moment the drape across the doorway parted and Miriam came in. Iscariot paused and a frown momentarily crossed his face. Then recognition of who might follow quickly dawned. "We are the witnesses to his presence, and its coming." He slipped out of the chair to sit on the rug by the others.

It always amazed me that however much time we spent with the master every time he came into the room it was special. His presence never failed to uplift the moment, and the same was becoming true of Miriam too.

She came and sat on the cushioned bench beside me just as Yeheshua himself appeared in the doorway and moved quietly to his chair.

"God is Love," Yeheshua said, after a quick scan of his audience; "and as I have come as witness to that Love, so all of you have been witnesses to me..."

"Now the time is coming for you to be witnesses to the Love itself; that shines within you, and for you; and can shine forth for all those you encounter in your life."

"The love we have comes from the One, and we are called to join with that oneness again, bring ourselves back to where we belong...

And what I need to know is whether this is what you... each and every one of you, really wants? And whether you are ready to look after the seed I will give to you, and allow it every chance to grow?"

Yeheshua turned this enquiry to each candidate, one after the other and each responded in his own way, that he was ready.

To Johannus he asked: "Can you yet distinguish the real from the unreal? That which changes not from that which does?"

"I don't think quite yet; but with your gift I hope that I shall be able to," answered Johannus and the master smiled a little. "Well ... maybe so," he said, "but you also have to really, really want that. Otherwise, it cannot do anything."

Finally, he returned to address everyone in the room. "I invite you all to come to the villa tomorrow morning, in the hour before sunrise. You need bring nothing, only yourselves, rested and alert; so please go and get a good night's sleep."

"And Judas, please be at the entrance hall tomorrow by the beginning of that hour, to see everyone in; only the people present now in this room... except that is for my mother as well, if she wishes it."

*

CHAPTER 22.

The path was overgrown but he managed to avoid the worst of the thorns that clawed at him. The light was dark, bluish green, and the surrounding foliage was high about him.

A frog or something hopped across the path but he ignored it, pulling back the last whippy branch that blocked his way. Beyond it the path widened and a hillside opened out in front of him.

He thought he knew the look of that slope but still didn't quite recognise where he was. There was a lake to his right, behind high bulrushes, where starlight gleamed.

He looked up to the sky … a constellation shone out like a tiara … and he wondered at it, never having seen it before.

The name came unbidden to his lips: "Kaella," he said, turning from the lake towards the sloping hillside, bordered here by the tall trees of a seemingly immense forest.

He scrabbled up what path he could find between huge boulders, looking for a cave entrance somewhere up ahead that he thought he would recognise, but only the crown of stars, still high above him in the night sky, answered his gaze.

"Kaella," he called softly, thinking of the impish smile of the young immortal he had known.

A cold wind came from the lake and in some other part of his mind he couldn't help remembering a contrastingly hot desert wind blowing across a plain, where shapes chased him but he couldn't flee; and his first encounter with the crone aspect of Hecate.

"Kaella," he whispered again between his breaths, hoping that he wasn't calling that last Hecate to him; but he still quailed rather when he saw a tall, queenly figure stood above him on the hillside, looking down.

She spoke with calm power, her vibrant voice caressing the air. "What do you want? Why are you here?"

Johannus struggled to think clearly. 'What do I want? Why am I here?' Any answers that came didn't seem to fit properly with Hecate's question. Caught in mental paralysis, the sense of the Goddess' presence grew in intensity.

Eventually his answer came, transformed into a sort of plea. "What should I want, great Goddess?"

The element of unexpectedness in this caused the onslaught of Hecate's attention to pause, creating a moment into which other answers formed on Johannus lips, unintentionally mirroring the questions of the Goddess. "To know what you want; why you are here?" he said; both an answer and a question.

As Hecate seemed to consider this the severity of her demeanour softened, and for a few seconds Johannus looked into the face and mind of the young Kaella and the story she had once told him flashed like lightening through his thoughts… but then she was in the deep heavens and a war was crashing all around, across the entire Vortex-Arch, and she joined into it, her power helping to shackle the enemies of reason that threatened a reign of chaos in the planes of Life.

Even as Johannus heard the cosmic groaning fade, Kaella had changed and the space which held her being had changed as well; for little half baked human children were forming their scribbled impressions on the walls within Hecate's hall of dreams.

Something about the little silver threads of moonlight entwining in the darkness of his mind discomforted Johannus, but he could not quite turn away, held to the vision by the will of Hecate.

*

He was there… Haldrun, walking on a wide green slope in the bright morning light, making his way with a party of seven others, onwards and downwards towards the destined land, set like a jewel in the deepest of blue seas.

He could remember first catching sight of this wonder when they had exited the ice heights, warmed by the light that had awoken them. There Gaia had been, far in the distance, visible beyond the high places of the Elohim.

They had followed the path through those beautiful lands where the presence of the Eloi was felt in every rock, in every blade of grass. The sparkling streams, the shady woods, the flower strewn meadows were a real part of those who had formed them, brushed by the breezes of their very spirits, uplifting all who passed through.

Occasionally one of the Elohim themselves had appeared to talk to them of the task they faced, and these meetings too merged into the joy of being there.

Glimpses of their distant goal between the green hills of the Eloi showed them they were getting nearer. The pool of blue that held the living pearl had grown wider, more distinct; the beauty calling to them more and more.

On and on they walked till eventually only a rocky ridge that flanked a wide bowl-like plain of sand and stone seemed to stand in their way.

Even as they finally reached this place it seemed as if a touch of weariness had entered them; drowsiness even.

Their way led them down through dunes to where they were surprised to find a young boy playing by the path. He smiled at them as they approached, and dipped his slim brown hand into the rocky ground that turned to water at his touch.

Laughing at their amazement he held a shining pebble in the air which grew in his hand to become a bright disk, spinning around his upraised finger.

"Where are you going?" he asked them as they continued to stare.

"Gaia calls to us," said Haldrun and the boy looked back hard at him.

The dark brown eyes melted Haldrun's thoughts and suddenly he realised that he had no idea which direction they needed to go. It all looked the same; like a wide round golden bowl.

"That way," said the boy to this unasked question, sending his spinning disk into a lazy arc that crashed it against a rocky outcrop, exploding it into a sheet of light.

The blast sliced across the plain, just above their heads, the heat of it scorching their thoughts and hair, out to the other edge, then back again, accelerating outwards, upwards, expanding and contracting as its speed was countered only by its bright heat; too fierce to continue watching as it sped upwards.

The boy was gone. Haldrun looked for some sign of him but all he could find from what had happened was smoke from the impact between the disk and the peak gathering itself up into billowing clouds; and somehow the ridge and the whole plain it encompassed had grown. Suddenly their surroundings were immense, imposing a new scale of their presence upon the travellers.

Nevertheless, it was as if the blast had just awoken Haldrun, for he felt his appetite refreshed; to be on this journey, to have this incredible chance of life… on Gaia. All they had to do was cross the great ridge barrier.

They set out towards it, aware now of the strong heat in the sky above and the shadows that its light caused on the ground under them; and they were grateful when they got close enough that the spreading clouds shaded them from the harsh brightness.

The mountain heights were gathering the storm power around them like a mantle of their majesty and it was none too soon that Haldrun and his companions eventually ducked into the ravine that had been rent by the fiery disk of light.

Ahead was a darkness that was itself full of the deep afterglow of the disk's might; more profound than any colour; where Haldrun's ears perceived what his eyes couldn't; a wall of high pitched sound like a million, million fireflies.

With room for only one person at a time the path became a narrow tunnel, and as Haldrun pressed on the tenor of what he could hear changed. The sound of a billion falling, splashing drops of water came from his left and he instinctively moved that way, finding that the tunnel had opened out into a wide cavern, that led to another and then another, into the heart of the rock.

Warm air wafted from the right and Haldrun could have gone that way but he had liked the coolness of the water on his feet, after the heat of the sun-disk. He had kept to the left and didn't know where the others were. Nor did they think to call each other; each being entranced in the magic of their passage through the mountain halls, echoing to the drip or gushing sounds of water.

Somewhere there was light, but so soft that it was impossible to tell where it came from. In fact, it seemed to be everywhere but nowhere in particular; hard to focus on, such that by turning all around Haldrun had almost completely lost his sense of which way was forward.

But now water was flowing over his bare toes, up to his ankles even. Looking down Haldrun realised he could not only feel the stream flowing, but he could see his feet as well. It was the water itself that contained the glimmerings of light.

He splashed along in it, the flow gaining strength as more and more and more little rivulets joined its course.

Haldrun laughed and the echo of it tinkled around him and he laughed again.

It wasn't long before the stream grew deep enough for him to be able to sit and be swept gently along over its smooth bed, winding a bit this way and that, down into pools and out the other side, the light getting a little stronger all the while.

The water washed all over and about him. Her... the water was a feminine presence all around him... her; she knew him and he let himself go with her, loving the accepted intimacy.

The excitingly gentle journey took Haldrun suddenly out of the mountain's side where the released water quickly spread wide across a slope of reedy grasses, golden green in the bright sunlight.

At first, the steepness made anything other than a wild foot-first slide impossible, but gradually the gradient lessened and Haldrun turned and allowed his hands to trail through the long strands of water grass.

He grasped hold of a bunch and his descent halted, surprisingly.

He held himself still, enjoying the flow of the water around him whilst the hot sun beat down, warming his languid body.

Lying on his side Haldrun could survey the wide grassy apron that spread from the base of the banded cliffs with their hundreds of layers of red and brown and yellow and orange, that stretched in a great arc away into the distance, fronting the towering peaks above and behind them.

Screwing up his eyes Haldrun was able to make out several figures that had exited those cliffs at different places, making their way over to a white line of a path that snaked its way down into a hidden valley.

The path disappeared somewhere between the slope where Haldrun was spread out under the early sun and a long green hill that had a fine white pillared pavilion at its top, unlike anything that Haldrun had ever seen.

He knew he could work his way over to the edge of the water slope and find a way to meet his companions but he didn't want to.

Looking down the water flow, he could see it divide around a wide smooth rock as it tumbled into a dell of silvery trees whose leaves shimmered in the light breeze. This would be his way down to Gaia.

There were many large rocks amongst the trees around the dell and as Haldrun craned his neck around he could see that the woods and rocks fell down and away, giving the impression of a there being a deep ravine to the other side, behind him.

Turning his attention back to his stream-bed he let go of the water-grass and allowed the water to take him once again, down towards the dell.

The rounded rock was coming up in front of him and with a little twist Haldrun steered himself round it and over a lip where he became part of a watery fall towards a wide pool, half full of swaying water lillies and lotuses. He plunged right into it.

Opening his eyes under the surface of the sweet-tasting water, he was shocked to find himself looking at a tangle of women's bare legs; slim ankles, shapely calves, long thighs and rounded bottoms.

Spluttering, Haldrun came up for air and to see what was happening. Where the water lilies had been many radiant maidens sported within a dazzle of rainbows.

His eyes went to one, most beautiful, in the middle of the play, naked as they all were, and… suddenly they had vanished, and there were only water lilies, pushing their pink-tinged white flower heads up through their rounded greenery, either side of where the flow still drew Haldrun on, rainbow showers falling in from above; but the maidens had gone.

A loud splashing sounded ahead and suddenly Haldrun collided with a curtain of water, not fierce, but enough to send him sprawling over the lip of the dell, back into the flowing stream and on through wooded slopes of the lower mountainside, coursing again around rocks and through gullies.

Down, down Haldrun was swept with the stream and, as its flow slowed and deepened, Haldrun was drawn under into fathomless dark water.

Fear crowded in on him as he sought to rise to the surface for breath, but was being pulled inexorably down into darkness and pressure that squeezed all thoughts out of him, any sense of what, who or where he was, leaving only the fiery need to take another breath.

Sparks of light were inside and outside, and the possibility of breath that had to be taken, whirling as another stream, through him, neither fire nor water, but something he gave everything he had… to both grasp and let go to… become …

*

"Not mine, not my dream; not mine…" shouted Johannus inside himself, disengaging somehow from the vision he had been caught into…

A watery way had formed, widening as a myriad other streamlets joined the flow, that Johannus unwittingly recognised as the beginnings of the river that wound through the Shadowland; where Hecate ruled supreme.

The queen that Johannus had bent onto his knees before.

He dared to glance up at her regal features, hoping she would be looking favourably on him but saw that her attention was absorbed by the happenings within the tide of humanity, drawing him in, to witness it as well.

Darkness was tarnishing the threads and a sadness emanated from the goddess as she tried in vain to keep it out; but somehow the thread essences cut deeper still than she could clean, allowing this contamination to seep back into them.

Fear of death was what brought this about, causing humans to delve into reserves of greed and cruelty that spoilt so much of good that they could bring about, Johannus thought; or was it Hecate telling him?

A fiery anger had built and built in Hecate, from witnessing the lusts for power and wealth that ate at human beings and drove them to destroy each other, caring so little for anything else, even for Gaia herself who supported them.

Only the shortness of the span of human life kept this from happening. This and the efforts of the Divine to help them, teach them, lead them on the way to higher goals.

But the Goddess had started to change again, contorted by the pain of enduring this all.

The third face of Hecate, that Johannus hoped he'd not meet again, forced its dominance upon the hillside, and Johannus saw in a few brief moments the part that Hecate was called to play in those efforts to contain or help these spirit-kin that had fallen into mortal flesh and walked on roads that fanned in front of her.

Fear crept into and up his spine, for her gaze had come to rest on him.

Though the queen of sorceries could take on any aspect that she chose, Johannus faced now the crone whose insight could not be denied.

She skinned him alive with the look in her eye, pinning Johannus' mind like an insect she might devour, knowing his history and the weakness of his choices, the paths of his desires; and then even those of some redemption too.

Hope at this last brought to Johannus memories of his best associations… his struggle to bring the abominated Mary Magdalene to Rachel's house of healing in Tyre; yet even as this came to his mind he felt Hecate probe ever deeper, uncovering his discipleship to the black magus Simon.

A huge jolt rocked Johannus: the realisation that this was when he first had called upon the mistress of sorcery, eager to uncover the secrets of her magic. That was the moment that had finally led him here, tied him to this fateful examination. Hopes and desires he had managed to forget were dissected by the Crone-goddess' knifelike sight and Johannus further paled before her.

But the Goddess' mind did not dwell with this discomfort of Johannus, going further still into the layers of intimate choices that had taken Johannus to the court of the magus.

Layers that were closest to Johannus and he struggled hard to keep these spaces of his heart from her gaze, to keep the Goddess from dissecting the deepest places and loves of his earlier being.

A hundred demons flanked the visage of the crone goddess, shaped like flying beasts of every kind, a company of terrible wasps, and her awesomeness threatened to overcome Johannus completely. He managed to lower his head, clamping his eyes shut against her, even as her face transformed into the fanged maw of a terrible serpent, agape and ready to strike.

No bite came, but Johannus felt the rush of stinging winds pass about him; causing no more hurt than the hot pricking of his own embarrassment and the un-named shame at its core. His limbs trembled as though they had been turned to dust.

Finally, a kind of quietness returned and when he dared to open his eyes once more it was the queenly figure the Goddess that faced him on the hillside; mighty in her magnificence.

Her presence exuded calm and though Johannus searched her face for the young Kaella he found little trace there or anywhere around. The whole hillside resided in the fullness of Queen Hecate's control, with a great hound sat on either side of her.

The air between them was full of a tension that in its own way shocked Johannus; that he had some sort of relationship with this immortal being. How their interaction had become such a strong thread in his life was hard to imagine but he had to cope with it somehow.

He felt that an onslaught was about to be unleashed against him but he wasn't sure why. He stood there… empty.

When the Goddess did finally speak it was in answer to the questions that Johannus had forgotten he had posed.

"I am the mistress of the myriad pathways, and the use of them that you call magic."

"I am the watcher of the crossroads, witness to all choices made; the shapers of Fate and Destiny."

"I am here to see that all the ways are clear to be navigated by the souls who cross between the worlds; and I will remain until the winds of change dictate to me a different path. For even I have a destiny that I must be ready to go and meet."

If the tension softened between them with these words, it also deepened, and for a long moment Johannus thought that she might be about to unveil further personal insights… but then it passed.

"You have called me as witness and I have sought to know the worth of what you seek; though you may not have intended this to be; even so it is."

Johannus understood that this resolution was needed; tangled strands needed unravelling.

"Choices lead to habits, that become a tide, that take you to a destined end.

This I know and witness all the time; how humans often slip down the slopes into the darkness."

"It is rare to find any who seek to climb towards the heights and rarer still to come by the extraordinary intervention that can change the tide around."

"If you wish to be such a hero then there is so much to be done to turn your path away from crashing onto the rocks of carnal life."

Johannus bowed his head for a moment as he felt the inevitability of the castigation that was about to come.

"… for you have been found to be unable to face the basic truths of your living;" her words sounded disdainful to Johannus, mirroring his gauge of his own worth, and he braced himself to receive more well earned harshness.

"How can you therefore aspire to greater truths?"

Her voice had changed, turning from her attack on his character… to pose that question.

He looked up… into the face of another Kaella, and found himself disarmed again by her youthful playfulness and beauty.

This was Kaella he related to as the real person and he was relieved to be with her again, though still nervous that things could change at any moment.

She already knew the story of his early life and loves so he realised there was no use to try to hide them. The naked imperfections of his heart's desires were laid in front of her. Would she take his offering as she sometimes had?

Not this time. She was sensitive to Johannus holding back from her and in this moment was aware that every nuance between them was pregnant with meaning; and her instincts were never wrong.

"You seek something else, don't you?"

"I seek… I seek… I seek that love, that beauty, which will not fade or change or die."

"You think she can give it to you?"

"Who?"

"Aphrodite."

"I don't know."

"No, you don't. Go then; see if you can find such a love that is untainted by lust; for only such a love…"

Kaella turned her head away, her sentence unfinished and Johannus felt the hurt and recrimination in her voice.

"I won't ever leave you Kaella," said Johannus in a desperate attempt to keep her happy and from changing again.

"Don't say such things… you are but a mortal man and I am of the starry race beyond your understanding. You know so little of anything you speak about."

Johannus sensed that she was angered, but though she didn't change her aspect, her voice was harsh when she spoke again. "Go. Go and see if you can find that love that has no taint; no lust in it that you seem to fear."

"No, I don't…" protested Johannus but she had gone now, and the queen stood over him. "Go now," she said firmly but not unkindly.

"Where?" asked Johannus, perplexed, looking around for anywhere to go.

"Go back," said the crone that Johannus turned back to find. She spoke with the sweet voice of the young Kaella but her smile was crooked, mocking him.

In her hand a knife flashed through the air beside Johannus' head, cutting an opening in space itself.

Sharp nails had grabbed his upper arm and she propelled him into the rent. "Go there…"

CHAPTER 24.

Johannus was arguing with his father about his wanting to go and train in sculpture and philosophy.

There was a boat in the harbour that was sailing for Rhodes on the next tide. Johannus wanted to be on it but his father forbade it. He told him that he had to stay and complete his training as a silversmith instead.

Allowing oneself to be seduced by the whimsical attractions of the Hellenic gods and their cults was no profession for a Jewish boy.

"Why then," rounded Johannus, "did you give me the Romanised name of Johannus, instead of good plain Jewish John?"

Not waiting for an answer, he turned and stomped out of the room and the house as well, but with no clear idea of where he was going; just needing to get away.

Inevitably he found himself outside the house of the one girl who soothed his ruffled feathers on days like this.

They weren't very close but she had a dark world of soft curvaceous flesh that easily accepted his unmasked desires and let him go as easily again.

She wasn't there and Johannus stood outside what suddenly seemed to be an unfamiliar door, wondering where he was. He wasn't sure he was in the right place at all.

Gradually it came to him that he did recognise this road; he realised it led down to the beach where he and his friends went.

There were several low fishermen's cottages beside the track and then another larger house where there was music playing. He didn't remember this; it must have been newly built.

As he stood outside the gate two girls came the other way up the track and swayed their scantily clad hips past him. They had been down at the beach.

One smiled at the quite handsome young man who stood, apparently undecided, on the path. "It's her birthday, Johannus," she said; "come in".

She was pertly pretty and he smiled back, wondering why he couldn't remember either her name or the girl who lived here, whose birthday it apparently was.

He stood there a few seconds and then decided it must be alright for him to go in as well. There was nowhere else he wanted to be anyway.

He recognised a few people inside, some engaged in drinking and talking and others gathered around where two musicians were playing in a darkened area of the house; set up atmospherically in the modern way.

One girl, quite short with curly black hair, spotted Johannus hovering by the entrance door and she grabbed another drink off the table beside her before going over to him.

Already emboldened by the free-flowing wine, she wound her arm around Johannus', guiding him into the darkened room.

Several couples were dancing and others sat or lay together on mats and cushions around the edges. Johannus drank, watching, and the girl snuggled into his side.

The music, the wine, the scent and warmth of the girl beside him all worked their effects on Johannus and they soon were engaged in a dreamy embrace.

Her mouth and body was open to him and he was momentarily shocked by the wetness there, ready for him. This wasn't what he wanted, was not why he has here.

Disengaging himself after giving her as much attention as he was able, Johannus told her needed to go visit the washroom. Lying, he told her he would be back soon.

There were several people gathered around someone he couldn't quite see, and he skirted around the group, looking for either the washroom or something that would tell him whose house he was in.

He felt like an outsider, out of sorts with the party happening here.

Then a lovely infectious laugh from amidst the people he had just passed stopped him short, like a jab of pain in his side.

He whirled around, just in time to see the back of a shock of blond hair disappearing out of the further door, into the garden.

Celeste was here; that was why he was; she was the reason.

Hurrying over to and then out of the same door he looked around in vain. There was no sign of her, or which way she might have gone.

Puzzled, Johannus looked back at the house … now he recognised it. *Her* house; this was *her* family home.

She must have gone down to the beach, he thought, noticing a path that led beside a wide bank of myrtle bushes, down towards the blue sea he could glimpse between the pine boughs.

He sped up his pace, careless of the sharp rocks that fringed the downward leading steps and, rounding the corner of the cliff path, encountered the full vista of blue and white; sea, sky, fluffy clouds and wide beach.

Sauntering down the now gentler slope, Johannus scanned the way ahead for any sign of the girl he was searching for.

A few people were on another path that crossed this one a little further down the hill, and sitting beside that spot was a bent figure which could have been either a man or woman, all cloaked in grey.

But there was no sign of Celeste; yet he felt sure she had to be here somewhere.

The old man sat within his shady robe studying everything and everyone who passed by. "There is no swimming in the sea today; there have been attacks," he warned ominously.

Startled, Johannus looked round at the grey-beard who repeated the warning; "there have been attacks; it is not safe to swim today," and turning back down to the sea it was plain to see; no-one was swimming.

But there was something else going on instead; people were dipping buckets into the water and carrying it up the beach to pour over their companions, lying on the sand.

More people than Johannus could ever remember seeing here were assembled on the sands, and too many for him to be able to pick out Celeste; his own sweet Aphrodite.

The woman beside a small wagon was selling buckets to anyone going onto the beach. She had specimens of every description piled in her wagon; from fancy little metal buckets down to crude wooden ones.

She eyed Johannus up and down and asked, "You will be wanting a nice metal bucket, I think. Copper or silver perhaps?"

"I have no money on me," answered her prey.

"You must have something. You cannot expect success without one."

Somehow this didn't seem at all odd to Johannus, despite it being unlike anything he'd ever known before. He searched around his pockets and found three small coins of insignificant value. He presented them to the woman; "this is all I have."

She turned up her lip, sneering at him unpleasantly. "Take this then," she said, handing him a poor excuse for a bucket.

Johannus took it despite it obviously being almost useless, with numerous gaps between the bits of wood it was made from. He looked at the woman dubiously; there was something about her as well…

"What would you expect?" she shrugged, turning away from him.

Johannus picked his way across the hot sand, and just as he was wondering whether he should throw away this ridiculous thing rather than wasting his energy carrying it around, a high pitched voice called out to him.

"Johannus, how wonderful to see you here." It was a large matronly woman, who Johannus regrettably recognised as being a friend of his parents. She had her daughter with her, and both were trying to take shade under a rickety awning, pushed on sticks into the sand.

"Ah, you have a bucket with you; marvellous. Perhaps you would be so kind as to collect some water for Miranda and I?"

Johannus looked at her daughter, thinking her even plainer than he remembered. She was one of the girls that his father had tried to interest him in. She looked back defiantly and their mutual dislike continued.

He started to stutter an apology that the mother immediately latched onto as the opposite. "Good, we shall wait here. Don't be long, we are depending on you."

Despondently he trudged towards the water's edge, wondering how he could make this disastrous bucket hold water. Pebbles, sand and some bits of driftwood was all he could find to mend it.

He was conscious that people were watching his efforts, which weren't turning out very successfully. The water flowed out through the gaps no matter how hard he tried to block them.

A couple of girls were vying to attract his attention, turning over and around provocatively, just on the edge of Johannus' vision.

Did he really care about this stupid bucket? Even though they seemed to be playing a large part in the general beach activity, he couldn't be bothered.

He stood up and in frustration, kicking it over. That woman and her daughter would have to find someone else.

One of the two girls was openly watching him now and he decided she was quite attractive, but only quite. There were others who were more so, and he started to wander down the waters edge, giving himself the chance to appraise the beauties on display.

Out of the several who seemed to want to court his attention with suggestive little movements and glances, there were definitely two or three that he wished he could try to approach.

But as the woman bucket-seller said, there seemed to be little prospect of success without an eligible bucket.

Something about the ridiculousness of the situation did grate on Johannus, but he attributed this to his own inadequacy, not the dream he was in. Instead of disbelieving it he started to think of a way to get hold of a suitable bucket.

Taking more notice of the buckets themselves Johannus realised that it wasn't only his that had been imperfect and leaky. Almost all of them leaked and most of them looked rough one way or another. The owners tended to carry them rather apologetically.

At the far end of the beach a high cliff caused there to be an area of shade where lots more people, appearing not to want to lie in the sun, were sitting eating or just chatting.

On the edge of the shade one girl was cleverly taking advantage of both the sun and the shade, moving around to suit herself.

She spotted Johannus as someone interesting, someone not involved in the bucket ritual, and as he got closer, she recognised him. Strangely they had been together a few years earlier. She called to him.

Johannus went over and was so surprised that this former girlfriend was on the beach. It seemed like ages ago that Carmina and he had been lovers.

They had both been very young and she had undergone an unwanted pregnancy that ended badly with the loss of the baby. Her parents made sure that they had no more contact.

He was genuinely pleased to see her, and she him; and as they sat and talked and Johannus couldn't help noticing that she had a rather elegant bucket by her side.

He took her hand and wondered what it would be like to kiss her full lips again. She let him find out because she knew the look in his eyes. She wanted him, and thought that this time she would have him as her husband.

The taste of her was intoxicating; as it always had been. He could see them getting back together too.

He also couldn't help himself thinking that by staying with her he could use her bucket to have access to all the other beauties of the beach.

He hated himself for thinking this but the thought itself was seductive. Possibilities opened to his mind that should have been brushed away but he couldn't quite manage it.

A girl walked up from the water and Johannus thought her the most attractive he had seen yet. She sat down in the sun, nearby. He could easily watch her, and he wondered whether this was perhaps what she intended.

Even though he was here with Carmina, he was already being torn this way and that.

Somewhere a bell sounded; a gong; mournful rather than joyous, and Johannus felt it more than he heard it; the recurring pain under his heart and this time it had come like a warning from outside of himself.

He looked up in response and, in the distance, walking down the beach, a figure in white caught his attention. The blond hair, the walk; he knew it was her; it was Celeste.

Anguish poured in on him, waking him from his own stupidity.

How could he have forgotten? The very reason that he had come to the beach at all. The person he was searching for. How had he forgotten?

She had reached the waters edge and was carrying on, slipping down into the sea's waves. No-one was taking any notice of her or trying to warn her.

Johannus jumped up, oblivious to the others around him, appalled to see that the girl he cared so deeply for was swimming out into terrible danger; and the anguish he felt for what he hadn't done, as well as what he had, redoubled.

Without thought of explanation he ran across the sand and down to where the small waves were washing up to the people stood there, and splashing through them he pushed on as swiftly as the deepening water would allow, diving forward to swim across to his love.

It was all becoming clear now. He had been duped; into what everyone else was doing. There had never been a real need to buy the bucket or get involved in any of those things. How easily he had forgotten …

He swam hard, trying to keep Celeste's blond hair in sight, but it kept dipping in and out of view as he swam through the gentle swells.

His heart's pain was a comfort now, keeping him aware of his personal mission, and he took no thought or care that he was swimming into danger himself.

And soon he was alone, out in the deep water.

He strained to catch sight of Celeste again and eventually was rewarded to see her climbing up some steps in the rocks on the furthest side of the small bay.

Those rocks were a favourite place for young people to jump, swim and dive from but there was only one other person there now, a boy and he was helping her up; she had clearly swum over to him; they clung together.

The bottom fell out of Johannus' world of dreams.

Stupid upon stupid, and he could distinctly hear laughter all around.

Kaella's laughter, though the face in his mind was that of the bucket-seller; except he realised her hooded eyes clearly belonged to the crone goddess.

Fear gripped him. An attack would surely be immanent.

He knew he was in a dream now, but also that such a dream with Hecate was not like any other: he could be affected; he might not awake from it.

The worst thing for Johannus was still that his 'special' love for… his own sweet Aphrodite, appeared not to be so different from the others; he just thought that it had been.

All of this so-called love turned round and bit you in the end… not so unlike Hecate herself.

Darkness swam around Johannus, sea and sky both, like a vortex, ready to take him down.

Why?… why?… why?… and the laughter continued to echo around him as the light faded. Voices and faces like ghosts were coming at him, and a wickedly curved knife glinted in what light there was. All was lost.

Hecate had won; nothing was left, and he was scared.

"Johannus; help!" The cry reached him, cutting through the waves of his self-pity. "Johannus."

He lifted his head to search for the source which seemed to be up the other end of the long dim tunnel he was in.

Struggling both with himself and to respond to the call, Johannus did his best to swim towards the light. For what seemed an age he got nowhere and then suddenly and to his surprise he found he was back in the same bay again.

Rocks around and underneath him still held nameless menace but the person who's cry he was answering was somewhere out of the water ... she called again, "Johnny, Johnny; over here .."

There was only one person who ever called him that, and she didn't belong in this... he searched the shore and couldn't see her at first, but then he did, on the path beyond the rocks... "Johnny, come out of the water... come on out!"

It was Magdalene, Mary Magdalene.

That side of the bay had two ways out through those rocks.

The first were the steps that Celeste had used, in the diving area.

The second was a slipway for getting small boats in and out of the water. It was covered with slimy green seaweed and lots of little limpets. Some people liked it but Johannus didn't. In particular he hated the black sea urchins that lurked in every crack, ready to spike the feet of unwary bathers.

"Which way shall I come out?" he asked.

"It doesn't matter," replied the distant Magdalene; "just come out."

Johannus only ever used the diving steps and he had no idea why he was making an issue of which way to use now.

He swam around and shouted out again. "Which way Mary?" but her reply was faint and distant. "Just come out Johannus; I have to go."

He could easily go over to the diving steps; they were so much cleaner and better than the other way, but horribly he felt he was going to have to use the slipway; he had delayed too long already.

Maybe it was because of Celeste, but he forced himself to swim over to the shallow, slimy slope, checking beneath himself to try to avoid the dark areas and whatever they might contain.

It took a monumental act of will for Johannus to crawl on hands and feet up the seaweed covered rock, but finally, getting to his feet, he realised that it hadn't been that hard at all.

He was out, out of the water; though still feeling somehow vulnerable in the subdued light.

Looking around Johannus realised it was not yet dawn and there was no-one else about yet. Where was Magdalene?

She was no longer over by the bushes at the back of the beach.

"Mary, Mary?" No answer came, but there was a path there, quiet in the semi-darkness; and standing before it, Johannus hesitated.

He heard something; birdsong; and listening intently realised there were several different birds punctuating the song, at intervals, announcing the day ahead; wonderfully.

Tentative, he started down the shadowy path, feeling his way and listening hard to compensate for the lack of being able to see much.

It led him to what was the first of many rows of vines, arranged on the side of the hill. As he climbed it came to him that the singing had changed as well.

He wondered at himself for not having realised it before; she was someone who's beautiful singing he loved to listen to.

It was Miriam.

Trying hard to see and hear better he pushed forward into the vines, struggling towards where the singer was, and managed to open his eyes...

Early light was filtering through the shutters.

The warmth of his bed was around him and he closed his heavy eyes again. What a strange night it had been, he thought and wondered about the dreams, thinking to sink back into them, to make sense of what they had been about, but... somewhere outside Miriam really was singing.

Johannus threw back the covers.

He had to get up early; this was a special day.

*

I had slipped out of bed quietly, careful to make as little noise as possible. Anna was still asleep on the other bed in the room, and I knew she had been up late, with mother.

Then I heard Miriam singing; calling to the sun, as yet to rise. Quite softly, as though for herself alone.

It was one of my favourite songs, that Miriam had sung a lot when they had been travelling together, to Kadesh and back. It celebrated both the new day and a new age; hope for the future being the truth for today.

I stopped to listen and saw that others had done the same.

Thomas and Philip were standing in the trackway beside the vineyard. They were also walking to join the instruction-session, to play their part in helping the master, when Miriam came out onto the flat roof to sing with the dawning day.

They had been entranced; having never heard that song before.

I came up beside them and Thomas turned for a second, nodding to me as I caught his eye, and when the song finished, we all waited a moment longer, wondering if she would sing another; but she didn't.

Judas Iscariot had been up earlier than anyone, relieving the night watch at the front of the villa. The master wanted him to secure the access for the session that day.

He was sitting inside the front door, attentive for every movement and noise,

374

and though he didn't see or hear Miriam going out onto the roof, he could just hear her song.

He was as ever moved by the beauty of them.

She was the master's companion and she played that part well. As long as she wasn't aspiring to be anything more, like Magdalene appeared to be, then Iscariot thought her inspirational singing could serve greatly in the times that lay ahead.

Thomas, Philip and I came in. Judas nearly frowning at the sight of me, but he didn't; rather he greeted us all very amiably.

I knew he didn't approve of me and had probably been glad when I had left with Miriam these months past. 'That woman wants to be one of us' I had heard him say when he didn't know I was nearby, and to Judas' annoyance the master had done nothing to discourage me.

Judas debated within himself, 'maybe the best thing that could happen is for events to move too quickly for her to make a real nuisance of herself.'

He couldn't see what part I could have when the whole of Israel united around their true and spiritual King.

Whilst he was musing like this, Johannus arrived and Judas smiled more generously. He thought of this young man as his protégé, and so reflected that perhaps Magdalene's role had been to bring him to the master.

Judas had hopes that Johannus would prove to be useful in aiding whatever his own part would be in establishing the master's kingdom.

Anyway, many of the participants were arriving now and Judas made sure that the right people had come and knew where to go. Yeheshua had asked for them to await him in the lower anteroom.

Johannus walked down the short stairs to a fairly sparsely furnished room that was cleverly situated so that it never got too hot or cold. It had high level windows that took light from the house's inner garden court where the window openings were under the stone seating, set around the colonnaded edge.

Miriam was already there and greeted each of them as they came in, and something relaxed in Johannus for he felt that he was in the right place; at last.

Some warm flatbreads had been cut up and set out on a table; Miriam told them to help themselves to one, and then the girl called Hestia brought in mint tea on a tray which she served to anyone who wanted it.

Johannus sipped his tea and looking around saw that there was a door that led to another room. As more people came in it became clear to Johannus that it must be in that inner room where the master would give the teaching.

And once Miriam knew everyone that was expected had arrived, she slipped out to let Yeheshua know.

Seeing her go, strangely disjointed snatches from his last night's dreaming came into Johannus' thoughts; memories of swimming in a dangerous bay but then also of splashing into a pool where Miriam was. No, it wasn't Miriam… but he couldn't quite remember who it had been.

More unexpected memories of Kaella, of Hecate, came to him, worrying him, but then all these thoughts vanished for Yeheshua had arrived, followed by Miriam, mother Mary and Judas immediately behind.

Judas went to open the inner door, but the master signalled 'not yet' to him, and instead went over to Hestia and asked to have some tea as well.

He turned back to the group, smiling and relaxed, enjoying this informal moment with them all.

"Before we go in and start," he said, "are there any last questions any of you have that you would like to get out of the way?"

I looked around; I couldn't imagine that anyone would ask anything at this point; I thought they had been thoroughly prepared already.

To my surprise Johannus was looking very thoughtful and the master's gaze was resting on him with a look of patient kindness.

Johannus was struggling with what he wanted to ask the master because for a flickering moment he had remembered having been in front of the goddess Hecate, and a question she was telling him to ask himself, but this was different; this time he really wanted to frame the question that he had hid from Hecate.

"Does lust always taint the love we have?"

A shocked pause in the anteroom followed this question; quite a long one.

The master looked for a moment to Miriam who raised her eyes to meet his gaze and then to his mother Mary, who smiled.

Returning to answer, Yeheshua's glance swept us into his attention; he leaned forward to address us.

"Bring your passions, all of them; bring them and they will be transformed; and in doing so, you will be transformed too.

Touch, feel, the Breath of Life, and all of what you have will become more…

More valuable; better understood.

Even that which you think of as unworthy.

The lust, the anger, the jealousy, the frustration too: all that is in you. Offer it up, with true sincerity, and in return you will be given a ladder to climb.

But if instead you hold these back in the secret recesses of your heart, it would be like having the ladder with missing rungs, and so very difficult to climb.

Open the channels to your heart and you will witness the Great Harmony.

Lay bear the true thirst that you have, so the Water of Life can flow through you, assuaging it.

Do not be ashamed or fearful for anything you have done, because whatever it is, your soul cannot be tainted or tarnished.

Any bad that has happened, can and will be washed away, in the great river, of time.

But neither should you deliberately do anything that you will then be ashamed of, for these are the things that keep us separate from where we should be, and wish to be.

Understand and remember this and you shall be able to walk in the Light that I have been tasked to bring."

Johannus breathed deep, accepting the master, what he was telling him, and let go of everything else.

Yeheshua turned towards the inner room. "Come; it is your time to receive the seeds to plant within, and practice."

BOOK 4: THE CRUX

PROLOGUE.

The Summoner had come.

Queen Ashera stayed a moment longer, looking down the long, long slope towards the borderlands, before turning to answer the call.

He had come in the night when the lower kingdom was arrayed in its glorious counterpane of stars; the time Ashera loved the best.

She walked across towards the council circle still mulling over the problems of the netherworlds where her daughter Kaella held the reins of power.

Darkness was erupting there and Kaella was struggling to hold it all at bay.

Change was upon them. They knew it had been coming and now the Summoner called them to council.

The court where the council was held was part of their pillared palace of graceful simplicity set atop a green grassed hill.

He sat, full cloaked in deepest indigo, in the 'reserved place' that Queen Ashera had never seen taken before.

She was the last to arrive, taking her seat around the central pool of Seeming; the pool that was there long before the Elohim had ever set their outer palace here.

From within the dark hood the Summoner's vibrant voice was clear as crystal, deep as night. "All are invited to come and witness the turning of the wheel of the Law, the changing over of the Ages," he said.

Ashera looked around at her court. She and they had already discussed what they were going to do in these restless times.

The king had gone as emissary to the Lord on earth, on Gaia, and the Elohim had all agreed to accept the changes wrought on them, whatever the cost; except for Hecate alone; who was her daughter Kaella. She kept her own council in her own place.

The lord of might, her brother-son, stood tall amongst the court and declared to the Summoner of their afore agreed intent. That they would retreat behind the banded cliffs and hold the heights, leaving these lower lands to what the coming age must bring.

He had no doubt that the Eloi could and would hold their homelands against any who might challenge them there.

"Perhaps you do not understand," answered the Summoner quietly. "You all are invited to come and be witness to the change; in the Way of Souls."

This Way was known to be found through the waters of Seeming; yet anyone who ever went did not come back as they had left, but by another route, where they and their memories were both washed smooth, like pebbles in a swiftly flowing streambed.

Ashera got to her feet, her height only slightly less than that of Maichel.

"What we have to weigh Lord Summoner, is the effects of our decisions on all of our people."

The burden was heavy on her shoulders but her demeanour showed she bore it proudly.

The Summoner rose in his turn and stretched a sceptred hand over the face of the waters; "Come, let me show you," he said, drawing his sigil on the surface.

The waters swirled and rose about them like mist, transforming all, lifting them to the Elohim's high seats of power.

Standing tall upon their Pinnacles of Sight amidst the wheeling galaxy of stars that paints the arch of heaven a violet glow, the Elohim watched the children of their breath, their spirit and their love, circulate the golden bowl beneath whence came the Call of indigo:

"Come be witness to the lamp of ages that brings the Light for all to know, the Love that holds the planes of life in place."

"Come if you will; you are each and all invited."

And responding, this host of heaven was joyfully accepting.

One thousand after another donned the proffered robes to enter within, the way of soul.

Heaven was emptying her realm to bless and be blessed.

Ashera winced at the temerity she had shown; to believe that her decisions would affect the fate of all she cared for. Rather it was the simplicity of their love that was making her now take heed.

Once back around the circle, freshly enlightened council members turned to accept the gift that the Summoner had brought and knowing that they followed those they thought to lead, one by one humbly took from his hand the semblance of the void.

Fair Amriel was the first to step through the waters and great Maichel was the last, excepting for Ashera herself.

She stood alone across from the Summoner and then at the last she knew him.

"What of our daughter Kaella, my lord?"

"She has her own lands and her own decisions to make, my lady...
What do *you* wish to do?"

"Can you give me just a few moments Lord Summoner?"

"Only that; the opening remains but not for much longer."

Alone again on the grassy hill Ashera turns her gaze to the arch of heaven above... but now the spread of stars has gone... except for just one small group; Hecate's own; low on the horizon.

Loss, like nothing else she has ever felt rushes in upon her mind, her soul, her very senses. All she has loved and cared for, nurtured and enjoyed: has gone; gone to nothing.

She staggers to her knees, groaning aloud, her mind trying to find a way to comprehend the emptiness.

Grasping around she sees again the little tiara of remaining stars... all that is left, each feeling like a stab to her heart. All else, all else... none of it will ever be.

Ashera's sobs are not for herself but the love that she has no home for now.

She turns her hurting thoughts towards her daughter, wondering for the first time whether she could join her in her fight to save her world. Yet even before she can wish for it, she knows it cannot be.

Their paths have been set on separate courses for much too long to change. Even if she tried with all her strength of will it wouldn't be real and wouldn't work.

She trembled, shaking. Thoughts of the Shadowland and its dangers had given half a moment's pause to the stream of grief, the awful press of nothingness.

Within that inch of space and time... one breath, and in it Ashera felt a tilting back to some semblance of balance. For indeed there was something else... as well as the welling up of that other unfathomable hurt that was the loss of her daughter's trust... something else, that she had forgotten was there.

Had always been there, even at the moments of greatest loss... and joy...

The call...

In every breath, behind every heartbeat ...

The call, that even the Summoner was only come as a reminder of.

That call which kept everything together, in contact, yet was so easily missed.

But she could not ignore it now... now it was the only thing she could hold to.

And opening herself... she turned, and went back to accept the Summons.

CHAPTER 1.

Miriam answered me. "If I were to tell it as I really see it, this is what I would say…"

We were sitting together in her room of the villa, out in the Ephraim hills.

I was mending the hem of my best robe and Miriam was sitting on the window seat, glancing out at the garden through the gap between half closed shutters.

The master had gathered the twelve to him and was talking to them under a tree that had spread its shade into one corner of this garden where springtime was blossoming.

A friend of Susannah's had lent the villa for Yeheshua and us, his followers, to enjoy in the weeks leading up to the Passover festival; as much as anything to be able to be away from the hornet nest that had been stirred up by the Pharisees and other leaders of Jewish life in Jerusalem.

That Lazarus had been brought back to life after being pronounced dead for days hadn't calmed anything down, quite the opposite.

We would be leaving again for Bethany in the next day or so and I was glad to have this time with she who is my dearest friend, and my Master's beloved.

I had asked her about this special time; these few days away from the crowds, their marriage week, some said; their private time.

The mid-morning sunlight was streaming through the shutters, bringing welcome warmth and making striped patterns across the floor.

"Very few of us get this chance to be with the Master as he walks the earth. It is most precious and yet so hard to take in, to take to heart, especially whilst it is actually happening."

"When he has gone the whole world will be ready to gather together to sing his praises, but who can love him when he is amongst us? And yet somehow, his gift has been given to us."

I knew it was true and wondered what more could be done, wishing that this moment could stand still…

"And the only thing that makes it possible for us is when we really want to listen and understand the experience that he brings to us, showing us who we are, and enjoying the home-coming of our souls."

My thoughts turned momentarily to our journey back from Kadesh-Barnea and the quest that the master had sent his dearest companion on, to find …. whatever it was that Miriam had found.

Little motes of dust were floating about randomly in the shafts of light, sparkling. 'We are like these motes of dust,' I thought; 'sometimes in the light and sometimes not.'

Then after our return from Kadesh there had been the parting festival in Galilee, with Yeheshua urging us to take on his purpose, and his work; to keep the lamp of inner truth alight.

If that was the marriage, here was the honeymoon and I couldn't, in my life, imagine a more fitting bride for the master than Miriam.

But in between had come the death and resurrection of Lazarus, and the inevitable confrontation with the Jews, in and around Jerusalem.

A light breeze brought the fresh scents of spring wafting through the windows. Miriam kept watching what was happening outside.

Yeheshua had brought her even closer to him than before her quest, and somehow they managed this without changing the way the he was with the rest of his disciples.

It seemed to me that her place was always meant to be by his side; she was the perfume of his love.

"What was it that you found at Miriam's tomb?" I asked, unintentionally blurting the words from out of my reverie.

I had wanted to ask this for so long but had never found the right time.

Miriam looked at me for a long moment and I thought she wasn't going to answer. She closed her eyes and, as I watched, her face set into a look of grave concern, showing lines of deep-felt pain.

"I'm sorry," I said. "I didn't mean…" my hands tightened around the hem of my robe, pricking my finger with the needle I was holding. "Ow!" I gasped involuntarily.

I looked down at the drop of dark red blood that had gathered and sucked the base of my forefinger there, to help alleviate the throbbing.

Miriam was watching me now. "It's all right," she said. "You have the right, my sweet; you are the one he sent with me after all. Perhaps I should have told you more already, but it isn't easy… to know how to…"

The pause lengthened and I sensed her gathering herself and her memories from deep within. It was obviously hard and I wanted to tell her not to worry; I wanted so much to retract my question.

In my mind's eye I could still feel the rough surface of the low tunnel in the tomb, where I had crawled towards the burial chamber of that Miriam of old and where this Miriam was sat in silence with the soft starlight of Venus playing gently on her face, channelled through a crevice in the walls of rock.

"I know it was a vision about these times to come," I said. "You needn't tell me, for I saw enough myself that spoke of the way that we must tread."

She no longer looked worried and even smiled at me then. "It was indeed about these times to come; for in his kindness, he knew that I would need to know this for myself: so that I can live through it, at his side."

I could hear sounds of something happening in the garden which made me want to get up and look outside but Miriam was still seemingly concentrating on how she was going to answer me.

For several seconds we sat in deepening quiet.

The song of a bird reached into the room reminding me again of the question

I had asked; for that had been prompted by Miriam's own singing.

At the festival in Galilee, she had sung about things I hadn't understood, that seemed to be about things she alone had seen, presaging events still to happen; 'what had they been?'

She half-smiled at me again and opened her mouth to speak... "there are great difficulties ahead... but we... but he... he will..."

Fresh sounds of movement came from directly outside our door and now it was my turn to smile for I felt such a wave of love filling the room.

Their love; such as I had felt like this once before, when he had sent her upon her quest and I had found them crying together, each knowing the separation that was to come.

That was when he asked me to go with Miriam and bring her safely back to him.

He was outside the door now, I knew; and Miriam was already up and moving towards it.

He entered even as she opened it.

He took her in his arms and she lifted her face to his.

Their mouths met. He kissed her and she kissed him too and they remained thus enjoined.

There were several disciples outside the door; some that looked and others that turned their gaze away. I closed my eyes.

The feeling was somehow brought even closer, as though I had been drawn into their embrace.

Bright stars of light out of the darkness; light that resolved into flower clouds of creamy white petals and the black turned indigo to deepest blue, that was the sky behind an almond tree in blossom.

I opened my eyes and Yeheshua had gentle arms about me, holding me from falling. He looked into my eyes as he let me go. "It's time to get ready," he said. "We are leaving for Jericho today."

CHAPTER 2.

Rachel, the healer from Tyre, drove her mule cart along behind the disciples that were accompanying the master Yeheshua down the track towards the Jordan road.

The day's heat was already strong but a breeze blowing across their faces from the north-east made it seem less so.

Rachel glanced back around the side of the cart, noting that Johannus was still guarding the rear. She smiled to herself, knowing how seriously he took such duties.

Mother Mary was sitting on the driving bench beside Rachel, whilst Miriam and I were walking just ahead of the mule.

Yeheshua stopped at the side of the track, allowing his disciples to gather around him; and Rachel pulled back on the reins, bringing the cart to a halt.

The master turned his face her way for a moment, catching her eye. She cupped her hand to her mouth in the sign for a drink and he nodded in response.

Fetching a water-skin from behind her seat she called to Johannus, who took it from her and poured some of its precious water into the jugs that Miriam and I were holding up.

Judas had come over to the cart: "Johannus, once you have had a drink, could you make sure Lew has enough? Looking out on the slope ahead, at the bend in the road."

"Yes, fine," he replied.

The way Judas liked to organise him had rankled a bit with Johannus but since having stayed with the master in the Ephraim hills, things had changed.

He had received instruction and Yeheshua had also insisted he be given time to himself, for practice in quietness.

Practice that could have been easy, but that his own unceasing mental commentary tended to make hard work.

He had just enough faith to believe that if he kept applying himself, the experience would grow for him. He was determined to persevere.

And here, walking along this dusty road in the burning sun, he felt in tune with everything, even Judas. All was good.

He knew Lew would be most grateful for the extra water, so he was glad to take it to him, out there on his own.

They sat together looking to where the river Jordan was a tiny sliver of silver in the glinting sunlight. "Is it far to Jericho?" he asked, and Lew shrugged. "We should be there later today," was all he offered, and Johannus asked no more, content to sit quiet by the older man's side, watching the hillside.

Lew fished out a small packet from a pouch on his belt and offered Johannus a couple of dried figs from it, which he accepted with thanks.

Shading his eyes against the glare, Johnannus stared for a while along and beside the road ahead, but there were no movements anywhere he could see. "I shall get back to the cart," he said.

Lew nodded, "see you later."

Miriam smiled at him as he rejoined the party that were loading things back into the mule cart, for moving on. "Come and walk with Mary and I, Johnannus; like in Kadesh."

He joined us, and I smiled at the memory of all that time we spent in the wilderness, each of us sharing the one aim; to get back to the master as soon as we could.

Now that seemed so long ago; now that we were accompanying him here into the den of his enemies; and still there was nowhere else we would be.

"If I were choosing the destination," I said, "I think we would be going as fast as possible in the opposite direction."

"That is the difference he makes," Miriam answered. "His courage, always to love."

Johannus and I said nothing, but we felt the truth of it. With him, we could brave anything.

As we walked and walked, silently together, I fell into a kind of reverie, my eyes closing.

Peace was in me, filling me.

I saw all of us on that road together; felt the master, the twelve, his mother, and many more, and his peace spreading out from us; stretching and stretching across the whole world.

Then something happened. I think I kicked a stone poking out of the track and stumbled; falling to one side; eyes flying open; my peace shattered.

Miriam and Johannus put arms out to grab me, to stop me crashing into the ground, but one of my knees hit the stony dust anyway.

I sat on the ground and mother was standing over me. "Are you alright Mary dearest?" she said, earnestly studying me, one of my hands held in both of hers.

"Yes mother, I only tripped. Careless of me, but I am fine."

"Come back into the mule-cart with Rachel and I anyway. Get out of the sun for a bit," she said, stroking my hand; and I complied.

Yeheshua had looked around questioningly, but mother shook her head, then nodded; "She is alright."

Sitting in the back, I mused on it all, trying to get back into that beautiful feeling of peace. Broken up but not gone...

I must have dozed off then for the next thing was that we had reached the Jordan road and found Christines approaching from Jericho, having heard that the master was coming. Apparently, there were many hundreds crowded there, believing the master would be returning through for the Passover in Jerusalem.

Yeheshua greeted them and after a short recuperation break for everyone, he directed them to go back to ask the people gathered at Jericho to keep as calm and orderly as possible, so that he would have a chance to come amongst them without giving those who professed to hate him reason to cause trouble.

Simon and Judas decided to go swiftly on to Jericho too, to help with these preparations. Yeheshua didn't say anything more, but then Judas called to Johannus telling him to get ready to go as well.

Johannus reacted with almost a jolt. He had his duties, to be a guard to the women, given to him by the master Yeheshua himself, when Miriam, Mary and himself, got back from the difficulties of the quest.

Judas was in the habit of believing Johannus was his aide or lieutenant or something, ignoring Johannus' other duties, which annoyed him. Now though he was just a little confused as to what he should do.

He looked over to the master whose smiling eyes were watching him. Yeheshua nodded and said something quietly to Thomas at his side.

Thomas came over to the mule-cart where they were standing. "The master said that you can go with Judas, Johannus, to find out what it is needful to know. I shall walk with Miriam and Mary... if they will allow?"

"OK, that is good," said Johannus relieved, and found himself thinking 'I wonder what he meant by, "find out what it is needful to know"...?'

He said nothing though, just got on and collected his blanket-pack from the back of the cart, making sure his leather water bottle was full, before joining Judas and Simon.

"Let's get going then," he said, and Judas nodded, turning towards Jericho.

The crowds were thick and excitedly expectant as Simon Zelotes, Judas and the others reached the city, and it was easy to see how the numbers could cause a crush and a problem.

Simon had spoken at length with those who had travelled up from Jericho, and knew there were some from his former sect there who might be useful now. So, whilst the others did as the master had bid them, he, Judas and Johannus sought out these zealots that were well respected and listened to by the authorities of Jericho.

Some of the zealots were easy to find, being close to the edge of the crowd, near a passage through to the central square of the city; and Simon recognised one of them called Jeremy, who in turn greeted him as a friend.

"Perhaps the safest thing would be to get the rabbi quickly through to the citadel where there can be rooms made available and talks arranged with the city elders. They could certainly assist him in his mission."

Simon agreed on this course and Judas was interested, asking what kind of help they believed could be offered.

"You can come and meet one of them yourself," said Jeremy. "He is a colleague of the high priest Caiaphas himself, passing through on his way to Jerusalem too."

They followed Jeremy through the long passage and turned right up the sloping street past several stores whose wares were set out in front of bead-curtain covered openings, till they neared a corner where two richly dressed men were standing. The one with his back to them was clearly a Pharisee.

The other saw them coming and stepped forward to greet Jeremy and his companions. "Ananias," said Jeremy, "Simon, Judas and… er, Johannus here, are hoping to consult with you concerning the well-being of the rabbi Yeshua. He is on his way here now, as you can see by the crowds that are gathered."

Ananias greeted Simon and Judas, but Johannus was looking at the second man, the Pharisee. He had started to turn as if to stand beside the other, but apparently had changed his mind. For a moment Johannus saw his profile, eyes glancing over Simon and Judas; before he turned quietly away and headed off around the corner.

Not before Johannus had recognised him as being one of the conspirators who had been at the inn; where the ambush of Miriam and Mary had been attempted, on their way to back to Yeheshua in Galilee.

The shock of it was like a blow to his chest and by the time he recovered Ananias was discussing the upcoming arrival of Ye'shua with Simon and Judas.

"We would very much like to discuss his visit to the Paschal festive-time, whilst there is this chance," Ananias was saying. "We have so much that we can do together, don't you think? and make it all go smoothly."

"His work is… for every person." Simon stopped, realising this wasn't perhaps the best approach, but Judas continued in his place, "for in the spiritual realm he holds the keys, but in this physical world there is much that you could do to help him and us, we are sure."

"Yes Judas, I think there is business we can do. We shall have some rooms ready where we can talk tonight."

Johannus froze at this, thinking of the Pharisee he had seen disappearing.

Ananias looked at him. "Are you all right young man? You look unwell."

"F… fine thank you. I'm just trying to understand… so I can be of some use …" he said rather lamely; but he was glad not to be more deeply involved.

"Listen," said Simon, turning to where they had come from. "He has come, I am sure," and they could clearly hear the renewed cheering of the crowds. They hurried back down to the passageway.

Judas and Simon sought their way around the outside of the crowd followed by Johannus, with Jeremy joining his other comrades; and some way behind was Ananias.

The press kept them apart from the master, but they could just see his head covered by a pale shawl across the heads of the throng.

Others were finding it even harder and one man, of shorter stature, had climbed a tree to be able to see Yeheshua who laughed, asking "What are you doing up there, dear friend?"

"Master, I wanted to be able to invite you to stay at my house tonight. I have an inn where many of your company could stay as well."

Yeheshua responded; "your good heart and deeds are well known to me and our father God. I would be glad to come and stay under your roof. Is there somewhere I can address this throng now though? If so, climb down that tree and come and show me where to go."

Simon, Judas, Jeremy and Ananias heard this exchange and realised that the plans they had discussed were not going to happen. Simon shrugged but Johannus noticed Judas' scowl. Looking back at where the zealot Jeremy and his friends were muttering and shaking their heads, he also saw the smirking smile of the priest called Ananias. A shiver ran up Johannus' back, and he hurried away to find Miriam and Magdalene.

What he didn't see was Ananias going over to Judas and pull him to one side to continue their earlier discussions.

CHAPTER 3.

The road to Bethany from her village was familiar to Yresmin now; and visiting the community there had become part of her routine since the return of its leader Lazarus from death itself.

She liked the Christines she had met, including Beor the blacksmith who she discovered was a friend of the Johannus that had been with Miriam and Mary in Kaddesh.

Yresmin had been high priestess of the Goddess Manat in Kaddesh until she realised that the 'star' she had followed as a girl to get there was still calling her; drawing her now to the master Yeheshua.

Nothing though could have prepared her for what happened on the road from Rekem to Judea, where 'Ghoster' Djinn worshippers happened upon her and dragged her off to their desert encampment.

Miraculously, she escaped alive from that horrendous ordeal but was still left with an awful message to deliver to the master that she hadn't even met yet.

'His circle is breached and he is doomed; the powers of Darkness have penetrated his inmost defences.'

She knocked on the door of Beor's workshop, peeking her head into the open work-area to see if she could see the blacksmith, but all was quiet so she went no further.

Retracing her steps back up to the road, she stopped again as a couple of heavily adorned priests crossed the start of the smithy's track, on the road ahead.

Wary of all like these she shrank back into the shadows.

To her they felt just like Ghosters, dressed up in black finery. Wealthy and respectable perhaps, but filled with a darkness inside.

She might not have been so sensitive about them if it hadn't been for her desert nightmare; but their every encounter was keeping that memory alive; making her task as messenger the more imperative; and unwanted.

The master had disappeared in the furore that followed Lazarus' return and no-one had known exactly when he would be back but everyone was ready. They were sure he would be in Jerusalem for the feast of the Passover and almost certainly staying here in Bethany too.

Meanwhile the urbane Ghosters were everywhere, so Yresmin didn't stay any longer, even though there were also more and more ordinary folk gathering to greet the master's expected arrival.

She had already picked up the few provisions her landlady Jermina had asked her to collect; from a stall where she also found out that the master Yeheshua had arrived in Jericho yesterday, and stayed on there last night.

Tomorrow was the Jewish Sabbath day and she would come back then; but now she would get back to her donkeys who meant so much to her.

Her 'Sella' had been the one who had got her out of the desert when she had collapsed even though, unbeknown to Yresmin, Sella already had her unborn colt growing inside her.

That was Indy. Born in a tremendous thunderstorm, she had named him after Indra, an Eastern God of rain and storms and he had been growing strong and beautiful ever since.

Yresmin loved to just sit and watch them together. He was more playful than she thought a young donkey would ever be and Sella responded with what Yresmin could only see as love.

They made her feel humble, knowing how badly so many of their kind were treated by many of hers.

Waking on the Sabbath, Yresmin had no work to do for her landlady, so she set off again for Bethany.

Before she even got close, she knew the master must be there because of the increased activity of all types of people on the road, and soon the crowd outside the Synagogue made it clear that he was inside.

Not being Jewish, she stayed respectfully on the outskirt of the crowd, not withstanding that these edges were dotted with small groups of those very people she feared the most.

She was grateful though, that she was managing to feel inconspicuous; not as she had the day before. Her patience was rewarded by getting a glimpse of the master as he exited the synagogue and made his way to Lazarus' house. She followed along with many others.

Yeheshua stopped and turned at the house's entrance. "The time has come," he told the crowd, "for mankind to know the way to get back home, for this world is our house for only a little while and we must know our actions here are taken as part of a greater plan."

"Go and prepare yourselves, make yourselves ready for the way ahead, for all will be called to know that the Almighty truly is our father, our refuge and our goal."

He made a sign of blessing and turned and went inside.

So short a time but Yresmin's heart had lightened, lifted, and was flying.

She would do as the master said; prepare herself, and decided to go and check again on the way home whether Beor might be at his workplace.

She knew it was unlikely on the Sabbath but still she followed some instinct that took her there, glad to get off the main road again.

His doors were closed as she knew they must be, but suddenly she saw what she had been hoping to collect the day before, hanging on a hook beside them; a small harness that she had asked him to fix together for the colt.

She smiled broadly, recognising the corded leather strapping that she had given him to make it with and then there was a sprig of jasmine put with it.

Beor called her that, in his jokey way. She had already paid for it so he knew she would wish her to take it.

She had wrapped some bread she had baked the night before and now left it there for him as a thank you; and with renewed warmth inside, she set off again to get back to Sella and Indy.

Yresmin groomed her friends most meticulously, glorying in the fact that she had no reason to follow the strict Sabbath rules of the Jews. Indy's coat was so soft and she brushed and combed it through till there was no possibility of a knot anywhere to be found.

Sella's was naturally short but she brushed her thoroughly and tried the new blanket she had got from Ruth, the married sister of Lazarus.

The stable area was spotless too by the time she finished with her cleaning. The more she worked the more she wanted to make everything as perfect as she could. She even polished Indy's harness rings, though they didn't need it.

She slept well but at one point she had a dream: the Goddess calling to her but not finding her, and though she had been unworried in the dream, she now somehow felt she should be.

She woke up feeling this vague unease as the light was growing in the eastern sky over the flat rooftop of her landlady's side of the house. She got up and washed herself in the cold water from a tub in the corner of their living area.

Her job for the day was cleaning the outer areas around the whole house and she started it early, glad to have the task to put her pent-up energies into. It occurred to her that all the cleaning she had been doing was to somehow wipe away the necessity of delivering the message and she shivered at the reminder.

She took Sella out of the stable and tied her in the yard and then half-grown Indy next to her. Brushing them out had been easy after her work of the day before and she put Sella's new blanket across her back, smiling to herself, 'how fine they looked' and 'how happy she felt'.

She hummed her favourite chanting song as she started preparing herself something to go with some flatbread that she had leftover from the day before, and goat's curd from the farm.

There were often people on the road, that Yresmin could watch go by through a slit window in the thick outer wall, and there were voices outside now as she chopped some herbs from Jermina's vegetable garden.

She looked to up to see them walk past; but they didn't.

She listened out because she could still hear them, but she had the feeling they weren't on the road. Had they gone into the yard she wondered?

Wiping her hands on her apron she untied it from around her waist, put it on the table beside her and turned towards the big double door of the stable-barn.

They were definitely in the yard, and her heart quickened because she could see them standing by Sella and Indy. One appeared to be looking at how he might untie Sella's leading rein.

"Hello, can I help you?" she asked with a level voice, her senses giving her mixed messages. She didn't recognise either of them but she felt that they were somehow familiar.

"The master sent us," one of them said. "He said to tell you that he had

393

need of her." His hand was stroking the fine blanket Ruth had given for Sella.

"The master Yeheshua?" Yresmin whispered incredulously; her pulses racing again for different reasons and she believed one of the messengers nodded in reply.

"I'll come," she said quickly. "The colt needs to stay with his mother, I'll bring him too." The man nodded again, smiling broadly at her enthusiasm.

This time the trip towards Bethany was a total excitement, she couldn't have cared if there were a hundred 'ghoster priests' trying to intimidate her.

They arrived at Lazarus' house just as Yeheshua and his close disciples were coming out. It seemed to Yresmin he emanated a softness in contrast to the harsh sunshine and she felt at ease immediately as he came up to her and the donkeys.

He stroked Sella's neck as though they were old friends and she nudged his knee with her nose.

Indy looked as though he wanted to jump around like a young lamb, but thankfully he was managing to behave, and Yeheshua scratched the springy curls on top of the colt's head.

"Let us get going then. I won't be riding till we get nearer to the outskirts of Jerusalem. What is your name?" he asked her.

"Yresmin" she said, looking into eyes that seemed to know her entire story. He asked her to lead her donkeys and keep close behind him; and he smiled. Everything but happiness fled away.

Miriam came up beside her and hugged her in welcome and Yresmin felt her world had come together, making total sense at last. Without having met Miriam in Rekem, she wouldn't have been here now.

Looking around she could see Mary as well, and Johannus not far behind; it seemed they hadn't recognised her with her head covered like a Jewish woman, and as they walked the crowd following was growing bigger.

Every step was taking them closer to the Holy City, the city that had been waiting for this moment, this day, for millennia. The day the Lord himself would enter in, showing his glory there.

Yeheshua slowed, turning to Peter at his side. "I shall ride from here Peter; can you hear the singing?"

Peter looked at him; he couldn't hear any. "No," he said but the master replied, "I can."

James and John came with their best coats to add on top of Ruth's blanket, but Yeheshua waved them away, and climbed to sit sideways on the donkey's sure, wide back.

Yresmin was close behind, holding Indy back as he pushed forward to be with his mother and the human master, and she had heard Yeheshua's words to Peter that made her strain to see if she could hear the singing too.

She loved all music and as they walked, she thought perhaps she could…

And then a chanting song of praising 'Hosannas' started up amongst the disciples following; and all along the way more and more people joined the throngs, to witness what was happening.

Someone in the crowd started it… recognising the wonder of the moment and taking off his cloak, had laid in front of the Lord's procession. Soon many more did the same and others, further back from the road, waved palm tresses and whatever they could find to express their joy.

Yresmin was amazed at the simplicity of the unfolding splendour, centred so completely on the figure on Sella's back. Her donkey carrying the master, the King that she had spent her entire life trying to believe would come.

Then she did hear the singing. They had climbed a small hill and the gates of Jerusalem had come directly into view but Yresmin was looking further still, to where she thought the music was coming from; higher, higher even than the hills around.

The sky had changed, for above the clouds that crowned the hills its blueness was pierced with violet light and brighter points of stars that shone there, though it was full day.

Starlight singing out the glory sent Yresmin into wonderment. Her eyes and ears drank it all in until it grew so loud that everyone must surely hear it too…

.. and there it was all around her as well, pure sweet children's voices singing the praises of the King of Kings coming.

Yresmin felt transported into a realm far more real than this world of doubts, hates and pains.

Tears were streaming down her face as the master turned to look back at her and she half laughed, half cried. He made a motion for her to come forward or rather to let Indy come forward to be beside him, she realised; so she did.

The children were singing their spontaneous praises all around as Indy came up beside his mother, placing his head and shoulders under the sandals of the master, matching every movement of his mother as though he was a living footstool for Yeheshua.

No-one would even notice such a normal thing as the colt staying close to his mother, but for Yresmin, walking into Jerusalem just beside them, it was a miracle, meant just for her.

Her heart overflowed with love.

Stepping out into a sound filled void; the diaphanous robe spread around Ashera, floating her into the wide space above endless valleys of gold flecked trees.

Light streamed up from the trees like a breeze, buoying her up, whilst out in front, a tide of star-souls were gliding in a wide arc, curling towards this valley's heart, where one tree bloomed much higher than the others.

The closer they flew into its embrace the wider and taller it became, filling the universe with its mighty boughs; tips to the highest heights and roots to the unfathomable depths.

The canopy above abounded in rainbow showers of celestial song, whilst in the mid-heights waterfalls played into pools among the green hill mounds where birds and animals were sporting.

Circling around and down into the deep beneath, their robes became as flaming circles of fire and air, and they… a shower of gently falling sparks within the tree's magnificence.

Through indigo again they stepped onto the clouds in a sky that held their celestial forms with ease… just above the tree's base, that now is a splendorous walled city, whence roads splay out like mighty roots.

Drawn here to the pivot point of the age where once again the seeds of Love are being renewed, to form the basis of a future forest; for beneath and beyond the great tree is a churning space of dense darkness, where those seeds must make the future bright with life. Darkness, through which the roots of the tree penetrate, seeking and finding that water which is beyond all telling.

At the very crux, on a road into the city, rides a man upon a donkey, a master soul of souls, living his life here amongst mortal human kind, bringing his love to the centre of the world's need.

Some men and women clearly were his disciples, around the centre of a great processional crowd that sang in joy; but others around about were not, and many of these seethed with dark and deadly hostility.

The Lord of Love rode upon a donkey, feet resting on her young colt's head… that Ashera recognised… and that somehow, heaven was bowing down to greet the King as well.

*

Kaella prowled the edges of the twilight knowing she was being drawn into events beyond her control and she was not happy about it.

There was something terribly wrong, for what was good and true and full of love was being taken into a ring of dark force that nothing could escape from.

Was she not Hecate and Manat too, queen of her own domain, peerless mistress of all magic arts? Yet powerless now to protect her own from what was happening.

Kaella knew the poisoned chalice that awaited the master Yeheshua and those that followed him into the Darkness.

What earthly use were angelic powers that applauded and stood watching as the worlds spiralled into the abyss?

She at least would not sit by doing nothing.

What was it about this mortal human world that placed it at the centre of the turning wheel of fate?

Why did the behaviour of these mean and frail beings matter so much that everything was risked like this?

What could even be achieved there... where pain and suffering robbed meaning from those brief lives just as death took from them any permanence?

Now it seemed she herself would need to step into the circle of fate, for only she who ruled the crossroads could yet stave off that outcome which would ruin all; to let the Powers of Hell take Love itself away in chains.

How would that help anything?

At least she had influence amongst certain humans, and two of these were with Yeheshua... and, if all else should fail... she herself would block the way.

CHAPTER 5.

Yresmin knew she still had to deliver the message to the master, to warn him of the trap the Devil infested Darkness had set, if she could.

All day he taught and healed at the temple in Jerusalem, fearing nothing, and Yresmin saw for herself that love in action that Miriam had described.

Saw too the powers of hate that she had encountered herself, in priestly garb, coagulating like dark clots of evil, never far away.

Then all in one moment she had her chance to tell him, for the master turned to her to speak of the colt that she had brought along with dear Sella, to bear him here.

"Mistress Yresmin, if you could allow me a request, could the colt be given as a gift to my Lady Miriam? That the one who has borne my feet hither will bear her also, whither she may choose to go."

"Lord, I need to tell you that your inner circle is breached by the Darkness that seeks to destroy your mission," she whispered quickly, fearful lest she didn't get another chance.

He looked long and almost solemnly into her earnest face.

"Fear not Yresmin, priestess of Fate, for Darkness cannot comprehend the Light or even fathom what its mission truly is; and if you would give Miriam your donkey colt, then Darkness will ever fail to follow where she goes as well. That would make me very happy."

Yresmin was amazed that she would be able to do this for the master, having lived for so long with her burden of being the deliverer of evil news.

"Y... es," she stammered at first, and then the words tumbled out; "yes of course, it would make me so very happy too; that I have this chance to serve you."

He smiled now and she knew everything was all right at last.

*

Johannus also witnessed Yeheshua working in the temple court, this day and the next, and saw the reaction amongst the priests and Pharisees; how much they hated what he did because the people loved him and what he brought to them; what all the priests and Scribes and Pharisees had never done or even wanted to.

Yet that hate could not touch the master, for just when it boiled-over against him and they tried to seize hold of him, Yeheshua was no longer where they thought.

Johannus marvelled to see their frustrated anger failing to affect the many others who were so happy and rejoicing from being in contact with Yeheshua's love. The contrast was so marked it made him laugh but he knew that others worried deeply about what was happening.

Judas was amongst these and he didn't hide it from Johannus. "Nothing is coming from this work," he said; "except undoing all the possibilities we have opened up with them."

"With who?" asked Johannus.

"The ones we will need to help make the Kingdom come about."

"Oh."

"Yet, the Lord know what he is doing, and it will work out. I just find it difficult to see how sometimes, when it goes on like this."

*

On the evening of the second day after the Sabbath Yeheshua asked the women to remain in Bethany the next day; and for Johannus to stay with them too.

That night he dreamt of Kaella for the first time in many weeks. He was staying at the forge because there were guests at his aunt and uncle's house; including Rebecca and her father, who were here for the Passover feast.

It was easier not to be there and try to answer their questions about what was happening between Yeheshua and the Jewish authorities, but sometimes he had to.

Kaella came to him as the beguiling girl he had first met in the cave, not as the mighty Queen of magic or fearsome goddess-hag he had come to know also dwelt within her.

She knew all his weaknesses and played on them, searching for something else, he knew not what.

Johannus was better protected than of times before, having Yeheshua as his master, and his time with the false Magi Simon being only a distant memory.

He woke, uncomfortable but otherwise fine, and got himself ready for the day ahead, as usual. Last of all though, he couldn't shift the thought that it was going to be an even tougher day in Jerusalem if the master wished the women to stay in Bethany.

He was torn both ways about it, glad to have his duty but knowing great events were afoot such that even Judas would have a part in but not himself.

And thinking this, he suddenly remembered something Kaella had said to him in his dream, that he must stop Judas; but from what he didn't know… and nor did she, it seemed.

*

Yresmin dreamt of the goddess Manat as well, who hadn't taken too well to her priestess leaving her service, but now had come to ask her help again.

Like Johannus, Yresmin awoke without clear recollection of her dream, only that the goddess had come to her in need, in fear for all her realm as well.

Yresmin set about her familiar walk to Bethany, this time taking Sella and Indy with her.

"Please lady Miriam, may he be yours now; this sweet and blessed colt Indy," she said to Miriam. "It is my greatest wish for you to have him; and the master's also," she added, as Miriam looked slightly puzzled. "He said that when Indy would bear you no Darkness could follow."

We were in the courtyard at Lazarus' house with mother Mary and Lazarus' sisters Martha, Mary and Ruth as well as Susannah, Rachel and other of his women disciples too.

There was much work to be done because we had spent days following the Lord from place to place, whilst he taught and healed the people, with no thought of other things.

Washing, cleaning, cooking and all the things we took a pride in not being forgotten and left undone, and whilst we worked Yresmin again asked Miriam that question that I had asked in the Ephraim hills.

"What did you find at your quest's end Miriam? In Kaddesh Barnea?"

Silence fell and nobody moved. Miriam looked up from what she was doing and wiped a lock of hair back from her face.

Beyond all my expectations, she laughed and the tension broke.

She looked at me and smiled, motioning for me to sit beside her as she sat on the bench that ran down one wall of the courtyard.

"It is right to tell you all, because it is about these times we are living through, these events that lead up to the Paschal feast and beyond, far beyond."

Despite her near levity in saying this a great hush fell upon us because we knew full well that many times our Lord had warned us of evil people taking him and killing him.

We women took these warnings seriously though the male disciples seemed to think it was some kind of parable of a future time; not an imminent danger like we feared.

"In Miriam's tomb I lived within the prophetess' vision, walking with our Lord on every step and with every breath, able to feel his loving focus all the way to the Most High."

"Even as the most terrible things were heaped upon his human frame, he felt them not, or not as they were meant, for he changed them into his will and love for Life, to be overcome; even unto Death itself."

She said nothing for a little while as we digested what she had said.

"Even today he will drive forward in goodness his messiah-ship, into the very heart of Jerusalem; scattering the vendors in the temple courtyard, like he did before I'm told."

"The enemies of Light will cringe and crumble as he shines truth into their lives; lives that cannot find a place for their Lord; and so, he will not go back to them. This I have seen."

".. and seen too that he will then give everything over to us his disciples, and even as he teaches us will be plucked from out of our midst by our own hand… our own inability to hold to his Word."

"Yet the evil that stalks him will find no way to reach and defile his soul, though it tries in every way it can. Even the cruel death it hands to him cannot sway him from his path… This I have seen and felt and known."

I listened in shock, feeling the blood draining away from my limbs, but somewhere heard my own voice answer hers: "Yet in Galilee you sang of the broken cross Miriam, and the open tomb and his victory over Death. What was the meaning of that?"

She smiled at me briefly, coming close and squeezing my hand.

"Death will take him from us, yes it will; but only for a little while, for truly he will triumph over it to show to all who can see… the greatness of the Life Divine. Yes, these things you shall see as well, even as I have seen in shadow-vision."

There was silence amongst us… and very quietly she spoke into it, "and it will also come to pass that God Almighty will take his dear form from our sight, but only to increase its presence in our hearts… for we will need to carry on what he has started."

Somehow the telling of it left little joy in my heart, knowing the things that would come to pass was hard indeed, and must have been so hard for Miriam.

As though she read my thoughts, she turned to me again. "Harder if I had not known, for truly I have these hours of every day to celebrate and cherish his being with me, with us. We need to celebrate him with all our hearts," she said; and Mary, mother to the Lord, said "Amen" and all of us "Amen" again.

CHAPTER 6.

Johannus sat in the lengthening shadows of the doorway to Lazarus' house, wondering what time he should have to go for dinner at his aunt and uncle's.

Tomorrow there was a feast at Bar-Simon's house for the master. Johannus was invited and had to be there, and the day after was the Pascal feast-day itself, so he couldn't commit that day to his aunt either.

Instead, he had told her he would go tonight.

The day had been a long hot stint especially as he knew in his bones that incredible events had been happening in Jerusalem. He was on the point of feeling regret at being stuck where he was, when the master himself came round the corner.

Yeheshua paused by the hastily rising Johannus, asking "is everything all right here?" and in that moment it absolutely was. "Yes Lord" said Johannus.

Peter, James and John followed a few paces behind.

He had missed nothing; it was all happening right here.

Other disciples followed but only the twelve came to go into the house; and the women were already inside.

Judas came back out to check how the day had gone here in Bethany, and Johnanus himself hoped to hear about events in Jerusalem.

Judas was more pensive that Johannus could remember; he was normally so certain about himself and his opinions. Johannus thought better of asking him what the problem was.

Judas did relate of some of the events of the day, and how the people loved everything the master did and said, but the priests didn't. "They haven't changed yet, and there is not much time," he said.

"He did so many miracles of healing and told clear parables, like about being invited to a wedding feast, but guests not coming properly prepared, showing no respect, and it felt so awful that I wanted to shake them. When would they wake up?"

"They were enraged but the common people rejoiced; and that is how it lies still. He won't go back to teach there after today."

"There aren't many avenues to explore now."

Johannus knew that was right.

"But you are going to your aunt's tonight, aren't you? You can get going when you want; I'll stay here."

Johannus had mixed feelings about going to his aunt and uncle's house. He knew Rebecca and her father would be there and he remembered their last meeting, wondering what their thinking was now. But he also knew that his aunt would try to pressure him about Rebecca.

And especially today, outside Lazarus' house, he had been thinking about Rebecca quite a lot.

She smiled at him like that had only been yesterday and Johannus' heart jumped a beat in his stuttered response.

Then her father stepped up, obviously pleased to have the chance to ask him about Yeshua, who so much talk was about everywhere.

"You should get him away from Jerusalem Johannus, whilst you still can."

Johannus listened closely to what the older man was telling him, keen to gather any information that might help.

"It can only end one way. They will destroy him, even if thet have to cut down their own mothers to do it."

"He knows sir," responded Johannus, "and he chooses to stay. He will always challenge hypocrisy practiced in the name of the Almighty, and never turn his back on the people he loves." Then added, "He will prevail; maybe we don't know how, but just that he will."

"Well, I do admire him greatly, and your faith in him," Petrakis said quietly, "but I think it might be wiser to retreat."

Aunt Jessica called them to eat and during the meal Petrakis told them how he had been able to corroborate Johannus' stories about Kaddesh and the battle against the 'ghosters' there. His contacts had been impressed by the details of his knowledge of the affair.

"There were accounts of the companion to Al-Uzza and Al-Lat recovering an important bethel stone as had been foretold. Was that you?"

Johannus spent most of the meal down-playing his role in Kaddesh, and afterwards his aunt contrived that he and Rebecca were left alone for a little while.

They were quite easy in each other's company which was pleasant for them both and Rebecca asked him whether he might take a job with her father if he were offered one. "So much depends; I have to stay and..." he couldn't explain, but wanted to try. "I have never been given such an attractive possibility though," and as she blushed, so did he.

It seemed strange that their relationship was somehow growing, alongside all the other things happening, yet so separate.

By the time Johannus left to go to the forge where he was sleeping an unspoken bond had been created, that Petrakis seemed to tacitly approve of.

*

I got up early but found that Yeheshua had already left with the twelve, before first light even. I was sharing a room with the sisters Martha and Mary, who had given one of theirs to mother Mary and Susannah.

The front door was locked and it was out the back in the small garden that I found Stephen, keeping watch. Yeheshua had met with the twelve here before they had slipped away along Lazarus' private path to where his married sister Ruth lived; and from there who knows where he went.

Stephen let me out a side gate and I found Lew around the front, keeping an eye on the streets about the house. He told me that there were some unsavoury characters around, probably priest-spies trying to track down the master's movements, but all was quiet for the moment.

Miriam would stay in their rooms a while longer. I knew how much she valued her quiet time; and there would be plenty of work to do for the feast later on, where all the Bethany and surrounding community would be at Bar-Simon's.

I went out into the streets, keeping mindful of the warnings that Lew had given me and walked to the forge where I knew Johannus was staying. I was curious to hear how he had got on with the guests that he had told me about.

The flat roof off to one side of the forge was a favourite place of mine and I climbed the hidden ladder to sit on my own there.

It was still quite early when Johannus discovered me on his roof, shocked that the rats he thought he heard had turned out to be rather bigger than expected.

"What is happening at Lazarus'? I should be over there."

"Lew and Stephen are there; they are keeping it locked up till after noon when the feast preparations get underway. There are spies and Pharisees around but Yeheshua was up and away in secret with the twelve, well before first light."

"What are you doing out and about Mary?"

"Well, the master's out and I don't like the feeling that I am hiding."

"I'll come with you if you are walking around but you can stay here if you want? There is food and drink here."

"I want to go and see Yresmin; I know where she is staying," I said. "But I'd like it if you came along."

The walk to Yresmin's was uneventful and though there were more of the rats above ground than either of us were comfortable with, none of them appeared concerned with us.

"Mary, Johannus, how wonderful to have you visit me. I expect you have come to see Indy, haven't you?"

"Of course we have… but you too, haha. How is the little wonder-colt?"

Yresmin shared her breakfast with us and we enjoyed her company, and that of both donkeys.

Somehow it came out that both Johannus and Yresmin were getting pressure from the goddesses Manat and Hecate through their dreams… to stop the Lord from walking into the trap, the poisoned trap that would be the end of everything, everything that was good.

"What does she think you can do?" I asked.

"I think she believes that Miriam can stop what is happening and expects me to get to her." She paused, then continued "but I am not her priestess any more; I am with my true king at last and I trust him even if she doesn't…"

"I would that I could be with him today," I said, "more than anything."

"He is on Mount Olivet," said Johannus, and I looked at him. "Really, who told you that?"

"Judas, told me last night."

Unspoken thoughts were broken by Yresmin. "If you go then, take these things I have, they will disguise you," and she pulled out some clothes from a box she had under her bed.

To Johannus she gave a tunic thing that she had been given at the army guard post, when she had escaped from the ghosters. He put it on and it did make him look a bit like one of the mercenary guards that rich people had.

"That is better Johannus, and here is a shawl for you Mary. Very Nabatean; look, here is the sign of Al-Uzza woven into it."

I swapped my own for the more colourful patterned head-shawl that Yresmin was holding out, and was excited at how different it was from mine. "Yes, that makes you look quite different too," said Yresmin, as I tried it for style.

Johannus and I set out for Mount Olivet, confident now that no-one would take us for Christines. Because I so wanted to be as close as I could to Yeheshua, knowing there were only a few days left to us.

Johannus was telling me about the doubts he was having about Judas; ever since the meeting at Jericho with a priest called Ananias, and the other, a Pharisee, who had walked away, but who he was pretty sure had been at that inn...

"Not one of them? Really?" I was horrified.

"Yeheshua had said 'I would see what was needful to know', and I can only think it was about that. And that Pharisee left, wothout speaking to either Simon or Judas."

".. but you told me he sorted it himself, by going with Zacharius." I objected.

"Yes, he did; he made his own plans that had nothing to do with Ananias or the city elders. But there was something Judas said after yesterday's events at the temple; about 'running out of options.' What did he mean by that?"

We had turned off the Jerusalem road and were heading towards Mount Olivet. I quickly checked behind; there was no-one about to see us go. "What do *you* think Judas meant?" I asked.

".. I think he is convinced that acceptance of the master's Messiahship by the priesthood is what is needed. I think he believed he had the right contact in Ananias. Now I don't think he is so sure."

"He cannot think that it is up to him to make it happen; surely?"

We walked along in silence and more than ever I just wanted to be close to the master.

The olive groves we walked beside suddenly gave way to a bare stretch of stony hillside. The main track swung to the left, staying alongside the trees but a lesser goat-path carried on up ahead and I took it without even thinking.

Over the brow the path continued up a little way further to another, rockier ridge, and where we found a little dell nestled among the rocks.

Johannus sat down amongst the rocks and took the water bottle out that he always carried in his pack.

I climbed between the rocks and up to the ridge-top to have a look at the hillside beyond, and was surprised to find an almost hidden vale just below, and in it an orchard filled with fruiting trees.

Surprised; and even more delighted to see that Yeheshua was sat under one of the nearest trees, with the twelve sat in an arc about him.

He spotted me immediately as well, and made a little raised hand gesture that said both 'hello' and signalled me to 'stay where you are'.

I ducked down and clambered back to where Johannus was. "He is here," I whispered and he said, "what... the master?"

"Yes, he signed me to stay here."

"Best that we do then," said Johannus. "I will keep look-out on the way we came up."

Grateful that I had the chance, I sat amongst the rocks and felt how beautiful it was to be in the company of my Lord, feeling our connection in my heart and breath, as I focussed there.

I lost track of time, entering the world of contemplation inside. I wanted nothing more than to soak my being in this feeling of peace, of heaven, of connection to everything.

So I did; letting go to it completely.

Johannus sat and kept watch over the way back to the main road, hoping that on this day peacefulness would reign over the hillside; and for a long, long time it did. He was glad of the bit of shade we had found amongst the rocks.

He stayed at his post, lulled and content... but eventually there were signs of movement that gave him cause to worry.

A group of what he could only describe as ruffians came along the way that he and Mary had followed, only they carried on round the bend, following the grove edge. He sighed in relief, but his concerns remained.

The group returned along the same track a little while later, and on back to the road; all except for two of them, who stayed by the grove. Johannus kept low and watched.

Just when he thought they might give up and go away, another group came over the hillside making a more complete search of the area and met with the two men. There were clearly a couple of Pharisees with this bunch that Johannus particularly disliked the look of. They appeared to be forcing some method into what the others were doing.

One of them noticed the goat-track that led up to where Johannus was, and the master beyond and they set the search off again.

Disaster, thought Johannus, turning quickly to go back up to where I was sat.

He woke me with some anxious apologies and gentle urgings. "Mary, Mary, quick. There are the worst sort of rats coming up this way. What do you want to do. Can you warn the master?"

I struggled momentarily to take in what he was saying, then, "how long till they find us?"

"Not enough for us to get quietly away. I think we are caught."

I looked at Johannus and thought 'what can we say we are doing?' but it was obvious what we must do. "OK Johannus, we must act at being lovers, getting away from everyone. Come here, this is no time to be shy."

I took Johannus' hands and slipped them round me as mine went around him. He looked really worried. I winked at him and grasped his bottom before landing a smacker of a kiss on his mouth.

I had just managed to pull him to the ground at the same time as ruck my skirts up a bit when we were discovered in a clear state of growing passion.

Raucous noise accompanied by angry commands broke our hurried embracing, that had been risking turning into laughter between us.

"Who are you? What are you doing here?" said one of the young Pharisees, invoking more raucous tittering from their attendant thugs.

"Is there a law against us being together?" I said, perhaps unwisely, but he must see that we weren't Jewish.

He went a nasty shade of purple and for a moment I thought I had risked our lives, but his bluster ended with only a kick to Johannus leg, safe in the knowledge of having his gang around him.

Johannus did really well. He pulled me to him and made a show of not being cowed by the intrusion. He glared at the man who had kicked him and appeared ready to fight any man who got too close, pack in hand like a weapon.

The other Pharisee was less aggressive but also very assertive. "There are dangerous people about," he said. "It would be best if you came back away from here."

I almost laughed but between us we were glad to be able to walk quietly back to the main road, drawing this bunch of unpleasantness away from the holy slopes of Olivet.

Thanking God.

CHAPTER 7.

What a precious feeling to the day. Despite that late interruption I have never felt so much love in my heart; dancing in me.

Even those thugs had served to sharpen the focus, especially for Johannus, I think. The way he had stood up to them and led them away from Yeheshua had made the incident into a gift, as if just for him.

We got back to Yresmin without incident, leaving that rough gang going along the road to Jerusalem. She was shocked by our account and insisted that Johannus keep the tunic for disguise. Nor would she accept back her shawl from me, saying that Al-Uzza suited me, laughing.

"Are you ready to come to Bethany with us?" I asked, as it was well into the afternoon now.

"Yes," she replied, "Sella and Indy are coming as well, to try out the stable that Lazarus has made."

I was honoured to ride on Sella whilst Johannus was given the leading roper of young Indy, and so we arrived in style in Bethany.

Miriam greeted me with a hug that completely fitted the poignancy I was feeling. "Martha and Mary are already over at Bar-Simon's house; and mother as well; are you alright?"

"I found myself close by to where Yeheshua was with the twelve," I answered. "It was such a privilege; being in that timeless place."

"Yes, it has been like that here today, too".

Yresmin reappeared from out of the side gate and we went with her to see the donkeys in the new stable attached to the back of the house. Indy seemed genuinely excited to see Miriam and she made a big fuss of them both.

"The community is working really hard to make this feast special. Shall we go over to Bar-Simon's house?"

Thankfully there were very few of the spies and Pharisees around, that had become commonplace wherever Yeheshua stayed; but instead there were many Passover visitors eager to get a sight of the Messianic healer in their midst. A real festival spirit abounded.

Beor was there and greeted Johannus by getting him to help construct a couple of extra tables that would be needed.

Mother Mary seemed to be everywhere, encouraging everyone and amongst all the women there was an intensity that I recognised in myself. We didn't want to waste a moment of this time.

I joined Susannah and Mary preparing vegetables whilst Miriam found where Bar-Simon was making serving arrangements with Martha and Ruth. It was all coming together.

We didn't talk much; the feelings of the moment's enormity were so strong. Mary shook with sobs at one point and Susannah and I comforted her, knowing the current of passion she was struggling with.

As the time for the start of the feast approached, I needed to go and get dressed and ready for it. Susannah had already been back to Lazarus' with mother and when they came back Mary and Martha had gone. Everything was nearly ready and I went and found Miriam. We left together.

Martha and Mary were coming back, looking beautiful and I noticed Mary was carrying an alabaster bottle of perfumed oil. It gave me such a memory jolt to that feast in Capernaum when I had washed the feet of the Lord with my tears and a similar oil, and my heart went out to Mary; so glad that she was doing this.

Miriam pressed my hand, knowing my thoughts.

It didn't take us long to prepare ourselves and get back to the feast, just in time for the arrival of Yeheshua and the twelve that were with him. He stopped briefly outside before entering Bar-Simon's house, acknowledging the crowd that was outside.

"My friends," he said, "I gladly welcome you on behalf of our host, to celebrate this time of renewal of our commitment; to the greatness and preciousness of this life we have been given. You people of Bethany are deserving of so much thanks for tireless supporting the efforts to promote the truth. Gladly now let us confirm our bond with it."

There were many tables outside the house as well as inside and Martha and Ruth in particular were already busy in serving the food to these, as Yeheshua ducked inside to be greeted inside by Bar-Simon and Lazarus.

The mood inside the feast was complex, with us women perhaps feeling more protective of the master than the brethren did, or at least displayed.

Yeheshua was particularly gracious and Miriam sang the songs of Israel's release from its Egyptian bondage. Songs that touched the heart of what the moment held without the explicit references she had used in Galilee.

After she had finished Mary came forward with her oil and knelt at his feet and anointed them and his head as well, for he leaned forward to accept her loving care.

Judas complained of the expense and others muttered as well until Yeheshua rebuked them firmly, praising Mary for her understanding of facing the trials to come.

Clearly, despite the numerous hints and warnings that Yeheshua had given, many still couldn't comprehend or wouldn't give credence to the master's prophecy.

*

Johannus was outside, near the outer door; feasting happening both in the rooms behind him and on the tables set outside.

He saw his uncle and aunt with Rebecca and Petrakis in the crowd, and wondered how long they had been there. He decided he would try to get some food to them.

They stayed, entranced like everyone else to hear Miriam's singing and Rebecca had seen him too, pointing him out to her father who raised a hand in greeting.

Martha was passing with a tray of food and Johannus was able to take two plates of meat from her and took them to an unused corner where he improvised a bench and table from planks leftover from his work earlier in the day.

He found a bowl of water for hand-washing as well and took it over to Petrakis with a towel, smiling. "Please join us in this meal of celebration and renewal" he said and they came over and sat where Johannus had made ready for them.

Quickly he went and searched for some wine and goblets for them, and as he did he noticed Judas exit the house and walk around to the edge of the crowd, led by a young messenger.

Johannus stopped what he was doing and watched. There was clearly someone waiting for him in the fringes of the crowd.

Quickly putting down the gobletss he made it over to where he could see that Judas was in close discussion with a man, walking away into the shadows.

The man was not dressed in any formal style to be recognised by but as he turned his head Johannus saw the profile that he knew. It was Ananias.

Shock of recognition flowed through Johannus and further dread crept up his spine and neck. 'What was Judas doing?' he thought, but at the same time knew there was nothing he could do about it. He went back quickly to resume getting the drinks for those who had become his guests.

… and it wasn't too long after that Yeheshua left with his mother, Miriam and others to go back to Lazarus' house, pausing for several long moments to thank and bless everyone outside, as he went.

*

I was so fortunate to be the one of those staying where the master was, with even 'the twelve' being based in other houses of the Bethany community, including Bar-Simon's, but with Martha and Mary living here it was much easier for us women to swell the household than the men.

Lazarus had had an apartment built within the upper part of the house, just for Yeheshua and Miriam, that had access to a wide flat roof area as well.

Tonight, Yeheshua beckoned to us that we should follow them through their bedroom and out to the flat roof where there were seats and cushions set about.

Martha, Mary, Susannah, mother Mary and myself, as well as Miriam of course, but also Ruth, Rachel, Sarah and Hestia had come along as well, drawn by the magnetism of the master and the night.

The moon was almost full and riding into the canopy of stars above, spread bright above our heads and the night was warm and welcoming.

We were back again in the same timeless place in the Lord's presence.

There were places for us to sit around as Yeheshua smiled, taking his seat amongst us with Miriam sliding to a cushion by his side. The mood was as intimate as he used to share with us, some evenings at Mirimion; more so.

I closed my eyes for a second and looked up to where the stars shone closer than I had ever seen... and thought I was on a steep hillside with a cliff high up behind me.

And in this vision-dream I looked across far time and space to the master... somewhere on a distant mountain; one of many, reaching high into a violet sky and a whorl of stars; Miriam at his side.

Yet clearly, as though he was just nearby, I could see him sat serene and smiling; radiant in his glory there amongst the white crowned peaks as time stood still.

King of kings with heaven at his feet, master of the ages that were changing all around him, yet his golden face and dark eyes that always drank in my gaze remained, and I opend my eyes and saw the same.

Blinking I could almost see the other scenes again, each being as true as the other, and each being equally welcome to my heart.

"This age to come will not be easy, for humankind has much to learn, men needing to stretch the wings of intellect and faith to reach their full potential... and womankind will mostly take the inner, hidden role... representing the union with Almighty God, and teaching man to know, how to accept...

And by the ending of this age to come, all this will change, and when the master of the ages is come again to bring the knowledge of life within, to all mankind, women will step up and take their rightful place in every sphere... and especially in helping to spread the seeds of heavenly peace on earth."

My ears drank in his words, which had for so long been the ones I'd longed to hear, needed to. How long I had been struggling to swim against this tide.

For many minutes he sat with us, revealing the secrets of our hearts; pouring his own strength into our beings.

The night was done and we were filled, complete.

"To you has been given all you need... to guide the steps of man with love and patience. It will not be easy to reach that point of change.

Neither does the master soul ever cease in striving... though you may not always see it.

CHAPTER 8.

Johannus found himself on a hillside that he knew... except that the weight of the sky was crushing down on it. He couldn't look up even though it was only void.

Somewhere ahead this void was concentrated to a single point... that he knew was there but couldn't see because of the dense fog spread out everywhere.

A pull was coming to him through the fog, to come forward; but looking down was so much worse than up; the dense darkness there wanting to drag him in.

The hillside itself was a slim strip of safety on a ground of oozing bog-lands. Noxious fumes full of hate and fear rose into the mists... that told Johannus something of the terror that awaited under the bog.

He tried to take a step towards the pinnacle of light but the ground threatened to open and engulf him into its poisoned darkness; he couldn't move.

Kaella's call came from within the fog, voicing an urgency, but still he couldn't go forward.

Dark and light swirled within the mist and suddenly from behind Johannus another figure strode past him, cloaked all in darkness.

He retracted in fear but heard Hecate's insistent command out of the mist: "Follow..."

A sudden sharp pain in his hip wouldn't allow him to stand still and he stumbled forward into the mist where the dark figure had gone...

No looking up or down; no way forward and no going back; shapes writhing in darkness all around but somewhere there was light... but also an aching in his side, spreading through him.

*

Johannus awoke with the ache in his hip making it impossible for him to lie there comfortably.

He got off the pallet and went to find some water to drink and splash on his face and head.

Walking helped ease his hip and he rubbed and worked on it some more, sitting on his pallet; leaning against the wall, with his left leg stretched out; almost comfortable again.

Though the ache had subsided, the after-taste of his night's dreaming remained; so he sat quietly in the company of his own breathing till all else was washed away.

At ease at last he finally decided he had to get up, so went to fetch his half loaf of bread from the little oven beside the forge fire where he kept it, even though no fire was lit.

He broke off some and chewed it; it was really tasty he thought, wondering what Martha had baked into it.

Thoughts of the dream had gone but memories of what he had seen the night before came back to him; Judas and Ananias talking.

This is what the dream had come from … he realised heavily; always those hate-filled priests and worse, stirring trouble.

But before going to Lazarus' house he suddenly thought of something else; something that his aching hip had brought back to him.

He went into the corner of the smithy where they kept the rough work and pulled out a wrapped object from among the bits of iron there.

Undoing the package Johannus pulled out the short sword that he had made himself when working here with Beor, and that had become part of his role as guard to Miriam and Magdalene on the journey to Kaddesh and back.

He smiled at the memories and ran his thumb along the blade's edge. It was sharp and true.

A ridiculous fancy Beor had called it, but it still meant something to Johannus.

He pushed the blade back into its leather sheath and was about to wrap it in the cloth again when he changed his mind. Instead, he rolled it up into the tunic that Yresmin had given him and placed it like an offering on the forge's sill.

Foolishness he knew but Beor was not working today so he indulged himself.

Dressing and readying himself for the day as usual he went to Lazarus house.

*

The twelve had come around and were sitting in the front downstairs room, except for Thomas who was helping me make the tea.

I liked the unpretentious way he had about him, happy to do the most menial tasks, unlike some of the others.

He seemed particularly thoughtful this morning but I enjoyed his company as ever.

"It must be wonderful to spend so much time with the master as you do," I ventured, half-whispering, to draw him out.

"Yes, it is," he answered quietly, "especially now but…."

"but… what?" The hush in the other room was almost audible which was why we were keeping our voices down low.

"He seems to be preparing us for his going; and I couldn't bear that. I don't think any of the others understand either. Yet… yet we must hold true to him now. True to everything, if you know what I mean?"

"Yes, I think I do, Thomas."

"We feel very small and helpless; at least I do."

I thought about it. Yes, there was something different about the twelve's behaviour. As though they were more attentive somehow; like now, waiting for Yeheshua to come down to them.

We took out the tea and I took some out to Johannus who had started his duty on the front door.

*

413

Johannus accepted the drink gladly, wondering whether he should try to discuss his fears with Magdalene. Yet, he had spoken with Judas and he seemed fine this morning. Maybe he had over-blown things in his mind.

But the problem he wrestled with didn't go away when Magdalene went back into the house. He thought he should tell someone of his fears.

*

Then the master came downstairs and asked the twelve if they would walk with him a while, setting off along the road to the south, away from Jerusalem.

Miriam had followed him down, taking my arm as we watched the master go off the road and up towards the rocky hillside where Lazarus had been buried. She turned to Johannus and sighed. "He will be back soon," she said.

When they did get back to the house Yeheshua turned to Peter, James and John and gave them instructions to go and speak with a man they would meet at Jerusalem's Fountain Gate; who would prepare a paschal meal for the master and the twelve, for later that day.

The other disciples had gone into the house and for a few moments, as the three set off to do the master's bidding. Johannus found himself alone with Yeheshua.

'Shouldn't I warn him about what I've seen?' thought Johannus as he turned towards his master with a questioning expression.

"Yes," said Yeheshua, "please go after those three and speak to the man called Nicodemus as well; after they have made our arrangements with him.

Please ask him if the master's mother Mary, Miriam his wife, and their companion Mary Magdalene, can stay with him for a little while? and then you will need to know the way to his house as well. Can you do that?"

"Yes Lord, I will do it right away," he said, feeling relief that he had been given directions that seemed to override the problem he had been wrestling with.

"All right then, I will sort it out with Judas," Yeheshua said, adding lightly after a tiny pause…,"to see your duty on this door is covered."

*

Johannus took his time catching up with the three disciples, happy to be doing this errand and savouring the time spent on it. When he reached them, he explained he had some things to ask Nicodemus for the master as well; about the women.

"Have you seen how many little groups of thugs there are as we get nearer Jerusalem?" asked Peter preoccupied, changing the subject abruptly, and Johannus couldn't help but agree.

There were none of these around the Fountain Gate though, nor did they have any trouble recognising Nicodemus. He was a distinguished looking man, older than any of the four disciples and with a presence that well suited his age. A man to trust Johannus thought.

James relayed Yeheshua's request and Nicodemus didn't seem surprised, as

414

though he had come here just to receive this request; but he was slightly more surprised when Johannus stayed behind to put the other request about the three women staying in his household.

He looked away thoughtfully for a few moments and then turned back to Johannus. "Yes," he said, "that is no problem and I can see it would be very sensible in this current situation…" he didn't need to say more, but he took Johannus by the shoulder and pointed out the way to reach his house.

"Ask for my wife Lily, if you are bringing them," he added, and then set me off back to Bethany.

On the way back Johannus stopped in at the forge and picked up a few things and when he got to Lazarus house was surprised to find Beor sitting at the door.

"What are you doing here?" he asked as he sat down beside his friend.

"I was passing by and that friend of yours, Judas, asked me if I would stay till you got back. Well, what could I say …?"

Johannus laughed dryly at his use of the term friend for Judas.

"Then the master Yeheshua himself came out and we sat and talked; it was like we'd known each other for ever," he chuckled. "Asked me about the other routes to Jerusalem from here and I think he has taken the little-known shepherds path I suggested, with the twelve; just a few minutes ago."

"Gosh, did he say anything else? Anything about his mother and Miriam… and Magdalene?"

"Yes, he did," and one of Beor's great hands clapped him on the shoulder. "He asked me to go with you and them when they were ready to join him in Jerusalem. He said that you would know the way to the house there."

Johannus put down his pack beside the short shepherds crook that Beor had leaned against the wall; he rather liked the look of the spiral wire-work around its outside.

Beor eyed the pack, smiling … "I'd wager you have that sword of yours in there," he said.

Johannus laughed it off and said nothing. Then on impulse replied that he hadn't seen Beor use a stick before.

Beor chuckled, seeing the irony of it; the way he had always teased Johannus about the sword. "That isn't really a stick at all, Johannus. Pick it up…"

Johannus picked up the crook and was immediately shocked by the weight of it. It clearly wasn't wood. His ran his eyes and hands over its surface and realised that it was the thin leather covering that looked like wood, held tightly to the core by the spiral wire binding.

He looked closer … bronze and silver wires turned together into one … and the core must have been iron judging by its weight.

Beor took it from Johannus and it sat lightly in the smith's massive grip. "I'd prefer it to a sword any day," he said and added, "I made it when I was about your age. Never had to use it, even in defence; but I could if needed."

Johannus reflected on all the jibes he'd had to put up with from Beor about his sword and shook his head. "You big, old… child," he said, punching the older man's shoulder.

*

I finished packing the few things I needed and went downstairs to where Lazarus was talking to mother.

The master had been gone a while and Miriam, mother and I were going to follow soon. Lazarus was concerned of course and would have liked us to stay in Bethany.

"Thankyou Laz, but if he is going to be in Jerusalem for the feast day then so will we," said mother. He has made this provision for us, so Johannus says."

I noticed then that Johannus was standing quietly just inside the front door.

"We can take the path the master took if you will; Beor is coming too and he knows the paths."

I knew Beor well and was glad the burly blacksmith would be coming with us; not only had were there reports of increased numbers of 'trained thugs' around, but I had encountered them myself only yesterday.

"We shall go along the main road," said mother; "there are plenty of others travelling by for the feast tomorrow; we shall be quite safe."

Miriam had joined us. "Then we shall take the donkeys back to Yresmin on the way," she added, "and they can help us with our luggage."

"We can carry that," laughed Johannus, "but travelling with the donkeys would make it easy all around; if you wish."

Beor was doubtful when we told him that we weren't going on the back route but conceded with a good grace and soon we had mother set on Sella's back, and her baggage too.

Indy was allowed to take Miriam's light pack and Beor insisted on taking mine. Johannus made a joke, "and now I see the sense in bringing you…" to which we all laughed, making Beor glower at Johannus, who hopped back out of his way.

There was a mixture of all sorts of people along the route but we got to Yresmin's barn in Bethphage without incident.

There she greeted us and was worried at the same time. "Come in, come in," she said ushering us and the donkeys through the yard into the barn-stable.

We discovered that there had been troubles on the road ahead into Jerusalem; some robberies apparently but Yresmin's landlady had been round to tell her the someone had apparently been killed in a fight as well and that she should be careful.

Yresmin agreed with Beor that the best route would be from the other side of Jermina's farm, where a narrow track snaked out to join the road to Jericho. She went to ask Jermina's permission for her friends to go across her land.

There was a walled orchard of overgrown trees with a path down the middle, leading to a sturdy gate at the far end. From there we turned into a narrow passage between the high walls of the orchard on one side and a profusion of prickly pear bushes one on the other, where a low wall ran along beside the next door field.

Johannus was carrying his and Miriam's packs and Beor had mother Mary's and mine, and we went as quickly and as quietly as we could.

We didn't see anyone till we reached the Jericho road and the travellers we met first were a family who were glad of our joining them.

Even so we did come across a band of men beside the road, quite close to the city, unpleasant looking and who seemed intent on scrutinising us as we passed. For a moment I thought Beor was going to challenge them, but he was content to shield us from them as we went by.

It would take more than a few ruffians to intimidate Beor, and Johannus dropped back to cover our rear. Neither were taking any risks.

We were glad when between them they got us to a pleasant looking house in what, for being within the city, was a wide and well cared for street.

Johannus knocked, and the mistress of the house herself appeared to take us in. Her name was Lily and they were clearly expecting us.

*

Johannus and Beor set off back towards Bethany, making a little circuit of the different roads. There was definitely something going on and the Pharisees in particular seemed to have a hand in it all; the way they were moving around with purpose... often trailing unsavoury hangers on.

"Come," said Beor, "let's go and see Yresmin again; see if she is all right; she seemed a bit nervous I thought."

Yresmin was glad of their return and made them tea and asked them both to stay to eat. Johannus readily agreed, but Beor said "I really have to be getting back to Mabel. We haven't long been married, and I don't want her to worry."

Johannus looked askance at him, "You sly old ox," he chided his friend; "how did you keep that so quiet?"

"We got married just before Lazarus was taken ill... to death, and then there was so much commotion when you came with Yeheshua; and then went on again, really soon after... But you must visit and eat with us. How about tonight if you wish? And you too of course, Yresmin."

Johannus laughed, "I think you might give Mabel a bit more warning, don't you? And besides I have just accepted Yresmin's offer of the Nabatean stew she has made."

Beor looked a bit bemused, but Johannus assured him that he was right to get back to his bride, saying he would love to come around and eat with them, just as soon as he could. "Things will be better in a day or so," he said, more confidently than he felt.

Yresmin's stew was very good and she was glad of Johannus' company too. They talked about how things had worked out in Kaddesh and she told him how Bishmi was now priestess to Manat, and of her journey here to Jerusalem.

Johannus was amazed at her tale and shocked at what had happened with the Ghosters. She told him of the message of the Djinn and of the burden it had been… but also how easily Yeheshua had lifted that from her.

"That 'the Darkness has pierced his inner-circle' did you say?" Johannus asked, and shivered at how this fitted his own premonitions.

"I've got to go back to Jerusalem before it gets dark," he said; Yresmin nodding as he continued, "I can't do nothing, but there is not anything I can do either."

She shrugged, "I know, but there is nothing any of us can do, except to take courage against any kind of troubles. Look; I am making places for anybody to come and stay here with me. There is room for quite a few."

Johannus smiled and saw that it was true; she had made some bed areas raised off the ground, which he realised might be really vital for some, the way things were around Jerusalem. "I shall make sure that the women know at least," he said, and it was her turn to smile.

"You should dress as a Nabatean," she said suddenly, her grey eyes fixing his. "You have the tunic; is it with you still?"

"Yes, in my pack," and for the first time Johannus felt quite free to show that he was also carrying his short sword as well.

"Good," was all she said and then went to fetch a couple of items from amongst her things.

The first was a sturdy belt and the second a hard leather Nabatean cap that had a flap that covered the back of the neck; he put it in his pack.

"Come on let's dress you properly" she said and Johannus found he was soon attired in Nabatean fashion, with his sword cleverly concealed under the outer tunic.

She took a couple of steps back, looking him up and down. "You'll do," she said, smiling broadly. "No-one will think you a Christine, I think; but maybe a hired guard."

Johannus laughed, and then, "Is that thunder?" he asked, for he thought he heard a low rumbling.

"Maybe," Yresmin replied. "There is a storm coming, one way or another."

"The goddess be with you as well," she said as she saw him off at the orchard gate; "and do your best for our King ,won't you?"

CHAPTER 9.

Everything that Yresmin had told him was buzzing around Johannus' head as he walked back to the street where Nicodemus' house was.

He couldn't help equating what she had said about the master's inner circle being breached with what he had seen Judas doing, and his thoughts were churning...

.. and amongst all the permutations there was one thing that was niggling away at the back of his mind... that in many ways he was quite similar to Judas.

Judas had definite ideas of very big things being about to happen and he was obviously very caught up with trying to bring these about; Johannus could see that.

Maybe the ideas weren't either right or wrong but clearly a time came to let them go. That point had surely been crossed but it seemed Judas was still holding on ...

The idea that seemed to dominate him was for a holy empire to come on earth but even Johannus had heard Yeheshua say so many times that his kingdom was not of this world. Surely Judas realised this, having been so much closer to the master?

He found a bench between two palm trees in a kind of street alcove near Nicodemus' house and sat there whilst he worried, and tried hard not to.

*

Hecate's world, her kingdom, was in tatters. The darkness had boiled out of the underworld in more places than she could possibly fix herself. All she could do was watch events unfold but at least she had the power to do that quite accurately.

The darkness had taken on the persona of evil... the Satan that would bring ruination upon this Divine coming. This was his age, his time, his territory and now was the moment for heaven and earth to tremble... and he to rule.

Hecate saw this but was struggling to do anything to change it.

Satan's design had been to insinuate himself into the councils of the high priest Caiaphas, flattering him with offers to share the power over heaven and earth that would be yielded to him.

Perverting the Divine within humanity was Satan's speciality and this would be the apex of his efforts... to destroy the mission of his opponent's beloved son.

It would be his greatest satisfaction.

*

Mother Mary, Miriam and I could feel the world gone out of control. That was the way I described it as we helped Lily clearing up in Nicodemus' kitchen; and they agreed.

Mother nodded. "Yes," said Miriam, "it is frightening and there is nothing we can do now, except pray with him. The change is happening."

Lily came in carrying a tray of glass goblets. Fine blue Roman glass that had been used in the paschal meal. She selected one in particular and gave it to Miriam, saying it had been the one the master used and she wanted her to have it.

Miriam paused and not wanting to reject the offer whispered to Lily. "Give it to his priestess; she should have the care of it."

She was looking at me and somehow when Lily then gave it into my hand it felt as though the Lord was saying to me… it would all be all right. The world may change but it would be for the better.

*

As Johannus kept his watch the door to Nicodemus' house opened and Judas appeared, looking quickly up and down the street before he stepped off in the opposite direction.

Johannus inhaled sharply; Judas was acting out what he had feared, in front of him. Without even thinking he got up and followed, careful to keep a sensible distance between them.

Judas was preoccupied with his own turbulent thoughts but probably wouldn't have recognised Johannus in his Nabatean cap and tunic even if he had seen him.

Judas was going to Caiaphas' palace; the Lord had told him to get on and do it quickly; what he had to do. And so, he was.

Someone had to cross the gulf, to spark things into life, in this world, and somehow Judas always knew it was going to have to be him. The master said 'betray' but what he meant was show them who he was. Yeheshua would do the rest.

Judas had seen many times just how capable the master was of eluding their grasp if he wanted; so, this was hardly a risk for so great a prize.

If Caiaphas himself were to see; then surely…

A few people crossed the road in front of him, down the way he was about to go. He fell in behind them.

"Will the fool take the bait?" said one and another answered: "Has already by the sound of it."

Judas knew they were talking about the master, and felt a hot anger envelop him. 'Ignorant pigs' he thought, but slowed down and moved away to the other side of the street.

Johannus saw this and wondered what was happening. For a moment he felt he knew what Judas was feeling and wanted to go over to him.

He started to speed up, focussing his thoughts on what he would say… when suddenly another figure stepped out of the shadows ahead, as Judas passed.

Ananias, meeting his man half way to the palace. He grasped Judas' hand warmly, placing an arm around his shoulder as he guided him to a short-cut.

The opportunity had gone and Johannus feared to go into the narrow alley they had taken. He knew where they were going surely but, after a few seconds standing there undecided, he forced himself to follow them into the shadows.

Judas wasn't reassured by Ananias apparent friendliness but he knew this man was highly trusted by Caiaphas and the money he was giving him would help the Christine cause as well; whatever else did or didn't transpire from the meeting he was arranging.

Johannus felt himself sweating with a cold sweat; just as Judas must be. He realised now just how well he had come to know him over the few months he had been with the master. There was a kind of arrogant bravery in the man… but this was beyond any kind of reason. Johannus' stomach churned, but he slipped on quietly anyway, some way behind them.

There was a guarded side gate to Caiaphas' palace that Ananias guided Judas through. Outside, the street had widened into a kind of square where quite a few people were milling about. Unpleasant looking hangers-on mostly and Johannus wasn't sure what he would do next.

Then he noticed a blind beggar-man sitting to the side of one of the front gates, and decided that would be the easiest place to hide, out in the open.

He crossed over to him and crouched down, addressing him as a guard might. "This isn't the best place to stay old man. Don't you have anywhere to go?"

"No-one cares what I do," replied the beggar, "so you needn't either."

Johannus smiled knowing the man couldn't see him. "I'm not here to move you on friend, just passing the time."

"You are no friend of mine that I know of; but you can stay and talk if you have to."

Johannus needed to keep a sharp eye on what was going on, and even get through the gate if he could, but perhaps this man would know something about the goings on.

"There are a lot of people around for this time in the evening," he said, trying to sound casual. "More than normal would you say?"

"Where have you been? Haven't you heard what is happening? They have been collecting for days, weeks even. You think I don't know anything, but I hear it all. The big thing is happening; that they have been planning for a long time."

"What is that then?"

"You stupid or something. Don't you know anything?" and he spat into the dirt and wouldn't say anything more.

Just then a large band came into the square and after a short discussion between the gate guard and two Pharisees that were with them, they started filing into the palace courtyard.

Johannus realised some were dressed quite like he was, with foreign looking clothes or makeshift helmets and he got up quickly with a parting "make yourself scarce!" to the old man and walked away across the square to melt into the file of men entering the palace. It was easier than he imagined.

Inside there was an open courtyard where there was nothing more to do than take some water on offer, next to a tabletop of food; but the food he didn't want. He stood sipping from the wooden cup, trying to be inconspicuous.

'Malach's men' he heard someone refer to them as, and he moved to the fringe, listening for any information that he could.

He didn't learn much except they were needed to do an important task and were expecting trouble. It seemed like an age and he squatted on some steps between pillars down one side of the court, like some of the others, waiting.

Just as he was thinking he should have stayed outside for Judas to reappear, and was wondering how he would now get away from the palace, the same two Pharisees came back into the courtyard and called over the man who must have been Malach.

Soon more priests came out of a side door and with an arm-tingling shock Johannus realised Judas was with them. Whatever was happening was happening now.

Malach got his men into some kind of order and Johannus had no difficulty in becoming a part of his mercenary band; no-one was counting. He had no idea what he was thinking of doing though.

Judas was looking pale Johannus thought, but he knew that the disciple was too involved to pull back now. Johannus felt an indescribable sorrow; whether it was for Judas or for what was about to happen he didn't know. He just felt dreadful.

Judas used every ounce of his strength to tell himself that this would result in a victory for his master, as Yeheshua had said himself it would… but it was a struggle to believe it.

Suddenly the other terrible warnings the master had given came to him mind, just as Ananias went to him. "This is just to protect him you know. Caiaphas is very anxious to speak with him; get everything sorted out. Just as you and I both are…"

For a moment Judas almost turned his back and walked away but his courage failed him. He noticed that Ananias was carrying a heavy pouch of money and the Satan in his mind told him this was proof of their sincerity… and he let himself believe the lie; it was easier.

*

Hecate watched the spider's web that Satan cast pull in his victims. Caiaphas was like a wrapped fly hanging in his larder and now Judas was bitten too.

"This is my winning piece," she heard Satan whisper into the mind of his high priest; "he will bring me the victory."

"You must crush the impostor Yeshua, must let my minions get at him and expose him for what he isn't; and your reward will be great indeed. No other high priest will ever attain such fame in heaven."

Ashera and the heavenly host looked on from within the way of souls, horrified lest this breath of hell might overcome the Lord of Life in human form, and them with him.

They could not intervene from where they were, though their fate hung in the balance with that of the human master-soul.

Hecate railed at her helplessness and that of the host above, unable to give the trust they showed.

Glowering in her fiercest form she managed to elicit an evil laugh from the Satan who could see her just as she could him. "Over there," he said, pointing at Hecate's hill, "is where we shall conclude this business, and yon witch will seal my case."

"Never…" shouted Kaella into her own mind.

Satan laughed the more.

*

I held the glass Lily had given me whilst Miriam's words rang echoing in my memory like a dream… 'mother, sister-wife and priestess'

Then Nicodemus came in.

"The master has gone and all the disciples with him." Nicodemus looked worried, and hadn't finished. "First Judas went, all alone, and afterwards some others were muttering about betrayal when they left …"

Miriam closed her eyes, looking pale. Mother put an arm around her and I went over and took mother's other hand in mine.

"He is stronger than ever," mother said. "He has known all along this night would come and yet he faces it moment by moment in calm acceptance. We should not be afraid for him, only ready to do what he may yet ask of us. That is all."

"Yes," said Nicodemus. "Everything in our power to do and give, so shall we do."

"Amen," we answered, all as one.

CHAPTER 10.

Johannus followed Judas in amongst the mob of ruffian soldiers, carrying a torch that had been thrust into his hand.

Despite their torches and lanterns, the hills started to close around them the moment they got outside the city gates.

He had the feeling that he must do something, and do it now.

The lights flickered and darkness enclosed about them, full of small noises; the clinking of metal on metal, a grunt from stumbling on a rock and the swearing of one ruffian being pushed into by another. Somewhere close by a dog started barking.

The urgency to act was almost like a force outside of himself and it seemed like he was walking in two worlds together; one rough, hard, physical and the other like the dream he had experienced the night before: into the darkness with no way back.

"Stop him…" came the commanding tones of Hecate in his head. "You have your sword; cut him down!"

He shook his head, as much to clear it as in denial. Should he? Could he? get to Judas? He shivered at the horrendous thought of murdering his comrade but forced himself to consider the possibility.

Any chance he may have had to reason with Judas had certainly gone; this was the only option to keep him from leading them to Yeheshua; but in the quiet he remembered the master's voice too; 'I shall deal with Judas' he had said.

For certain Judas was taking them to the private orchard where the master liked to spend time with his closest disciples… and in his heart Johannus knew Yeheshua would be there too, that he wasn't trying to escape this terrible moment.

"Kill him now… he is already dead," came the insistent voice from the dream half of his world. He moved the torch to his left hand and pulled his sword from out of its scabbard, but only to protect…

This wasn't right and his heart ached at the prospect of what he might yet do. Yet, this pain was helpful somehow, and he opened himself to it.

Rippling sounds of running water reached him as they approached the ford to cross the Kidron stream, and it reminded him of Miriam's singing.

She was like the water, following her course with immeasurable grace and thinking of her calmed him; she had helped him before.

*

Kaella who is Hecate sat on her hillside and wept, but whether it was for herself, her world, or for this young human master-soul she wasn't sure.

Miriam standing by the stream below was blocking her way to Johannus; but since he hadn't sought the connection Kaella had no cause to argue.

Moreover, Miriam had more love for Yeheshua than she could comprehend…

and Hecate felt strangely envious of her.

Kaella wanted to know this love and looked down upon the scene below where Yeheshua and his disciples stood within a circle of holy light.

*

The dream-world receded and Hecate's voice with it, replaced instead by the feeling that Miriam was walking beside him. "Keep with your heart," he thought of her saying. "He will pull us all through this with him. Trust him and the love he shows us."

They crossed the water and Johannus glanced around at the mob of guards. No chances were being taken. There were many of them, strung in a long line in single file or two abreast. The way had got narrower and Judas was far ahead where the trees started ...

And Judas was concentrating hard on getting the job done quickly, just as the master had told him to. He didn't like the rough gang that Caiaphas' man Malachus had brought with him; Judas wished only to get Yeheshua safely to the meeting with the high priest.

This show of force was not the right way to be going about it; they were making entirely the wrong approach.

Didn't Ananias understand this? Didn't he understand that was why he said he was going to kiss Yeheshua's cheek; to show in the darkness who the master was...

.. but now Judas was finding it increasingly hard to feel the composure he needed. He wanted to go to the master as a disciple, not a betrayer. His self-imposed task of kissing Yeheshua was becoming unmanageably hard. He had to screw up his courage just to think of it. Not because he didn't love the master; of course he did.

Suddenly they had reached the gate to the garden and they paused because Judas had stopped. 'Were they here as he believed they would be?'

For a moment he hoped they weren't but then he saw the figures gathered under some trees, illuminated in the moonlight.

Seeing Judas' hesitation, Ananias grasped him by the arm and steered him through the gate, with Caiaphas' hired mob of guards following behind.

As they poured into the orchard one man rose from the group and stood forward to meet them. Judas knew that it was Yeheshua.

He felt the power of his presence and stood in awe but other darkened minds coming behind were struck into chaos, some throwing themselves to the ground as if a blaze of light had cast them down.

Many of Malachus' less hardened guards turned and fled past Johannus who took advantage of the confusion to get nearer to the front ... where the master was plainly telling Malachus that he was the one they sought.

Johannus had got close to Judas and Ananias, just behind a couple of the disciples who were trying to shield their Lord against the intruding ruffians.

Malachus suspected that the man that had come forward was not the renegade rabbi but a trick to mislead them, but then Judas came around beside Yeheshua and kissed his cheek, the sign that this was indeed 'He'... and the signal for several of the guards to push through and put chains around the master's arms and wrists.

"Must you betray your master with a kiss, Judas?" Yeheshua asked and Judas' heart quailed.

Anger rose hard within Johannus seeing and hearing this but Yeheshua raised his arms and with a word the chains broke away.

This enraged Malachus and, as the band's leader, he went forward with his cudgel, preparing to strike this Galilean in the face; to knock him down.

It was Peter who reacted with the greatest speed and alarm, fists bunched as he searched for some weapon, and Johannus behind him quickly thrust his unsheathed sword into the elder disciple's hand.

Peter looked at him for a bare instant, unrecognising, before he sprang to his master's aid, striking at Malachus' cudgel arm. Everyone froze.

Incredibly, Yeheshua rebuked Peter for this violence and put instead his hand upon Malachus' shoulder; staunching the blood, healing the wound.

"The Almighty would send the legions of heaven to protect me if I were to ask," he said, "but this is in fulfilment of the prophesies, and it is my greatest love to do His will."

Johannus broke down at this and several of the other guards crowded forward to surround the master, whilst his disciples turned to attack Judas instead.

"Leave him alone," Yeheshua told them, "It is not for you to judge him; he will do that himself, far more than any other can..."

Plenty more of the thugs were ready and eager to arrest the disciples and they tried to grab at them, would have knocked or even cut them down; hadn't they scattered before them.

Johannus stood there bemused, not knowing which way to turn but decided to follow Ananias and Judas and the ones who held Yeheshua, leaving the sword where Peter had dropped it.

Judas was trailing a little way behind them, anything but reassured by the way things had turned out. A gulf was opening beneath him.

Johannus could have caught up with his former comrade but he didn't know what he could say to him; not now. His heart had dropped out of his world.

Judas got to Caiaphas' palace, standing hesitantly before the gates and Johannus stopped in the middle of the square, watching him.

Judas eventually went on through, though the master's words did nothing to suggest that the meeting with the high priest was going to be fruitful. Judas' high hopes were replaced by the dread of what was about to happen.

Johannus decided instead to return to Nicodemus house with all haste and to tell them what he had seen.

There were many people scurrying about carrying the news of Yeshua's arrest. Some were official messengers of Caiaphas and the priests but there were others trying to flush out any fleeing disciples, to gain their price as well.

Johannus paid them no attention but as he approached Nicodemus house, he saw someone stood outside knocking on the door. He slid as close as he dared, staying unseen within the shadows.

Nicodemus himself answered and quickly took in what the messenger was telling him. He bade the man stay outside and turned and closed the door, but quite soon returned with a sturdy man who was clearly a trusted servant.

Nicodemus was speaking to several people just inside the house that Johannus couldn't see; but from the way he was asking them, pleading with them to remain inside till morning light, and that 'there was absolutely no use in them coming', he guessed it must be Miriam and the others.

Johannus crossed to the other side and quickly went by for he knew there was no point in trying to talk to Nicodemus; he already knew what had happened.

By the same token he felt he couldn't try to talk to the women, for he hadn't anything in his heart left to give them. But nor should he hang around either, risking drawing attention to them in some way; in any way. His keeping away was their best protection.

He thought of going back to the palace, aching to be comforted himself, but there was nothing there to go for now, and wrapping his hurt close about him like a cloak he headed down the road out of Jerusalem.

The commotion of everything going on made it possible for him to pass out of the gates and he went in the only direction he knew; towards Bethany and on the way Bethphage where Yresmin lived.

He saw other figures here and there but he wasn't sure he could recognise anyone. Horrible loss was giving way to an all-pervading feeling of failure.

He remembered Yresmin's words when they left; about looking after their king. He couldn't go there either, not to tell her what had happened.

He paused and saw someone ahead go into her yard, and in the moonlight, he recognised Nathaniel who had escaped from the garden.

Johannus carried on by; and eventually he got to the entrance track that went to the smithy, and turned down into it.

Sitting on a step outside he tried to think about going to bed and sleep but with so much horror broiling around inside him all he wanted to do was shout, and cry, and hit out; at something, or someone; at everything that was happening.

Even the sanctuary of this familiar place was closed off him it seemed. Too much shame and anger was pumping these frustrations around him; for him to go inside.

Once again, he wearily got to his feet and trudged out onto the road. He wandered past Lazarus' house where he had felt so happy to be able to be useful but which now lay hushed and closed, dead to him.

He carried on, along the road out; out into the wilderness. Away from everything he had loved, loved still.

This was the way he had watched the master and his disciples go that very morning he remembered, increasing the poignancy of the moment. Then just as he had seen the master do, he climbed over a low wall to join a path that went up the rocky hillside to where the tombs were.

But there was no comfort in the black hole of the open tomb he found there, only the maw of unspoken horror. He walked on by, glad to be back into the moonlight on the hillside.

He sat there with his head in his hands and unexpectedly his thoughts went to Judas, the one who had tried to get him to join him in what he hoped to do.

In his mind he saw that disciple wandering in an utter state of loss and guilt, knowing that what he had done could never be taken back; that he had to finish the destruction he had started… of himself… and Johannus finally broke down and wept at the senselessness of it.

Cried until he lay there exhausted… and Kaella on her hillside finally took pity on him, and passing her hands over him let him pass into sleep.

CHAPTER 11.

When Nicodemus became alerted to the situation and was told that his presence would soon be required, we were stunned and shocked. What we knew could happen was happening; the threatened nightmare had turned real.

Miriam came from her bedroom looking pale and drawn but determined to help us face what she knew was coming.

"This will be our hardest day to bear," she said, "and more than ever we will need to stick together."

Mother comforted her dearest daughter, her own beloved Lord's beloved, and I was so grateful that I had them both with me in the gaping hole that was opening in the world.

This became the pattern of that next terrible day.

Word got back to us that Nicodemus was to represent the master in front of the Sanhedrin. We knew no-one would be more able in this than he, and we took it as a signal that we must get there to be with him.

*

Johannus woke on the hillside, stiff and cold, with all his feelings wrung out.

He started the walk back to Beor's workshop rubbing his arms to help get some warmth into himself and rounding the corner off the road, to his great surprise met Petrakis coming up from the smithy.

They stood facing each other with one great unspoken question between them, clearly written in each of their faces. 'He knows' they both thought.

"I must get back to Jerusalem," Johannus said, and Petrakis nodded. "We shall be here for a few more days," he said, "If there is anything..." and he trailed off.

Johannus nodded, looking down. "Yes, thank you," he said looking back up into the older man's eyes. There was no falseness there and he nodded again. "Thank you, I am grateful, really. I will let you know as soon as I can ... whatever."

*

Satan brooded over the situation in Caiaphas' palace. The trumped up charges were destined to fail and had been duly discredited in front of the Sanhedrin... but that had never been the real aim.

His aim was to find the chink in the human's defences that would lead to a denial. Denial of himself and of his belief in his inherent divinity; but if he hadn't got that then at least Yeshua had condemned himself to death, enraging the priests with his refusal to deny it.

If denial was his aim, then doubt was his best weapon. A weapon that he would back up with every kind of humiliation and physical abuse that his demonic forces could muster.

That way the instruments of Satan's dominion would worm their way into

Yeshua's human psyche, even whilst agonising Death tore it apart.

… and that would only be the beginning of his triumph.

*

"He has set his course," said Miriam, "and no power on earth can divert him from it; or any from Hell either. Yet you must know how much he values our being here with him."

We were pushing through the edges of the crowd to get to the square in front of the Roman governor's palace. I looked around and the thought came was that these people were certainly not the ones that would have come to hear the master preach or see him heal the sick…

Except for the groups of Pharisees and the like… they were here and were leading this huge mob. This was 'their' crowd I realised, trained and taught and certainly bought to do their bidding.

*

Johannus got into Jerusalem to find that there was only one thing happening; the drama displayed by execution of plans that had been long in the making.

Caiaphas and his priests were making sure that everything was being done properly according to Roman and Jewish law, but at the same time raising the stakes of pain and humiliation as they shuffled the master from one set of judges to another.

Many of the ordinary people of Jerusalem watched as the huge hate-fed crowd engulfed the central places of their city; a crowd eager for every chance to condemn the chosen foe.

Johannus had already stopped at Nicodemus' house and been told that mother Mary, Miriam and Magdalene had gone into town earlier. He knew they would want to be as close to Yeheshua as they could.

He searched for the women but although he couldn't find them at first, he did see several other of the disciples including a glimpse he thought of Judas, looking desperate. 'Did he believe Yeheshua might still unleash his power against this mob?'

Pilate had finished with the case, Johannus heard; apparently he had tried to release Yeshua as the 'scapegoat' to be driven away but the mob had become so frenzied that he had given in to them, and was sending the master back the Jews to do as they wished.

The worst had come.

*

They had wanted the Romans to crucify him but Pilate had refused the use of his own soldiers. So, Caiaphas approved a stoning instead.

The crowd surged towards the city gate that led to Calgary, the place of skulls pushing striking and shoving the already bleeding Yeshua before them.

It was hard for us to keep up with their frenzied pace but Miriam in particular wouldn't be left behind even when a Pharisee thug pushed her down to the rocky ground.

430

Mother helped her up and wanted to check her for injuries but she wouldn't wait and I took mother's arm as Miriam pressed ahead again.

Johannus appeared from somewhere behind me and took mother's other arm.

They couldn't wait to get to the place of skulls and not content to strike the Lord with their fists someone picked up a fist sized stone and hit him with that.

Soon many of them had rocks in their hands and were striking him with them until people further away started to throw the rocks and they left him where he had fallen.

Miriam was on her knees quite close to Yeheshua when a rock hit her in the back. Mother and I cried out in unison at this outrage and Miriam sagged in pain; harsh hands pulled her out of the way.

In the momentary pause someone shouted that soldiers were coming and quickly we realised it was a small troop of Herod's guards. A priest cried out that these could crucify him; they could get the death they wanted.

Caiaphas was apparently somewhere close by, watching for word to come that these soldiers would be allowed to crucify our master. Then it did; they were to use the spared bandit Barabas' cross that lay nearby.

Johannus scanned over the crowd and saw Judas again, looking at the broken body of the one he had betrayed… and his face had collapsed into misery as he turned to run away.

Seeing Yeheshua lying stunned and broken dashed Judas' last hope that the master would demonstrate his powers and scatter the crazed mob.

His hand was on the silver pieces lying heavy in the pouch at his belt as the unbearable clarity of what he had done fully dawned.

He had been so sure that the master would avoid their efforts to hurt him like he always had before. That he had been so sure of all his own ideas had been his undoing.

He ran as fast as he could from the scene, desperate to change what he had done. With nowhere to go… except to give the money back.

His brain told him long before he got there that doing this would make no difference but he had nothing else left. They didn't care one jot about him; why should they? but he threw the silver pieces on their floor anyway.

His brain was racing in circles, pumping emotional conflict through his veins.

'Why hadn't you seen what you were doing? You had been given enough warnings, hadn't you?'

'Thought you were 'chosen' didn't you? One of the 'great ones' who could do no wrong.'

'So much time has been spent on you and look what you are now; the most despicable person… everyone should and will spit on you; worse; you are finished.'

Judas pushes his head forward into talon-like hands that rake through his hair, scraping his scalp. 'Why? Why? Why?'

'You wanted to bring in the money; it would be useful even if the Lord evaded the trap.' His mind wouldn't stop; didn't give him any room to recover.

'Trap? Trap? You knew all along it was a trap!'

'Yeheshua knew as well. He let you spring it and walked knowingly into it. It is his fault this is happening to you. His fault and you are having to pay!'

"No, no, he warned me not to do that," cried Judas but no-one was there to hear him. "Satan !"

'You are Satan's tool and always will be now…' the full horror of spiritual darkness crushed in on Judas.

He looked around and saw he had wandered onto the edge of a building works, outside the city walls. There were many bits and pieces lying around the place and he found he had picked up a length of rope.

Satan was in his head, he was evil…

unintentionally; surely unintentionally? but that made no difference; he had let it happen and for how long had he nurtured it? God help me.

"He washed my feet; he loves me," he cried out aloud, the desperation of his heart fighting the darkness that had flooded his brain.

'You traded that; you traded it all, for what? Thirty pieces of silver?'

"Thirty-two."

'You counted them and were proud you had got more than they said, weren't you?'

"Aaaaiiiyyh" Judas wailed, seeing his own mind laid open in front of him with all its little prejudices and hates. He saw how superior he thought himself to 'common' people; how much greed and sheer unpleasantness he had stored inside of himself. Satan made sure he saw it all and he couldn't take it.

"Stop! Stop! Stop! I can't bear this. Let me go."

'You are eternally mine now. That was your choice and nothing can change that. Nothing!'

Judas' body was trembling and sweating. He knew he had brought himself to this as his hands made a loop in the rope and worked the knot.

He wasn't sure whether this was his will or that of Satan. They seemed to agree on this one thing and his hands completed the rough noose that he knew he was making to hang himself; moving as if in a dream.

Cold dread and the desire to rip all this traitorous thought from the rest of him propelled him to tie the other end of the rope to a tree branch that overhung a rocky gulf.

As he placed the rope over his head, tightened it and prepared to jump, one thought surfaced into the total emotional bitterness; "I betrayed my Lord... who was everything good."

He jumped.

Satan laughed. He had his winning piece now; safely fallen to the death of despair and the deepest of hells.

And the one who thought he would have the victory was trailing up a hill behind a 'friend' who carried the cross they would nail him to; and Satan laughed the more.

*

We wept uncontrollably to see Yeheshua having to work so hard to just stagger up the slope.

He stopped for a moment to talk to us but rough hands pushed him on, making him fall again onto his cut and bruised hands and knees.

"Don't weep for me," he said as the soldiers forced him back up, enabling him to smile at us bloodily for a second. "My gateway of the cross awaits and I shall meet you at the sepulchre when the sun rises the day after."

The demonic crowd hated his ability to take every pain and humiliation they piled on him with equanimity; it drove them to even greater hatred.

A friendly hand on Johannus shoulder made him turn around. It was John and there were a number of women with him.

"Well done friend," he said, "you have done your best."

"John," cried mother Mary. "He struggles so and we cannot help..." she hugged him as he came up to her but only briefly, for we had to continue to try to stay with the master, however hard the crowd hustled us about as well.

He had reached the place where two crosses were already raised with their wretched human burdens attached and nothing but nailing Yeheshua to the third was going to satisfy the mob's lust for evilness, their hunger for his pain.

Miriam fell and her hands were bleeding where they had broken her fall on sharp rocks. John sprang to her side to help her up, quickly followed by mother and so I suppose I was the first to see the nails being driven into Yeheshua's hands, one after another, forcing a wailing cry from me as my whole body was flooded with emotional horror.

And then his feet... and both Miriam and mother Mary fainted at that.

I heard myself wailing again as if from a long way away... then "He will come to no harm," I heard a voice saying: "Love is a greater force than you can comprehend." I came back to myself and blinked, looking around for the speaker but there was no-one.

But Mary and Ruth were here, weeping that they couldn't change what was being done to our Lord. Martha was there as well and we huddled together, the four of us, tears flowing.

Johannus saw Yresmin and went to her. They stayed back a bit where a few other of the women were.

Yeheshua drew all our attention to him. He let the hatred that they threw at him wash right past. We could feel that; that he was still giving himself willingly, and with total compassion.

Pharisees came and went, trying to mock him but they were like hollow empty vessels compared to the man on the cross, expressing all his love into these last moments of his life; his death.

Caiaphas' priests came and argued about a sign Pilate had written about this being the 'King of the Jews' but they were like a meaningless ghosts; only our master was real for us.

Johannus noticed that once any person in the mob had vented all the hate they had, they could no longer stay to watch; but went away as if in guilt.

More came and all went; it was only the Lord's disciples and the soldier guards themselves that stayed the whole course of it… and these soldiers themselves were changed through the hours of Yeheshua's passion.

They had driven the nails into his hands and feet and callously cast lots for his clothes, including the seamless coat that Martha and Mary had painstakingly made for him as a wedding gift, but by the end they were clearly deeply affected by being with him through all of it.

They stayed on guard, not letting anyone too close till very near the end when Yeheshua asked John to take care of his mother and Miriam.

Hearing her name Miriam stepped forward to her beloved and though one guard went to stop her, his comrade put a hand upon his arm and drew him back.

She stepped forward to the cross, reaching up to gently swathe him with the tears that had been streaming down her face; from her fingers to the toes of his poor feet.

He raised his head, speaking to his father God. "Into your hands I commend my spirit, " he said, and the one guard most affected by it all took his spear and thrust it deftly towards the master's heart, to make a quick release for him.

In all the hours our Lord had not spoken much, all his attention going within, to the life-essence ebbing from his battered body.

He spoke to the other men on their crosses and he said he thirsted to the guards, and maybe a few snatches to others that I didn't catch, but in one extrorinary moment he looked at me, and it was as if his face was at the other end of a tunnel between us, down which the whispered words came: "Go to Tobias'; go to Tobias," and that was it.

I didn't understand, except there was a work for me to do, and I answered 'I will," with all the love I could put into those words.

*

Satan watched the failure of his minions to affect any kind of weakness in the human on the cross.

Any self pity, doubt or denial would have been enough of an opening for the full force of Satan's powers to pounce, but none came.

He frowned in anger and the ground shook about Jerusalem, but to himself he said, "this changes nothing."

CHAPTER 14.

The light grew at the back of the cave and with it came the sounds of singing and music that might have been the sea. An infinitely blue sky stretched up and out above the glimpsed surface glistening far below.

A fresh breeze wafted ambrosial laden aromas in and around the cave, welcoming Yeheshua's etheric spirit up from the broken body laid out upon a stone shelf.

Hecate stood by the opening way, the first to honour Yeheshua's triumph over Satan and his human minions.

She had seen things no human eyes could see, that were designed to test and break the spirit of the human who had allowed himself to be taken into their grasp.

She had watched throughout the crucifixion because it was the crossroads of an age for all the worlds, and she was the goddess of crossroads. It was on her ground... as was this tomb, her cave.

She had done everything to try to stop it but in the end this human had won the day all alone, staying true to his divinity within, never doubting, never giving ground to his most fearsome adversary.

He came forward to where the light was streaming into the cave and gazed out for few moments, listening to the clarion call of a new day beckoning his spirit forward into the limitless expanse of joy and glory, before he turned away. "There is another path that I must travel first," he said, his eyes peering into the furthest, darkest recess of the tomb.

Hecate started for she knew this path of which he spoke and a premonition of dread filled her, that his merest glance and wish should unlock the seal she had so carefully placed upon that way, that nothing thence could enter her abode.

"No!" she almost screamed, "I cannot allow that;" then added, more quietly: "souls do not go there except when dragged by the chains of actions that you have broken free of forever." She moved to block his path.

"Don't oppose me now Kaella, for you and I are not opposed. Remember instead what has brought you here, what it is that you are searching for. Can you remember?"

That threw her off guard, him calling her by her child name; for here she was the peerless Queen of her realm, but he saw through all that, knowing her in all her guises; and for an instant the dread hag in her threatened to flare up to engulf the cave, with the ugliness she herself hated so much.

"Yes, I can," she said instead.

"The mirror that you sought is nearer than you know, for it can be found in human life, within all human hearts."

"The mirror that shows the unaltered truth, the real divine, is in the hearts of every living thing, but in the human life is given the possibility of knowing it."

"Humans are so weak…" Hecate started in reply, "and their lives so limited and mean." She sounded almost disgusted.

"Maybe it seems so," answered Yeheshua, "but the jewel without price is also theirs if, when they understand their need, let their true thirst be felt…

"This coming age is not an age of peace but one in which the thirst for peace will gather strength… in all the world."

"And then the Lord of Peace will come, even when the darkest hour is here and thirst is deepest. Then the time will come for you to be there too Kaella, for indeed he'll bring the gift for you as well."

Queen Hecate considered all that the master was telling her and wondered at these choices she might have to make.

Something in his words echoed others she had used herself, she remembered. He smiled, and taking human birth might indeed be a possibility.

"But still," she pleaded, "you are not able to go down to darkest Hades as you are; without dire cause or reason…"

"Ahh, but there is!" said another voice, from deep in the shadows of the cave. Hecate was shocked but Yeheshua did not seem surprised…

She whirled around on the intruder to find an old man sitting on a rock at the other side from the stone shelf. He looked quite similar to Yeheshua except his long hair and beard were white, with just a few streaks of black.

"There was a human in his care he let fall to utter ruin; is that not so?"

Yeheshua said nothing, so Hecate replied for him. "Judas was given every warning and teaching too; he had free will… and followed it with help at every turn from…" she recognised him then, with a shudder of horror, " from YOU!"

"Hahaha," laughed Satan, eyes glinting red: "I can help you though; that is my realm, this is my time, and it is my powers that you need."

"What is it you are saying?" Yeheshua asked quietly.

"I will give you up the soul of he who betrayed everything he knew was good. Yes, he knew all right, and chose to turn from it for a few worthless pence. Haha… but… but I can give him back to you."

"Have I asked for that?"

"You know you have to. I know you have to."

"Give him then, if that is what you wish," said Hecate and the red eyes whirled on her, pinning her to silence.

"I will give him up if you give to me a key you have. That is my price."

"The keys of heaven and hell are for mankind and not for you."

His adversary's mouth opened and stayed that way for several moments. A key to enter Heaven was what he wanted but Hell's were already his. How could this… ghost… think to take them from him?

"Go then… and leave your disciple in my care. I will enjoy that!"

Hecate flared into the form of a fiery snake to strike at the evil one but Yeheshua raised his hand; "Peace Kaella, this is not your fight, but thank you." He turned back to the other: "I will do what I must do."

The older man remained unmoved. "You cannot enter Hades as you are, unless I expressly wish it; even if you think you have cause to do so."

"Nevertheless, I will walk this path; it is my father's wish."

The cavern echoed with Satan's roars of rage and laughter both together.

"He has no say there. That realm has been given over to me and this age belongs to my… inspiration."

"Go back to him; you have no place here, insubstantial like you are. Bring the might of heaven with you and maybe… who knows?"

He threw back his head and laughed again.

"You are welcome to try, but remember… this is my time, my age, my time of strength; come uninvited into my realm and the slaves of my adversary will not find it unprepared or undefended."

"No armies," said Yeheshua. "In my human body lies the way to enter in."

Hecate blanched at what this human spirit was saying; divine though he was. The dense matter of that body would be defenceless against the hunger of Hell's demons to devour it's flesh, and him with it. It couldn't be contemplated; ever.

She couldn't even speak though, standing rooted to the spot.

Satan looked at her with such an evil smile she herself almost fainted. "Yes indeed, that would be fine," he said, returning his gaze back to the human ghost of his adversary. "Come in that way by all means."

*

Judas' mind span into the darkness of the crushing void, leaving the familiarity of his body in drawn out suddenness.

There was nothing; especially nothing for his mind or soul or spirit to orientate to, spinning out of control.

Bigger or smaller; further out or further down; nothing to hold to; nothing to measure his existence against; no way to even hold his mind together.

No form, just spinning into the enveloping madness; and the presence of an evil that overcomes him; a madness more terrifying than death itself.

Satan's world is taking him in and only one fine thread of thought remains: "I betrayed my Lord."

"I betrayed the good; brought this evil on myself."

"I am the betrayer…"

"Betr… aaiii…yyyyyyyyyyyy…" scream ears back, and everywhere.

The thread of that noiseless scream becomes a line, a pipe, a tube that Judas is falling through and the sides of that tube are all covered in… in human excrement; all over what he is as well; his face, his eyes and ears, his nose … the foul smell, he becomes it, the revolting feel of it making him retch as though he still had a body but he hasn't, only this; this is his; this is him.

Utter darkness; madness congealed into an excrement he belongs to… except the excrement itself turns on him and starts to bite and sting:

"We don't belong with you; once we were beautiful; you did this to us;"

come the thought words of the biting insects; the swarming, stinging flies that the faeces have become.

Stinging that is burning; burning coals all over and through him; biting and stinging.

"You don't belong with us." They were driving him away... even this; no place to go... all of it filling him: the madness, the filth, the biting, but no becoming, so much of that which has no place for him, crushing him into blackness where the burning is expanding into an unbearable cold... without... without anything

*

CHAPTER 15.

The entry point is in and out and up and down; it is the Way of Soul.

And back into that body is going to be infinitely harder than leaving it.

Every bit of strength and knowledge will be needed just to squeeze his spirit back through the cells and bones and sinews of that strangely thick and liquid denseness, whose only remaining Destiny was to feed the worms.

'Even if he can succeed,' thought Hecate, 'he will become supremely vulnerable, and to enter Hell with his spirit drained by that endeavour is nothing else but madness.' The hardest thing is that she will be forced to witness it… for her seal has been removed, opening the lowest gate from her domain.

Over by the cloth wrapped body, Yeheshua extends his great compassion, even to his own broken corpse that he needs to call back into service. He gathers all his being, and love of life into one small flame divine, set upon the bridge of the nose that once he breathed the breath of life himself through.

Everything that is, is hushed as he crosses into a cave within the cave, surrounding him with nameless horror.

His clear light shines into the fabric of that enclosure, driving out the dead demon of mind, banished out beyond the radius… until, in the clarity, there is no doubt, no tiredness, just the light of his being… and here he can rest secure, and stay indefinitely.

That is but the first step however, and now he must find the strength to take the next, and trust to whatever is, awaiting him…

Hecate is rooted to the spot as Satan moves over to the dead master's head and caresses the temples with his fingertips, smiling almost tenderly, beckoning his victim further in.

Hecate tries in desperation to move and feels a wind of quietness brush past her shoulder, recognises there the presence of the spirit of Miriam within it.

"I go to play the part of all mankind," she whispers close to Kaella's ear, "and yours as well;" and in those words Hecate finds the hope she ferverently wishes can be true.

Maybe it is that hope that reaches an almost faltering spirit, for with renewed strength Yeheshua moves further within and finds himself beside a pool of purest water, and vapour, that is the form of Miriam, his sister soul; joining him.

The breath of love and peace flows between them with an agelessness of one eternal moment, and yet which they both know has another purpose too.

Breath alone can fill a void that lies somewhere beyond from where they are, and they follow whence the need of it draws them, deeper and deeper till they can hear the groaning sounds of those, already once banished, now heralding their view of a dark tunnel to nothingness.

The least inviting place to go but the one that Yeheshua knows that he at least must now attempt.

The groaning itself is enough to inhibit any thinking but Yeheshua starts up a wordless song of hope and joy and Miriam quickly joins in with him, taking notes to the greatest heights as he to the deepest places, winging the breathless sound before them towards the void, the tunnel hole that stretches into a spreading gap, growing ever wider with their song.

Clear to each becomes a path of sound around the edge where they can tread; her to the left and him to the right, with the veil of breath that could be, strung between them like a mist.

Their paths cross at the furthest end of void and spiral downwards but it is hard to go there without the density of of even air.

With each step his energy is draining out into the surrounding flesh and bone and blood that needs to be enlivened.

And it gets no easier; as still descending the ways widens hugely again, demanding Yeheshua give all his power and strength and, like a dove swimming down into the sea, he labours with everything to bring breath to the heart of his being.

Superhuman efforts that Miriam following, helps him with; wrapped in her caring love and thinking, enabling him to slip downwards like a dolphin rather than a feathered dove, until together they find they do slide, completely exhausted, into a pure receptiveness which they can fill with warmth and happiness.

Lying side by side, they marvel at the magic, the love that is eternally theirs. No need for anything more, or else; truly content.

She knows he is going to tell her that he must go on, and she demands of herself not to try to hold him back, though everything in her wants that; just as when they first met in the temple of Heliopolis.

"I can come with you," she said at last; "there is nothing in you that I am fearful of."

"I know you would, but this is just a way for me alone. Please stay and receive from me that which is the essence of the age to come; the key to all you found and saw in Miriam's tomb in Kaddesh…

And when I have done what I have to do, then sweet nectar will rain down from on high, and that will be the sign… for you to come forth… whole and free… a master soul."

Miriam bows her head and Yeheshua slips back beyond, where there is a hidden way that leads to the very depths of all that is.

No longer is it an effort to go downwards, instead the way pulls at him relentlessly, taking all he is… a one-way path in bone squeezing darkness; no coming back.

Down, down, down; forever denser and deeper till only the blackness remains; and ahead he knows… a final low, dead-end passage.

Alone he enters and in, even as it closes behind; this is the ending place.

There, he knows, lies the coiled serpent, though he cannot see it; yet he places his foot with mercy on its cold head.

It is the beginning and ending of mortality, neither dead nor alive itself, but with a frailty that cracks open to receive the tenderest touch of its own foot …

Mercy awakens and his spark enters into it.

A spark that is… and becomes again… a fire within the crucible… a fire that grows and rages into a thirst that cannot be quenched; by anything other than the river of all life… Fire becoming wings that drive the serpent upwards, a fire-feathered dragon-bird calling down the rains of heaven.

*

Miriam, feeling the sweetness of that promised rain and the heat in the wind rising, drums across the cavern with her feet, unfolds her spirit and alights onto the rising warmth, climbing through the veil of purity, and she is out once more into the cave of Hecate, pulling loose the death shroud as she comes.

*

He is breathing and opens his eyes and tries to rise, his arms clasped by Miriam's spirit as he does, sitting now upon the cold stone bed.

He can remember nothing, only that he has one task to do and that this is his moment to accomplish it.

Hecate sees the colour returning to his cheeks as he clambers to his feet, and more than ever she feels the strength of love within the mortal master, making her wish she could follow where he leads… one day.

*

Yeheshua knows the place in the deep shadows where his adversary is mentally pulling him forward, and though weak in a body still filled with pain, he moves towards the entrance to the Lower Way of Soul.

Only his eyes look heavenward as his silent prayer flows from his heart; a moment alone before he enters the gate of Hell.

*

The numberless host of heaven are gathered around the Way of Soul, witness to the Lord's ordeal but powerless to intervene, unless he asks them for their help.

Even now they recognise that moment has arrived and they are poised and ready to respond, but no unbinding call reaches them… until Miriam steps forward to the entranceway her Lord is crossing over.

She clearly heard the prayer from her Lord Yeheshua's heart, and grasping under his armpits as he falls, calls in her heart to the heavenly watching throng:

"Pour forth your love to aid our Lord, you that are blessed with so much to give. Pour it forth now and I will take it to his need."

And together they fall into the blackness, one of Miriam's arms tightly around his chest, the other trailing upwards, grasping the invisible line to heaven.

*

Demons rush forward to grasp and wrench and tear at Yeheshua to feed their fearful hunger for such mortal flesh.

442

Hunger that never leaves them, always driving and gnawing at them. And here was the promised prize... finally to end the frustrated desperation.

Their numbers were completely overwhelming for they knew he had great magic powers and no chances were being taken. All the demons of hell would get their share.

Yeheshua felt the unbreakable ring of darkness advancing on him, understanding their uncountable numbers and something of the pain filling that host.

He exerts all the power he has, all he has learnt of material forms; not to oppose, but rather to have more of himself to give, to answer the demonic need; shrinking them to snakes and rats, and even worms and mice.

Even as they sink their claws and fangs into Yeheshua's divinely human flesh Miriam's spirit pierces the gash in his side, bearing the powers and energy of heaven's lovers to his heart.

To Yeheshua the pain he feels within those demons is no different from that of their tearing biting efforts to fulfil their hunger. He lets it all go, all the pain and hate, all the frustration and madness, all the darkness, letting his flesh and blood be taken to assuage that terrible hunger and thirst.

And as the flesh is ripped from his face and arms and legs, his back and front, and even all his inner and outer organs, so the divine energies of heaven restore and replace that flesh, flowing like an endless river from above and through the spring of Miriam's love and purity into his very veins.

The demons of Hell reel backwards as they devour the master's mortal flesh, falling to the ground in a stupefaction ending in oblivion.

Piled high all around, until finally there are no more, excepting Satan's most evil lieutenant, and nothing left of Yeheshua's former earthly body either, other than his still beating heart.

Miriam is distracted for a moment, by Satan himself crushing out the connecting line of soul; so that then, his last, most powerful, most evil servant, can step forward to take the master's heart...

Yet which, though taken, is renewed in celebration by Miriam's very own, her power to gift into their 'two in one bliss', united.

And the last demon fades away like all the others; slaked into finality.

With all of them gone only Satan himself remains, sitting motionless on his throne, and Miriam raises her hand, straight from within Yeheshua's heart, holding up the sigil of the New Age, shining bright against this Satan's face.

He tries to turn away, but in frustration cannot move, as thus she stands erect, indomitable, in front of him.

"Thus, the gates of Hell collapse" Yeheshua states, turning to stride off down those very Halls, empty of demon devils, but still inhabited by countless moaning and suffering humanity.

Full of reborn light and vigour Yeheshua steps forward, going amongst the damned; to renew their hope.

"Come to the light and give up your misery; it benefits you not at all," he calls, and again: "the light is come to dispel your darkness, give up your hatred of yourself; come and take a better way."

With little response; minimal returning to the master, Satan moves to take his throne once more; sitting there, exuding his power; dominating his own domain, smirking in victory.

But the master has not finished, and calling upon all his compassion and power together, shakes the very foundation of that hall and throne; with light and sound and heart-spoken words that no-one could ignore.

"I have not come this way to let you drown in your own self pity. Arise! Arise! Come seek your way to reach the light, for it is here and you are free of any but your home-made demons. Come… now! Take hold of this freedom!"

Repeating his call here, there and all through the halls, he goes on relentless.

Eventually the wretched captives realise their chains are gone and hope has come where none should be. Gradually, they stretch and move, harkening to the master's words, and move towards his light.

"There is a path being forged" he says to them, "that leads out of this fearful place. Look you well upon my footsteps hence, that the love of heaven lights for you. Follow where they lead and you shall gain release from here."

"Help each other! Help each other rise and you shall rise yourself as well. Push each other down to get advantage and you shall have that snatched away from you. It is a simple law: Seek the light and help each other to do the same, and you will gain your freedom once again!"

The damned souls of humankind start to work now for their newly given right and climb the steep, steep way upwards; but Satan is not going to sit there and let it happen.

For the power of Beelzebub and Lucifer and of every Devil are combined in him, to wield against this foe, to crush him now and stop this exodus.

He stands to his full height with wings of darkness stretching out to touch each wall of this, his hall… mighty in his own domain.

Yeheshua does not even turn, but continues his walk amongst the suddenly shrinking, erstwhile damned, but Miriam steps out from by his side and back to face the Devil, the Satan, revealed in all his might.

She faces him full square and with one hand forbids him move by the seal and sigil of the age that has come, and with the other picks up the rope created out of the footsteps of heavenly light.

Satan stares with deepest hate, a single glance of which might once have slain a dozen hosts of men, but now it just gnaws back at him, within his mind. He can plainly see the game has changed; the rules are not the same, and he is powerless now to move against this slim female spirit holding the seal of time against him.

Frustration thrice-fold eats at him, forced as he is to watch his foe going further and further on amongst his victims to set them free, and watch as well this new pretender hand the rope of light to help those victims climb back up and out of Hell.

Frustration that he turns back on itself, knowing he must find another way now, learn to pervert the hope that is dawning here, make other plans to deepen the human despair in this coming age.

The power of Darkness is growing in him still and he will learn fresh ways and means to bring his will to bear on all mankind, but for now his mind can only seethe and rage within him … for now.

EPILOGUE.

The master walked on beyond the lowest regions of the Halls of Hell, out into the utter outer darkness where the crushing density of cold emptiness is as the wailing and gnashing of teeth.

And there Yeheshua found one ruined person, all alone.

"Judas…"

Judas cannot see or move or speak, and the cold has taken away all feeling, but somehow he can still hear the words of the master, spoken heart to heart.

"Judas, you are not alone nor ever will be. Existence is all one, connected in the Word within. Within you and all around, even here where nothing else at all can be, that is the utter nothingness of created form."

Judas is numb; the makeup of his mind has been crushed and his heart is pain.

"The Word is movement within stillness, the heart and basis of all that is… that is the feeling within."

Still, Judas cannot respond.

"Light, movement, feeling… all are because of the Word. I have come to bring its healing balm to you… here and now."

A spark of recognition flowers momentarily in Judas, leaving an imprint of hope which he tries to cling to.

"Come with me and I will show you the way to your renewal."

Judas finds that the spark of feeling he has become has grown, and can move as though attached to the presence of Yeheshua.

He cannot see but feels the timeless, space-defying gap being crossed.

"The age has changed and the gates of heaven and hell are being opened to mankind, to own the paths to their redemption."

"You must start from the beginning, but if you can be true to who you are and what you have learnt then we shall meet again at the changing of the age."

The semblance of sight returns to Judas, the sight of the Lord himself, as he carries the infant Judas far beyond the lake of tartarus to where another shore awaits them.

"This is the pool of innocence that leads into the sea of all beginnings. I go to the one who is holding back my adversary, to give you this chance to start anew… and until we meet again, she holds you too."

The sound of falling water comes from beyond, and once Judas drinks into himself this vision of his Lord, the light that is Yeheshua pulls back, merging into the myriad drops of water flowing into the pool … as he passes behind, leaving only sparks of his light, circulating in the dark waters.

Judas pauses for one moment only, amazed to be feeling thankfulness in his heart, before stepping forward into the waters of soul, that receive his spark, like the mother does her child.

BOOK 5: THE CAULDRON OF CHANGES

PROLOGUE.

Kaella knew everything had changed.

She had been there in the tomb where the mortal had dared to descend into the mouth of hell… and Miriam alone had followed… whence had been emanating those eruptions of foul disease and death, even into Hecate's own kingdom, Kaella's garden.

But Satan had cowered… and the most ravenous of his demons had fallen away, poisoned by Yeheshua's greatest kindness, and heaven herself had replaced his flesh engorged.

Darkness was overturned, like freshly ploughed earth, ready for renewing, for re-seeding.

Kaella breathed the cool fresh breezes of a new day, a new age, clasping her arms about her knees. A mist still settled over much of her country, but it held no menace, not anymore.

She listened to the bird song and laughed within.

*

CHAPTER 1.

Johannus noticed one face amongst the others, leering at him; triumphant in its hatred.

He couldn't put a name to it but he knew the person, the face burnt into his memory, always seeming to be part of the darkest moments…

He reached for his sword, thinking to destroy the evil.

The Inn was crowded and someone pulled at his arm, Magdalene saying they must get away; 'Miriam was the one they wanted'; they had to get her away.

Except that they were on a hillside and it was the goddess Hecate, his Kaella, demanding that he 'kill, kill'; use his sword, to strike against the evil hunting them!

Miriam and Magdalene were up ahead and he struggled to go up the hill, feet making no progress despite his every effort.

There was the face again, the one who had been at the inn… but now he was the mob raiser which Johannus was struggling to get away from; up to Mary and Miriam… where stones were hitting Miriam as she bent to help her fallen love, trying to protect him from the hate.

And the man laughed as he urged the crowd on… gazing evilly on the hurt he was orchestrating… Satan himself shining through that twisted face.

A storm of barely controllable rage rises in Johannus… his blood boiling as Satanic jibes pointing him out, across the crowd.

Heedless of risk, he grabs at where his short sword is hidden under his outer robe… but it is not there.

He has given it to Peter, but the master had forbidden it's use… and he has nothing to make the horror stop or go away…

For now he is coming straight at Johannus, eager to strike him in his help-lessness; and bringing others with him… to grab him. Men with hammers and nails, to take hold of him, to drag him…

harshly dragging him over the rough ground…

*

The pain of sharp stones digging into him was real, no nightmare figment…

And nor was the anguish of wanting to kill the taunting demon.

He remembered, even as he struggled between waking and dreaming, of how he really had ached to go beserk as he had caught sight of that devil in the crowd, so eagerly watching the results of all his planning.

An anger that had never been far below the surface he realised, that he had nurtured even… believing it contained somehow the power to destroy, to wash away the worst that could be…

Yet he had failed, had been unable to be anything but pathetic; nor had he any real idea of what it was about; why Yeheshua was accepting this… almost as Judas himself hadn't understood…

And the pain of that in his brain, his heart, was much worse than the discomfort of the ground he was trying to lie on, sleep, hide... anything but wake to what had really happened.

*

Haltingly Johannus struggled to get up and look about the hillside where he had slept, recognizing the slope near Bethany where Lazarus had been entombed.

He stared at the places of death as the memories of the day before came back, as if streaming out of the hillside holes like smoke, engulfing him with choking, fuming visions.

It hadn't been a dream, as he was trying hard to make-believe.

The Jewish leaders and their paid rabble had taken the master Yeheshua; beaten, brutalized and finally crucified him.

For no reason other than he could bring healing and peace to every person that sought him for it.

They couldn't stomach this; and that he said he did it by his Father God's will and mercy.

Their God; not his, they raged. Nothing like that could be done without their sanction.

*

Johannus sat back down, head in hands, grieving and trying to think why he had come back here.

All of his involvement in the events paraded past his mind and he searched for something more he could and should have done, or done differently. See if he could lessen the feeling of guilt that weighed so heavy in him.

He had been on to Judas; his suspicions roused and confirmed he had followed him and tried to foil his plans and those of the High Priest.

And, like living out some heroic fantasy, he had handed his sword to Simon Peter, from amongst the arresting guards...

And somewhere in the back of his mind he felt that Hecate had been involved, who had used to trouble his dreams so much.

Dimly he thought it was she that had brought him to this hillside and wondered if it was by spite or kindness, for he had felt both sides of her nature.

Wondered too if he could be free of it? Or whether he wanted to?

The need for human comforts made him rise and stumble his way haltingly, back over the wild ground to where the day of the Passover was beginning.

Johannus reached the Bethany road as a few others were making their way to morning Synagogue. He kept away, back from the road's edge to let a couple pass; he felt dirty and unkempt.

Getting closer, further into town, he recognized with a shock Rebecca and her father standing together outside the Synagogue, whilst Johannus' uncle, at whose house they stayed, was talking with a dark robed man Johannus didn't recognize.

He couldn't have faced any of them today, maybe never the way he felt, with what had happened. He stared rigidly to the front as he skirted well around the outside of the synagogue square.

Before anything he must get to the smithy where he had worked with Beor, and who had made sure Johannus could always have access if he needed. He would be able to wash and drink and maybe find some bread as well. He couldn't help but realise how hungry he was.

He was momentarily surprised that he hadn't slept there last night, but then remembered how he hadn't been looking for rest and sleep, but rather to dash out the memory of events of the day... on the wild hillside.

*

Getting into the smithy wasn't the problem, or finding water and some paschal bread to eat, but beyond that he felt caught in a slough of inertia, his energy gone, his mood entirely depressed.

Nothing would make any difference, there was no use in doing anything.

He did manage to wash himself... enough so that he could feel a bit more comfortable; and he searched around for sacks and blankets that could make a half decent bed. But, the idea of sleep did not entice him at all; not with the dreams that were surely awaiting him.

He prevaricated, doing nothing, but that just took him further down the bleak dark slope. Eventually he knew he had to sit or lie down and practice feeling what was within, having no expectation or relish for the task.

Try to focus, not listening to the incessant moaning of his thoughts, but trying to lean all his weight on the simplest blessing of being; being alive.

Wrapping himself in whatever feelings of gratitude he could muster, if only for breathing, like a comfort blanket wrapped tight around him; and he vented his grief there.

Being just sorry for himself, or something more, it must have worked; because he slipped gradually, exhausted, into dreamless sleep.

CHAPTER 2.

"Mary, Mary… Magdalene." I heard from somewhere, must have been my dream, as I struggled for sleep and waking both; neither wanting to dwell in the thoughts of what I had witnessed, nor able to let them go either. Any rest had been horribly fitful, choked with grief inside me, and others weeping outside too.

I was half lying sideways on a wide pallet with my knees hanging off the front, my head resting against the legs of Susannah who was lying across the other way, behind me, breathing evenly now.

I pushed myself up, my eyes feeling full of grit as I dragged them open, blearily peering around the room.

It was the main reception room in Joseph's merchant premise and there were other women disciples scattered around on hastily prepared sleeping places.

Rachel was on another temporary palette like ours; Salome lay almost cat-like on a pile of various folded blankets and cushions, whilst Ruth was stretched out on the sturdy kitchen bench that had been placed against Joseph's cabinet-desk. I remembered her sisters Martha and Mary had gone home late to Lazarus.

I had expected to see Miriam, slumped in Joseph's chair. It was set to one side with a footstool in front; to allow her to stretch out. I had looked over to her during the night and she had been sitting there, upright, eyes closed; but now she was not.

Probably with mother I thought, or perhaps outside where steps in a small courtyard led up to the flat roof.

Joseph had a bed made up in the only extra room, which he gave to mother Mary, and I wondered perhaps if that was even harder for her there, lying alone, without having the other women around her. This wasn't Joseph's main house; that was outside the city but had been thought too close to what had been happening for them to be safe there.

There was a rustling from somewhere within the house, and I saw Joseph himself moving across an opening to the small room which doubled as a kitchen; going no doubt to set the fire and to prepare some drinks and breakfast for his guests… in this hour of greatest need.

He had obtained permission to take Yeheshua's body to a tomb that had been prepared for himself. That was before a servant had brought us here, to his merchant offices. I don't know when he came in; he can hardly have slept.

I got up, wrapping my shawl close about me and stepped barefoot after where Joseph had gone. There was one question that had been recurring in my mind throughout the night, and if there was a person to ask about it, it would be him.

He turned his head as I entered the kitchen, the undisguised lines of sorrow clearly straining his face. He seemed too old and full of wisdom to be bearing such grief; but he rallied somewhat and forced a smile of recognition to a fellow disciple of our dear…

My thoughts faltered, and my answering smile brought tears to my eyes.

"Come sit down my dear," he said, "I don't think you have slept any better than I have."

"Thankyou grandfather," I answered, for this is how he liked being addressed, "though I would prefer to do something to help you if I could."

"Well, if you wish. Do you think you could get these embers going again?"

"Gladly…" I said, taking the bag of kindling scraps from him, and kneeling down, I settled in front of the fire pit.

My hands worked of their own volition, selecting the best twigs to catch the sparks I would blow into them, but the thoughts of the night were still circulating round my mind.

It seems Joseph sensed something in me, for he stood beside me, receptive.

"Do you know anybody called Tobias, grandfather?" I asked, as his silence encouraged me to speak.

He stood still in thought a moment. "Mmm, maybe yes," he said. "What makes you ask?"

"Yesterday at Golgatha," I replied. "He looked straight into my face for a moment, close to the end, and said 'Go to Tobias', softly, but it carried to me like down a tunnel, and again, 'go to Tobias'. Just that and then his gaze was turned elsewhere. I keep wondering if I had been mistaken or that he wasn't saying it to me at all, but I cannot shake it off, or deny it happened."

"Ahhh…" and the pause lengthened before Joseph answered. "Your friend Thomas' uncle is called Tobias," and then, "I think this is who our Lord meant. This Tobias is a lawyer, and has a house in the upper city, off Ararat street, I think. Mary may know better than I."

*

The fire was going and a water-pot stood over it before I got up and went to look for Miriam.

She wasn't in mother's room. Mary was curled around with her hands up to her head, but seemed to be deeply asleep; I wouldn't waken her.

The air was very close, as though another storm was preparing itself to strike. There had been several bouts of severe lightning through the night, but as yet no rain had followed.

Miriam wasn't in the courtyard either, and as I leaned against the ancient vine there, another series of flashes lit the sky overhead. Could she be up on the roof, despite the lightening?

I dug into my resrves of courage and climbed the steps that went up around two sides of the courtyard to the flat roof; where indeed the body of Miriam was stretched out, as though struck down.

I went across and kneeled beside her, feeling to discover if she was still breathing and her heart beating. It was. Thankful, I half sat, half lent sideways down beside her; feeling I had done this before somewhere. Then, when more lightning crackled, seemingly all around us, I started to get up, to go get help; to bring her safely down from the roof.

Getting to my knees again, I raised my head to see mother coming up the final steps to the roof; with Joseph following.

Without need of words, Mary and I turned and lifted Miriam up, as far as we could, whilst Joseph had fetched Susannah and Rachel; and between us we took a still unconscious Miriam down to what had been Mary's room and laid her on the bed.

We left her there and Joseph started answering questions about the placing of our Master's body in the tomb. How it was closed up and had soldiers guarding the entrance, lest anyone should try to steal his body away and claim him 'risen'.

Outside peals of thunder were were now accompanying the lightening and getting closer, to suddenly crash directly overhead as we were trying to eat some of the breakfast that Joseph had put out, but without much appetite.

Suddenly Mother herself stood up to speak. "Dear friends," she said. "We must not be down-hearted. This is the culmination of everything our Lord has done. How many times has he said that this would happen, but we didn't believe it really would? So too he said he would rise from the dead again… somehow. Today is our day for prayer and maybe fasting if you wish… but above all kindness, to ourselves and to each other. Open the tombs of our hearts to give and feel the love that is there, that he gives for us."

As she was saying this, the first drops of rain could be heard splashing into the courtyard, growing stronger until they rapidly increased into a torrent streaming out of the sky, breaking the tension like sheets of descending mercy.

*

It poured down for what seemed a long time, but when the last drops were only coming from the roof edges, I set out along the route that Mother had given me to Tobias' house.

The housemaid who opened the door a little told me that the master Tobias was not at home, but that his nephew Thomas was in the garden.

I told her that I was known to Thomas and would be grateful if she would tell him I was here.

She said that he had asked her not to go to him, but that he had said nothing about his friends. Her eyes showed concern, and I accepted her invitation to go inside.

*

Thomas sat slumped on a bench beside an arbor in the walled garden, where the ground had been somewhat sheltered from the downpour.

His mind was known for its clear lucid thought, like the Greek philosophers he much admired, but now it was just a cloud of confusions, doubts and deep personal pain.

Grief seemed to have robbed him of his power to think, to know, to act. Grief for the loss of his dearest friend and master, yes… and for the loss of his

454

own certainty, his direction, purpose, his joy of being alive.

Better to die now, quickly, decisively, he told himself; rather than to live without the purpose he had known. Go; follow where his master had led, out of this world that had killed the one who had made sense of it all; the sense and the master that Thomas loved.

He shied away from this course though, that seemed against all he had learnt from his Lord. The supreme value of life; kindness; compassion, peace…

But where was that now? What was the good?

Socrates had chosen death rather than speak untruth, and live a lie.

Follow him there; be a man; be true to something.

His heart ached with such a grief… that he would gladly drown in death's final embrace.

He cried, ashamed of his trembling weakness; but his will was becoming set.

Just as he saw a figure coming down some steps towards him from the house, a woman but it wasn't Tobias' housekeeper, whom he had bid leave him be.

Of all the people he might have expected to seek him out… he hadn't expected it to be Mary… Mary Magdalene.

They did share a bond, that he hadn't quite yet fathomed. Except that it had no place in what he was feeling now. Why was she here for pity's sake?

I shivered despite the sun as I went out down the courtyard steps and across the garden to where I could see Thomas, doubled over in his despair.

He who I had first encountered in Antioch, even though just passing in the street… noticing him from amongst his student friends, laughing; and myself in a group of novice priestesses. I didn't forget him.

How surprised I had been to meet him again with the master Yeheshua and though we never spoke of being in Antioch, he knew I had come from there and had always been friendly.

I couldn't deny that he felt special to me, but if it wasn't for the words of Yeheshua on the cross, I would never come to him here. My heart beat a little faster as I removed the head shawl, allowing my hair the freedom of the morning sunshine.

He struggled to his feet, wiping his face on his robe as he got up but unable to hide where the streams of tears had flowed, or bring his face into equanimity.

I was shocked to see the state he was in, and just how close he felt to seeking his own end, but he held out his arms to me and we hugged, feeling our grief like twin rivers that had broken their banks.

He must have heard that some of us had been able to stay close to the Lord at that terrible killing place, for "Mary," he said, "did you witness what they did to him? Please tell me what happened?"

I looked into his pleading eyes and realised how much worse it must have been not to have been there; not to have been able to see the giving of love even at the gates of Death itself.

I sat beside him on the bench and tried to tell him everything:

How humility and dignity had won through all the trials of humiliation.

How unbounded Love had dissolved the cruelty of so much pain.

How Light and Hope had dimmed in all the world except for in the face of that one man, and how the soldier had finally ended it with the thrust of his spear.

These last words seemed to crush the breath out of Thomas, his face turn visibly greyer than it already was.

"At least you were with him," he said, looking into my face. "You stayed."

"Remember Lazarus" I said, but he responded that now he himself had gone who was there with the power to call him back. I had no answer.

I felt I had to ask, but we both admitted we hadn't been able to practice, and one of my hands went to his shoulder... where the tensions were fiercely knotted...

"Get some rest" I said, thinking he really needed to try to sleep, so I started to rise, but he held me back. "Please don't leave me" he said, "I don't think I could bear to be alone.

So instead, I gently turned him round from me, to allow my hands to work upon the knotted regions of his back and shoulders; helping him to let the tensions go.

Little by little it seemed to be having some effect as I followed the lines of my work around to the hollows of his upper chest and shoulders, opening him up to receive the sun's warmth as he relaxed back against me.

Perhaps sleep could come for him at last.

His eyes were closed and his face had regained some of its aspect of clarity, which was so easy to admire in him.

I leaned around a little, and kissed him affectionately on the forehead.

He turned and looked at me. The sun was shining in his face and my heart missed a beat. We were like as one, not two.

Still, I was shocked when he put his arms around me and held me close, burying his face in the curve of my neck, kissing me there.

"Thomas" I said, holding his face in both my hands. "Thomas."

He blinked... conflicting emotions sweeping through him. Suddenly he drew away...

"I am sorry... so sorry... I mustn't... Please forgive me."

I wished I had said nothing.

Then it hit me, remembering why I had come here; that he had sent me... 'To Tobias'.

"He sent me to find you, on the cross... that is why I have come."

"What?" said Thomas, dumbfounded. "What do you mean?"

As I told Thomas the details of what I had experienced, an understanding dawned about the significance of being alive. The gift it is, not a burden.

I took Thomas' hand and led him to the back recess of the arbour... where we embrased each other tenderly, and kissed sweetly, deeply... opening to the wonder, of giving ourselves into a timeless merging.

I spread my cloak on some seat pads there and we knelt together as I undid the ties of our clothes; mouths still holding us together, lest any pause should dare come between us; his hands searching to find and caress, express, everything to all of me; both the pull and pulling, achingly, we fitting our bodies to each other's need; riding and moving and moving together on the tide of a wondrously growing ecstacy, to fulfil what our hearts sanctified; of knowing and giving, incredibly piercingly, life's bliss, together…

As the power to bring new life and fulfilment spread through us.

*

We lay together for a long while, enjoying the sweet contentment we found ourselves bathed in.

I was the first to get up and I sat entranced by Thomas side, setting myself to feel and enjoy the flow and stillness joined, within. Peace that is naturally present, always, but we ignore so much; but now I bathed in it gratefully.

By the time I opened my eyes again, Thomas was sleeping deeply, half propped against the base of an ancient fig that stretched up and across the garden wall.

I bent and kissed the top of his head, murmering my goodbyes.

The same maid greeted me as I re-entered the house and told me that Tobias was still not back.

I asked her to prepare some food for Thomas in an about an hour, and take it to him in the arbour.

Then quietly left.

CHAPTER 3.

Through all the oppressive closeness, lightning flashes and crashings of thunder Yresmin felt the rain's approach, and her thoughts went to the donkey colt she had named Indra after a great eastern God of storms; for a huge storm had been raging when her beloved Sella had been giving birth to him.

That Yeheshua had now asked that she give this colt to Miriam was like a mercy to Yresmin.

She had only been a little while in Jerusalem, a foreigner knowing no-one, when he had brought her into his circle… sending disciples to request the use of Sella and Indy for his 'entry' into Jerusalem.

How honored she had been; and then had found that Miriam, Mary and Johannus, who she had met and helped in Kaddesh were here with the master too… and in these few short days she had been included into his life, even as he was snatched away; the warning she had brought being no use in the end.

She mused on this, remembering how he had looked at her so knowingly when she told him of his impending betrayal. He knew, he knew; of that she was sure. He had faced that betrayal and the hatred of his enemies with acceptance, with calmness and unassailable love.

*

Yresmin had been the singular priestess of Manat, Nabatean Goddess of Fate, of death and rebirth.

She was no stranger to the fears and grief that Yeheshua's disciples were being subjected to.

She knew it for she had been captured by the desert Ghosters on her way to Jerusalem; Djinn worshippers, human blood drinkers; murderers from whom she had barely escaped with her life… and with the awful, Djinn-given message of betrayal and death for the Hebrew master.

And now, just as the crashing of thunder and lightning finally gave way to the downpour of relieving rain, so Yresmin felt the need to give more… for even as she could feel the balance of fate and was comfortable of her place in it … now perhaps she could be of some help.

Before the rain had completely stopped its drumming on the makeshift barn roof, giving way to rays of intermittent sunshine, she set out to visit Lazarus and his sisters. She always felt at ease with him, and them; wanted to check they were all alright.

Unlike so many other of Yeheshua's followers Yresmin felt a great weight had been lifted… for, since coming to Jerusalem she had felt paralysed by the presence of predatory groups of Pharisees, reminding her so deeply of the desert Ghosters, ready to swoop and punish… but now that was gone.

The worst had happened, and she was released from fear of them; nothing worse could come.

Walking along the road from Bethphage to Bethany everything smelt fresh after the rain and she feel free and happy, despite her wet hair and outer garments; she was of the desert world and always relished the feeling of rain, especially now with the sun beating down again.

Passing by the track down to Beor's smithy her eyes followed the rivulets of water still coursing down the little stony tracks on either side of the centre, and noticed that the door was unbarred, that someone was in.

She turned down just as Johannus' head popped around from inside, almost comically, making her laugh.

"Johannus," she called down to where the smithy's doors faced back from between two larger houses. "How are you? I am so glad to see you."

He had dropped in at her barn the night before, but hadn't stayed longer than to give back the things she had lent him. His distress and agitation had been beyond anything he could have shared with others.

Sometimes Johannus felt that Yresmin didn't really approve of him and so now he was doubly thankful for her friendliness. "Yresmin, I am sorry I didn't stop last night... it... it..."

"I know," she cut in. "No need to try to explain. I am on my way to Lazarus' house. Do you want to come?"

"Yes, thank you; yes, I would." He had been thinking of going the other way, to brave going back to Jerusalem, but changed his mind to accompany her instead.

Martha hesitantly opened the door to them, clearly worried as she peered around outside. Ruth's husband had accompanied her and Mary back last night, leaving Ruth to stay at Joseph's offices in town.

"You are soaking, Yresmin," she remonstrated with her. "Come in and take that wet cloak off and let me get you a towel for your hair. What were you thinking of?"

Yresmin didn't mind being fussed over a little and allowed Martha to sit her down and towel dry her slightly graying but mostly dark curly hair, as Mary brought in a tray of refreshments.

Johannus couldn't think how to broach the awful subject of Yeheshua's death, his crucifixion, but Yresmin was much more candid. "It is not over," she said to Mary and Martha. "You know that, don't you? He had to do this, but it is not over."

"We were there," said Mary. "I cannot get it out of my mind." They were quiet and she continued, "but you are right Yresmin, his love, that he has given... our love... it is not broken, only getting stronger. I feel that too."

"I was thinking to go back into Jerusalem, to try to find some of the others," said Johannus.

"Everyone seemed to be scattering last night," said Yresmin. "Quite a few came by my barn, but not to stay for very long. Only a couple stayed till morning and they left early too. Afraid of the authorities searching for them, I think."

"We know where Miriam, Mother, Magdalene and a few other of the women stayed," Martha put in, "but we came back for Lazarus; he was not there, at the end, and is in his room still …"

The silence shared was a great comfort and eventually it was Yresmin who broke it, softly, "I would go to Miriam and Mother if I could," she said.

"I will come with you," said Johannus, and Mary, "I too; and can show you the way there."

*

I arrived back at Joseph's premises soon after Yresmin, Johannus and Mary got there too.

I had slept a bit, and left Thomas sleeping still. We had shared more than either of us had probably intended, shedding all fear of judgment to know that closeness which is sacred to life itself.

Yresmin hugged me close and looked me in the face, seeing not the grief that had battered us all, but new life gathering… taking it to her bosom.

Miriam was always constant… filled with grace, yes… and Mother and Lazarus' sister Mary too. Suddenly it seemed so important that each of us were here, to have each other; all of us.

Johannus sat over by the fire, and I joined him. "How are you?" I asked, clasping his outstretched hand.

"All right; I think," he replied. "At least a whole lot better than last night. How about you? You do look better." Then added "I am very grateful to be here. Have you seen any of the twelve?"

I felt my cheeks blush and was cross with myself. "Yes, I have in fact. I found Thomas in his uncle Tobias' garden this morning, and he was in a bad way. I think they blame themselves more than we women, partly because they had not been able to protect him, and partly because they were not there at the end… except John of course. Have you?"

"I haven't seen any of them since the Garden of Gethsemane, other than John who was there as well. No, that is not right, I saw Peter in Caiaphas' palace, but kept away from him. It was a terrible time."

*

Yresmin had the strangest feeling that the Goddess was sat at her shoulder…

"Nothing is over… it has only just begun". Her words? No, it was the goddess.

She saw vistas opening to her mind's eye… deserts and moutains, with lakes in the mountains; green forests stretching for miles, filling the air with smells of the earth and rain.

Flying over it all on something greater than any bird; a dragon… out of fable, swooping low across the surface of a lake and lifting high in the up-draught off the mountain side that climbed from its further shore.

460

Exhilaration filled her but she said nothing... only lent back and closed her eyes and let the vision come to her.

The dragon alighted on a ridge near the top of the mountain, and stood there as the Goddess, in woman's form again.

Yresmin bowed down, but the woman spoke in her mind that those days of her servitude were gone... all changed

And in another moment, she was awake, finding Miriam looking concernedly at her. "Are you alright?" Miriam asked. "I have seen and known the power of trance myself," she added softly. "It can be quite daunting."

"Yes, fine," Yresmin replied smiling a bit shakily. "Another old friend seeing that I was alright."

*

Philip and Nathaniel of the twelve arrived just in time to join us for the evening meal. James and John had been there earlier in the day as well but had gone back to Nicodemus house where a few of the others were; clearly trying to keep in touch with everyone; to know we were all okay.

Philip was very strained but Nathaniel talked as cheerfully as was possible, asking about as many details from Joseph as he could; but he didn't eat much.

They stayed on, making some rudimentary plans for getting a meeting together for disciples from Galilee that were staying on... the Paschal week. It took courage to try and mother was particularly supportive of their efforts.

The night looked like it was going to be warm and dry after the lightning storms of the night before and the rains of the morning, but there was still a sense of expectancy in the air, of something unfinished, waiting.

I went up to the flat rooftop and Johannus came up too, checking whether he might be able to sleep up there. Then Miriam came up and told us that Joseph had invited us to his house, to stay there as everything had quietened down.

"He will come back," she whispered, taking my hand. "That is what I saw in Miriam's tomb in Kaddesh. I could never tell you... that I saw his death, in every cruel detail... but saw too he will come back to us."

That is all she would say, but it fitted... fitted what the setting sun was saying to me. "Going, and yet to be coming again." We could always feel when he was near.

CHAPTER 4.

Kaella stared out of her cave entrance at the sun setting on the sea and felt the warm breath of the dragon that slept somewhere in the cavern behind.

Herakaphon, that being the shortened version of her name… was a queen of her kind.

Kaella had set out that morning to explore the extent of the changes in her world. It was bright and the sunshine permeated the air throughout her domain from the green, flower strewn, vine trailed garden that she often enjoyed to the far distant scintillating desert of rocks and sands that she was walking towards.

She turned right before the toughest grasses and thistles would be replaced by only the occasional cacti in the sandy, rock packed ground, and followed the winding path that led uphill…

Across a little rock ravine where sometimes a stream flowed down into the now dry river bed at the edge of the plain, and up a steep rough slope leading up the side of the escarpment on a path that only Kaella and the mountain goats knew, even with eyes closed and in the dark.

Climbing and climbing, the air changed its texture as the stillness of a stifling heat was replaced with breezes that swept around the higher slopes.

Kaella didn't know tiredness but she turned anyway and sat and drank from a flask she had with her, and looked out over the vista of the world where the red brown desert met the wide blue-green expanse of the sea, glinting in the sun.

The thin valley of her green garden that led from the sea entrances of her multi-complex of caves was still visible around the shore. She drank in the myriad flavours of the world and the air of the heights, thinking about where she was going.

Up behind her over the cliff-top were the long, long grassy inclines that eventually became thickly clad with dense woods of oak and birch and beech, ash, alder, rowan and many others that were the border between hers and her step-mother's kingdoms.

Sitting still on the cliff side Kaella felt the changes in her being, and knew that Ashera was no longer there either. Kaella's heart told her that she would not be able to reach her, not as she had used to do, along this way that led to the kingdoms of the Eloi and the Elohim.

Nevertheless, she roused herself to continue her journey to her people, she who had chosen the more solitary way, living in the borderlands between Gaia and the so-called immortal planes.

'Whatever that meant', thought Kaella… for change touched everything.

She reached the woods and felt the familiar presences of deer and smaller mammals there, touching her mind with the Eloi imprinted notes that were everywhere, though they themselves were not.

'Where were they?' "Close-by" Kaella felt, but as though a veil had been set between them and here. As if they had flown higher and this wood had become part of her land... her borderlands to Gaia.

She spent a long while glorying in the touch of the scents and glances in the undergrowth and leaves, the soft noises from the trees, and birds that flitted from branch to branch within them. She welcomed every part of it into her care, somewhat sad that the Eloi were gone but at the same time happy that their world continued on its way, crossing with hers.

Beyond the woods lay more tree strewn grasslands but these were cut and punctuated by rounded boulder groups and greater rocky outcrops jutting skywards. Between these the path steadily rose, bordered sometimes by walls and buildings that now lay bare and broken, but somehow still elegantly part of their surroundings.

Some things remained; like the simple bridges that crossed over the winding streams Kaella came to, moving ever up and closer to her goal. The lower kingdom palaces of her mother; of the Elohim.

She wasn't surprised. Saddened perhaps, yes... a bit, but not surprised. The great palaces lay in ruins as if they had been deserted for thousands of Gaia years, for that is what would be needed to bring such changes here.

She walked between the buildings, walls and colonnades sometimes intact but more often tumbled, great columns reaching skywards to support the arch of a disappeared roof and slender ones that still retained their place inside the empty halls. Magnificent in their ruin, the clear designs picked clean by the ages.

Again, Kaella had the strange feeling that this whole land was sliding into collision or merger with some future point in Gaia's time, like a legacy from the Elohim themselves.

She searched her mind and heart for her brethren, her father, mother, sisters and all her kin... and felt them strongly, calling with laughter to her, and hard as she tried, she could neither see them, nor feel sorrow for it. They were with her, but she was alone as well.

Her heart ached though, with trying to encompass what it was she felt, and so came at last to the lake set beside and between the highest places; hid in a marvellous dell of a small valley that seemed somehow to be too great to be contained where she found it.

Nor did she remember it, but something nagged at her brain that it was familiar. She walked down the shallow slope towards its edge, rimmed by a kind of balustraded path with openings where wide steps led down to clear, water-washed pebbly fringes.

Kaella sat on the lowest step with her bare feet in the water entranced by the coolness of its touch. Somewhat sleepy and a bit thirsty she thought to drink a little from the lake... and leaning forward she saw the great dragon being reflected back at her. Mesmerised by its beauty, power and majesty she leaned ever forward, seeing the worlds and galaxies spin within the eyes, her eyes, and she sipped the sweet waters of the lake as they reached her lips.

When she awoke, she was no longer at the lakeside, but could still see it glimmering below, a pool of indigo in the shadow of its surrounding palace topped hills.

Magical, extraordinary, and one of the only pools for dragons to drink from she knew, although she somehow also knew it existed in hundreds of different places at the same time.

She looked down at herself and saw both the skin she wore and that of the dragon within her human form, and marvelled at it, not knowing what it meant except that she could become that within her as easily as she had used to give herself over to the other sides of her triple-facetted self.

No longer; it seemed that these two had now fused into Herakaphon… that with her became Heraikaliphon … and she rose and shook out the great wings that extended and stretched diaphanous from her wrists, and arching her back she dived forward and up into the air, catching the wave to swim out across the gulf, letting it lift her with the undulations of her being, up into the sky.

She, the great dragon, circled the hilltops of the lower palaces and rose higher and circled wider like the greatest of eagles and was enmeshed, embracing the wild glory of her flight.

Kaella saw and took it all in, the weathered heights of the banded cliffs, perhaps not quite so impregnable as once she remembered, worn down by the thousands and millions of years passing … and beyond … beyond were a fabulously high and distant range of snow clad mountains, now seemingly part of this world, descended from where the Gods had become, higher and beyond any sight or understanding of even the Elohim…

… but part of the history of every living soul.

CHAPTER 5.

Thomas woke, lying in the arbour of his uncle's garden. Mary was gone; he looked around; found no sign of her; of her having even been there.

It had been real; he was certain of that. He could still feel her all around him, the scent of her, the sweetness … everything.

He shook himself; of course it had been. He had heard stories, from Yeheshua too, of people having dreams and not knowing whether they were real or not, but surely this was different.

He searched more thoroughly and found the shoeprints on the still damp path; a woman's print. His heart returned to normal, allowing him to enjoy the happiness he felt… but his mind said that it could have been Tobias' maid coming to check on him.

He would have cursed himself, but he started to remember some of the things Mary had been telling him, and then the grief flooded back like a swollen river raging with storm water.

Somehow, he managed to hold his balance, the balance of his mind that reeled from so many punches. Yeheshua gone… but she had come to him, and she said…

He stopped himself; there was life, he felt the spark of it in his heart, a tiny lamp still burning and this was because Mary had come to him… the master had sent her. Dream or no dream, and for the first time in several days he laughed; grimly but nevertheless…

He got up again; he had collapsed back onto the stone bench at the very back. He dusted off his clothes, thinking what he must do now.

He must go to Nicodemus' house, for that is where Peter and John and some of the others were. Had she said that or did he just know it? No matter, he must see how his brethren were faring, how he might help.

'How strong the women were, when we thought them weak'. How much stronger was their love it seemed to Thomas. Maybe it was different for them, but he had his love too and now he knew he would find the strength he needed. He must.

He went back into the house and asked the maid if there was some Passover food he could have. He said nothing about Mary and nor did she.

He ate and it helped bolster his will.

"Please tell my uncle I am going away for a few days," he said to Ishmaelia, "and thank him for all his kindness, which I will strive to repay." His uncle had insisted that he accept some money for while he was in Jerusalem, knowing that his studying with Yeheshua had curtailed his means of other employment.

Tobias was an admirer, a follower of the master in his own way too. "He will be back soon," Ishmaelia had replied, but Thomas knew he needed to go while the moment beckoned.

Walking to Nicodemus house helped him further, pumping the blood around him, raising the energy of his thinking and if not his hopes, then at least dispelling some of the horror from his mood. Something like equanimity returned; but a brittle balance.

He knocked on the door of where that last, fateful meal had been and Nicodemus himself answered, opening it to him and clasping the outstretched hands of the younger man.

"Yes" he said, reading the question correctly in Thomas' face. "They are here; at least Peter, James, John and a few others are. Not all…" his words faded mid-sentence, remembering.

Thomas nodded, not being able to get any words through the strictures of his throat. He shook his head and tried to say "Thank you…" but Nicodemus stopped him by pulling him gently into the house .. "Come," he said, "come and join the others and have something to eat."

Kindness struck him softly, but powerfully. He went into the room and immediately Peter turned to him and their eyes met. Hard to hold them, feeling his own inner pain mirrored in Peter's eyes, but he managed to. They both bowed or nodded slightly as he did to each of his brother souls as their troubled gazes met his own.

He sat down in silence where a place of cushions was hastily made on the floor. They were sitting around a floor table where some food and drinks were set. Peter broke off a corner of unleavened bread and gave it to him. Tears welled in Thomas' eyes but he received it, even though he had eaten at Tobias' house; and then some wine from James… but no-one said anything.

Few words were spoken but Thomas gathered that James and John had been to Joseph's place where mother Mary and other women were. They were all alright and Nathaniel and Philip were there now giving what help they could .

"I am going away for a little," Thomas said after a while, breaking one of the shared silences; and many eyes turned to him, excepting Peter who continued his slow stare at the plate he was cleaning.

"We need to stick together," said Peter, not looking up.

"I shall be back shortly, and keep you all in my mind and heart, but I need to face this in the best way I have. I want to pray and think and the rhythm of a long walk is what I need, or wish for at least. There and back again. I wanted you to know."

John nodded, and one or two of the others as well. "Do you want a companion for the way?" he asked.

Thomas smiled. "Thank you John, but I think I want to walk with my thoughts and memories alone, just now."

"Where will you go?" asked James, and Peter looked up at him as well.

"Towards the hills, the wild…" he answered; "but not so far as all that. Maybe out past Bethany, but I don't quite think…" he trailed off, getting to his feet.

"This is only the second day," said John, as he got up as well. "Don't be too long brother," and he clasped Thomas to him for a long moment.

Many hands gripped his and he gave everything back that his heart could. He smiled. "Thank you all," he said, "and don't worry for me; your strength is making me strong. I shall be back before too long," and he left the room to thank the host as well.

Out on the street he felt the resolve strengthen in him. He needed to get out of this city. His mind had returned to memories of the Ephraim hills, and that was the direction he struck out for.

*

Johannus wasn't sure that he should go with the women to Joseph's family house, as there were already two servants with Joseph himself to take them there; and he hated the idea of pushing to be invited.

He wouldn't stay at these offices either so he went in from the courtyard to pick up the pack and cloak he had brought with him

Yresmin was in the front room talking with Miriam about the donkey colt Indy, who was back with his mother Sella in Bethphage. "I had better go back to brush and feed and water them…" she was saying, obviously a bit reluctant to leave… and Johannus found himself offering his help. "I could go and do that for you Yresmin. I am going back that way anyway."

Yresmin turned and looked at him in surprise and Miriam, beyond her, smiled at him despite his interrupting them. "Sorry," he said, "I didn't mean to break in, but I am just getting my things to go, so…" his explanation trailed away but Yresmin's face had lit up changing the moment on its head.

"My place where the donkeys are…?" she began; "would you, could you Johannus? That would be so kind of you. I mean you should stay there if that would be good for you and have any of the food, and…"

"Would it be alright with your farm-owners if I did?" he asked and Yresmin nodded vigorously "Oh yes fine, but if you let them know you are there, they will probably have you mending something, tomorrow, haha…"

Some time later Johannus walked up to the gate, going through in his mind the instructions that Yresmin had given him. 'The third vertical slat from the middle; in the right gate; push it forward at the bottom where it meets the cross-bar, just in line with your waist'.

He did this and as Yresmin had said no-one watching would be able to see what he was doing … 'now move the bottom of that slat to the right, it has a nail protruding from the bottom into a groove in the crossbar. Allow the groove to guide the nail around until you are pushing leftwards and this will trip a lever which releases a weight.'

Johannus felt the dull clunk as the weight dropped, pulling up a wooden stake from a stone-hole where the gates met and which had been keeping them closed together. Pretty simple, but really effective. The gates were high enough so no-one could see in but they opened into a closed yard that had outbuildings on two sides. One a stable-barn where Yresmin and the donkeys lived with all they needed, as well as being for hay storage; and opposite a storehouse for every other kind of farm produce, materials and implements, as well as a heavy workbench and tools for making and mending.

The third, middle side, opened through onto a field that led to other walled fields and round to the farmhouse itself, on the further side of the barn-stable.

He closed the gates, re-lifting the weight that allowed the stake to drop back into the hole, pushing the gates to align them with it.

He knew the layout of the barn quite well and went to where the donkeys were in a stall together. Sella looked at him but gave no sign of being pleased or not.

He murmured some friendly words and she turned away to nuzzle the colt. He looked inside their stall for the wooden barred food-holder set a couple of feet up a wall and saw that there was no hay in it, though there was plenty of water in the heavy stone trough in the corner.

"Okay, I'll get you some hay now, and do your brush-down later," he said, but realised that actions were undoubtedly better than words for the donkeys.

The hay was stored on a raised floor along the side of the barn that had wide doors opening out to the field, and he picked up a long handled wooden fork that was leant beside the short ladder leading to the stacks of hay bundles.

Johannus collected some hay with the fork, reached it over to the feeder and then went back for more. Sella ignored his efforts but the colt went over to pull some through the wooden bars.

Johannus climbed into the stall and as Sella turned her head to watch him, he remembered Yresmin had tucked something into a pocket of his pack for her.

She seemed to have already guessed this for she was poking her muzzle into the pack hanging from his shoulder. The root vegetable tops he fished from inside were well received.

As he gave them, he patted her strong neck with his other hand. She was quite docile and steady and not so pushy as some donkeys… and the colt was delightful and very friendly.

He clambered back out of their area, went to get himself some water to wash with and drink, from a rain tub in the yard; and then came back inside to rest awhile whilst the daylight faded.

"I will groom you in the morning," he called to the donkeys as he crossed to find a place where some straw filled sacks and a few blankets gave him a good place to rest at the back of the barn. He was feeling drowsy, and in a while he had dozed off.

The dusk had turned to darkness when Johannus awoke and it was a few moments before he could remember where he was. His first jarring thoughts were of the crucifixion and its awfulness, and it was a little while before the other events of the day came back to him.

It was rather cold and he felt quite alone in the dark, though the donkeys were nearby. He shivered, pulling the slipped blankets back over him as he lay listening into the space around.

There was nothing but a few distant and indistinct noises, and he turned his focus to his own rather achy body and much too jumpy thoughts.

For no obvious reason Beor's working forge came to his mind and he could almost smell the heat of the softened iron being beaten into shape. Holding, controlling.

In the darkness he felt an eye watching him, like the open hole before the forge's fire where a great head lay on the smithy's floor, pushed in from the blackness.

He shook his head to free his mind, for he was led to thinking of great beasts of myth, the dragons that the black mage in Antioch had told tales of. Not a good way to go he decided and pulled himself back to the barn...

This place where Yresmin had kindly let him stay, and where the donkeys Sella and Indy gave him their solid, dependable company. Immediately he felt a lot better and his vision of the dragon's head merged comfortingly with thoughts of the donkey Sella's.

He laughed gently to himself, finding the shapes of them swapping around in his mind, dragon and donkey, the colt jumping, the dragon flying, off across and into the starry night.

He slept then, and peaceably.

Yresmin was so happy to be with Miriam and Mary, even in this most terrible of situations; but when Yeheshua's mother came up to her and was asking her to tell her about her life and the things that brought her to Yeheshua, it was like coming home, her real home.

Mary and her were about the same age and they felt like sisters in so many ways. Mary had studied in the Isis temple of Heliopolis which had so many similarities to those in Qadesh, where Isis was known as Al-Lat or sometimes Al-Uzza; but not so much Manat.

When Yresmin told of her journey and capture by the Ghosters, Mary gripped her arm, feeling everything like it was happening to her. The Djiinn's warning, the desert storm, their escape, the wonderful donkey Sella's fortitude, the vision dreams and finally her arrival in Jerusalem where the proud Pharisees seemed to her like city versions those desert Ghosters.

Then Yeheshua: his disciples coming to seek out Sella and her colt, for the master's entrance into Jerusalem; that incredible day when the sky sang to her. Everything had changed, never to be the same.

Mary knew what this meant to Yresmin. Heard how she had travelled to Qadesh following the same star that had brought those Magi to her lord's birth; knew the sacrifices she had made and the years spent making preparations to receive her lord herself.

Even though she had found and lost him again all in one week, Mary saw Yresmin's faith in her Hebrew master to be stronger even than death. Death was clearly just another Chapter to this extraordinary woman who had spent her life as lone priestess to the Nabatean Goddess of Fate.

They talked late into the night in Joseph's house, near to Yeheshua's tomb itself. Such a powerful feeling had built up, as though the night itself was bursting open. No-one could sleep much; just an hour here or there.

Yresmin heard some of the stories of us other women too. Miriam told of her meeting Yeheshua in the temple in Heliopolis where she had sung to him the songs of Israel, but he had put on hold their love to do his Father's work; and then how she had found him again in Magdala.

I told of how I had come to be inhabited by the seven devils that the master had driven out of me. Not an easy story to tell but the part that Johannus had played in getting me to Rachel, the healer near Tyre, explained much to the others of our connection, especially Yresmin who had met us both in Qadesh.

Susannah gave thanks for the wonder of being in a position to help the master's work; being the wife of the Governor in Caesarea-Philippi she had the funds to give him, and others who shared this priviledge agreed whole-heartedly.

Then the moment came that some great tension broke and to Yresmin it was as if the sky was sounding a great deep note like a vast gong ringing, though they were inside the house.

She got up and ran outside, others following. Something that we all felt but could not describe was lifting us up and up, a breath filling and filling us.

Almost too much to bear... Yresmin slumped against a wall and found herself being held between Miriam and mother Mary. "It has happened, praises to the All highest," she cried out, though she knew not quite why or how, and others sang "Alleluia, Alleluia."

*

Kaella was sitting at the entrance to a cave where there was neither only-night nor only-day, but both together.

Outwards, the sun shone on paths that spread in a mighty web around the world, and inwards the mysterious caverns of the night, all tunnels, caves and tombs were joined in deepest void whose portals shone as the very stars of heaven, magically present but impossibly distant at the same time.

Even here, where Kaella sat on the edge of possibilities, the impossible bloomed. Behind where the dragon lay asleep, a great light expanded in the void, like sun and moon together, coming neither from above nor below but from itself, in the heart of all.

Kaella saw, but blinded into darkness, felt rather the wave of what she knew as love to sweep outwards through her... every fibre, and then the stillness before another wave and a third, thrilling every part of her, rippled throughout universal being, keeping and leaving a greater, deeper stillness in its wake.

Even as her one-time priestess did on Gaia, she collapsed swooning, on the undulated surface of warm sands by the ocean's edge.

*

Miriam's was the face I saw as I awoke, not knowing when or how sleep had taken me. It was almost morning, the first light of day spreading almost imperceptibly upwards over the horizon.

We were on the flat roof space and others of our sisters were also asleep or just awakening. Miriam, sitting next to where I lay, stared over me into the growing light, breathing it in, eyes softly closing even as I turned to look as well.

The hillside was a pale grey-green with its wide scattering of olive trees over what would become the red-brown earth, once the sun had gathered its strength to heat the day.

The base of the hillside was still wreathed in the thinnest of mists but at the top the new light picked out contrasting yellows and purples, shining above all, through the new dawned blue.

I raised myself enough to lean with my cushion against the low wall to one side and allow the birth of the day to permeate through and into me as well... my inner spaces of thought and feeling.

Mother Mary it was this time, with one of Joseph's maids, who brought fruit and water up to where the early risers wrapped in blankets were sitting like I was, meeting life anew.

Yresmin stood up and joined mother, going back down to return carrying a tray of little cups and a tall, spouted pot from which wisps of heated vapour curled.

I opened my eyes again and stretched my limbs, wondering what Thomas was doing now and whether he was all right; I felt that he was. Miriam saw me and poured out a cup of the small mint tea and brought it over to me.

"We are going over to his tomb soon" she whispered, "I am not sure if everyone will want to come but I thought you might?"

"Ooh," I responded. "Yes, a thousand times yes; I would stay and live there as a hermit if we could."

"Ha, Yes, I think we would have a community of women hermits living there before too long," and she smiled as she hugged me to her. I felt all my tensions leave me.

In fact everyone came as Mother Mary and Miriam led the way to the gardens where Joseph had given the tomb over to our lord.

I was a few paces behind them and quite a few followed further back, Salome and Rachel, Mary, Johanna and Ruth, Susannah, Sarah and others as well.

There was a great commotion in the garden, guards scattered and leaving in some distress, even as we arrived.

Others had come as well, serene figures entirely unaffected by the guards' panic. A panic which became apparent emanated from the heavy stone having been somehow rolled away from the tomb's entrance, even as they guarded it.

Serenity outlasted the fleeing panic, leaving the quietness of the morning to permeate everything with its natural magic.

Only two or three watching persons remained, totally unperturbed and emanating a feeling of boundless caring.

We waited too, in wonder and a certain amount of trepidation. What was happening, had happened?

Miriam and mother moved into the garden together, approaching one of the watchers. I didn't hear what they said but felt myself drawn by the powerful fact of the opened tomb…

And that I had just missed someone stepping from it.

I couldn't move any further but was stood rooted as the figure clad in white joined Mother, Miriam and the other watcher. They all seemed to shine to me, lit by the first sunlight slanting through the trees.

The third angel, for I felt they must be angels, was asking me what I was looking for, and I answered, "the body of our lord Yeheshua" and he said, "why look for the living amongst the dead?" and turning I found it was the figure from the tomb, though I couldn't focus my sight clearly because of the light.

Then I could, and Yeheshua's smiling face was right in front of me, eyes laughing. Amazed, I reached out to hold him and he said "Yes, it is me, Mary; but don't grasp me, I am not ready yet; but the immortal you can always have.

Go tell Peter, John and the others that I am risen and come to meet with them again."

*

Thomas had walked and walked until he had come to a convenient inn on the road to Jericho.

He had paid in advance and woken early, eating only some of the paschal bread he had carried with him and some watery wine that served as his drink supply.

Setting off before the sun had risen, he stood awhile outside the inn, listening to the countryside awakening before eventually launching himself onto and along the dusty road. A cock crowed somewhere behind and a dog barked nearby, but otherwise it was the sounds of his own making that kept him company.

His sleep had been mercifully dreamless and the evening before he had felt strangely exultant in his walking, travelling as if into the evening sky, above where his thoughts could catch up with him.

Now in contrast his thoughts joined in with the steady slap, slap of his travel sandals, but not altogether unwelcomed companions to the dawning day and its richly laced air.

He thought of Magdalene and of Yeheshua, starkly contrasting thoughts and yet strangely in concert with each other. Left leg, right leg, independent but together making his progress down the road.

His lord was gone and Mary had come to him, lifting him from his grief, but he needed now the space to think, more than anything.

The space not to think as well. The space to be free from thought's chains, to propel himself forward and upward, like the small birds he just disturbed from a roadside bush.

What if…? what if…? No number of what if's made any difference, not to this moment. He had to focus all of himself on the task he had taken on; to go more deeply into this now, easy with the rhythm of his body, full of strength; propelled by the purpose to feel more and more in every stride, to leave his doubts behind.

Doubts. How people loved to wallow in them. How could there be doubt about the glory of being alive? None when you felt it coursing through you, giving all its love into you. How could you ever doubt when you felt that, the glory?

But when those clamouring thoughts crowded in on you and clouded your heart from that sun, how then could you escape…?

Argument and debate worked well for Thomas, finding a cutting edge keen enough to point out that feeling anew, trusting to his power to know and feel the truth. But in truth he knew it wasn't his power, but came from within as inspiration, the breath of life and heart.

Yeheheshua had shown him that.

He had known the same thoughts as others, 'I don't want to know', 'I am doing fine', and most basically 'why do I need a teacher?'; but he had been lucky for he had realised he was looking for something.

Well, Yeheshua had set him free and not chained him down as people seemed to imagine. He felt that freedom, had known it deeply and now he must prove it, beyond all doubt, now... that he could follow the course of his own heart, this way; this day.

Contentment rose within him and he refreshed his heart and mind with it, settling down in the shade of a tree as the heat of the sun started to really break through.

He loved the cut and thrust of his art as a lawyer, but loved more this contentment of seeing and feeling everything to be in harmony.

Doubts dispelled, he would continue on this journey up to the hills where they had spent that honeymoon week, of Yeheshua and Miriam together.

Of all the brethren Thomas thought he felt her worth most keenly, how she leant her strength and love to the master and his work. How much Yeheshua loved to have her near as well.

Others he knew were not so happy and found the pairing a distraction... to the teaching.

Well, how they could think or sometimes even say that was beyond him and many times he had struggled to hold his tongue, knowing he would regret the sharpness it could achieve.

He had kept his peace.

*

His way took Thomas up alongside the Jordan river and he rejoiced in its flow, coming down from Galilee, like Yeheshua and his followers, bringing water to this desert land.

He laughed as the river seemed to and stopped awhile on its banks to eat the last of his rations. He would need to find some more to buy, today.

When he did, he stocked up with as much as he could easily carry, grateful to his Uncle Tobias for the means to do so. Grateful for a lot of things and that felt good as well.

Amongst the things he managed to buy were a shepherd's long, thick winter hooded-cloak, that he would use to sleep in when he had gone beyond the last inn; and an ironstone striker to make a fire with.

Simple pleasures keenly felt, giving himself the way to be and sleep amongst the stars.

CHAPTER 7.

When Yeheshua asked me to go and find the twelve my heart swelled with joy, filling me with energy.

An energy that soon found its expression in a fast and happy run to Nicodemus' house.

Simon Peter himself answered the door and his somewhat severe expression at my arrival changed into curious disbelief as I tried to explain it was no spirit vision we had seen for I had touched the risen lord's arm and felt its solidity.

I could almost hear Peter's practiced disapproval of my temerity, but with it the simultaneous hoping that it could be possible, and in the next moment John was there at Peter's shoulder asking me, "where was this? when was it?"

"He waits to see you there, in the gardens where the tomb is; Siloam's garden."

Believing or not, they didn't wait to question further, but set off at a fast pace.

There were others in the house as well, Andrew, James and Bartholemew, and I spent a few more minutes explaining what I could to them before stepping once again outside to run to Tobias' house.

I couldn't help but remember and feel the kisses that Thomas and I had shared when I was there yesterday, that led to so much more, but it was the kisses that remained etched in my being.

But seeming an age away now, as Tobias opened the door to his smart town house.

He was a tall imposing figure, thickset but slightly stooped as he leant on a polished black stick, eyes sharp and enquiring with bushy dark eyebrows contrasting his flat grey hair; all topped by a cap worked with a few pearls.

We had never met individually but I recognized him as having sometimes been close-by when Yeheshua was teaching in the temple. I remembered that Thomas said he was a baptized Christine and liked to contribute financially to the master's work.

"Sir, my name is Mary, known as Magdalene and I am looking to give a message to Thomas... from our master Yeheshua."

His eyes went wide, brows jumping in surprise. "What can you mean?" he answered and then, "but Thomas is not here... and the Rabbi has been crucified, as you must certainly know."

"Yes indeed, but he is risen from the dead, I have spoken with him in Siloam's garden." Tobias still looked completely shocked, and I continued, "just a few minutes back, and mother Mary and Miriam there too. He told me to come and tell the twelve, and I had already heard Thomas was here with you."

His eyes pierced me for a moment but this examination was quickly replaced by a look of great wonder. "Thomas left last evening, but said he would be back by the end of the festive week," he said, adding kindly, "would you come inside and have some refreshment Mary? You have not spared any effort I think, to get this message to us."

"Thank you," I said, seeing in that moment what it meant to him, just how deeply the master had touched him in his life too.

I spent only a little while telling Tobias as much of what we had seen the last few days that he might not have known. The wonder I had seen in him remained and a smile eventually broke across his face, lighting it up as I spoke.

"My dear this is most wonderful, amazing. I had heard about Lazarus' return and had been a legal witness to his death as well, so perhaps I should not be surprised, but this is most, most astonishing, wonderful news. How was he, the master?"

"I didn't recognise him at first, because of the light … the sunlight streamed in most brightly, but it was more than that, and then he spoke to me and it seemed that his voice brought my mind, my heart into focus; and he was standing there with me, just as you are sat here now."

*

Thomas managed to light a fire on the hillside he had chosen. Not without a lot of failed attempts, but eventually he got a loose ball of fine woollen strands to catch alight and take, together with some dried-out bark bits, blowing softly, coaxingly into them; with extra kindling more carefully prepared and placed each time.

He hadn't collected a lot of wood; just enough to keep the fire going for his frugal meal, and give him warmth as he made a place to sleep under the night sky. But first he would look within, scrying the sky of his heart and soul.

Even as he did, Yeheshua was in Simon's house in Bethany, where all the other ten were gathered, and the master was asking after him… or so it was in his dream vision. He woke, and though only a dream, felt the warmth of this blessing as greater by far than what the fire had been able to afford him.

Long into the night he gazed up into the counterpane of the brightest stars he'd ever seen, with a keen, sweetly painful longing for the dream to be real, again; but slipped instead into sleep long before the first light grew in the east.

That next day Thomas reached the house where they had all stayed only a couple of weeks ago, but it was closed up and he didn't try to go within the gates, but turned instead to traverse the rough, semi-arid hillside where a few goats were roaming, seemingly untended.

As the day wore on the weather changed, venting moisture filled air from towering cloudbanks, advancing over the hills, from the west.

He was in a wild part of these hills, where almost nothing but rocks, punctuated by occasional thornbushes, lay up and down the broken slopes. And then the real rain began.

Beginning to get quite soaked, he was trying hard to find some cover when, on impulse, he skirted back and down from the rocky outcrop he was climbing, and fortuitously came round upon a shallow overhang indented into the hill, half filled with thorn and completed by a massive fallen boulder.

It looked to be nothing more than where the boulder had cracked and fallen away from the cliff, allowing enough space for the thorn trees to grow.

Getting scratched ducking under those thorn branches, Thomas found the overhang to be just enough shelter from the worst of the rain; and thought himself fortunate, for it had continued to hammer down, even as he looked around for the best place to keep his things dry.

Behind the fallen rock, against the cliff face, was a dark gap going into the hill; just big enough to squeeze through, thought Thomas; but he felt no inclination to try, until the steady drizzle following on from the initial downpour made the prospect of an exploration more enticing.

Once past the narrow entrance, the passage opened a bit wider until Thomas found a second space, squeezed around behind the wall of rock on his right; but after which the passage disappeared to a crack.

Examining this, Thomas realised a huge slab had probably split and fallen from the roof above, and the first boulder he had found was but a small outlier of that ancient fall.

He looked for a way to climb the side of the slab, for if he could, there might be a better space above. Going back a little along the passage, he found a possible way up which, climbing with difficulty, he was then committed to… for he could only really go on sideways, and upwards.

Thankfully managing to scramble up onto what was a wide flat shelf, he crawled forward on all fours, till the gap above to the roof was high enough to stand; nearer to the cliff front.

Sitting on this shelf Thomas looked out across the hillsides to where, in the distance, he knew the Jordan river must be, though he couldn't make it out.

He stayed for a while, enjoying the exhilarating evening views, before sliding back to where he had climbed and a crack running across the shelf showed how this massive block was actually three bits, the innermost section sloping back into the darkness and the back wall.

Thomas had a strong feeling that he would not have been the first person to find this natural place of shelter, and if he could bring some more light, he would have loved to have explored it more.

'Perhaps in the morning' he thought, when sunlight should be streaming directly into the cave; for he had already decided this would be the place to spend the coming night.

He wanted to find a better way to go up and down from this shelf before daylight faded though, and so searched for the most likely places; at either end of the central crack across. There was nothing promising on the side he had just managed to come up, but on the further edge a lot of rock had broken away, getting crushed and smashed into a tumbled mass between the slab and the cliff. Pieces of all sizes, that didn't look promising to climb down until, on trying tentatively, Thomas found an almost invisible path of stepping places, that went this way and that, round and down to the front.

Turning around from where he had clambered down to, Thomas could see no sign of the cave above the high shelf; for its opening was set back from the front, and it looked to be just a rocky faced cliff. Therefore, no reason for anyone who didn't know better, to try to climb up the scree.

He knew that it must be as easy a way to go up, as it had been down; so, before he did anything else, he tried it again; up and down a couple more times, till he could remember the steps and handholds quite well.

*

Kaella had been watching the mortal climbing the hillside to Hecate's cave. She could tell he was a high-minded soul, recognising him as one of Yeheshua's closest disciples, but wasn't sure of his name.

That he found the cave, explored it, and had decided to stay, gave her some clear insights into his past choices, and future possibilities; the strands that wove his being together.

Hecate's power to help or hinder was in some way being invoked. But so much had changed, and Kaella didn't understand the changes herself yet.

She watched and waited patiently, hoping she would discover…

CHAPTER 8.

Yresmin arrived home in a state of great animation soon after Johannus had finished brushing down the donkeys and making sure they had everything they needed.

Her excitement spilled over immediately, so pleased to be able to tell Johannus about seeing Yeheshua in the garden... of the empty tomb; the scattered guards, everything.

"Seeing him? A vision?" asked Johannus and Yresmin answered "I don't know, but he seemed just like you and me, talking with us, saying he would meet with us again soon... but then he was gone. So, I don't know exactly, but I saw Magdalene touch his arm and I am sure he was here, just as we are."

Johannus didn't know what to think. Except that if this was true everything was changed again, and his heart skipped. He had no reason to doubt Yresmin, who seemed to him one of the most practical and capable people in the world.

He had been there when the spear was driven up into Yeheshua's side on the cross; had seen the master hang lifeless there, and heard that Joseph had had his dead master's body prepared, and laid within the tomb.

Those things which he believed the powers of darkness would never achieve had happened; so why should he not now dare to believe that the Lord of love had overcome that darkness and returned to us, as he had said he would?

How much wouldn't he love to see him alive again.

"I should like to go and tell Beor at the smithy in Bethany; would you come too?" he asked. "For you have seen him alive, now... and Beor would believe you."

"The twelve, or eleven rather, are planning a meeting tonight. Probably in Bethany I think, because the Jewish leaders are encouraging Galileeans to be hunted out of Jerusalem. It is not safe there. Neither is Bethany because that will be next but let's take the donkeys with us; it will look more normal... and Sella can give a mighty good kick and bite, if she has the mind to," and Yresmin laughed defiantly.

*

Beor was not at the smithy but they went and visited him at his house, which Johannus never would have done had Yresmin not been with him. The bluff ironsmith looked askance and disbelieving until he suddenly burst out laughing; "he had known this would happen all along," he wheezed; "led them on a merry dance, thinking they could snuff him out like a wax candle. Ha ha, well that has put spike in their wheels... hurrah."

He ushered us into his house and wouldn't let us leave till we had told him everything at least once, and got us to tell his wife as well.

Finally, we had to say we needed to get the donkeys to Lazarus' house and that the streets were not safe either.

"Oh, don't worry yourselves, let me come with you and I shall go on to visit Simon too… I think he will be involved in anything going on tonight."

So they went, Yresmin and Johannus staying at Lazarus' house and Beor going on to Simon's house. They might try to make trouble there but I wouldn't dare if I were them.

Martha was amazed at what Yresmin told them, wondering just what it would mean… for all of them.

"The Jews are enraged and claiming that we have stolen the master's body from the tomb, to make it look that he has risen from the dead. They say all the guards are swearing that is what happened and they are hounding as many Galileeans out of Jerusalem as they can find." Yresmin paused; "it is all coming new, again."

Johannus suggested that they bar the front door against trouble and that he would guard the back way where the donkeys were housed, in case Mary and Miriam and some of the others came out here.

"Good gracious," said Lazarus coming out from his room. "The master returned from the dead as well?" he mused, smilingly. "No wonder I feel so much better;" and a great laughter spilled from him; "I had been thinking that he brought me back just to leave me again."

As soon as it got dark Johannus did go out the back, keeping Sella nearby, though the colt Indy was safely tucked away in his stall. He found a convenient spot where he could see everyone approaching, in readiness for anything.

A few people did indeed stop across the road and stare intently at the house, but seeing it hard shuttered and closed, with no obvious activity, moved on.

At another time a couple of dark swathed men came close to where Johannus stood tensed and ready to challenge, when obligingly Sella gave out a harsh bray that sent them scuttling away, and left Johannus chuckling; 'maybe I should practice my braying.'

Then a man was at the gate and Johannus hardly had time to react, just managing to step across the path saying "who comes…?"

"Johannus it is me, Yeheshua," said the man and Johannus peering forward in shocked surprise suddenly recognised his master, and fell to his knees in mixed bewilderment and joy.

"Get up, or you cannot do your job," laughed the master. "The way is long and there will always be much needing doing, but we shall meet along the way. Fear not anything; for the future is opened up, for men and women with hearts that are true."

…and the Lord passed on inside the house,

A few minutes later Yresmin came out and pulled Johannus inside, whispering, "come, guard the door from inside; it will be just as good. Look, stand here where you can see and hear the master." and she hugged him briefly before slipping inside the front room herself.

The night was long and there were many comings and goings; some strange and others welcomed, and by the morning Johannus was on the outside again, sleeping beside the little colt, remembering that Miriam, mother Mary and Magdalene were happily inside; Yresmin too.

CHAPTER 9.

We were all so happy, and the only thing that made me worry was that Thomas had not been there; at Simon's house, when our Lord had come.

That is what I learnt that next day. All other ten from the twelve were there, but why was Thomas not?

I worried for him, and worried that it was because of what I… that we… had been together, but I couldn't ask anyone.

It was like I had to breathe the harder to make it all be true, what was happening. Breathe for him too so that he should know and come and join in our joy. The harder to make my heart sing with the feeling of our Lord's return. 'Oh Thomas, Thomas, come back, come home.'

Yeheshua had asked after him and Peter had said he had needed to go walking and the Lord had smiled, apparently. They used to walk together sometimes and talk the way philosophers loved to do, and Yeheshua had once admitted how he enjoyed the flying of their minds like birds together in the clear blue sky.

"Don't worry, he will be back, in his own time," the master said.

*

More rain came that next day and we stayed mainly inside, glad as well that the trouble makers kept away. We heard that other disciples had seen the master again, walked with him. Not just us; but here and there and hopefully everywhere his followers were finding out.

We would try to spread the news as well.

*

Thomas thought he might make a fire again but realised all the wood he had was wet and that he was unlikely to find dry stuff, after the rain.

Anyway, when he unrolled his pack the woolen cloak-blanket it hardly seemed damp at all. Perhaps he would need no fire; and the sky still had cloud covering, which should keep in the warmth of the day.

He ate the food that he had largely been given, in the village where he had bought the cloak and striking iron, for it was Paschal food and kindly shared. One or two bits he had insisted on buying, fresh vegetables uncooked, but that had mainly been to pay for something.

He found a well sheltered part of the wide shelf, in case of any winds or further rain and settled down to think, to contemplate, to sleep and in fact to dream.

He was a young boy again and on the hillside below, except it was much greener and had many wide boughed trees.

He climbed up through the wood and had a strong feeling of being watched, and not just any watcher, not fox or deer or bird, but something greater.

He thought he glimpsed it between the trees, crouched, stock still; yet gone before he blinked; but there again if he could be as still as it.

'Dragon' his subconscious mind rang out and his heart raced. He dared not move a muscle; held his breath, and still the eye caught his, yellow-green like a cat's, and a gaze more weightily intense than the light between the great trees.

Gone, done, no escape... but then he was standing here on the cave's shelf, no longer a boy, but still feeling the presence of the dragon, close by.

Thomas could not decide whether that presence issued from deep within or round outside the cave; and he stood there a long while, undecided.

Eventually he was drawn to the back of the cave, as much as anything because he had wanted to explore it, and found himself looking at the wall there, seemingly illuminated by its own light, within the rocks themselves.

He stared at it and saw there were lines engraved on the surface of the rock, lines that made a sort of staircase, and putting out his hand to touch one of those lines, found only space... for there were indeed steps, cut there; and that the light was coming down from where they led.

Mesmerised and intrigued beyond fear, Thomas put his left foot forward and started to walk upon the stone stairs. The way was neither narrow nor wide, the steps neither steep nor shallow and it wasn't hard to climb them.

The rock-light was in fact starlight he realised, as he neared a rectangular opening that framed them, and as his head almost drew level a great shape flew overhead, blotting out everything... all light, all thought, almost even breath...

Thomas crouched down and it was gone.

It took him a long while before he could poke his head ever so slowly and gingerly through the gap, but he knew he couldn't have gone back, so he screwed up his courage and went on up.

The hillside was completely grassy and the sky full of stars, if anything seeming closer than the night before, and turning around found he was on the bank of a dark lake reflecting the same stars as above.

The steps he had just come up were gone, and yet somehow he felt no surprise, only wondered where the dragon was.

"Here" said a voice, and looking around found himself only a couple of dozen paces from a young woman, hardly more than a girl.

"I am Heraikaliphon," she said, and for a moment Thomas saw the dragon, massive and indistinguishable from the dark sky, and then he couldn't; only a line of mighty trees on the slope behind the girl. "What do you want? What are you doing here mortal human?"

Thomas thought about it, but unusually for him had no real answer, except "nothing ... unless to find my way forward, and to get home."

"Home?" queried the girl.

"Yes" said Thomas... his heart yearning for rest, love and... coming home.

"And is forward the way home?" she asked.

"Can you tell me?" replied Thomas, "this place here seems to be a crossroads for me."

She laughed then, a sound like gravel being lashed with waves, not like a girl but the dragon he faced, with breath of fire. "Indeed, you are at a crossroads Thomas," and the girl stepped forward from the great shadowy beast which settled, crouching on the hill behind.

"Kaella is also my name," she said, crossing half the ground between them; "and that is my cave where you are sleeping and this is the crossroads of Hecate where you stand."

A shiver went through Thomas but he held his ground… "and can you help me then?" he asked, knowing the name of the triple goddess Hecate of whom she spoke.

She closed her eyes and seemed to grow in his vision then, but it was only for a few moments.

Kaella looked straight into Thomas and spoke like an Oracle… "Mother from the country of Thoth; father of Hermes' stock; Thomas, your life is as a bow stretched from Thrace to Thebes and drawn back by the mighty Hebrew Sage, pointing into the dawning light; and you the arrow."

*

She had gone… and Thomas woke on the shelf again and indeed there was light dawning into the mouth of the cave; but that didn't make the rock any softer under his body's weight.

He remembered the girl Kaella's words, though some of the other details started to fade as he readjusted to the needs of cold physical reality.

She was almost right, in that his mother Judith had been living in Alexandria when she had met his father Isaac, the son of a Macedonian engineer, Philip; married to Thomas' dark-skinned, Jewish-Egyptian grandmother, Manneh.

Isaac died in a building accident when Thomas was quite young and it was Philip, together with Judith's brother Tobias who had filled that gap for the young Thomas, ensuring that he got the widest possible education; quite a bit of which had been in Antioch, but some with his great 'uncle' Elias in Jericho.

If the oracle Kaella had been insightful about his past, maybe she could also be so for his future too; and that had seemed to promise great hope.

He smiled to himself and went back to sit and consider the whole: days past and path forward; and the gradually growing heat of the present hour of the present day warmed him there, sitting on the cave front.

About an hour later he got up, packed his things and left the cave.

Feeling decided, he ambled down the sun-kissed hillside in a generally south-eastern direction, towards the great river and the road back to Jerusalem.

CHAPTER 10.

Johannus and I stayed around Bethany after Mother, Miriam and Yresmin left with Sella and the colt Indy; to see Joseph and Nicodemus and Tobias and others, still in the turmoil of Jerusalem.

Mother was sat upon Sella's broad back with Yresmin leading, and Indy followed Miriam, swaggering happily, and almost full grown it seemed to me, watching them go.

I wanted to visit Beor again and ask him about all the other Christine followers in Bethany; he would know everyone, I was sure. Martha, Mary and Lazarus had asked me to stay.

"Are you going to visit your aunt and uncle, Johannus?" I asked, remembering it like yesterday, when Miriam he and I, had set out for our quest to Kadesh; and returned here again, still somehow with his uncle's horse.

"Yes, I think I will," Johannus answered. "I saw them a few days back, on the Sabbath after... but couldn't face them. How things have changed."

"Ha... yes; let's go via the forge then; it is on the way and I want to catch up with Beor."

I knew how much Johannus valued the friendship that had developed between us and Miriam too, but it was Beor that had originally helped him, giving him work when he had arrived from Antioch.

In fact, Beor had been the first to tell Johannus about the master and his deeds... things almost beyond comprehension, but that happened right here. Healing Bar-Simon, controlling the fire... and many others.

Beor was working in the forge when Johannus and I turned down the track to hear the singing of his hammer as he beat the metal into shape. Hot sparks flying and sweat jumping from his arms, it was amazing to see how delicate work could emerge from the mighty blows.

"Don't stop," I said as we approached, "I love to see your crucible of forces at work."

"Mary," he smiled out of the side of his face, not turning... "so you are bringing my wayward apprentice back to me I see." He laughed, and Johannus did too, watching the concentration of the master smith as he turned the iron to receive a few last delicately deft blows to the tip of what he was conjuring...

"It is for a chariot shaft," he said, wiping his arms down with the towel he used to hold the piece he had been working. "I am expected to deliver it to their barracks, this afternoon."

He judged it was time to quench the heat of the pole, plunging its end in the water bath.

Steam fizzed, combining in that confined space with the charcoal heated fumes of the furnace, a mix so familiar and welcome to Johannus' flaring nostrils.

We hugged and Beor sat down, inviting us to join him, sharing each other's news on the huge changes from a couple of days ago… and eventually we took pause, savouring the texture of the silence and company of each other's thoughts.

"I wonder what they know The soldiers; of the lies that the Jews are spreading about us stealing his body form the tomb," I asked, glancing towards the chariot piece he needed to deliver.

"They do say that a Centurian was overseeing the Jewish guards…" Johannus added.

"Why don't you come and see what you can find out Mary? If anyone could, you could."

I gave him my best effort at a withering look, but Beor only laughed. "What about you Johannus?"

"I think it is time I visited my aunt and uncle," said Johannus, "unless you need my help with carrying stuff of course?"

Beor growled something under his breath I couldn't hear, and took a friendly swipe at Johannus, that would have knocked a slower man, unready for it, from his seat …

"Ha…, I can come, and carry as well," I said, completely straight-faced, and Beor threw up his hands in mock despair. "OK, okay, your help would be greatly appreciated."

We set off a little while later, after such food and refreshments as Beor had to share, and Johannus went to visit his relatives.

"See you later at Lazarus' house," I said to him. "Yes?"

"Probably yes, depends on what is happening at uncle Mikael's; but soon anyway. I shall definitely come over tomorrow, or meet you here after breakfast, as I need to ask the smithy whether he needs a good helper for a while?"

"Fine chance," said Beor. "I can't find a decent worker for even half of a good wage."

"Done then," we all agreed.

*

Johannus walked with a spring in his step up to his uncle and aunt's house, without any plan of what he might say, only knowing he would be pleased to see them and share whatever might seem best. How different from a just a couple of days ago.

He would also be glad to see Rebecca again, for he had thought of her a lot and felt he had neglected … what? He wasn't sure. Would she and her father still be there? He suddenly hoped he hadn't missed them.

There was no answer when he knocked. 'Damn' he thought, 'but no hurry,' trying to convince himself, thinking to sit down and wait awhile.

He knocked again, just in case they had been out of hearing, and then got up after a few minutes to try once more, with no result.

He sighed, thinking of what he would do instead… just as his aunt called out "Johannus... what are you doing here?"

She was coming up the path arm in arm with Rebecca, both with head coverings but that was the only similarity. Jessica was short, wirily solid and walked with a certain dogged determination whilst Rebecca was curvaceous and gracious, moving with a slight sway that caught Johannus in the pit of his stomach.

Suddenly he felt both happy and nervous at the same time, a desire to impress being quickly overwritten with a genuine gladness to see them.

"Aunt Jessica, Rebecca, I feel I have been ignoring you badly but I think you must know that strange things have been happening, which... which have sort of kept me away."

They both knew of his being with Yeheshua so naturally were not sure what to say. "Awful, awful..." his aunt was saying, shaking her head, but Johannus took her other arm to Rebecca, saying, "let's go inside aunty, and get some drinks." and as he looked to Rebecca over his aunt's head, she smiled back in a way that transformed his world ... again.

"Are uncle Mikael and Rebecca's father not with you today then?" asked Johannus as he helped his aunt inside, Rebecca coming close around beside him, brushing his side as they moved a chair to a better position for her.

Jessica complained they were fussing, so he went out; "I'll get the kitchen fire stoked up. You rest your feet aunty; then we can talk."

His aunt liked to be in charge, arranging things, but Johannus knew he had to tell her now, before he found himself agreeing to do all sorts of things just to placate her.

"Yes, it was truly terrible," he said, coming back into the main room, seeing the wood he had added was now taking quite well; "but haven't you heard? He has come back? Returned afresh, even from death; just as he said he would, but not even we could believe."

Aunt Jessica looked at him incredulously for long moments. "What...?" she said eventually, gathering all of her incomprehension into that one word.

"Can that really be true," said Rebecca "How? Who has seen him?" Then staring into Johannus' hugely spreading smile; "You?... you have seen him, have you?"

"Yes," he answered, "I have; at Lazarus' last night. He came when I was keeping an eye out for trouble out the back. Suddenly he was there and I didn't realize who he was at first."

"Well how do you know it was really him then," asked his aunt, "and not someone pretending to be... if you couldn't recognise him? Or perhaps a ghost; yes, surely a ghost. How frightening."

"Oh, it was him all right," said Johannus laughing, but not knowing any way to explain how Yeheshua could do what he did; to explain how the master had always seemed able to slip away without people knowing; especially when his enemies had tried to get hold of him.

Now, even more so; and for us as much as anyone it seemed. Where he came from and how he would disappear. Then again, we didn't care, but it did keep us a bit off balance; not knowing.

Maybe that was the point.

"Remember Lazarus? How he came back after being dead for three days? And the master told us what would happen to him as well… but we couldn't take it in either."

"Did he go inside?" asked Rebecca. "At Lazarus house the other night?

Johannus realized that he wasn't doing a very good job of telling the story. "Oh yes… and he talked for a long time with quite a few of us there. His mother and Miriam and Mary Magdalene were all there. It was most marvellous… Changing, has changed everything.

And just then Johannus' uncle Mikael arrived with Rebecca's dad Petrakis, opening the front door with a cheery "Hello?"

"Dearest, guess who is here?" answered aunt Jessica pushing herself up and quite nimbly getting to the doorway. "Johannus is here and telling us how he has seen the ghost of the poor crucified Rabbi Yeshua. Isn't that strange?"

Mikael and Petrakis came into the room and both Rebecca and Johannus had risen as well. Johannus was not quite sure how to respond to what his aunt had said, but stepped forward to greet his uncle with a hug before grasping Petrakis' outstretched hand.

The older man looked querulously into Johannus face, who half shrugged, but smiled as well. "Not a ghost, no" he said. "But truly, yes… I have seen the master, alive and in the flesh; at Lazarus' house."

CHAPTER 11

Kaella sat in deep wonderment after her encounter with Thomas.

She was thinking of whether there could be something to taking the path of a mortal human that she had missed.

Certainly she had been told that it was in a human life that she could attain the 'True-mirror' she had always craved... that could show her the Divine; in her, within.

The mirror that had led to her expulsion from her mother's house in the beginning times, for her attempted theft ... except she had been searching for that special treasure that her father was the guardian of, not her mother's beauty compact.

Her mother had gone mad with rage and her father had not gainsaid her, telling Kaella that she had to leave... but that would be the first step on her path to finding her answers.

Yet having passed through almost every descending plane of being Kaella still found that the mortal life of humans seemed probably the least desirable...

Though both Yeheshua and Miriam had demonstrated something else, something that had not only caught Kaella's attention, but her admiration and desire to be involved.

She sat thinking, in her caves that networked her domain, and felt the desire for freshness... of water falling into a smooth rocky pool, its coolness drenching her; before changing to a sun-heated, fine-sanded beach, with little lapping waves delighting her... and so it was.

Languidly she stretched, being back in her cave where the walls glowed translucent, with warm breezes wrapping around her, like layers of the finest fabrics drying her.

She walked over to another entrance again, overlooking the mortal world. How hard they had to physically work to achieve anything... even the simplest things, the basic needs.

Yet that Thomas had found an inner strength and calmness she wondered at, so there must be something, something?

She thought of Johannus as well, who she had taken for a dream lover for a while, even protecting him with her 'other fierceness' when the darkness had erupted into his nightmares.

That nightmare darkness that had come into her kingdom too... but the Hebrew teacher had been able to master it, somehow. Changing everything, everything.

What? was what she must find out, and even then, looking across the world, could see Johannus with that girl from Egypt... and Kaella frowned.

*

Johannus felt the shadow of cold touch him and shivered. "I must be going," he said to his aunt, as they sat all together in her parlour, "but it has been so good to meet with you again," he added, turning to Petrakis and his daughter. "I hope you are staying a bit longer, and we can meet again this week maybe?"

"Well, yes, we are staying till the end of the festive time," answered Petrakis, looking over to where Johannus' uncle was nodding vigorously. "Yes, yes of course; that was always understood," replied Mikael smiling, dismissive of any possible suggestion to the contrary.

"I really want to see what becomes of this affair," Petrakis added; "can't leave it like this."

"Come for dinner tomorrow, John," insisted his aunt, and Johannus was happy to agree.

*

Thomas for his part was glad to be staying in Zachias' Inn in Jericho, hearing the rumours of the Lord's return from death as well.

He couldn't dare believe it, didn't want to place his hopes in rumours that could have come from anywhere, though Zachias believed them to be true.

"I shall set out back to Jerusalem then, tomorrow morning," he told his host, thanking him for his kind hospitality.

Unexpectedly this made him think of Mary and the closeness they had, the intimacy, the sweet moments of ecstacy shared right in-amidst the torment. 'Had he been avoiding her too?' he wondered, not knowing how it all fitted together, except that she had undoubtedly saved him from killing himself.

*

I did think of Thomas of course, felt the connection between us, wondering if he had too; he must, mustn't he? I worried that he had not come back, but our connectedness told me he was all right and would be back… soon.

I sought out Yresmin in Bethphage, needing to know as much news of things in Jerusalem as possible. Johannus had started helping Beor around his forge again and I wanted to be useful too. We hadn't learnt anything much at the Roman barracks, except how impressed they had been in Yeheshua's calm acceptance, in such contrast to the madness of his tormentors.

No one would talk about the empty tomb.

There were still great tensions in Jerusalem with the circulation of claims, lies and confusion, and Yresmin seemed best placed for many of us to visit. Miriam was already there, looking after Indy. Salome had come with her and one of Joseph's friends.

We were in buoyant mood; tomorrow was the Sabbath day and many Christines were planning to meet both in and around Jerusalem, all hoping to hear more about the master's return, and maybe even have the chance to glimpse him.

How incredibly lucky I had been to witness his return at such close hand. I didn't deserve it when I thought of all those who wanted it so badly. Why had I been so fortunate. "Don't try to hold onto the mortal," is roughly what he

490

had said, "but rather the immortal, that is always with you."

Had he been referring to me with Thomas as well, when he had said that I wondered?

"What are you thinking, sweet?" asked Miriam as I daydreamed at the vegetable chopping. I shook my head, rather to clear my thoughts than anything else. "Just wondering how things can develop from here. Have you any idea?" I asked, returning my concentration to the task in hand.

"He leads the way, in all things I think," she answered; "but the time is coming for us to walk it as well. He has done all that anyone can possibly do, gone beyond everything that can be gone beyond. Are we ready too?"

Salome answered something I missed, as I stopped to think, but I didn't find an answer.

*

Kaella decided to spread her wings, literally, taking the dragon form to see how far she as Heraikaliphon could go; testing the changes.

Kaella's own powers were not just limited to her own domain, but in uniting with Herakopha they were best equipped to discover what they might.

She soared into the evening sky, following the setting sun and the magic of where lands merged into the sky. Banks upon banks of hills and rolling clouds that were fired up into the colours of the heavens beyond.

Higher and higher she flew, the pinks turning into purples and the light of distant stars sparking into life.

Faint at first but all the time growing greater and brighter, out across the wide expanse of coming night, knit together in singing the song of the universe.

Kaella heard the song in ways she never had before , caught into a double-noted harmony that drew her... more than any other part.

Soaring into the spaces of the music, Heraikaliphon crossed towards those notes, feeling her sinuous being vibrate to their call; into the wide timelessness of the void, letting the pull take her to its source.

Kaella sensed the presences ahead, as the mighty dragon she was opened herself to the warmth and breezes of a massive world, glowing golden... the world of lion people.

Two towering lion-beings stood upright on the hill ahead and Kaella knew to glide gently down to the slope before them, alighting from Herakopha in her human form, much less than half the height of either magnificently maned lion, though she was tall.

No threat came from them, only the aura of wisdom, courage and an indomitable strength of caring.

She bowed to their majesty and they smiled warmly on her. "Do you come to tell us of the changes, young queen?" one of them spoke into her thoughts.

Kaella didn't need to speak herself for the answers to come, "it is to understand the changes myself that I am come."

There seemed to be a soft humming all around her... like lion minds and hearts considering this.

"The changes have just begun, Kaella… " the other lion spoke, the female one Kaella realised; "and we must hold the heart-space for these, the changes we feel too."

"What …?" Kaella begun, and the first was already responding "changes for humankind on Gaia to grow and learn; in preparation to coming into their heritage… if they can."

"And your way has choices too, daughter," continued the other, "with an age ahead to work through those, before the time comes that has been awaited down the ages."

*

Herakopha was sleeping when two young male lions came to Kaella, with a tall, cream-maned elder female.

Neither of the young ones looked like lions, having amazing patterns in their soft fur more reminiscent of leopards or tigers perhaps; maybe 'felines' would have been a better word, except for the beautiful manes of many adults.

Manes that grew on both the males and females.

"We are not the same as your Gaia lions," said the beautiful pale female, "but we are from the same people, though much changed through the countless march of days in this world."

The young ones were very friendly, wanting to play with Kaella. She felt the urge to reach forward and touch the one closest, who reciprocated, allowing her to brush the silky soft fur of his patterned shoulder while the tip of his tail curled round to stroke over her hand.

She laughed and the other feline, blue to silver coated with darker trimming looked curiously to the sleeping Herakopha.

"Come with us to have some food and drink if you will…" said the elder, "and we shall bring some back for your dragon partner, later. She will be hungry when she awakes."

"Thank you… ?", "Lilsa," said the other.

"Thank you Lilsa, I would love that. My name is Kaella."

"Yes… let's go then, I hope we can show you something more too."

Kaella was curious about what these lion-kind would eat and was surprised when she was brought to where four great aphora-like jars stood around a wide circular table of polished stone in an open-air dining area.

Each of the tall jars contained a different liquid and Lilsa poured some from each into four stone bowls, beautifully decorated in different patterns of inlaid metals and stones.

"Taste some," said Lilsa, "and tell me what you think, which you like best … if you would."

Kaella stepped up to the bowls, peering at their contents in turn. The first was brown, almost red, and smelt of all the earthy aromas Kaella could imagine, and in her mind's eye she saw a wide plain beneath rolling hills, and tasted the depth of a hundred streams cascading down and through rocky inclines and canyons, back into the earth again to finally snake out to join a mighty river; its waters red with minerals.

She put down the tasting ladle and told Lilsa what she had experienced, thinking how much Herakopha would love that.

The second liquid was greenish, almost blue, depending on the light and the tastes changing from sip to sip as Kaella seemed to taste the varied leaves, roots and fruits of a huge forest, like to many on Gaia but different too. Mighty woods, stretching from white topped mountains to a vast, unending desert, shimmering with heat under a white blue sun, still low in the sky.

The third bowl had the clearest purest water Kaella had ever tasted and she knew this came directly from the snow mountains beyond the forest, and the fourth contained a golden yellow liquid, so sweet that Kaella couldn't find an end to tasting it, but instead had a vision of astonishment…

"Bee people…" said Lilsa, for Kaella was looking at faces that kept changing, catlike but not, wings beating so fast she couldn't see them. Bright beings and full of the sweet light and heat that they infused the liquid with; and behind them the golden desert covered with a multitude of flowers, the kind that bloomed suddenly in a few days after the rains.

"From these four we can make anything we want to eat and drink, just depending how you mix them," explained Lilsa, stirring a ladle of red-brown liquid with half as much green blue until with a few added golden drops the mix congealed into an almost solid paste.

Lilsa took the paste, showing it to Kaella. "See how hot it has become and if I work it with this spatula it becomes quite solid too, and a drop more yellow fluid will burn the edge." She smiled at Kaella, "this is one of my favourites; try it if you like."

Kaella did, mesmerised by the mix of flavours, textures and hot spiciness that reminded her of a kind of filled flatbread; her mouth bulged as she bit another hunk from it. "Oh, it is quite delicious," she said whilst Lilsa's laugh purred from deep inside her.

*

The young lions had had their fill of quaffing their water, laced with some of the brown-red liquid and just a few drops of desert-honeydew, and were carolling around the hillside beyond, sometimes on two paws, sometimes four, chasing deer-like beasts that pranced and ran and charged back at the lions as well.

"Come Berittas; come Halfren;" called Lilsa, "help us please carrying this to the dragon Herakopha", and aside to Kaella, "she's stirring, I think. Yes?"

She had poured two much larger bowls, one filled mostly from the red-brown aphora, though grown solid, and the other a mixture that Kaella didn't see prepared, but it was an almost clear liquid that bubbled heavily.

Herakopha stretched and smelt the approaching food, appreciative with a

493

hunger come from her inter-stellar flight.

The young lions were strong; strong enough to carry the large and heavy food-filled stone bowls, sufficient in size to satiate a large dragon's hunger

She ate and drank and bowed in thanks, her mighty head touching to the ground near to the lioness' soft-pawed feet.

Lisla spoke in both Kaella and Herakopha's mind-as-one. "Let us alight the air, for there is a place that you surely still seek, above and beyond the heights of snow, and on the way, I would show you something of this world as well; that is the labour of our love."

CHAPTER 12.

Yresmin came back to Bethphage, her long strides making a measured pace, trying hard to contain her excitement and joy.

She had seen it happen; she had seen him at the temple court; seen the darkness quail in front of him.

Because of what she had already heard, she had dared to go the temple, to see how the the city's powerful, their scribes and priests would react; but she had stayed outside, with many others; whence the lies were being relayed, that were meant to quash the rumours of the risen Christ.

Then he was there, stood beside her; only for fleeting moments, but he had smiled at her and she knew him; though others only saw a simple fisherman come to town.

He went within the court and was asking after the Galilean who was want to preach there, and they told him lies; everything bad to heap upon the master, especially about the open tomb and his disciples stealing the body.

But when he had challenged their stories, demanding someone who had been there to speak out truly, no-one could; and they had got furious that he would not shut up and just accept their lies.

But then he said that he had been there, knew the truth of it; and throwing off his outer fisherman's garb had stood there as the teacher they could all recognise. This only made many of them madder, trying to lay hold on him again; but a bright light came between them, defeating them and shining about the master, so that they cowered away.

But even then, he spoke to them of truth, to dispel the darkness of their fear and hatred, to uplift their hearts... and many did see that he truly cared for all, and unlike others, didn't judge, but offered hope for everyone.

Then he was quite suddenly gone again.

When Yresmin got back home she busied around, talking all about it to Sella who was close by, making ready for guests who might come tonight. Her barn had become a sort of meeting place for some Christines, mainly the women and those wanting to get a bit away from the anger in Jerusalem.

Her place; she who was not even a Jew, but Nabatean. She had learnt to fit in and it didn't seem to matter, particularly amongst the women where mother Mary and Miriam were well loved, and Yresmin thanked them so much in the fullness of her heart.

She thought Mary would pass by this evening, as the eleven Galilean close disciples, would be meeting again in Simon's house in Bethany.

The end of the Jewish festive time was fast approaching, after which... she didn't know, it must depend upon Yeheshua.

She hummed a song, a hymn of her temple, of the coming of the rain in the desert, and for a moment she thought of her Goddess Manat... and a half remembered flight across the sky, upon a winged beast of fable… 'dragon'.

*

Thomas walked back into Jerusalem, up the hard streets that would always be awash with blood to his mind's eye.

He knocked on Nicodemus' door first, but only a servant answered his knocking and she didn't seem to know anything, which Thomas grudgingly admitted was probably a sensible precaution.

So, he walked over to his uncle's house and found Tobias in the garden. He told Thomas something of what he had heard about the commotion in the Temple that day, though he had not been there himself.

"There is a meeting tonight in Bethany, I was told to tell you if I saw you. Simon's house; they believe he may come there, and he has been asking for you they said."

"I cannot believe that," said Thomas. "It's all just too fantastical."

*

Johannus sat at his uncle's table where Petrakis was describing the events at the temple that day.

He had been there when Caiaphas had thought to silence a nuisance fisherman but had got the biggest surprise of his life.

Petrakis laughed long and deep till tears ran from his eyes. "I wish you could have been there Mikael; seen it for yourself. I am sure you know what I must mean, Johannus. You have seen what his strength is, and now I have too. Haha… ha ha, how will we go on now? How will they?"

"We and they must learn to walk the path of light, as he does, I think," answered Johannus.

"Yes," said Rebecca, surprising everyone; "I think we must too."

*

I was with Miriam and mother when we all left Yresmin's place, walking to Bethany, again to visit Lazarus' house, like the week before.

We knew of course of the meeting at Simon's house, and I knew that I had to go there, whatever Peter might say, or think.

Thomas might be there too; my conviction being almost equal to my hope.

Miriam sensed my mood for she said that they would come along a little later as well, even before I told her I was going.

Beor was on the door and let me go in without comment or hesitation.

I hadn't the nerve to go into where all the 'twelve', who were no longer twelve, were, but instead went through to where I could hear voices in the kitchen.

Simon looked up, a little surprised, but smiled in welcome. "Do you need any help?" I asked, the hope clear in my expression and he nodded in answer.

"Thank you, sister," I would. "I still get the shakes when carrying things like this."

I put a hand gently on his arm in acknowledgement, picking up the tray of drinks he had made to take through to the inner room.

Peter predictably arched an eyebrow at me as I entered but I ignored him, presenting the cups to each in turn, as meekly as any serving girl.

My heart almost stopped for there was Thomas in a corner being berated it seemed by Nathaniel and Philip, his closest friends.

I left serving them to last and just as I was reaching there, another man entered the room, and suddenly I realised it wasn't just any other man… though his features were hard to see under the head cloth that was still laid shoulder to shoulder over his head.

All attention went to Yeheshua, for I could see him clearly now and glanced over to Thomas who was peering across at him, the light in the room not being strong.

"Thomas," he said, pulling the shadowing cloth back, "do you not know me?"

Thomas went forward, "I could not believe what my brothers said," falling to his knees and his hands and eyes going to the sandaled feet, seeing the wounds but not touching them.

"Come, get up, see and feel my hands and side as well; so, you can know that I am really flesh and blood, bone and sinew, just as you are…"

"Lord," Thomas said getting to his feet, trembling. "I can still scarce believe that it is true; but you are wholly real and living," his hand being taken by Yehseshua and pressed to his side where the spear had pierced up towards his heart; "this I now know, not just believe."

"Blessed are you Thomas, but how blessed are those that shall believe without even seeing me?" He sat down where his seat was prepared, "And that is the job that you can do for them and me… to let men know that life is ever with them and that the love of the Almighty is not a breath's distance away from them."

"I come as witness of that love and of the holy breath that holds us close inside."

I had moved prudently to the back of the room and sat listening, entranced.

More than once one or other of the senior disciples looked my way, disapproving; and I thought to maybe go outside the door, but found I couldn't move.

Then I realised that there must be a meal being readied and got up to help the host Simon again, just as Simon himself came in with a choice of drinks for Yeheshua, and a bowl for him to wash his hands.

The meal was plentiful and conforming to the Paschal rules, and I slipped in and out as much as possible, serving the Lord and his disciples, remembering how I had come to him once before, asking for instruction at just such a celebratory meal.

He smiled briefly up at me as though he shared this memory, and I swung my hips a little more pronouncedly as I left the room that time.

I stayed inside the outer door, so happy to just be there, soaking up every bit of it, and eventually Yeheshua came out to go, talking with Thomas close on the other side from me.

"We shall walk long and often Thomas, in places that you cannot even yet imagine," he said, and unexpectedly turned to me, "and I shall always be there for you, with you Mary. Know that in truth," he said, and my heart leapt in my breast, words for once failing me… and then he was gone, outside.

I looked around for a long second at Thomas whose eyes were shining after Yeheshua, then hurried outside myself, but the master was nowhere to be seen.

There were a few disciples outside, mostly women, who had clearly just witnessed Yeheshua passing, judging by the happiness in their faces.

Beor was still here by the door like a bulwark of steadfastness, filled to over-brimming.

"He went with Miriam and his mother, towards Lazarus' house; moving quicker than I could run … much! How did they?" and he shrugged, almost unsurprised by his own amazement.

I agonised for a second, wanting to go back inside and say hello or something, anything, to Thomas.

I poked my head inside the door and saw Thomas surrounded by several of the others. I think he looked over towards me as I turned to go back outside but I dared not look back again.

By the time I got to Lazarus' house Yeheshua had gone and Johannus was on the door this time, standing almost as a mirror image of his friend Beor. I ducked inside and joined the happy group of my friends inside, greeting and asking me after all that had happened at Simon's house.

I was happy to tell them that Thomas was back and everything I had heard and seen, and found myself being hugged in Miriam's arms, holding me close.

I could not admit it then, but some little thing in my heart wanted to weep as well, and silently I did, taking it for joy, despite the little stab of un-answered questions.

CHAPTER 13.

Herakopha rose into the air with both Lisla and Kaella on her back, which seemed the most friendly way for Kaella to converse with her hostess as they flew over the wonderful world of the lion people.

Ahead and around beneath them Kaella perceived many of the features she had sensed in the 'liquid tasting', the vast desert to their left, and bordering it a wide plain that became more and more covered with a mighty forest that rose into the hills, and still higher rolling hills, that stretched towards the very distant white peaks of mountain heights.

And under them the wide snake of a river moved languidly towards the world's darker side, away from the desert, and along its banks all sorts of herding animals could be seen, and leonines too, enjoying it.

Darker side, but not altogether dark for there was a shimmering of lights out to the right of their flight path, like strings of jewels, shining, scattered out beyond the line of shadow.

"This world turns, but not as your Gaia does," said Lilsa, answering one of my as yet unasked questions. "Our sun always shines out there, over the desert, and it rises and sets in an arc across that horizon. But it never shines directly on this other side, which is why we do our great labour there…"

"What labour?" asked Kaella.

Lilsa pointed, "look at these elongated hillsides we are coming to; do you see the lines of rock terraces constructed on their slopes?"

Kaella's sharp eyes could see what looked like lion-made pillared avenues, peppered with varying structures, running along the sides of the two opposing ridges, encompassing a massive ravine-like valley between them.

The valley stretched as far as her eye could see to left and right, and lions were busy here and there on their terraces of rock that were separated by green swathes of what Kaella took to be grassy hillsides.

Herakopha swooped a bit lower to see them more closely, revealing the scale of the stone-works edging the ravine, and gradually gliding down, down, down, inside.

"Fly left," said Lilsa, pointing along the valley. "Follow the escarpment to the desert; but we won't go far because it becomes intensely hot out there."

They flew gently, circling side to side as they watched several gangs of large lions working, carrying huge rock-blocks between them as though made of some light wood, humming deeply as they went.

One group were bringing them to a place where smaller, colourfully patterned felines were working on the blocks, cutting them to size, shaping some, and polishing others to an almost mirror smoothness.

"What will they do with those?" asked Kaella and Lilsa indicated the side of the valley, this time where a zig-zag of paths led right down into the wide cleft.

Herakopha circled towards the dipping paths and sure enough another gang of the mighty carrying lions were lowering blocks to the very deepest depths … that unexpectedly were bathed in brightness, somewhere within.

"Fly on up to that ledge ahead," said Lilsa; "it is a good place to view from."

Herahopha climbed to land neatly on the wide apron space laid out before a huge deep cavern where many lion people were relaxing and enjoying the food and drinks stored in the inner coolness.

There was a wide variety of sizes and colours of these lion folk and many were obviously fascinated by the visiting dragon and her riders. Some waved towards Lilsa and she responded in kind, but Kaella couldn't help but be drawn by the view onwards, out into the desert.

Pinnacles of dazzling golds and reds and yellows shone out there, with attendant purple shadows stretching back in line with the low-slung but nevertheless intensely bright sun.

Shading her eyes Kaella followed the line of the twin escarpments sinking gradually into the sand washed desert.

Lilsa was at her shoulder again. "Can you see, if you follow the lines of this valley far out into the desert, how a low ridge rises gradually up again to form an arch of hill going over the far horizon?"

"Is that a continuation of this …?" asked Kaella, turning back to look up the wide ravine to where the light sprung up here and there from down inside. She was amazed at the scale of the work that must be involved in what the lion people seemed to be constructing.

"This is one of many light-tunnels we have dug and lined with the polished stone-work, funnelling light from an always lit ring of the desert, right up through these valleys, to spill out into the shadow side."

As they were talking a lion figure exploded onto the apron, seemingly from nowhere.

Herakopha and Kaella both started, and Lilsa apologised to her guests. "Sorry," she said, "I should have told you how some of us travel here. We can all do it to some extent but the Hansuae are masters of the art. They have the ability to shrink their size and weight, and grow it back again, which turns a leap into something akin to flight."

There was a conversation being had along the terrace and another lion turned to go back the way of the arriving messenger, running with a mighty leap to disappear from view.

"Ha…" exclaimed Kaella, "I think I saw something of that shrinking, just as he disappeared."

"Yes, you can see it if you try" said Lisla, as a group of young lions brought out a selection of bowls for the guests to have refreshments.

"Drink your fill," said their hostess, "for the Elders told me that your way leads back along this ravine into the cold of shadow and thence up beyond the mountains to reach our sister world. You and Herakopha will need the warmth of these inside you."

Kaella somehow knew that she had further to go and so didn't question Lisla, but instead, enjoyed exploring the drinks that had been brought, and meeting those who brought them.

Older than the first youngsters she had met, these had full grown manes and deepset eyes, that gazed into her with friendly amusement.

And Herakopha too seemed to like them, and they her. A couple of them moving to her head and scratching the ridges for her where that great head met her neck.

Kaella knew she liked that, her dragon self.

In fact, Kaella felt really at home amongst these people, these extraordinary lion people…

*

And Miriam laughed, deeply and happily.

Mother Mary and her were walking together back towards Joseph of Arimathea's house, flanking the young colt donkey between them.

His long, quite furry ears was silky to the touch. She stroked one, and scratched the place behind it.

The master had been with them that day and both her and Mother felt full of wonder for the new world of possibility laid out before them.

Mother remarked how calmly Miriam was managing to deal with the turmoil, just when she had become married to Yeheshua; now all this, all this?

"Change yes, but so full of hope, for all;" the younger woman replied

Mary bent forward, looking into the face of Indy who whinnied softly. "He says: can you scratch him just above his shoulder?" she said seriously. Miriam laughed and tried to oblige.

It was Mary's turn to laugh for the donkey closed his eye in satisfaction. "He really did want that scratch," she said.

"I never doubted it," rejoined Miriam; "and I think he is almost grown ready to be ridden… and earn his grooming!"

Sella whinnied from behind them, as if in agreement, for she was being led by Yresmin, not far to the rear.

Yresmin had been watching, thinking how difficult it was to assess the colt. Sometimes he seemed quite young, but at others quite different; tall and strong and knowing.

That Yeheshua had asked for the colt to be given to Miriam was a wonderful choice she thought, stopping to lean against Sella as she did… and not only because Yresmin knew that Indy would serve her with the bravery and steadfastness as great as any other could; but something more besides. She couldn't quite put her finger on it.

She was just glad, and hoped to get the chance to be around and see.

A trick of the light, the sun shining low, throwing deep shadows across the road and the travellers on it; but for a moment she swore there was a third person there, a figure of light upon the donkey, or was it just the donkey swaying slightly between the two lovely 'human goddesses' Yresmin thought.

   She blinked and the vision was gone, and she hurried to catch up.

CHAPTER 14.

Most of us were going back to Galilee now that the Passover festive period was over.

I was thinking to travel up too, carrying on as normal, hoping for the master to take us along the new path, but not knowing yet how that would be; when and where he would go or come; maybe he didn't want us to think like we had before.

The whole world seemed affected, and we were unsure how to go forward either.

Miriam and mother were staying with Joseph a while longer, and there were one or two others staying in or around Jerusalem as well.

It seemed Thomas was one of these, being keen to sound out the attitudes of the authorities, and having lawyer training he was well placed for this, working alongside his uncle Tobias.

I felt divided, wanting to stay in Jerusalem but having already made arrangements to travel north; and why was I thinking about Thomas like a stupid girl?

I decided to walk to Jerusalem, to Joseph's house, to talk to Miriam, and as I was coming from Bethany I passed by the track down to the smithy, hearing an intermittent hammering.

'Would Johannus be staying in Jerusalem?' I wondered and almost went down to ask, but decided to press on. I would find out next time.

Tracing the road from Bethany through Bethphage towards the city, I looked in on Yresmin but she was not in.

Sparrows were chirping and playing in the bushes by the farm wall and I thought to take the cross-country route from Yresmin's barn. It was so quiet and low key compared to the last time I had come this way.

Martha had baked me some fresh spicy bread and packed this with a stoppered jar of watered wine to serve as lunch on the way, and when I stopped to sit at a place where I could see the hills of Jerusalem ahead, I was grateful for it.

I would have liked to have stayed longer with Lazarus, Martha and Mary; if it were not for there being things I really needed to sort out in Magdala; for they had invited me to, and I hoped I might one day.

The sun was pleasantly hot and I lingered enjoying the warmth until a wide cloud edged its way between it and where I sat, musing. Suddenly a bit of a wind blew into the cool shadow and I got up to continue on, wishing that I might bump into Thomas in the city.

Thoughts were tugging me this way and that as I walked through the city streets and, out of character, I looked into the temple outer court, just in case... but there was nothing that I wanted to do or see there.

Eventually reaching Joseph's house my enquiry was greeted by one of his servants, a girl called Celine, a few years younger than myself.

"No, the ladies are out at the moment. Would you like to come inside and take some refreshment? It must have been a long walk."

"Thank you; but do you know where they have gone?"

"They went with the master," she said, and my heart leapt, but I realised she was talking about Joseph, the master of the house. I think she realised my thought and she added, "I think they may have gone to his merchant house, in the city."

Again, I found myself a little torn, uncertain. "Thank you, I think I might go there myself then?"

"Are you sure? they should be back soon."

"Well alright; maybe I'll stay," and suddenly I thought of Yresmin. "Was the Nabatean lady with them?"

Celine nodded. "Yes, she was, and they took the donkeys too."

"Ahhh, yes; okay. I will go then; thank you for your kind offer, and the information Celine," I said, happy with my mind made up. If Yresmin was going back to Bethphage I would walk with her.

When I got to the city house, I found them sitting under an awning area on the flat roof, and was welcomed warmly to join them, and share the fruit and drink that Joseph had left them.

Yresmin took and squeezed my hand as I sat down on a cushion beside her, turning back to ask mother her question, "So all those years ago you were taught in the same temple that Miriam met the master?"

"Yes," Mother answered, "It seems like lifetimes ago…" then laughed. "Perhaps it was."

She looked content. "What will you be doing now, Mary?" she asked me after a pause. "Do you think we should be going back to Galilee yet?"

"I was thinking that I must, to check things through with Jacob, who said he would need my help, and I said I would go back, as soon as… "

"He asked me to meet him here in Jerusalem," said Miriam quietly, "so I don't think I will be going."

"I get the feeling there is going to be a lot more work to be done here yet," Mother mused "and he said something to me about we would need to rent a house, but I am not sure who he thought could be doing that."

"That decides it then," I said. "I can send funds once I have settled the accounts with Jacob. So, you all can look for a suitable house to rent here."

"You cannot go alone," broke in Yresmin, "I shall come with you." Then, "I would love to see Galilee and the sea and everything. So much happened there."

"We could ask Johannus to come with us." I said; "like old times."

"Hmmm… then be very careful. You know how many bandits are about," said Miriam, reminding me of the journey back from Kaddesh.

"I think they were trying to get to you Miriam," I said softly, seriously. "I am sure we shall be safe. I shall ask Johannus if we might borrow his uncle's horse again."

"And we can take Sella," offered Yresmin, "will you be all right to look after Indy, Miriam?"

'I think between us we should manage," put in Mother, laughing.

"You can stay at my place any time you need, with the stable and everything."

"Or with Lazarus," I added, "they were hoping that you might."

"If there is some money coming, we can start looking for a place," said Mother, "I am sure Joseph and Nicodemus will be able to help find somewhere suitable."

Suddenly things were moving.

Yresmin got up and said that we better start right away, and with parting hugs to mother and Miriam we were on our way back to Bethphage and Bethany.

*

Johannus had just about finished up for the day, working the forge for his old friend when to both their surprise Yresmin and I suddenly appeared.

Yresmin knew Beor quite well by this time too so it wasn't long before the blacksmith was enjoying the fun, perceiving that we had come for Johannus.

"Watch out now lad," he said, "or they will have you going off down the spice trail again before you know it."

"Well; maybe not the spice trail exactly" I replied.

"Oh; where then?" asked a startled Johannus.

"Just Magdala, and back. We would only want to borrow him for a little while Beor. Then you can have him back."

"Just as he was beginning to be useful again," grumbled the blacksmith.

"And hopefully bring your uncle's horse?" suggested Yresmin.

"Whoa, whoa," answered Johannus, "and I suppose you want me to do this tonight, and leave tomorrow? Just as I was getting comfortable here with the old fellow."

Beor was too quick for him, landing a clout around his ears before he could dodge it. "Not so slow or old as all that, you soft boy. Take him girls, by all means; a walk up north would do him good; sooner the better."

"Thank you," I laughed. "Well, the sooner gone the sooner back they say. Yes, it would be good to leave tomorrow, if possible. What do you think Johannus? Would it help if I came round and thanked you aunt and uncle for all their help as well?"

Johannus perked up. "I think Petrakis and Rebecca will still be there. They would love to meet you. Would you stay to eat as well? That would really please my aunt."

"And would you like to come and meet my family, Yresmin?" asked Beor, before I could answer Johannus, "and stay for some dinner? I know my wife would love to hear about your time and travels from Kadesh. She was amazed when I told her."

Yresmin happily agreed, and so I did to Johannus too.

CHAPTER 15.

Transferring the funds would be done by the olive oil merchant that we worked with in Capernaum. My brother had built a large, modern olive press to take all the excess from the groves around Magdala as well as his own, and had made the business very successful.

The merchant had offices in Jerusalem as well and he would get word there to release the agreed money to Joseph, once Jacob and I had worked it out.

Mother thought Joseph would want to put the money up but Miriam felt that he had already done so much for us since the crucifixion that he shouldn't be burdened with this.

"At least let's keep Joseph clear from our requests, but if Peter and James wish to approach him for help, so be it."

"Let's hope that the fishing is good then," said mother and Miriam smiled,

That evening I went with Johannus to his uncle's house as I had promised, not certain what to expect.

I had encountered his aunt and uncle briefly in the town but hadn't been formally introduced.

His aunt Jessica was like so many of the women of her age and she was happy as soon as I agreed to stay for a meal, which actually turned out to be really tasty.

Johannus uncle was much more perceptive than Johannus had led me to believe, complimenting me on our successful journey to Kadesh before offering us the use of his horse again, long before we got anywhere near asking him.

Petrakis was charming and clever too, and I had the feeling he was sizing me up as a business contact, even though his questions were almost all about Yeheshua and the turning of events.

"The message he brings is what he cares about most," I said, "which is why we are so keen to get a proper base here in Jerusalem, whilst the door is open."

"Mmm, yes I see that," said Petrakis. "He has really rocked Caiaphas and his lot. All eyes are on him and you; and will be for as long as this goes on."

I don't know why I hadn't been expecting to like Rebecca, but when we met I did.

Her wide set green eyes looked directly back from a clear face framed with silky black hair, and her smile in meeting me was genuinely warm.

I could see that their attraction to each other was mutual and I was glad for Johannus. "I am hoping not to borrow Johannus for too long," I said to her, and then to her father, "the worst problems we encountered on the road back from Kadedsh were between here and Galilee."

"What I heard you managed to do about the deep desert raiders was remarkable," said Petrakis in reply, "but I understand what you are saying about the forces that have been working here, right under the noses of the Romans."

"Yes, those that organised the capture, public humiliation and execution of

Yeheshua are still out there, though maybe unsure of quite what has happened," I agreed.

"Do you think he might come to Alexandria?" Rebecca surprised me by asking. "I think he would be very well received, especially by the circle of us that listen to the teacher Philo."

Petrakis nodded to that and I had to say I didn't know, but couldn't say it was impossible. "Maybe if he goes to Heliopolis which is where he first met Miriam, he might also go to Alexandria, I suppose;" and Rebecca's eyes glistened.

What was certain was that none of us had an idea of what the master was planning next.

*

Kaella felt the presence of the lion-folk as a kind of warmth; not the same as Herakopha's, who had a great heat within her that powered and sustained her, even in the greatest cold… not the same as that, for the lions' warmth was all the way through, coming through their fur and surrounding them too.

Maybe it wasn't exactly a physical warmth for Kaella felt it was a part of their communication… and as one lioness, Simeone, gave Kaella some sweet yet earthy liquid food, she somehow understood how it had been created. Saw a clear vitreous rock, collected from the deep desert, being pulled into hollow tubes, then coiled; and the loaded waters of earth or forest circulating round and round in brightest sunlight; till the fluids were concentrated into essences; deep in the ravine tunnels.

She understood how this created the lions remarkable sustaining food; and these ravines with their rocky shelves is where they lived in a comfortable balance of heat and shade as they made another tunnel from the desert's heat across to the cold, starlit side of their planet.

'Starlit side'… a vision came into Kaella of the other side of the planet she had glimpsed in flight, realising that as it pointed always away from the Sirian sun so it must always face out into the starry heavens, ever revolving, always changing… travelling around their sun, spinning along its course.

She had a great wish to see that starry side of the lion world, and Simeone understood, offering her another drink, this time of blue crystal water, and a pack of solid food which she indicated Kaella should take. 'For when you feel the cold' sent Simeone. And Kaella felt it like a warmth spreading through her as she tasted it.

Lilsa came over, joining their meal and Kaella had the feeling that Simeone was Lilsa's grown-up daughter; though their colouring was so different, their heart-minds were very close.

"Yes," spoke Lilsa, as if in answer; "and now you know the how, it is nearly time to see to where and why we bring the sun's light through our world."

Reluctantly Kaella said goodbye to her newfound friends, because she did indeed feel their warmth as friendship.

Once Lilsa had mounted behind Kaella, Herakopha leapt off the ledge and with strong rhythmic undulations of her back, worked her stretching wings, climbing higher to glide back up along the ravine, the sunlight at their backs.

Easy as swimming the dragon flew and glided up the length of the terraces, mile after mile of lion country, until the sun gradually set over the horizon behind them.

Then again Herakopha settled into more strong, rhythmic undulations, driving to go higher and still higher as the shadow spread on the land beneath, but she could keep their flight within the spread of the sun's rays.

From the height they reached Kaella could see lights sprinkled ahead in the darkness, and in the deepening violet sky, stars sparkling.

Eventually Herakopha began a shallow gliding dive towards the jewel-like spread of lights beneath and Kaella felt a great sigh of wonderment going through her.

The warmth of having Lilsa close behind her enabled her to enjoy the sight, despite the cold. She had never seen anything like it… perhaps most closely resembling stars being reflected in the sea, but magnified by some great magic.

Herakopha circled lower and they were able to make out details of the brightest lit area below, growing broader and more distinct as they floated downwards.

It was an immense bowel, drawn in pure light, the inside rim being faced with mighty polished slabs and the ring punctuated by patterns of huge monolithic crytsals that threw light all around, mainly towards a central, flat-topped mountain of crystalline rocks.

As they descended Lisla pointed out how the crystals themselves were floating on giant rafts revolving slowly in the flow of a broad river.

The dark crown of the central crag itself overhung its cliffs, so that the light was diverted back downwards upon a canopy of surrounding woodland trees and grassy slopes, where several streams of silvery water wound their way down dales and over waterfalls to cross the plain and reach the river.

"Where does the water of the hill come from?" Kaella asked, and Lisla pointed to the further, darker side of the hill.

"The light and water join over there," she said, "in kind of cauldrons that release copious clouds of steam, running up the cliffs there, and turning back into those icy streams within its crown."

Kaella could see the clouds of deepest indigo now, issuing from patches of redness underneath them, and as they floated down towards what appeared to be a landing place, she could see lions working over there. "The residue left after the water reduction enriches the soil," Lilsa said; "which is what the lions are collecting."

Lilsa dismounted lightly from the dragon and step-jumped easily down into the circle, despite the considerable height of the outer wall they had landed on.

She invited Kaella to follow, which she did, slightly more cautiously; but Herakopha leapt into the air and winged her way over to the cauldron heat, rising effortlessly skywards beside the rising steam.

"Watch her," said Lisla in Kaella's inner ear. "She is of 'the others'."

Having circled up the thermal as we might run down a hillside the great dragon alighted on the edge of the crown, neatly folding herself into the darkness of its contours, watching all below her.

Kaella's heart almost missed a beat, witnessing the other-wordliness of her companion, and felt an answering beat from her as well.

The cold had disappeared in the warmth of the landing aera and Kaella waved skywards as she followed her guide into the plains, towards where the light and water entered the ring together.

But any time for observations was cut short as their attention was drawn into a kind of music that was growing around them...which gradually Kaella realised was a chorus of welcome, ululating in waves from various groups of the animals and bird-kind gathered there; led by a few of the great ones that Kaella recognised as elephants.

"You are the first they have seen, to come..." Lilsa was saying to her, "from Gaia;" and suddenly Kaella felt overwhelmed with mixed honour and humility. She bowed deeply.

The music continued to rise as the waves travelled around and around the circle until it ended with one great shouted exultation into the sky.

"It is what we wait for... for humankind to come to claim their destiny amongst us all as well."

"When, when?" asked Kaella hopefully, but Lilsa shook her maned head.

"Not yet, not yet," she answered quickly. "We know that. They are too deeply embroiled in struggles with their own darkness. They themselves are the front line, the battlefield... and no-one knows how that will work out yet."

Thomas was working hard with Tobias and Nicodemus to follow up what had happened in the temple when Yeheshua had confronted Caiaphas and his nest of liars.

True, he wanted to make up for his doubt that the master could come back from death; but whatever the reason he showed a tireless energy and desire to snuff out those lies.

He was prepared to challenge anyone. His own experience brought him a fearlessness that reminded Caiaphas' pack of their last confrontation with Yeheshua, which none of them would forget.

Nicodemus and Tobias were able to open the way to the Roman Governor Pilate who was in fact grateful that the master Yeheshua had shown no desire to try to create an insurrection against the Rule of Rome.

Clearly, he had the popular backing to be able to have done so, and rebellion had been what the Jewish leaders seemed determined to prove him guilty of; yet Pilate now thought it much more likely they were simply scared that the young sage would displace their authority, not Rome's.

What if that had happened? Perhaps the best for everyone he thought, unhappy that he hadn't been able to do more.

He granted an audience to the lawyer Thomas whose calmness impressed him, reminding Pilate of Yeheshua himself when he had attempted to persuade the teacher to flee the city.

"What is your problem?" he asked Thomas bluntly. "What do you want of me?"

"Nothing on either count except that our voice should be able to be heard without fear of violent reprisals."

"What would your voices say that should bring about such fear and hatred?"

Thomas sighed. "Indeed, I do not understand that myself; but I have thought about it, especially since his crucifixion." Pilate winced inwardly but Thomas continued, "... clearly the Jewish priests fear that their power can be shaken by our master's teaching, but I don't see that. He never wished for anything that they have... only to help people appreciate the gift of their own life, of being alive."

There was a long pause, for the Roman governor had no answer to that. Eventually he asked another question, "... and what about his return from death? I have heard myself from the man who ended his suffering on the cross by running a spear to his heart. There was no coming back from that ..."

"Sir," replied Thomas, "I do not understand how any more than you, but I asked him and this is what he said to me: that his father God wanted him to demonstrate the supremacy of life above all else, even beyond death itself; that it continues and we do too in so far as we believe in life, in truth and his being witness to that."

"I can almost believe you Thomas, for I met with him too and tried to convince him to go away, avoid the hatred, but he would not. He knew what they would do, and I was powerless to stop it. But if he has really come back despite everything, should not the earthly powers fear what might happen next?"

"He could have avoided it, I believe that too," agreed Thomas. "But if he had wished ill of Roman rule there was so much else he could have done to undermine it, other than healing the sick and suffering. His teaching concerns the kingdom of the heart that we all belong in, nothing else."

"Well," answered Pilate, sighing deeply himself. "It seems to me that there is nothing but hope in that message." He paused, thinking; "I shall make sure that jealous priests do not have the law on their side in trying to silence his voice. If that is what you are asking from me, lawyer Thomas?"

"Thank you then a hundred times over. It seems you have perceived my hopes better than I do myself. That would be a great blessing to many who find themselves sore pressed at this time."

"I shall work on the best way to achieve it, you have my word on this," said Pilate,

And Thomas left amazed at the workings of truth, which he loved.

*

Yresmin loved to be with Miriam and Mother, knowing the great effort they put into seeing the master's vision play out, searching for the right place that could serve all the community around Jerusalem; and she went with Miriam to visit every follower of Yeheshua in person, not only to tell them of his return but to draw them in, to celebrate this moment of greatest joy.

She saw how hard Miriam worked to make sure that everyone understood the real meaning of Yeheshua's ministry, and to follow his loving example rather than thinking he had returned to lead them in some kind of righteous war.

There were plenty who still wanted to twist everything around, to stir up hatred; on both sides.

With Miriam, Yresmin saw how so many problems intruded on people, weighing them down, and she was glad to be able to help with some of these, finding herself looking after more children than she had ever imagined.

She had an unexpected gift for it, for there was something about her that they responded to; the natural authority of a high priestess perhaps, and the thought made her laugh.

Mother and Miriam often discussed what the possibilities of a real Christine community in Jerusalem might have; how they could help Yeheshua create it; and amidst one such deliberation Thomas came knocking on Nicodemus' door where they were staying.

Yresmin answered and let him in.

"Is Nicodemus in?" he asked.

"Not at the moment," she said, "but mother Mary and Miriam are."

"I have some quite good news that they might like to hear," he said as they climbed the steps, then asked, "is Mary here too; Magdalene?"

"She has gone back to Galilee... to release some funds for a place here in Jerusalem," she said; "which Mary and Miriam are looking for."

Thomas looked thoughtful and Yresmin continued, "I was going to go as well until I realised I could help more with what they are trying to do here; Miriam and Mother... they are taking on so much."

"Yes," said Thomas, "that is just what I felt too... about the work here being needed to be continued."

"Someone has arrived from Galilee I think, and is with Miriam and Mother now; but we can go in."

In Nicodemius' main room the disciple Jeremy was relating how he had dreamed of Yeheshua by the seashore, when Peter, James and John had been out fishing.

"The master said to me that the eleven would be coming back to Jerusalem soon and that whatever preparations that could be made, should be and then he would come as well."

"When did that happen?" asked Miriam.

"I don't know if it has. I was at the Zach's Inn in Jericho last night when this happened, and when I told him this morning, he thought I should come to find you as the dream suggested."

"Thank you so much Jeremy," said Mother; "this confirms everything we have been doing."

Thomas was silent, realising he was one of the eleven who should be there, to be able to be coming back.

"You can get up there if you are quick; borrow a horse," said Miriam to him, seeing clearly what he was thinking.

Thomas beamed, "I will; because I think I have done all I can here. I had an audience with Pontius Pilate and he promised to make an edict that there would be no violence allowed against us for giving our witness to what has happened."

"That is marvellous," said Mother; "too many people have been attacked."

"It was Nicodemus. He got me the audience, and Pilate already seemed to want to do it. I hardly needed to persuade him, if at all."

*

Aaron and I had finished making our arrangement.

He gave the third copy to a runner who took these short notes from various people, mostly merchants, taking the leather pouch to a particular Inn at Beth-Shean in the Jordan valley, where many roads joined.

Several runners met there every evening and sorted the notes for onward journeys, there being three riders who rode overnight down to Jericho together where the pouches were taken on again the next morning by other runners.

Bandits never bothered these messengers, having no use for the cryptic business notes, but occasionally they got the riders to deliver their own notes as well.

Aaron had given me the second copy of our arrangement and kept the last for himself, before settling back to take refreshment, when Johannus arrived, clearly bursting with news.

Johannus tried to conform to the greetings of expected business protocols but I stopped him quickly, asking him what his news was.

"The master Yeheshua has been seen on the shore with Peter, James and John and the others too," said Johannus, "and now they have gone into the hills. Many, many people have heard the news and are starting to gather by the sea, hoping to see him."

*

Kaella wandered around the great basin filled with warmth and life with Lilsa who showed her where the light entered through a wide tunnel, feeding down an avenue of deflection stones, allowing only a part to reach the floating rings of crystal monoliths where it blossomed out all around.

"It changes constantly as the position of the sun moves in relation to the other end; sometimes getting quite dark if the sun's angle is wide form the axis; but never completely"

Some of the diverted light went out through a few polished exits channels around the outer curving walls, whilst water fell splashing back in from some high cracks creating the streams that ran under foliage and alongside paths, some also winding down the side tunnels and out of sight.

"Where do those tunnels go?" asked Kaella.

"The light brought from the desert side is enough to feed many 'pockets of life'. This is the brightest but the tunnels lead to others that have all manner of different kinds of vegetation and places that we all enjoy. It is our pleasure to create them in this otherwise barren side of the planet."

"Barren perhaps but the stars are most incredible… it is almost that we are in amongst them here." And as Kaella said this, a flock of large, long-tailed birds circled around and disappeared in a flurry of sound.

"We are yes, and the stars have special relationships with each circle too, and with the animals and birds here… connecting us to all the heavens."

"It is marvellous what you have done… are doing," said Kaella. "I wish the people of Gaia could see this."

"They will, Kaella. One day, when they have discovered themselves in the true majesty of this universe. We look forward to being with them then."

"There are some that do, already."

"Yes, and each one is another spark. The fire will catch once the wood is dry and ready."

"That may take an age, or more."

"Yes, it might."

Thomas got up to Capernaum just in time to witness the preparations of impromptu celebrations for the reported return of the master.

Yeheshua had asked that half of the fish from the great catch he had helped his apostles land be given out to the many people who were starting to gather at the site on the shore where he so often used to preach.

The same apostles that had gone with him into the solitude of the surrounding hills.

Celebrations started early with people setting up in their selected spots before joining together to prepare food or make music and sing songs.

Thomas wove his way around the many little encampments on the shore and could hear the songs of Miriam springing up here and there... before he was irresistibly drawn to the favoured path towards the hills. One they had often walked together.

He was pretty certain the master would come back this way. The others would for sure anyway.

*

When Johannus and I got to the festive site we were struck by the feeling that something very precious was happening, and no-one wanted to spill a drop.

Someone pressed a plate of deliciously cooked fish into my hands and another gave me a loaf to break some bread from, which I did before passing it on to Johannus.

We were sitting with a family group from Nazareth that I hadn't met before but felt that I had. Jonathan, his wife Sarah, two small children, his mother and another, who turned out to be Sarah's brother.

Suddenly the master was close by, talking casually to people eating, though we hadn't seen him coming; I don't think anyone did.

Before I had hardly taken this in, he had turned to me. "Mary, I want to tell you of this house I saw, on the outskirts of Jerusalem. I think it would suit our needs perfectly."

"Where?" I asked, astonished. "Mother and Miriam are looking for somewhere."

"At the end of the path where Beor led us into Jerusalem from Bethany on that day; over the pastures."

"I think I know," said Johannus. "A rambling old deserted farmhouse; Beor has mentioned it."

"Yes," Yeheshua said, "that's the place. I have been thinking we might be able to get that."

"It would be really good if we could; the eleven will be coming down; and soon it will be Pentecost."

*

Johannus and I didn't want to waste any time getting the master's message to Mother and Miriam in Jerusalem, the mood of Yeheshua himself being so full of optimism for the times that were coming.

It was impossible not to feel it as well when he was there with us, stirring us into action.

I was thinking of finding Thomas to ask to borrow his horse as I was sure he would be coming back with the others, and I realised just how much I wanted to see him.

Easy not to think about it when we were with Yeheshua.

I sighed inwardly.

Which is how it must be for Thomas now.

I understood that.

Instead, I said to Johannus, "Aaron has always been offering me the use of his daughter's pony; a sturdy animal by his account; but apparently she has had no use for it since she has got married. Let's go and ask him if I can borrow it."

"Of course, of course," said Aaron. "I am sure she would want you to have her."

"Well, if we get along, I shall make Sarah an offer for her. She would be useful and I am wanting to get around more. What is her name?"

"Sarah called her Freedom," Aaron laughed, "but I just call her Freida."

I saw Thomas coming back into Capernaum with the other apostles, but Yeheshua was not with them.

I tried not to dwell on it as Johannus and I rode down to Beth-Shean, from where the overnight post riders left for Jericho.

It was hard to be riding away when I wanted to be with him so much.

CHAPTER 18.

Thomas and I hadn't had the chance to really speak since our meeting in Tobias's garden. Maybe he had tried, but been unsuccessful, even as I had.

I had felt close to him all the time he had been away, and still so now; but we just seemed to miss out being together.

Events kept overtaking us, but they were wonderful events. Perhaps it was just anxiety but I was late and my monthly times were generally very regular.

Any such thoughts vanished when we met up again with Mother and Miriam at Nicodemus' house, the morning after a stop with Zacchius.

They were excited to hear all that had happened in Capernaum and more so to get the message about the house they were looking for.

Having his personal direction was like being right there with him and we wasted no time to go and have a look for it.

Johannus thought he could find where it must be but when we came to the right road we couldn't find anything that could have inspired Yeheshua's comments; nothing.

There was one deserted old house whose windowless back-wall ran along the side of the road to a rather broken looking the gate which we peered over. It appeared to be a severely dilapidated place; not very promising at all.

Johannus wouldn't be put off so easily, determined to find the path that came across the pastures. He searched up and down until he located an almost invisible sheep track that came out onto the road through some scrubby trees.

"It would be more obvious from the pastures side," he said, trying to sound convincing.

We waited on the road watching him disappear into the trees, only to as quickly re-appear and beckon us enthusiastically to follow.

We looked at each other dubiously, but Miriam shrugged and started off gingerly along the narrow track. Mother and I followed.

Johannus had found a place where we could see through the scrub to what must have been the other side of the house from the blank wall we had seen on the road, and indeed we could see that there were a row at least three decent looking windows on the upper storey. Was that it?

"It does look better than from the other side," agreed Mother.

"The roof dips badly at the other end," said Miriam .. "and that outbuilding is no more than a ruin," I added.

We retraced our steps to the road. "Why don't we go and check with Joseph and Nicodemus?" suggested Miriam. "They will know who to ask; and if it is for sale we shall find the agent. I think it must be the place."

"You two go Miriam," I said. "It doesn't need the four of us for that. Johannus and I will go and see some of the others; Beor at least should know if this is the one."

"Good idea Mary," smiled Mother and Miriam nodded, "Yresmin has been visiting lots of people with me, and Beor knows everyone." "Let's meet back here midday tomorrow then," suggested Miriam, "and if you find anyone who knows about repairing buildings, bring them too," laughed Mother.

*

Kaella knew it would be time soon to leave the world of the lion people and was saddened by it. Herakopha however, seemed to have seen further than her somehow.

Lilsa read her mood and came over to sit beside her.

"It is almost time for you to journey on," she said; "but before you go there is one more place you need to know, for Herakopha to make the leap; the place where our ancient elders started what we do; and yours too."

"Is it very far?" asked Kaella.

"Not as your dragon can fly and Herakopha will be drawn there like a bee the flowers. It is at the base of the great mountains of ice and snow that you could see. Come let us eat some of the food you brought and get ready;" and a little tremble of anticipation ran through Kaella.

Herakopha rose out of the circle of brightness, up into the star encrusted purple-black sky and from a height Kaella looked down to a dark plain with scattered patches of blue and green.

Herakopha needed no directions, drawn inexorably towards the awe inspiring heights that crowned the planets central ridge, half its slopes that faced sunward sparkling in clearest light, those that turned away glowing in icy blue and indigo.

Freezing updrafts of ice filled winds drawn in from the blackness were ever building up those shadowed slopes, even as the sun's heat across the desert melted the sheer front face in a myriad of cascading rivulets, falling to join and fill the rivers that fed the planet's hills and valleys, forests and plains.

Long ridges rose before the towering ice mountains and Herakopha's skill in flight just breasted the first high line.

The ridge face was scored with deepcut ravines and its profile punctuated by ancient worn-down peaks, the greatest of which were topped by attendant clouds, and Herakopha soared towards the base of one of these that Lilsa spoke to her of, and as they crested the ridge a sight of amazement greeted Kaella, even in this planet of wonders.

Beyond the ridge, and between them and the ice heights stretched a wide blue sea that had been completely hidden from where they had approached, and it's incredible luminescent beauty was like nothing that could be imagined or expected.

Herakopha glided in to alight on the lawn-like slope that stretched down from the mist enshrouded peak, down to the shore of the sea below.

The shock of finding the place was that there was so much light coming up from the sea and which was what caused the ice slopes beyond to shine ice blue as well; lit without an apparent source.

Kaella felt immediately this to be the home of the lion elders, and the rocks that faced the seashore confirmed this in the grandeur of ancient carved columns climbing up out of sight, but mostly she could feel it in the presence of the place itself.

Gazing out over the sea, Lilsa was explaining it to her through the touch of her own presence. "The light you see, filling the waters and the cliffs themselves comes through the first mighty tunnels that the elders cut through from the desert, in earliest times."

"Light that melted the sheets of ice to make this sea over time, till now it has accomplished the great balance that you can see, and fills the waters still."

Lilsa could sense her questions… "Some little water flows back to the desert side but most of the tunnels are capped with the clear vitrified glass from the deep desert; and it is from here too that the water comes that you saw flowing through the ring of light, and into all those other places beyond."

Herakopha was craning her neck out towards the sea and Lilsa laughed; "she senses the great whales and other kinds that swim out there. She hears their song in her own great body and I can hear or feel her answer too."

Without thinking Kaella joined with Herakapha, merging into that great one, becoming a part of Heraikaliphon, standing arched, all four legs ready to spring and mighty wings to stretch for her to soar out over the sea that glowed with light, calling with life.

"Wait!" commanded a great clear thought within Heraikaliphon, that brought her up short and drew all her excitement into focussed calmness. "You shall fly the sea and the mountains beyond as well, but first stay a while, we need to talk."

Kaella was back standing on the grass looking to see where that thought-voice had come from, half expecting one of the great lion elders to be there. None were. Instead, there was a long-beaked, black-headed, white-bodied bird standing almost upright on a small knoll, staring at her from one bright yellow eye.

But in the form of Heraikaliphon she had recognised that voice with it's ancient depths that nevertheless sprung always fresh and true as a mountain spring… of purest thought.

"Yes, thought I am and joined here with bravery and strength," it said in her.

"And these you need in some measure for the final stretch…"

Behind the bird, the mist curled into a myriad of swirling shapes, like a vision of another mountainous world in smaller scale.

If Kaella expected lions, she saw rather dragons flying there. Herakopha was staring out of one of her great golden-green eyes at it as well.

"Yes; that is our sister world and as Herakaphon drinks in the vision so you must drink from the waters of the lake, the sea below, to give you strength to take you there. Go with Lilsa and I will talk with Herakaphon here.

Lilsa offered an arm saying, "come, let me…" and Kaella took it, finding

518

that bounding down the slope with Lilsa was astonishingly easy and fun.

It took them only seconds seemingly, but Kaella found it made her very thirsty. Gratefully she knelt down where a little stream was channelling off amongst the shore-side rocks, and cupped her hands in the light filled water, bent her head and drank from them.

And again, a long draught.

The water more than quenched her thirst, it filled her once and beckoned her to take more to feel it saturate every part of her with its strength and fullness.

Happy she sat back on her haunches and looked across the surface of the sea-lake to where mountain ice-cliffs rose impossibly high on the other side.

"Yes," spoke Lilsa in her, who also had bent to drink, "Those are the heights you will fly when joined with Herakopha. Your spirit has the strength and she knows the pull to where she has to go. Together you will fly... where you both must go."

CHAPTER 19.

Yresmin was excited when Johannus and I told her about all that had happened and that we had found the house that Yeheshua had told me of in Capernaum. She could hardly wait to go and tell Beor.

"Yes, there are others we can go and see," she agreed as we set out. "Beor will probably know lots of people would like to be involved, don't you think?"

"Yes I do," I said, "and I think that's just what Yeheshua has in mind; to get people involved."

It was, I was sure; and it was as though everyone had just been waiting for this moment; to be able to join in and help with something; something we could all be doing for Yeheshua and ourselves too.

Beor was already working his forge as his unexpected guests arrived and when I told him of the house Yeheshua had said Beor would remember, he slapped his thigh with a tremendous thwack.

"Yes, yes of course," he said, "that is just what has been bothering me but I couldn't think of… he said to me to remember the place, when we were off to Nicodemus' house, that fateful day."

"Could you take us there, tomorrow? or will you need to do things here?" I asked, knowing full well wild horses wouldn't stop him.

"No, no; there is nothing that won't wait a few hours."

"I'm sure Martha and Mary will want to come," I said. "I shall go round to tell them tonight."

"There is another couple I would like to tell," said Yresmin. "Miriam and I were with them the other day. "Her name is Sanyata, and she has three children. Her husband is a stone mason."

"I know them, his name is Jason," said Beor. "He hasn't been very well recently, but I would value his opinion on the place. Never thought we might actually buy it."

"I will drop the horse back to my uncle tonight," said Johannus. "Maybe Petrakis and Rebecca will want to come. They seemed so interested."

An hour or so later we were back at Yresmin's.

Petrakis cannot come because of business, but Rebecca had been glad to be asked.

I heard from Beor that Sanyata and her husband would come with the children, and a widow called Grelsa that Sanyata had said needed to get out more.

Quite a mixed party met mid next morning at Simon's house to start our trek off across the hills on a sunny day in early summer.

Sanyata's children running ahead with Simon's dog, but not too far; we could see them.

And suddenly we saw the farmhouse, nestled on the edge of the town, slightly out of place amongst the expansion of the city, its fields invaded with newer houses.

"That's it," said Beor, "the one with the old byre to the right and the higher storage bits on the left, set around the yard"

It was certainly the same as we had seen last night and we stood and gazed for a few seconds before hurrying on down the hill, through a sheep gate coming out beyond a wall of tangled vines and scrubby bushes,

The closer we got the more dilapidated it seemed, almost as if to put off potential buyers like us.

It was Jason who was the first to speak. "… could easily do something for those," he said, pointing to the overgrown and deserted looking buildings on the left, "if I were able to take from the byre that has had its day I would say."

"The main house looks in need of repairs too," said Beor; "but I believe there is one long room above, that is still rather nice and in good order." I wondered how he knew, but said nothing.

An undergrowth of prickly pears and impenetrably thorny bushes blocked off the approach from where had once been the farm fields, so we carried on along the same track we had the evening before.

There inside the gate the old farm stood empty and forlorn, having outlived its original purpose and descended into near desolation.

My heart sank as I tried to imagine the work to be done to bring it back, but I seemed to be in the minority. Beor was pointing out how strong the main gate hinges still were and Jason the stone labourer how only half the roof would need redoing, and that many of the fallen tiles could be re-used; once the roof timbers were replaced.

"I know just the man for that," said Simon; ".. repaired my house and is very clever at re-using bits and pieces. He has quite a store of wood himself and could use some from the byre as Jason would the stone."

"My dad would love to see this… " said Rebecca unexpectedly. "He loves seeing things like this brought back to life. I can imagine him wanting to help buy materials that would be needed."

As we were talking on about the possibilities, Mother and Mary came up from the town way with a man in tow.

"This is Isaac, the owner's agent," mother said by way of introduction, clearly surprised but not at all unhappy by the size of our reception party. "He will show us around and answer any of our questions."

Isaac was keen to take us to see the room that Beor had spoken of as 'rather fine', and indeed it was. "Yes, this will be perfect for the master and the twelve," said Miriam, "we needed this to be able to welcome him here."

There was plenty more to see as well, both in the main and surrounding buildings. Unused and half ruined, the agent seemed almost embarrassed, but I was beginning to be able to see through the eyes of those like Jason and Beor, who went around touching this and lifting that, seeking out the sound amongst it all.

"It is a good price, a fair price," the agent was saying, but no-one said anything, knowing it was not for us to comment. I went to Mother and Miriam to ask about it.

Miriam smiled at me a little, holding my arm, whilst Mother stroked her chin and looked gravely at Isaac. "The well needs to be working, not full of rubbish," she said, "to get near the price you ask for."

"Of course, of course," replied the reddening agent, slightly flustered by so many of us showing knowledgeable interest in his dilapidated charge. "That is one thing I can give absolute assurance of as I have kept a check of it myself. Please come, let me show you."

The well was nothing remarkable to look at but was appropriately shut off, having a locked wooden entrance lid under the pile of stones that covered and hid it.

With help from Jason and Beor, the lid was soon opened and the cool smell of the water deep beneath unlocked.

There was a cross spar with a rope attached and a bucket on the other end, now hanging on a peg between the two rocks that held one end of the spar.

"Look, look," said Isaac, letting the bucket down till we heard the splash of it hitting water. It took a few seconds until Isaac felt the tug he sought and started raising the small bucket again, hand over hand.

"Try some," he said, selecting Beor's outstretched hands as the best candidate to pour some into.

The smith took the water almost reverently to his lips, and turning to Mother and Miriam pronounced it good.

Pleased, the agent was nodding from one to the other, and Mother sighed a little. "Good, good," she said. "Then I think we may be able to come to a deal Isaac, if you are able to help us in some way over the cost of renewing the roof?"

"Only half the roof, dear lady," replied the now happy looking agent, "and my client has allowed me some discretion in this matter. Please come back to my offices and we shall see what can be arranged."

Miriam whispered in my ear. "Would you and Johannus be able to go with mother, whilst I stay here? I really want to have a better look at it, and catch some time with everyone else here…" then, when I happily assented, she checked whether it was alright with Isaac if they started clearing it up a bit, whilst there were many hands to help.

He looked a bit startled, but when Mother said that I was the one who had arranged the funds and that I was coming to the office, he could do little but agree. "All right, if you wish, and then I will bring you down the keys later, or hand them over to you ladies perhaps," he said including me into his business circle for the first time.

"Some tea perhaps," I said taking an interest in negotiations, "it has been a walk over the hills to reach the house."

"Of course, of course," he said, relieved to be moving into familiar territory. "Let's return into the city then."

CHAPTER 20.

A few hours later we returned to the farmstead as the proud new owners.

The news had obviously spread fast for there were quite a few more people there than when we had left, and a tremendous amount of clearing up work had already been done.

Now almost everyone seemed to be gathered in the shade of a large tree that overhung the back wall from the field; sitting around Miriam, who was speaking.

Johannus had been a little reluctant to leave Rebecca to come with us but I noticed that she was near to Miriam, listening closely.

The scene had a feeling of great familiarity to me. It could have been Yeheshua.

Johannus made his way quietly to squeeze in beside Rebecca; Mother and I stayed at the back.

Miriam was answering… for the question of whether or not Yeheshua would now establish his kingdom had been broached again.

"Not like that," she said. "Not a new Judah or something, taking on the Romans. His is the kingdom of the heart; this is where heaven is, can be for everyone."

"This is about you; your life," she continued, "and when we live it well it becomes a fine thread in the story of this world too, that carries on. And a time will come when these threads will make a beautiful and worthy garment and then it shall be said His Kingdom is come to Earth. This comes from us, from living it, every day."

There was real freshness in the way she spoke, reaching the nub of what our hearts needed to hear.

"… So here today we have started something new, a place where we can find about that way of living, and help each other too. Together we can make things so much better and everything that has been done here already shows that."

She pointed to the other corner of the yard, where Salome and Martha were stirring a large pot over a fire that had been made for that, and had just given the 'ready' sign across to Miriam. "Come, let us eat of what we have brought, that Salome and Martha have cooked."

And as I watched, Rebecca turned, stretching out, and smiled directly into Johannus face, that lit up in response. He reached out a hand and she took it in both hers, eyes laughing.

*

Heraikaliphon stretched her wings wide and launched herself into a glide that took her down the grassy slope Kaella had just walked back up, and out across the surface of the light-filled waters.

Sounds and song and trills rang up, some almost bird-like and others deeper and longer than any such, and Heraikaliphon, out over the deeps, swung to her right to wing her way along the length, parallel to the shore, following the trail of the magic sounds.

For many long entranced moments the great dragon flew, feeling the breadth and depth of the calls, recognising the notes of the planet herself coming through, those that had guided her flight hence so easily.

Now she swept around in a giant arc to her left as she sensed the approach of a great ice shelf ahead and knew that she must gather all her energy to fly, climb the heights, up and up to where another call was reaching her, from the rock and snow and ice and clouds of the greatest of mountains above.

The warm breezes coming off the sea sped her easily up the blue ice cliffs that plummeted down from the heights, and beyond these, further mighty slopes of snow and rock beckoned the great dragon to try her strength, find her glory.

Roiling at the highest, furthest ends of these slopes were great banks of cloud and mist such as the ibis bird had revealed, and the Kaella within knew this was the way, the focus of all the strength and power she as Heraikaliphon possessed. Harder and faster she arched, to beat her wings, propelling her ever upwards.

The searing cold of the clouds froze her breath but the great inner heat of the dragon-being thrust her onwards.

Ice needles bit into her, enveloping her in their stinging net, but she endured, relishing their enlivening effect, driving her higher, towards the brightest, darkest void. She jumped.

Needles of ice turned to needles of sound, unendurably high, impenetrable…

Somewhere the words came to Kaella "… only with humility can you enter in;" and they hit her like past and future colliding; her father's words and those of a Hebrew sage, and she accepted, realised, fell back, dropped, fell, shrank…

Falling, falling, the wall of impenetrability cascading down with her like mighty rushing water, she recoiling, returning, seeking within, so much smaller, becoming like nothing, a tiny drop of conscious nothing, within the womb, her own womb; and just one moment… one more… and the rushing water eases in that, and softens into a great flurry, all about her, of wings; the dragon wings of Herakopha who is beneath her, catching her, gliding into the softening mists ahead, between massive trees in a canyon filled with rocks and jumping streams that steam up into the mist… and moss, and deep rich smells, and soft branches all around, where the dragon comes to land.

*

Thomas knew. He knew when Yeheshua talked of a house with a wide long room for them to stay, close by Jerusalem, that it was one that the women there would have found now.

He had noticed Yeheshua taking to Magdalene… he had been looking for her too, but then she was gone; and Thomas knew she would be taking the information to Miriam and Mother Mary.

The next day he turned to Peter and John, together with James too. "Let me go ahead to Jerusalem and make sure of this house the Lord has told us of, to go to. And I will come back again with news of it."

Peter nodded and John said, "we shall start off soon, so will meet you on the road. Look out for us."

Thomas took the horse that he had hired through his uncle Tobias and made haste to get down to Jerusalem.

He inquired at Nicodemus' house and then Joseph's when he found Nicodemus to be away from home.

Joseph told him of the house that Magdalene had enabled the purchase of, and gave him directions to get there.

Thomas found the place and was amazed. It was quite late on but there was still enough light to see how scrupulously clean the yard was… and wondered how the inside must be.

There were a few people still there, doing jobs or sitting by the fire in the yard but Thomas couldn't see Miriam, Mother or Magdalene. Instead, he found Johannus inside the main building.

Johannus greeted him warmly. "Come in, come in; are the others here as well?"

"No, I have come ahead to check what is happening, and then get back to tell them. The Lord has told them of a large upper room. Is there such a room?"

"Yes indeed; it was the only part of the house in pretty good condition. We haven't had to do much to it. Come up and see."

The room took up most of the first floor of the main house.

Thomas looked up and down, noticing the southerly windows looking out towards the pastures and hills beyond. The floor was soundly made and had a few rugs scattered along the length. The walls were freshly cleaned but there wasn't much more to see, hardly a stick of furniture yet.

Johannus almost read his thoughts. "We don't know what furniture will be needed, but we have a carpenter making up some pallets and Yresmin with other ladies making mattresses. Good for sitting and lying on both."

Thomas nodded, almost dumbstruck. He could hardly believe how quickly this had been brought together. "You all have done an incredible job," he said, then "have the women all gone?"

"Yes," said Johannus, "you must have just missed them." He had the feeling Thomas wanted to know more, but Johannus didn't know who had gone where. He had been asked to stay as caretaker and had agreed willingly. So, he said nothing.

"The others are coming, will be on the road tomorrow. Can I stay here tonight and set off back in the morning?"

"Of course," said Johannus. "Many people have been drawn to help here; but this upper room will always be quiet and ready for the twelve… or eleven rather."

Thomas spent time looking around all of what had once been a thriving farm, but now had found a greater purpose. There was still one small field attached at the back, though all the rest had gone. It was almost a paddock or once an orchard maybe; a good space for tents or such like, Thomas thought.

The rest of the outbuildings needed much work doing, though a lot of rubble had seemingly already been cleared judging by the great but orderly pile in one corner. Thomas could see that it would have posed a bit of a quandary for most buyers, but was proving wonderful for us.

He slept in a small room on the lower floor, where Johannus had set a spare pallet.

In the morning he waited as long as he dared, hoping Magdalene would arrive before he had to get going. He found some food and heated some water to make sweet tea, but eventually knew he had to get going.

"Give them all my love," he said to Johannus, "it is amazing what they have done here. I have to go and let the others know, as I promised."

*

I heard from Johannus that Thomas had been there the night before, and he seemed to be studying me for my response.

I must have blushed, for he looked away quickly. Mentally I kicked myself again, but I really wished I had come down earlier. It wasn't Thomas' fault and I had the strangest feeling Johannus wanted to tell me something if he could; but I wasn't about to tell him anything.

"How long before the eleven arrive do you think?" I said instead. "Will Yeheshua be with them?"

"I don't know," said Johannus, "but we must think that he will be. How do you think we should prepare."

"That is why I am here," I answered, "and Miriam is arranging with Martha and Mary for as many things as he might need to be here for him, just in case he stays."

Together we explored further into all the house, seeing if there could be a separate part for Yeheshua or whether it would be better to screen off one end of the upper room for him. We decided on the latter, thinking cloth screens would be the best way. A tented area within the upper room, with its own window.

I went off to Bethany without delay, to make recommendations to the others at Lazarus' house.

Mist surrounded everything in the valley and the great dark pines faded up into it, leaving wispy patches around their bases and across the rock-strewn floor; patches that thinned or thickened beguilingly as the sunlight tried to find a way through.

Herakopha had gone into it and Kaella let her go, for it had the call of dragons to it. She didn't mind at all being alone, if indeed she was; for every part of the wood was full of nature's life.

Water ran in rivulets everywhere, round and over rocks, between which reedy growth poked, sporting little yellow flowers.

A dragonfly rushed past, darting and hovering here and there until it skimmed off to find a bigger pool.

Kaella spied a large flat-topped rock that looked a dry place to sit and she worked her way across to it, enjoying the rough prodding of the rocks and the cool of the water on her feet. She reached down and cupped her hands to drink some, rich and earthy, before scooping up more to splash over her face and neck.

She had some food left from that which Lilsa had given her and she took it out of her little pack.

Thoughts seemed superfluous sitting there listening to the water coursing in its myriad little falls down the steep valley-side behind, lulling the mind.

Sudden noisy bird song broke through Kaella's reverie, and she roused herself.

She knew that there must be a purpose to being here which she thought unlikely to be achieved by going to sleep, so resolved instead to climb the cliff behind and get above this enchanting mist, if she could.

There were a pair of long laced sandals in her little pack that would serve the purpose.

She loved to test the power of her legs to crest such slopes as these, often following wild goat paths and delighting in the flowering plants she could recognise along the way or anything else to catch her interest.

The mist was swirling and steaming off rocks above the valley floor; and nearer the sunlight the tang of the minute water droplets made every other smell more vibrant somehow; the moss, the tree bark, pine needles and cones, wetness and earthiness, and life in everything. Then... eyes in the mist; here, there, then gone.

A dozen or so tiny birds with long black tails flitted from branch to branch as if calling Kaella to rise higher as they were, travelling along to the tops of the pines.

Soon these tall dark pines gave way to lighter larch and birch before the mist dissipated completely and there was just bright sunshine streaming through the branches of sparse woodlands.

Familiarity abounded; trees, birds, flowers, everything; this puzzled some part of Kaella but lulled her too.

Higher still the trees grew fewer and stubbier, replaced by boulders and bushes that Kaella not only recognised but that flanked a way along the side of the hill she knew very well.

Around the large outcrop ahead would be her cave…

And there was no cave; which jarred her mind to wonder what made her think there would be? This was somewhere different, but it was almost playing with her, confusing her.

She sat, steeped in sunshine, on the large apron in front of where her cave should have been but wasn't and looked out across the now broad valley emerging out of the remains of the mists.

The pines had given way to broad-leaved oaks, wild cherry, beech, maple and many others, chestnut, elm and dark doughty yew trees, and beyond the woods gave way to meadow-land and fields she felt she should know; but not in this here, this now.

What was really strange was she felt there were memories of things yet to come laid here, as well of those already remembered. Confusing and disorientating.

She opened her pack again and finished the food and wished she had brought some water.

Suddenly a great commotion grabbed her attention.

From somewhere higher up the hillside there was a noisy beating of mighty wings just as from behind a dense copse in the valley below a large dragon rose into the air.

Long and lean and red-gold with arching back it swam up into the air with remarkable ease just as the sky disappeared above Kaella. She ducked quickly and the golden-green body of Herakopha slid overhead to accelerate down towards her counterpart in the valley beneath.

Straight under the larger red-gold beast she swooped and he turned and dived after her, beating hard to try to match her speed and she flipped and turned and rose high in her turn, stretching and arching, catching the wind and sailing with it.

Kaella watched entranced as they sported off into the distance, never having seen two dragons playing together.

She was quite thirsty now and decided to retrace her steps to where the water was cascading down into the mists, but as she followed the path it stubbornly led upwards and differently to how it was before, yielding up none of the streams Kaella sought.

Instead, the path led to a rustic wooden gate, sturdy with uprights on either side and an overhead cross-beam between them carved with clouds that seemed to be shifting and moving slightly, like real ones.

Kaella studied them for a while and found she really liked them, so decided to go on through.

It swung open easily to her touch.

The path became wider and better defined, with steps cut here and there into the rock and stones packed in where the broken structure of the hill needed them.

Gradually the way flattened out, the steps becoming shallower and wider, with more and more areas of intervening gravel, until just ahead there loomed a dark green close-cut hedge flanking a stone archway that the gravel path ran up to.

The archway contained high double-doors, made mainly of wood but fitted with bronze caps, hinges and crosspieces beaten into remarkable patterned surfaces, fascinating to the eye and smooth to the touch.

There was no handle Kaella could see so she pushed at the gate doors, tentatively and then much harder, but they remained firmly shut.

Looking around she found at length a thick woven silky rope hanging down half hidden in a slot in the hedge, and ending in a big knotted tassle.

She pulled on this to no effect; then harder but still nothing, till at last her thirst overcame her caution and she pulled it down strongly with both arms.

The rope finally moved convincingly, sounding a deep gong inside the hedged walls and simultaneously the gates swung wide inwards to reveal the garden within.

For inside there was a most remarkable garden, set out as if created just by natural beauty, neither formal nor at all wild but a harmony of rock and streams, shapely trees and flowering bushes, grassy banks and swathes of bright flowerings all set about a small lake that had at its centre an island pavilion of stone and wood, and metal fastened swathes of cloth across wide window gaps.

Kaella moved cautiously into the garden, looking around as the quietness encouraged her.

Another higher sounding gong rang over by the lake and the figure of a girl appeared, or rather moved upon the path beside it. Lovely, with straight black hair falling to her waist where her loose gown was fastened with a wide embroidered girdle, the girl moved gracefully towards Kaella, hands out, palms together, bowing slightly in greeting.

"Welcome; my name is Polliendra," she said, and Kaella sensed the aura around her.

'Dragon,' echoed her mind of its own accord and then… 'Daughter of the most ancient.'

Kaella had a question in her mind as yet unasked but Polliendra answered. "Nothing is quite as it seems, no; for we walk the borderline between reality and illusion."

Kaella returned the greeting of folded hands and bowed head, "I am Kaella," she said.

The girl smiled, "or maybe Heraikaliphon as well?" and something that Kaella hadn't realised was all tensed up, relaxed inside. She smiled back.

"Everything has changed," she said, "and I think that is what has brought me here."

"Come," she said, "there is need for you to see…" and she turned to glide to where Kaella now saw the arch of a graceful bridge stretched out from the garden to the island in the lake.

She followed the girl and as they approached Polliendra held out her hand. Dark eyes looked deep into Kaella's.

"Don't be afraid, just keep hold of me," she said, and Kaella gave her trust and her hand both.

As she stepped onto the bridge, the scene changed and changed again, one vision following upon another.

She looked on unafraid, for though all else changed the bridge remained, and fresh images came more rapidly as they advanced. Some she knew from her own past and many were beautiful, though some others violent and chaotic.

The constant changing became a source of difficulty for Kaella for a kaleidoscope of reactions swirled inside her bringing on a great nausea and feeling of falling.

She fought it and held hard onto Polliendra but the nausea contained a debilitating fear and this started to lick about her in the visions, like a fire.

She needed to let go but to hold on as well; conflicting needs that fed the fear and increased the nausea. She had to let go, but couldn't.

She felt her mind falling away, rushing towards and into the cauldron of her fears… but her hand remained gripped in Polliendra's and suddenly she was being lifted, lifted clear of the sick cacophony of visions and into a wide dark void, immense and immovably still, the hugeness of space itself.

Kaela was a tiny point in the vastness.

Around the very edges were a thousand, thousand, pinprick stars, all emanating the needle points of sound that together made a symphony of surprising, random music.

Within the boundary of those stars stretched a vast outline of darkness, deep back into seeming infinity, overbearing Kaella by the might of its presence, pressing into her through two fire red orbs, eyes that were the source of mind and thought, holding her effortlessly tight in their glare.

"I am Pomandres," spoke the void into Kaella. "First of all dragons, the primal cause; progenitor of both thought and thirst, the twin offspring of the mirror mind."

Fear spread all around Kaella but not consuming her because of an awe that wrapped her too.

"What is…?" but Kaella didn't know if this question was from herself or Pomandres.

"What are you here for?" and this time the weight of the pause clearly demanded something real from her, to give herself meaning.

"I am seeking to understand the changes and … what they, what I…"

530

Pomandres: "You...?"

"The choice I have to make."

Silence; resounding and deafening; blotting out everything, but not unpleasantly...

"You have made the choice," said the dragons voice, softly in her ear now, "and now you need to understand something more."

Kaella felt the breath of the dragon's fire going through her brain, blasting it to nothing; no cinders, no heat even... just a blessed emptiness into which she collapsed, falling again but softly; no spinning, more like the cherry blossom... held in Polliendra's hands.

CHAPTER 22.

It was late afternoon when the eleven got down from Galilee but Mother and Miriam were still there to greet them. Johannus was always there now, and I stayed a little while too.

Yeheshua had told them of the place and Thomas knew the way there.

Mother showed them all the arrangements that had been made with pallets and cloth screens and everything in the longroom, the upper room of the main house.

Many hands had worked hard to make sure there was enough warm water in the big barrel that was hung in one of the outhouses; enough for washing in the small stream that turning a plug-tap in one corner released.

Salome had organised cooking dinner in the large pot, but she had left earlier so Mother and Miriam prepared to serve it to the eleven in the longroom; but most came out to the courtyard once they knew it was ready, feeling a kind of contentment out there, with the sunset radiating the last warmth of the day.

Once everyone was ready to retire Johannus was set to escort Mother and Miriam back to Nicodemus' house, but Thomas stepped up to go instead.

He and I had swapped glances when the eleven of them had first got there but I knew the time was not right to talk with him. We left instead for Bethany, to tell there of the arrival, and the chance of Yeheshua's coming soon, hopefully tomorrow.

Yresmin was already at Lazarus' house and asked if I would go back with her to see if there was cleaning up or anything that needed doing, and I agreed quite happily.

It ended up being a little later than we anticipated and when we got there Miriam and Mary had just left, going into the city; the other direction.

Johannus knew I wanted to speak to Thomas, I could tell, and I tried to not let it show but we had known each other a long time and he was clearly concerned. Still, I wasn't going to say anything just now and I gave him a big hug instead.

"Are you alright Johannus? You look worried."

"I am fine Mary; and if I am worried it is only about an old friend. Maybe it is nothing? I am sure it is."

"Then find us some things to do to keep us busy and not in the way, would you?" I said, smiling at him, "because you have been here bathing in the fun and glory, but we haven't"

He laughed and we helped a bit. The mixed collection of community dishes had already been washed up and put away, but there were lots of garments and sundry lengths of cloth still strung out upon the clothes lines stretched across the yard, from earlier in the day; finally dry and ready to be brought down, folded and brought inside.

Eventually we knew it was time to get on back. I toyed with the idea of going to Nicodemus' house, but Yresmin wanted to go home, so I went with her. If there was anyone who maybe I could talk to it would be her; and as we walked we talked, and it just kind of spilled out.

She wasn't the least bit shocked; thought indeed it was the most normal thing in the world, which it doubtless was in Nabatea, but not so here.

"You have to tell him," she said. "It is important for him as well."

"We keep missing each other, like tonight, and he is very tied up too; but I will try."

"Do you want me to?" she asked. "It might make it a lot easier if I broached it to him, as a friend of yours who was concerned."

"Oh no; please don't. This is something I need to tackle myself. I just had to talk to someone; and thank you for being the one ..." and we had reached her place and she worked on her door-locks.

"Mother might be even better you know. She would know how to deal with it. Look what happened when Yeheshua was born. That was..."

"Quite different," I said firmly, but thought maybe she was right.

When it came to it, I found I couldn't quite broach the subject with mother though.

We were all down at the house the next day and everything felt perfect, and I wasn't going to spoil that.

Johannus was on the door of where the stairs led to the upper room. He said that Yeheshua had arrived earlier and was up there with the eleven now; and had asked that they could be left undisturbed.

Philip appeared at noon and he and Nathaniel took drinks and some bread back up with them.

There were quite a few other Christines here by then, working in the yard or outbuildings, just soaking up the chance to be here; just as I was, and Miriam and Mother, Martha and Mary, Yresmin, Salome and many other women too.

Miriam reported he had said that at the Pentecost, the fiftieth day after the Passover, he wanted all of us to be ready. That his tasks on earth were nearly done, and that the presence of the true love would come to us, to know, even as he did.

All of us must be ready and not just the twelve, for we all had his work to do.

She spoke with great power, but softly and we knew it was true. We felt that this would be how it had to be. We would be ready.

As the afternoon wore on suddenly a few came out from the longroom and said that Yeheshua was going to the Mount of Olives and that we should follow there.

We didn't know if he had already gone or not, but those few had quickly disappeared out the front and so we hurried after them, seeing them disappear around a far corner, for we had paused to get the word spread of what they had told us quickly as we could.

Mary knew a better way to the mount and so we women followed her, gathering our robes and running sometimes, not wanting to be left behind.

Suddenly Yeheshua was with us, just where we had left the city behind and were starting to climb. He was serene, shining and stood away from the road, inviting us all together…

"You won't be asked to do the same things my apostles must," he said, "because the world is not ready for that yet; but yours it will be to keep the inner truth alive, for that is the vital yet hidden thing. You must nurture it just as you would your own child, and help others to do so too, even though no-one tells you that you should."

"This will not always be so, for the time will come at the ending of this age when many women will be at the forefront, helping bring the world to Peace; and I will be working at your side and you at mine."

"I will always be with you, and the Pentecost will be a demonstration of the power of that; the living proof; for the world is not the reality it seems. It changes as all creations must, but that which we know… within, will never fade, but always is."

He hugged Miriam and Mother and would have hugged us all I think but instead turned and strode away fast uphill and we followed as quickly as we could.

Others were with us now, and up ahead a few of the apostles where Yeheshua had caught up to them.

"I have done all that I have come to do," he said so that all could hear, "and go to bring what you will need. Wait in the place you have prepared."

*

I don't know what anyone else saw, for I was gazing at him and he seemed so bright that I closed my eyes and he was still there, and beautiful beyond belief because the quality of the light inside was full of life and more real than anything.

CHAPTER 23.

Kaella allowed herself to be pulled, still trembling like a falling leaf, gently into the centre of the pavilion where cushions piled on a rug of finest silk invited her to collapse amongst them.

Polliendra poured her some tea from the steaming spout of a slumbering dragon-teapot.

Pulling herself up to take the drink Kaella sipped from the delicate cup-bowl cradled between her hands savouring its subtle exquisiteness even as it soothed and cleared her mind.

Gradually the image of the dark dragon and the red orbs that knew so much... released its grip on her.

The space in which she sat was an intimate setting; clearly this was Polliedra's personal pavilion with a low platform bed at the garden side against which Kaella sat, cross legged.

Behind the bed were fine embroidered drapes set at intervals across the inside of the wide wall opening, additional to those framed heavy ones she had seen from the outside.

To the left was the entrance they had come through, over the bridge, the last few paces of which she could still see from where she sat.

On her right side there were sliding screens covering the entrances to two further rooms, and somewhere beyond she knew another bridge stretched over the lake into the garden again.

Polliendra sat across from her, an ankle high wooden table between them, and despite the captivating beauty of her hostess, Kaella couldn't help her gaze being drawn now and again to the open fourth side of the room where a balcony faced out onto a vast and open space.

From where Kaella sat, she could just see white peaks punctuating the horizon beyond, sparkling in the sunshine and attended by an occasional cloud.

Polliendra laughed, a surprisingly deep and vibrant laugh that belied her slenderness. Her dark almond eyes surveyed her guest who seemed so young, and though this could be illusion Polliendra didn't think so.

This goddess was an enigma; one who didn't know her own way.

She smiled at Kaella seeing her having recovered from her encounter with Pomandres.

She rose and offering her hand again to her guest led her out onto the balcony.

Kaella felt a tingling run through her body at Polliendra's touch, aware of the magnetic attraction of the girl-woman-dragon... a kindred spirit such as Kaella had not met before.

Stepping onto the balcony revealed an even more wondrous panorama than she ever could have imagined. The sunlit peaks she had glimpsed were mere tips of vast mountains, unbelievably high, sharp and distant, set around a mighty ocean of gently churning white clouds and blue waters, difficult to clearly separate.

Kaella almost stepped back from the parapet, but the inner vision of her Heraikaliphon-self held her steady and allowed her mind to fly instead upon the mental wings of that mighty beast.

Vision that could pick out other dragon kind gliding here and there and everywhere amongst the clouds below that otherwise the keenest eyes might just about have seen as far scudding birds.

And even on the distant peaks Kaella could see the occasional glint of gold that told her of some majestic dragon kind being perched or flying there as well.

Instinctively Kaella sought out Herakopha.

Her mind knew that a tiny motion of red and gold was where she was, and diving down her sightline to her dragon self the clouds and waters opened for her to sweep through into another world beneath.

Fascinated, Kaella landed on the familiar shoulders of Herakopha, flying a wide circle opposite the great red-gold dragon, but on again her vision drove down to even more familiarity, where events around the city of Jerusalem, in Gaia, were rising to a climactic head.

The risen Lord Yeheshua had gathered back his close-knit circle, ready to launch forth his power in them, and the many, many others that were part of it all as well, including Johannus with whom she had an attachment; but of all beings there it was Miriam that she noticed most.

She had a magnetism grown so strong that it seemed her form would not contain it.

They were on a hill called the Mount of Olives and Kaella felt waves of love filled light spreading out from there, washing her through with the vitality of being alive.

Faster and brighter the rings of light pulsed out into all of space, renewing and invigorating everything. She closed her eyes and felt it more, saw it still, and heard the chiming of the stars like high pitched temple bells above; clear and pure from all cross the sky.

Herakopha circled up in the waves of energy, elating in the uplift of power and light and love. She and her mate circled ever further apart but the feeling holding them together grew stronger still.

Kaella arched backwards, rolling over and round to float and dive into the waves rising through her and up and out and all around.

For a moment she was completely free of everything and in the next felt that her hands were gripping onto something smooth and hard and cool. She opened her eyes and found herself holding the stone balustrade again, gazing once more across the ocean to the distant peaks. Somehow they seemed even further off, but clearer at the same time.

'How can something be nearer and further at the same time?' she thought, and laughed at herself because of the joy that she was feeling.

She looked around to where Polliendra was gazing up into the deepest blue that ever could be; a multitude of glittering stars scattered across it in fullest daylight; shining back the love, re-emphasised within them.

For a second Kaella was sure she was looking at Miriam because of the similarity to the magnetism she had felt below… and yet when Polliendra turned her head, though her beauty was indeed enhanced .. she still was the dragon girl glorying in the reflected wash of love.

Kaella smiled at Polliendra as they watched in amazement the softly falling snow dancing in the air around them.

Looking down she saw Herakopha below, perched now on the lower ledge of one of the great mountains, by a cave there, and looking closer Kaella saw two golden eggs that she was guarding, so beautiful and full of promise that she felt an overwhelming feeling of pride for her.

Further down Kaella saw the glow of what had happened all around the followers of the Christ, risen indeed, and sending back what made him that… and she noticed Johannus there with the girl called Rebecca, kissing and holding each other close…

For a second Kaella felt a strange little stab of jealousy, somehow slipping underneath her guard, catching her by surprise, and however incongruous it was to everything else, she couldn't turn away the sight and feeling by force of will.

But Polliendra had noticed, felt it happen and understanding better than Kaella touched her hand to try to lovingly drew out the hurt from her, for such small human feelings were new to Kaella, hard to fathom.

Dawn herself into the loving contact, Polliendra slipped her arm through Kaella's and led her back into the pavilion and to her bed, laying her down and lying herself beside her, holding her close, not letting anything else be between them, just the comfort of their loving touch.

Absorbed into the press and touch of their bodies Kaella gazed into the face so beautiful and eyes that drew her loving into them so that Kaella could no longer feel a difference, who was who, a merging that she gave herself into, completely.

Images of herself, of Kaella, daughter of the Lord High King, so young and innocent as she still was, danced in her heart-space, joined in Polliendra's own, and despite all of her knowing, her experience and undoubted power, Polliendra was touched more deeply than even she could fully understand.

Tenderly Polliendra let Kaella float free within her embrace, recognising and following the deepest thing they shared… the ageless thirst, that had become their quest to fulfil and be fulfilled, eternally renewed and renewing.

Images of Johannus and Rebecca returned between them, Kaella and Polliendra, a clue to what Kaella and Polliendra now both knew, and which the great Dragon Pomandres had asserted; that Kaella had indeed chosen her path, the mortal human path.

Polliendra kissed Kaella deeply, so sweetly giving back that love Kaella had abandoned to her so completely that it had awoken Polliendra's own remembrance.

And Kaella returned the kisses knowing now that which was between her and Polliendra, or Johannus, or Rebecca was a thing beyond the jealousy she had struggled with, undone now in the revelation of the one sharing they all possessed, was indeed just one, the one, always holding and letting go, even as the breath herself.

CHAPTER 24.

Johannus awoke to the feeling of falling snow and got up from his pallet-bed to see if it could perhaps be true. It was very early, just on the cusp of night and day.

The day before had been momentous, as every day seemed to be, for the eleven had gathered together in their long room to choose another to join them, to make them twelve again.

Matthias Levi was a brave choice, a stalwart disciple from the very start, right at the ford where John had received the master, and he had earlier studied and taught the Egyptian mysteries of the Ennead, learnt near Heliopolis where Miriam and Yeheshua had first met.

It was Miriam that earlier in the day had stepped forward to uplift the brethren lost in grief and uncertainty, for once again they had been gripped by the growing loss at their master having gone.

She gave of her strength and understanding, answering their need for encouragement and love, only to be rebuffed in turn by Andrew and Peter. It had been at their request she had revealed to them a vision she had received of her Lord and love; and related to them his teaching to her, of the soul's journey home; of its release from the mortal planes of being.

But they had doubted; both her and that they should have listened to her.

Johannus had felt her pain at such unwarranted treatment, and was grateful that a couple of the others had stood up to rebuke Peter for being so unjust and unfeeling.

Johannus had been sitting near the door as he often did, as he was when the eleven had drawn lots to choose Matthias to be their twelfth.

Yet for Johannus the highlight of the day had been when Miriam had sung in the evening by the great tree where the community liked to gather; and had sung a new song of thanks for all the blessings they had received, both great and small; bringing them together; for one, for all.

Reaching the window, he looked out into a half light, and at softly falling flakes of snow.

Amazed that they could come now when the heat of summer seemed to be growing every day; and though they mostly settled only for a moment before disappearing, there were a few hidden places where little piles of whiteness had gathered.

Johannus hastily pulled on a robe to go outside and have the snow falling all about him. Stretching back his neck he felt the individual flakes spotting onto his face… and he laughed with joy.

He had experienced plenty of stronger snowfalls but never one like this, when least expected, and looking around found a patch of white at the base of the courtyard tree where there was enough to scoop up a little handful of the soft magical stuff.

Clouds had cleared from the horizon where the sun would soon be rising, even as the snow ceased falling and Johannus spread the cold wetness in his fingers and palms across his eyes and cheeks.

He wondered briefly if anyone else might have seen the snow… it was still so early.

Sitting back upon his bed he remembered this was the day called Pentecost, the fiftieth day after the Passover, and much had been said about being ready; but how and for what he did not know. He gladly took the precious time to gather himself inside.

Breakfast was soon being readied in the barn, where already some small secure sleeping rooms had been made for a few of the women, and more were being worked on by Beor and Simon from Bethany, and their friends and other disciples with such skills to lend a hand.

Mother, Miriam, Lazarus, his sisters and many more arrived quite early as well to join in the making of this day, what it would be. Mother in her favourite pale blue robe and Miriam all in stunning creamy white.

Magdalene had been unusually quiet Johannus thought, though close with Mother Mary and Miriam as she often was. Maybe this wasn't her moment to be the boisterous rebel she so often could appear to be.

Johannus looked out for Rebecca, but couldn't see her in the courtyard as he went out to join the queue for breakfast. Nor in the barn itself, so he went to sit with Beor and a couple of the others that had come to help.

Several of the twelve were quietly eating at one end of the barn and every-where there was a feeling of focus, fuelled by the appreciation of a new day and to be sharing this communal breakfast.

Johannus asked Beor if he had seen the snowfall earlier and the burly black-smith laughed. "Snow? You are joking… "

"It wouldn't have waited around for you to get out of your marriage bed," quipped Johannus and the two sitting with them laughed. Beor reddened; "Pah," he said, making others look around at his gruffness; "so there was snow coming down in this month of the year, yet only you saw it… haw haw."

"I saw it too," said Salome who was just sitting down nearby, having completed all her work making the breakfast. "and I did too," said a shepherd called Jesse, "just a little before dawn, and it reminded me of the stories," he added before leaving the thought unfinished, but they all knew what he was talking of.

Philip spoke into the following hush, from the far end of the barn. "What a wonderful thing that was Jesse; this is the dawning of a very special day. He has promised to come to us in another way, and this must surely be a sign."

"Amen, amen," with murmuring agreement and some happy laughter echo-ing around the barn.

*

What a day it proved to be. We sat in what was to become the orchard but then was just a small piece of field.

Miriam and Mary sat beneath the tree by the wall and Yresmin and many women, and not a few men too, sat around under cloth awnings that had hastily been set up to shade us from sun's heat. More were coming all the time.

The twelve were all together in the upstairs long room and the intensity of the focus, the waiting, could be felt all around the compound. Three disciples were sat on the steps that led up to it, and others, preferring a solitary vigil occupied the recesses of the barn across the yard.

Johannus was here with us though, across the circle from where Rebecca and Beor's wife sat, having just arrived with Lazarus and his sisters. All the Christines within the area were gathering here today.

"What we are waiting for is already with us," Miriam was saying, sat at the heart of us all. "We do not have to wait but only feel its power already in us. He doesn't ever leave us, our hearts would stop from beating if he were to; it is just we that fail to see, and fail to hear, what he has always been telling us."

"Will you sing a song for us Miriam?" asked one of the women that I didn't recognise.

"The song that shall be sung this day is like no other," answered Miriam, "for it is the one that comes spontaneously from our hearts in unison, of longing and fulfilment both together, recognising we are all one with him, the Lord within our hearts, and sung within as joy. This is the news he brought that we will feel in certainty today."

It was so natural to be listening to Miriam, having her tell us what we already knew and were already feeling. Only she could express it so completely and I saw mother's eyes were filled with tears… of joy.

We sat in silent acceptance, not needing any further words, even from Miriam, because I know we were all feeling it; just as it was in the growing day all around us, the warmth of the sun and the coolness of the wafting air, mirroring the play of heart and breath inside.

The hush was palpable and spread through every attentive part of us, joined within to everything and everyone, the twelve, the cat crossing the yard in the sun, birds sitting in quiet anticipation, the wind, the tree, the very earth itself was in our breath.

How long it was in coming I don't know because I lost myself in the feeling, sunk deep into the waves of coming and going, but when it did it was not to me as an individual sitting there but rather as the tide comes to the shore and washes all up along the beach reaching higher than any barriers the sand has made, swirling through around and over, covering everything.

Through me, through us all, a kind of quake shook away habitual thinking, an inner wind blowing through petty distractions from the light of certainty of what being alive could be, and is… and always will be.

*

The door at the top of the steps to the upper room opened a crack and then wide open, two figures standing there that seemed lit by their own light within though the sun was shining too, and whether it was in my seeing or their being I couldn't know, nor did it actually matter.

It was Thomas and Nathaniel first but soon then Matthias and Andrew, Simon Zelotes and Philip too, all coming down into the yard, hugging each other and the other disciples that were there.

Peter, James and John were the last to come out, standing framed by the door at the top of the steps, filled with inner power emanating from them like a fire; but a fire of inspiration and overflowing love.

Peter came down slowly but so transformed in demeanour from the figure of uncertainty he had displayed the day before, when challenging Miriam's experience, that today he went over to her and Mother, holding out his hands, one to mother Mary, one to Miriam.

"Now we shall go into Jerusalem," he said "and truly tell the people of this promise of our Lord fulfilled, that he has sent the spirit of heaven itself to inhabit our mortal frames ..." and Miriam gave her blessings too, back to him as he set off across the yard, leading the way into the city, with lots of others and apostles following.

CHAPTER 25.

When Thomas came down from the upper room he shone with a happiness and clarity that struck me the more forcibly because of the effect the wave of glory that had washed through us, the touch of its beauty stirring the heart of my womb where a new life was growing.

Thomas' smile was so full of the contentment he seemed to have been missing of late that I didn't seek out his eyes but bowed my head towards the preciousness that I was carrying instead.

He didn't seek me out especially either though he may have seen me; I am sure he did. But as he turned to leave the yard it did seem that his glance and smile fell full on me as I lifted my head, and though he didn't pause even for a moment I felt all the warmth and love there that I could have ever wished for.

Miriam being already on her feet was the first to follow after Peter and the other apostles out into the city, and most of us were soon in her wake too, glad that some great barrier had been breached and we could now share our love with all who had come to celebrate Pentecost, or just wanted to know the truth of what we had seen and felt.

So many, many people stopped what they were doing to listen to these men full of the passion of inspiration that day and of those very many wanted to come back to our new communal home to receive more of what we had to teach and give.

Mother had stayed behind to be ready and indeed Peter asked Matthias to go back to receive these newcomers into our midst, which he did with the aid of several others, Johannus and myself amongst them.

Salome too decided that she would start preparing the meal early and more of it than usual, so I helped her get started washing and cutting the vegetables whilst Johannus helped Matthias to organise a simple baptising arrangement, bringing the shower out to a position in the yard by the overhanging branch of the tree.

Soon there was quite a queue of people lining up to receive a small dowsing of the water as they found their way, accompanied or not by some beaming disciple into the compound; the level of activity was growing by the minute.

The whole of the little field was getting filled with groups of people sitting around, either listening to Nathaniel by the tree, who had come back with Peter's brother Andrew to help us, or else just taking in and absorbing their part in the whole thing happening.

But despite all the activity there was also tremendous calm, a going about what was to be done in the simplest of harmony, there being no need for rushing or anything else other than what we wanted to be doing, which we were.

Mother was at the heart of it and seemed to be greeting the newcomers in person like friends come for a wedding feast and Matthias doing the baptismal duties with a warmth and humour enjoyed by all whom he pulled through the steady trickle of water into his welcoming embrace.

Johannus had found Beor and got his help in filling an emptied barrel from the little stream that ran beside the footpath from the hillside towards Bethany, the very reason that the farm had once been situated where it was; a godsend, literally as the need for more water became steadily more apparent.

I found eventually that everything had or was being taken care of and decided to go back up into the city again and see how my friends and brothers were doing.

I met one or two groups here and there as I walked up the narrow ways into sudden little squares and on again, that formed the route up to the centre from this side of town. There was a buzz of excitement in the air and in the discussions going on, and more and more I felt drawn up towards the temple court itself, that had been the site of so many dramas in recent weeks.

As I came to the arch that led from my way into the wide, open space before the temple itself, I encountered a couple of Roman guards lounging against the pillars on one side; quite relaxed. All was well.

The crowds were quite large but it wasn't hard to see where Peter, James and John were standing in different parts of the outer court each talking with the many people who had gathered around them.

It surprised me that I wanted to go and hear what Peter was saying most of all, normally thinking him to be rather abrupt and difficult, but when I got close enough to see and hear him properly, I was so glad I had.

He was speaking to all sorts of people, from many different parts of the Roman world, come to experience this festival in Jerusalem, and was managing it by expressing what meant so much to him in the simplest terms. It moved me to see how he had found the deep humility that enabled him to cross any barrier, language or cultural, to communicate so eloquently, just from one human to another, the love the risen Lord Yeheshua had brought into his life, and could into anybody else's too. If they wanted…

Suddenly I had the vision of Moses striking the rock in the desert, that had cracked it open, just wide enough to allow a stream of purest water to issue out … a source that didn't fail, even in that desert place. Peter the rock, ahhh and so he is.

Looking around I saw people asking questions to those they realised must be Christines too; and them answering as much as they could, despite being taken by surprise.

Then someone was pushing past behind me, none too gently or carefully and I looked around to see an unpleasant looking man barging his way towards the front of those listening to Peter.

'Troublemaker!' I thought and looking over the shoulders of people behind me I saw others of that type pushing through the crowds here and there, and a few arch looking Pharisees standing back as well.

As I pondered what this would mean an unmistakable glint of white caught my eye at the archway I had entered the square by, framing Miriam for a moment as she said something to the guards there.

Even as I thought how it would take rather more than them to solve the brewing trouble, they jumped to attention, for following around the corner came a troop of soldiers, half Roman legionnaires and half 'Palace' guards; the mix that had met with most success in policing days like these.

I counted sixteen of them, not including the Roman officer who I realised with a start was the man at the garrison barracks I had talked with some weeks back.

The mixed platoon fanned out around the back of the square as he got up on a plinth at the foot of one large pillar where he could see and be heard.

Clearly Thomas recognised him as well for I saw him disengage from a couple of Greek looking men and made his way quickly over to the officer.

I remembered then how Thomas had done so well to get an audience with the Roman Governor Pontius Pilate, who had promised to put a stop to the harassment that Christines were getting after Yeheshua's crucifixion.

Not only had he met with Thomas but Pilate had been true to his promise and put out an edict that forbade any molestation or harassment of Christines for declaring the master Yeheshua had arisen from the dead, because so many others had witnessed having seen him too, and Pilate greatly wished to make some amends for his previous inaction.

I watched fascinated as Thomas and Julian, as I remembered him to be called, discussed very briefly what was happening before Julian waved Thomas away with a brief sweep of his right arm.

Discordant voices were being raised around the court and nodding to one of the Palace guards near to him, Julian let out a shrill couple of whistle blasts from a small metal instrument he was holding to his lips.

The guard gestured to others on either side to move forward with him to where they could see the troubles being brewed; even as everyone went silent.

I turned back to look for the troublemaker and found that everyone had instinctively stepped away from him, leaving him exposed and isolated.

And just the same seemed to be happening at many other points around the court too.

Julian signalled over to one of the Pharisees with his rolled-up edict scroll who got the message. Very soon all three of them had left the court taking their bullies and hecklers with them.

Such a sweet victory I thought, looking around for Miriam.

I couldn't see her and then she tapped me on the shoulder with a sweet "Mary, here you are; I was wondering where you had got to".

I laughed. "How did you do that? I was looking for you."

In sudden clarity I remembered her when we were both kids in Magdala.

She had been two or three years older than me, and had left with her father when her mother died; he had been a merchant who plied the routes from the East, and south to Egypt. Spices, frankincense, myrrh; those kinds of thing.

She had always liked to sing, even then.

"We have been arranging things back at the compound," I said. "So many people are there. Matthias is doing tremendously baptising newcomers and Mother is mother of course; it is lovely, and there is lots of food being prepared too."

"Let's go around and visit John and James before we go back," she said taking my hand. "They don't need our support but it is lovely to hear them speak."

Peter was in full flow, conversing happily with a couple of older men who appeared to be loving what he was telling them. "How come we never heard of this?" said one, as we wandered away; along to where John was surrounded by an even bigger crowd, some of which were women.

"Did he ever get married?" one middle-aged lady asked, quite near in front of us.

John's eyes had flicked up to see us arriving as this question came and his face creased into a big smile. "Yes, indeed he did," he answered, "a most beautiful and accomplished lady."

Miriam's hand squeezed mine and I felt the warmth rush through me, the blush that didn't show on her face.

"How awful that they did what they did to him, and with a wife as well. It seems unbelievable."

Softly Miriam answered for John, being right next to the lady now. "But he is risen and will always be so; in the hearts and lives of us that know."

The lady's face melted into tears as she looked into Miriam's. "Oh, how wonderful. I wish I could have known him."

"You still can, that is the wonderful truth. It is just who we are when the layers get peeled back. Always has been and always will be. For those who want to know it here, in our hearts. For those who don't... well, maybe they will one day."

She took the lady's hand. "If you want, we are going back to where many of us are celebrating the Pentecost, and you can come too."

"I am a widow now," she said, "but my daughter is over there," she pointed to the other group around James, where we were going anyway.

Her daughter turned to her, her face shining. "Oh, we have been waiting for and wanting this day for so long, mother." They hugged each other.

"We are going to where his mother is right now, with many others," I said. "Do you want to come?"

By the time Miriam and I got back to the celebrations there were quite a few others with us as well.

CHAPTER 26.

In the days after Pentecost enormous efforts were made in making what had been a ramshackle but spacious farmhouse and outbuildings into a community and welcoming centre for Christines and any who wanted to come.

Andrew was given the task of co-ordinating all of the building and other works that could make this place 'suitable', as Yeheshua had said it should.

The large upper room was kept as a place of worship, teaching, or quiet meditation, and much was done to create other rooms for any apostle staying, for they would come and go as the demands of different, new communities called out to them.

John insisted that mother should have her permanent rooms and this was done right at the start.

Johannus moved out of the main building, staying camped in the field for a couple of days before Yresmin asked if he would like to stay with her, which he did, or sometimes at the forge or with his aunt and uncle, and in these days his formal betrothal to Rebecca was arranged, much to the pleasure of us, his friends; before she would travel with her father back to Alexandria.

Miriam stayed with Martha, Mary and Lazarus in the suite they had made for her and Yeheshua, and she asked me if I would share it with her, at least for a while, to which I happily agreed. I had the feeling she wasn't going to be resting anywhere permanently.

The barn was made into accommodation for any women coming from further afield, like the many of us that had and would visit from Galilee. Which just left the renovation and expansion of the other outhouses, for everyone and everything the main house couldn't manage.

Luckily there was a surge of volunteers after the Pentecost celebrations, and of much needed funds as well, for all we were doing.

Miriam and I went over the hill route each morning, almost always with Yresmin and Johannus too, and often Rebecca and sometimes Beor. We called it Miriam way, harking jokingly back to Galilee, and the compound we called 'Yeheshua's Inn' or just 'the Inn' which kind of caught on, though some apostles called it 'the churchyard'.

Miriam had amazing energy. She liked nothing better than to be travelling around the nearby villages, visiting the people like the mother Anne and her daughter Jasmine whom we had met in temple court. Yet she also spent plenty of time at the Inn, helping out and being around for anyone who might want to talk to her; but always quietly, a comforting presence in the background, especially for visitors from around and those often being women.

Her singing was much sought after and I think she preferred doing that of an evening in the field, now fast being spaciously planted into becoming the orchard, both for fruit and the shade it would give to outside gatherings.

The coming of the promised 'comforter' at Pentecost, whilst a sweeping clean of thinking and being the presence we had all experienced in the company of Yeheshua, it was not new exactly; rather the understanding it was truly in us.

So, when Johannus said at one meal, sitting with Yresmin and me, that he felt the presence of the Comforter to be the company of everything of the feminine he had ever sought, Peter overheard whilst walking by behind us and quickly cut Johannus down.

"The Holy Spirit is not female, Johannus. You should never say such things."

Johannus was mortified that his experience had been overheard and censored by the chief apostle. He stammered, "n… no of course not. It is just the way I…" and he trailed off, but Miriam had heard as well and came to his defence.

"Peter, that is not fair to attack his experience. You must know how often Yeheshua referred to the Holy Breath as 'she', and I am sure he referred to 'the Comforter' in that way too? He did to me. Not the only way, but you cannot imagine the Almighty is wholly masculine, just because he said 'his Father God'."

Peter went red with fury at being challenged so, but before he could reply James had stepped in. "Yes, you know that is so Peter, and it is just as you say Miriam, a figure of speech that kept the balance of feeling for our understanding."

Peter opened his mouth, his anger still showing, but Miriam answered, "Yes, we know the Almighty is so far beyond what we think of in these ways," and James agreed, "I think that was what Peter was trying to say too, that we shouldn't put our own ideas up for this, but then nor should we deny another's experience either."

Peter took a few breaths, managing to say nothing, then went back to his seat shrugging his shoulders, but we all knew that he wasn't a man to let such things go easily.

We were all very human, still a mix of very different people and opinions; there was no magic change in this. Every day we were trying to apply what we had learnt and could gather as we sought to grow in the life within.

*

Johannus was horrified that he might have caused a rift between Miriam and Peter, though he also knew that Peter had always struggled with Miriam being so close to the lord, and in ways he never could be.

She didn't interfere in any of the activities or decisions of the twelve and was wholly supportive of all that they did or asked of her, yet her time was clearly devoted to all the people who maybe had not had the same chance as they had to be close to Yeheshua.

And Peter never tried to impose any duties on her, knowing that was not his place to try nor ever could he do so. They worked on forging the way forward in unspoken goodwill if not complete harmony.

Miriam would travel quite far and sometimes Johannus would go with her, and often Yresmin and sometimes me, yet she had the energy to outstrip us all. And of course, she always took the colt Indra who was nearly strong enough to bear her now, though she ever only loaded a bag or two onto him.

I had started to feel the nausea and I still hadn't even talked of anything with Thomas; I must soon if... but this is where my doubt was; would he want to know?

Johannus was taken up for a couple of days with Rebecca's return to Alexandria, and I was hiding any unease and sickness I felt by catching up with business affairs in Jerusalem, staying at Joseph's house.

Miriam told mother that she was going to go up to Galilee to spend time around the communities there, particularly Tiberius, Magdala, Capernaum and Nazareth, to see how everyone was faring since Pentecost.

When Peter heard of this, he decided to send apostles with her, for support.

Thomas, Nathaniel and Philip were chosen and she readily agreed, but then she never waited around once she had made her decision so the next day set off up the road to Jericho for the first leg of what we called her tour. John went instead of Thomas, who was still in Bethlehem.

Some saw her dynamism as a potential challenge to the Apostles authority but we knew it was her singular closeness to Yeheshua and everything he had been about that drove her to walk the path of her love; his love.

I was glad that I hadn't gone, though I would have liked to have, but the daily bouts of sickness were getting worse, and I knew it as confirmation of what was happening inside, being no stranger to childbirth as a priestess in Antioch.

Yresmin was worried about Mary, knowing she hadn't told anyone about being pregnant, and was quick to spot the 'early sickness'; though they had said nothing of it between them yet.

Johannus had noticed something, but he was so happy in his relationship with Rebecca, on top of everything else happening, that he hadn't thought too much of it.

Yresmin felt she at least had to tell him; after all he was staying in her barn.

When she did Johannus thought it amazing but couldn't quite understand why Mary hadn't yet told Thomas.

"They have been all so tight amongst themselves Johan," she said. "You know… 'the twelve'. I don't think she can break into what is going on for them right now. I know it is different for her, that she has been almost one of them, but Yeheshua is not here so I think I understand how it must be…"

Johannus shrugged. "Maybe, but of them all I really like Thomas." Yresmin looked surprised. "No that is not what I meant. I really respect all of them, and like many of them in ways. John, Nathaniel, Philip; yes, all of them in different ways. That is just it, they are all different, and I think Thomas would be really good with Mary…"

Yresmin cocked an eyebrow at him. "It is more about Thomas being really good with Mary AND their baby," she said. "But he needs a chance to be the father that he doesn't know he is."

Johannus thought on it for a while. "I shall go and find him."

"Is that wise Johannus?" came back Yresmin quickly, wishing she hadn't said anything. "Wouldn't it be much better to do it through Mother? That is what we would do in Qadesh. Many came to me that way."

It seemed Johannus had not heard her, or not properly, for he muttered, "it has been a half thought in the back of my head; that she has been asking… if I have seen him, and more than once too. I best go find him and tell him that, at least."

He got up and started to put on his coat and sandals. "Are you going there now?" she asked.

"Yes; I will only regret it if I don't do anything; and if I don't do it now, I never will."

"Then I am coming too."

"No need, Yresmin. I am only going to talk to Thomas. We can't both do that."

"I am coming."

Johannus shrugged and said, "thank you, it will be nice to have your company and support; and anyway, maybe we will see Magdalene first and it will all be done without us."

Yresmin looked slightly puzzled but it was her turn to shrug, "Yes, maybe."

*

They went along the road route form Bethphage rather than back via Bethany, coming out through the front gates into the hive of life that 'the Inn' had become.

They stopped, looking around first for Thomas and then for who might help. The building work was going on apace in the outhouses and Johannus wasn't sure where Thomas's room was now.

Yresmin could see that mother wasn't in the barn or 'orchard' but at least she knew where her rooms were, and nudged Johannus's arm, letting him know she was going to see if Mary was in.

Spurred into action Johannus turned and followed her towards the main house-block, veering towards the steps that led to the upper room; to see who might be there.

Just as Peter came out from the downstairs door, heading for the steps as well.

Their eyes met, and Johannus mind sprang back to their last encounter where Miriam had come to his defence. He felt his neck prickle slightly but there was nothing but beneficence in Peter's gaze, despite his somewhat stern bearded face; his presence spilled around with warm good grace.

For a moment Johannus hesitated, wanting to ask after Thomas but feeling reticence as well.

The moment would have passed, but several other things happened in quick succession.

The door opened from the upper room and hearing someone on the top steps, Peter looked around; up. Simon Zelotes stretched out a hand as though he would ask Peter something, just as Yresmin came up behind Johannus, having found the way to Mother's rooms locked.

"Er...?" said Simon, seeing he might be interrupting.

Peter turned back to Johannus noticing as well that the Nabatean priestess had joined them.

"What?" he asked. "Is there something I can help with?

Johannus relaxed. "I was wondering where I could find Thomas?"

"Ahh," said Peter. "He is still in Bethlehem, should be back later today, I think. Can I help?"

Johannus was about to say 'don't worry it is fine;' but instead Yresmin asked, "Rabbi, could you tell me where Mother might be perhaps?"

Johannus frowned slightly, and Peter looked from one to the other, mildly puzzled.

"Are the two things related?" he asked them both, and whilst Johannus said nothing, Yresmin answered. "Yes," and then, "well yes, in a way; but I was hoping to see Mother about some women's matters."

"Johannus?" asked Peter mildly, and Johannus stammered trying to avoid connecting Thomas to women's matters "er... well I just wanted to talk to Thomas... and Yresmin... ummm, was hoping to talk to mother Mary."

"Mother is out visiting Joseph; I think she went to see Mary Magdalene."

Maybe it was nothing, maybe just the mention of her name at that moment, or maybe that Johannus flushed slightly, or maybe Yresmin flinched, but anyway Simon coughed softly to clear his throat.

Peter turned from them to Simon, who was looking meaningfully back at him. There was a pause in which Peter decided to leave whatever it might be to Mother Mary; he nodded a smile to Johannus and Yresmin and with the slightest of shrugs went on up the steps.

Johannus turned quickly to look at Yresmin who seemed equally perplexed, and then back up at the disappearing back of Peter.

To his discomfiture he saw Simon touch Peter's shoulder, looking questioningly down at the pair of them in the courtyard. He spoke softly something to Peter which Johannus couldn't hear, except perhaps '… Magdalene'; or hopefully he imagined it.

But he could almost read what it might have been from the fixed expression on Simon's face.

His skin seemed to tingle for the flash of a moment and then it was gone, even as the door closed to the upper room. He turned and took Yresmin by her arm, feeling worried but not blaming the older woman. "At least we know a bit more; about where both Magdalene and Mother might be," he said. "Why don't we go to Joseph's house?"

"Good idea," answered Yresmin, despite her own misgivings about what had just happened.

*

I opened the door of Joseph's offices when I saw that mother was the one knocking.

"Come in, come in; what happy coincidence brings you here?"

"Mary dear; I was visiting Joseph's house and he said you were here, so I thought I would pop in and say hello whilst I was over. Is everything all right?"

"Yeess, just using Joseph's kindness to sort out some business without having to go back to Magdala. He has been a great help."

"Yes, he said. I had wondered whether we should have gone with Miriam. Did you think that?"

We chatted on for a little while… and I could see she was a bit worried about something. I had finished all the accounts I needed to do, so had no reason to stay. "I have pretty much finished here;" I said as she sat there thinking, in a long pause, "and will be going back to the compound and on to Bethany later. Do you want to come?"

"Thank you," mother said, brightening up and smiling as she also got to her feet, "but I promised Joseph I would stay for the meal and then accompany him over to our Inn. He wants to see all the work that is being done." She moved with me towards the door. "Would you like to join us. I am sure that Joseph would love you to."

I would have liked that but was hoping to catch Thomas who I had heard was

552

coming back from Bethlehem today. I really didn't want to put it off any longer.

"Mmmm lovely idea, but I simply must get on back to the Inn. There is much I have to catch up on… and then get back to Bethany afterwards."

*

Winding my way through the streets of Jerusalem, my mind scouted ahead, not for the first time trying to decide on the best way to broach the subject with Thomas.

Most vitally I didn't want any of the other apostles around, and didn't really want to call him away from them. It was them that had made it so hard to find a time together.

Today nothing would put me off; I would find a way.

Passing through the gates I scanned around at all the activity going on, not seeing Thomas; nor Johannus either, or others I thought might know whether Thomas had returned from Bethlehem.

'Is he here?' I thought, wandering down into the orchard where there was a corner set aside for a horse or donkey. Neither were there now and I think Thomas had taken the grey mare that had been lent for the Apostles' use; so maybe he wasn't back yet.

I couldn't see anyone to ask so turned back, deciding to wander close to the house and see if I could pick up any news.

On impulse I decided not to go up to the upper room, instead heading towards Mother's rooms though I knew for certain she was not there. As I passed by the steps Simon and Matthias were walking towards them and I thought to greet them except that Simon threw me a very strange look, and may have even nudged Matthias, for he seemed to smirk without looking my way.

Unpleasant tingles ran up my spine and I veered off my path and headed back towards the outer gates instead. Suddenly I felt uncontrollably sick as well and was grateful that I got out and found a patch of scrubby ground next to the outer wall where I heaved up anything I had eaten earlier.

Leaning against the wall I closed my eyes following inside the calming breaths, even as my mind started to remember and wonder at the look from Simon Zelotes and Matthias's odd response.

My skin felt cold and I hugged myself, leaning back against the stones where the sun's warmth was still pooling, allowing me some welcome numbness.

Two voices that I vaguely recognised skirted the periphery of my silence which I paid no attention to until, with a shock I heard my name "Magdalene… could have been anyone."

My attention was sucked into their faint conversation, not knowing whether they were inside the walls or in the street nearby, but clearly recognising Levi talking to Simon but not catching many words. "…it is too bad that… ing Thomas… …ather whoring prieste…" Simon was saying and Levi's response, "… hoPeter …can… vent it …ing to… any unpleasa…"

Shock hit me in the guts and I doubled over to retch out the emptiness inside.

CHAPTER 28.

Panic flooded through my brain as I wondered desperately what had happened to shatter my world into pieces.

How could they be talking like that? Simon had never liked me I knew, ever since Yeheshua had cut down his objections... to me, as a woman, joining them; but we had always managed to tolerate each other since.

And Jude... why would he call me a whoring priestess? Why were they talking about me like this?

The sickness felt like it was all through my body, and my head buzzed horribly. I needed to sit down, but get away from here as well. There was a grassy bank a little way along the road, around a corner and I struggled to get myself to go there, wanting to crawl rather than walk, but somehow I got there and was sick again when I did.

Breathing was my lifeline, steadying me in those horrible shivery minutes that seemed like hours.

I don't know how long I lay there but I realised I had to move and my mind was once again functioning, thinking about what might have happened and what and where I was going.

Was that why mother had sought me out and seemed worried? Surely, she would have warned me if she knew they were thinking those things? But why were they? How could this be happening?

Yresmin was the only person I had told; not even Miriam, but I was certain that she wouldn't have allowed anything to slip like this; unless she had wanted me to talk to Mother, or maybe she had, and someone had overheard?

What difference did it make? Everything was ruined, destroyed before we even had a chance.

God, why? Why? Why take this from me like this?

I walked faster, the urge to get away overcoming the sickness. But a different sickness was getting to me, closing in on me. Rage and horror mingled, broiling in me.

Bethphage was not far now but I could not think of seeing Yresmin for my heart and mind was filled with pain of an approaching storm of doubts and hatred.

I looked briefly into her yard, but it was shut and no-one about.

Strangely, this is like the last place of refuge, sanity, before heading on to... God only knows where.

I leave nevertheless, inexorably going towards Bethany and what should be the welcoming refuge of Martha, Mary and Lazarus's home; my home in Judea too now.

But I cannot go there. Something stronger even than my desperation; some pride; some stubborn stupid pride won't let me approach the safety... I have to stay and envelop myself in this awfulness, all alone.

Nowhere to go; except that as I pass the alley to Beor's smithy I turn almost involuntarily and go down there without thought, tears of frustration, misery and utter dejection streaming down my face.

There is no question in my mind that I can ever talk to Thomas now; he is forever snatched away from me. The pain of despair cuts deeper than any knife.

Why is this being done to me? I am sitting on a pile of sacking inside the smithy, not remembering how I got there, but that have taken a couple of the sacks to cover myself over with.

A terrible thought starts to eat into me; that I was never meant to have this, not really. I wasn't worthy of what had been given to me.

I could have been perhaps, but my pride had undone it all, like Judas… and I could feel it gone; snatched away by my own non-worth.

And the demonic buzzing was starting to come back into me; distant… but inexorably coming back for me.

*

Kaella watched all that was happening, particularly between Rebecca and Johannus.

She didn't want that to happen, couldn't let it be; not when she had just decided upon him, herself.

She brooded and was thinking of trying to penetrate the wall, into his dreams again, as once she used to… when she perceived something terrible unfolding for Mary… called Magdalene.

The Hecate that Magdalene had once called out to in the subterranean temple of Astarte, was not really the same Kaella as now, not as she had been.

She and Magdalene had never known each other, though Kaella had followed Johannus closely in those times when they: he, Miriam and Mary, had journeyed to Qadesh.

It was Miriam that had recognised and blocked her way, not Mary. And Miriam that she recognised now as maybe no-one else yet could.

But seeing what was happening to Magdalene she felt an awful kinship to her need, for here was darkness seeping into the world again; and too close to Magdalene for Kaella to influence.

Horror dawned on her, not wishing this on anyone and she sought around for help, instinctively sending out to Miriam, but she was not close-by; Kaella could feel that.

She shuddered, watching the smokes of darkness whispering up and about Mary, inside her defences, but Kaella turned to leave the sight nevertheless.

Miriam had gone to Galilee and she flew as quickly as any dragon could, searching out the light of Miriam's beauty and kindness.

Magnetism that surrounded her in deep-seated certainty; a clarity that was too real for Kaella's form to engage with directly.

She circled around and about and over, high as Heraikaliphon could still to no avail; could find no way

Cold to her heart, almost sharing the despair she sought to alleviate, Kaella fell to her knees, outside of Miriam's promised ring of warmth, and prayed to the Master Yeheshua for help.

How long she stayed in that darkness she did not know; had no way to tell.

*

I cowered in horrible anticipation, praying desperately to Yeheshua for his help, but knowing that wasn't quite right, for answers came in Yeheshua's words themselves, spoken in my house in Magdala.

'If the door is not locked against the devils of evil thought now rooted out, would they not surely return sevenfold stronger?'

And, as I digested that first deadener: 'If that which has been given is not respected, why would it stay unwanted there, for what was once known can be taken away, and the door locked again that had been opened.'

That there was no redemption for one who turned from the gift of life, the knowing of oneself.

That .. and I knew these devils all too personally.

The horrid buzzing grew inside me whilst I thought these things, certain now that where once Yeheshua had helped me, now I had invited back my pride and wilfulness, and given full rein to my carnality, there was no second chance, no returning to innocence.

Had not Yeheshua himself said to me just a few weeks back 'Do not touch me;' in the garden of Siloam? Had I already strayed onto this path into the abyss, even then?

Buzzing, taunting thoughts out of my control were returning for me and I knew no defence to keep them at bay, excepting one; that could also be my uttermost undoing.

My child that lived within my womb; they would not have her. I would fight them with every last fibre of my heart and soul to keep her safe, for I knew in that moment I was carrying a daughter.

That my sanity could be washed away and my soul plunged into fathomless, bottomless darkness, maybe yes it could; but not her.

That was already too unutterably fearful to contemplate, and I would not...

Not consign my unborn daughter of my love to the same...

No... I would not. Mother, help me please. Help your child, if not me, then this innocent in me, I beg... and beg, and beg thee again.

*

Kaella heard soft voices, just near enough to bring her back to thoughts of hope and help... for Magdalene. She opened her eyes.

She seemed to be lying in a garden and the voices had stopped but someone had seen her and was coming over to her.

She recognised it to be the Ka form of Miriam; she who had always had this power, and now was using it because of Kaella's need. Of this she was sure.

556

And that it was because Kaella's need was not for herself but for another; drawing her into the path of humanity.

"Speak your heart, daughter," said Miriam. "What brings you here to me in such need?"

"It is for Mary Magdalene I come my lady. She is in direst danger and I know no other that can help her. The forces of her soul's undoing are already within her mind. So, I have come to you to beg your aid."

"That is well done; thank you Kaella," answered Miriam. "Rest; your part is done. But pray for me; that I do not get there too late."

CHAPTER 29.

I had to get out, and quickly.

The shadows had grown inside the smithy as the day dropped into a quickly growing dusk, menacing me from the outside, as well as what was going on in my mind.

Each corner seemed to hold a demonic presence and the name Azrael-roth was echoing through me, like an appalling call into the darkness...

I had to escape it, so gathered myself and ran; not even shutting up the smithy properly, just heading wildly away from everything that seemed to hold menace.

Why couldn't I go to Martha and Mary? But I couldn't mix this madness up with all that was real and important to me... as I really am; had been. I had to run.

It seemed to help... the running. The effort, the hard breathing, the motion, leaving no room for anything else to get to me... but I knew I couldn't keep it up forever.

I had somewhere turned onto a road that I didn't recognise, going through mostly open land; passing a few buildings on the outskirts of Bethany. There was a tunnel of trees around the road ahead that I didn't like the look of, so I slowed to a walk, one hand holding my side as my breath heaved, following from the extra efforts.

Out to the left there were pasturelands leading up to some hills above which stars were just beginning to come out in the sky above.

My decision was made, almost made for me, and hitching up my dress I found a place where I could climb over the low wall. Scrub branches along the wall caught at my clothes, at me, like hands pulling me back, refuelling my panic.

I tore away and jumped into the field, nearly twisting my ankle, but instead fell to my knees, scratching them and my hands. I spat on my hands rubbing them together and down my dress as I got up again.

Slower, but with equal effort I started walking across the uneven ground, stumbling and gasping but so keen to get away from 'this world' that seemed bent on destroying me...

*

Yresmin and Johannus came upon Mother as she got back to Joseph's house and she invited them in after her.

They hadn't seen Magdalene and showed some surprise when Mary told them she had seen her at Joseph's offices in town, which she picked up on. "Is everything all right?"

"I had been wanting to talk with you about something mother, but maybe she spoke with you herself... Magdalene?" said Yresmin, and in a moment it was between the two women, and Johannus knew he had no place there.

"Come with me my dear," said mother, opening a door to invite Yresmin into a parlour room that led out towards the back garden, her expression questioning back to Johannus.

He nodded to say "Yes I am fine."

Johannus paced around the front entrance hall until, to his surprise, a servant came from out the back, and invited him to come to Joseph in the garden.

The beloved uncle of Yeheshua's family was working in his garden, tying some trailing branches, heavy laden with perfumed flowers onto a wooden frame that ran around one side of the outside courtyard. Joseph's house was lovely with much of his own personal care spent on it, like today.

"Aahhh," exclaimed Joseph, putting down the twine and turning to greet Johannus, "I heard you and Yresmin had come to visit; how very nice. Would you like a drink? I shall be having some as I know it is being made for Mary and Yresmin already."

"Thank you, grandfather; that would be very nice," he answered, though Joseph could tell something was bothering him. "You have a lovely place here. Do you do all the gardening yourself?"

"No, no," answered the older man, taking the tray from the servant who brought out the drinks, and over to a table where there were chairs. "I only do the bits and pieces that I like these days, but I do love having this garden."

They talked about this and that, the work at the Inn, Miriam's tour in Galilee and after a while Joseph concluded there was something else bothering the young man, but that he had best not try to pursue it.

"Would you like to stay for our meal, you would be most welcome?" said Joseph, giving Johannus the chance to either ask for his help, or follow his own way.

"I would love to sire," started Johannus, "though I need to get back to the Inn quite soon," he said, thinking of when he might see Thomas or Magdalene. "But if Yresmin could be included in your kind invitation, I would be most grateful; rather than my just deserting her?"

"Of course," answered Joseph, "that goes without saying."

"And please give her my apologies too."

Joseph saw that it must be something important, and gave his hand to Johannus as they both got up. "Keep well Johannus, there is much for you to do in these times. If you need to get back to the Inn, I am sure it will be for the best. We shall look after Yresmin, and come that way a little later."

*

Johannus was grateful, for he had been eager to get going.

Something was wrong; his heart told him he should be back.

He quickly navigated the now well-known route to the Inn, arriving with everything seeming normal. He slowed his gait, regaining his breath and looking for someone...

Seeing neither Magdalene nor Thomas he wanders along beside the barn down to the orchard, instinctively keeping away from the main house after the earlier encounter.

No sign of anyone, but then he spots Beor helping in an outhouse, his great strength being used to hold a beam being worked into place.

"Have you seen Magdalene?" asked Johannus as he passed, and Beor's face spoke volumes in reply, the little shake being all Johannus needed.

This time Johannus steered closer to the house, deciding to make certain whether or not Thomas was around.

His sense of anxiety was still high when the last person he wanted to see came out of the lower door… Zelotes, looking smug.

Johannus thought to turn away but a surge of rage came through him and he found himself walking straight up towards Zelotes.

The look on Johannus face jolted Simon to a halt. Despite himself he felt a guilt creep up his neck making it prickle.

The anger flowed through Johannus without his being able to stop it. "What have you done Simon? Why are you looking so smug and so guilty?"

Johannus was standing face on to Simon and the apostle was stuttering; "Nothing, nothing … what are you talking about?" But he was backing away and turned to go back into the door he had come from.

Johannus wanted to shout after him and was shocked at himself. What was releasing this in him?

Peter came out of the room above and Johannus quickly realised there was no advantage to what he was doing. Meekly he asked the elder, "Sir, have you seen Magdalene? Mother said she was coming back here?"

"I haven't seen her for a few days Johannus. I hope everything is alright?" answered Peter with real concern.

"I am sure everything is well; but I will know better when I find her, sire. Thank you though."

"Maybe she went to Bethany instead of here?" suggested Peter and Johannus agreed, nodding gratefully as he turned, heading off to the front gate.

*

Normally he would have gone over the field path, but today opted for the road instead and barely had he got outside the gate than the grey mare carrying Thomas turned the corner.

Johannus was caught by indecision, his main aim having become to find Mary, but his brain told him that he had to say something to Thomas too.

Thomas was glad to have made it back to the Inn. It felt like it had been a long journey today and he was tired. Clumping along the last stretch he saw Johannus coming his way, looking slightly agitated.

Thomas liked the man, so slowed Hera down to a walk to greet him on passing., and Johannus came up close to Hera's neck.

"Thomas," Johannus spoke as quietly as he could; but without preamble rather blurting, "Mary… Magdalene, she is with child, your child."

Thomas was shocked at this though he knew it might be true, but Johannus continued, "… the others; Simon and others are acting rather strangely, as though they know something that they can't. I am going to try to find Mary."

Thomas didn't know what to do. Turn around and follow, or rather ride ahead and find her himself? Or go back to the Inn and see what was going on with his brethren?

If he hadn't been so tired, he might have chosen the first option, but equally he needed to find out, sort out, what had happened at the Inn; and Johannus was already going after Mary. "Take Hera, Johannus. I shall go and sort out whatever is going on with the twelve."

Dusk was drawing in… "I shall do better on foot, Thomas; but please follow quickly, when you are done."

"I will, and please tell her I shall meet with her as soon as I can, Johannus."

Johannus nodded, and hurried on along the road to Bethany, increasing his speed as daylight faded… passing Yresmin's barn; his place as well at the moment, and slowed, wondering if he should get a coat?

From somewhere in the back of his mind he half remembered his recurring dream of being in the desert with an empty water bottle and he decided he would make sure he didn't regret not taking this opportunity… just in case.

He put on his coat, filled a water bottle and one last impulse grabbed one of the blankets from the 'guest pile', and then carefully locked shut the yard gate after him… it was getting quite dark now.

Down the road he marched, thinking what he might say, either to Magdalene or to Lazarus and his sisters where she stayed… if she was not already there.

Past the alley to the smithy, looking down out of habit, and nearly passed on. Then suddenly thought, why are the door gates ajar? They shouldn't be.

He went back, and down the alley, and he was right. It looked as though someone had left in a hurry, or maybe was still inside.

Going quietly forward he called out her name, "Mary, Mary, are you there?"

There was no-one inside, but it looked as though someone had been. Nothing certain, maybe a lingering hint of her presence or the disarrangement of the pile of sacks. Could have been nothing in themselves, but with the door being left unlocked he was sure Mary had been here.

'Why?' he wondered, and then he thought why he liked to come here sometimes, to get away from everybody.

He was sure that's how it was for Mary. The same feeling that had made him anxious earlier; but stronger here.

He looked around to make sure that she had gone, and then left as well; carefully closing the gate doors in the prescribed way.

Where to now? He had no idea, but something told him that it wouldn't be to Lazarus' house. Nevertheless, he had to make sure.

CHAPTER 30.

She hadn't been to Lazarus's. The sisters asked Johannus if there was anything wrong and he could only shrug, trying to diffuse their concern, keeping it light. "No, no; I certainly hope not; just wanted to catch up with her. She was in the city with Joseph and I know she was coming back today. She must be at the Inn. I was out here so I thought I would ask you first."

Indeed, he could only think of the tombs, or to follow the hill path back to the Inn. He didn't want to go to the hillside of tombs again, and felt that she was wouldn't either. One or the other, he had to choose.

Unhappy, he trudged around to where the path went off the road and up into the pastures. Mary, Mary. What happened? He remembered of course everything that had happened in Antioch… and this made him more desperate not to let her down now.

Stars were shining high above the city already, and the hour was later than he would normally have come this way. But he sensed he was right, and carried quietly on; feeling and listening his way forward, just in case Mary was close by.

*

I hobbled over the rough ground, seeking a better path; so important to keep going because I couldn't help feeling the horror of being pursued. Mental images of these pursuers assailed my mind, driving me on…

… but somehow worse was the feeling that my own demons were waiting for me ahead, and that was where I was being driven. Except I knew that these didn't need to be on the hillside, for they were already inside, demons of doubt, self-hate, despair and death, growing closer to their inevitable goal of… claiming me.

I tried hard to think of Yeheshua, to call to him; but it was weak, desperately weak. I could remember him saying that he would always be with me but it didn't feel like that; rather that he was an infinity away in a heaven cut off from where I was … or could ever get to.

I wept. For myself and for everything I had lost. Uncontrolled sobs going through me, for I couldn't understand how this could be happening.

My utter fear of being possessed was not about some imagined thing for I had known its deep and intimate reality, that would have killed me had I not got to my master.

On up the hillside I went, finding a sheep path now that made the way a bit quicker but the tears were still streaming from me as my heart railed against this shock.

And railed against the horror that this would be the fate of my yet unborn girl, Sarah.

*

Kaella couldn't rest long after Miriam had left her, rising again on Heraikaliphon's wings into the night.

Circling higher and higher, she swooped southward once again towards the Jerusalem in her world, a jewel of pulsing life that was still stained with the blood of Yeheshua, but which had received blessings upon blessings in return, and these were the powers that drew her in.

Thomas was there she felt, the young lion who had stood before her might upon her own hilltop. He was in a bigger centre of power and light; there was no way for her to reach him there.

She knew that the child growing within Magdalene was Thomas's, could trace the connection across her world to where the mother was crawling her way across the countryside.

Kaella already knew that rescuing Mary was beyond her, it needed someone within her physical world to be able to reach her... before it was too late.

She circled higher again spreading the net of her vision all around.

Miriam was travelling on the road from Galilee, aided by the stout young donkey colt that was much more than he seemed, though quite how? was veiled from Kaella's sight.

Too late thought Kaella, she would be too late.

Only Johannus was close enough to make it to Mary, but he wasn't strong enough on his own to challenge... however willing he might be to try.

Kaella let her great form glide round towards her chosen human, fearful that this was not a good time for her own approach, but put that aside.

Down to alight in the shadow of a grove of trees high up the hillside that Johannus made his way along.

*

Johannus felt rather than saw the shadow dropping onto the hillside above him. He shivered slightly, sensing the power of night contained in it.

He stopped and peered in the direction of the copse, wondering what it could mean.

Was that a shimmer of light? A figure on the hillside? A ghostly glimmering?

His first inclination was to pull the blanket he carried around his shoulders, which gave him what he needed to hold his ground, even advance a pace or two towards the woods, gaze fixed on the glimmering.

The touch he felt within his mind was hauntingly familiar. Kaella was out on the hillside, had come to him... for what? What was her game?

'Magdalene,' came the reply, faint but out in the region of her presence.

He growled within himself, 'I know that, witch queen; what is she to you?'

'In danger; the darkness has reached her. You can help.'

The ghostly light had solidified somewhat into a more recognisable figure from out of his dreams, but now he could see behind her a massive crouching form.

Any other night Johannus could have coped with all of this, but in his

563

amplified sensitivity there was already a feeling of demonic interference and he didn't altogether trust Hecate in all this either, despite his always having liked Kaella, and more than that.

'Come' said Kaella. 'Come Johannus, I shall you the way;' and without waiting for his response the great Heraikaliphon had sprung up into the night, obliterating many stars from Johannus sight.

Kaella knew she didn't have much influence over Johannus anymore, but flew her dragonform in the direction she knew Magdalene to be anyway, and was gratified to see him moving after her, though so slowly it could make her weep in frustration.

*

Alone, hopelessly alone now, I trudged upwards, but feeling nevertheless I was descending… down, down to where there was no returning, my mind almost entirely engulfed in demonic thoughts, my heart broken and soul self-condemned.

Only Sarah kept me trying; my daughter yet to know what life could be, to breathe the air and have her heart beating with the glory of being given… everything.

But I was surrounded inside and out, with despair; even as I crested the hill nearby a mound of rocks and earth, no higher to go; and no hope to be found there either.

I tried to gather myself, the knowing inside, here at the end; but my heart was sunk so deep in pain that all I could do was weep for everything.

Somewhere, from somewhere I heard another voice, not like the clamouring of those within my mind, but soft and steady. "Why do you doubt so, Mary?"

She looked around but there was no-one. Yeheshua? Miriam? It could have been either, but there was no-one around, just a whisper of hope as I felt my own breath echo the touch of it.

I clasped Sarah's hand in mine, turning again to look for another way.

Shapes were all around, grey shadows of lifelessness that I could recognise from my own thoughts. Azrael-roth and the minions of death, exuding a dread mist that blotted out the stars above.

They didn't particularly bother me now, it was only that I had brought this knowingly upon myself, had courted my own downfall, having been given everything, yet somehow cast it away.

Above, a shape darker even than the evil mist itself flew overhead, circling once then veering off, pointing to where I must go, or so I felt; where sentence would be made and death received.

Our souls in chains, Sarah and I followed where we had to go.

*

Johannus trudged on, not having any idea what or where he was going, but neither could he think of a different course to follow, and just maybe Kaella was trying to help.

He couldn't see the dragon in the night sky anymore, but occasionally he thought a star or two would glint out of view, and so he followed on, seeming to skirt around the city of Jerusalem.

He stopped a little while for a drink from his water flask and was very glad he had brought it.

It seemed it was going to be a long strange night.

*

I didn't know whether the evil was inside or outside of me and it didn't seem to make any difference anyway.

It rushed around, through me, demented spirits shouting the obscenities I had once been trapped interminably with.

'Doubt?' Came my belated answer, torn out of the remains of my mind. 'Don't I have good reason? Wasn't I once the most wretched of creatures? and then given new life, somehow to think I had become worthy of the highest heights, the greatest honour.' Stupidity, 'Pah, only to topple headlong into the source of my wretchedness again. Not Doubt, no, just the realisation of my self-destined fall.'

All around me the same condemnation showered down, from my own head or from the demons I no longer knew. My end approached as slowly and inevitably as this long blind march through interminable night was claiming my mind and soul.

Except the one tiny part of me that had always been able to be separate, and that was now pressed into contact with Sarah, like the clasping warmth of our hands.

No thought involved, just the desperate determination to somehow get her to safety, and this spread a little way into me like a shoot of hope.

Not for myself, I would end it all myself. I had no doubt the demons would lead me to take my own life, cut my neck or wrists or simply plunge my body from some cliff. This was my path to damnation and I had already drunk the cup to take me there…

That brought on the unimaginable horror; being pitilessly driven into the endless torment of losing my own soul's way, my soul itself.

Bitter beyond tears and the howling of bestiality.

Stumbling on, under the combined weight of that, and a heart rent with dread.

Could I, in my ending, shield this awful dread from my lovely girl?

Yet that shoot of faintest hope was deliberately being torn from my hand, almost numb now.

Desperately I clutched on so hard that my nails dug deep into my palm, giving focus to my straining, till even that faded as a strange blackness descended over all we were.

I knew we were approaching the place.

A grey clad figure stood out in that darkness, dread power surrounding it and even the demons themselves, crowded close in on me, claiming me, were cowering at the same time.

The voice when it spoke was incredibly flat and neutral. "Give the child over to me."

Was it me or was it the devils around me that resisted like a crocodile on a baited line.

"Give the child to me," she said again, for it was a woman.

CHAPTER 31.

She was tall and shrouded, but carried the sharp curved knife of sacrifice.

Behind her was an even darker cleft into the depths of dark, and by her side a tiger beast, red eyed and whose growling maw revealed teeth to match the priestess's knife.

She took a step forward, knife raised and glinting. Everything stopped, even all the clamour inside of me.

"Drink this" she said in the same even tone, bringing the knife down to slice my mouth and neck, its blade cold as death,

Water trickled down my throat… not the blood my mind was conjuring up; and everything changed.

The veils of devilry dropped from my eyes. I had somehow found myself to be in a garden that I recognised: Siloam; and it was Miriam that was stood in front of me, pouring water into my hands and open mouth, from a small travel skin.

By her side was the donkey colt Indy, and behind her the tomb whose entrance stone was partly rolled away; the scene all lit by a waning half moon, newly risen in the east.

"Don't worry for the child," said Miriam. "You have your work to do. I shall look after her."

The demons within me still held an almost crippling grip on everything inside; my voice and thoughts and even my emotions, but I could still hear and understand Miriam's words. Azrael-roth and his kin were powerless as yet, outside of me, and seemingly in real fear of Indy.

"Go inside the master's tomb and sit upon his bed and practice what he showed to you and me both, that day in your house in Magdala. Distinguish the real from the unreal, the simple truths from the maelstrom of madness. You have the means to rid yourself of demons; they have no power over you, sister."

*

The tomb was nowhere I wished to go, not as prey meat.

Miriam had gone and I was all alone.

My mind, my body, everything in me froze.

Fear ran up the inside of my spine and doubt cast a blanket over my heart; devoid of hope.

Even Sarah was gone… all void.

Entering the tomb was the hardest thing I had ever done… drawn into the sheer terror of Azrael-roth's final victory over my soul.

Unfathomable sadness threatened to overcome me completely, but numbly I squeezed through the gap into the blackness, fumbling forward to find the shelf carved from the rock itself.

Sitting down I didn't think at all, just followed the simple instructions I had in my heart… indelible, without expectation.

The maelstrom of madness, never the same, never still, had erupted once more inside my head, but I couldn't afford to fear it or pay it any credence.

I just looked for one tiny glimmer of what was real in me; nothing vast and sweeping, but it was there… the place I could rest my attention and I knew that it was real.

Though it was almost nothing, somehow it had just the amount of comfort and rest I needed, and peace. I could sit there quietly whilst the storm raged on in me and it didn't touch me.

One after another I brought all my senses, my feeling, into focus on the gift of life happening within me.

Unheralded and unasked it continually gave itself into me and now I was attuned to that, just that.

The efforts of the demons to sweep me away into their domain continued unabated but something in me just dug deeper into the security of my life, in me.

I didn't need anything else, no approval, no relations, no other people, only the real in me. That in fact was everything.

Eventually the wailing of Azrael-roth and his creatures collapsed into their own non-reality; not in me any more, anyway.

Ever wider waves of peace swelled inside me and I came became their focus, rocking me in the gentle motion of my breathing.

In the relief of everything that had been happening I laid myself down along the shelf and slept with my head resting on my arm.

CHAPTER 32.

Johannus was tired and no longer quite knew why or where he was going; what had driven him to be trekking along these paths, unknown to him, beyond the city of Jerusalem.

Yes, he knew it was about Mary, Mary Magdalene; but why he thought her to be in such danger he couldn't quite any longer fathom.

Instead, with the need for sleep dragging stronger and stronger on him, the desire to find somewhere to lie down out of the cold of approaching dawn, became uppermost.

Kaella on the other hand could see the events unfolding; she saw that Miriam had got back in time, and she relayed this into the half dreaming mind of Johannus on the hillside.

He saw Mary, as if held in trance meeting with Miriam in the garden of the tomb that Joseph had given over to Yeheshua, and saw that Mary had gone herself into the tomb, whilst Miriam was sitting close by with the donkey colt.

Realising he wasn't too far from the garden, Johannus roused himself to action and gathering his strength like once he had those few years ago when he had taken Mary to the healer Rachel, he doggedly walked the lanes and ways, grateful that he had got there, to help his companions of the Qadesh Quest.

Half stumbling across the grass to where Miriam was, Johannus wondered how she had got there, back from Galilee.

"Is everything alright, Miriam? with Mary? I saw that she had got here, to you."

Miriam looked at him then glanced over his head to the way he would have come over the hills. She knew of the connection between Kaella and Johannus and sensed the dragon-girl's helping hand. "I think you need to sleep Johannus, more than anything else. Yes, everything will be alright for Mary."

"Yes… I am tired. This is a nice night to sleep out though, and I would stay here for her if you will?"

He closed his eyes, sitting down on the blanket he had laid on the ground, relieved that he could rest and that everything was somehow fine again.

"You have done well Johannus," said Miriam, and he looked up at her, for a moment seeing Yeheshua himself standing there. She gave him her travelling cloak. "Take this for your comfort and when the light grows, see if maybe Mary will have need of it. I am going to Joseph's now if you are staying for Magdalene."

*

I awoke from a sweet deep sleep to find Miriam's cloak laid over me and a water flask next to the shelf, that answered my thirst.

The night had been darker inside me than I could have ever dreamt but that had made the coming of the light into my heart and head all the more wonderful and complete; permeating into every part of me like water to a person thirsting in the desert.

I suddenly realised that this was the very same shelf that my Lord Yeheshua had woken on as well, and his presence was as if woven into Miriam's cloak that I hugged around me.

I knew there was nowhere I needed to go, nothing I needed to do except soak every part of my being in the understanding of myself, accepting this spark of the divine I had been shown, been allowed to know in me.

Yeheshua was closer to me, all around me; as he had promised; and filled me too, shining through all of me. I was just a garment of the glory within and being blessed to have and know this now.

And inside my womb was the most incredible gift of another life, my daughter yet to come forth into this world, still bound with me in the miracle of being created. As indeed I still was as well, being created anew by the miracle of life being breathed softly into me, again and again and again, and on, and no reason for being anywhere else, or anything else.

A miracle because sitting there I didn't need to do anything to make it happen, could do nothing anyway, nothing other than open my heart and mind in gratitude that it was, making the joy of it enveloping me all the more.

Strong sunlight striking through into the floor of the tomb roused my mind to acknowledge the world happening around me as well.

Memories of what must have transpired the night before slotted into place within my brain, belonging to me now and no longer holding me as victim to the thought forces and opinions, personified in those most demonic forms.

I would go to Magdala.

*

Thomas had gone back into the yard, taking the mare down to her stable in the corner of the orchard, spending time to feed and water her despite his thoughts whirling around.

Brushing her down helped him calm his mind from the anger bubbling up into it, but he knew he must face whatever it was that was going on.

Nevertheless, he wasn't going to pander to the game of their imaginings; he was first of all going to see if there was some food in the barn kitchen.

Salome was still clearing up and was able to give him some leftovers from the evening meal. He thanked her and sat down, deliberately clearing his mind of the babble of unhelpful thoughts.

Washing up his own plate, he thanked Salome again and made himself hold the feeling of Mary Magdalene foremost in his mind and heart as he went up into the upper room, where several of the brethren were; just as he knew they would be.

"Has anyone seen Mary Magdalene?" he asked straight out, watching the faces of the four of them inside. Jude shook his head and looked away whilst Matthias looked surprised and turned to Simon Zelotes who was talking with Andrew, Peter's brother.

Andrew looked at him steadily but Simon started noticeably, turning away a bit too late for Thomas to miss the smirk that crossed his face.

Thomas made a great effort to ignore that, instead addressing Andrew directly, "I heard some things that led me to believe she had been here, looking for me. Is that not the case?"

Andrew looked uncomfortable now, but it was Matthias that answered, "No-one has spoken to Magdalene today that I know of; only Johannus and the Nabatean woman came looking for you earlier today."

"Peter talked with them I think," said Andrew, "He is in his room if you want to ask him."

"Thank you, I will," Thomas replied and then called across, "Simon…? "

Simon Zelotes reddened slightly but turned to face Thomas who continued, his eyes boring into the face of the other man, "is there anything you want to say?"

"No… nothing," replied Zelotes looking distinctly shifty and Thomas knew he had found the source of whatever bad was going on.

"Well, if you do, please say it to my face, brother," and pausing long enough to ensure his words hit home he turned to go with Andrew, leaving in the direction of the outer stairs.

Peter was his usual thoughtful and caring self, looking at Thomas with concern from under full brows, his hand stroking his beard. "There seems to be the idea going around that Magdalene is pregnant with your child Thomas, though I don't know where this has come from."

Thomas nodded, "It is possible Peter, we were together soon after the crucifixion and if you can keep this between you and me?" Peter nodded, "without her coming to me I would have ended my life then and there; and, and it was me that initiated what happened after…"

Peter considered Thomas words as the younger man continued "I may not be able to help myself from damaging any man, brother or not, who I hear disrespecting her."

"I think you should go to her Thomas," said Peter not unkindly. "I believe she is staying at Lazarus' house; and I will deal with anything amongst the brothers. Don't worry on that score; you have my word."

Thomas thanked him and left the yard from out the front without looking back, walking fast with a purpose following where Johannus had gone before.

He also knocked at Lazarus' house asking after Magdalene, and Mary was worried now.

"Johannus was asking for her earlier," she said, "but we haven't seen her for days, though we are expecting her back; is everything alright?"

Thomas thought about opening himself to Mary but this was almost Magdalene's family, it was her territory to cover. He shook his head, "I just feel a bit tired," he said, "but Mary asked me to pop in when I got back from Bethlehem. I shall try at Yresmin's, I think she could be there. Please say I dropped by though if she comes back tonight," and he smiled at Mary as he backed away. "Thank you," he said.

It was dark as he headed back again, past Yresmin's barn at Bethphage where a light prompted him to go and knock on her door. She was there and ushered him in without accepting any argument to the contrary, even though Mary was not there.

So thankful to see him, and she couldn't help but give him a most unlikely hug, which he also returned gratefully. Suddenly he realised how he had been all over the place, and needed this chance to talk about it.

Yresmin couldn't help herself either; feeling completely emotional about all the day's events... and responsible for what had been said to Peter earlier; and then how kind Mother had been when she had talked it over, and now Thomas himself here with her; she told him everything.

Thomas understood how things could have happened and he was overcome with how Mary must have been affected, just from what he had gathered from seeing Johannus, and then with confronting Simon too. Something had been wrong. He wept quietly as Yresmin spoke, feelings welling up from deep inside that he needed so much to let out.

He wept later on, ever more, without respite; after having reassured Yresmin about all of it, and accepting her invitation to stay.

Wept about everything he had missed and wouldn't be able to make up for... for the pain and loneliness that Mary would be experiencing, knew she was, for he could feel her somewhere out there in the dark, her soul ranged against the hurt surrounding her; for there being nothing he could do but pour out his heart, his pain too, for her... for he did love her, and was very glad that she carried his child; for him, for her, for love.

If there had been a chance of finding her, he would have continued trying, but he could only hope that her friend Johannus would. Instead, he lay curled up neither sleeping nor waking, just holding onto Mary in his soul, till eventually he drifted into a half-sleep, dreaming he was on a hill where he had been once before... a girl... a mighty dragon... and going beyond.

And another girl, who was his daughter, striding out across the world.

*

Kaella looked on and knew she too would be joining the mortal path in the age to come...

And knew that she would bring daughters into this world as well; would become just as involved in these human relationships and dilemmas.

That she had thought human lives to be both mean and meaningless now seemed so wrong, for she could feel the intensity of all that was happening and how that could reach both the deepest and highest places.

Could and would bring her to where she needed to go; to know, to find, to reach... her goal.

*

And Thomas rallied beyond his tears and dreams, knowing the peace where everything was joined.

CHAPTER 33.

I would go to Magdala; not because I was running away or didn't want to face the brethren.

Magdala, because I was going to embrace this new start, this new life; because of my love for Yeheshua and the work I would do now.

And for Thomas, and the unborn baby too.

No, not to enable Thomas and myself to get together. I was beyond that now. I had the fruit of our union within me and would always have his love and he mine. I knew that, and also knew we both had work to do; the work that would forever hold us together, though perhaps seemingly apart.

First, I wanted to go and have a talk with Mother.

Johannus was wrapped up in a blanket, lying back against the side of a tree.

I looked at his face, head drooped against a shoulder and thought not to disturb his sleep, but he suddenly jerked awake and struggled to get to his feet.

I laughed and helped him up. "You are alright Mary?" he said or asked, and I laughed again. "Seems so, and thank you for the water; and this is Miriam's cloak isn't it?"

"Yes, she said you might need it."

"Would you take it to her and thank her for me. I am going to the Inn to see Mother as soon as I can."

Johannus caught my sense of purpose. "What are you going to do then?"

"Go back to Galilee and continue the master's work there."

There was a long pause between us; words not needed. "I have resources there, and a place to have my baby as well. I have been given everything, everything, and now I know how much."

"I hope you will allow occasional visitors?"

"Of course; you must come, very soon."

I gave him a big hug. "Please tell Miriam that I am going to be ready for her to visit anytime too. In case she is coming back up to Galilee. For as long as she wants; and you!"

"Thank you; I will tell her. Will you be coming over to Joseph's?

"If I have time, but I know there is an asses train leaving mid morning and I want to catch that. But send my love to grandfather for me as well. He has been so kind."

"I will. Go on then or you will miss breakfast; and count on it I will be coming up to Magdala soon." Final hug. "Seriously, it is wonderful to see you looking so good," he said.

We parted and I set off for the Inn and for the first time in days I didn't feel sick but was really looking forward to seeing all that was happening there."

At the barn I discovered that breakfast was being taken to Mother in her room, and managed to beg the chance to take it to her, plus a flatbread and a hot tea for myself.

I crossed towards her entrance, not even thinking of anyone else but enjoying the atmosphere and the early morning energy. John came out of the door into the yard, greeting me with an exclamation, "Oh Mary, how good to see you."

I had always liked John too, "Mother will be so pleased you are here. She has been asking after you."

He held the door open for me. "Thank you, John; and in case anyone asks, I am very well... "

He smiled, "I never thought otherwise Mary."

"And I think Yeheshua would be really happy with all that has been achieved here, John. Who could have thought?"

"I know; and it has all only just begun," and he laughed.

I grinned back and slipped through the door to get to Mother's rooms.

My knock was answered by Mary herself opening the door and taking the tray from me as I went through. She put it down on a small table and turned back to give me a massive hug, eyes glistening as we pulled apart.

It felt like Yeheshua was right there in the room with us and I found myself looking around for him.

"Peter came to see me last night," she said and added, "Thomas had been to see him it seems."

"Ahhh, well..."

"John told me this morning that Peter had called Simon Zelotes in to talk to him..."

".. and he kept him there most of the night. From what John told me Peter was getting Simon to explain himself again and again; to be really clear at just what he was saying, thinking, and telling other people. And never satisfied until he got the message completely and fully that it was really none of Simon's business, and never ever would be."

"Haah; well I have only told Yresmin to this point, although Johannus knows and now I think he told Thomas. I would have come to you mother but there was so much I was unsure of..."

"So, now you are? Sure of what you want?"

"Sure of what I must do; ever since the day you and my master made it possible for me; and now so much more so... to walk the path ahead. I plan be going up to Magdala today."

"What about Thomas?"

I stopped to think before answering. "I cannot answer for him, mother, but I think the master gave him work to do and I have mine too. My lord has opened my eyes; and Miriam too. I was in a bad, place, blind beyond, even beyond when we first met. Do you remember?"

"Yes sweetheart, you were very badly hurt then."

"So, I was indeed... abominated and possessed and yet our Lord took me into his heart, and the heart of what he was and is doing." I stopped, paused, "and Thomas has given me the most marvellous gift too, that I will treasure with my very life as well; but I don't want him to leave off from what he has to do; no, I really don't. I shall love him that he is following the footsteps of our Lord, even as I shall be trying to do."

"And I have been watching Miriam, mother, seeing how much she cares that all the work her beloved did is not wasted, visiting all the women in particular, in their homes, that they can keep the inner lamps he lit burning; and last night she helped me through a dark, dark place as well, to have the chance again to know... the simplicity of what I so often overlook; being real and true to that. That is what I must do and want to help others with, and Galilee is where I can do that best, especially with the baby coming."

Mother put out her hands to take mine. "You are right Mary, I feel it too," she said. "That we can be filled with the spirit of his love, our love, God's love, to such a depth that all the community will be our family, and any person seeking that real comfort. The brethren do have a path to follow, out in front of all the world, but ours is no lesser task, to secure the love of the truth within the hearts of those who have opened to it, if just for a moment. Yes, there may come a time, and I know he said more, but I am more than content in this time we have, to live out his love here."

"Yes, this is a time for gathering our strength. There will be many rocky times ahead, and the apostles will be the ones to take the brunt of so much, out in this world. I fully see that. And it is a fantastic start we have been able to make here; supporting that work and having a way for it to blossom." I laughed, "who could believe that such a thriving place to express that love could grow so quickly. It was only a few weeks ago we were thinking of it all in Nicodemus' house."

"Hah, yes it was. Drink your tea, it will be getting cold, haha, and have some of this fruit, it is good for you."

"I must get out to Bethany. I have to say good bye to them there."

"Martha stayed in my guest bed last night. They were worried after first Johannus and then Thomas knocked on their door looking for you. She came to see me quite late on and I convinced her to stay. I am sure she will have heard you are here by now..."

I got up and out to knock on the door of the small room next to Mother's and no-one was in, but as I turned back to Mother's room there was Martha with the broadest smile I had ever seen her wearing.

"How did you get here like that?" I asked astonished, disengaging from her hug.

"I heard you were here and was waiting just outside, in the yard, haha. Saw you come out of Mother's room."

"Moses! I have caused such trouble. Well, I am going to retreat up to my home in Magdala for a few weeks or months; and I was going to try to get out to Bethany first to let you all know. But there is an asses train I intend to join leaving by midday, so it was going to be tight."

"I would stop you if I could, but maybe Mary and myself will come up to visit you instead. Lazarus is getting stronger and stronger; he might come as well."

"Martha, I will be back and imposing myself on you all too soon. I hope you will be alright with a little one as well?"

"Oh, that will be so special, darling! I can't wait to tell Lazarus, Ruth and Mary."

"I want to keep it a bit quiet; in fact really quiet, but I suppose that is impossible now... Nevertheless, my wish is to try... to do this my own way."

I could see she was about to say 'Thomas?' and I shook my head. "I want to do this by myself, Martha. So, I must go today; in fact now, before..."

She nodded and we both went into Mother's room where we had a three-way hug before I left them quietly and disappeared quickly through the yard and out into the street.

Johannus took the cloak and message from Magdalene to Miriam in Joseph's house, which was quite close.

Miriam had not come from her room yet, but Joseph's manservant Aaron showed Johannus through to where the elder was having some breakfast in the secluded part of the garden, bathed in the morning light; the same spot he had sat with Joseph only the day before.

Joseph didn't rise but indicated that Johannus should join him, which he did.

"Aaron, please bring some watermelon," said Joseph to the other who was clearly more friend than servant, and only a few years younger than Joseph; "if I remember correctly that is our guest's favourite?" Johannus nodded, "and please join us, with some more tea too, Aoron. I think Miriam will be down soon."

Aaron looked at the cloak Johannus was still clutching, but thought better of offering to take it from him, and Johannus was quietly grateful.

"So did everything work out alright yesterday?" asked Joseph simply, but Johannus suspected he must already know. He was just working out how to answer when Miriam appeared with the watermelon slices that she had taken from Aaron.

Joseph and Johannus got up and Miriam placed the melon on the table before going around and kissing Joseph on the cheek.

"Good morning my dear," said Joseph. "I hope you slept soundly after your sudden journey? I was just asking Johannus here whether everything has worked out alright from yesterday."

Miriam looked radiant rather than tired, thought Johannus, and he found himself offering up the cloak as some kind of evidence. "Magdalene asked me to return this," he said to Miriam but also in answer to Joseph. "She surprised me this morning by being up so bright and early, and asked me to thank you for it."

"Ahh," said Joseph, "that sounds good news then," and Miriam smiled conspiratorially to Johannus.

"She also said she was going to Magdala today, and that she hoped you would go and stay as soon as you might like to; and for as long as you would like as well."

"That may be sooner than she thinks, hah; I am thinking of going right back today. I left a message for Philip and Nathaniel in Bethsaida, and there is much to be done there." She paused looking directly at Johannus. "Would you be able to come up too?"

Johannus didn't hesitate. "Yes, certainly." His mind raced thinking of what he would need to get, how quickly he could do it. "When?" he asked.

"Well, perhaps we could join the same train as Mary, so I was thinking to go to the market area before midday, with Indy; he will be well rested by then."

"I will be there. I shall go to Yresmin's to pick up my things, but will be there before midday."

Johannus rose to his feet again, "I beg your leave Grandfather to go; and I thank you for your hospitality again."

"Yes go, go, by all means, and God speed Johannus."

*

When Johannus got to Yresmin's he was surprised to hear that Thomas had stayed, and had been almost following after the way he had himself gone. And that he was now gone to visit Lazarus and his sisters in case Magdalene had got back there.

The story of the night before came out gradually as Yresmin pulled out one bit after another, being particularly fascinated at his reluctance in relating the influence of Kaella and the dragon, but Yresmin wasn't the least surprised.

"Sacred bearer of the Goddess Manat," was all she would say. "Dragons?" pressed Johannus and Yresmin nodded.

"I am going to Galilee today," he told Yresmin. "There is lots going on, and I am so happy to get this chance to go up with Miriam there."

Yresmin recognised his excitement and also felt a bit of envy herself.

Miriam seemed to be a couple of steps ahead of everyone, when considering her work in the communities of people who had already received Yeheshaua's message and love into their lives; as well as her frontline involvement in the new wave of inspiration for the risen Christ.

Yresmin wanted to join Miriam in what she was doing just as Johannus did and her envy was simply for the ease with which the younger man was able and ready to 'up sticks' and go wherever the call came from.

She could as well, she felt that; but it would take her a bit longer. Somewhere in her heart she knew that this change would be another big moment for her, and even as Johannus gave her a goodbye hug, her mind was working out how long she would need to make her arrangements, and possibly goodbyes.

She went out after Johannus into the barnyard, to the gate that led out onto the Jerusalem-Bethany road. "Tell them I shall be coming up in a week or so as well," she called after him as he set off towards Jerusalem, and turning back to see to Sella she found herself talking to her faithful donkey, scratching behind her ears. "I think we might be off on our journeys again soon my lovely girl."

*

Thomas decided to go over the pasture-way back to the Inn. He loved that name, Yeheshua's Inn, 'a stop along the way'.

Home was another place altogether, and after everything that had happened since the crucifixion Thomas felt that belonging so strongly; where the master had shown them, and still shone so brightly there, within his heart and mind.

He amongst all the brethren had been the least likely to accept what had happened, but now that he did, even though he couldn't fully comprehend it, he wanted to live his life in the fullness of what it meant.

578

His vision had grown to be a passion... to give other people the chance to open their eyes too. Even as the spirit of compassion had come to him and all the disciples together... to bouy them up along the way.

The energy coming from this passion had transformed him, and he loved nothing more than travelling from village to village to see who knew of what had happened, meeting those who did and taking any chances that came to share his love for what he had been given, the opportunity to fulfil his life.

And he never forgot the role that Mary Magdalene had played in keeping him from destroying this chance, and now he wanted to repay something.

Because, she was someone he really loved in so many ways, and she loved him too, he knew that.

Now that that episode had developed into another life coming into the world, he was caught between the currents of passion and other conflicting emotions coursing through him.

It was a lovely day to be on the pastures and he stopped to pray, to contemplate for a while in the shade of grove of trees he had walked up to.

He prayed for guidance about being the father to Magdalene's child, and cleared his mind to give himself to the light within.

Kaella saw Thomas sitting where she had been the night before, and he felt the presence he had met once out on the Ephraim hills. Recognised there had been a crisis for Magdalene the night before and had the strong sense that everything had worked out alright.

Kaella let him alone to his meditation and scried instead for signs of Johannus, Miriam and Magdalene, and found them together starting off from Jerusalem in a donkey train that would pass underneath her hills themselves. She relaxed, happy that she had been able to be of some value; in a different way to ever before.

Thomas stirred as sudden breeze followed the disappearance of the sun behind some clouds. Stretching himself he got up and brushed himself down.

He would wait for Magdalene at the Inn, but he wasn't sure she would come. But Mother would be there and he felt it to his core that she was the only other person he could or would talk to right now.

He breathed a great sigh of relief and set off into the returning sunshine.

CHAPTER 35

Thomas sat in the barn sipping a little cup of piping hot mint tea.

Salome had gone to request a talk for Thomas with Mother and had not come back yet. Mother was probably giving him time for his drink.

They had always been close, he mused, feeling she was almost his real mother. But anyway, many disciples had been in the way of bringing their questions to her before taking them to Yeheshua.

Some those same disciples were now busy making sure that everyone was going to hear about the Lord Yeheshua's victory over death and darkness. Mainly in and around the market places; and reports were spreading of miracles.

It was quiet here in the yard of his Inn, with the workers out in the fields bringing in the harvest. Thomas had seen the same happening too from Bethlehem to Jericho and had been proud to be a part of the rising tide.

He knew he would somehow be taking it further too. It needed to reach to the ends of the world.

Salome beckoned to him from Mother's entrance way across the yard and he quickly put the nearly finished drink down and walked over.

"Thank you," he said to Salome. "How is she?"

"Great," she replied. "Really been looking forward to your coming."

"She knew?"

"Of course," laughed Salome, making Thomas almost blush, but he shook his head at her instead.

When Mary answered his knock with a cheerful "come in", Thomas entered quickly crossing her ante-room and onto one knee beside the chair where she was sitting. He took her hand and kissed it and she ruffled his hair with her other one.

He loved the subtle radiance of her presence and sat back on the mat in front of her.

"Thomas, what have you been up to?" she smiled, laughing at him.

"Have you seen her? Magdalene?"

"Yes, earlier today. She is well, in case you were worried." Her deep vision encompassed him and he glowed, whether with embarrassment or gladness he wasn't sure. It was all the same

"Do you know where she is now?"

"Not exactly, no. But I know she is settled in herself, to take the child on in her own way. She is very content, Thomas. More than that, she now knows that she will be a gift, a task and a companion from God, to help her along the way ahead."

"She?"

"Yes Thomas. Mary has seen that she will be a little girl, and will call her Sarah."

"Aaahh." Thomas felt a yearning inside, but wasn't quite sure of its nature. "I would see her if I could," he said.

"I am not sure she will see you now; it might be too hard for her."

"What should I do then, mother?"

"Give her time, and do the work that you must do. She wants you to continue in that, more than anything. She told me so."

Thomas sighed and felt a weight dropping from him, leaving him to rest in the swell and fall of his breath. "There is so much that I would do, and need to try, for all the power I have been given… and glory shown."

"Yes, I know you do, and so you shall, Thomas; so you shall." There was a pause, and then she asked, "have you written down any of the things he said? For amongst us all you are the most gifted in that way."

"I have a few, yes; but not many. Do you think I should?"

"I would like it if you could," she said, with remarkable tenderness.

"I will try then." He suddenly realised something. "You know, I have been feeling the desire to go and visit my old teacher of Philosophy in Antioch. He was inspiring to me as a youth and now I would like to return the favour to him and any of those I knew then."

Mary looked at him. "And you should. Go and spread the light a little further, for I am sure many will follow soon after."

"I would like to make the writing into something that could help them on to be ready for when those disciples get there. I think it could be, for they love to wrestle with such thoughts, like Socrates and the others."

"And after that I feel I have another path to take too, but cannot quite see it yet."

"You will, when the time is right, my dear friend. You will."

"Then I must set about it without delay. Will you tell Peter, James and John for me?"

"John is in Jericho; you might stop and see him yourself. I will tell Peter and James that you are called to go to Antioch." She kissed his head that he had rested in his hands, beside her knees.

"Oh, and Mary has gone home to Magdala, with Miriam I think, and probably Johannus too. She will be fine."

"Aaahhh, very well. Thank you, mother. Thank you more than I can ever say. I will always have you in my heart, whatever way I go."

"And I have you in my heart, Thomas. God speed."

CHAPTER 36.

Johannus got to the caravan area and found that Miriam had just arrived, with Indy too.

It seemed that half of the asses had already left as there was business to do in Jericho. The remainder were to leave soon for Jericho as well, to spend the night there and get going again early in the morning.

"Mary has left with the first train," explained Miriam, "according to the train-master Al-Harim here. She had a couple of asses that were Jericho bound."

There were four men including Al-Harim himself to drive the train. Less than normal because of the split, and they were glad of Johannus joining them; he could help, and Indy and Miriam would naturally too, being joined at the head of a group of the asses.

Johannus looked at Indy, trying to see how he was different from the other donkeys. It wasn't just his age for he had grown fully higher than the pack donkeys. He seemed like a wild ass thought Johannus, sprightly, alive and kicking... hahaha.

"He knows who he is," said Miriam, seeing his wondering expression. "Doesn't have any doubts, not like us; and he is free, too."

Johannus turned to her. Though he had travelled to Kadesh and back with her and Magdalene, it was often like he was seeing her for the first time.

"Free?" he said.

"Yes, in his own way, he is," she said scratching him behind one of his long furry ears. "He is less complicated than us, but very clear about that."

Johannus remembered in a sudden moment being a small child. There had been a kitten that had liked to play with him. They had been best mates; but it was wild too.

He laughed. "Good then. That is very good, isn't it?"

"He is very good for me, yes. Which reminds me did you see Yresmin?"

"Yes, yes, I did. She asked me to tell you and Magdalene that she would be coming up to Magdala very soon. I got the impression that she wanted to sort out her affairs to be free to do and go wherever."

"What about you and Rebecca, Johannus? Have you arranged to go to Alexandria soon?"

Despite himself Johannus blushed, and Miriam laughed at him.

"Yes, I will be going there quite soon; before the Adonis harvest festival."

"Good," said Miriam, "that gives us a little time then."

They joined the train, Miriam leading Indy and Johannus helping bring up the rear line of four asses. Quite soon they were making a good pace, the liveliness of Indy seemed to be infectious. Al-Harim was delighted.

"Where did you get such a fine beast?" he asked Miriam.

"The Lord Yeheshua asked a friend who owned the mother to give him to me."

"Yeshua? who they say survived his crucifixion and has been seen in and around the city of Jerusalem?"

"The same; and he did indeed overcome death and bring back the news that life is so much more than just a round of toil. Even death cannot hold the human soul, and yet we make such a hardship of this life. It is not meant to be that, but so much more."

"They say he was a holy man who cured the sick and could banish evil spirits too."

"He was such a master soul, and only ever wanted to help others to have as good a life as he experienced, which he knew was meant for all. To know the kingdom of the heart that does not die and lives in us now, just the same."

"Terrible thing that he was murdered by the priests and their lackeys," said the train master. "A very terrible business."

"Yes, but he overcame all their hatred and came back to us. I have spoken with him many times, as have others too. There will be many at Jericho where we are going. Do you know Zaccheus who owns an Inn there?"

"Yes, I am hoping maybe to stay there tonight, if my luck is in," said Al-Harim.

"Good. Well, so are we, and I think it will be a very special evening. I am expecting that John, one of Yeheshua's closest disciples, will be there and will be speaking of him and his work, his message; and Yeheshua himself stayed on his way to Jerusalem, much to the annoyance of the town's leaders, who wanted to make a show of him being their guest."

"Ha ha... well I think we are making good time with that fine colt of yours leading the others. Maybe we shall have more time there than usual."

CHAPTER 37

Thomas didn't waste any time once he knew what he was going to do.

There were a few arrangements to be made and so set off to the townhouse of his Uncle Tobias, who had been so good to have here in Jerusalem these last few weeks. That he was himself a Christine too was a great help.

Thomas had been able to aid him occasionally in his work as a lawyer; a small return for all the material help he gave to Thomas.

Tobias house was where Thomas habitually did his writing, including recording some of Yeheshua's insights, 'his sayings'. Mother was right, this was the time to gather his memories before they lost any of their force.

He packed up his writing case and another bag of the most useful clothes for travelling. This journey would be longer than most, but he was hugely looking forward to it.

"You must take Elias's horse back to him in Jericho, Thomas. It would be great favour for me and Elias too."

Elias was Thomas's great uncle and one of those whom Thomas had worked under at the end of his lawyer's training. He was old now and loved to see his sister's grandson whenever he might visit; spoiling him frequently.

"Is he still active in the law, uncle?"

"Not much now, no; but he keeps up with everything that is going on. He will know all about what happened to Yeheshua, and has no sympathy for the Jewish leaders here in Jerusalem."

"Yes, I got that impression last time I saw him, just before we came back here for the Passover; but I didn't have long to talk to him then."

They were eating the evening meal in the quiet of the inner garden court, where Thomas memories of Magdalene were still so strong. He wondered where she was now and how long it would be before he would get his chance to speak with her. Maybe she would be at Jericho too.

"Is there anything I can do for you in Jericho, uncle?… or indeed anywhere on the way to Antioch?"

"I do have a letter for your aunt, my sister in Caesarea Philippi, if you would be so good to drop in on her for me. I will have it for you by breakfast."

*

Thomas set off after breakfast with Elias's horse, a steady mare that suited a less fiery spirit than Thomas's, but he was grateful nevertheless. He was used to relying on the kindness of others even though it still frustrated him a bit.

Tobias watched him off and wondered what his nephew's destiny would be? He was clearly a bright star in the firmament.

Thomas did stop at a couple of villages on the road to Jericho, visiting some friends from the days of his studies and arrived at Zach's Inn in the middle of the afternoon.

He spent some time looking after the mare; he would take her round to Elias in the morning. It would be too late today as his great uncle wasn't expecting him.

He needed a drink himself and wandered into the building to see who was staying there and was more than delighted to find both Miriam and John talking tgether, at one end where the Inn had window and doors that opened into a walled courtyard.

Zaccheus noticed Thomas's arrival and went quickly over to welcome him, soon joined by John and Miriam too. Zach took the bags himself to the room Thomas always had, for Zach knew him when he was doing his studies here in Jericho.

Miriam went to get another pitcher and cup for Thomas to join them.

There was going to be a big meeting tonight because the news had got about that the singer Miriam was here as well as John, Yeheshua's apostle.

"And now you are here," said Miriam. "You might be asked to speak too."

"That is fine," answered Thomas. "Nothing I would rather do than talk about Yeheshua and the work we have to do. Where will it be held?"

"Not here," put in John, "but there is a sizeable square not far away; you must know it, near Joshua's gate."

"Oh yes, with the raised steps up to the administration block that the Romans built. They call it Augustus Court. I believe it was Judith's market in the days before them."

"The Romans are quite sympathetic and are happy for us to be using it. Pilate's proclamation counts here as well."

"I think I shall take a rest then," said Thomas, "and get freshened up before we go."

*

Thomas emerged from his room, refreshed and buoyant and went down to find his friends who were out in the garden with another, who he recognised immediately as Matthias, the disciple they had voted to make up the numbers of the twelve.

"Matthias, how good to see you." he said. "What brings you to this pleasant Inn?"

"Peter sent me, Thomas. He heard of good things happening here."

"Indeed, they are," said John. "Just like at Jerusalem in some ways, and Galilee in others, from what Miriam is saying."

"Yes, the communities are already strong in Galilee," agreed Miriam. "Numbers are growing steadily there, but not like around Jerusalem. Here in Jericho, it seems to be somewhere in between."

"I heard that you are going up to Antioch, Thomas;" said Matthias.

"Yes, I am. There are a whole number of people there I want to tell what has happened, and there is no longer time to waste. I feel that there will never be times like these again; not for me, not for us." He paused. "How did you know?"

"Mother told us, that you have many friends up there, likely ready to hear the Master's message."

"Ahh, she is such an inspiration. John you must look after her so well, as the master asked."

"I will, with all my life Thomas. You know that."

"We have everything to do, everywhere to go, but he is always with us, every step and so much joy that it's hard to contain."

It was Miriam speaking and they all knew she was right, leading the way for all of them.

"Let's go and see what is happening in Judith's place then," she said.

*

They walked four together along to where the evening celebration would be held, Miriam in the familiar loose grey travelling robe she favoured and Matthias talking to John on his other side.

Thomas wondered why exactly Peter had asked Matthias to come, for it seemed it must be more than a coincidence, his having just had that run in with Simon Zelotes as well.

Was Matthias following him? Or much more probably was he sent to see how things were working between him and Mary. Well, he was out of luck there because she had gone on with Johannus and the asses train this morning, well before Thomas had even arrived.

She had business to get done with several of the asses which were carrying goods for her and grandfather Joseph, and had decided to travel with them.

But on the other hand, he couldn't believe that Peter was that concerned with Magdalene and himself to send Matthias. That wasn't the impression that he got when he talked with him. Who knows?

Still, Matthias was here and Thomas liked him anyway; the evening was feeling too magical already for him to thin of it more; it really didn't matter.

They had got to where the street turned left and went down into Augustus square and following it they found a group of Christine disciples working to set up some trestle tables, and on the ground beside them several large cloth covered trays, wide shallow bowls, boxes, and pitchers too.

"What are people going to drink from?" asked Miriam to a woman Thomas knew the face of but couldn't quite place.

"We have lots of cups from the Inn, in there…" she replied, pointing to one of the woven grass boxes, and suddenly Thomas recognised her; the girl who used to help sometimes in the Inn's kitchens a few years ago; her name was Shalima.

"Oh Shalima," he exclaimed, "how good to see you here," and then, "I don't suppose you recognise me. It has been a few years since I used to stay at the Inn."

"Don't be silly, of course I recognise you," she replied laughing, "and I was here when you came through with the master Yeheshua too."

"Ahhh yes, well and here we are gathered again for him, and he with us too."

"Yes. I know, it feels so strong… like he could walk into the square at any moment. Could you help me get this table flat?"

The arrangements continued with everyone helping, and gradually more and more people starting to drift into the square, into the central space; being either curious or having heard about the celebration. John and Matthias went to talk to one or two of them.

Thomas detached himself from the group and went over to sit on the steps at the end where the Roman office building was.

Surveying the scene, it looked so purposefully peaceful, just as the Lord might have wished; not a Pharisee in sight.

There were a couple of Roman soldiers unobtrusively standing guard by pillars at either end of the broad flight of steps and beyond them some as yet unlit torches and a couple of braziers running down the sides of the court.

He watched as Miriam went over to a couple of people who had just come into the square, carrying bags. They all came across to the steps near Thomas and started unpacking musical instruments… a harp, lute, drums and pipes or flute… and cymbals for good measure.

Unhurriedly they started playing and testing the pieces and then another man came over, a bit out of breath, and took over the pair of drums.

Miriam joked with them that she had forgotten most of the old songs they had played when she had met with them before, but soon she joined in with their impromptu rehearsals and very quickly the small group of attracted onlookers had grown into a small crowd.

Deftly they played through some of the favourite songs and psalms of olden days, of Moses' sister Miriam of course and later of the songs of David and Solomon. Small snatches mainly but it was soon clear by the reactions of the crowd which ones they favoured.

John had come over to join Thomas as he sat quite close to the side and Matthias was over beyond them on the further steps. The sun had just fallen behind the buildings on the western flank, but the warmth of it was still in the stones; and the coolness of the air and the softness of the light were at their sweetest.

Miriam turned to her musician friends and they quickly agreed this was the moment… and which songs they'd play.

Her voice was rich and spellbinding in the depths and heights she led her audience into, recreating scenes and feelings of the greatest and the best to have walked the earth; who had trod the same paths and met similar hardships and loves that they all knew too.

These who had recognised the gift, and the calling of the almighty power of life itself.

Thomas knew the story of how Miriam had met Yeheshua through her singing of these songs in the teaching temple of Heliopolis, when they had experienced the close bonding of their souls.

He saw as if almost through the eyes of Yeheshua himself a beauty in her that these stories were a mere dim reflection of, and even as he thought this, she started to sing the first of the songs that she had composed for her Lord Yeheshua, to celebrate his coming to be with them, back on the shores of the Galileean sea.

Tears were streaming down his face he realised and Miriam glanced his way and smiled.

CHAPTER 38.

They came to a natural pause in the singing where Miriam invited the audience to take some time to have some food and drink which had been brought; for afterwards there were two, no three of Yeheshua's apostles here, to speak of all these miraculous times through which they all lived.

One or people begged her to sing some more and others joined in the entreaties.

Looking over at John, she said she would sing again at the end of the night, and he was nodding vigorously in agreement.

John stood up and began to lead the way towards the tables covered now with all sorts of delicacies that could be eaten off the plate-like flatbreads that were set in piles at one end of each table.

There were a few crippled people sitting together on a wall at one side of the square and he went over to ask them what they might like and Matthias joined him, going over together to fill some flatbread plates for them.

Zaccheus was busy overseeing the food and drink, and Thomas asked him if he could help. Though Zach was short in stature he had amazing energy and commanded the respect of everyone who knew him. He had everything well under control.

"Here young Thomas, have some of this wine; I kept a flagon back because I liked it so much. Matthias, come and join us and let us celebrate your joining the exalted ranks…"

"May I take a little to those on the wall there," said Matthias, and Thomas helped him carry a few cups to them with Zach's blessing.

Little groups were sat around all over the place, eating; and Thomas sat with Miriam and the musicians, feeling a contentment seeping into every pore of him in the full silence of eating together.

All done, he got up and joined in collecting the rough pottery cups that had been finished with and then clearing away the food remnants and taking down the trestles as well. He liked to be involved and to be doing something to thank the givers of the supper.

John had now gone back to the centre of the steps being loosely surrounded with the crowd again, mostly sitting on the mats they had brought, but with more standing at the back.

He introduced Matthias as one of the twelve, who Yeheshua asked to lead the giving of his message to all peoples and then acknowledged Thomas as another, but who needed no introduction. Instead, John asked if Thomas would like to speak.

"John, please you speak to us rather, but if there is anything I can say as way of introduction then that would be my pleasure;" and so saying he stood up in front of everyone and allowed all the love he was feeling to come through him and the words he spoke.

"We are here because of the life and works of the greatest being I have ever, could ever, ever… not even have imagined. Yehehesua, the Lord who taught the true love of Life and each other, and who even overcame death as well; the master teacher and healer who many, many of you here will have had the chance to listen to, to feel his healing love at first hand."

"The love he has shown us lives in all our hearts, can light us up just as he was lit. Within every single one of us… what a miracle is that? The light and love that heals the inside of us. That is the gift we are asked to take up, use, feel every day in the simple way of acceptance he has shown and which we can help others have as well."

"We have this chance, this invitation to walk in his footsteps, allowing no one or thing to stop our joyful procession along the way through this life, in this world. Each tiny step one after the other to be our joy to take, whether hard or easy it matters not, because we are travelling on our journey into the heart's own kingdom and he is always right by our side."

"The marvel of the spirit filling us within, with every breath, is ours to hold onto and give out, both, time after time with no faltering from the spirit's side… to give into us the power of life itself, from the Almighty… and we learning to be taken… more and more."

Thomas paused, feeling himself drawn up within the inspiration coming to him, wonderful in its beauty, marvelling in the feeling of it flowing through him. He knew it was more than him, so much more.

"I am not saying that this path is easy, my friends, for like you I need every day to ensure that I am filled with enough strength to walk it, given in the quietness of contemplation within."

"We so often find ourselves in the middle of so many troubles and… yes suffering… in this life, but these are only the rocks and landscape of our journey, maybe obstacles even; but the path remains and will continue on, my friends, opening out to give unsurpassed views; all the marvels of this world outside as well of the glory of the kingdom within, always urging us on to meet, to reach… the indescribable answer to our thirsting hearts, the sweet water of Truth."

Thomas looked around at all the faces as he spoke, feeling the love he felt in himself, coming right back from them so much so that there was no difference, it was all merged into one gratitude.

"So here we are, and unbelievably fortunate that Miriam will sing to us of that love again, because no other can lift our hearts in celebration quite the way her singing can, for so the master has said many, many, times… but first I beg that John will share with us as well."

So saying, he sat back down and John himself stood up in his place, their hands grasped together for a second or two as they passed.

"Thank you, Thomas," he said, "what else indeed is there that can be said?"

He looked around the crowd and realised how much larger it had grown, even whilst Thomas was talking, having drawn in interested bystanders as well. Taking a deep breath, he opened himself to all of them, heart to heart.

"The marvel of this is that it is a living truth and has no end; nor can it ever be fully described, for it continues on in us, and there is no end in us opening ourselves to it, till it takes us beyond; this is our life happening and no words can ever fully tell its glory... though we love to have this chance to try."

"Our chance to try and give of that, praise of what we experience... of his love."

"Maybe some of you didn't get the chance to hear Yeheshua; maybe some of you are hearing of him having risen for the first time. That he was crucified at Golgatha, as witnessed by some here today, having the Roman soldier's spear thrust into him to end it there because even that soldier saw the purity of love being tortured for no reason."

"And I can witness too that he came back from out of the maw of death, that he walked and talked, ate and drank with us again, showing anyone and everyone that nothing, not even death itself could ever overcome that which is True. The life within us is eternal and we are bound into it when we realise it is the gift of the Almighty, direct to each of us, with each breath, yes... such as we all receive, moment after moment, day after day."

"He rose that so that we can too be in the love that we can feel, because it is in our hearts. That is the kingdom, that is all of our birthright... all people. Nothing could be simpler and more self evident than this. We share one world and are the children of one Life, one God."

"One Word dwells in all our hearts, for us to be fulfilled in the peace of knowing it therein."

"The baptism that Yeheshua gives is into knowing of that peace within, whereof the baptism by water is just a symbol."

"By believing in him, receiving the truth within and walking in the light of that truth, each of us can cross the immeasurable deserts and reach our goal."

"And see His coming, in Power and Glory again."

John sat down and to a chorus of alleluias from all around the square, packed now even more than before.

Thomas looked across and marvelled at how many people had come to hear, just as behind him the musicians started warming up their instruments and a hush fell across everyone... like being joined as one person.

Then Miriam stood forward, her soft grey headscarf still in place, and started singing a song that both Thomas and John knew they had heard before; that last time in Galilee... but had not then understood.

*

All hail the Day Star from on High!
All hail the Christ who ever was... and is... and evermore shall be!
All hail the darkness of the shadowland!

All hail the dawn of peace on earth… good will to all men!

All hail triumphant king who grapples with the tyrant Death… who conquers in the fight and brings to light immortal life for men!

All hail the broken cross… the mutilated spear!

All hail the triumph of the soul! All hail the empty tomb!

All hail to him despised by men, rejected by the multitudes; for he is seated on the throne of power!

Al hail! For he has called the pure in heart of every clime to sit with him upon the throne of power!

All hail the rending of the veil! The way into the highest courts of God is open to the sons of men!

Rejoice O men of earth… Rejoice and be exceeding glad!

Bring forth the harp and touch its highest strings; bring forth the lute and sound its sweetest notes!

For men who were made low are high exalted now… and they who walked in darkness and the vale of death are risen up and God and man are one for evermore;

Allelujah… praise the Lord for evermore… Amen

The crowd erupted in shouted approval, clapping and 'Allelujahs'!

John caught Thomas' eye, remembering. This song was true to this very time and moment and yet Miriam had sung it first before any of what it described had happened. She had always been a true prophet in their midst, and bride of the Lord in song and deed.

Thomas nodded his head; he was thinking of his Mary for he knew she and Miriam had gone together on a quest requested by Yeheshua. He wondered for a second what had occurred there… and then Miriam was singing the most familiar of her songs and all the crowd were once again transfixed by her, the words and the beauty of her singing.

Everyone in the court of Augustus, Judith's market, knew Miriam's next song by heart and as the music rang out, she started encouraging the crowd to join her in singing it.

Bring forth the harp, the vina and the lyre; bring forth the highest sounding cymbal, all ye choirs of heaven… join in the song… the new, new song.

And then she sang:

All ye choirs of heaven… and people of this mother earth, of Jericho… join in the song… this song for us and for our Lord… that is forever new.

And because people knew the words that were coming… some did join in, but quite softly at first, for none of them wanted to mask her singing with their own voices:

The lord of hosts has stooped to hear the cries of men, and lo, the citadel of Beelzebub is shaking as a leaf before the wind.

Feeling Miriam's power, they grew in confidence and their strength:

The sword of Gideon is again unsheathed.

The lord, with his own hand has pulled far back the curtains of the night; the sun of truth is flooding heaven and earth.

The demons of the dark, of ignorance and death are fleeing fast; are disappearing as the dew beneath the morning sun.

And now their voices were fully joined with Miriam's…

God is our strength and song; is our salvation and our hope, and we will build anew a house for him; will cleanse our hearts and purify their chambers every one.

We are the temple of the Holy Breath.

We need no more a tent within the wilderness; no more a temple built with hands.

We do not seek the Holy Land, nor yet Jerusalem.

We are the tent of God; we are his temple built without the sound of edged tools.

We are the Holy Land; we are the New Jerusalem; Allelujah, praise the Lord God.

At the end they were all laughing, jumping up and waving their arms and John had a sudden thought of the Isrealites bringing down the walls of Jericho… with their music and shouting.

The walls coming down here were just as difficult to break down, but he felt it happening.

Another couple of Roman soldiers came out into the square to light the torches and start the braziers. Miriam turned behind the musicians to readjust her outer dress, taking off her cloak.

She detached the headscarf from her folded cloak, rearranging it over her golden hair that glinted in the light of the setting sun, from between two buildings, low on the horizon.

Her dress was pale blue-grey with loose arms and a wide band around the middle where the long scarf had its ends tucked in. She was stunning Thomas thought, especially lit by the evening sunlight.

The crowd were swaying side to side with arms on each others shoulders in the spontaneity and the joy.

Miriam stepped back to face them and the energy was warmer than a hundred braziers and louder than surf crashing on the shore.

Her face mirrored the joy and with the motioning of her arms she lifted them further, urging them to sing with her some more.

"All the men should sing the first line: '*I have the Lord in my heart,*'
.. and all the women sing the second: '*We can never be divided.*'
Alright let's do it:"
'*I have the Lord in my heart,*'
'*We can never be divided.*'

So, Miriam sang, bringing in the men and then the women, repeating the lines again and again as they got to enjoy their participation.

Once she had got them going, she paused them in their rhythm to introduce another two lines, singing them herself for them first:

"Men: '*He gives me everything I need,*'
Women: '*for my soul to be delighted.*'... "

On they went as she got them to sing the four lines with her all, alternately the men and women:
'*I have the Lord in my heart,*'
'*we can never be divided.*'
'*He gives me everything I need,*'
'*for my soul to be delighted.*'

Thomas glanced across at John who was singing away happily… both parts Thomas noticed, laughing.

Out of the corner of his eye he noticed Matthias as well, singing a bit, but much less enthusiastically; even a bit of a frown showing his struggle with what was happening.

Thomas sighed momentarily but Miriam was singing now:
"*His love will always lift me, for we are one in Spirit now.*"
"*In being nothing is my pleasure, so Divine can be my life.*"
"*This is something known to those…*"
"*who open up the way within.*"

And then the chorus from the crowd: '*I have the Lord in my heart, we can never be divided.   He gives me everything I need, for my soul to be delighted.*'… and on, around again and again, Miriam finding ever new ways of praising the joy of knowing… until the sunset faded and the moon and stars came out above.

BOOK 6: 'AGAIN, AND AGAIN'

CHAPTER 1.

Thomas awoke later than usual, having spent the evening in the company of eager seekers of the Master's teaching, in a Jericho enlivened by the singing of Miriam.

Never had he known anything quite like how she had sung, getting the whole crowd to be a kind of chorus as she went along, to accompany the spontaneous outpouring of the spirit and her heart.

Something different to anything he had ever known, because she knitted together the divide between the inner and the outer worlds. She crossed the gulf within herself, and showed the way for them as well.

So many newcomers had then wanted to receive teaching from disciples that none had gone to bed very early. John had still been up when Thomas bade goodnight to the last of those who had come to him.

Awake again, Thomas spent his customary first hour focussing inside, getting filled with peace and clarity, before crossing to the Inn's communal wash area and then on to the kitchens to find some breakfast.

There was no sign of John or Miriam yet, but Matthias was already at a table and Thomas joined him with a hot flatbread and some pieces of fruit given by a girl who had, the evening before, been playing the lute on the steps in Augustus square.

Matthias said nothing of that so Thomas didn't either, having seen that the newly-chosen apostle had struggled rather with Miriam's unorthodox approach.

Instead, he asked his brother disciple how well he had slept and if he was staying a while in Jericho?

"No, indeed. I shall be returning to Peter today."

There was a slight pause as Thomas took this in. Matthias hadn't said he was returning to Jerusalem, rather that he was 'returning to Peter'.

He had thought that Matthias's arriving in Jericho so soon after he had got there was maybe something to do with Magdalene and himself; especially after Simon Zelotes had stirred things up; but that seemed unlikely, since Thomas had cleared the air with Peter.

Suddenly it dawned on him that that was just coincidental timing. Matthias had been sent by Peter on an altogether different mission, and Thomas saw now what that was.

Thomas pulled one side off his flatbread and chewed on it as his thoughts churned, and swallowing he responded to Matthias.

"Please send my love to Peter and the other brothers, especially Zelotes, who probably seeks it least, and tell them that though I travel north to Antioch I expect to return soon, just depending upon the success of my mission there."

"Oh, certainly I will, Thomas. I have heard you have strong connections there. Your boldness is well thought of…" and Thomas could almost hear

Matthias's follow-on thought… 'unlike that of Miriam, who is going far beyond the bounds seemly for a woman disciple.'

That was why Peter had sent Matthias, to see what Miriam was about, who had taken to touring the outlying communities whilst the twelve were centred in Jerusalem. Nathaniel and Philip had gone with her to Galilee this week past, but somehow, she had come back to Jerusalem and now was in Jericho.

Peter had never been comfortable with her being closer to Yeheshua than anyone else, so that now he might be feeling threatened by her. His position perhaps and the direction the work took them, Thomas realised.

"Safe journey then Matthias," said Thomas finishing his final mouthful of flatbread and selecting a piece of melon from his plate. "It is amazing how strongly our Lord's work is happening in Jerusalem, where he was so cruelly treated. And important too that his other followers don't get neglected; in his sight we are all equal. I am hoping to catch up with Nathaniel and Philip in Bethsaida."

"Hmmm, that's good Thomas," replied Matthias. "We do all need to pull together. The brothers shall be glad of your supporting influence there in Galilee."

Thomas got up. "I have to return the horse I rode up here to her owner; so, if I don't see you before you go… let us always be true in heart, for that alone should be the arbiter of what is good; and no other kind of rules."

"Truly spoken, brother," Matthias answered with genuine feeling. "Clear-sightedness comes from there indeed."

They embraced and Thomas felt some of the tensions melt away. He smiled, "go in the Spirit's care until we meet again."

*

Thomas strode across to the stables where he had left the dappled grey mare that his uncle Tobias had asked him to take back to Elias, a great uncle or cousin to Thomas, very old now, but who a few years ago Thomas had spent a year apprenticed to, in the law.

He had grown to like the horse, which at first he had thought rather too placid, but as they travelled up to Jericho had realised the value of her friendly nature. He would miss her on his journey, knowing he would have to find another mount… maybe in Galilee, for he had no funds here unless he asked Zack for help. Maybe that would be best, but it hurt his pride to beg; well, it wouldn't be the first or last time for that.

The stableman had made sure Meg was fed and watered and so he gave him some small coins he had and led the mare out of the yard and on across the city towards the mainly Levite quarter.

Tobias had told him that Elias had moved into a smaller house around there, behind a synagogue in Aaron street, and that his housekeeper lived next door and would be the best person to call on first.

Her name was Jessica and he would recognise her house by the bright colours she liked to paint her door and shutters.

Thomas held Meg's reins as he knocked on the orange door which was soon opened a crack and then a bit more to reveal a middle-aged woman who was eying him and the mare up and down uncertainly.

Then a slight smile came into her face as she realised… "Ahhhh, you will be wanting the Master Elias," she declared, and Thomas nodded his smile in return.

"There is nowhere here for your horse though master, unless you wish to leave him… her, at the synagogue; that is Meg, isn't it?" She nodded her head side to side in some pleasure. "There is a shaded place around the side that is quite well used for leaving horses."

"Right," said Thomas, "I will do that then. Please could you tell the master Elias that his niece's nephew and former pupil Thomas Didimus is here to see him, whenever may be a suitable time to call."

"I will that," said Jessica, "and give you his reply by the time you come back from the Synagogue."

When he came back Elias was there to greet Thomas with an enthusiasm that belied his years, and was soon asking him all about the events in Jerusalem as he ushered him into his main living room. Thomas hadn't realised how interested Elias would be. He told him all he could…

".. and now I am going up to Antioch and Tobias asked me to return Meg, the dappled grey mare to you."

Elias looked at him from heavily lidded eyes that seemed puzzled for a few moments, but which then lit up with a twinkle as the old man started to laugh, pause and laugh again.

"My dear boy," he said at last, patting his chest with one bony hand, "your uncle Tobias has played a great trick on you, and given me this fine joy as well."

Thomas had no idea what Elias was talking about. "Are you saying that Meg is not your horse sir?" he asked, following the only line of argument that made any sense.

Elias began to laugh and try to say something but then started coughing, which drew Jessica hurrying into the room to his side.

She fussed over her charge, frowning at a worried Thomas, but Elias recovered quite quickly.

"Jessica dear," he said patting her arm, "please get me the box that I pay you from, from the back of my desk."

She did but Thomas was unable to guess what was going on.

He had a key to open the little wooden box which had a quantity of small value coins in it, and he took a couple of these and passed them to Jessica. "Please go out and buy us some wine; and for you too, my dear."

When she had gone, he pulled a section out of the side of the box that was a flat metal key, the sort you pushed into a slot to release a lock.

Elias pulled at the edge of the seat he was sat upon, and a part came out

598

easily by a couple of finger widths from the frame.

Thomas watched fascinated and Elias held out a hand to him.

Pushing the key down into a slot in the wood enabled a small shelf to slide smoothly out from under him. It wasn't deep and only contained a flat tray covered with a black cloth, which when removed revealed a number of silver coins set into gaps in the tray.

Elias scooped out three of these and returning everything to its place, finally put the key back into its hidden slot in the box.

"These are for Meg," he said to an increasingly astonished Thomas, into whose hand he had pressed the coins.

"Whaaa… she is not mine, great-uncle. I cannot accept any money for giving her back."

Elias started to chortle now, enjoying himself. "No, that is true Thomas; she is indeed mine and your uncle Tobias has been kind enough to look after her for me these last few years."

"I have nowhere to keep her, but never wanted to sell her on to some uncertain fate. Tobias has been doing me a favour, but now has given me this lovely opportunity."

"I really want you to take her on, because I know you will need a mount for your journey to Antioch… and everywhere else you need to go. But you cannot do this without money for her upkeep and that is what these are for. So that you will always be able to look after her properly."

Thomas stammered, unable to find words or an answer, " .. I cannot… I don't know; what I… erm, you cannot."

"Oh, I can Thomas, and I am so glad that I am able to; and not just for you, though you are worth all of that to me, but for the work that you will do. That is a little to help you spread the message of hope of that great Rabbi Yeshua. That message of hope for all people, that is the true meaning of our nation."

Thomas was dumbfounded; that Elias was able to turn the tables on him so adroitly giving him no choice but to gratefully accept, both the money and the use of Meg.

"Sir, I am eternally grateful… ", but his words petered out because he had none to say; for he felt it being a gift from heaven.

"Just look after her well, that is all I wish. I am so happy to be able to do this."

CHAPTER 2.

Before Thomas got back to Zach's Inn, Matthias had already left for Jerusalem and Miriam was bidding John farewell after spending a couple of hours in close consultation with him.

"Are you going the same way as me, Thomas?" Miriam asked him easily and Thomas had to laugh that he was now that he had gained a horse to ride.

"What? Your great uncle gave her to you?" asked John.

"Not only that John, but he gave me money for her upkeep so that she could be used for spreading Yeheshua's message. It was such a shock, I was completely... humbled actually."

"Well, I hope she gets on well with Indy," said Miriam softly; "he was given to me for much the same reason. I was so honoured too."

*

Matthias rode happily along towards Jerusalem his thoughts flowing freely along the lines of what was being achieved, what was still to be achieved, and enjoying having a part to play in it.

His stay in his old haunt of Jericho had been pleasant, the evening event had been actually very exciting, but he also knew that it wasn't what was meant to be happening; not the way it was. It did need to be brought more under control, and he could help with that.

The Lord had given Peter the responsibility of taking his work forward, to establish his church on earth, and nothing was more important than that. Peter had sent him to be his eyes and ears, and so he was.

Matthias would bridge the gap because he knew he could. He had taught the mysteries of Egypt before coming to the master and recognised that Miriam had received training in the Temple of Isis; which showed in the way she was able to move the crowd.

An extremely powerful tool he knew, and not at odds with the work of the spirit either, but dangerous if it became the end in itself.

That could and would be avoided because he would give Peter all the help he might need.

Miriam should stay with Mother, not be running loose all over the country.

On a whim Matthias pulled up his mount and turned her around to ride the short way back to a track that they had just passed, that had reminded him of who lived down that way.

Kareem Aten-Akbah had been a top student of his when Matthias had been teaching the Mizraim mysteries of the ancient Ennead. Of Atum and Osiris, Isis and Nephthys, Set and the others.

As he rode his mind jumped ahead to the possibility that Kareem might have already taken on the teaching of Yeheshua, or that he might be open to this now.

At the same time something in him hoped that maybe Kareem wouldn't be; but he wasn't clear why this was. It would be marvellous if Kareem joined them.

*

Thomas and Miriam fetched their baggage and met in the stables where Indy and Meg both happened to be stalled, at opposite ends.

They agreed that they would set the baggage on Indy and that Miriam would ride Meg on the first part of their journey.

Thomas loved a good walk and at the same time he was impressed at the size and strength of the donkey colt. He seemed unusually mature; maybe it was that he was generally free of burdening and stood tall and proud, almost like a small wild horse.

Meg and Indy got along tremendously from the start, her placid nature being offset against the liveliness of Indy, making them good travelling companions. Soon they had got on the northward road out of Jericho, managing to tail a small caravan of camels that were moving on the road ahead at a reasonable pace.

Miriam and Thomas quite quickly shared the aims of their journeys, how Miriam was going to Magdala to stay at Mary's house for a while and Thomas to Antioch to fulfil a promise to his old philosophy teacher: that if he ever found the answers to what they sought he would come back and tell him; and he knew so many others too. Thomas felt greatly drawn to go and speak of Yeheshua and his work there.

That and to spend some time compiling and writing down the sayings he remembered most; of his master… to be somewhere he could have the clear perspective.

"Oh good, I hope you will, that sounds fantastic; and I want to write what I can as well," said Miriam. "I will ask for Mary's help in that, for she learnt the writing arts in Antioch too."

Miriam's talking of Mary and reminding Thomas of their shared history touched him deeply. He realised Miriam must know much of what had happened between them.

A little reluctantly he opened up about his feelings of it all to her, how he knew Magdalene to be pregnant with his child, from the time after the crucifixion, when she had found him and sought to repair his need to live again.

"We had always known there was something between us since we first met in Antioch, but I had chosen to ignore it. I am hoping that it is not too late, even after the way that Zelotes ruined everything, denouncing her to the apostles, or so it seems…" He trailed off.

"She has healed that wound, Thomas; though it was sore hard to do. She has found her course and I think may be reluctant to see you now."

Thomas felt the simple truth in Miriam's words and it felt to him that the master himself was with them, so natural was it to talk, like he used to do with Yeheshua.

"It must be awful for you Miriam, not having him here," he said in the silence.

"Every step I am with him, and he with me," she answered lightly.

*

Matthias came to the crossroads that comprised the heart of the village near to where Kareem had his house, and let his mount drink at the water trough in the shade of a great fig tree, cut back to allow easy access to the watering place.

He picked a ripe fig and tried to recall the way to Kareem's house as he bit into it, deciding at last that he wasn't going to need to ask any of the rag taggle of children that were gathering to peer at him. He had remembered.

Swinging back up into the saddle he guided the mare out across to the where the least of the roads went eastward past a couple of shops fronted by their beaded screen doorways that worked to keep out most of the flies.

At the far end of the village there were a small gang of dogs scrabbling over some rubbish by a wall with several large prickly pear plants, and Matthias was glad to get past them and hoped too that he might soon be at Kareem's and able to sit in the shade on his verandah.

The warmth of the spirit lit his heart and he felt beneficent as he got down to open the gate to Kareem's property, enjoying the dappled warmth as he led the horse up to the house between the wide-set olive trees on either side. Insects buzzed about lazily and Matthias breathed in the scents of jacaranda flowers and myrtle bushes that framed the space in the front of the house.

A servant girl opened the door to him and he asked after his old student who soon appeared in person, hugely delighted to see his former teacher. There was so much for them to catch up on.

*

In the bushes at the side of Kareem's house a man crouched in a place he had for spying, which was his main employment, along with dealing with the outcomes of the findings, which could sometimes be quite extreme.

His employers were a shadowy group of powerful men whose alignments were both religious and financial because those were the elements that best supported their power. It was a closed circle that did become viscous at times.

Kareem had both these elements too, being a rich Egyptian merchant and also a leading light in the religion and mysteries of that country. They wanted to know if his acticities were a threat to them.

Seth moved slightly to get his ear closer to the gap in the window frame which allowed the sound of even quite softly spoken conversations to reach him. Kareem had a visitor.

Not that Seth was limited to this form of information gathering, for he had already infiltrated the group that Kareem was the teacher of, becoming a keen and prominent student.

But spying enabled him to get to know an entirely different side of Kareem's activities; and he always enjoyed the thrill of this.

And most surprisingly, as he listened, he realised that this visitor was connected deeply with the last huge assignment he had been paid for; bringing about the destruction of the teacher-healer Yeshua.

The more he listened the more he knew that this was unfinished business, and more deeply and personally connected to his ambitions than even those of his employers. Different and well beyond theirs, in the way he thought really counted.

His mind-soul purred to him.

CHAPTER 3.

Thomas and Miriam passed the fork in the road where they had come down from that special week that they had spent in the Ephraim hills with Yeheshua, and his presence was with them like the warmth of the sun and freshness of the breeze around them.

They caught up with the camel caravan by the time they arrived at the stand of thorn trees that was a normal midday place to stop, with dappled shade for travellers to sit in and just enough scrubby vegetation to occupy the camels' attention.

They had been given good supplies by Zach which they were able to share with some of the caravaners, and that wouldn't do any harm to Zach's reputation either.

Thomas had taken all the bags and saddles off Meg and Indy and put water in one of the stone troughs that were placed here and there under the trees, just for that purpose.

When the time came to saddle up again Thomas decided that Indy was definitely strong enough to carry Miriam if he fixed their bags behind Meg's saddle. He set about arranging a makeshift side-saddle from blankets and strapping for Miriam to ride on Indy.

As soon as he was fully satisfied with it, they set off ahead of the caravan and as they rode, they talked of many things and of places visited; of Egypt, Sheba and beyond the eastern seas to where Miriam had gone with her father on the spice trail, and where the young Yeheshua had visited, studied and taught too.

"You have also lived outside of Palestine, in Antioch," she said; "and didn't someone say you had travelled to Greece?"

"Yes, I did a couple of times, with my grandfather. Once to the mainland, to Athens, and once because he wanted to visit Delphi before he died."

"I loved the islands in those azure seas," he added after a pause, and then told Miriam how wonderful he thought the event had been the night before; that he had never experienced anything like the way she had got the audience involved in the singing.

"Did Matthias say anything about it before he left?" he asked, almost by mistake.

Miriam gave him a little sideways glance and laughed. "I am well aware that not all the apostles approve of me Thomas; and that may include Peter. He has never been one to hide that, and I respect his frankness; but I do not look for their approval or to be a member of some club or cabal."

"Nor do they or you need my approval, Thomas," she added quickly. "Our Lord gives us his love in equal measure; the breath that comes to them and me and you is the same miracle for each and every one of us."

"I am really saddened that some seem to disapprove," said Thomas; "but not

John. He was gone completely into the singing, taking both chorus parts and would have joined in yours if he could, haa. It was so… liberating."

"Yes, that is why I love to sing. I can really let myself go into it. I am so thankful that I have it to give."

"And Thomas, it seems to me that we must reach out to every heart that is thirsty to know what this gift of life contains; wherever we shall find them. Quite probably some that have the greatest desire and capacity for it have not even heard yet, not even be in this country."

"Yes, I know, that is just how I feel too," he agreed.

"Well, you must promise to come back and tell me how things go in Antioch."

"I will yes;" and they rode on; each in the rhythm of their own mounts; Indy was proving to be every bit as sturdy as he was enthusiastic.

"Look there, the tops of those trees showing over the next rise are in the garden of the inn we are staying at. We have made good time."

*

Seth walked back along the country route to Jericho, musing on what he had heard.

Matthias had been visiting Kareem, his former pupil and yet it seemed to Seth that he was also seeking his assistance with something to do with the crucified Yeshua's consort Miriam.

The same Miriam who had somehow escaped his trap to kidnap her a few months back; he had failed; she and her two companions had escaped.

Nevertheless, he had played his full part in her Yeshua's ignominious death, nailed to a Roman cross; his greatest, sweetest success.

Yet this Matthias was insisting that the tales of him rising from the dead were true; inexplicably enflaming Seth with rage and hatred; bringing to life what he had learnt of the conflict between Set and Osiris, who Set had killed but who Isis, like this Miriam must have, somehow brought back to life.

Since being with Kareem, everything had changed. He had been Zeph, but now was Seth.

It was natural to him that he had imbibed the spirit of great Set, being the God of storms and chaos and the 'other side', that all the rest of the group seemed fearful of. Yet Kareem had approved; the Ennead needed Set and Kareem needed Seth, and Seth grew ever stronger in the group and in himself, feeling he had always had this role, was born to it.

He despised weakness, especially in those grown rich and bloated in deceit and who took power by abominating their religion. Religion that they had added their stink to.

Yes, he would take their money as always, but now he knew his own purpose, and the means to achieve his goal, in immortal Set; and his revenge.

He spat in the dust. She would not escape him twice; and this time she would be his.

*

Miriam and Thomas freshened up and met in the gardens of the inn which were irrigated from a thin but permanent stream that flowed from out from the northern ridges of the Ephraim hills down to the Jordan.

The evening sun was not yet set and they had some wine.

Thomas was remembering his walk out into those hills in the days after the crucifixion, his way of trying to clear his spirit, and his starlit meeting with the dragon girl. It seemed like an age ago and yet it wasn't that long really.

"I was walking in those hills a few weeks back, and had a dream, at least I can only think of it as a dream, but even now cannot say that I was asleep."

"What sort of a dream?"

"I found some hidden caves when I was looking for a place to camp and through a fissure came up onto a slope behind them, in the starlight. There was this girl there... a kind of spirit but not like out of any dream I have ever had, and in the rocks and trees behind her I saw or sensed the shape of a huge dragon. Awesomely powerful but not actually threatening me, or so I felt."

"Mmmmm..." said Miriam, but nothing more for a while, then "that would be Kaella."

"Who is she?"

"There is more to her than just dream-stuff; but she is of that world also. She is somehow involved in all that has been happening; been trying to help against the pall of darkness creeping out from Hades into the world."

"How can that be?" asked Thomas.

"There is much we do not see, or need to know about Thomas. Not normally. Angels and devils; and the spirits that possess. People's beliefs and the power of our minds are very powerful, but not compared to who we really are; what is real. We have been shown that Truth that is beyond all doubt. That is all we need."

"So, this Kaella is some kind of spirit?"

"She is the human side of the goddess Hecate I believe; something like that. Hecate that is the Goddess of the crossroads, yet is at the crossroads of her own path."

Thomas said nothing, but was questioning still. "There is much we shall come across that we won't understand, Thomas. You should ask Yresmin about the Djinn and the 'Ghosters' in Nabatea."

"Isn't she the one that gave you Indy?"

"Yes, and the donkey that Yeheshua rode into Jerusalem is hers too; Sella, Indy's mother. Yresmin was high priestess of the Nabatean Goddess Manat too, in Kadesh. Their Goddess of fate, like Hecate."

"Hmmm... The old Powers that people believe in; giving them existence. Yet I didn't believe in that Kaella, but she was there... and she said that my destiny lay in direction of the sun's rising, or something like that."

"Ahhh..." said Miriam, and the sun had now dipped below the western hills and the heat had gone out of the garden. "Let's go in and get some supper. It will be good to get an early start as well."

*

Tefnut, Nephthys and Isis. These were the influences that Matthias was asking Kareem to engage with, to help bring Miriam in line with what was happening; 'come into the fold'.

Seth had listened intently, understanding that because Miriam had been trained in the temples of Heliopolis, Matthias felt that Kareem and his group might be able to help Peter and the apostles. Kareem had been agreeable, even a little excited by the chance to exercise his group's training.

Tefnut, Nephthys, Isis... Tefnut, Nephthys, Isis... Tefnut, Nephthys, Isis... the names revolved in Seth's brain, finding a route for him into the action, where they would serve his purpose, even more than Matthias's.

Nephthys was Set's consort, though she had gone with Osiris, had his child. Seth was storing his hatred for that, but for now he could use their connection, to become a part of this.

He loved it where he could bring together random details into his planning; he excelled and revelled in it, squeezing the juice out.

Anna was the student for Nephthys and she definitely wanted to play the consort role to Seth, though he felt nothing for her.

Well, he would let her now, and he would get as close as he needed; and might even enjoy himself.

No time like the present; he would visit her house tonight.

*

Thomas shivered, feeling a chill run up his spine, and the sense of some intensely non-benvolent presence.

He was in his room at the inn and he suddenly felt a deep concern for Miriam.

He went out quietly and over to the part of the Inn where she was sharing a large room with several other ladies, as was the way. He stopped at the door; could hear the soft tones of conversation and gentle laughter coming from inside, and suddenly felt quite foolish.

He dismissed his earlier thoughts as being just of their evening's talk in the garden, but when he got back to his room, he still had the sense of some lingering evil.

There were two beds in his room, but only him staying there.

He sat on his bed and the light form the candle-lamp flickered around, creating shadows that played on his frame of mind.

Resolutely he decided to put out the candle, sit on his bed and focus within, on the Real.

It was not easy, because his mind fed freely on what he had felt and thought, projecting it into an overwhelming presence of menace, but he didn't run from it; mustn't.

607

He stayed and the malevolence prickled through his mind and spine, but he held steadfastly onto the stable pole of the breath, coming and going… coming and going, until he found himself; free and steady there. All was as it should be, breathing in calmness.

*

Anna opened the door to find Zeph, Seth rather, standing there in the twilight, looking as dark and dangerous as always, with the tight black beard she thought made him so attractive.

She was large, almost a tall as he was with fairish skin and hair that she dyed red. She was much closer in type to Set than he was, and he resented her for that as well, but he smiled as she showed her surprise at seeing him.

"Sorry to bother you, Anna; I was hoping you could tell me when the next Ennead meeting with Kareem-Atum is?

"Come in, Seth; so good to see you."

He stayed and heard about the happenings in Anna's recent days, particularly about the events in Augustus square where she had listened to Yeshua's Miriam singing and told Seth how special it had been.

He seethed with frustration but feigned pleasure at Anna's enthusiasm for the Christine message of Yeshua's return from death: "just like Osiris really."

Seth held his tongue behind the false smile; but possibilities wormed into his brain even beyond Miriam's annihilation, that had become his initial aim.

To use her to attain his own immortality.

Seth's rightful dues and her utter destruction; unless she were able to prove her devotion; to him.

Set's cruelty would give him revenge either way; making Yeshua's crucifixion look merely uncomfortable by comparison, and wipe out any trace of Miriam from the annals of history.

CHAPTER 4.

Johannus travelled on up to Galilee with me; Miriam asked us to go ahead; and said that she would be following in a day or so.

I knew he had hated leaving Miriam in Jericho but would respect her wishes beyond anything else; had always, ever since the three of us travelled to Kadesh and back.

I was glad that Miriam had asked him to be here for me though, for he knew the things I had been through better than anyone, but would make no judgement on me.

I knew that; from the history we had shared; both kind of outsiders in a way; and now it was a chance for renewal.

Yet it wouldn't be long till he would be going down to Egypt, to Rebecca his betrothed, in Alexandria.

She was so much what he needed. I could see that from a mile away, and I think he was almost shocked that she wanted him, and almost more so that she and her father had been so receptive to Yeheshua's message.

There were a few people in Alexandria that knew of Yeheshua from even before he started his ministry here in Judea and Galillee, and Petronius had spoken of one of them being a great teacher too; though I couldn't remember his name. Oh yes, it was Philo; Juilius Philo, whom I had heard of from Arianne in Antioch as well. I must follow that connection up.

Rebecca balanced Johannus so well, basking in his obvious admiration for her, as she fed off his boundless enthusiasm. They were well matched indeed and I loved teasing him about her.

"What presents will you take her?" I asked, knowing that he hadn't thought of that, being so bound up in all the recent events; my problems, and then coming to Jericho, and now on again.

Nor would he have the money to get anything worthwhile; it was quite mean of me.

"Wha... a .t .. ?" he stammered; "presents? Er... not really sure; what sort of things should I...?"

"And something for Petronius; and for her mother if she were still alive, of course," I added; his thoughts turning him ashen as he tried to fathom it out. He was such an innocent in so many ways.

I gave him a minute as I thought how much our blacksmith friend Beor would have loved the fun, and then couldn't help but take his arm and give it a tug... "Don't worry... I think I know just the things."

"You do?"

"Yes, I do; and you are lucky, for I cannot think of anyone better to help you than where we are going now."

It had been late when we neared the sea and decided to stop at an Inn on the outskirts of Tiberias, before travelling on to Magdala this morning.

It was the second day of our journey to Galilee with the asses train and we had shared the use of one of the donkeys as a mount, taking it in turns to walk.

It had given us the chance to talk of our many journeys together which made us realise just how much danger we had found, avoided, dodged or met head on, like these last months that had culminated in the crucifixion of our dearest Lord and Master.

Was that an end or just a beginning? It seemed that he walked almost closer with us now than he had before, when all the disciples were clustered around him.

Johannus had trod a very singular path, and I had shared much of it with him; right from the time that I had picked him out as the one of Simon the Magus' disciples I could perhaps work with.

God! how that had blown up in our faces, and yet, somehow we had been able to help each other to come to Yeheshua; in different ways, and Miriam had become central to both of our relationships; to Yeheshua even, in a way like for no other disciple.

Even just a few days, or was it weeks ago, Johannus had innocently likened the touch of the 'Comforter', the 'Holy Spirit', as to being the company of the Divine Feminine, which seemed to touch a raw nerve in the Apostle Peter who jumped down on Johannus; who in turn was defended by Miriam, reminding Peter how Yeheshua used to say 'Her' about the Holy Breath and Comforter, even as he used 'He' about the Father.

Even though surely he, Peter, understood how far beyond these terms the Almighty, All-Knowing, All-Loving, Omnipresent was?

I smiled slightly to myself remembering how Peter had looked like a small quarrelsome boy for a few moments before clearing his mind and nodding in recognition of the truth of what Miriam had said.

An interchange that had done much in setting me on the course I was on now; to be a force to help the women who are Yeheshua's followers; here in Galilee.

We rode on, that is I rode and Johannus walked, past the place where we had broken onto the Jordan road in their escape from the kidnap attempt on Miriam; when we had been returning to Yeheshua from Kadesh.

Seemed like a lifetime ago, and indeed it really was; Johannus had not yet met the master at that point. This was a new life he had now.

"Do you remember that inn where those people tried to kidnap us? well Miriam anyway," he asked.

I nodded, shivering slightly, remembering.

"What kind of people were they? Not regular bandits; do you remember? There was a Pharisee with them and I saw their ringleader once in Jericho; before the Passover week; travelling back from the Ephraim hills; a dangerous looking villain."

"Of course I remember, Johs; but their memory brings no pleasure. People hired to do the bad things for others. I remember the one you mean I think; smelt of evil-doing is how I would describe him; from out of darkness."

"The darkness that could not defeat Yeheshua, even by dealing death," Johannus affirmed, "and now he has given us his light to wield. Still, it will be so good to get to your place Mary."

We had a short rest beside the sea, north of Tiberias, taking welcome refreshment, but it was not long before we were back on the road. The journey had been longer than Johannus remembered.

"Nearly there," I said, "but first we need to make one visit, before going on to my steward, Jacob." We had taken my two asses and left the train already; that was going on to Capernaum and Bethsaida.

The day was hot as we went up a dusty track through a wide set olive grove, on up the rise to a small house all set about with bright flowering shrubs.

"Lenny, my half brother lives here," I surprised Johannus with. "My father's son by another woman; he has always been poorly but my father made sure he had a life. My mother was kind to him, but never told my brother of his existence."

Johannus tied up the asses to a heavy post set into the ground in a scrubby area of grass and bushes that offered them some shade and rough grazing; and I helped take off their bags before going up to the house.

Knocking briefly on the door, not really expecting a reply, I then went around the side to the back of the house where a kind of garden was set into the side of the hill. Johannus followed.

The garden perimeter consisted of piled up pieces of rock carved out from a crevice in the back slope creating a sheltered arbour where bushes on the slope above curved overhead.

Many of the rocks were rough hewn but some had received varied degrees of working, shaping and smoothing into what could be creatures of someone's wild imagination, peeping and creeping out of the stone.

The owner of that imagination was sitting cross-legged amid the semicircle of watching rocks, working on a much finer piece of sculpture, that was clearly a nearly completed stripy cat figure.

He was wearing only a loincloth as he chipped gently with absolute concentration at the neck of the beast, and for several long moments Johannus and I just watched in fascination.

A little voice chirped from inside the house and the sculptor looked around, seeing us there for the first time.

I stepped forward, arms outstretched towards my half-brother who unwound his legs to get up and greet me.

One leg was quite withered with a foot that pointed inwards from a twisted lower portion, but he could stand easily enough and we embraced. "Dear sister, how wonderful to see you. Are you well?"

"Very well thank you Lenny. I am sure you have had news of all that has been happening in Jerusalem; with Yeheshua crucified but then returning to us?" Then turning, "this is Johannus, the friend who brought me back from Antioch, amongst many other adventures since."

Lenny nodded towards Johannus, one calloused hand reaching out to grip Johannus' outstretched one. "Yes, I have, though I have been eager to hear the news from your own lips Mary. Let's go inside for a drink and something to eat, if you will?"

We saw a little face duck back away from the doorway as we turned to go into the house; clearly from where the little chirp had come on our arrival. How she had grown since I last saw her.

Lenny and I sat and talked for several minutes whilst Johannus looked in some wonder at the various pieces of sculpture around the living room. In pride of place was a beautiful pair of figures, lovers fit for a palace.

Johannus had trained as a silversmith in Antioch and could well appreciate the fine work of the pieces.

The little figure, who we found out was Lenny's daughter, came out carrying a large water jug with some difficulty, and then rushed off to get some cups. "Thank you, Jess;" said her father and I managed to get a hug from my little neice when she brought me my cup.

"Johannus," I asked as sweetly as I could, not wanting to move. "Could you get a bag for me out of the luggage? The bag of grain off the older donkey."

Johannus made no objection, but jumped up to go back out, returning round the back with the requested grain bag.

Thanking him, I started to undo the stitching along the top edge with one of Lenny's sharp wood-sculpting tools, pulling from inside another smaller bag that was hidden in the grain inside.

And opened this to reveal a series of spice bags inside that I delivered to my brother.

He smiled widely as he accepted them, holding them each in turn and smelling them through the bags, rolling them in his hands, assessing what their contents must be.

"And then there is this one," I said as I finally took the smallest bag, made of a soft black material, out of the spice bag and handed it to Lenny. "I think you need this."

"The grain is from Egypt and the spices from Kerala, but this one comes from somewhere even further afield" she said, as her brother took the little bag hesitantly from her, feeling its weight despite its small size.

"It's not, is it?" he said.

"Open it; find out," I replied, and gingerly, hesitantly he did, dipping his hand inside to bring out a piece of deepest blue stone. Johannus gasped.

"Lapis lazuli;" I said to Johannus rather than my brother, who was checking each of the stones from the bag with a look of wonder and delight on his face.

"Quite hard to get hold of, but I got lucky. A friend of Miriam's father brought them from somewhere north of Bharat."

"Mary, they are wonderful. So many too. I only need a few small pieces to complete this pair."

"For Herod's daughter," I said, aside to Johannus again; "and before you say anything she is a Christine sympathiser too, through knowing Susannah."

"Aaahh; well, the lovers are a beautiful work, Lenny; breathtaking. What are you doing with the lapis lazuli?"

"Their eyes, and her jewels," answered Lenny. "They will finish it completely. I will pay you fully Mary, once I get my final payment. I know they will be thrilled now I have these."

"No problem, Lenny, and you should have enough for any similar commission."

"It is amazing to have the most special materials for my work; which reminds me, I have a little something for you too sis;" and he got up and hobbled nimbly over to a chest in the corner that held many of his useful bits and pieces, and especially the tools he used for the most delicate work.

He picked out a little package and brought it over to me. Johannus was watching closely as I delicately as possible pulled open the fine cloth nestling in the palm of my hand. Inside was revealed a small piece of green stone, carved into the shape of two fishes, swimming together.

"Jade," said Johannus. "It is beautiful; they are beautiful."

"They just need a silver chain," said Lenny, "to go through this part. They should be well balanced enough."

I had no words but gave my brother the biggest of hugs; several. Then suddenly it reminded me of what I had been planning for Johannus presents for Rebecca.

"Lenny; do you still have that store of little stone beads and figures… a bit like this but not Jade? I remember them so well…"

"Yes I do; I just love to make them; sometimes as beads and sometimes as pendant bits, like the fishes. Jess loves to play with them and making them is a kind of relaxation for me; so I have lots!!"

"Can I buy some from you? Enough to make a necklace and some bracelets?"

"Of course, Mary. With what I owe you for the lapis lazuli you could have all I could produce for years to come; haha."

"Right; I will then, because we have to get Johannus here ready to go and meet his bride to be in Alexandria; and although her father is a rich merchant I feel sure he and she will appreciate the specialness of your work."

"I do have some funds actually, Mary;" chipped in an astonished Johannus, "but I love your idea, and this is what I can do myself. I have some fine silver chains that I was making with Beor's help and my Uncle's tools, and these I can make suitable both for neck chains and pendant attachments, and clasps for the bracelets… and make you a special one for your Jade fishes."

"They aren't much by themselves, but put together with your brother's work, they could be really special."

"Then I think you just found yourself some work," I smiled laughing, "just until you are ready to go to Alexandria of course, but I am hoping both you and Miriam will be able to stay a couple of weeks here with me?"

"That would be brilliant, Johannus," chimed in Lenny, "if you wanted to come and work here; that would be great for me."

"Okay, done;" said Johannus beaming.

Lenny's wife Anna worked at Jacob's farm, which was what we worked together for wine and olive oil in particular, having two largish presses that enabled a reasonable scale production, involving many of the local growers.

When she knew we were going there, Jess was desperate to come along too, and her father agreed that she could.

She was so excited that she was allowed to ride on a donkey to Jacob's with Aunty Mary, where her mother was, and she soon became quite chatty, even with Johannus.

"Are you staying, Aunty?" she asked and I conceded that I would be.

"Will you come and visit?"

"You can come and visit me as well Jess. My house is not far away."

"I know. I have been there, Aunty Mary…"

"Yes of course you have; well, you shall come again and as often as you like. Maybe your mummy will come too; I think I have some visitors coming and will need help with the house."

At Jacob's, Johannus helped unload the donkeys and getting them fed and watered, giving them a bit of a grooming by way of thanks as well, before going down to the steward's house where I was sorting the deliveries with him, and talking of other of our business matters.

It seemed the olive pressing business continued to go very well but they would need to get at least two more presses and people to work them by the autumn if they were going to keep up with demand; and to do that they ought to hire a carpenter and a wagonner to start on them now. It had taken a while for the last pair to understand how to make them, though Jacob had made sure he knew most of the problems they had encountered along the way.

"Very good Jacob. Let's do that then. There are business funds available aren't there?"

"Yes, there are Mistress; and I am glad you think it is worth doing."

"I shall probably be here for a few months at the least Jacob, but I shall not get in the way of you running things. I just like to help when and if you need me."

"There is no-one that can see a better trading deal than you Mary. No-one that has the connections in Jericho, Jerusalem, Tyre, everywhere."

"You have reminded me, Jacob. I shall want to go down to Tyre to see Rachel again sometime. Let me know if you have any need to ship our oil or anything soon."

And so, we went on and Johannus went to see what else was happening, but it wasn't long before I came looking for him and found him in the vegetable garden with Jess and her mother.

"I must go down to my house now Johs and was hoping you might help me get it ready? In case Miriam comes up tomorrow? I have a feeling she is on her way."

"Can we come too Aunty? Can we mummy?" Shrugged shoulders all around. "Yes, okay Jess, you know I said you could." And her mother caught her up in her arms as we all set off.

CHAPTER 5.

Seth rolled over on the bed; Anna's bed. She was sprawled naked and unconscious to the world on the other side.

She had done well to match and balance the ferocity of his 'love-making'; he had to give her credit for that. And he had enjoyed it much more than he had imagined he might; helpful for the weeks ahead.

He went to the basin and poured some water from the dark brown painted jug that was in the window where it would catch as much as possible of the sun's early heat. It was still cold but he thrilled to the tingling fierceness of it over his warm skin.

Dressed, he took the few morsels to eat that he found under a bushel, enough to keep him going for a while. He had his work to do; he wasn't going to hang around.

Anna woke to find him gone and marvelled at what had happened the night before, scarcely able to believe it hadn't been a dream; what with Seth having gone almost as though he had never been there.

Seth had heard all he could bear about the marvellous evening of celebration and Miriam's singing. Nevertheless, he needed to know what was happening now.

He understood that Zachharius of the New Inn was heavily involved; no doubt that was where they were all staying; John, Miriam and the others. Two more apostles of the crucified 'Christ' that Anna called him; Thomas and Matthias... and Seth spat twice in the dust.

He dared not go there because Zachharius knew more of him than most; they had crossed paths and Zeth avoided him as much as possible. A good stroke that... Zeth; that would serve better than Seth or Zeph.

But he was sure he was not known to the stableman, whom he had been careful to keep for a moment such as this; dangerously close to Zachharius but vital for his, Zeth's needs.

He saunterd off the road, having ruffled his hair and clothes as though he had just awoken; the most unguarded, the least dangerous.

He managed a genuine yawn as he wandered over to where the stableman was.

"What a summer this is proving to be," he said to the man brushing down a chestnut gelding. "That is beautiful animal you have there. Is that the inn-keeper's own?"

"No, but one of the guest's," replied the man, looking at him without hardly raising his head. "You are not staying here then?"

"Me? no," laughed Zeth. "I was passing through but met a lovely lady at that celebration in Augustus square the other night; I am happy to say. Did you hear about it?"

"Oh yes, many of them were staying here. Personal friends of Zachharius; the Innkeeper."

"I was wondering about the singer. Wasn't her name Miriam? Fantastic; do you think she will perform again?"

"She left yesterday morning."

"Oh." Seth let the silence lengthen but not to straining point. "The name's Zeth by the way; with a voice like that I suppose she is going to Jerusalem. Never mind, I am going the other way, if I can find a caravan to ride with. Have you heard of any that will be going north?"

The stableman looked at him closely, deciding he was the harmless traveller he seemed; one of those who liked to drift. "In a couple of days, I think there is one due in; going all the way to Persia from what I heard."

"Well, that would be some trip. Perhaps I could do a stage or two with them though. Thanks for your help."

"Nate; the name's Nathan, but most people call me Nate. Maybe you will be lucky with hearing the singer again though; she was going north too. With one of the apostles that spoke; Thomas."

"Ahhh, yes; he was very good," and a cloud passed over Zeth's mind like a warning. "Well maybe, who knows," and he was ready to walk away, but Nathan seemed determined to give him more information, now that he had started.

"I think Thomas was going all the way to Antioch." Zeth stopped himself turning away.

"Well, that is somewhere I would like to go one day, Nate. Have you travelled much yourself?" He didn't want to overdo the friendship bit, especially as someone might come who did recognise him; but he had to slide out of Nathan's day as naturally as possible.

"No. Always been a Jericho man myself. Expect you have been around a bit?"

"A bit, yes" said Zeth, "but one day I hope to settle down. When I find the right lady."

"Not the one from the other night? Haha."

"Hmmm… maybe, maybe not; hah. I think not, though. Lovely girl, but would want too many children. Not sure I could cope with that. Anyway, I had better go get the bread I came out for; or else."

"Two streets down on the right," said Nate.

"Thanks mate, and about the caravan, Nate." They laughed, and Zeth was gone.

North; Capernaum probably. At least that is where she had been going to meet that Yeshua a few months back. It would be a good starting place, and he had no doubt he could track her down.

But he still felt the warning in his brain, and he was good at paying attention to these. That is why he was the best.

There was no rush; he would play the long game. Make a proper job of it and clear up as much of the pollution as possible. That is how he thought of the religious groups; life pollution. He was going to do his best to cut this one down before… he couldn't quite put a finger on why he hated it particularly, but yes… before it got any more popular and unbearable.

He would make his report to his paymasters about Kareem, and recommend continued observation in relation to the Christines. They would pay; he always made them give what hurt them most.

Also, he would make them an offer that he knew they would pay almost anything for; to cut off the heads of the growing Christine threat to their influence; delivered without any stain on them; just internal strife; with a little help. He had been formulating a plan for that already.

*

Matthias reported on his journey to Peter, describing the unguardedly rousing nature of Miriam's approach to preaching; her way of seeing things.

"John and Thomas were both there though? Are they planning more of the same? With her?"

Matthias suddenly had the feeling he should have stayed longer; he had no idea of what was actually going on now. "Er, Thomas was definitely travelling on up to Antioch, and John I am sure was staying in Jericho a while longer."

"But you don't know what Miriam is planning?"

Matthias frowned.

Peter regarded him sagely. "She is a danger to herself I fear; and so maybe to us also; for she is strong-willed, for all her apparent gentleness."

He looked down into his cupped hands. "Not your fault Matthias, and better that she doesn't think that you are hanging around spying on her. I will deal with her soon enough myself, before the authorities force our hands."

Matthias looked at him questioningly. "Keep close to me on this Matthias, I will doubtless need your help, but the fewer that get involved the better. I want her back here with Mother; behaving as a good daughter-in-law should."

CHAPTER 6.

I opened the door. I was expecting someone to come from Jacob's house with some supplies.

There, stood Miriam.

Just like she had that first morning when she had come, two years ago.

It took me a second to recover as those memories came flooding back, to the time we were both there to receive the inner teaching from Yeheshua. And all that had happened in the meantime.

How she had blossomed I realised. She had always been beautiful and full of such promise; promise that she had now fulfilled, and yet was still completely uncomplicated.

I went forward and embraced her, welcoming her again into the house of the beginning of our great friendship.

I looked quickly out the door to make sure there was no-one else with Miriam, then closed it.

"My mother is not here," I said. "She is visiting her old friend in the centre of Magdala, probably for another week or so; but there is another family staying here. Let me introduce you to little Mary and her mother." We went in.

"This is Anna, and her daughter Mary. Her husband Hosea is working at Jacob's house."

Very soon we were taking drinks, honeyed nuts and some spiced cakes out into the garden to the shady place we used for sitting out in the heat of the summer.

Johannus joined us, really pleased to see Miriam.

"I hope you haven't come up alone, Miriam?" he asked, looking concerned.

"Actually, Thomas came with me. "

We looked at each other. "But I suggested he didn't come down here; he is staying back up on the road."

All sorts of feeling swirled around in me; I couldn't say anything.

"He would very, very, much like to see you Mary, but I said you must decide. He will wait for your word. He is travelling north to Antioch."

My mind was already made up. I was sure of my way, and sure he had his to follow too.

Yet, if I was so sure, then I could tell him so… because the love was still real; more so.

"He can come then," I said. "Would you go and say I would love to talk with him, Johs?"

Johannus winced as he raised himself from the low seat he was on.

"Are you alright? I can go," said Miriam.

"Just my hip, I am fine. Stiffened up a bit; will do me good to walk it off."

"I will come with you then," said Miriam, and they went off together to leave me alone with my turmoil of thoughts and emotions.

Except for little Mary who was playing unconcerned with the hem of my dress; and she smiled up a sweet smile that hit me just where I needed it; simplicity itself.

Antioch? Where we had first met, and so many other things had happened. I hadn't been back yet, but I would like to be going as well.

My heart was racing when Miriam returned with Thomas and Johannus following her. The two of them seemed to be chatting happily but the moment Thomas saw me he stopped and broke off from them.

I turned away to move towards the further end of the garden, but not before catching his eye and opening my hand towards him. He followed and his fingers touched mine as we left the sight of the others.

I would have taken him my arms and kissed him… and yet I didn't.

Not caution, or fear of rejection, but instead, a sudden wash of gratitude that finally, finally we were able to talk, and that was what I wanted. To explain so many things, and yet now he was here even that need seemed to be fading away, as his presence took over from everything.

"I know," he said, "it has been a kind of madness, and you have had to bear the brunt of it. I am so sorry."

"Hah, yes, you are right; but I am also bearing the very best of it too; and I am so glad. Our daughter will be…"

"Very blessed." we both said together, and laughed.

"How do you know the baby will be a girl?"

"I just do; there was a lot of things that happened back in Jerusalem, when I was thinking of ending my life; when the demons that returned sevenfold into me were leading me to that end; but knowing Sarah in me was one of the things that kept me from it."

"I could feel something dreadful happening, but I couldn't find you."

"Yes, I know. Miriam was there somehow and, and I was able to see through to the light, even in all the madness; but it couldn't really reach me in the end."

Thomas was holding my hands very tight. "Because it wasn't me. In the end I knew, completely."

He sighed deeply and suddenly realised he was still squeezing my hands, and let them go. "I am sorry."

I laughed, shaking my fingers loosely. "Don't be Tom, I love the place that this has brought me. There was probably no other way I could have reached this simple certainty I feel."

He looked down, and I wanted to put my arms around him again, but took one of his hands in mine instead. "I hear you are going to Antioch?"

*

CHAPTER 7.

Thomas rode his grey mare Meg along the road to Bethsaida, where he hoped to find Philip and Nathaniel; glad it was those two up here in Galilee, away from that boiling pot of Jerusalem.

The day was hot, but his waterskins were full and his heart was light.

He had asked Mary to marry him, not because he thought he had to, but because he felt they were truly partners in this path, this life.

And when he did, a great weight had lifted from him.

She had looked deeply into him and lifted his soul on wings of clarity, making him only able to feel that love; Heaven's gift, to them both.

Yet she had chosen not to answer in words but instead held him close so that he couldn't see the tears in her eyes, feeling that they had merged into one being.

Then suddenly she had grasped his arms and pushed herself far enough away so that she could smile tightly back into his face, seeing his tears mirroring hers.

"We have work to do my love," she had said. "Nothing will happen if we take our hand from the ploughshare now."

Thomas sighed as he slowed Meg to a stop under a couple of thorn trees that made just enough shade to make it worthwhile slipping from her back to take a break.

He poured out some water into a shallow wooden trough he had brought for Meg, and a cup for himself. She pushed her muzzle against his arm, as a thank you before dipping her neck over the trough.

He had changed his opinion of her from being rather pedestrian to being remarkably economic in what she did, never over-exerting but always seeming to have more energy left than he did.

In fact, she outlasted him in the very quality he thought he excelled in, stamina.

"Well, we shall both be tested on this journey girl," he said, patting the side of her neck. "We shall rest only a little while here though, and hopefully get you a proper stable for tonight.

They had passed Capernaum, stopping only briefly at Yeheshua's house there and Thomas asked the couple of ladies who were looking after it how things fared in with the Christine community in the town, and was grateful to hear that Miriam's influence had already spread its sweet balm there; a healing, making this house, her house, a central place for the community.

Of course, she was Yeheshua's partner from the time of his last celebration here, their marriage day. So right that she was ensuring the use of it to help fulfil all the work the Lord had done here.

By all accounts she was a dynamic influence still, particularly amongst the many women disciples, continuing the master's teachings with them.

Thomas wondered what Peter would make of that? And he also smiled to himself that Mary was joining her strength with Miriam's; a powerful pairing.

She was sunshine in his heart and had banished all the misgivings of darkness he had perceived earlier in the journey.

He mused these thoughts as he leaned his back against the tree. Meg had trotted easily along the road to Bethsaida and they were making good time. They should reach brothers Philip and Nathaniel's house this same day.

His mind returned to Mary, and how she had managed to leave him really happy, yet had said nothing by way of answer to his marriage proposal.

What had made him say those words he had no idea. It hadn't been in his plan to do so, but when he had, relief had flooded him; it was out of his hands now.

Somehow the encounter had renewed his energy and resolve to get quickly up to Antioch.

What she had given him were a couple of names of people he was going to visit on her behalf. Her friends Arianne at the temple of Astarte and Sarita, married to a rich Zoarostrian merchant.

Particularly Arianne, and she thought he might like to use the scriptorium of the temple which had been her and Arianne's domain those three years ago.

Bel was the name of the high priestess that had banished Magdalene on her becoming possessed, but Arianne had helped Mary to the utmost of her capabilities.

He would go, for Mary; but held out no hope of more than telling them how well Mary was now, through Yeheshua's love.

He pulled himself out of his reverie and went over to see how Meg was, and decided it was time to move off again. She had eaten the couple of handfuls of meal he had brought for her and drunk the water; there wasn't much else; she swished her tail to shoo away the flies.

"Right, let's go girl." The day was hot but he knew the road got more shaded again, where it passed close to the sea. Meg seemed glad to get a trot on as though she could smell the green life of trees and grass somewhere ahead too; where Jordan's stream came down to the Sea.

*

Seth made sure he went to Kareem's next Ennead meeting.

He had decided against going north just yet; better to make his plans and preparations carefully, having first gained more knowledge of the plans of the man called Matthias.

At the meeting Seth made sure he stayed close to Kareem; a neutral brooding strength and aid, as the teacher worked with his human representatives of the goddesses Nephthys, Tefnut and Isis; blending their magic into an irresistible call: the subtle chants of Ancient Egypt to be a tool for the hands of Kareem and Matthias.

Despite himself Seth was quite impressed with the results; the balm and strength of it. Like a massage to the mind and spirit; but to be resisted by him at all costs.

He shook himself free of the effects to make sure he had the presence of mind to discover everything he could of Matthias' plans and purpose, realising how well they could be married into his own.

He had maybe two, or at most three, weeks to make his. Hard for him to temper his impatience, but with a great effort of will he brought his mind to focus on what he would do; realising that he needed the time, and perfect timing.

The dark enemy of the Ennead would need to return, and he would need to be the one to bring that about.

Apep-Apophis the most ancient; the recurrent dark; the endless snake who undid all the Gods' work; bringing Ignorance against the Light they strove to spread. Ignorance called Darkness. Only great Set could keep it at bay; working with Isis's magic.

He could call the snake, but only at great danger to himself.

He would have to offer Isis, or Miriam, in exchange for sharing its power, and then attack the Christines, to take Miriam; forcing her to work with him to control Apophis instead; as only immortal Set can.

So yes, he had a lot of work, starting with the corpse that was disintegrating foully in the basement of one of his 'residences' on the other side of Jericho.

*

Kareem sent word to Matthias in Jerusalem that he would be welcome to join them for next week's meeting of the Ennead.

They would be ready to practice and work with him.

*

For a moment Thomas worried that he was riding away from something that he needed to be involved in; a nagging doubt that everything was not quite right, but meeting up with Philip and Nathaniel that evening made him feel much better again.

"Magdalene is back home?" they asked, declaring that they would go over and visit as soon as they could. There were a couple of family matters that they had pretty much sorted out and had spent all the time they needed with the Bethsaida Christines too; so maybe tomorrow or the next day they would go to Magdala.

Spurred on by this good result, because Thomas liked the brothers probably most of all the twelve, he set off early the next morning, heading North like a firebrand of clarity ready to burn up the darkness; the misery of ignorance that kept all the world in chains… no longer.

Meg matched him all the way, and he made sure she was properly rested fed, watered and groomed along the road, even as he felt the tide of his own passion readying him for Antioch, the city of his youth; to give the news of what Yeheshua brought; the living truth for all to know.

The journey invigorated him and the time to himself replenished him, feeling that it was he and Yeheshua together that rode into Antioch to meet his friends, and find those that Mary had told him of as well.

And when he found two of his friends, at the house they used all to share, he felt a great upsurge of love for them, but knew he couldn't tell them all the things he so much wanted to; not yet anyway. So, he asked after their philosophy teacher instead, who had been old even when he last saw him; older still by several years now.

"He is still here, yes," his friends replied, "but living with a family who care for him now; near the centre. We can take you there if you like."

"I would like that very much," answered Thomas. "Can we go there today?" And so, they did.

The old man was lying in his bed, dozing, when Thomas was let into his room, his two friends just behind him; but on hearing them he opened bleary eyes to see who they were.

Thomas dropped forward onto his knees by his old master's bed, taking one of his hands in both of his; tears streaming down his face as he felt their connection, brother spirits who had sought the truth in this life.

No words were needed, but for the benefit of the others the old man spoke, his face lit up in reflection of Thomas. "So, you did find it; it was not a false hope." A statement of fact, looking into the young man's heart because his own was wide open and ready in the hope of it.

"Yes," said Thomas. "I did, and it is here in us all, already."

"The Truth? Thank the Gods then, because if it wasn't I could never find it now;" and he half laughed and half coughed, prolonged-ly, which took a lot out of him.

CHAPTER 8.

Thomas stayed at Philestres side or nearby, for three whole days and in that time, he told his old teacher the whole story of all that had befallen since he had last seen him; fearful that the old man, being frail and sick, might leave this world before he knew as much as Thomas could tell him.

Instead though, all of Thomas' story or maybe his vibrant presence had a near miraculous effect on Philestres, renewed light and life coursing through his ancient skin and bones.

So much so that by the end Philestres was determined and strong enough to ask Thomas to impart to him the inner teachings of the Master Yeheshua, if he would; for knowing the Truth within was still upmost in his Socratic mind and heart.

So, Thomas did; happily.

Philestres's young students and some older associates were not oblivious to what had happened and didn't need Philestres recommendation to make them also listen to what Thomas was telling them, but the old teacher told them anyway: to pay heed and do as the young sage asked, if they valued his advice.

Thomas also told them about all that was happening now in Jerusalem and Galilee and that doubtless other Christine disciples would follow Thomas up to Antioch.

And how glad he was to have been able to meet with them first and let them hear the news from him; especially as many of them knew him from before.

He asked after Kasver the wealthy Zoarastrian merchant Mary had told him had married her friend Sarita, and was slightly surprised to hear how well he was known to them, and held in high regard too; because of the generosity of his works, especially amongst the lepers of the city.

And he enquired after the Temple of Astarte, which raised some eyebrows all around as he spoke, making him boldly ask for someone to show him the way there, for he had business with the keeper of their library.

Two younger men he did not know stepped forward and he accepted their offer to go that very day without delay, for he did not know how much time he could be staying in Antioch.

As they walked Gregorius and Aeshel told Thomas of the destructive earthquake that had collapsed the front part of the temple under a year before, killing Bel their High Priestess.

Thomas was shocked that he hadn't heard, and rather more that Mary hadn't. Maybe she had but hadn't seen the need to tell him. She certainly seemed to have thought that her friend Arianne was all right.

Musing on these as things they knocked on the side door, opened by a wizened but tough looking older man, Thomas asked this doorkeeper after the priestess Arianne.

"Who is asking?" came the reply; dry and even.

"Thomas Didimus," he said, then added, "er… er, who is also a friend of one of hers; Mary Magdalene."

The man jolted noticeably at that name. "Magdalene? Really?" His face lit up briefly then settled into a hard questioning look.

"Yes, you know her then?"

"Of course, I did. Arianne told me she had survived but not much more."

"She went on a long journey south; has only recently returned. Not surprising that you haven't heard more. There has been a lot going on, hah… yes, I see that now."

The doorkeeper stood aside, making room for Thomas to go in, but putting out a hand to stop his two companions. "These two can wait for you with me in the guardhouse if you like." Then to them, "stay here and I will come back for you." His voice brooked no argument and Thomas nodded briefly to them.

"My name is Gaius," said the older man as he led Thomas around some of the large piles of debris still littering the front temple site. It must have been a terrible time; almost all of one half of the building had come down. Thomas guessed that this was the man Mary had told him was consort to Bel.

"High Priestess Bel lived here," said Gaius. "She never stood a chance; was killed outright." Then quietly, "she was a very close friend of mine."

Thomas felt Gaius' enduring grief, probably as much as anything for not dying with her. He felt sorry for the hardened ex-soldier.

They walked past what must have once been a fine water-filled rectangle running inside along the building, but was now a jagged-angled pit. Light shone strongly onto some remaining water nearest where the building had stood, half covering pieces of fresco and smooth sided stones from broken columns that had fallen into it. Strangely beautiful still amongst all the ruination.

Gaius touched Thomas' shoulder, as he stood staring down into the water. "We go up these stairs here," he said.

Thomas climbed after Gaius, noticing the signs of reparation work all around this side of the building, filling cracked arches and bolstering leaning walls; strengthening what could be saved.

They went down a corridor to a heavy wooden door where Gaius stopped and knocked twice, waiting respectfully for an answer.

In a few long moments the door was opened enough to reveal a brown robed women with curly black hair drawn back and held by a gold clasped band behind her head that reflected the sunshine as she glanced from Gaius to Thomas.

"A friend of Magdalene to see you mistress Arianne," said Gaius simply, and the look of astonishment that spread across the woman's face was most marvellous to Thomas' eyes.

He wondered for a moment whether he had met her before when he was living in Antioch, but realised quickly it was the bond of both of them knowing

Mary that made him feel like that.

He smiled involuntarily and she asked quickly, wide-eyed, "Mary! Is she well? She is not here I suppose." Then, "come in, come in. Gaius could you ask Maddie to bring us some mint tea and sweetmeats?"

Thomas found himself in a long wooden-floored room lit by a row of arched windows down one side and lined with racks of scrolls and shelves of tablets down the other, whilst dotted with writing desks in the middle and more comfortable chairs down the far end.

"I am Thomas, called Didimus," he found himself telling the brown robed priestess as she led him down to the comfortable seating, "and Mary sends her heartfelt greetings, though she cannot come up to Antioch quite yet, she said to tell you she longs to see you again."

"And I her; we spent many hours over many days, years, working here together," responded Arianne. "Please, you must tell me what has been happening since the time I heard from Rachel of Tyre that the healer Yeheshua had cast out those evil demons from her."

Thomas was nodding, and drew in a deep breath... "Yes, rather a lot has happened."

He sketched for her in vivid the wonders of the past year or two, from when Mary fought to be a disciple equal to the men and Yeheshua had supported her cause (which made Arianne smile broadly and knowingly) to the marriage of Yeheshua to Miriam in Galilee, when she and Magdalene returned from the master's given quest; to the Master's tireless teaching and many miracles that culminated in bringing Lazarus back from death; and the unabated fury of the Jewish leaders and Pharisees that resulted, because of all of that.

Then told of Yeheshua's trials and crucifixion (which made Arianne cry out in horror) but also his return from death itself.

Arianne gasped, scarce able to believe that what she was being told could be real.

"Neither did I," answered Thomas to the look of bewilderment on her face. "I could not believe it when they told me they had seen our Lord returned from death; nor would I till I had touched his broken hands and felt where the spear had entered his side at the end."

"And did you?"

"I did." Thomas paused, looking at the clear faced priestess, "and I will tell you what I felt at that time, that I have told no other, not even Mary."

"It really was my beloved Lord, returned; but I felt also that he had finished, or nearly finished the work that he had been set to do on Earth; and was ready to hand the Earthly Master's mantle over to another."

A silence between them grew and Thomas saw how deep and dark Arianne's eyes were.

He flushed. "For an instant the question came to my mind like a moth to the candle's flame; 'could I be that one?' but I thankfully swept it aside with the greater love he had shown me; seeing for a stark moment who it was that could truly bear that Greater Love, in and for this life."

The walls around them seemed to want to lean in and hear what she was about ask, and he to reply. Hers was a soft "who?" and Thomas in reply leaned forward and whispered a few words in her ear, fearful lest the walls indeed had ears.

*

Zeth-Seth arrived at his 'other' place, situated in the most wretched outskirt of North-eastern Jericho, as close to the desert he had been able to find.

It was early dusk but the reek would have guided him to it in darkest night. The houses on either side were deserted which neither surprised nor worried Seth.

He unloaded some of what he needed from the donkey that carried it and, heedless of the animal's discomfort, tied it tightly to a post around the back of the house.

This place was part of what he did and who he had been, a place of poison, torture, death and decay, but things were changing. He was changing; he was the change.

No longer would he be at the beck and call of polluted and weak-minded humans. He knew now, he could do better.

The study of the Ennead had triggered something very deep in him, had made the pieces fall into place; about himself.

He knew the tales and roles of those Gods: Osiris and Isis and the others, high minded, noble ones, that were not like humankind at all, who were weak and selfish and most often cruel.

And how the 'players' liked to pretend to those godly vanities; all except to Set, feared for his raw chaotic power, which they thought of as evil.

They were afraid of him and the strength he had; could not or would not enter his dark realm of thought and being; though none of their 'games' worked without him.

All that is, except Zeth. He alone embraced Set entirely, and had been rewarded hundredfold. He alone understood the whole story and had been given the key to bring it about.

The energy rising through him gave him such a focus that he could do anything. He had already delivered the new Osiris to Death and was under no illusions as to who his Isis was.

She has tricked him before, into pity and weakness; but would not do so again.

Concentrating on the job in hand, he carried bundles of wood and bags of other things through a well locked back door into the inner room of his domain.

It was not large, being blocked off from the front of the house by a wall into which Zeth had put a fire pit and chimney. There were a couple of stained wooden seats and a large cupboard on one side wall.

But most ominously, at the back end, near where Zeth had just come in, were stone steps leading down into darkness and the cellar from which the putrid stench exuded.

Leaving the door open to let in the rapidly fading light, Seth set the baggage down on the floor and moved quickly to the firepit with the bits and pieces he needed to get a fire going, followed swiftly by two fat-greased rag-torches, that he put in the sconces on either side of the fire.

Once done and the coals were burning well Seth added brimstone-sulphur on top of them, bringing more foul-smelling fumes to fill the room, mixing oddly with the reek from below.

Seth liked working alone, and the darkness below held no fears for him, but even so he wrapped a sweeter smelling headscarf around his face before carrying first a torch and then armfuls of dry wood down there, which he spread around the centre of the dark space that rustled with little noises, certainly rats and probably snakes as well.

Once he had spread his load of kindling wood around in as a wide disk he went back to the fire and raked the lit coals into a shallow bucket that he also spread over all as well, so that quite soon there was a wide low fire spreading around the central cellar area, cleansing the living filth with Set's clean fire. He sprinkled some more brimstone over it and got back out and closed the door and back up the steps, before the fumes would become overpowering.

Under where the fire had been there was a hinged rectangular metal plate, the same size as the fire opening, which had a handle on it that Seth pulled with a hooked bar, lifting it to fit snuggly against the front, opening a large hole from the cellar below up into the fireplace flue above.

Going outside Seth lifted two heavy sacks that were still tied onto the donkey, carrying them into the house, then reluctantly went back and poured some water for the donkey into a trough there before taking the rest of the water-skin back into the house and locked the door.

He was nearly ready; ready to open to the most forbidden… the oldest, deepest, ugly beyond evil; fathomless. He was nearly ready, who alone could bring this change; had to… to stamp out the spread of all that Seth hated most; all of it.

He had the granules of what people thought most precious, the frankincense and myrrh he would protect and anoint himself as bringer of the dark; the Lord of the new age, and sacks of the sand which he would cover over the sulphurous ashes with.

He waited a little longer, poised, totally concentrated until he felt the pull to go; that the moment of his power was here, and being filled, carried down first one and then the second sack and a small rake.

The fumes were still almost overpowering in the cellar but most of the fire had turned to ashes enabling Seth to pour sand onto the middle part, step there and rake any still living embers into two piles, out on either side.

Whilst these still had enough heat Seth added the gum nodules of frankincense to one and myrrh to the other and then spread the rest of the sand into a wide disk between the two, for him to sit and then lie on, blowing the incense piles to life.

Light flickered from outside the door, which would go out in a little while, leaving him in his anointed throne of darkness. All he had with him was a little stoppered phial and the part-filled water-skin that he knew he would need after he had done.

Starting to intone the name of darkness he let his mind embroil itself into it's meaning, it's reality, unstoppering the phial and drinking its bitter contents.

"Apep come, Apophis come; Apep come to me, come to your destined world, Apep Apophis, come… Apophis come…" he intoned on, as the drugs took final effect on him.

CHAPTER 9.

The snake came, tongue licking out; dead black eyes staring straight into Seth's drug filled mind.

The incense glowed slightly, smoke curling distastefully into Apep's senses… but Seth in between them drew the snake's hunger onto him…

Opening wide his jaws, striking swiftly; taking all Seth's head in one bite of pain, of fear, and horror.

Sucking, re-biting and drawing Seth's shaking mind-body further into him.

*

Peter prayed for guidance.

He was uncertain of the wisdom in Matthias employing the mysteries of Egypt towards Miriam.

He knew the story of Miriam and Yeheshua first meeting in the temple of Heliopolis, and that she was undoubtedly trained in their mysteries too, so he understood the argument of appealing to all of her and not relying just on his, Peter's, own authority to bring her into line.

Maybe he should have consulted with Mother, who herself had fled to, and studied in, those same temples; when Herod had tried to kill her newborn child.

He dismissed this thought though; the task was his; he must make the decision.

So, he prayed, but got no answer; meaning to him that he would let the situation continue, but step in himself decisively when the need arose.

*

Seth felt his mind-soul being digested by the reborn snake, holding only to his unshakeable focus of desire and hate: a blackness as strong as Apep's.

Felt the mindless greed to absorb all his cruelty and dark desires, feed on the life that had been Zeth's, sucking the juice out of his fears and hates as well, magnifying the horror back, to sustain the snake's own greed for it.

Only the thought of Miriam, of his one-pointed desire to do to her what he allowed Apep do to him, remained, and was more than Apep could yet digest.

That was the remnant of Seth's mind, his eyes seeing through the snake's dead ones, his thoughts flickering beyond the greed, the ignorance.

He saw signs of Apep's slithering weaving progress through the dark ahead, felt the overwhelming gnawing need to feed; to grow and grow; to spread all of itself; it's awful inhuman, soulless greed of ignorance.

To draw all life down into it.

Felt it all, through his entrapped mind-soul; Apep knowing what he held back.

*

Herakaphon sensed the approach of the deathless snake as well…

Knew it from the ancient conflicts with his kind, before the birth of

631

humankind; impressed upon the great beast's heart-soul.

Kaella, resting in the twilight nearby didn't; not until her soul-twin Herakapha had dived, as Herakaphon, down towards the darkness, rising like a tide beneath.

Didn't see until the fire from Herakaphon burned into that dark; highlighting the approach of the huge snake through the roiling blackness.

Apep lunged up underneath the fire to sink his fangs into the dragon's neck, but he was caught by iron talons instead, just short.

Whipping around, coils flailing, the snake's fangs managed to connect with the dragon's softer underarm just as the fury of Kaella exploded into the fray.

Herakaphon screamed, talons clawing at the giant snake's head; the smoking eyes being target too, for Kaella's bursting brightness...

*

Seth screamed uncontrollably, the brightness of the light and pain of sharpest talon ripping through him, throwing half of his mind, bodily unconscious from the head of Apep.

Apep recoiled and fled, and Herakaphon sank, poison-filled to the dark ground.

Kaella wept, seeing the life-spirit was draining from her half-self.

*

The keening of a goddess losing her heart soul-beast, even in those changing times, is hard to ignore around the universe where it is joined to her plane, and Miriam responded to her friend's grief, for so she had become.

Placing a consoling arm around Kaella she stroked Herakaphon's head, feeling his distress; he was too far gone to bring him back...

"He needs to go to the world he took you to Kaella, where he will live anew... forgetting all of this, for a while at least."

Kaella said nothing, also stroking her heart-friend's neck. "He will forget me then," she said at last.

"He is not bound by the same laws as us Kaella, that travel the human path. He can recover his memories in time."

Kaella had known for a little time that she must chose the human road, but had not declared her heart on this, even to Miriam. Now the decision was made for her, and poor Herakaphon too.

"He has uncovered and wounded my enemy, Kaella. He has done a great service and I am most grateful, and to you for the blow you have struck here for the Light. It will not be forgotten ever, by me."

Miriam let go Kaella then and took Herakaphon's huge head in both her arms, laying her head against his brow, whispering in a language even Kaella did not know.

"Once I was a priestess on that world you saw," Miriam said. "This is their rite of transfer; he needs it given quickly to minimise the harm to him."

So saying, she carried on her lilting words that started to weave pictures into

Kaella's mind as well: of other flying dragons around distant snowy peaks; and a great bowl of the making, where the wind of breath was born, for dragonkind; for Herakaphon, and he was suddenly gone, to join the other tiny, tiny dots in the soft mists there.

CHAPTER 10

The snake went on into the dark; angry at the pain.

With Seth, half awaking to a thirst even more immediate; both seemed to be trying to dominate him.

He scrabbled around for the water skin, even though he knew he was going to vomit.

Vomit out the snake in him? or himself out of the snake? Not that easy.

He retched convulsively and his mind reeled in coils of hate; back at him.

Pulling the stopper from the waterskin; feverishly trying to drink; spilling more and swallowing back acid vomit; retching again, Seth crawled towards the faint light that came from where the steps were. Desperate.

Clawing the door open he made it to the bottom step, feeling a rush of coolness flowing down onto his already cold sweating neck, aiding him. He tried to drink, only to retch again.

He felt some small separation between him sitting on the step and him in the snake, swimming in the dark; between his thirst and that other dread, owning him.

A couple more steps gained and he was able to stop and drink without retching but never far from it; his throat though, relaxed its stricture and he could think a bit.

By the time he got to the top of the steps he felt miraculously that the snake had curled up and gone to sleep. He almost laughed except he knew...

*

Thomas stayed and talked with Arianne a while longer, telling her of his wish to write down the things he remembered Yeheshua saying best, that might trigger others to seek as well, and Arianne begged that he would return to the scriptorium and use their materials and allow that she could copy too from what he wrote.

Amazed at this response, though why he should have been from Mary's greatest friend he couldn't say, he readily agreed to come back and start the next day.

Which he did, having stayed with the two students Gregorius and Aeshel overnight, and visited Philestres in the morning, recounting to him the success of the day before. Philestres had been slightly astonished but beamed contentedly nevertheless. "Never turn your back on the Gods' blessings," the old man chimed in, "or the Goddesses', haha."

Arianne allowed Thomas all the space he needed to think and get into his writing before she ventured to join him with some simple lunch of spicy soup and bread, which he readily accepted and enjoyed.

He had completed a page and offered it over to Arianne who studied it thoughtfully, smiling occasionally and obviously intrigued at what she was reading. "Is it alright if I make a copy of this?" she asked.

"Please do," said Thomas, "that would be wonderful."

They worked away together and after completing a couple more pages he put the stylus down and watched, admiring her skill and easy concentration into what she was doing. She quite soon caught up.

"Do you know of Kasver and Sarita?" he asked as she looked up, realising he was being stupid and that she must, for his wife had been a priestess.

"I hardly knew Sarita as a priestess," answered Arianne, seemingly reading his thoughts. "She was a year-friend of Magdalene's and didn't spend time here, where I had been spending almost all mine for three years before they came," she explained.

".. but yes, I have come to know both her and Kasver quite well since her marriage, because Kasver helped Mary with the leper-caring project that had been very dear to Mary, and which Kasver carried on running after her... her abomination."

Thomas said nothing for a while, then simply, "I should like to meet them if I could."

*

Arianne said she would see what she could do and sent one of the younger priestesses to seek Sarita and tell her that a friend of Magdalene's was here with their friend's love and request to meet with her and Kasver.

The girl came back with the invitation for Thomas and Arianne to dine with them the next day.

"They are a really lovely couple," she told Thomas. "It is Kasver who has been organising the work here, since the earthquake; with Sarita of course."

"It must have been horrendous," said Thomas, "were there very many killed?"

"Only a few really, but mostly senior priestesses who were in that building collapse; and Bel of course. Everything changed."

"How so? I can see that there doesn't seem to be a High Priestess now."

"No, we didn't want to replace Bel. She was a driving force and there was no-one who could fill her place, especially with the other senior priestesses that died too." She stopped talking for a while, but then continued. "Three of us decided to split the running of the temple and the work we do between us, but quite a few had already left, maybe out of fear or just the chance to go; become army followers, as like as not. There was a bond..."

Thomas nodded. "Will the temple recover fully do you think?"

"Not as it was, no. Feels like the change was coming, meant to be. But we shall continue much of what we have always done, but it is changing. Like the work that Magdalene started with the lepers, and wanted to do with people possessed. It will come as it is meant to be," and she brightened up with a new thought, "maybe Mary will come back and help in ways we never expected." She smiled at Thomas and he beamed back.

"She might, yes, and others too," he said musingly. "I would love you to meet Yeheshua's mother, and Miriam too, of course."

CHAPTER 11.

The dinner with Kasver and Sarita came quickly, though there was enough time for Thomas and Arianne to copy out another couple of copies each of what he had written, one of which they took to Kasver's house with them.

It was a lovely place, almost a small palace, with an outstanding view across the city.

Sarita had arranged and personally involved herself in cooking the food for the evening and Kasver was a gracious host, himself offering the best wine he had to his guests as they arrived.

Sarita hugged Arianne who then introduced Thomas to them.

"Surely we have met before," said Sarita. "Did you once live in Antioch?"

"I did, that is true," answered Thomas, a little taken aback, "though I am sure we never met here…"

"Haha, I know," laughed Sarita; "Magdalene pointed you out to me, when you were passing with your student friends, all laughing. You may not have noticed us."

Thomas flushed involuntarily and Sarita laughed again but Kasver scolded her, though lovingly.

"You must tell us, please," she continued earnestly, "how is our dearest Magdalene? It was such a terrible time when she was attacked by that black magus and his evil. We were so happy and amazed to hear about her release. Did you know her then?"

"Soon after, when she had recovered, I did," said Thomas. "She was like no other woman amongst the master's followers; became a leading light and still is so now."

He told them something more of recent events as they sat and ate on the balcony in the warm summer evening, and as he did he couldn't help remembering all that had transpired between himself and Magdalene.

"I have asked her to marry me actually," he said, as his story had reached a point he could no longer seem to avoid it, "and she is pregnant with my child," he added, surprising himself more than a little, but happy to have said it too.

"That is tremendous news," said Kasver, taking the lead from the slightly nonplussed women, "there is nothing that would surprise me about Magdalene. She is a remarkable person. When do you think you may marry?"

"Well, she hasn't actually accepted my proposal," said Thomas, to which both Sarita and Arianne answered together, "oh, she will;" and giggled.

After that the conversation turned to how they could all meet up again with Mary as soon as possible, and Thomas admitted that he would be going back within the week.

"There is a music week happening in Capernaum, like there was two years ago in Nazareth where Miriam's singing caused a huge stir. She will again I am sure, and I wouldn't want not to be there. Miriam was, is, our Master's wife and sister soul, and the greatest friend of Magdalene."

"If you are going, then we would like to come as well," stated Kasver. "There is nothing holding us here in Antioch is there Sarita dearest? For a while?"

"A fantastic idea. Could you come as well Arianne?"

*

That night Thomas dreamt, and in the dream a great dragon passed over him like a shadow, flying and he knew it from another time, soon after the Lord's crucifixion, and a familiar voice was talking, from just behind him, a woman of power. "You must go to where the sun will rise, Thomas. You must go there."

He woke and was troubled as though a ripple of darkness had travelled through the earth, seeking him out. He felt it and wondered if the dream was connected.

He lay for a long time trying to dismiss it, until the light started to rise in the eastern sky and he settled himself to welcome the new day, give himself into the rising light that was inside him."

*

...and Seth shuddered at the knowledge that the sickness was in him and he in it, irretrievably entwined, even though it seemed to sleep, giving him a little reprieve.

He also knew that what he had awoken would bring the destruction to all the petty efforts of those he so despised, even as he would be for Yeheshua's Miriam, who could not escape him.

He went over to the cupboard where he pulled out some of the things he needed; a wide lidded dish or shallow bowl, glass-like but heavy and dull grey coloured; a roll of what contained his poison knives, eleven in all, that had a thin grooved channel on either side, running up to their sharp points; and most horribly, a pair of skin gloves that he had made from the still warm flesh, flailed from the back of the dead man, from the corpse that was rotting in the cellar beneath.

He lit another fat-smoky torch, put on the long, carefully sewn gloves, and quickly, before he could even think of the snake other than a fleeting horror of it, with iron nerved resolve took the torch, the knives and dish back down the steps, into the cellar.

*

Matthias greeted Peter as they sat down to eat in the converted barn of 'Yeheshua's Inn', on the outskirts of Jerusalem; the enlarged farmhouse that had become the hub of the Christine activity in the city, growing stronger every day.

"I have heard," he said, "that there is going to be a week of holy music and singing in Capernaum, in just a few days time. This is a most portentous moment for us."

Peter raised an eyebrow over the piece of flatbread he was placing in his mouth, stopping in mid-motion. "Portentous moment?"

"The timing couldn't be better. Kareem and his women are all ready and eager to perform, having tailored what they will sing for… for us."

Peter considered it. He had woken with a horrible feeling in the pit of his stomach and had only just managed to bring himself around to eating. It took all his willpower to say nothing hasty back to Matthias but let him have his say.

"Miriam will be singing for certain and I am hoping we could ask her to join in with us, later in the week."

"Kareem has been baptised and so have the women taking part," he added, knowing that Peter had his doubts about the enterprise.

"That is good," said Peter, feeling more hopeful at least. "Perhaps you would ask them to come and sing here first?" That way he could at least have a say, knowing what it would be. "This Thursday maybe?"

Matthias nodded, thinking. This would give them just enough time. He would leave immediately to talk to Kareem, 'to strike whilst the iron was hot.'

"Yes Peter, I think that would be ideal. Can I borrow the mare again? We need to get organised."

Peter agreed; he would be very happy if Miriam became, well… not an issue.

*

CHAPTER 12.

The body in the cellar had been a man he had known; had meant to be working for him, but had betrayed him.

Seth mused on that for just a second before the deathly feeling of the snake's presence engulfed him again. Not completely, as it had when he had taken the drugs but like a blanket of evil darkness dragging him into it; from somewhere nearby.

Thrusting the evil smelling torch in front of him Seth pushed forward into the circle and set it into the pile of now dead coals and ashes where the myrrh had been, repressing a cry from inside of himself.

He was finding it hard to think, but knew exactly what he had to do, so screwing up his face he put down the dish, removed the lid and with his gloved hands dug into the rotting sludge that were the remains of the man who had let Miriam and her companions escape him, those few months ago.

It wasn't too hard to deposit enough off his skin gloves to lay across the bottom of the dish, but it did seem to want to stick, and he came very close to vomiting again, blacking out.

Had to be strong, and holding onto the last vestiges of Set's strength of will, he dipped his hands into the ashes of the other incense pile, noticing for the first time damp black stain on it, like congealing blood.

Dragon's blood, or Apep's blood; both. It didn't really matter and he couldn't have said how he knew this, but the horror of the night was still fresh in him; he knew.

He dragged the gloves across it, getting as much of it onto them as he could.

This was harder to get off than the human remains and he had to use one of the poison knives to scrape it off onto the sludge in the dish.

Then as carefully as his throbbing head allowed, he took each of his knives from their iron shod sheaths in the roll, and stuck them into certain portions of the stinking mess, laying the handles around the rim of the dish.

Nearly done; just the poisonous slime to spread on top, from the evil-smelling plant matter that produced it in one corner of the cellar.

Seth felt the dead eyes of the snake on him, and the tongue licking the darkness, seeking him from the corner he was trying to get to. Couldn't... couldn't move.

Something was hissing softly ahead of him and he knew he had to hear, had to get on his knees and crawl a bit forward.

'Take it Ssssethh' the darkness hissed in Seth's brain; 'bring me hher..sssss.'

Trembling uncontrollably Seth stretched forward a skin-gloved fingers to scrape slimy mould off the edge of stuff in the dark; out of range of the guttering torchlight.

And quickly as he could he edged back onto the sand and deposited both the gloves and the slime on top of the mess in the dish.

It was done.

He put the lid on it, like the jaws of the snake snapping shut and managed somehow to get back to the steps and out of the hell-hole.

*

Thomas woke early, feeling an urgency within; but to do what he didn't know.

His dreams had been strange again; a decapitated snake had been there but full of poison that had to be squashed out of it; every bit or else it would regenerate. He had succeeded somehow in his dream, standing on it with his riding boots, getting every bit exuded from it.

And he now sat down to focus to the same end inside; immersing himself in light and holy breath.

Breath that lifted him, filling him with a joy so that soon an hour had passed and Thomas went outside to wash in the cubicle, set up for just this, and follow on out to find his breakfast.

Several students were at the same bread shop he used to go to before, and had gone back to now, and soon they were sitting together and enjoying their repast.

One of them had already heard him speaking with master Philestres and he asked Thomas to explain to the others the teaching of the master Yeheshua.

"It is a practical teaching, not a theoretical philosophy," answered Thomas. "Not different from Socrates's either."

"I have just been writing down some of the sayings that I can remember and this was one of those:

… "If people seek to lead you saying '… the heavenly realm is in the sky,' then the birds of the sky would get there before you. If they say to you, ' … it is in the sea,' then the fish will be there first. But instead, know that realm is within you and outside as well … and when you know yourselves, then you will know and be known, and understand that you are the children of the Power of Life itself. But if you do not know yourselves, then you live in poverty, and are the poverty."

Silence settled as Thomas' breakfast companions took in his words. He spoke again…

"My Lord Yeheshua said: 'I took my stand in the midst of the world, and in flesh I appeared to them. I found them all drunk, and did not find any of them thirsty. My soul ached for the children of humanity, because they are blind in their hearts and do not see, for they came into the world empty, and they also seek to depart from the world empty… but meanwhile they are drunk. When they shake off their wine, then they will change their ways."

Silence fell, even deeper, then the student called Bartholomew asked: "What was he like to be with?"

Thomas thought for a moment before answering. "He gave so much that sometimes it feels like he is more with me now than even when I was with him. He left the whole of his love inside us. He will never die, and nor will we that know him."

"Can we know him too?" asked another.

"You can and will," said Thomas. "There is no shortage of riches of the heart, of knowing the self, for those who want; unlike the riches of this world."

And Thomas understood then the urgency within him and realised that it wasn't going to be hard to fill the few days he still had in Antioch.

So much to do and many willing people to help too; he was genuinely excited by the goodwill he found.

Then going back to see Philestres in the afternoon there was a small crowd outside the house, and he was slightly shocked to find out he was what, who they were there to see.

He would have ducked through into the house but one lady caught his attention, it was like she was draped in cloud of sadness, and the child in her arms too.

The day had been, and still was, very hot and Thomas was burning with enthusiasm for the work ahead, but the chill around this woman was palpable, and he went over to where she stood, a little away from the others.

She had heard that a young master from Judea had brought life back to her son's ailing master Philestres and she hoped beyond all else that he could do something for her daughter.

Thomas felt his skin prickling with energy all up his back as he asked the woman what ailed the child?

She shook her head but held the little girl out to Thomas, who took her in his arms. "What is her name?" he asked; she was so cold.

"Aileesha."

Thomas murmered her name and Yeheshua's too, and he felt a great rush of heat flowing through his arms to her; driving off the chill.

"Aileesha, are you alright?" and the girl opened her eyes for the first time since he had seen her. "Tired," she answered and Thomas smiled.

"That's alright, you should have a good sleep and you will be fine," he said brightly, feeling every word to be true, for he could feel life's warmth had stayed with her. The chill gone.

She smiled back.

People were crying and some shouting, and the woman was so happy, thanking him, that Thomas was amazed. He really hadn't done anything, other than feel compassion for them; something more than him had done the rest.

"We are meant to be well," he told the people gathering around him, "it is just how we are meant to be; and happy too, that is our natural estate. We should not be so surprised."

Many in the crowd were shouting out his name and he felt unsure of what to tell them. "Go home good people, but know that the master Yeheshua has brought this truth for us to know, that we are the citizens of heaven when we

641

recognise that happiness, that joy within us, that is our natural state. No greater truth needs there be than that..."

He did talk on for a few minutes before bidding them to go in peace, as he finally ducked into the house where Philestres was staying.

"They will be back and more," said his old master, coming up behind him and placing a hand on his former student's shoulder.

"It will not be fair if I stay here with you then," said Thomas. "But I have an offer to stay..."

"Don't tell me who or where," said Philestres smiling, "for I shall be telling everyone I have no idea where you have gone."

Thomas laughed, "You can tell anyone that wants though, that I shall be in the forum tomorrow morning, an hour or two before the sun is at its height. To tell about Yeheshua and the love of the Almighty.

CHAPTER 13.

I am so happy that Miriam is staying with me, and we travelled round Galilee with Johannus too, like when we had set off for Kadesh. It seems so long ago.

It was in the front room of the house in Capernaum that she asked me.

We had been meeting with some of the women disciples that recently Miriam had worked with on the inner teachings, like Yeheshua used to do, especially with the twelve.

"You can give the instructions too, Mary; you know that don't you? For those you are sure are ready and will benefit most?"

She was talking of entering the quietness, the silence that was totally inclusive, all embracing.

I said nothing, only wanting to soak it in, but I nodded, grateful for her confidence in me.

I felt it too or I could not have agreed; so much had changed and moved for me, yet here we were, almost at the beginning again; the simplicity of it all laid out clearly.

"Yes, they must know how much the Love is with them still; must know the comfort of feeling that, like we do. Growing, in and for each of them; not gone anywhere."

"We shall travel far you and I," she said; "and though I may go one way and you another, yet always that love will hold us together, just as it does now."

I was glad, happy that it could; that we could. Then she asked me:

"Would you help me write something? I am not very accomplished in writing."

It caught me by surprise, but I don't know why it should have done. Maybe because we were talking directly to so many people there hardly seemed a need to write things down.

"Of course," I answered, and then slightly stupidly, "what kind of thing?"

"Not anything hugely long," she answered smiling, "but do you remember that one exchange when our risen Yeheshua came amongst us to answer our questions and then urged us to get out and spread his message; and how reticent we were when he had gone?"

"God, yes," I answered irreverently, "when you urged us on as well and Peter asked you for any teaching that Yeheshua had given you but not to them; yet when you did both he and Andrew turned on you. How could I forget that?"

"I realised then that what I must do might not be possible for the Apostles to swallow. Some things are set too strong, not only in them but in their world all around, reinforcing that."

"You mean about us women and our 'place' in things," I said more forcefully than I intended, for this has been the very thing I have spent my life struggling against.

"Yes," she replied gently, "that, and because of that I will go my own way, so that they can also fulfil what has been given them to do."

I was taking in the implications of this when she added, "and I want Johannus to have a copy to take to Alexandria with him too, and to the temple at Heliopolis where Yeheshua and I met."

"Where are you thinking of going?" I asked with a heavy heart.

"There are many places that Yeheshua told me about; their people, some great and some simple, palaces and small villages; places where he sowed seeds and I would like to see their growth as well, and tend to them; and sow more too if I can."

I was thinking of saying something, probably something to blame Peter and the others, but she got in first. "We have to spread the light as far as possible Mary; take his Word as wide and far as possible. This is my task and destiny to do, for I can go where others wouldn't; and you shall too. Once your daughter is old enough…"

She had jogged me once more out of my usual thinking, lifting me to see a greater view.

"You needn't worry about anything Mary; just following the path you know is right will take you through, for there is no power on earth that can resist Life's purpose."

"Well, I hope I can follow that purpose like you describe," I found myself moving into enthusiasm, brightening again, "I have been working on things for Johannus to take to Rebecca and Petronius and his wife too, but writing something like what you are saying, that he could also take, would be so much more again, for all that he will need to do."

*

Johannus was sitting in the shade, leaning his back against a tree outside, at the front corner of Miriam's house in Capernaum; the community's centre now.

He was working with some fine silver wire that he had made when working with Beor in Bethany; using some of the simplest skills of the silversmith, but which he could do whilst still keeping an eye out on all the comings and goings.

He wasn't sure exactly why he felt the need to be more vigilant than ever, but he did.

Particularly for Miriam, and as he mused on this, he realised it was because she had been doing more public singing and public speaking, becoming known and so potentially a target for some, and he was worried too about leaving them and going to Alexandria.

Anyway, right now he was going to do as good a job as he possibly could, especially with the singing festival coming up, right here in Capernaum.

Women came and went into the side door, hardly noticing him sitting there but he had come to know them all now; which ones worked in the kitchen and sometimes asked him for a hand with something heavy; which were more involved in laundry or maybe just there to be with Miriam; and Mary now too.

644

It was mainly women but some men came; often one of the women's husbands, but one or two others too. Johannus recognised all who had been before. He made it his business to get up and ask any new person what they did at the house, because he was here with Miriam and Mary.

No-one minded and many were friendly when they went past.

His fingers worked the few thin silver strands he was twisting into a 'rope', making little knots at intervals that made it attractive and manageable.

He could do this without thinking hardly at all, and would leave the ends for joining to another length, or adding a hook or eye at some future time; so his senses were free to notice anything around, though he seemed not to.

He had learnt a lot since first he had accompanied Miriam and Mary into Nabatea, from many more experienced than he, and now he was quite comfortable that he would spot any trouble before it brewed; as much as anyone might.

He could feel it coming in the air, he thought; knew that there were bad people out there but none immediately threatening.

A small noise out the back caught his attention though, and he got up, feeling the stiffness pain that still troubled his left hip, and he rubbed it vigorously as he turned round to search back to where the noise had come.

Just a cat being a tiny bit clumsy in jumping off the wall, dislodging a stone.

I stopped writing for a bit. I had been copying the first text that Miriam and I had put together.

Re-living that special time as Miriam described it was amazing because it is still the core of everything I do; try to live, every day.

And writing the words, copying them, brings that home so deeply that sometimes I can hardly write; shaking with the import of it.

Miriam has gone out for a walk with several of today's visitors and Johannus went with them too; and I want to get a bit more copied.

She keeps saying it is 'our gospel': the Gospel of Miriam of Magdala, which written down could just as well be read as Mary Magdalene; her little joke I think, that it can be attributed to me. "Well, you are the one writing it, Mary," she said, "and it is truly ours to give to the world, for anyone who can understand."

"That it is the possibility of every single human being, to rise above the rules and circumstances of this world, to experience who and what we really are, a part of. Once all those 'goods' and 'bads', 'haves' and 'have-nots' that we live with all the time; the opinions and fears, can be put aside, for us to rise into our true being."

"And experience the Divine; Divinity. Everything."

I bent over again to lovingly write each word down, allowing it to resonate through me; thinking that maybe down the ages others would get this experience too.

I sighed, once again knowing that our paths ahead would need to try to reach out in every direction. The apostles, so few really; and others like Johannus and Yresmin too.

Writing this was another start though, and I bent to my task again with relish.

*

Thomas collected up some of the copies he and Arianne had written and took them to Kasver's house where a group of young men, and a few women too, were gathered.

He had dreamt again of the necessity of going eastward, and this time it was not the woman of the dragon, but a cry of help; a demand almost.

Of all the people that knew those places, those lands, Kasver and Sarita were the best placed and he wondered if he should confide in them.

When he did talk to Kasver he got a better impression of the huge extent of the lands involved, that as a merchant Kasver knew tales of, if not from personal experience.

Sarita knew the lands beyond Persia slightly better than Kasver, though not with the merchant's knowledge that he had. Hers was more about the customs of her people. She had slightly darker skin than Kasver but said it was lighter than most in that land, where much of the year was baking hot, punctuated by the yearly monsoon-drenching rains.

But also, that it was cooler in the mountains of the north, and both of them talked of a king Gondophares ruling there.

Thomas pondered on that name, feeling he had heard it before, but knew not from where. His dreams? He shook his head.

"If I must go east then all of what we are doing now may be a part of that as well," he said. "But first I know I will be going south to Capernaum."

"Edessa is a great city," said Kasver, "if east you are talking of, that is on the boundary of the Roman world with that of the East."

"Maybe, yes." That made some kind of sense to Thomas, though why he couldn't yet say.

*

Yresmin had packed all her things and sorted out her affairs in Bethphage, ready now for her and Sella to get on the road again.

She knew she was going up to Galilee to join up with Miriam if she could, who Johannus said would either be with Mary in Magdala or possibly in Capernaum. So, here she was, following the star again.

What surprised her most however was that Lazarus had said he wanted to travel up as well. He and his sisters had heard of the music festival by the Sea of Galilee and he was well enough now to travel and felt an urgency to be there.

They, Lazarus and his sisters, had been her best friends here, always welcoming her into their home, and she was excited and somewhat relieved with the prospect of travelling together with them.

Then Beor had insisted that he was coming too, as much to keep them safe she thought, but when he heard that Miriam would doubtless be singing at the festival too, nothing would stop him.

CHAPTER 15.

Matthias managed to arrange for Kareem and his ladies to come down from Jericho to Jerusalem for the Thursday rehearsal at Yeheshua's Inn, with Peter.

He travelled with them, feeling more buoyant about everything than he had for a while, so glad to have brought over Kareem to see the whole picture, of Yeheshua's mission.

Peter greeted them himself and showed them to guest rooms that had been readied.

They sang their enchantments in the long room that evening, being transformed from Goddesses of the Ennead to three angels: 'Love', 'Hope' and 'Charity', and there wasn't one person who wasn't singing halleluiahs at the end; even Peter was impressed.

Afterwards he was given a more private rendering and was able to make some suggestions that would make certain verses even more personal to his own feelings and experience.

Kareem liked his ideas and Matthias was exceedingly pleased.

'Maybe too much,' thought Peter in a flash of insight, which he turned back upon himself. 'I hope I am not trying to compete with Miriam, rather than calling her home.'

He could not and would not compete, he chastised himself. He being a rough fisherman and she his Lord's beautiful partner; but Yeheshua did love him he knew, and he had seen Him in a moment brighter than any light, a flash, a glimpse of the Divine, that had left an indelible mark upon his soul.

"Don't change anything you have done," he said after his musings, "but maybe add another verse in the middle just for me ... "those phrases of:

The Light and Holy Word made manifest ... for us to follow, us to know and take us home ... I of us all, the least worthy ... but only Him that saves."

Peter shot Matthias a warning look before he could say anything, offer his praises, but Kareem and the three women got together and sang a few working attempts together until they thought they'd caught the essence in a verse which they sang back to Peter, once then once again and on the third time it almost made him cry.

CHAPTER 16.

Seth was having a hard time sleeping.

Every time he approached the edge it felt like he was being drawn down into dark depths with no hope of release, so he fought it off; like Set did Apep, with his spear.

And when he did sleep it was invariably unpleasant and often littered with human or animal faeces. Nowhere to rest, to relieve himself, to let go.

Two things drove him on. That this was the plan he had concocted for his enemies, that he would bring it to them, let them drown in it.

Secondly, but more urgently, was that Miriam was his way out, his way to Immortality and to be forever clear of the dross of this existence.

Nothing had changed; he would still wipe her from history, and in doing so combine with her, extract from her, the life of the gods for himself.

And now he had the tools.

He re-entered the house of death as he thought of it and prepared himself to go down into the cellar again; this time with much brighter torches in his hands, fire in his brain, fierce determination in his heart.

He also had a small bundle of wood which he set in the middle of the cellar room before bending down to extract his knives one by one from the poison bowl, ensuring each grooved blade tip was well poison-laden before sliding it into its tight metal ended sheath.

All eleven blades collected and set into their place in the fabric roll, Seth turned and placed one torch into the spread of wood, which took very little time to get burning well.

Before turning to leave he skilfully kicked the poison bowl into the fire. He was freeing himself now, almost. Definitely not coming back here anyway.

Crossing the cellar quickly with his knives, he ran up the stairs and took the axe out of the cupboard, with a few other bits he intended to keep, and started smashing everything else to bits, like he was possessed, which in fact he knew he was, but a possession he welcomed this time...

Set, Set, Set, I will make you greatest of all. This world will burn for you.

Gathering up armfuls of smashed wood he carried them down the steps and laid a trail from the fire inside, out to the steps where he laid the other torch amongst the bits.

Upstairs again he picked up all he could and threw it over and down the steps, pulled fabric from wherever he found it and trailed that down as well, working himself into such a rage that he would have pulled down the whole house if he could have, in one noiseless scream.

Instead, he saw that the fire had started to take good hold and he was heavily, breathlessly content with his work. Picking up the axe and other things he had withheld from the flames, he went outside to where the donkey was tied.

He watched and laughed; whereas the donkey grew very frightened.

Behind him, as he kicked the beast into motion down the road, the fire was already reaching around the outside door and out of the high up window.

*

Seth didn't need to follow Kareem's singers any more. He knew where it was happening and when. He hadn't any time to lose himself though.

He didn't have to see Anna, though part of that thought pained him; he would make it up to himself later.

He couldn't act well enough for all of that; he had lost too much of himself to Apep. Spending too much energy just not to be completely swamped in the ignorance of its greed.

There were going to be many people at the singing festival, and he would need to find out where Miriam was staying. He had discovered that the one called Mary Magdalene had a house in nearby Magdala, and that she and Miriam were close friends. He realised also that this Magdalene was the other woman at the Inn that night. She must suffer too; he would go there first.

There were three poisons for the knife blades, each working in a different way. Two of them he had worked with, had experience of. The first paralysed, the second killed... inevitably, sometimes very quick and sometimes very slow and painfully, but inescapably...

The third was new, but he had a gut feel, an instinct, an insight, about how adding the bloods of Apophis and the dragon to the first paralysing poison, would open the victim's mind and soul to him, and to the snake.

He would claim Miriam... and leave the others to the snake.

*

CHAPTER 17.

Pharos was another who was looking for the house of Magdalene in Galilee. He was Mary's merchant captain who had brought her cargo from the Eastern lands, and especially this time the lapis lazuli stone from the northern realm; and with it came one sea captain of their King Gondaphres, a man called Habban.

This Habban was on a mission too, and somehow Pharos had found himself locked in with it, although he had only agreed to guide him to Jerusalem.

For the captain had the task to find a man who knew about the building of the famous temple of Solomon here, and bring him back to Gondaphres to aid the king in his own building plans.

So, when they had made enquiries about the temple and the building of it, all Habban was getting were the stories of the master Yeheshua who had been crucified but apparently had risen from the dead... but HE had said that he could destroy the temple and rebuild it again in three days.

To Habban this could be no coincidence, that all this had recently occurred and once he discovered that one of Pharos's most valued friends and business partners was deeply involved, there was no backing out.

Furthermore Pharos had unwittingly let slip that the lapis lazuli for Magdalene was actually for a sculptor of King Herod, or his daughter. So, now they were on the road to Magdala, for Pharos and Mary's older merchant friend, Joseph, had told him that was where she had gone.

He wrung his hands and heart both. He liked Habban, who was not only very personable and dangerous at the same time, but also virtually owned the sea routes around northern India as well as many of the inland ones too; but he wished he wasn't getting Mary so deeply and unwittingly involved.

Habban had hired two horses in Jerusalem where he left his men, and insisted that Pharos accompanied him on this venture to find this Mary who could solve his mission, he knew.

Habban was clearly not a man to mess with, and in addition he had a letter from his king to say he was on important business for him, which now had been counter-signed and sealed by none other than Pilate's legate, so no-one would dare question that.

They stopped at an Inn on the road to Galilee and enjoyed a quite reasonable evening meal of surprisingly delicious spiced goat stew and local wine.

As they sat relaxed, chatting about the virtues of various trading routes and whether it was better to work for the king or be your own man to chose your partners as you pleased, a man who had obviously been listening nearby coughed slightly to attract Habban's attention and claimed he couldn't help hearing they were looking for Mary Magdalene's house, and that maybe he could help them.

Pharos immediately disliked something about the man, mistrusting him, but Habban seemed oblivious to his obsequiousness, and let him explain that her house was on the right, going down the hill towards the seaport on the inland road.

"Not a real sea such as you great captains would know" he said, "but a good one for fishing in, and if you like fish… then …"

"Fish be damned," snorted Habban, "but thank you for the directions. You know this Mary Magdalene then?"

"Only a little," he answered, "more her friend, Miriam."

Seth couldn't quite work out why he had said that, but it just came out.

Pharos froze at the mention of Miriam. Her father was one of his, and his father's, greatest friends. And it was because of Miriam that he was in business now with Mary. But to hear this unpleasant character claim to be her friend rankled like food gone bad and the hair prickled on the back of his neck.

"You know Miriam do you then?" he shot his question at the man adding, "what did you say your name was?"

Habban looked at his seafriend; he had never heard him be so brusque before, he was always such an amiable and hospitable fellow.

"I didn't, but it is Zeth," said the other, starting to hold out his hand but then thinking better of it. He was a bit too deep in now but he had carried off harder deceptions before. "Met her on her way back from Nabatea with Mary, to be with the Rabbi Yeheshua. Did you know him?"

The man was being so urbane yet underneath he just smelt wrong to Pharos. He wanted to close the conversation as quickly as possible. "Only through friends; good friends," he said. "People I would believe and go a long way for."

Seth could tell which way the wind was blowing, but couldn't help one last prod. "So, you are going up to Capernaum for the music festival I take it?"

Habban could sense his companion's growing discomfiture and stepped in. "Our business is other than that, but not that I wish to discuss it, if you don't mind," and said with such finality that Seth knew he had no option than to back off quickly. "I bid you good night then."

CHAPTER 18.

This was the third day since they had set out from Antioch, riding along with a southerly bound caravan; Thomas, Kasver and Sarita.

Arianne had been unable to get away because of the temple's upcoming summer Adonis festival which she had a big part in organising, but promised to travel to join them and Mary as soon as she could.

Thomas planned that they would stay this night with Suzanne in Caesarea Philippi if she was there and he had paid for a letter to go ahead of them.

Kasver and Sarita were charming companions and time and again the conversations seemed to turn towards Gandhara, because Thomas was fascinated with his being seemingly pointed there, one way or another.

Sarita told how her mother came from a village some distance to the south of where her father lived, who was of Greek origin living in Bactria, his ancestors having connections to Alexander's army.

Her mother's family strongly followed Durga ji and the mother Devi and were very unhappy about her alliance with this Gandharan suitor; but it made no difference because he succeeded in getting her to run away with him, if not actually abducting her.

Sarita had been born quite soon after and her father had allowed Sarita's mother to return to her family village for a few years, thinking it better for his daughter that way, for never had he been able to sway his wife from the customs of her birth. He paid for their life there though and visited frequently when his work allowed. He was a master carpenter.

He longed to travel to Greece to see the lands that had given birth to his heritage and when he deemed that Sarita was old enough, he brought her mother and her, not unwillingly northwards, first to Taxilia and then further on to his own town of Alexandria in Bactria.

The journey that had led to Sarita being taken to be a priestess at Astarte's temple in Antioch had been long and arduous, largely because the caravans were frequently disrupted by the Roman - Parthian wars.

But particularly because her mother had died at a city called Hecatomapolus where a plague had suddenly broken out. Her father was inconsolable and for a whole six months hardly did anything but mourn, until eventually he stirred enough, worked enough, to get him and his daughter travelling west again.

The temple in Antioch turned out to be a very temporary school for Sarita, the young Persian merchant Kasver falling in love with her as he had, and being rich enough to pay her bridal price to the temple; but her sojourn there had been long enough to have made some very good friends, of which Mary had been her best, and Arianne had followed later.

Perhaps it was not surprising then that the night gone by Thomas had dreamt of travelling there, to Taxilia.

Though not like Sarita had, by donkey and sometimes camel over steppe and semi desert lands, but rather up along a huge broad river from the sea, and under some compulsion he could not explain even to himself.

What amazed him most was the clarity of his dreams, not like any others that he was used to having.

"Is there a big river in that country of King Gondaphres?" he had asked and both Kasver and Sarita had looked at him very wide-eyed. "Yes indeed," they had answered in unison, but he declined to go further than saying he dreamt of one.

But he did say that the master Yeheshua had travelled and taught in those lands, not many years earlier, and had a special place in his heart for the people of those high hills and mountains.

"Miriam knows more of it than I do though," he said. "Maybe you will get the chance to ask her about it."

And he thought of Mary a lot and wondered what her answer was going to be, to his proposal. Sarita and Arianne had been so sure, but he wasn't. He was sure she loved him but he felt she was stronger than he, more certain now, not needing marriage.

She had their child in her, a daughter she reckoned, but she was wealthy enough to not need him for money that was certain.

But they shared a destiny. That is how it seemed to him, and one that he could or would not dislodge from his head and heart.

So, what all this stuff about the Eastern lands was he couldn't fathom; nor did he need to.

Nevertheless, nevertheless, he was very happy and felt overwhelmingly grateful to be able to give himself... and Mary was a part of that.

*

I was so happy; didn't want anything to change. Having Miriam here and working with her was such a marvel.

I often thought back to that first morning when she had come down the path to my house, to receive Yeheshua's inner teaching.

Mother had been on a donkey up on the road, and she too had come back later.

There had been a pure delight in that meeting, that had never really left us, underneath everything else.

Today we were visiting Nazareth, reminding us of when we had set out from there on her quest. After the singing festival, two years ago.

There was a growing community of Yeheshua's followers in Nazareth and they repeatedly had invited her, and me as well, to come and share her inspiration with them. They always remembered her having sung there, and sometimes she would again.

Miriam's presence anywhere was enough to know that it was possible to immerse oneself in the riches of the heart. That was her strength and nothing would hold her back from that; nothing.

I relished every day and walked high.

Thomas would be back soon, I knew; but couldn't see clearly what would become of us.

Miriam surprised me. She said she thought I should not reject him.

"Trust the Almighty within you, Mary sweetheart," she said, "not the 'limiter'. You know, the one that wants definitions and allows only certain outcomes."

"I think I do," I replied; "but does that mean marriage?"

"What does marriage mean? Not what we think, and some want. Not a bond other than the strength of shared love? I don't say you should marry him, just accept how you both feel."

I thought back again to when, on returning to Galilee from that quest to Kadesh Barnea, how Miriam had embraced her marriage to Yeheshua, full knowing of the trials that were to come, where he would be ripped away from her and crucified, a reviled and beaten criminal.

That was what she had seen in the tomb of Moses's sister Miriam, a prophetess herself.

" .. but we are never been separated, and that is the beauty," she said, in answer to my thoughts. "Even if he had not conquered death itself; for death cannot take away the riches we have in our hearts. The only things it cannot."

*

The stay with Suzanne was greatly welcome after the long journey. Her husband the Governor was away and she was planning to go down to Capernaum as well, so was able to join them in their journey.

She looked after them very well and seemed to enjoy Kasver and Sarita as guests, and they her company for the onward way.

Thomas did dream that night, an amazing and most welcome dream of being with Yeheshua by the sea, watching the sun rising over the water. He thought the sea of Galilee, and Yeheshua was saying, "I have crossed this sea Thomas, and you must cross it too."

"Yes master" Thomas replied. "When should I leave, and where to?"

"Very soon Thomas. A boat has come to take you."

Thomas was surprised by this. "A boat to take me over?"

"… to Gondaphres kingdom in the north Thomas."

CHAPTER 19

Johannus dreamed as well.

He was with Kaella and she was grieving.

Johannus sensed that she was alone, and somehow more vulnerable than he had known her to be; not in command of the situation.

She was the maiden aspect of the goddess Hecate, and he had learned to be careful of any entanglement.

In his dream though he approached her, asking what was wrong, but she only looked at him with red-rimmed eyes, mouthing sorrowful words he couldn't hear.

Moved deeply, Johannus stretched a hand towards her... and she responded with her own, touching.

*

Johannus was flying, his great wings brought beating out and down by the arching up of his long muscular back;

.. and then they folded back up as he pushed his chest and loins down, preparing for another stroke... like a long thin boat, rowing through the air.

Then he saw another, flying like him... a dragon.

Higher than he, circling up and around the side of a great mountain, in a range of majestic snow and ice tipped peaks.

It was natural and invigorating to be a dragon, Herakaphon; but then suddenly he remembered his own body and instead of flying he was standing on the balcony of a high viewpoint; and there was someone else there.

Miriam: but different; long dark hair framing her beautiful exotic face; yet to Johannus in his dream it was still Miriam.

"She will need your help Johannus."

"Who? How?" he asked.

"Kaella," she said. "She will need you."

"She will have your children when she takes the human path, as she must now. Her dragon soul has left her plane, is the one you became a part of in coming here, Johannus. I tell you this to help you understand..."

*

Johannus was in a palace and there were many beautiful women there too, serving him; dragon women... he knew that.

He knew too that these magical creatures were both; the combined energies of male and female; highly evolved creatures.

Knew that they could sometimes have the gift of human birth for their young.

Knew that Kaella's daughters would come from this world, and he would be their father somehow; at some time, in some life; the only way she would survive, the girl he had loved... crying grief stricken back on another world.

Johannus awoke, feeling determined, for the new day to count for something.

They had stayed the night at an Inn in Nazareth; Miriam, Mary and he.

Just as they might have when they had been on Miriam's quest.

He realised it was quite early and was glad he had the time for readying himself.

His dream had lingered on in bits and pieces and though he tried to bring it back to fuller meaning it faded into the fabric of his being, yet leaving some sense of purpose in him as well.

Gratefully received.

Breakfast was in a garden room; Miriam and Mary were already there.

As he entered Miriam got up smiling and asked him to join them, which is not something he normally would have done.

"Mary and I have something for you," she said and he almost blushed. He might have done in the old days, but much had changed; not least since Rebecca had come into his life.

She picked up a cloth package from the table and handed it to him as he sat down.

Slightly shocked and mumbling words of thanks Johannus took it from her, realising there was something hard inside. He couln't imagine what it might be.

Undoing the cloth ties, with some fascination, revealed two small scrolls held in pockets inside.

"Wow," as all he could say as he gingerly picked one of the scrolls out.

"We have written something and would like you to have a copy of it," said Mary.

"Two copies in fact; one from each of us if you like," laughed Miriam.

Johannus didn't read very quickly but as he started to, he realised it was something very special, about the time, maybe the last time that Yeheshua had been teaching.

"Something for you to take to Alexandria with you, Johannus," said Miriam, laying her hand gently on his forearm holding the scroll. "One for you, and one that hopefully can be used to make copies of, for those people who want to understand his teaching."

"Wow," he said again, "this is so special. I don't know what to say. I will treasure them."

"I hope it will mean something to you, like it has been for us writing it. And is a thank you for all the care you give, and can pass on to others. Come now, let us have something to eat, we have another long day ahead."

Pharos and Habban trudged along the road to Magdala, having left their horses at the inn, each wishing they could feel the rise and dip of the waves under their feet rather than the relentless dust and stones of a road in the heat of the day.

"Didn't that man say her house was on the right going down into the town?" said Habbban, wishing he hadn't suggested the walk would be invigorating.

Pharos glowered at him, not liking the mention of the unpleasant character; but at least they had come amongst trees as they had crested the rise, and their most welcome shade.

"Yes, he did," answered Pharos, "and I must say that I am glad of these trees."

Seth was glad that they had gone over the rise and into the tree lined part of the route because staying out of sight whilst following them had been a bit of a pain and though it meant there was a long way to catch up, at least he could get a lot closer now.

He had a hunch that these were going to be useful contacts when it came to getting close to his quarry; such a big help that the Egyptian sea captain knew Miriam well, and he almost laughed aloud at the irony of it.

He could feel the loop tightening on his quarry, something he had experienced many times and it excited him tremendously.

By the time he had slipped into the line of trees beside the road they were out of sight again, but that was not a problem.

Caution was his guide and his game, and he felt the slithering of the snake somewhere out in the darkness of shadows.

*

Anna opened the slider in the front door of Magdalene's house, viewing the two men outside who had pulled the bell-chain.

"I am Pharos, Mary Magdalene's captain for the spice run, and this is a messenger from… from a distant place," said Pharos indicating Habban, who was holding his letter of passage; slightly foolishly, as he realised it would probably mean nothing to this woman.

They both expected to have to cajole her…

"Okay," said Anna brusquely. "Stay there and I will come round to you. Mistress Mary is not here but I shall take you to her business partner."

Before Pharos could say anything the slider had shut and the two men looked at each other and shrugged.

Anna left the front door bolted, took Jess' hand, who had been hiding behind her, and went to the garden room door. "Go tell Dan I am locking the house up early today and then meet me at the side door. Go on, run, quick as you can."

Jess bounded off, the kind of errand she loved because it took her straight back to her mummy.

Anna checked and shut up the shutters that had been opened and then went to the side door, treading on the lever pedal that lifted the drop bolt, opened the door and then moved the hidden block on the outside that allowed the bolt on the inside to drop back into place.

Jess did not keep her mum waiting for hardly any time before catching her skirts again and Anna hoisted her into her arms, where little Jess stayed, arms around Anna's neck, head tucked in there too, just able to look around her mother's head-shawl.

"Come with me," she said to Pharos and Habban at the front, "Mary's business partner will help you."

They walked down the hill a short way before turning left up a path that led to Jacob's farm and other buildings.

"Is it Jacob that we are going to see?" asked Pharos, trying to indicate that he was well acquainted with Mary and her business.

Anna said nothing.

"Over there," she said finally as they reached a courtyard between three buildings. "I shall knock first and tell him."

Jacob was impressed with Habban's letter with the Roman legate's added seal, and therefore was also convinced that this was indeed the Pharos that was Mary and Miriam's sea captain; though he supposed sea captains were not really that much different from fishermen after all.

"Do you get to do any fishing whilst crossing on the spice trade," he asked Pharos absently, and Habban laughed uproariously.

"What!?!"

"Sorry," said Jacob, "but it something I have always wanted to ask. It seems like such a simple opportunity to get some great food; and my being a farmer, I suppose. Anyway, how can I help you since Mary is away travelling with Miriam."

"Ahhh," said Habban, and Pharos frowned slightly before brightening. "Have they gone far? Are you expecting her back soon?"

"They will be at the Capernaum singing festival that starts in a couple of days," said Jacob. "I understand they will be over in Nazareth about now."

"Someone mentioned a sculptor," put in Habban, "that has done some work for King Herod's daughter. Do you know where I could find him?"

Jacob started. "Well, I do in fact, but can I ask what you may want with our Lenny?"

"I am asking for someone who knows about building; the building of King Soloman's Temple in particular; on behalf of my King. And thought the sculptor might have inside knowledge of that."

"I doubt Lenny would know, but you can ask him yourself. His wife is the lady who brought you over, and it seems you are lucky; she seems to be waiting outside."

*

"Excuse me sir," said Anna, as Pharos and Habban came out from Jacob's office, "but I think there something you should know."

"Really?" said Habban, trying to think how possibly she could have known.

"Jess thinks she saw someone following us when we brought you up here?"

"Jess?" said Habban.

"My daughter. She was looking behind over my shoulder and thought she saw a face poking around corners as we came up here."

Habban's face became serious very quickly on hearing this, glancing across at the listening Pharos.

"What did he look like?" asked Pharos, dropping to one knee on spotting the little girl peeking around her mother's skirts.

Jess shook her head, then made a grimace at which Habban laughed.

"Okay," said King Gondaphares's captain, "Let us see, I don't like the sound or look of that. I was going to ask your mother to show us the way to her husband's house, but I might change that."

Anna started, wondering what the great big captain would want with Lenny.

"Don't worry," he told her, realising her concern, "but would you carry your daughter like you did along the road with us, the way we came. Not too far, I think."

"Yes, I shall be going that way anyway," said Anna.

*

Seth had waited patiently in a copse behind a bank and was just wondering if he should give up on this particular line of his enquiries when the group came back down the path, completely unaware of him.

He saw them turn right at the bottom but didn't follow them; instead, he crossed into the woods on the other side of the track, following a goat path that was roughly parallel to theirs.

Once he saw that they didn't go back into Mary Magdalene's house he sidled down to the road they were on, catching sight of them as they went around the next bend.

Glancing both ways up and down the road he saw it was clear and stepped out onto it, hurrying quickly up the way they had gone.

He realised they were dangerous men to cross and slipped one of his daggers out of its hiding place in his travelling cloak, setting its sheath into a matching strap on his left forearm. Just in case.

He approached the bend cautiously, gauging how far they would have got, for he could remember details like the distance to the next corner without difficulty.

He looked all around and behind before cutting through the trees at the bend, sighting their backs walking steadily on ahead.

This was standard work for him, especially when he was searching for weaknesses and connections. He thought the woman and her child might well be such for Mary Magdalene and Miriam if he needed one.

Knowledge was power and anyway he always liked to tie up loose ends. Now he wondered where she was taking the sea captains.

*

Pharos asked Jess, as he walked behind Anna but not obstructing her view, "did you see anyone behind?"

She nodded. "Just at the last minute. He just poked out from behind a tree."

"You have sharp sight," said Pharos, "I could use you on my ship."

"She does," said Anna, smiling grimly, "but please don't encourage such thoughts."

Habban laughed softly, but a touch grimly too. "Let's hurry on quickly. I want to get off the road just over the rise. There is a long straight behind us there."

Going over the crest the trees stopped, giving way to uneven ground with boulders and some scrubby vegetation.

"Come over here," said Habban, leaving the road and circling back into the trees where some larger boulders were. "Sit down back here Anna, and you Jess. Keep really quiet, not a noise. Pharos and I will watch."

Crouching behind the boulders the captains kept a good eye on the road, not too far away.

Suddenly they got a shock.

The man from the Inn the night before was moving through the trees, much closer to them than the he was to the road, and he was looking, ahead mostly, but they had the feeling he could almost sense them as well.

Pharos shivered and touched the dagger at the belt on his waist, but Habban laid a hand on his arm, watching intently as the man, probably a professional killer by the look of the dagger at his sleeve, worked his way out of the wood and down the hill beside the road.

Bad tidings indeed.

The journey down from Caesarea was uneventful and Thomas found himself wondering about the dream.

Did they count in the same way as real conversations? Talking with Yeheshua had seemed so real.

Was he expected to go to Gandhara because of what was said in a dream?

Kasver was riding by his side; Susannah and Sarita were behind them, talking about the festival which was starting tomorrow. The rest of the caravan was ahead.

"You are deep in thought, my friend," observed Kasver, "is everything all right?"

Thomas laughed. "More than all right Kasver, sorry. But you are right, I have been trying to think my way through something that I know is impossible."

Kasver said nothing whilst Thomas debated within himself, then explained: "I maybe have to go to the eastern lands, yet I have asked Mary to marry me. If she says no, I can go, but I don't want her to say no. But neither do I want her to come with me if I do go. I know that she should be carrying forward all she is doing here."

"Ahhh, I see," said Kasver, still slightly puzzled. "Why are you so sure you have to go.?"

"My lord Yeheshua said as much to me in a dream last night."

"Maybe you will go there one day then."

"He said very soon. A boat is coming or has come to take me there; or so he said."

"Well, you only have to worry if that really happens," said Kasver.

Thomas was silent. He didn't know why he was so certain, him 'the doubter'; but he was.

"It will," he whispered, smiling across at his new friend.

*

Sarita pulled her horse up beside Kasver, as Susannah did to Thomas. They were nearing the turning they would take for Capernaum.

"Where will you be staying Thomas?" Susannah asked.

"I don't know yet," he replied. "I shall go to Miriam's, the community house, and see what is happening before I can tell. You?"

"I would too but there is a villa that Seb and I sometimes stay at, where they rent nice apartments. I shall go there and rent a small one for myself, and Sarita thinks this will suit them best as well."

"OK, right. I know the ones you mean. Outside town next to where the Roman prefect stays, with his guards."

"Yes. I think the Inns will already be pretty full for this week."

"You are probably right; a good idea. I will still ride on into town, but come with you first."

"Fine. Maybe you would come back after and give us any news? Even if you don't need to rent, but it would be great to hear."

"Yes, of course. And I shall be more than happy to bow to your experience on the renting." They all laughed and Susannah would have poked him in the ribs if she could have reached.

*

A couple of the musicians from Jericho had come up to Miriam's house and were practicing in the back yard, along with a couple more local players. They were not the only ones that Thomas could hear as he led the mare across town to the house, where Johannus appeared out from the side and greeted him.

"Thomas; fantastic, you made it. Things are really hotting up."

"So I can hear. Who is here?"

"Mother arrived not long ago, with John, and Peter was here earlier too with some others, but he is staying at his own house, and I think John may be going there. Miriam and Mary are here of course. Where will you be staying?"

"I don't know yet, but have some options. Where should I tie Meg?"

"Just here," said Johannus, leading the mare to a post under a tree and looping her reins to one of the ropes there. "I shall get her some water and feed. Don't worry, you go inside."

*

I was in the front room. Miriam was outside the back listening to the players practice together and Mother was upstairs and John too, when the door from the kitchen opened.

Thomas came in, and my heart did a flip.

His smile lit my world afresh, sending warmth all through me.

"Welcome," I said, arms spreading wide involuntarily.

"So…" he said, as we disengaged from our embrace.

"Mmmm… so, so good to see you," I said, laying my head on his chest, then, "You must be hungry and thirsty; have you just got down from Antioch?"

"So…" he said again, trying to look severe. "I have, yes. Rode from Caesarea with Susannah today," and he held me at arm's length. "Guess who else, as well?"

I hadn't got an idea; I was flummoxed.

"Sarita and Kasver," he said, "and I promised I would go back to them with the answer to a certain question…"

I was amazed, excited and all in disarray at the same time. However, I thought this moment would play out, was ripped into tiny pieces.

".. where I would be staying? They are at the villa by the Prefect's house."

"I have a small business house here; where you can have my room," I said, mixing my trembling into a rush of words. "But I want to come with you to meet them now; as soon as possible," I said, having recovered into a ball of happiness. "Let them know the answer to a certain other question that they may be interested in…", and I held hard onto Thomas again. "Yes, yes, yes," I whispered into his ear, kissing him there.

Just then there was the noise outside of other people arriving at the house, being guided round the side to the back, by Johannus; bless him.

I recognised Mary's voice and her brother Lazarus; and a door opening upstairs.

Thomas held me, ignoring the potential intrusions. "What was that, my love?"

I held his hands and looked back deeply into his face, his eyes, his soul. "I love you, Thomas. I love you very, very much," and leant forward, kissing him again.

"Yes, I will; marry you. If you still wish it."

CHAPTER 22.

Yresmin was as happy as ever she could remember, since being a little girl in her home in Mecca, having travelled up to Capernaum with her special friend Lazarus and his sisters, and Beor as well.

Martha and Beor had stopped off at a house belonging to a couple who were long-time followers of Yeheshua, and who Mary and Martha always stayed with up here; helping them with setting up for the extra guests.

Yresmin's faithful donkey Sella had come on with her, bearing Lazarus on to the house, where everything was happening; everyone was…

She was talking to Johannus outside, taking in the duties he was doing, when Thomas came out of the side door. They turned to him, taking in his beaming smile. I was close behind.

"Can I borrow Meg, Thomas? To go up and meet Sarita and Kasver. Johannus, would you show Thomas where you are staying? Thomas is having my room."

Johannus, turned to Yresmin, "Would you be able to take over here for a little while, just keeping an eye on coming and goings?"

"Yes, fine," said Yresmin, "and could you take Sella with you as well? Miriam just told me that is where Indy is."

"Perfect, okay," said Johannus, untying Meg for me, and setting off with Thomas and Sella to where they would be staying.

*

Seth was watching from down the street, not hanging around, just passing along casually and crossing over to a road that went into town, carrying a half-sack of maise flour on his shoulder that hid his face, and was wondering where was the best place for him to stay.

He was not in a rush; he would bide his time, find his best opening.

He had discovered where the festival was being held, on the shore of the Galileean sea, apparently where that Yeshua had used to teach. There was a big Nazarene influence in the arrangements that didn't seem to bother the local Pharisees even; which surprised him.

Now he had seen where Miriam was staying, and the Magdalene woman; definitely the centre of attention with all the comings and goings; and he noticed Johannus with the Nabatean woman, being quite well organised.

He wondered about Anna, Kareem and the others. They would be here somewhere but hadn't seen them yet. He must be careful; they would recognise him easily and he didn't want that.

Perhaps he would sleep out by the festival site. The nights were very warm, it wouldn't be hard. In fact, that would be the best place, get to see the rhythm of everything without being seen himself.

Right now then, he would find a place to have a drink and become invisible in the goings on in the town itself. Good plan, for he was feeling thirsty as well, thirsty for all he could achieve.

*

Pharos and Habban decided that they needed to report who they had seen following them, the same man who had tried to befriend them at the Inn; agreeing it best to go to the Roman authorities.

They discovered there was a presence outside of town, where the Galileean Prefect often stayed, and Pilate himself, if he was passing through.

The letter from King Gondaphres had the instant effect of the Roman guards taking the captains very seriously; their 'principale' called Tiberius, spending much time in trying to get a picture of the man.

They wouldn't want any trouble on their patch, but the description Habban and Pharos were able to give could have fitted almost anyone; making their view of him being professional quite credible.

Like any of the spies in every country, he would be hard to find.

"You could stay here if you like," said Tiberius. "How long are you planning to stay?"

"Thank you but that won't be necessary. We don't believe we are the target for the man, but probably some of the people at the singing festival may be."

"Well, we shall do what we can to find him and stop any trouble; but it will be difficult with so many people come for the event." He sighed, then told them of the next-door villa that might be a good place to stay, as they let out rooms.

They thanked him and took him up on his advice to look next door for rooms to stay the week.

*

Kasver noticed the captains arrive outside, having just said goodbye to Magdalene after a tearful and emotional get together, catch-up, and promises to come and meet Miriam, Mother and all the others too. With Thomas; and he smiled inside.

He couldn't help but recognise that Habban was from the north of Bharat. The clothes he wore being a clear indication to Kasver's practiced eye, but he couldn't place Pharos so easily.

He could guess they were both seafaring men; something about the way they moved, and held themselves; he could almost picture the ship's deck and waves all around.

Of course, his conversations with Thomas were still fresh in his mind and he could scarcely believe that the protagonists in Thomas' quandary, his problem, could be right here in the same villa as they were.

No doubt he would meet them, or that he would find out the answers, but it was not for him to mention, just to witness what was a remarkable, almost miraculous story, apparently unfolding.

He wondered what Sarita would make of them.

666

CHAPTER 23.

Seth sat at the side of the back of a bar with his rough wine, eyes apparently unfocussed, like most of the others there, except his weren't. They flicked across the view outside at regular intervals, but not that anyone would notice.

There was a square and people were crossing and re-crossing it, nothing unusual. Perhaps busier than normal for the first day after the Sabbath he mused; almost certainly.

Suddenly someone came and stood almost directly in front of the shop-bar where Seth was. Someone he clearly recognised; Kareem.

He wasn't looking into the bar, but had his back to it. What was he doing there?

Seth turned sideways, shrinking into his clothing, pulling his collars up a bit, watching intently over one.

It didn't take long to see why Kareem was there as first one and then two other women of his singing group came to join him. The last was Anna; Kareem must have brought a spare person. Only three were needed for the Ennead chants.

Kareem led them off and as they reached the other side of the square Seth couldn't resist getting up and doing a long-distance follow, which was like food and drink to him.

One corner to another Seth not only followed just in view, but so casually that no one noticed what he was doing.

Except at one point Anna suddenly turned her head to look back. He saw it happening and was able to nod his head forward as he dropped a small package he was carrying on the ground, and bent down to pick it up. Props of the trade; at which he was one of the best.

He imagined she hadn't seen anything of him but wasn't absolutely sure.

He turned back and went another way, giving up the follow, but making a guess at their direction. Even more now he needed to see where they were going. He might have to do something about Anna; sooner rather than later.

Then there was that aborted follow the other day. Frustrating; he reckoned at the time they had just turned off into the scrub, along an animal track, back up into the wood again. He had backtracked and found such a one, but it was getting too late by then to locate them again.

He had dismissed it; but now this.

He knew that some of his sharpness had originally been blunted by the connection with Apep-Apophis, but since he had been able to get working on his 'kill', able to be focussed again on Miriam, his target, the snake of ignorance had been almost a helpful shadow.

Something he might be able to make work, for the moment anyway; like every kind of darkness.

He shivered, but at the same time caught sight of Kareem and the women again, crossing the end of a side-street from the road he was on.

Trusting to the gathering dark, Seth worked around a different way, moving fast like a snake over sand, this way, that, this, that, until he knew he was ahead of his quarry; and also through the glowering eye in a different skull did he know they were close, he had them.

Saw the house they went into, not an Inn, nor Peter's house either; but both noted it carefully.

*

Thomas and Johannus sorted out the house to their satisfaction for the few days, Thomas being secretly thrilled to have Mary's room, remembering how she had said 'yes', had whispered 'YES'; and it resounded around his brain… YES, YES, YES.

A great weight had lifted from his heart and plonked itself right in his head, destroying all orderliness there, which he prized very highly.

What did this mean? He had no idea; but he was so very happy that she had accepted him.

So unlike him, but maybe not?

"I am going back to the house; are you coming?" It was Johannus from the shared office space.

"Yes; ye-hes," Thomas all but laughed all through it. "Yes."

"Is that what she said?" asked Johannus perceptively. Only Miriam was more in tune with what had been going on. "I don't think you have said hello to Mother or Miriam yet."

"God, you are right. What are we doing here?"

"Well, I have just fed the animals. Not sure about you."

"Fluff off Johannus. You are such a neck-ache"…"Thanks."

*

Seth collected his stuff from the Inn where he had stayed the night before. It didn't suit him at all, but the girl he had effectively paid to look after his luggage for him had, momentarily.

He made his way out to the festival site, in the early dark, skirting the places where fires were burning for a few people out there, and he set up his own camp off to the back, behind a ridge and bushes, where he wouldn't be observed.

He lit a fire from wood that was plentiful and dead, quite a reasonable fire, more than he should have needed now, but he did need to think what he should do, and the presence of the dark within him was oppressive.

Within him and around him, looking at him; and the fire hurt his eyes, and Seth took the pain for pleasure.

He decided he must kill her, tonight if possible. It was a risk either way, but better to get rid of Anna before she spoilt his plans. The snake was whispering in him, wanting to spread its death and despair everywhere.

'It will help you with getting Miriam.' The thought hissed in his brain, and for a fraction of a moment Seth realised it was not his own, but pretending to be. He grabbed a piece of wood out of the fire, not the burning end, but it still burnt his hand.

He didn't let go, but waved the burning wood around in fierce defiance then used it to spread bits of the fire's burning embers out into a rough circle, wide enough to sleep inside …

But then he realised he couldn't sleep here now, anyhow… he had to go back into town and do whatever he was going to do.

The snake followed, or was with him and connected with him again; he couldn't tell the difference.

*

Thomas came back, full of fire; with Johannus too.

Kneeling before mother he wept that he hadn't greeted her earlier and when she pulled him up, he cried again in front of Miriam, so that she smothered him in her greeting.

He knew that they knew, and he sweetly came to me and took my hand, and turning to face them asked for their blessings, which made them both laugh, much to his bewilderment.

"Of course you do, Thomas; and you Mary," said Mother and Miriam clapped her hands in nodding agreement.

"We shall arrange a ceremony," said Lazarus, who had entered the room whilst this was going on, with his sister Mary. "Not, for tomorrow, but the day after, in the afternoon and evening. Mixed with the singing too."

I was myself astonished at this and could only nod my head in wonder, thinking stupidly 'but I cannot sing' and saw both Miriam and Mother smiling as though I had said it aloud, which maybe I had. "Of course you can my darling; most perfectly," said Miriam.

*

Johannus had taken over from Yresmin again, who went inside to join in and find out what was happening; not long after coming back to tell Johannus about it too.

"The day after tomorrow, that is quick," he said. "No time like now though," then, "Oh Yresmin, I am so relieved that they have finally sorted it out."

She looked at him with her dark deep eyes, and laid a hand on his arm. "It has a little way to go yet I think Johannus," just as Lazarus's sister Mary came out to join them.

She told Yresmin that she and Lazarus had been squeezed into a room in the house, but that Thomas was going to walk back with her to Martha and Beor.

He came out a few minutes later. "You needn't worry about me," Yresmin insisted in her most final way. "I am very well able to look after myself." But Thomas wouldn't be dissuaded at any cost. "I cannot let you have all the fun of telling them; besides I need to speak to Beor as well." Yresmin arched her eyebrows. "Yes, tonight," he said.

669

As they walked along Thomas found they had the easiness of travelling companions who were each comfortable with themselves and didn't feel the need to make conversation to cover silence.

The cicadas were still making a lot of noise and the night was laid around them in velvet beauty. "You are very lucky," Yresmin said, "but it is not luck you shall need most but strength, for every day. I know you have all that and so does Mary too; you have made your own luck. Like Yeheshua and Miriam have."

The thought of Yeheshua and Miriam brought Thomas up straight, thinking 'they were separated and yet are together in a very real way.' He could feel that when he was with Miriam, stronger than anything.

He had stopped where they were crossing the bit of town, approaching the house where she was staying.

As he stood looking down a road to where the full moon, barely risen, was shining back from low in the sky above, a figure scurried across that road and stopped as well, looking first at the moon and then quickly back up to where Thomas was. Their eyes seems to meet, even though it was too great a distance to see, and the light was behind the man, but... then he was gone.

Thomas thought he recognised something about him, the way he stood and moved, scuttling even though he had a carrying a bag on his shoulder. Maybe because of that; something not good, but that was connected to his own story in some way. He couldn't put his finger on it but his thoughts pierced the night; seeking clarity.

It made him wonder why he had said what he had earlier, about needing to talk to Beor, but now he knew. He had to tell him; they needed to be on their guard, and no-one was better for this than the big blacksmith.

*

Clarity flooded into Seth's brain for a moment.

He was close to the street where Anna was; where he could watch and listen invisibly, and find out where she was sleeping. How to get to her and, that is where the confusion of his thinking lifted, between the moon and the sight of his enemy; Horus.

He knew him, just as he knew Miriam.

Miriam was his target, not Anna; even though his mind and body told him the things he wanted to do with Anna, to Anna.

This was the snake; so entwined in his mind that he could hardly tell.

Except now. He knew that Apep wanted to destroy the Ennead and that he Seth, had to keep completely focussed on his own mission, on Miriam. Only in her ruin would he gain the freedom he sought.

The snake retreated. Seth felt that and decided instead to walk along the street where Miriam was. Just a little test, for although he was in no hurry, tonight had taught him he couldn't relax for a moment. He needed to spring his trap soon.

He knew Johannus would be on guard now, but he wouldn't even notice the old bent widow woman hobbling along on the other side of the road. He pulled the simple black cloth from his bag and wrapped it around him as he had a hundred times before.

He didn't even look up or around as he passed the house, but took everything in anyway. Closing in; nearly there.

It was the first morning of the singing and music festival and Kasver accompanied Sarita down into the communal hall of the villa where breakfast had been set out for the guests; quite a few by the look of it; different seating and tables being spread around the hall.

Several people were already down and eating including the two sea captains, as Kasver thought of them. Certainly, the one from the north was an imposing looking fellow, and the other also but in a different, composed kind of way.

Sarita noticed them as well and tugged on Kasver's arm, not herself having seen them the day before; Kasver had decided to let her discover them in her own time.

"Do you see that man over there, sweetheart," she said, "the bigger one? He is from my country!"

"Yes," replied her husband. "Looks almost like some sort of emissary by the clothes he is wearing. Maybe just a merchant, but used to having power. Gondaphares's man, would you think?"

"Gosh, I don't know," said Sarita. "He could be I suppose."

Habban looked up and saw them; guessed that they might be talking about him and also noticed Sarita. He smiled at them for a moment then carried on eating.

More by chance than design Sarita and Kasver started talking to Pharos and Habban as they stayed on in the hall after breakfast. Both captains were charming and naturally the talk went to the festival starting that very day.

"I know someone here from my youth who is the best friend of one of the foremost singers," said Sarita, and Habban asked politely, "was that in Gandhara?"

"No, no, in Antioch, just before I met and married Kasver." She was a little worried that she was going further than Kasver would like, so changed tack; "I did live there as a little girl, yes. Some distance south of Taxilia, and I think you must know that country far better than I?"

Habban chortled. "Yes, you are right, I do come from there, and am on business for the King, Gondaphares; but right now, Pharos and myself are hoping to meet up with a friend and business partner of his, who lives here too."

"Ahh," said Kasver, "well we are both on the same mission, haha."

Pharos had been quiet, but taking it all in. "The singer who is a friend of your friend, madam," he started. "She wouldn't be called Miriam by any chance would she?"

Sarita paled slightly. "Why yes, she is."

"Oh, and we are looking for a friend of hers too. Mary, called Magdalene."

All were amazed, but the shock of it hit Kasver more than the others because of his conversations with Thomas whilst riding down from Antioch; so that he almost missed what the others were saying.

"Don't you think we shall Kasver darling?"

"Sorry, what?"

"Be meeting up with Mary again today?"

"Oh yes; I surely hope so."

*

Seth had spent the whole night in restless motion around the town, snatching some sleep here and there, but by the time the light was growing in the east he was on his way back to his chosen spot at the festival site.

He didn't need to watch or partake in any of the organisation going on, so just took the opportunity to catch up on some much needed sleep; having first cleared his space of all unwanted little rocks and stones.

And filling the gaps with extra sandy soil, and spreading grasses over it; no point in being uncomfortable.

But he did dream, and it was of the poison of the snake; exuding from it everywhere it went. It was swimming in the sea, and under the land, and around the streets of the town… following Seth, wherever he was going… and Seth jerked awake, in a sweat.

Feeling the dark around him even though the sun had climbed high into the sky.

The music had started, and this at least provided him some distraction, but the singing of the psalms didn't really do anything for him, until… he heard Miriam singing.

She sang some of Yeheshua's favourite psalms and it nearly destroyed Seth's focus, until he knew this singing was not for him, never would be, and a strange jealousy like nothing he had ever known before surged through him.

He had to leave, but couldn't leave, he was eaten up inside with worms of disgust with himself, and her for doing this to him.

She would pay.

Nothing changed, he was just getting closer and he screwed up all his reserves, trying harder to hate.

*

Peter and the Ennead team were there as well, watching and listening, entranced as well by the beauty of Miriam's singing, especially when she moved on to sing some of the songs of the Miriam that had been Moses's sister; singing about the exodus from Egypt.

Not the time yet for the Ennead Goddesses to join her, whispered Matthias by Peter's side; that would be later in the day. She had practiced a bit with them and would again in the long midday break.

Peter nodded; he knew that, he just loved listening to her singing, and was looking forward to those about Yeheshua.

And just when he thought she wasn't going to, she did. Sang the one he loved

673

the best, Gideon's sword flashing through the light in his mind; the darkness shattered; the Lord conquering all his enemies.

An image that resounded in Seth's mind as well. He could be that… Lord.

*

Pharos, Habban, Sarita and Kasver were entranced no less than any; hoping to pay their respects to the singer at her house that lunchtime.

Susannah was with them and had gone ahead to the house to check the situation. She had been able to pass on their sincere admiration and desire to meet Miriam, but the singer herself was involved in rehersals.

Maybe Magdalene or Thomas could though she told them.

"Thomas?" asked Habban, for that name had come up several times, but he couldn't quite recall…

"Thomas is one of the close disciples of the master Yeheshua you have heard talked about," said Sarita. "A good friend of Mary and Miriam, and the one who came to Antioch, and with whom we travelled down here."

"Ahh, I thought you came with Susannah," queried Habban.

"We are," put in Kasver. "Magdalene and Thomas know her very well and we stopped over at Caeserea with her, where she joined us to travel down from there."

"If I remember rightly," said Habban, "this Thomas is a very capable man; trained both in the law and philosophy. No doubt the great arts and holy mysteries as well?"

"Quite probably," said Kasver with an element of finality.

*

Seth observed it all from the very back, seeing Habban and Pharos with the other foreigners, wondering what was going on with them; they were quite near the back as well, on a little mound.

He saw Thomas and Mary at one side of the stage, going off with Miriam when she left.

'Horus' spoke Set in his mind; 'Horus, my enemy,' and he notched up his hate for him as well, helping him whet his appetite. Revenge was due, for so many humiliations.

Johannus had dreamed, and he knew that Kaella was in them but couldn't remember how or seeing her, just felt her presence with him now as he got ready to go and see how Yresmin had got on overnight, at the house.

Yresmin had been awake all through, keeping watch inside because Thomas had brought her and Beor in, to help Johannus.

She had assured him that she was used to doing the night watch as Manat's priestess, where the night hours counted for so much; and dreams as well.

Beor and he were going to swap around through the day and evening hours, locking and shuttering the house up when no-one was there, with a few other measures as well.

Thomas had mentioned that he had seen someone who had disquieted him.

From the description given Johannus had felt shivers of cold go through him.

Thus, he welcomed the feeling of the goddess' presence in him that morning, boosting his courage and inner strength, with an energy, a warmth, and determination.

He could not deny that feeling, but nor did he forget Rebecca, wanting only to do his best, be worthy in both their eyes.

His step was light and his heart full as he greeted Yresmin with a hug and a smile; she had come outside, taking his customary place by the side gate.

Everyone left later to go to the festival site, but Johannus didn't. He stayed for quite a while before going inside and closing and locking every shutter and door.

Then he did leave and made to go to the festival site, but in fact didn't. He was concerned that someone may have been watching for him to leave, and so he doubled around by another street and came back onto the avenue, down in the other direction from which he had left.

He had decided on a spot to watch from and stayed there long enough to ensure himself anyone watching would have made their move, if they wanted to try to break into the house.

No one did, so he allowed himself to go and listen to the festival, managing to hear all of Miriam's singing, which filled his heart, like nothing else.

He had kept to the side and back, where the track around the shore of the sea joined the site, and he left very quickly at the end of the morning, before anyone else did.

He saw nothing worrying on the way back, and at the house checked all around for any little disturbances to his 'tells', that he had learnt from Kardun, their Nabatean desert guide around Qadesh.

Then he unlocked the side door and checked everything inside, opening shutters again before resuming his place outside.

*

Miriam, and Mary with Thomas were the first to get back, followed quite soon by Mother and John, all smiling at Johannus and expressing some concern at him being stuck there. But he assured them he had got to hear the singing and thought it had been very beautiful.

A little after came Lazarus and Mary with Beor as well, the Bethany blacksmith who and stayed to keep him company as the other two went in.

"You have been doing your special tracking things then have you?" he said softly. "Hope you put some sand and leaves and stuff over by the back wall where the cacti are least on the other side?" And he laughed good-naturedly.

"All right, all right," laughed Johannus back "but that is to someone else's back yard, not a path."

"Does that mean you didn't?"

"Not saying," he whispered, "but you can do it if you like; if you think you will remember how you set your leaves and twigs, haha."

Beor slapped him fairly gently on the shoulder, which would have sent Johannus sprawling if he hadn't been ready for it. Beor grunted approval.

Thomas came out and eyed the pair with amusement. He particularly loved the bluff blacksmith who he had known in Bethany and around over several years.

"Beor, are you able to come with me for a little while? Would that be okay Johannus? To give me some help with some... er... preparations."

"For a wedding by any chance?" prodded Beor. "Of course, no worries at all."

"Mother asked me to make sure that no one disturbed Miriam, Mary and her, in Yeheshua's room." Thomas told Johannus, "No-one at all, until they come out. They need some time... Is that okay? You know best how that is worked."

"Fine," said Johannus, knowing that it could be tricky, but glad about being asked. "Everyone else already in the house knows that, I take it?"

"Yes, they do. John is in his room; Mary is preparing the lunch and Lazarus just wanted to rest in the downstairs front room; but said he would ask anyone else not to go up."

"Okay fine," said Johannus again, and Beor tipped him a wink as he and Thomas set off for town. "I'll be back as soon as; to take over"

*

Susannah arrived at the house with Sarita and Kasver, and then Pharos and Habban, following a bit further behind them.

"Hi Johannus," said Susannah, "Is it all right to go inside? This is Sarita... a friend of Mary's from Antioch, and her husband Kasver. Magdalene asked for them to come today."

Susannah had regularly stayed at the house when Yeheshua had lived there and knew the ways of it intimately; and here was Sarita and Kasver who Mary had told him so much about over the last two years. Extraordinary.

"Yes Susannah, of course, no problem. Mother, Mary and Miriam are in

Yeheshua's room and have asked on no account should they be disturbed. I am sure you understand." Johannus felt in many ways the situation was beyond him to control. He held fast inside, and let go of his worries, as far as he could.

"So nice to meet you, Lady Sarita; Magdalene has spoken often about you, in our travels; and you sir, too," as he turned to Kasver. "If you would like to stay and wait in the front room where Lazarus is, the man claimed back from death by Yeheshua, they will come down, but I don't know how soon."

Johannus was grateful that words were almost coming by their own accord.

"Or else there is a nice courtyard around the back here, with seats in the shade; and either way I am sure Susannah and Lazarus's sister Mary will be making refreshments for us all at some point."

"Thank you," said Kasver; "and these gentlemen coming behind are captains Pharos, a business partner of Mary's, and Habban, an envoy from the court of King Gondaphres. Both hoping to meet with Mary and Miriam too."

Johannus's heart was beating with all the fine introductions, and knowing that Mother, Miriam and Mary really did not wish be disturbed, made him feel like a puppet in a bigger picture, and a glorious picture of great things.

He looked up slightly wearily at the two sea captains waiting patiently, and took a few paces towards them. Pharos began, "this is captain Habban who has come a long way on the business of his king; and I am Pharos, a captain and business partner of Joseph of Arimathea and Mary Magdalene, and have been his guide here. We ask the chance to meet with Mary."

Habban nodded in agreement and Johannus surpressed a little sigh, but then felt his own interest in these two hardened travellers come alive. "That is amazing that you have come all this way, and meet here now. Such an auspicious time, and with Miriam singing. Did you enjoy this morning?"

"Very much so," said Habban, "I also want to express my admiration for the Lady Miriam's singing, and am hoping to be here a few days longer."

"Do you have somewhere satisfactory to stay?" Johannus asked Pharos, aware he was staying in one of Mary's business premises, as Pharos might have expected to do.

"We do," said Pharos, "the Lady Susannah has been most helpful, and Sarita and Kasver, who we met this morning too. A most welcome coincidence, that we were all wanting to come here."

At that moment Beor returned, and Johannus was happy to have been able to engage the captains, without having felt the need to block their access.

"Beor," he said, "these two sea captains have sailed all the way from Gandhara, in the north of the eastern spice lands. Pharos here is a partner of Joseph and Magdalene's, and captain Habban, an ambassador of King Gondaphares."

Johannus waited the few moments it took for Beor to get drawn into an animated conversation with the captains, before offering to go and get them something to drink.

"Water would be fine," said Habban, "or maybe some red wine if… Pharos?"

"Wine would be most welcome," said Pharos, and Beor concurred that he could help them with it also.

Johannus glowered at him, and shot a reminder as he left to go into the house "Thomas all right? We have a full house here now…"

*

The conversation had got round to how the captains had been followed on the way to Magdala and back again, and that they had reported this to the Roman Guard, next to the villa they were staying in.

Another shiver ran through Johannus as Beor explained how Thomas had seen a suspicious person who met the same description.

"This Thomas," said Habban, "seems to be useful to have around; a perceptive man of learning I have heard… but practical too, would you say?"

Beor couldn't praise Thomas highly enough. "Indeed sir, I would say that Thomas is the most widely learned man I know, but with few of the airs and graces like other clever folk I have met."

"So practical? In things like knowledge of buildings, perhaps?"

"Quite possibly," responded Johannus; "he studied in Antioch, in philosophy and law, as well as other arts and sciences, like astronomy and geometry and quite possibly including building too; but has his roots here in Judea and Galillee; being one of the foremost disciples of the master Yehashua."

"So, I have heard," agreed Habban. "The master who said he could destroy the Jewish temple and rebuild it three days, some said? And others say he himself came back to life after being crucified. Truly remarkable…"

"Yes," said Beor firmly. "One of a long line of quite amazing things done by the master Yeheshua." His tone left no room for doubt…

"The man Lazarus, who is a neighbour of mine, was himself brought back to life by the Lord Yeheshua, having been dead in his tomb for three days. He is here inside and I am sure he would be glad to tell you himself."

This caught even the doughty Habban by surprise, especially from such a down to earth man as the blacksmith, and he nodded his head thoughtfully. "Well, I am certain I have come to the right place," he said, and smiled broadly all around. "I am so glad to have got here."

John had come into the kitchen where I was making some tea and said that Mother was asking if I could join her and Miriam in Yeheshua's room.

"I am just making us drinks; I will take them up now. Here, this one is for you."

"Thanks," he said, taking the cup in both hands.

I took the tray up and the door was slightly ajar so I pushed it open with my foot and went in.

Miriam was sitting on the bed and Mother was sat in a comfy cane chair to one side, both accepting of the offered tea with murmured thanks.

I set the tray, with my cup, down on the floor, arranging and sitting on some cushions that were there on a lovely rug.

The silence was like sitting out in the country on a balmy day, leaning back and letting the beauty soak into you, and there was even the song of a bird I didn't recognise coming through the open window.

Mother put out a hand and closed the shutter slightly, not to keep the song out, just us in together.

Words were not needed and we sat in the quiet, cups abandoned as we opened our hearts to His presence, the moment's presence, eyes closed but all senses alive... within.

*

Thomas had made a start on all the things he needed to do but the more he did the more there seemed to be.

Money wasn't exactly the issue, more keeping all the threads together, and seeing the Rabbi who Lazarus and Mother knew, and who had been a friend of Yeheshua too, had been very helpful, if not a little daunting.

Money would become an issue in some ways, because although Mary was quite wealthy in her own right, Thomas was not prepared to live off that alone.

But he wasn't thinking about that now.

Lazarus had talked with Martha as well, who were doing most of the practical arrangements it seemed to Thomas. He was grateful, and Martha seemed very happy to be so involved.

Beor had gone back to the house, and Thomas took to one of his walks, that he always liked to do when his mind was fully laden.

He walked back out along the shore to the festival site, enjoying the day, but careful to keep to the shade where there was some, dotted along the way.

By the time he got there he was ready for a drink and took out the couple of farthings that he had in his pocket for a drink at the stall a man had set up.

As he approached, another man turned and walked away quite quickly, but before Thomas could see his face.

He wasn't walking like Thomas had seen him the night before, sloping with the bag slung across his shoulder, but something made Thomas wonder; a cold kind of shiver; but even as his eyes followed him the man disappeared into or past a group of people, and was gone.

*

Seth knew it was a narrow escape; he hadn't seen his enemy approaching as he was taking his drink, but had made the best of the moments he had, and was now watching from a hollow, a little way beyond the group of people he had melted into.

No one had seen anything remarkable about a man slipping down into the shade of scrubby thorn bush to take a midday nap or had noticed him move further round to get a view back to the drinking stall.

Horus must have seen something with his hawk vision eyes but Set was used to that.

*

Thomas wouldn't have done anything, other than get a good view of who the man was, but he knew this was another warning sign, and he decided to go back to the house, and then his own room after.

Sarita and Kesver might be there now, and he didn't want to miss them meeting up with Mary this time.

When he got to the house, he found Johannus and Beor talking to a couple of equally robust looking visitors, one of whom was quite richly attired in a foreign kind of way, but Thomas quite liked the look of him.

"Here he is now," said Beor, catching sight of Thomas's approach.

"Here is who?" said Thomas joining the group.

"Thomas, this is captain Habban," said Johannus, "come from King Gondaphares. Habban, this is the man Thomas Didimus of whom we were telling you." They nodded cordially and shook hands.

"And this is captain Pharos, a captain who does much business with Mary and grandfather Joseph as well. And he knew Miriam's father, who sailed with his own father too. Amazing."

"Ahh," said Thomas, greeting him as well. "Well met gentleman, a great time to be here."

"Is it true sir," asked Habban, perceiving that Thomas would be disappearing quickly into the house, and he didn't want to miss the moment, "that you know about and have an interest in the building of the temple of Solomon in Jerusalem?"

This caught Thomas momentarily off guard, for no one here would have known that before he came to Yeheshua he had been interested in the form of how the temple was constructed to give access to the presence of the holy of holies there, for worshippers to be able to read the words kept within the Ark, though keeping the Ark of the Covenant itself safe.

Yet, how over time this way to the presence had been cut off and jealously guarded to keep out everyone, except for only the one or two, the very, very

680

few, who had clearly themselves lost the truth of it.

"Indeed sir," replied Thomas, "but that was before I came to understand the real meaning of it. It isn't something that concerns me now."

"Nevertheless," pressed Habban, happy to have found this out, "please be kind enough to let me talk of it with you sometime."

At that moment Thomas caught sight of another little group coming up the road, Simon Peter and an Egyptian looking fellow, followed by couple of ladies, well wrapped up against the midday sun.

"Here comes the man most likely to be able to help you captain Habban," said Thomas. "This is Simon Peter, the foremost disciple of the master Yeheshua."

"Johannus, Beor, would you introduce the good captains to our revered friend? Please excuse me gentlemen, but I have urgent need to catch some friends inside. I hope we shall indeed have the chance to talk of that again."

"Ahh; why of course," said Habban, caught between the desire to continue the conversation with Thomas, but conscious of the advantage in making the acquaintance of Peter as well. "Another time, when we shall have plenty of ease I hope."

Thomas smiled and nodded to them both, as he turned to go inside.

CHAPTER 27.

Mother had the little scroll we had given her in her hand.

"This is very beautiful," she said. "It tells me clearly so much of what I need to understand. What we all need, but maybe we women especially, who care to tend the plants he has put so much of himself into growing."

"I must follow in the steps he made, yes," joined in Miriam; "to water the seeds and tend those that have sprouted, wherever I find them; and sow more as well. His message needs to find all who are thirsty for it… as far as we can."

We had been like one being, breathing in the truth together, as one… in one love, and I was included, completely.

"I think he enabled me to work within the circle of the brethren for a reason," I said. "To work across the barriers for others too."

Mother laughed. "They are not all so bad," she said. "Even Peter under his gruff exterior has a true heart."

"Yes, I know mother, but I am not sure that they value the part women play. And they mustn't get away with that too much. Isn't that why the Pharisees have become as they are?"

"It could be so," said Miriam; "but mustn't be allowed to become a problem. They have been given their tasks, and we have ours too. That is all that counts, to follow our path day by day as it unfolds."

She stopped, saying nothing more and it was Mother who eventually broke our silence:

"The time will come…" and I heard 'for women' in my head.

"It will," said Miriam, "for all; all the ignored and downtrodden too."

"Good," I responded, "then the meek can really inherit the earth."

We hugged each other, for a long time, knowing, I don't know how, that we might not meet like this, all three together, many more times in this life. Mother, sister-wife and disciple-priestess.

*

Thomas entered the front room where Sarita and Kasver were sitting quietly and Lazarus too, though he had nodded off to sleep.

Sarita put her finger to her lips to let Thomas know and got up to come over to him. "He has been so sweet to us, making us feel like we belong in all of this; but he is still frail after all his illnesses."

Kasver got up as well and came over to Thomas too, hands outstretched.

"I am sorry I have deserted you so badly," said Thomas. "It seems that I am to be married tomorrow, and have been busy trying to play my part in it."

"Yes, Lazarus told us", said Kasver. "He is very happy for both of you."

"In truth he has arranged more of it behind the scenes than anybody; and his sisters. Is Mary here? His sister."

"She and John are out in the back courtyard, getting lunch ready for how many people they are not sure. Practicing for tomorrow, she said," and Sarita laughed.

*

I was first out of the room towards the stairs, and down below were two of my oldest friends, Sarita and her lovely husband Kasver, talking with the man I loved, my betrothed.

But to my surprise it was Lazarus who saw me first, gracefully rising from sleep to greet me as though I had been in his dream. "At last daughter beloved, how much we have been hoping you might come."

"There you are!" cried Sarita. "You are a hard lady to keep up with."

There was a lot going on, and no explanation needed. "I was privileged to be at your and Kasver's wedding, and now I feel so happy you are able to come to Thomas's and mine."

We had already discussed their children being back in Antioch and I couldn't help now adding, "I hope I can come up and visit you soon again. God willing with a little one too."

"Yes," put in Kasver, "We so hope you can." And Sarita and I hugged.

Mother and Miriam had both come down the stairs, and as I introduced my friends to them, Kasver responded eloquently, "Thomas has told us so much about you both, as we travelled down from Antioch. It is our great good fortune to be here, and we thank you for allowing us to join with you now."

"As Magdalene has told us of you too," answered Mother, "of all the good things you are doing in Antioch."

I didn't realise that mother would have remembered me telling her of the work with the lepers that Kasver had taken on with me, and after I had gone, but she was amazing like that, how she retained so much.

"There were two sea captains that came with us too," said Sarita, mainly to me. "One, your Pharos," she said, "and the other a man called Habban from King Gondaphares in northern Bharat, where I was born."

"Pharos, really? Shouldn't we invite them in to eat with us?" I asked mother. "Do we know who is eating here today?"

Mary, Lazarus's sister, came bustling into the room at that moment, having heard my question, followed by a smiling John.

"They have gone with Peter," said John. "He invited them to eat with him, and his family, and the man Kareem who brought the singers with him."

"Two singers, Ruth and Anna, have stayed," said Mary, "so they would be here to rehearse with you when you want Miriam."

"Right," said Thomas, "and Beor and Johannus are still out the front. Just twelve then."

"I make it thirteen," said Mary. Thomas recounted, "you are right, thirteen."

"Twelve," said John, "I think Johannus has gone to check on the animals; but we should keep some food for him."

"Let's all eat then," said mother. "I see you have set the tables out in the courtyard. Thank you so much Mary for your hard work."

"I only did the final putting together, you had prepared most of it yourself, mother."

We heard all the news from Antioch, of Thomas's ailing former teacher Philestres, the impact of his recovery with the great ensuing interest in Yeheshua's teaching; of Arianne; the results of the earthquake on the temple, of Thomas and Arianne's writing together, which made Miriam and I smile at each other…

Then much of the meal was spent discussing Thomas and my marriage arrangements at this time tomorrow, when many more people would be coming here briefly to eat and celebrate; before the singing in the afternoon.

"Martha and Yresmin are working on it already at the other house," said Mary. "Mary, you have arranged the wine yourself you said?"

"Yes, I saw Jacob this morning, and he is looking after that,"

The conversation had just moved on to the captain of King Gondaphares and what his mission was when Matthias arrived with the other two singers, who had been having their dress costumes adjusted in town.

We had finished eating but Miriam still apologised for having to get up to go over their singing plans; the topic of Gondaphares stayed in the air.

"He seems interested in the temple in Jerusalem," said Thomas.

"He is, I believe," said Kasver, "on a mission from his king to find someone who knows of its construction, to return to Taxila with him." He looked at Thomas as all the pieces of Habban's arrival slipped into place.

"Oh," said Thomas, looking back into Kasver's face, remembering the details of their conversation. "I was right then; the ship has come," he added softly.

"Maybe you would like to come to the villa where we are staying tonight, to talk it over. As our welcomed guest…"

"I think maybe I should," said Thomas.

CHAPTER 28

Miriam went over the songs with the four Ennead singers.

She herself had been trained in Heliopolis so their musical chants were second nature to her, and she understood the subtleties of its rhythms and wordings better than anyone.

"Once we have the rhythm of those phrases, those exchanges, established, I shall start improvising over them, around them and with them, coming back each time to the chorus phrases that you have kept going. Do you see?"

They did, at least after they had practiced a few times and quite soon Miriam knew they were ready. "Rest here and I shall make you some tea, or what you would like; and then we should get going over to the site."

*

Peter was fascinated by captain Habban, a man at home both with the politics of a king's court and the rough conditions of the high seas.

A man who knew his place with his master but had command of men as well.

A courteous man but not one ever to be crossed, with impunity.

Peter saw their similarities; captains each, yet the kingdom of his own Lord wasn't so easy to define, or how to be a captain of it. He could learn much from this Habban he thought.

Habban for his part recognised in Peter the same qualities that had taken him to where he had got. He had respect for him; more than he often found.

Habban told him of his mission and all that he had found, about Yeheshua, his crucifixion and resurrection too, about the temple and what the meaning of that was as well.

Peter raised an eyebrow. "Who has been telling you all these things?"

"Many people have been giving me the fragments that have built up a picture. The last bits about Solomon's temple came from your Thomas; it seems he made a study of it before he met the Master Yeheshua."

"Yes, that doesn't surprise me, hah," laughed Peter. "He is very astute. I was making studies of the movements of the fish in this little sea we have here."

"My friend you mustn't diminish yourself, not to any man; that is a considerable skill that many envy. But let me tell you why I believe it is that King Gondaphares has sent me on this mission; then you will understand."

Peter leant forward in interest; Habban had lowered his voice as though the walls were listening:

"They say that in his youth Gondaphares was a seeker after wisdom, even coming to this land, but in becoming King he rather left that path, and only now seeks to regain it...

And I have been told that the same Yeheshua you speak of came travelling in our lands, teaching; but that as King, Gondaphares did not know him. I believe that is what is driving him now, to make amends, seeking to build a

Holy Temple, like unto Solomon's."

Peter sat back and exhaled his breath, not realising he had been holding it.

He felt like whispering too, but didn't: "I think you are right that Thomas may be the man you seek. I shall speak to him."

Even as he said this, Peter was sure that his telling Thomas he should go to Taxila would have little effect. Just as trying to rein in Miriam was having very little effect that he could see; almost the reverse.

At least John had brought Mother here which was probably a better way, but were they expected to spend their time running after this woman, however accomplished? Not what he had thought he would ever be doing.

Pharos had been quietly watching and listening to the exchange as well, and came in with a perceptive observation of his own;

"I think the times are changing for us all. What was a rule may no longer be so; what was thought true may have to be looked at again, from our own experience. Miriam and Magdalene seem to do that, and you with them too."

This surprised Peter almost more than that which Habban had said, almost as though this man had read his mind. Perhaps there was something in what he said, but he knew not what exactly.

"Ahhh, Matthias is back," he said, grateful that his brother apostle had returned, and showing Peter and his guests great deference; which made Peter almost uncomfortable in a different way. "Does this mean it is time to go to hear how well Kareem's singers can perform?"

*

Miriam and all at the house set off together and this time Johannus was with them, following, whilst Beor remained behind to see the house was secured properly.

He had his own methods and was happy to shut and lock the house up, and take a nap in the back courtyard, in the shade, out of sight; but seeing everything that passed.

Very few people did, mainly the odd cart along the road, and an old woman dressed in black.

He saw her twice, which surprised him, the second time on this side of the road, stopping to peer down the path beside the house.

For a second Beor thought she was going to come down the path to the side door, but she didn't. Instead, she turned back and carried on, almost quicker than she had come.

Beor got up and very quietly went up to the road and looked up and down; she had gone.

*

Seth had seen Johannus go off with Miriam, but hadn't known Beor was still there.

He wanted to investigate the house for weaknesses to his methods and went past once, seeing that there was no one still on guard there.

Overcoming his natural caution in these dealings he returned a little later the way he had come, closer this time, stopping even to look down to the door that everyone used to go in and out.

Tempted to check it for a second, he held back, having half a feeling that he might be being watched, from down there. Not the snake Apep that had been nagging at him all through the previous night, not helping but draining his energies. This was different and much more familiar to him.

He trusted these slight sensings, they having saved his life over the years.

Turning like any other nosy old widow might, thinking better of something, he made off again scurrying more than he meant at the last, off around a corner.

Catching up with himself, calming his breathing, he took off and put away the black 'shawl' at a suitable quiet spot and ambled on down into town, thinking.

There were more ways of finding weaknesses than testing doors and windows, and Seth would search for all of them.

Walking out to the festival site he mingled with the other visitors, even apparently happily donating a few coins, along with others, to the man collecting for the costs of running it.

Seth's face had formed into a kind of set smile, but as he concentrated on Miriam being up ahead, the smile became more real, and more devious. Realising this he carefully relaxed back, looking around at some of the others. Impossible for him to imitate the actually happy demeanour that many had.

So, he decided not to try too hard, just to focus on Miriam like he had been, walking faster to be catching up on others and not have them coming up on him. At least Apep couldn't get near.

Suddenly he realised that the captains he had tried to follow in Magdala were not far ahead, and walking along with none others than Matthias and Peter.

He knew Peter from Jerusalem with Yeheshua of course, but this was the first he had seen of him here. What a strange coming together he thought, but maybe not.

He would have to be extra careful; they were all dangerous in their own way.

Quietly he split off left as they reached the back of the crowd, and made his way round to his little camp, still undisturbed and out of sight, discreetly checking the rocks that covered where he had buried his things.

All was fine, the nine knives would still be there, even as the two he was carrying were in their sheaths under his robes.

The afternoon music and singing had already started, but he wouldn't go closer till Miriam was singing.

Making doubly sure there was no-one around or remotely aware of him he collected another two knives from their hiding place. He knew the time was coming; his mind had started to form a view of where the weakness was, he could attack through.

*

Miriam went out on the stage to much applause, remembering herself being here on such an evening with Yeheshua, not so long ago; their own marriage time.

Her little band from Jericho and Nazareth were already set up and had played some of the things they liked and had practiced together,

And now were warmed up for those which Miriam liked to sing the most, the ones composed for Yeheshua himself and his disciples, when he had been teaching and healing and confronting evil; the morning star, the light in the darkness.

In fact, it seemed these were the most popular with almost all of the crowd too, judging by the way they clapped and sang along as well.

That she could express the feelings of her heart was such a freedom, always.

Peter was close to the front, with Thomas and John too, in an area that had been roped off especially, though he didn't know by whom. Habban, Matthias and the others were close behind.

Magdalene and Mother and other women were at the side, backstage.

Listening to Miriam brought so much flooding back, of being here with Yeheshua so many times and tears involuntarily streamed down Peter's face. And all of the songs that they had lived with as their joy.

Almost more than that; Miriam was somehow with Yeheshua still… in the power of her presence; as they had been, together.

The band played and Miriam sang. This was when she could live the truth most completely, living and giving, always changing and growing but always yet the same feeling. New words and phrasings, born of the present, to reach the hearts of the people there, with them, being alive.

Peter noticed; everyone must be feeling it. More than just singing songs, but being full of being alive.

Miriam finished and went back off stage to tumultuous applause.

*

Seth watched and listened as well, from the furthest edge close to his lair.

Saw all the people there and made his plans against them.

The weakness he must find would be in the timing, when he would catch them unawares.

Even with all his weapons he would only survive against relatively few in numbers.

But his information on what was happening, what they were doing, was not good enough.

He would need to have an opportunistic opening.

And hard as he was focussed on Miriam it took all his effort to close his mind and soul to her words, instead piling up the jealous hate against those she was singing for, who were not him.

She had left the stage and he noticed now a couple of little groups of Pharisees that had joined at the back of the crowd as well.

How he hated these, he realised; that had bled him of everything, his life, for their own ends.

He would never work with them anymore, but nor needed to. He had awoken a greater power.

He shivered though at the touch that this thought brought at the back of his head, or in his eyes, for through him he felt the snake was watching too, watching him, waiting for its time... just as he was.

*

The Ennead singers were up on the stage, and Miriam had arranged for her band to join in with them too...

Which worked really well, making the style of their chanting closer to the songs the people already knew and loved...

And the words and phrasing had been adapted by Matthias and Peter himself, which made Peter's heart swell a little with a creator's pride, knowing it was real and true.

Songs that spoke of the wonder of the Truth in flesh, in every heart that opened to Him; of the marvel of overcoming death, by life given for every one of us; the knowing of not being worthy, but the wonder of being forgiven.

Songs praising the Almighty in all Majesty, but also of coming together and being a part of the whole.

Songs to bring Miriam home to take her true place in the family.

Then Miriam stood forward, getting ready to join them, as the song of the Ennead called directly to her:

"Come to join us that sing the praises of the Lord;" ... "Come to us all who hunger and thirst;" ... "Come to us who are tired and heavy laden;" ... "Come to us that we may sing His praises together" ... "Come to us, come to us."

And she stepped up to join them, the great applause breaking out anew.

As Miriam sang with them, she directed the words and thoughts in gestures out to the crowd, to join in the singing. "Come to us, come to us," they sang, again and again at every chance, soon swaying in unison as well.

With the Ennead keeping the verses going round, and the crowd punctuating too, Miriam stepped away slightly and began to put in her own additions, in her strong, true and heart touching voice... each improvisation that she did working in with the other singers but gaining their own momentum too, pulling in further an already involved crowd.

"Oh seeker... climb the stairs within... to where the holy of holies is;"

"Oh seeker... find the true resting place... of the Ark of the Covenant;"

"Oh seeker... read the words of sweetest love... that lie in your own true heart and soul:"

"We are the seekers, Lord; Come to us, come to us... within."

And everyone was entranced, singing the verses of the Ennead too, punctuated now by Miriam and John, and Thomas, and even Peter found himself at one with it; albeit holding fast to the Spirit of the Comforter in him, lest there be any contradiction… but he found none.

Excepting Matthias, who was somehow infuriated, and couldn't believe that Miriam was going so far beyond the bounds, using his songs as a platform for delivering her own teachings.

Unable to contain himself he leaned forward and tapped Peter on the shoulder, whispering louder than he intended: "Surely Peter, she takes this too far; too far!" which was noticed by the captains standing next to Matthias too.

*

Apep-Apophis looking through Seth seethed and hissed, engulfing Seth's mind in a suffocating darkness.

Anathema to it that the Ennead were sounding their songs again, here; right now.

Seth staggered, but the snake's distaste was not different from his own thinking, yet all-compelling.

Miriam was a light that burnt in its eyes and brain, but the others could be wiped out, quickly.

Seth felt his own jealous hate, amplified by greed and a different hate, until he could listen no longer to the singing.

He slid away to his lair and got ready to make their moves.

Thomas made good on his promise to visit Kasver and Sarita at the end of the evening.

They had been sitting with me, so we all walked back to their villa together, joined by Pharos and Habban, all enjoying the aftermath of the day's festivities.

It was so good to finally meet up with Pharos too, for I had heard the surprising news of his being here, and with the other big sea captain as well, who sported a fine sword at his belt; obviously a man approved of by the Roman authorities, I realised.

"What brings you all this way sir?" I asked the man called Habban; aware that everyone else probably already knew.

"My King commanded me madam," he replied soberly. "He seeks someone who knows of the constructing of the temple of Solomon."

"I don't think we know of many masons, do we?" I said to anyone in our group, adding "although perhaps someone I know who sculpts in stone, and sometimes for the daughter of King Herod might know more."

"We have heard of such a one," said Pharos.

No-one added to this but I was already surprised; 'did they somehow know of Lenny?' I asked myself.

We had turned away from the shore track, in favour of another way that led to the villas, and as if in answer to an unseen agenda, someone quickly crossed the way ahead, a scurrying figure that made me shiver, unwelcome memories returning.

*

Seth didn't see them in the dusk, focussed on where he was going and never having met anyone on this track.

But the snake felt the ripples of their presences and pushed Seth on faster, not enjoying the group's proximity.

Seth's Apophis driven plan was to get near to the house and lie low, watching what was going on till he knew when and where he could strike.

*

Our conversation on the road turned to the figure I had seen, for both Thomas and the Captains seemed to have recognised something about it too, and it posed an immediate possible threat that could not be ignored.

Habban cleared his throat, almost nervously. "I think madam that we may have seen that person before, on the road to your house in Magdala."

"Or rather on the way to going to see Lenny," put in Pharos, and I realised that it was Pharos that had taken them there, or probably through Jacob.

"Did he follow you there?" I was suddenly worried, chilled to the bone in fact, as I thought of the vulnerability of Lenny, Jess and Anna. If this was the same man that had been involved in trying to kidnap Miriam and myself, I didn't bear to think of it.

"He was behind us when we left your Jacob's farm, it is true," said the captain Habban, "but Jess had spotted him, being carried by Anna."

"Which gave us the chance to give him the slip; not going anywhere near Lenny's house," completed Pharos, making me feel a bit better. Brilliant little Jess, I thought.

"But," said Habban, and paused, obviously considering whether this was something he should say in front of me. "This man had already approached us in an inn the night before, pretending to be a friend of yours, and Miriam too."

"I knew it could not be true," said Pharos. "He was a suave operator. Totally unpleasant."

I shivered again, seeing slithering darkness. "Are you sure you gave him the slip? He doesn't know where they live?"

"Assuredly madam," said Habban, "he went past us where we were hiding, but definitely didn't see us; in the wood at the top of the ridge. He went on downhill towards where he thought we had gone."

He didn't say about seeing him fingering an assassin's knife up his sleeve; that it was so close that Habban had been able see that clearly.

Thomas decided that as soon as they got Sarita and Kasver back to the villa he would ask Pharos to accompany him and Mary back to the house. Nowhere was safe.

"I shall come too," said Habban, even though he knew that there was no way now he could ask for Thomas to come to Taxila with him; not in front of his bride to be with their marriage happening in the morning.

*

He was stood behind a bush, pushed back against a wall, watching from round the back of the house as the Ennead singers returned. Everything was dark, but gradually lamps were lit inside whose light filtered through the closed shutters.

He had plenty of patience and a certain freedom from the snake's mind, though he was sure it was still right there, watching.

It was just that they were in close alignment.

He could wait all night if needs be; he just needed one moment.

It was a long wait and the night was oppressively hot. He hoped this was going to work for him.

He already knew which windows belonged to who, so when one of the upstairs shutters was opened from the inside, he knew whose bedroom it went into.

He didn't lose time. He had endlessly rehearsed in his mind the exact holds and movements that would take him up and through the window, noiselessly.

Leaving the bush, he stretched and shook loose his arms and legs, checked the knives were properly secured, crossed to the house and began the climb.

He had seen through the opened widow one of the girls leaving the room. Either Ruth or Anna, and the old cruelty in him decided he wanted Anna. So did the snake.

*

692

Thomas had left Mary at the house and thanked the captains for their help, letting them walk back to their villa knowing they had done all they could.

Beor was still outside by the side gate, and having heard from Thomas about the man they had seen, Beor told him of the old bent widow who had peered down that very path a few hours earlier.

Thomas took a long deep breath letting it all sink in. "Beor, please would you bring that staff of yours with you, to be doubly on guard here? No, not now, but tomorrow? And for the wedding too? We need to be on maximum alert. I shall speak to the Roman guards first thing in the morning."

"What about tonight?"

"I shall keep watch, with Yresmin, inside,"

"Well, I shall join you too then. We can take alternate naps to make it easier. I am not having you asleep at your wedding," and they laughed.

The night passed uneventfully and at first light Thomas went and washed himself where he was staying, letting Johannus know what he thought the problems might be before he headed on back to the Praetorian villa.

What he discovered when he got there and started talking to the Roman guard in charge, shocked him to the core.

A woman had been found dead earlier, but more horrible was the story of the ones who had survived. There were three, and they had come from Jericho to sing in the festival.

It was the girl called Ruth who had told them what had happened in the night.

She had got up to go to the toilet, in a separate area, and because the night was so hot, had opened a shutter in the room she shared with a girl called Anna, also a singer.

When she got back, she knew immediately something was wrong, something awful.

She could hear something inside her room but barely dared look inside because she 'knew'…

She hadn't been able to say what she 'knew' or what it was she actually saw when she plucked up her courage to look inside, only that there was a writhing of shapes on Anna's bed.

She couldn't see clearly because there seemed to be an obscuring darkness, horrible to perceive or feel even, but she knew that she had to get away, and also warn the other two girls.

Having gone into their room she found she could hardly speak much less explain, but quickly started barricading the door and windows, terrifying the other two with her frantic intensity.

It wasn't necessary to try to explain because they could feel the evil in the house too, but eventually she told them enough so that after they had fixed every gap and wedged closed every opening, many times over they prayed together, mainly to Yeheshua as they were newly baptised.

Maybe they should have run or something, but they couldn't. What they had been able to do was sing softly with each other the songs they sang with Miriam, and this raised their spirits to the point they felt the evilness had gone.

At first light they had dared to go outside and see, and found Anna dead upon her bed.

The bed was very ruffled but not much other sign of a struggle except two stab wounds in her side, one in her belly and the other just under her heart, almost like the fang marks of a huge snake.

Nor was there hardly any of the blood you might have expected by stabbing, and their friend was very grey; clearly dead, with eyes still staring wildly sideways.

They had turned, horrified, and fled downstairs to find the man called Kareem, who was their teacher and organiser of the trip, but there was no sign of him, or him having been there that night. Yet he had come back with them from the festival and bade them good night after locking the door from the inside. It was still locked.

The guard was as mystified as they were shocked, obviously from the terror. But there was a window still open in the dead girl's room, so presumably Kareem had somehow been responsible for whatever had happened and gone out of the window.

Thomas didn't say too much about that theory, only telling the guard about the suspicious man who had been seen repeatedly, both here and at Magdala, and was heartened that they took him seriously, mostly because of the report that Habban had made. They seemed to give the big captain considerable credence.

One final thing he asked was whether they could spare a guard for the house that Miriam was in, because of the closeness of both the murder and the unknown assassin.

The guard-in-charge thought about it. "Tonight; I shall spare a guard to be there through the night, as that appears to be his method. One night whilst we apprehend the killer."

Thomas was grateful and set back to the house himself, wondering how this would affect his marriage, realising that he couldn't let it. He had to tell them because they would find out anyway, but not until after the wedding. He would only tell Beor, Johannus and Yresmin now.

*

Peter got to hear a bit later that morning through a panicked Matthias, who now had three women to be responsible for.

"Bring them here," said Peter. "I shall make sure of their safety." His wife would make them welcome, and was the most comforting influence he could

694

imagine.

Kareem had not been found and was on the wanted list now of both the Roman and the local authorities. Matthias had already spent an hour explaining his connection to Kareem to the Roman guard and would have to do so again to the local official, no doubt.

He thanked Peter profusely for his help, aware again just why he was called the rock. Nothing seemed to shake him.

Which was not quite how Peter saw himself. Nothing was going right it seemed, especially this thing with the Ennead.

All he could do now was to be true to his Lord. Nothing else worked.

Miriam would do what she would do and Thomas too. It was far too late to stop him and Mary Magdalene from getting married, and he now couldn't even see why he would want to.

The mission of Captain Habban? Not exactly his business, was it? Would he be glad if he succeeded? If his king was truly wanting to understand… maybe. And then there was talk of Yeheshua's requesting Thomas to go.

"Go fetch the women, Matthias. As soon as they are settled safely here the better."

Seth woke up next to the horribly mutilated body of Kareem, not at all sure of how they had got where they were, amongst the rocks in a piece of the wilderness.

Someone or something had stabbed and torn at Kareem repeatedly, from face and neck down to his legs; his garments ripped and partly removed revealed the extent of it.

Seth looked at the body with a kind of professional interest, quite detachedly, although he was well aware that he himself was the hand that must have done this.

He remembered little of the night, except killing Anna, and nothing else, which was almost refreshing.

He first checked his daggers, and found that two of them had definitely been used; one paralyser type and the other a most deadly. Both from his forearm sheathes; he would have to change those as soon as possible.

Next, he looked for evidence of a trail of blood, but found none, so he roughly buried the body by piling as many rocks as possible over it. In a kind of gully he found nearby.

Glad of the good night, sleep and work, he made his way as circuitously as possible back to his lair-camp, keeping well clear of the town.

He knew what his plan was now and almost laughed aloud.

*

Thomas got back to the house to find Beor, Johannus and Yresmin already waiting for him outside.

Quickly he told them the bones of what had happened, feeling the shock waves spreading through them. Two murders they thought, just as he did.

They were not going to spread the news to anyone yet, and hoped neither Matthias nor Peter would either, assuming they would soon find out as well.

Johannus went with him to Mary's business place and Yresmin returned to the inside of the house to keep close to Miriam and Magdalene. She was totally fearless Thomas realized.

Beor had his staff, the iron one that he had covered in a skin of leather, distressed to make it look just like wood. Yet the blacksmith was as nimble in wielding it as another man might a wooden one, such was the uncanny strength of his forearms and wrists.

Thomas and Johannus went to get Thomas ready for the wedding, which had two stages. First the formal betrothal part where Thomas would give Mary his gift and the blessings would be said. This would be done with a few guests in the synagogue under the directions of Rabbi Joseph; Thomas had asked Miriam to read the blessings.

Then they would all come back to the house where the tent canopy would be and the feast given out to all the guests, and the dancing and singing; he didn't know how these arrangements were being done, but he was worried about the assassin as he now thought of him.

"Beor, Yresmin and I will be there all the time," said Johannus, and there may be a couple of others we could find.

Suddenly Thomas saw the answer: Pharos and Habban; who could be better? and as witnesses too? "You go back to the house now and I shall meet you all at the synagogue at the arranged time."

To be sure that he had the time, Thomas saddled up Meg and rode her over to the villa. He would ride her to the synagogue too he smiled to himself. He liked a good entrance.

*

Seth wasn't going to bother with the wedding, that he now knew about from Anna.

She had told him everything she could to save herself, but that was never going to help her.

Everyone would be on guard there, especially once his activities of the night before were uncovered. Except for Kareem of course; he liked his messier work to be kept for himself.

No, he knew the hour he would strike; let them sweat and worry till he was ready.

Instead, he was resting up at his camp-lair, just as many others at the festival were; there were little tents dotted all over the site; but not near him though.

After the evening concert of last night, I had gone back to the house; what a day it had been; so exciting how Miriam's singing took us the way it had; into Divinity's heart and soul.

Refreshments were made and gratefully received; Susannah with Mary taking the lead, and now all sitting around and talking about the day gone by, as we often had.

Mother said she had loved the new form of song, with the crowd joining the chorus lines and Miriam's spontaneous expressions; and Miriam was delighted how happy Peter had been with it too.

I found out then that Miriam had moved out of her and Yeheshua's room; for Thomas and I to have it for our wedding day.

She and the other girls took me up to see how they had arrayed it with a canopy of many long and multicoloured cotton ribbons; so beautiful; and everything fresh and set about with little bowls of all manner of tasty or subtly scented offerings.

I was amazed, and after letting me explore it they took the lamps and left me there to rest for the coming day.

Grateful for this I lay on Yeheshua and Miriam's bed and closed my eyes as the last light of the day faded outside, and my thoughts with it.

I dreamt that I was listening to Miriam singing again, with Yeheshua; seeing through his eyes; into a place I had never seen, and they were deeply in love.

And then suddenly came to me the greatest pain, of separation; for he had to choose between a life of earthly love with her… or else to do what only he could do, had come to do. To bring Peace and Truth for those who thirsted. Not closing his heart, but opening it further, to face the way ahead.

Leaving Miriam devastated, distraught, inconsolable.

Then it was the time I saw her first in Magdala, finding again her love, to aid him in his teaching and all he had to do.

Re-joined; rejoicing.

And I saw too, there at the festival time in Nazareth, where Miriam's singing had stunned the crowds.

But witnessed again their love and pain, when the master set her on that quest; and was asking me to go with her as well…

Except that it was me asking Thomas. No, Yeheshua asking Thomas to take the ship to go to Gondaphares.

And suddenly I was awake again; but it wasn't late, I could still hear voices murmuring downstairs.

*

I sat listening to them, not able to pick up the words and must have dozed off again, for I was travelling with Miriam and Johannus too.

There was a wonderful city of rock-cut temples, where Yresmin was the high priestess. And we were fleeing from the attentions of their king, away into the wilderness, always the wilderness.

Then I was in another temple rough hewn into the rock, but this was an ancient tomb and Miriam was sat with eyes closed in a spot where the light of the morning star shone through a fissure in the rock wall, playing on her face.

I remembered wanting to ask her, but now I saw...

The earth herself, riding in the firmament of stars; the bride of heaven...

Felt their union.

*

When I awoke all was quiet in the house, and the height of the moon shining her beams through the closed shutters told me it was close to midnight.

I snuggled down under the thin coverlet, it being a very warm night, content; but my dream vision wasn't finished yet.

Drifting in the rocking rhythm of the horse I was riding, suddenly all my senses were alive to the sound of a woman's screams. Soundless but somehow pressed on my consciousness, and I flew towards where it must have come from, an Inn on the road to Galilee.

Miriam was just behind and I knew this to be where we had been ambushed and an awful fear fell on me, of the oppressive evil happening somewhere.

All at once I was floating above my own body, the disciples of the magus abominating me with devils again.

But it wasn't me down on the bed, but the singer Anna struggling against her attacker that was about to stab her in the belly as he raped her from behind.

I cried out to her in the soundless world we shared, my hand reaching out as she floated up, free in the moment.

Even as her murderer drove his dagger home, his face turning as if he saw his victim was escaping him.

That face, leering and grinning horribly, was known to me; and I hugged Anna close to me fiercely, willing myself to awake from this nightmare.

*

On stage, underneath the canopy that was Miriam and Yeheshua's, where Anna had sang with Miriam, I was alone, gazing across to where the sun would rise, over the sea. Weeping tears for Anna, feeling her having gone through me from this world.

Except that Yeheshua was beside me, though I had not seen or heard his arrival.

*

Lying here with the morning light growing in the east, I cannot remember all the things he said to me.

I know it is my wedding morning, and I can remember how he smiled with deep compassion.

"Thomas must come to Gondaphares, Mary," he said, and I knew it too.

"Yes, but may he be wedded first, Lord?"

I awoke as he hugged me, and felt the meaning of complete love.

Peter stayed with Ruth and the other two singers, Melanie and Hirani, all that morning, doing whatever he could to heal the shock and horror they were feeling; sharing his simple fullness of spirit with them; a heartfelt love that poured from him, despite anything he might think or even sometimes say.

They felt it, even when he was sternly telling Matthias that he had to go and search for Kareem and help the guards find out the truth of what had happened. He, Peter would take sole responsibility for the singers now, but that he, Matthias must not rest until the killer or killers were apprehended.

They rested and even slept awhile, the three huddled together, in sanctuary.

Peter knew that the wedding was probably already underway and that it had been his intention to try to dissuade Thomas from this course, even to backing king Gondaphares' requests, but he no longer cared about that.

The need of the three singers to understand that their lives had not become entwined with evil was paramount, and he sat like the rock he was in the way of anything that sought to make it otherwise; his enemy; the enemy of life and light.

He stood firm, shining life's beacon in the other darkness, unperturbed.

And at the time for the marriage canopy ceremony, he rose and set out with the three to Miriam's house as if nothing bad had happened, to add his blessings to Thomas and Mary's union.

*

Mary and Susannah had fussed over getting me ready for the formal betrothal at the Synagogue, whilst Miriam and mother fought my case for simplicity, saying there was time enough for this when I got back, which forced a glare from me, much to their delight.

Johannus, Yresmin and Lazarus joined Miriam and myself to go to the ceremony, whilst Beor stayed with Mother, Mary, Susannah and many local disciples bringing food and wine, led by Martha of course.

Miriam went ahead with Yresmin, leading her donkey which Lazarus rode, and I was mounted just behind, on Sella's foal Indy.

Johannus followed ever watchful, just as Yresmin was too, I noticed.

Before we had got far, Pharos joined us as well, to say that Thomas had asked Sarita and Kasver to come to the Synagogue. I was glad yet didn't need to know; but he stepped behind to walk along with Johannus.

As we got in sight of the Synagogue, there was Thomas dismounting from his grey mare Meg, flanked himself by Sarita, Kasver and the captain from the East with his sword at his belt, looking splendidly exotic in contrast to the plain grey and white chosen by Thomas which made my heart jump about like the foal I was sat was sometimes want to do.

*

Peter was the first to greet us back at the house, side by side with Mother, and I was thankful that he looked so happy for us.

The blessings had been beautiful with Lazarus playing the part of my father, and Miriam our closest friend to give the blessings.

Johannus had come inside and I was glad of that, supporting Thomas's side along with Kasver.

Sarita stayed close to me as my oldest friend.

The honour guard of Captains Pharos and Habban stayed outside.

*

We held hands, all through, for once I was holding his we neither of us seemed to want to let go, but would always be connected.

We were still holding each other when we arrived at the house with the canopy set up outside where the front of the house had been opened completely, like it frequently was when Yeheshua used to teach the people who came there.

Miriam led us up to Peter and Mary who in turn led us to sit on the seat of honour together, in the timeless way; the marriage seat, and all the guests came round to give their presents and blessings, receiving our heartfelt thanks in return.

The first thing I noticed was that there really was no Anna here, that the dream had been about a real event. I knew it was, because she had left through me and I felt her passing even now within me.

If I could make it happen, she would be taking all this love with her too, not memories of abomination.

The guests danced and sang, after I had expressed that this was as much in memory of Anna, as it was for Thomas and I. That she was now with the boundless love, for which we all aspired.

Miriam matched my mood with her song and the other singers followed.

"Oh my heart, oh my heart, where are you taking me? Oh my heart, oh my heart, for I know not the way."

"Oh my love, oh my Lord, never forsaking me; Oh my love, oh my Lord, you are carrying me home."

I looked at Thomas and whispered in his ear as I kissed his cheek "I knew about Anna, my love. In my dream-vision she escaped the horror through me; being there for her, and Miriam too."

He looked back at me with an incredible tenderness that nearly broke my heart; that we had both been reminded of the transitory nature of our earthly dream was clear; clearer too as I remembered my Lord Yeheshua's words, concerning Thomas.

The tenderness continued as he carried me up to the master bedroom; the guests continuing the celebrations below.

"Love me Thomas," I said, fearing that my mentioning Anna's death might affect him badly. "Even as we loved when Yeheshua had been killed on the cross, love me now that Anna may know the beauty of it within me too."

He took his time in a most masterful and gratifying way; removing my clothes one by one and allowing me to do the same for him, until we were kneeling naked on the bed, facing one another, my hair being the last thing that he released, his arms being around me undoing the pins and bows, my body being soft against his hard muscled one, framed in timelessness.

Laying me down Thomas kissed me on the forehead first, and down to my mouth and left not a part unloved of me this way, and I gave back of the feeling he gave me, my hands following his head, fingers through his hair, and his strong shoulders, aching in my being for all of him and I to be united, which bit by bit we were.

Even in the joy of it, I cried for Anna; not sadness but release, of all the cares of this world and into the caring of the lover…

Lover and beloved entwined, giving each into the other, and receiving gifts of pleasure and love in every wave our bodies moving together made.

*

"Oh my heart, oh my heart, where are you taking me? Oh my heart, oh my heart, for I know not the way."

"Oh my love, oh my Lord, never forsaking me; Oh my love, oh my Lord, you are carrying me home."

Later in the afternoon we joined Miriam and Peter with the three singers following after our portable bridal canopy being carried by Beor and Johannus; Mother and the others came behind too. Neither Thomas nor I would sit on the seat provided like an impromptu litter, and even eventually convinced Beor and Johannus that the canopy itself was just an encumbrance.

Beor rolled it up and carried it along as though it weighed nothing to him, which it probably didn't. I laughed at the thought and Thomas turned as my hand went to pull my scarf across by face.

"It is lighter than his staff for sure," I whispered to Thomas, but Beor heard as well and did a blacksmith's impersonation of an embarrassed blush, which made Thomas guffaw with laughter, and a tiny smile crept across Johannus' face as well.

"You are right my lady," smiled Beor, his recovery spurred on by Thomas laughter and set even firmer by Johannus' smirk, "but I reckon it could still be useful enough to floor these buffoons you have chosen here, before they even knew what hit them."

No-one doubted that, and we all knew an enemy would suffer badly from him. Thomas answered soberly. "Point taken, old friend, and I hope you don't need to use it, but if you should, none other could like you."

*

Matthias was crushed when he left Peter's house; devastated and horrified that this must in some way be all his fault.

It burned in his heart and brain; all clarity gone; just ashes, foul tasting, shaking what faith he had.

He tried to pray, in vain; because his mind was racing at the same time, in circles.

How could this have happened? Where was Kareem? Who would want to kill Anna? She probably had had the loveliest nature of the singers? Who could have?… and where was Kareem?

Kareem had been his oldest student, when Matthias used to teach the Egyptian mysteries, before he met John at the ford, and then the master Yeheshua.

He tried hard to focus his thoughts. Kareem was basically a good man; maybe ambitious, but only to make the best things happen. He couldn't be the one to have done that to Anna as the Roman Guard captain seemed to be suggesting. Could he? No, but Matthias had to find him first, to prove that.

He trudged back to the house they had been staying at, but it was all locked up now, not even a guard there.

He decided to look around outside anyway, just in case he could find a clue. There was not much to find amongst the trampling of the heavily studded sandals the Romans favoured. He searched around nevertheless, sure that someone or something else had been involved here.

There must be. He prayed he might find... something.

Anything, like this trampled bit of ground being significantly different? Just behind a bush by the outer wall. Nothing special, but maybe not like the other heavy trampling; just a small area somewhat imprinted on, smooth, with flattened grasses and shallow indents in the rough soil.

Nothing much, but a start, and he tried to feel what would make it like this. Someone had stood here for a long time probably by the look of the different prints; each about the same in depth but in slightly different places or angles; someone waiting a long time and changing their position slightly, but only one person, he was sure.

This couldn't be Kareem; the girls said he had locked the house from the inside and the only window unlocked was the one Ruth had opened.

But here clearly there had been another person, and somehow he must have killed or drugged or done something to Kareem to take him out.

He remembered the captain saying there was clear evidence of someone jumping from the window and falling over on the gravel, even a little blood from it; and they had escaped by opening the back gate from the inside and closing it again, but where Kareem had gone from there, they couldn't say. The road surface behind was hard and stony, not given to leaving tracks.

One thing Matthias could see immediately was that the window in question was clearly visible from this position behind the bush.

Maybe Kareem had been pushed out of the window, and his attacker got down less clumsily? Then dragged or carried him away. Possibly...

Matthias went out the back gate as many Roman and local guards had done before him, destroying any evidence. He couldn't see any blood, and this kept nagging at his mind.

'Why hadn't there been more blood on Anna's body or around it? He had seen her earlier, been shown her body as part of the questioning, to see how he would react. There had been some blood around the two patches where the knife had been thrust into her, but not nearly as much as would be expected.

"Poisoned like a huge snake bite," the captain had pointed out, and such an idea was easily dismissed until a horrible prickly feeling broke out all over Matthias and the hair stood out on the back of his neck.

'Apep,' he said half aloud, half in his thoughts. The enemy that could never be fully vanquished, because it was the darkness of ignorance itself. A soon as the light of knowing, of appreciation, of loving, dimmed; before the thought could even be forgotten, ignorance with its poisoned fangs of greed and hate would automatically be back. It was part of the Law.

He shivered. Was this really a snake, that snake, or something different? Clearly to his mind those were human prints on the ground by the bush; but what if the snake could transform itself from snake to human and back again?

705

His mind baulked at the thought.

If the poison was such that it congealed the blood inside - his brain forced Matthias down the road of logic - then it would kill and staunch the flow of blood out at the same time.

The horror of it could only be gathered in little bursts or Matthias would never have carried on. But it would make perfect sense for Apep to attack the Ennead singers; its ancient enemies; and Kareem more so.

And himself most of all, excepting Peter, thought Matthias, belatedly.

None of them were safe at all; and he had brought this upon them.

Yet wondered at it.

Surely, something more was needed, was involved, for this ancient evil to have manifested here and now? If indeed, that is what it was.

*

When we got out to the festival site, Beor set the canopy up again, unobtrusively to one side of the stage; and it being useful shade, we agreed to sit or stand under it together, enjoying the music that was playing.

It was a wild kind of music from a band of travelling folk that mostly kept away from towns but loved the beauty of the desert wilderness, finding their inspiration in the natural world and all the songs about it handed down through their tribe from ancient times.

My mind was transported back to a square in Antioch where just such a group of players had come and performed some strange but clearly meaningful dance or play. The memory made me look over towards Sarita and our eyes caught and locked, 'hadn't that been the very day she had met Kasver in the town temple of Aphrodite?'

She smiled and squeezed her husband's arm and he bent to kiss her face, just as Thomas, noticing… did to me.

No-one knew where from or where to these groups wandered, or when they would appear, but clearly they had been attracted here and Miriam and the Ennead singers were particularly interested, swaying and clapping in time near the front of the onlookers.

I abandoned the bridal seat and pulled Thomas over to where Miriam and the girls were entering into the spirit of the strange but lovely music, with its unusual rhythms and tones, pulling at some otherworldly part in me.

The 'new girl' Ruth in particular seemed very involved, and Miriam whispered in my ear that Ruth had met and sang with them before.

As she said this, one of the musicians beckoned and called to Ruth to join them and their own singers, who were waiting for their moment to join in.

With a glance to Miriam who smiled nodding, Ruth stepped into the circle joining the wild tribe singers as they began their song.

Her voice was lovely I saw and powerful too as I could distinguish it from the other women who made a fuss of her, dancing around her.

It was beautiful and one by one the other two singers and finally Miriam herself were called into the circle, to join in with Ruth. Miriam pulled me in with her.

Suddenly I had an insight; they were singing a kind of tribute to life and death and renewed life; the cycles in nature, and within my heart I knew it was for Anna, and my beloved Thomas, and me, and our little unborn Sarah, and all people. A tribute, a celebration and a keening, all together.

*

Seth was watching from a distance as the Ennead singers joined the wild tribe dancers in their music. He scowled, simultaneously feeling a hiss of foul displeasure shaking him like he might have shook a rug free of dust. Apep was always close, though Seth didn't realise it much of the time.

The unseen snake's anger was greater than Seth could control, hauling him, pushing him closer, urging him to take out his poisoned knives and attack.

This was not his chosen moment though, and before he got to the back of the crowd Apep's influence waned, being unable to endure the joy, enabling Seth to regain his composure, to slip into his ultra cautious mode, checking all around that he hadn't been noticed.

And with a shock he found himself looking across the edge of the crowd into the eyes of Matthias.

*

Much earlier Matthias had left the road, thinking what he would have done, where he would have gone if he was hauling a body with him.

Unlike the Roman guards and local officials, who were thinking of how a lone person would have run to get away quickest, Matthias realised the attacker would leave the open road as soon as possible, heading into the relative wilderness that bordered the other side.

He didn't find clear evidence of where to go but instead found himself wandering side to side, following his intuition further into the rocks and scrubby land.

Thorn and other bushes were scraping at his skin as he passed, careless of any pain.

Tears were pouring down his cheeks and anguish squeezed his heart. 'What had he done? What had happened?'

Before long he was a distance from the road amongst more broken terrain, more rocks and better places to hide; and places where he found the ground disturbed. He would have been tired carrying or dragging a body by now.

Suddenly the hair on the back of his head and neck was prickling hotly as he realised he was in the worst possible place; but wasn't truly ready to die.

Something told him this was the area, near to here, that he would find what he needed; Kareem.

He knew Kareem must be dead, but despite his fear Matthias tried his best to search where he might be; hidden, or maybe not.

And after seemingly aimless rambling, criss-crossing back and forth, around the back of some large rocks, he saw the shallow depression with many smaller rocks piled into it, and knew that was the spot.

Looking around fearfully Matthias searched for any other eyes watching him, but not feeling any immediate threat he quickly stepped over to the stones and started pulling a few away, enough to find a sleeve and a hand, that he knew to be Kareem's.

*

He hadn't stayed longer, grief could wait, but he knew now, and so would the Guardia soon enough when he directed them there; but first, first he had more to do, to try to stop any further outrage... further killings.

So, he had come to where the festival was starting its afternoon sessions and celebrations, drawn by some invisible connection with the perpetrator he was tracking; Apep or not.

All was quiet, except for the music and sometimes singing; people milling around the edges, getting drinks or going to relieve themselves, out beyond.

Matthias passed all around the back searching for who or what he did not know, but at least he had clear purpose now. He waited and watched.

He was just wondering whether this was the right thing to be doing when Miriam, Peter and the marriage celebration arrived to join in, and Matthias knew he needed to be here now; he stayed, watchful.

And then the wild tribe started their ancient dancesongs, chiming with the odd wildness Matthias was now feeling, setting his senses onto high alert.

Then suddenly he saw someone moving in from the side of the ground where there were small ridges and many rocks and bushes spreading out into the wild.

Moving with a purpose, Matthias stared as the man slowed and stood on the edge of the crowd, quite far from Matthias but close enough to make out his features.

There was something about him; something unappealing; and then he was looking around and looking straight at Matthias... And Matthias knew.

*

Seth thought for only a couple of moments before instinctively ducking down and away from the man he knew had recognised something, moving around the back of the crowd.

Matthias, Kareem's contact. He had glimpsed him and heard them talking from where he had been hidden outside Kareem's house. He knew it was him; and somehow Matthias knew too.

Ducking into the crowd rather than back away, Seth used one of his most practiced skills; to slip around and past people, through crowds, causing minimal disruption but being able to always maintain a fix on where his target, or as in this case, his pursuer was.

Matthias searched hard for the assassin, as he knew him to be, jumping up to try to see more, but he had no idea which direction he had gone.

He had moved quickly around to where the man been, but was no longer, or anywhere Matthias could see.

He scanned the ground behind, shading his eyes against the setting sun, but he hadn't gone back, he was pretty sure.

Seth had worked his way back around through the watching people, past

709

where Matthias had come from, who was searching mostly beyond, and the other way.

Seth kept his eyes fixed on Matthias and nearly made the mistake of leaving the crowd's edge as Matthias turned to search the outlying ground.

He was thinking that the angle of the sun would have hidden him, but he now waited a minute or two to be sure, edging around and away back towards the town all the time. Finally, he was satisfied, and keeping his eyes on Matthias made the quick break into cover and was away.

*

Matthias knew he had to do something different and went quickly around behind the back of the stage area, aiming for Peter, who was still listening and enjoying his singers joining in with Miriam and the wild tribe players.

Peter remembered Yeheshua telling him about such musicians from the desert places, in another country Peter didn't remember now; but he did feel the touch of the music and celebrated with it, even the keening.

Matthias came up next to him, reminding him instantly of Anna's dreadful loss.

"Peter, I have found him; both of them."

"What? Who?" responded his elder.

"Kareem is dead, and I have seen the one who did it. He is, was, here."

Peter took Matthias by the arm and reluctantly took them away from where the music was swirling and dancers following it; turning and turning, working round in a circle.

"Tell me everything," he said and as briefly and completely as he could Matthias did.

"We have to take this to the Guards," Peter said. "You have done extremely well," he added, hugging Matthias who was still very agitated. "Now we must get it finished."

Ruth had been the one to first tell Anna about Miriam's singing, back in Jericho.

She hadn't been one of Kareem's Ennead, but she had a talent for singing and picking up and learning different styles and words, such as when she had met the wild tribe people, out beyond Jordan's ford.

Anna had recognised her talent and brought her to meet Kareem, who agreed she could be an excellent backup for any of the singers, and so she had come up with them but would have done anyway, excited to be there and loving Miriam's singing, many of whose songs she already knew by heart.

Now Anna was gone, and Ruth had been there, but because she had kept her head, she had probably saved Melanie and Hirani as well as herself. She didn't believe though that Kareem had any part in it; it wasn't him she had seen in her room.

It was still too raw to think about. She hadn't been able to tell the guards properly, who had already made their minds up anyway, about Kareem.

Peter had been amazing with all three of the singers, 'a proper rock' she thought, laughing at the known reference.

He was still just being there for them, nothing if not a wall of solid kindness.

She looked across the singers to see him talking with Matthias, nodding and trying to calm the other man down, who was clearly agitated.

Miriam had noticed as well and she took Ruth's hand to spin her round again as they were paired up in the dancing circle, and Ruth felt the tensions run from her, sending once more her sweet-sour keening cry into the evening sky, of love and loss and desire too, to become whole again.

Mourning Anna was what she needed so much to do, and Miriam knew; and together they sang to the beat of the drummers, the song of the wild night wind.

Peter came over to them when they finally came out of the circle, the sun having slipped down below the horizon.

He took Miriam aside and explained what Matthias had done and discovered, and he called Habban over to tell him too, as he understood the captain had reported such an assassin earlier to the Guards; but no one had then known his target. Now they did it seemed.

Ruth took her cloak from Hirani as Peter concluded what he thought needed to be done. He went off to talk privately with Thomas, whilst Miriam came back to her and the other two girls, telling them what they had decided.

"If you agree to this Melanie, Hirani, you shall stay with Peter and his wife till this is all over, sooner than later hopefully. Ruth, would you be agreeable to come and stay at my house for tonight at least?"

Ruth nodded, surprised and pleased; Miriam continued, "There are some special songs I would like to tell you of, that you would like as well, I think.

Can you read and write at all?"

"Yes, a bit, I can," Ruth said blushing, never liking to revealing that.

"Wonderful, because I have a little scroll I would like to give you; from Magdalene too; and for Anna…"

*

Thomas listened to Peter's tale, nodding soberly and frowning through much of it.

He would try to keep as much of it as possible from Mary, but would have to share what he could he realised.

His plan to take her tonight to the villa where Sarita and Kasver were, with the sea captains having taken rooms there too, was still best he thought. Susannah had given him her suite there because she was staying at the house now.

It was very secure in itself, and had the Roman guards next door too. They were on high alert now and would be sending a guard overnight for both Miriam's and Peter's houses, he was sure.

"We shall go back to Miriam's house now," he said, and make sure all the arrangements are good, before riding to the villas. See you tomorrow then."

Peter had thought he might say something about Habban and the call to go to King Gondaphares, but he knew in his heart this was not for him to say, he had best keep his own council and make sure that the singers would be safe.

*

CHAPTER 38.

Seth made off into the night but in doing so found himself in the maw of Apep, alone in the blank cold darkness, no strength to resist, even as it had been the night before.

Matthias went to the combined guardia and told them he had found the body of Kareem and seen who he thought was the assassin at the festival, ready to strike at them again. It was too late to take them to the body now but he begged the captain for a guard at Peter's house where the singers were now staying, and the captain agreed.

He had decided the festival must be wound up tomorrow; the killer flushed out.

Seth was drawn inevitably towards Peter's house, being able to beat the snake back out of his mind as he got closer, one half of him at least. It seemed that there were people already there, one of who was Beor.

Seth watched, trying to block out snake thoughts urging him to destroy Peter and his household first, and then move on to Miriam. Then Matthias appeared with a Roman guard, clearly preparing for a night siege.

Shutting out the hissing, Seth also realised that Matthias was now sensitised to his face, his appearance, his presence; it would be doubly hard to get past him; clearly maddened by what Apep had done to Kareem, and Anna.

There were three others that could recognise him clearly. Miriam, the one called Magdalene and their 'sort of' guard Johannus, all of whom had seen him and escaped from him, at the inn ambush.

Unlike with Matthias though, things had become personal about Johannus, the one who had tried to baulk the plan to take Yeheshua. He knew about that and considered him to be a rank nuisance, deserving to be snuffed out.

Even as he thought this, Beor came out and started talking to the guard who pointed a direction out to him and Beor set off quickly, passing perilously close to Seth's hiding place.

He was one to be avoided, that one. He had noticed that the staff he often carried was not wooden; it held an unhealthy sense of steely power in the blacksmith's hands.

He stayed for several minutes before moving from his position, careful as ever that no one would see him or where he went, guessing that Beor had gone to the Roman barrack house, to accompany another sentry to the other house. He had to think that.

He smiled to himself; his plan had been long in the making, though opportunistic by necessity. Experience told him that his opportunity would come, and he just needed to be ready to take it.

His main problem at this point was the snake itself, clouding his thoughts.

His weapon was complete focus on Miriam; his and only his.

Everyone else would be extras, on the side, though he did admit to himself there would be a certain satisfaction in killing Johannus on the way in; the weakest link.

Back up near the main road, Seth heard the 'clip, clip' of the Roman legionnaire's sandals long before he saw him and Beor go past the side track he was hiding down.

Quietly, gently he sneaked down to the road and crossed over to another passage on the other side. He knew every part of these ways now like the hairs on the back of his fingers, and this would lead him on a similar course, moving swiftly and invisibly through the dark, around towards Miriam's house.

It was no longer just about wiping her out of history, though that would be most gratifying. In a kind of desperation, he plainly saw that she was his only way to escape the ruinous Apep.

Its company had finally sickened him beyond even the depravity of his own thoughts.

His thoughts; so much more exciting than those of ignorance and greed.

But by gaining Miriam, forcing what he wanted from her, Seth would gain immortality, and that was what he gave himself to, admitting nothing else.

Approaching the road again up the path he had selected, suddenly he heard a galloping horse.

He tensed, feeling the coiling of the snake about him, for it had not gone anywhere, was just was biding its time… but now was angry, vengeful, hating, and Seth was coiled too.

'Strike it; ssstrike now!!' But it was too late, even if Seth had wanted.

With a clatter of hooves and sharp rush of wind the beast was past, on back up the road.

It had been beautiful, the wild dance, the sounds, the notes that came from deep within me, released as song, full of feeling. I didn't want it to end.

I could see that little fires were being lit here and there around the edge of the site, because the sun had finally sunk down.

Thomas and Miriam came and took me, words no longer needed.

Thomas laid a shawl around my shoulders and then his arm around me too, pulling me into his chest. And mine slipped around his waist as we made our way out and back along the track with so many others, in a kind of human river.

I knew that I didn't have him for very long but now was savouring every moment, as I sensed he was too.

Knew he had to go, that he must follow to where he was called to go, and I couldn't resent the fact.

He would be back, but only for a short time before he would have to go again. I knew this but didn't know exactly how I did; but it helped. The time we had would always be just enough; if I could trust.

Back at the house Thomas surprised me that he had arranged somewhere else to take me that night; to celebrate our new status.

I collected the few things I would need and spent a few minutes looking at all the lovely little touches that my friends had done for me, for us; quickly wrote a note of heartfelt thanks on a tablet, picked up my reed bag and, a little reluctantly, left Miriam and Yeheshua's room.

Thomas took my bag and we went out the front door where our remaining guests were waiting to see us off on our new journey, and I was touched once again at the kindness shown, soft-skipping past them to where Johannus was holding the bridle of Meg.

To the side I noticed that Beor and a Roman guard were there as well.

Thomas helped me up into the saddle and quickly mounted himself behind me, allowing me to hold my bag whilst he held onto me and the reins as well.

Gently he nudged Meg in the sides and we started off to waves and cheers from everyone and I waved back, laughing.

Thomas urged Meg forward into a trot and she responded, going gently down the road until we came to the turning for the road that went out to the villa.

Thomas pulled her to go that way but she became a little skittish which I knew was most unlike her. I leaned forward and patted her neck, whispering in her ear, "come on Meg girl, it's alright."

Her eyes turned, showing white, but Thomas calmed her. "You can run if you want to girl," he said.

She did it seemed, quickly getting into a canter down the softer verge, then all of a sudden verging into the hardened middle, and with a clattering of hooves, galloped for all she was worth until she felt that the danger was past, slowing back down to a fast trot instead.

"Well done girl," said Thomas, and I had to agree; whatever had spooked her was gone, it felt a whole lot better now.

We arrived at the villa feeling happy but sobered by the fright; I think we both were.

There was a Roman guard on the gate and beside him stood Habban, still with his ceremonial looking sword at his side.

He smiled broadly and with a gesture of greeting swept the gates open for us.

Thomas jumped down and extended a hand back up to me. I took it though I didn't need help and enjoyed the little jump to make him catch me.

Habban laughed and took the reins from Thomas. "Her stall is ready, next to Susannah's horse. I'll take her there; it isn't far, just round the side." Then, "and I think you know where your apartment is," he added adroitly.

"Thank you, captain," Thomas answered, taking me in his arms and sweeping me off my feet, to carry me into the building.

I was most unused to anything like this and just held onto him, feeling his strength sending shivers through me.

Quickly he made our way through the lamp lit hall and we were at the door we needed, Thomas pushing the door open with his back.

"Don't worry," he said, picking up my thought on how easy it was to get inside. "The front door is the only way in; the back way is kept bolted on the inside and all the windows have secure bars as well as shutters. I have checked it all out," and he bolted our door as he set me down.

Susannah must have done some extra work, making it welcoming like coming home, but I didn't have much chance to take it in because Thomas had lifted me up again to carry me through and lay me gently down on a big bed in the softly painted bedroom, where someone had already lit another lamp.

Our space; always. Any room where we could be together; just us.

We were married. We had all our lives as man and wife, whatever else we did as well. And I wanted to luxuriate in the knowledge, because the awful events of last night highlighted the preciousness of this one.

We kissed and allowed ourselves to explore being as one, in two people. Experience the giving and receiving, flowing between us.

"I shall never let you go, my love," I said. "Even though we might be at the furthest ends of the earth from one another."

He looked at me and we both knew this could be very real.

"We shall be closer than this even, because we shall each be doing the work of our Lord, strengthening this bond beyond what anything else could."

"We shall," said Thomas. "That is how I can give myself completely. And is what I have seen also between the master and Miriam. The eternal, expressed in living moments."

We said no more, not wishing to waste any of the precious time we were being given, to make our presence felt in each other's being; making indelible impressions to be stored in our hearts.

*

Later, when we had eaten the tasty bread and drunk the fine wine left for us and bathed our bodies in the small hypocaust heated pool the villa had for guests, in the Roman way, we returned to our rooms, relaxed and happy.

Somewhere at the back of both our minds though I knew there was the issue of the call to go to King Gondaphares. Strangely it had been John that had mentioned something of it to me, and I had somehow gathered the rest.

Then of course I had dreamt of Yeheshua just last night… telling me what?

I couldn't quite recall but I would never ignore his words, even from a dream.

Knew it was somewhere in Thomas' thoughts too, for John had said he knew and had refused to go.

It mustn't lie between us; must be the thing that made us whole. "He must do the work set out for him, Mary" the Master had said, "and only you can bring him to it."

I held his hand and led him back to the bed.

"Lie on your tummy my husband, and I will give you what I was trained to do, as Astarte-Aphrodite's priestess."

CHAPTER 40.

Seth wandered between the two houses, Miriam's and Peter's, keeping his eye out for their weaknesses and strengths, knowing their rhythms and what they did, better than they did.

Knew the exact time that the Roman guard at Peter's house would cave in to sleep, could count him out and did.

Knew how well the Nabatean priestess kept her watch, always bringing a drink or conversation to the guard placed outside, just when he needed it; to be of continuing use, sitting at the place Beor and Johannus did, mostly out of sight.

Knew the fierce determination of Matthias who had seen the guard sleeping but would not himself succumb this night, remembering his friends who Apep and Seth together had devoured.

Knew how much the snake wanted to destroy Simon Peter's house and guests, but Seth also knew that Peter's brother Andrew had arrived late in the evening, making the task harder still with the three of them.

And knew how close the snake could get before feeling the need to slide away, which Seth used carefully to his advantage.

Knew that Beor was awake and about, sometimes inside one house and sometimes outside talking to the guard, swapping stories before going on a tour, a walk on the streets; and that was most dangerous for Seth.

Had to know where he was and what he was doing, always at a good distance, using his new detailed knowledge of the neighbourhood.

Saw Beor find the sleeping guard at Peter's house and talk to Matthias instead, but only for a while.

Noticed that the blacksmith was also getting tired, but Seth knew he would see the job through to the morning light and smiled; Beor would finish then.

Seth felt no such need for sleep; had taken his in the middle of the day before, and didn't need more.

Knew that there would come a point when they felt they had done the night, the day was come, Beor would go and the Roman guards with him, even Matthias and the Nabatean woman would relax a bit, get some rest.

Knew there would come a time to strike, when the weakness showed; always did.

*

He revelled and excelled in deviousness; admired deviation to excess.

They were the tools of his masterpieces, and he was the yet uncrowned master.

Was there a limit to this power? No, for there were always more things that could be twisted to need; every bit of knowing used to his ends; and he ever sought those.

Apep was opposite, sought to drain power, knowledge; everything getting engulfed, into the dark pain of ignorance.

Together there was nothing they could not challenge and overcome.

When the brightness grew too great, the monstrous Apep hid in the dark of unknowing, resorting to people's fear of what might be there.

The fear that could never quite be removed from ever restless minds, for the snake laid in wait just behind their thoughts.

And when preparedness was too steady for cleverness to disturb, Seth could resort to pure directed hate, like the nails to drive through flesh and bone in a crucifixion…

Or his poisoned knives to drive the pain and death home just the same; and he had a fifth one with him now, one of those that both paralysed and opened the victim's mind to his,

For Miriam, when the others were rid of.

*

CHAPTER 41.

The night of loving surpassed anything I could have hoped or dreamt of, leaving me as a pile of sleepy smiles, laughing inwardly.

And understandung what real peace was like, spread through my entire universe.

We had climbed our hill together, ignored all signposts to go the other way, any way other than to ourselves… doubly, magically singular, yet each containing everything.

How could that be? Yet the masters had always said it was so…

'Know thyself'

The moon had shined on us and the stars were our canopy.

And we knew the way up the hill to join them, and Yeheshua and Miriam and Mother Mary and all the lights that had and were always shining in this world, as Love and Kindness.

Thomas pulled a pillow round and the cover back, and suddenly sprang from the bed.

"I have to go," he said, wide awake and energised. "Something is happening that must be stopped."

'He must come now,' our Lord's words echoed in me. 'He must come with Habban, Mary; to where his work lies.'

I nodded rather sleepily, ready to do what was needed.

But this urgency was for now… and I started, trying to catch up with it.

Not waiting for anything other than grabbing his outer robe, Thomas ran out of our room. I thought he was heading out of the building, but am not sure why.

I went to a window undoing the shutter and throwing it open, in time to catch sight of Thomas leading Meg from her stable and hoisting himself onto her unsaddled back.

"Thomas," I called out and he looked for me, waving back, "I must go… now," he said, the urgency carrying back to me across the yard.

*

Seth did make time to follow where Mary and Thomas had gone; out to the villa and Guardia barracks; he went in the early hours before the dawn.

It was part of what he needed to know; the others; what was happening, and he had plenty of time through the night to check them out; he never knew what chance might give and it helped keep him focussed, out of the grasp of the snake's darkness.

He didn't go close in; the Roman Guardia had lit torches and placed a sentry, close to the gated entrance of the villa whose outer wall was topped with unpleasant looking spikes.

From a distance he was just able to make out the villa's inner entrance, 'where Magdalene would be', hissed Apep; but Thomas too, and there would be someone on watch tonight, able to rouse the guards next door if needed.

Seth's mind in Apep's dead eye saw the captain with his sword drawn, ready.

He didn't stay but slipped gliding back round to Peter's house and it's sleeping guard, needing to attack, now… in the darkest hour of pre-dawn.

Circled closer in, gnawing hunger pulling him; into the teeth of the courage of the humans inside, driving darkness away. Back… giving Seth some control again.

He watched the house and after a long while was pretty sure Beor was not one of those inside.

Seth was worried by Beor who liked to keep active, moving about. He might well be on his way here at any time, and the light was almost beginning to come up.

He turned and scanned every detail of the approaches before slipping silently and almost invisible out onto the footpath again, searching about whilst he made his way towards Miriam's house, keeping well hidden, moving from viewpoint to viewpoint quickly, quietly, always ready to run or attack, knowing every place to hide or flee.

He saw Beor coming without the big blacksmith having any idea, and Seth melted away along a side path, round onto the road behind where Beor had come from.

For a long moment he had wanted to kill, coming at Beor from behind but even Apep was wary of that spear-like staff, so similar to what Set himself had used, in the days of his ancient power.

Seth struggled for his life, desperately seeking the intensity of focus on his own desires, separating him a fraction from this nightmare.

Was it his imagination or were the circling vultures of his mind becoming reluctant, to swoop down for his moment of approaching victory?

Was weakness seeping into him? Just as when Isis had tricked him into pity?

Not this time; never. He steeled himself against any of Miriam's Isis wiles, seeing now how even just hearing her singing had softened him. He seethed inwardly that this could be.

He glimpsed a vision of the game, the enmity between him and Horus and Osiris, no, Thomas and Yeheshua stretching back through time. A vision such as Isis gave. Miriam again; he spat.

Of course he wanted her for his own, but he would make her pay with everything she had finally, and nothing would change that. Pay for the millennia of hatred and humiliation heaped on him.

Reinstated. Ready. Set in his mind, he waited patiently again at the place down the road from where he could gradually see the Roman guard in the growing light, nodding and jerking back to semi-wakefullness, again and then again.

This was his time, nearly, nearly, and here was Beor returning for the handover.

*

Johannus enjoyed the morning walk to the Residence, feeling the glory of a new day, the birds, their song, everything adding to the feeling. Mary's wedding and the singing with the wild tribe had gone a long way to blotting out the other terrible things that had happened.

Reaching the house, he found Beor chatting with the Roman guard and Johannus asked them if they would like a drink, as he was going inside anyway to do a check of everyone about before he took over from Beor.

Most people seemed to have had or were having breakfast. Susannah was in the kitchen where he begged three cups of tea. Mother and Miriam were in the front room as were John and the new singer Ruth too. Mary and Lazarus were in the back courtyard.

Finally, Yresmin was sitting on the lower steps of the stairs, obviously very tired and Johannus said her she should get some rest. "Have my bed," said Susannah bringing out a tray with three steaming cups for Johannus.

Thanking Susannah, he took the drinks out the side door to Beor and Julius, the guard. They were clearly tired having been up all night and Johannus left them to their drinks for a couple of minutes, taking a tour of the outside of the front, appearing nonchalant but shooting sharp glances in every direction he had identified as being from where a possible threat might come.

"Has it been a quiet night?" he asked, rejoining the two who had been enjoying the last of their mint teas.

"I suppose so," the big blacksmith answered, "quiet but very tense, at least in my view."

Julius was nodding, exhausted. "Come friend," said Beor, "I am walking your way. Johannus, be careful won't you," he was unusually serious, talking low, no joking. "I don't think this is over yet, by any means."

Beor noticed Peter and Matthius in the distance, coming along with the two singers. He urged Julius on, feeling the need to go and meet them.

Striding almost jauntily ahead Beor met the apostles with a cheery "good morning", very aware that the two had taken turns in staying up through the night with Peter's brother Andrew.

He scanned the roadside, unaware he was almost opposite Seth's hiding place. Maybe he felt something, just wanted to see this last duty through. "Well met," he said, "the household will be glad to see you today. Ruth is up already and has been practicing with Miriam," he said to the two young women following.

He walked a few paces back with the little group and, when satisfied again, turned around to catch up with Julius, looking hard all around... Seth held his breath, and then Beor had gone.

Johannus watched the senior apostle's company approach, a little weary looking and he took a few paces out onto the avenue to greet them.

"Good morning friend Johannus," said Peter taking and leaning rather on the younger man's arm as they turned towards the side door to the house. "It has been a long night, but we have joined a new day."

Johannus allowed Peter to lead him into the house, and he held the door open for Melanie and Hirani too, ushering them through the hall to join Mother and Miriam in the front room.

Closing the door, he turned back to go outside... just as Seth slipped in the side entrance, seizing his moment which he had followed, unfolding from down the way, moving in very swiftly.

Johannus saw the specialist knives, one held in either hand; saw the intense look in Seth's sallow bearded face, the surprisingly slight build and easy balance; but most of all he recognised who the intruder was, from the inn on the road to Galilee; and the man sneaking away in the street in Jericho those months ago. A very dangerous and unpleasant adversary.

Seth didn't hesitate, didn't give Johannus a chance to snatch up a weapon or shout for help. He dived quickly forward, leading with the knife in his right hand, bringing it around in a scything curve, up under the guard of the startled Johannus.

Johannus parried, aiming a chop at Seth's swiftly moving forearm, managing a glancing blow, trying to grab Seth's wrist, whilst also keeping an eye on the other knife, drawn back, ready for a low jabbing blow.

The smaller knife in Seth's right hand was highly poisoned but the most manoeuvrable, and being twisted against grasping fingers it found its mark, slicing across Johannus' left hip, knocking him backwards as much by the shock as the power of the rush.

Seth stood over the half-fallen guard, driving his knee viciously into Johannus solar plexus, laughing. "You are dying now anyway..." he said.

Somehow Johannus was still holding his right wrist, so Seth pushed down on him with his knee again, bringing the other dagger to bear over Johannus' flailing right arm. "Let me put you out of your little misery," he gloated.

Johannus looked at his attacker, his death, and felt only that he must some-how warn Miriam, mother and the others. He had tried to shout but only managed a wheezing grunt because of the wind having been knocked out of him.

He breathed hard, feeling the poison in his left hip, the cold spreading there .. and for a moment Seth was panting too, and their eyes locked.

Gone was all the history, just this bare moment, joined in their focus on Miriam, one to protect, the other to attack; opposite sides of the same coin.

Left hand knife poised to strike, Seth's stare pierced Johannus gaze, finding a soul that mirrored his, not so very different, not the fear he sought.

Johannus broke it, his eyes flicking away as Seth brought the killing stroke down… but another hand held his tighter, dragging it away as he was jerked backwards and the most poisoned knife twisted in its path, missing its aim and plunged deep into Seth's own stomach flesh instead.

Thomas dragged Seth single-handedly off the sprawled Johannus and threw him across the room, the dagger still sticking from his side.

Thomas had ridden Meg down the beaten earth track, robe flapping about him, bare heels digging into her barrel body.

He passed a startled looking Beor and Roman guard, scattering them, but knew that he dare not stop; riding hard, and rounding the last bend, joining the avenue, he knew why…

Down the way he saw a sinister figure scuttling across the road towards the house, too far for him to catch him but he knew he must try.

Urging Meg to go faster they careered up the softer grass verge and pulling as best he could on her mane to slow her down again, Thomas slid off her back in front of the path going down beside the house. There was no one there; the side door was open.

Heedless of his bare feet on the sharp stones Thomas gained the entrance to see a struggle happening inside… an attacker laying into a fallen Johannus, raising a knife to strike!

Thomas crossed the hall in two lunging strides, managing to grasp the hand that held the descending knife at the wrist, pulling it sharply back, feeling it slice into Seth's body even as Thomas yanked him with all his might backwards with his other arm, fingers clenched into the robe at his neck.

*

Johannus lay back against the wall, feeling the cold darkness penetrating his being, disjointedly wondering whether he could ever get to be with Rebecca, as the poisons started to take hold of his systems.

Thomas looked between Johannus and his attacker, whose open eyes stared from a contorted, rictus smiling face, chest heaving but otherwise unmoving, and Thomas was momentarily uncertain of what to do.

The knife that had cut Johannus was lying on the floor and Thomas bent to pick it up, smelling the blade-tip, realising it was a poisoned weapon, just as Miriam burst through from the front room…

Miriam quickly realised what had happened, dropping down beside Johannus looking for the wound, gently lifting his one hand that was clasped over the hurt.

Seth had clamped his wild undying gaze on her and Thomas approached him wondering whether he should pull the other knife from him, or what? Surely, he should be dead or dying by the way the knife was plunged deep into his body.

But somehow, he seemed to be clinging on, fixated.

Miriam glanced at Thomas and shook her head. "Leave him," she said, without explanation, closing her eyes and placing her hands on the near unconscious Johannus; one on the back of his neck and the other on the purple-black skin around the wound itself.

*

725

Johannus was entering the cold dark sea, seeking to let go from pain, to sleep, when a sudden warm wave flowed into him and a dolphin splash of phosphorescence sparkled in his darkness.

His heart beat loudly in his ears as his sight followed the stream of light and the path of the marvellous creature that had entered his passage into deathly darkness.

Even as he watched another stream of light detached from his thoughts, saying 'be grateful you are still alive'. The voice of Kaella from a mermaid diving after the porpoise.

And the darkness wavered and thrashed and sought to outrun the light that pursued it through the depths.

Suddenly something awful out there turned and reared up, something blacker than darkness itself, except for one glowing red eye, enough to light the huge fangs of its poisonous mouth.

Miriam stood where the dolphin stopped and held up her hand, holding forth the sigil of the master of the age, flaring into such a brightness that directed itself directly at and into the one glowing eye of the monstrous snake.

The eye's explosion threw shock waves through all of Johannus and the deadness itself fell away into the depths, wriggling out of his fading vision, as the mermaid Kaella seemed to slap at him with her tail "he will be fine, just needs to sleep."

*

Mother had come to Miriam and was holding her in her arms, exhausted as she clearly was.

Thomas had felt something of the invisible struggle that had just occurred and watched as Seth had suddenly arched back and collapsed, a broken rag, lifeless.

'Thank God Almighty' he mouthed silently, never having seen such living unnaturalness, finally extinguished.

CHAPTER 43.

I went and washed and quickly dressed, I knew what I had to do.

There was a small papyrus roll, ink and a stylus supplied in the apartment.

I sat down, dipping the stylus in the ink and flattened out the paper, writing down the words that had been given me in my dream-vision, just exactly as he had said, rolled it up, tied the ribbon and without delay went down into the main hall.

Habban and Pharos were both already eating breakfast and by the look of them neither had had a full amount of sleep.

"Very good morning, I hope you both slept well," I said with a broad smile. "I am going over to the house now; Thomas has already left."

I waved away their protests that I must stay for breakfast first. "This matter does concern you though, Captain Habban. I would like you to read this whilst I take some bread and dried fruit, to eat on the way."

The wording was short and to the point, and in a matter of seconds Habban was on his feet and reaching for his coat and sword belt, at the peg rack.

"Pharos, come quickly," he said to my captain, and we all raised eyebrows and shrugged, laughing, as Pharos rolled up the parchment; he had read it too.

Just as we were leaving Beor arrived, looking very concerned, but obviously relieved to see that I was all right. "Thomas galloped past," he said, by way of explanation, "barefoot and mostly undressed. Didn't stop either. I am worried."

"Where was he headed?" asked Habban quickly, pointedly.

"To the house I would say... that way, and he hadn't far to go at the speed he was doing. I thought I better find out what he was riding from though; I had not long come from the house myself."

"Come on then," I said. "We are going back there if you want to come? You can tell us all that has been happening."

It didn't seem to take long to get to the house with Beor telling us all he could; that the night had been uneventful but with a great tension in it, it seemed to him. Peter had Andrew, Matthias and two of the singers staying with him; and he shot me a glance, not wanting to upset me, I knew, by mentioning what had happened to Anna.

"Go on," I said.

He described how the Roman guards had been at both houses but were affected by great drowsiness. He had felt it himself but all were very determined, Matthias probably most of all. And of course, Yresmin was completely unaffected; he laughed, "tougher than any man I know that one," he said.

"Including you two," he said jokingly at Pharos and Habban, who laughed with him.

"Still," he said, "there was the feeling that something was afoot, some mischief; but I wasn't able to put my staff to it."

727

When we got to the house, we found out just what that mischief had been.

All of the household, excepting Miriam and Johannus who were resting upstairs, were discussing the dead body in the side hall, along with Peter Matthias and the singers too.

They were talking about him as one who had been one of Kareem's students, particularly a friend of Anna's. They were shocked.

I was too, because I recognised him immediately, from somewhere completely different.

He had been one of the leaders of those at the inn, who had tried to ambush and capture us, Miriam in particular, when Miriam, Johannus and myself had been returning from Qadesh to Yeheshua, here; only a few months ago.

It seemed like lifetimes away; and for this man it truly was… and I could not say I was sorry.

"I know him; he is a murderer and many other things. How did he come to be here?"

"We don't kn..know," stammered Matthias. "He seems to have been a friend of these singers, but wasn't meant to have any part of this."

"Of what?" I asked, grimly. "Not meant to have had any part of what?"

"Singing," whispered Matthias, clearly distraught.

"This man attacked Johannus," said Thomas, "cutting him with a poisoned knife. I was lucky to get here just before he used his second knife, and dragged him off. He stabbed himself in the process, and eventually died…

when Miriam came and somehow staunched the effects of the poison in Johannus."

"Johannus is all right?" I asked, worried. "And Miriam?"

The man had probably been deeply involved in everything against Yeheshua, and now Miriam too, I thought. It had got obsessively personal.

At this Thomas glanced over at Matthias and so did I. He had turned pale grey.

"He is the same man that followed us to your house, Mary," said Habban, "and tried to follow us to your brother's. He was carrying knives then too."

"He had five here," said mother quietly, "it looks as though he was going to kill as many as he could. Amazing what Johannus and you saved us from, Thomas"

"That Miriam has…" Thomas started, but syopped. realising that Miriam had quietly come downstairs.

She walked over to mother and me, greeting me with a great hug, whilst mother turned and spoke out. "Someone should go and tell the Guardia."

"I'll go," said the indefatigable Beor; then Pharos, "I'll come with you," for Habban had stepped forward too. "You are needed here," Pharos added to the ever willing captain.

Miriam turned directly to face the still blanched Matthias, and Peter moved closer to support him.

"The problem is opposite to what you think," she said, mostly to Peter. "In fact, there are no real problems, only the solutions," and turning again to Matthias said, "You shall be an example… a beautifully shining example," she said, bringing compassion to rain down upon his fearfulness.

"You shall not teach or preach or have any need to organise," she said, glancing squarely at Peter. "You will not need to speak even. Silence will be your dearest companion, for you will be so completely engaged in practicing the teaching that he gave to you; inside."

"This is your mission Matthias, to be that which you are… made already," she paused; "and I have a gift for you in this as well."

She picked out from a fold in her robe one of the scrolls we had written; it must have been the last one, and gave it to him.

"This is especially for you; I don't think you were there;" and she left her hand on his arm when he took it. "When the time comes that you laugh, and laugh so much that you cry… and cry out all the pain with that pure laughter; then, then that will be the time when you will be able to answer any question people will put to you, though you have sought them not."

She turned again to Peter. "We are not the designers or architects, dear brother; at best we can make our hands competent to do some labouring."

"It is in the hearts of humans everywhere that the kingdom lies, has always been and will always be."

"If we can uncover some of the dust and dirt that has been laid over ours, then others can do the same?"

"Each person is a kingdom. We must never try to create a counterfeit; never."

"I have my task to be me, as completely as I can; just as you have yours to be you, as you really are."

"And the master always comes to show us how. Has and always will. Again, and again."

"Again, and again. Different ways, different times but always to the heart of things, of life."

Peter bowed his head and I think would have knelt before her had Miriam not stepped forward and grasped him in a rough embrace. I think he cried, but Miriam released him and turned to me.

"His message of hope will be taken to the furthest corners of the world, that we can reach, for everyone and not some kabal. In that hope we go forward into this new day, every new day."

"And I think we have some contractual business to do as well; is that not so beloved?" she said, not brusquely but quickly as though if she delayed a second her courage might have failed her.

Her eyes locked with mine and I saw her tears.

I was shocked for a second and then realised I was holding the little papyrus roll.

"Thomas, you need this," she said as I handed it gently to her; and undoing

729

the ribbons she went over to the desk in the corner; Yeheshua's desk; Thomas and I following.

She opened a drawer and took a seal-ring from the very back together with a flat little box.

Opening the tight-fitting lid Miriam pushed the seal-ring down into the red-inked pad inside and then transferred it to the papyrus, rolling the seal around, printing YHShVH in a tight circle (Yod He Shin Vau He).

"There," she said showing the paper to Thomas, squeezing his arm. "You are given over into the keeping of Captain Habban," who she beckoned over.

I had written that as his wife I gave Thomas over into the safe keeping of Captain Habban, to take to the Kingdom of Gondaphares, on the strict understanding that Habban was also responsible for bringing him safely back again, Almighty willing.

And Miriam had sealed the promise note in Yeheshua's name, with his personal seal.

Captain Habban took out his sword and went down on one knee in front of Miriam. "I swear on my sword and my honour to you, that I will carry out all that is written here."

Thomas was completely dumbstruck as the captain got up and took him by the arm, saying "It will be a fine adventure sir," but Thomas was looking only at me.

"It has to be, beloved. We have to trust our master's word. I cannot live if we do not."

He took me in his arms and kissed me deeply, there in front of everyone, oblivious to them.

*

CHAPTER 44.

I feel overcome with riches; connected into everything and complete in ways I cannot express or could have known to have wanted.

Thomas and I stayed on at the house to wait for Johannus to recover, whilst most others went out to join the last day of the festival.

What Miriam hadn't said immediately but which I already knew, was that she was also going East with Thomas and Captain Habban...

And that Yresmin would join her as well, travelling with Sella and Indy; at least as far as Yresmin's original home, inland from the port of Jeddah.

Miriam had waited till all the fuss over Thomas and myself had calmed down, and Peter was the one she had addressed.

"There are people and places that our Lord Yeheshua told me of Peter, that I want to take his message to again; in the lands of the East. And as Captain Habban and Thomas going that way, this is the time."

Peter hadn't known quite how to respond.

Up until recently he would have been relieved, but things had changed, he had changed.

"More than anything, I ask you to support our dear sister Magdalene in all the work she will be doing. Thomas will obviously be away for a while, and she with his baby...

The fact that Thomas and I were now married had changed everything, and him being away on the request of King Gondaphares was a kind of political coup for us Christines; especially with Pilate and his legate having taken positive interest in Habban's quest.

Peter smiled and hugged me with genuine warmth, and I knew I would have his support for what I so much wanted to do here in Galilee; and in who knows where else this would take us.

All had changed for Thomas with Miriam going into the East too.

I don't think he could have articulated his feelings, but I knew. If it had been me going with Miriam, I would have felt uplifted and blessed, and I felt that for him, with him; it made me so happy.

Miriam had come over to where I was sitting with mother, the three of us again. I rose and she hugged me, knowing that so much must be churning around inside me, despite my knowing this was coming.

"Dearest, there is one thing that I have seen in you," she said, "that I cannot take any credit for; just a gift we share."

I knew what she was talking about, for not only had I been having the vision dreams, but there was my waking vision of Anna and her coming and going out through me at her end.

"It is sometimes called 'far-seeing', but it is more 'vital' than that. But because of this in you, and it may be to do with Sarah too, I think we shall be closer than ever, despite the great distances that may come between us."

As if in answer to this there came to my mind a picture of my daughter Sarah and myself travelling to a distant land, arriving on a different shore, shipwrecked but living, and Lazarus and his sisters too.

"Ahh yes."

More came to me as well, that Miriam herself was carrying Yeheshua's son. "I don't think anything can come between us, or Thomas either; I am so happy."

Mother joined in. "There are many, many lands and places for his disciples to get to; once we know and trust ourselves a little more." Then adding, "I really like Sarita and Kasver, Mary. With everything they said that Thomas has achieved in Antioch, she says you shall be going back up there sometime?"

"Yes, I am hoping to, soon." There was a pause and I knew "And if you and John might like to come as well, that would give me great joy, and them too I know."

She beamed and I felt how much of a staunch ally and friend I had in her. And more; so much, much more.

Miriam got up. "I must go and seek out Ruth, for I have promised her that we shall go and sing with the wild tribe again. She has a great talent you know."

"She has, but not to replace you," I said.

She smiled and came back at me, with a request. "I am hoping you and Peter will take her under your patronage; and maybe could travel a bit as well? It would mean a lot to me if she retained her, independent spirit."

She was looking at me and I felt it in my heart; that she had been my second saviour, as Yeheshua was my first, and that I might not see her again on this earth, in this life; not quite like we were here.

"Again, and again," she said. "This goes on and so do we."

EPILOGUE.

Johannus and Pharos rode down towards the Tyre coast with a donkey in tow.

Johannus knew he was taking more baggage than he ever had on a journey, which was partly because he was setting up trade relations between Magdalene and Petronius, but also because of presents heaped on him for his formal betrothal and marriage to Rebecca.

More surprisingly he had found that his left hip seemed to have improved beyond belief; and not just from the poisoning, but from an earlier injury too.

Pharos was enjoying it all, delivering Johannus just as Habban was Thomas. He laughed aloud at the thought.

Habban and Thomas had started their journey back to Jerusalem where the captain's men were awaiting him, but Pharos was sailing down from Tyre with Johannus to pick up his vessel at Mios hormos in Egypt.

As passengers on one of Rachel the healer's coasters, that she now shared the use of with Mary and one or two other traders.

Pharos looked forward to meeting Petronius; it was always good to have more potential partners, especially in Alexandria, and striking up this friendship with Johannus boded well for future links.

So much had come from Pharos' father being close friends with Miriam's, who often sailed the spice and incense routes, and with the young Miriam sometimes along as well.

So times rolled on and around…

And there was something Miriam had said to them on their passing that had puzzled and intrigued him.

He turned to ask Johannus. "What had Miriam meant when she said watch out for you and wayward goddesses?"

"Oh haha," laughed Johnannus, "she would mean Kaella I would think."

"Kaella?"

"Ahh well, hers is a long story, and as she is a goddess it has probably got a way to go yet…"